A ROGUE FOR CHRISTMAS

A Regency Holiday Collection

LAUREN SMITH

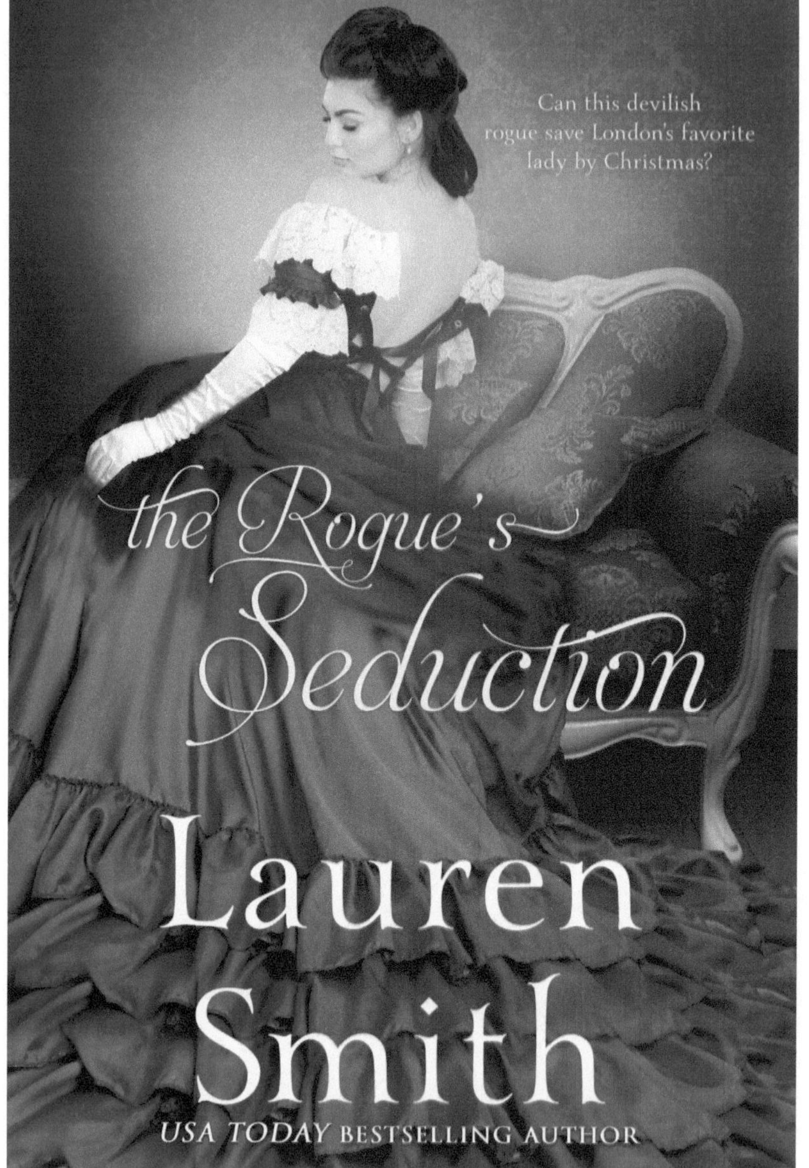
Can this devilish
rogue save London's favorite
lady by Christmas?

the Rogue's
Seduction

LAUREN
SMITH

USA TODAY BESTSELLING AUTHOR

THE ROGUE'S SEDUCTION

THE SEDUCTION SERIES BOOK 3

~ 1 ~

ondon, December 1821

Perdita Darby tugged the hood of her cloak close about her face, shielding herself not just from the bitter wind that battered the hackney coach she'd hired, but from any watchful eyes lurking in the shadows. The street was empty, twilight and the cold having chased even the most dedicated late-night strollers to their homes. Even the street urchins, usually desperate for coin, were tucked away in their alleyways on a bitingly cold night such as this, seeking what warmth they could. Perdita feared the darkness might hide someone who would realize who she was or what she was going to do. That could spell ruin.

"M'lady?" The driver of the hired coach stood by the door and closed it as she tugged her skirts free. He began to doff his cap at her, but she waved for him to keep it on. The night was too cold for such things. He smiled gratefully and kicked the snow off his boots.

"Please wait for me here." She pressed a few coins in his palm, and he nodded.

"Of course." The driver pocketed the coins and climbed back

up onto his seat. He bundled his heavy brown cloak over his body and huddled down for warmth.

Perdita faced the door of the townhouse in front of her. It was a lovely home, one that had been on Duke Street for many years. The noble arches were framed with ivy that grew up from the flower beds bordering the windows, even though the leaves had dropped away to expose the skeletal webbing of vines beneath. But in spring when the ivy was bright and sprawling, it would make this house look almost like a cottage deep in the Cotswolds, not a stately townhouse in the midst of a bustling city.

It was clear the owner of this house didn't bother with a gardener who would have kept the ivy from spreading. But that shouldn't have surprised her. She knew the owner of this house. Perdita planned to throw herself at his feet and beg for his help if she had to, and it didn't matter if ballroom whispers called him the Devil of London.

She squared her shoulders.

Be brave. He's the only one who can help you. Don't let him know how frightened you are.

She marched up the steps and rapped the metal knocker mounted on the stout oak door. Suddenly doubt assailed her. This was a terrible idea. Her mind screamed at her to flee as she stood upon the threshold to the underworld.

Perhaps she could beg her parents to let her go to the continent for a few years and avoid the fate that had driven her to this door at such an hour. Yet that would only spare her, not her family, of the consequences of running away from the blackmail she was facing.

The door creaked, the old oak protesting as the hinges grudgingly gave in. A middle-aged butler stood there, his beady eyes peering down at her over his long, thin nose and pointed chin. His professional demeanor lacked the politeness expected of a servant in a decent household. His shoulders were broad, and he seemed far too muscular for a refined position of a butler. But this wasn't a decent household. This was the devil's own home.

"Er…" He blinked at her, apparently startled by her appearance. It was a risk to be seen standing on this particular doorstep after midnight, a fact of which she was all too aware.

"I must see Lord Darlington at once," she told the man, praying he would let her inside. She could not take the risk of being seen and starting a scandal. Or rather, a different scandal than the one she was meticulously planning already.

The man hesitated, his body barring her entrance through the still partially closed door. "This is late, even for my master."

Perdita didn't back down. "I am aware of the hour, but he will want to see me." She raised her chin and announced this with such regal bearing that he would not dare question her. He sighed and stepped away from the doorway. Her mother's lessons, it seemed, hadn't been wasted on her after all.

"This way, madam." He waved a hand for her to step inside. She entered the townhouse, her body relaxing, but only just. She may have been out of view of the street, but she was still in very dangerous territory.

Two dim lamps illuminated the hall and staircase. She was surprised they were still lit. Was the master of the house still awake? She had assumed he would be, but the house was hushed and ghostly quiet. She took a moment to study her surroundings with open curiosity. The foyer was bare of any decorations, paintings, or even end tables. The starkness of it surprised her.

So this is where the Devil of London resides.

The furniture she glimpsed through a cracked-open door a few feet away—the drawing room perhaps—was outdated and threadbare. It made sense. The master of this house was rumored to be a desperate fortune hunter in dire straits. His desperation was no fault of his own, but rather due to his parents' untimely deaths and their accumulated debts.

It had to be a heavy burden to enter adulthood with the responsibilities of maintaining title and lands held in one's own family without any money by which to do so. Any man in such a position was a *dangerous* man—particularly when it came to rich, unmarried heiresses.

Like me...

"Please wait while I speak to the master. Who shall I say is calling?" the butler asked.

"Perdita Darby," she said, trying to still her trembling as she watched the butler go upstairs.

Perdita swallowed the knot of fear in her throat. This man had been desperate enough to kidnap her dearest friend, Alexandra Rockford, in order to win a five-thousand-pound wager by seducing her. That alone earned him his nickname in her eyes. To treat a woman's virtue as something to be wagered on! In the end, however, he had failed. Alexandra had been rescued by Ambrose Worthing, a man so in love with her he had fought his best friend to free her.

Alexandra had assured Perdita that Lord Darlington hadn't been *entirely* wicked—he'd only planned to convince the men involved in the wager that he had bedded her when he had not. But that did not make the Devil of London a hero, by any means. At best, he was a villain with a conscience. But Perdita was desperate enough to risk herself in his house tonight, knowing the danger and scandal that could fall upon her.

This is a terrible idea. Unfortunately, she had no other option. Only Lord Darlington could help her. She was prepared to do just about anything to escape her situation.

"Madam." The butler appeared at the top of the stairs. "His Lordship will see you now."

Perdita stared up at him, startled. "Upstairs? Not the drawing room?"

The old codger had the audacity to grin at her. "He insisted you meet upstairs, or I was to show you out."

The nerve of the man, demanding she meet him upstairs! Did he treat all gentle-bred ladies like this? Or, knowing who was paying a call upon him, he was perhaps doing his best to frighten her off. Yes, that must be it. He thought she would be too afraid to go upstairs.

I'm not afraid. Well, I am, but I'll be damned if I let him know that.

She lifted her skirts and ascended the stairs, her heart hammering. She followed the butler to a room where the door was slightly ajar. She glanced at the servant, but he was already departing.

Perdita pushed the door open and froze when she realized it was a bedchamber. Darlington had the audacity to call her to his *bedchamber*? Did he believe she had come for amorous reasons, or that she would condone such a brazen attempt at seduction? It was entirely possible, given the scandalous hour and the fact she was without a chaperone, but she would set him straight if he dared to try to seduce her.

She wished for the hundredth time it would have been possible to visit him during the day, but there had been no alternative. People would have seen her enter his home, and that would be the end of her carefully kept reputation. She tensed when a dark, rich voice spoke.

Vaughn Darlington, the viscount dubbed by *ton* as the Devil of London. His voice sent tingles of excitement and fear through her. She took an instinctive step back toward the door.

"Fleeing so soon? I would have wagered you were braver than that, Miss Darby. Or perhaps, given the lateness of the hour and the method of this meeting, I should call you Perdita?"

She bristled and pushed the hood of her cloak back to better peer around the room. There was a four-poster bed against one wall and a fire crackling in the hearth. The wood floor showed dusty outlines of where carpets had recently been. The dark-green brocaded curtains about the bed were faded, and a few rings were missing, letting the fabric gape in odd places. Worn and peeling silk wallpapers depicting men hunting in the forest covered the walls. A once beautiful wardrobe stood in one corner, a door missing. The shaving stand held a white china basin with a large crack down its side.

The masculine air of the room was overpowering, just as the man himself was, but the circumstances and the condition of his rooms filled her with a strange pity that made her go still as she turned her focus on the man himself.

Leaning against one worn, ancient chair was Lord Darlington. He was tall, broad shouldered, and had a dangerous look about his all too beautiful face. With piercing blue eyes and light-blond hair, Darlington could have passed for an angel if it weren't for the sensual, wicked curve of his lips. He wore buff trousers and a white lawn shirt, with a dark-blue waistcoat. His cravat had been untied and lay loose over the back of one chair.

Perdita's heart quickened. She had never stood in a room with a man in a state of partial undress like this. She forced herself to rally to the task at hand.

"Lord Darlington, I come here with a proposal." Her tone was brusque with a manner of business about it. This was not about seduction, no matter how sinful he made her feel. Though she'd rehearsed this speech a dozen times on her own, she had not been prepared for the strange and frightening feelings that assaulted her now as she spoke to him alone.

He crossed his arms as he studied her with that wicked twist of his lips, making her breath quicken. She shifted in place, and her boots scraped softly against the wood floor.

"Do go on." He chuckled, seeming to enjoy her discomfort.

"Well, you see..." She spoke haltingly, still mortified that she was here begging him for his help. "I need to stop an unwanted marriage proposal." She twined her fingers nervously as she removed her gloves. "My mother has convinced a certain gentleman that I am willing to consider his offer, when I most certainly am not."

She tried not to think of Mr. Samuel Milburn and how that man had made it clear he would imprison her in a life that would slowly kill her. She could still see him leaning in close to her and whispering: *"The women I care for know better than to seek the company of others, when I should be enough. My home has all you will need, so I will hear no talk of travel or nights out. They would only distract you from your duty, which would be pleasing me."*

He was a brute and a tyrant and worse, but Perdita's mother, despite her ambitious nature, didn't usually believe in society gossip.

Perdita did. She'd heard that Milburn had thrown a woman to her death from a window, but because the woman was his mistress, no questions were asked. It had been dismissed as an unfortunate accident. All Perdita knew for sure was that this man was a monster. She had tried to tell her father and mother what she'd heard, but her words had been dismissed as idle talk. If her older brother Thomas hadn't been away at sea serving in His Majesty's royal navy, she would have sought his help.

In Perdita's experience, being a wealthy heiress was a terrible burden. It put a mark on her. She'd fought off fortune hunters for the last few years, but a man like Milburn was dangerous in other ways. He didn't care about her money—he cared about breaking her spirit and possibly even killing her if she didn't give him what he desired. She was *sport*.

She'd made the mistake of meeting him at a dinner party last fall, and he had immediately shown an interest in her once he'd learned she was none other than Miss Darby, the beloved lady of the *ton* who all sought to please with their praise and their many invitations.

Perdita had not wished to cultivate such a favored reputation on purpose, but it had happened quite naturally. But to Milburn she became a prize he wished to win—and then suffocate and destroy. Once he had her in his sights, he had been able to contrive a scheme that could destroy her family and blackmail her into accepting his proposal.

"What does this have to do with me? Or did you merely wish to tumble in my sheets to avoid marrying some silly young buck? I don't care much for ruining innocents, but in your case I might make an exception," Darlington said, his sharp gaze on her.

Perdita considered reminding him he had in fact attempted to ruin her innocent friend over a wager, but she thought better of it. Quarreling with him now would not aid her in acquiring his help.

"I wish to engage your services." She still couldn't say the words. It was too humiliating.

"My services?" He shifted slightly, a frown curving his lips. "What *services* do you require?" When Darlington said *services*, it sounded sinful, wicked.

"I wish to hire your cooperation in appearing to be engaged to me, publicly. Not a true engagement, just for a few months, to deter the other gentleman so he will leave me be." She glanced down, playing with her gloves. She was betting that Milburn would lose interest if he believed he had another challenger for her hand.

His eyes turned wintry, almost chilling as they settled on her fidgeting hands. "So I'm to play your fiancé? What's to be my reward in scaring the bounder off?" Darlington still leaned against the side of the chair, but Perdita was more aware of him than ever. The small distance between them seemed to shrink every second.

"I will pay you. I have access to some of my dowry. It is invested in a private bank with Lady Rosalind Lennox. My father put the funds in his name, but he allows me to have some control over them."

Darlington stroked his chin. "I require a more permanent solution than a temporary flow of money. You said you bank with Lady Lennox?" He continued to stare at her with that assessing gaze, and she suddenly feared he might not agree, that he might consider blackmailing her directly for her funds in the bank by exposing her visit to his townhouse. Surely he wouldn't dare.

When he still gazed at her expectantly, she realized he awaited some response to his question. She nodded.

"Then you are acquainted with Lord Lennox, her husband? He is a selective but successful investor. I wish to be involved in whatever scheme he chooses to invest in next."

Perdita nodded again. She was well acquainted with Rosalind Lennox, but she only knew of her husband, Ashton Lennox, in passing. Perhaps she could persuade Rosalind to allow Darlington to invest with her husband. She only hoped such a request wouldn't seem inappropriate to her friend. It was a risk she had to take to avoid marriage to a man like Samuel Milburn.

"I believe I can arrange a meeting. As to whether he allows you to invest..." There was no way she could guarantee that.

Darlington pushed away from the chair and came up to her. The simple action seemed to change everything between them. Before he hadn't seemed so threatening. But now with his towering frame so close, she felt very much like a tiny rabbit facing a very large wolf. She knew he was tall, but standing inches away from him made her feel small and feminine in a way she never had before. It took a moment for her to catch her breath. She had to tilt her face back to look up at him.

"I suppose that would be good enough. But you know once we have begun this charade, everyone will expect us to marry." It sounded like he was warning her. They would never marry. If there was one thing she was certain of, she would *not* marry the Devil of London.

"I am aware of that. After a time I deem prudent, you may cry off our engagement and go on as you please." She had to be completely sure Samuel Milburn was no longer interested in her, and only then could she risk a public break with Lord Darlington. Otherwise, her family's reputation would be ruined, and her father might be facing penalties under English law.

His lips twitched in an amused smile. "And you are ready to

brave the *ton* after being jilted by me?" The wolfish smile that stole across his lips was not reassuring. "I doubt any other man would have you once I've been your lover."

"We would not be lovers, only engaged."

Darlington laughed softly. "Any woman I asked to marry me would certainly be my lover beforehand. I wouldn't wish to marry a woman unless I was positive I enjoyed my time with her in bed."

She ignored his scandalous words. "Being jilted by the likes of you, even if some assume we've been lovers, is better than having a man like Samuel Milburn find a way to compromise me. I know the sort of man he is, and as unbelievable as it is, he is *worse* than you." She threw her shoulders back and glared at him, daring him to argue the point.

"Milburn?" Darlington's eyes widened. "That's the man who is chasing your skirts?"

"Yes. Do you know him?"

He nodded slowly. "Unfortunately, I do. We've run into each other at various clubs." He paused as though choosing his words carefully, weighing what she ought to hear or not as the case might be. "Most of the *ton* see him as a delightful gentleman who could do no wrong. Others know him as I do. Some would say he and I have similar tastes in pain—not in receiving it but causing it."

"A taste for pain?" Perdita shuddered. She'd heard Milburn had thrown his mistress out of a window. Any future with a man like that would seal her fate, but she hadn't heard the same of Darlington. He wasn't cruel, though she'd heard he was impossibly *wicked*. Even a fleeting kiss upon the hand during an introduction had been known to cause such scandals that ladies in the ballroom took flight to escape, like a flock of birds dressed in silk and tulle.

"Yes." Darlington's eyes were on her face again. "We require something a little different in our bed play." He paused again, his eyes dark and fathomless as he stared at her. "But unlike him, my goal is *always* pleasure. A crying, hurting woman is not arousing to me. But for Milburn, it makes his blood turn to fire."

Darlington's bold words on such a subject made her take another step back.

"You like to cause *pain* in bed?" She hated how her words trembled as they escaped her. Surely whispers of this would have reached her if that were true. "This was a mistake. I should—"

He reached up and cupped her cheek when she tried to pull away, then wound a strong arm around her waist, her cloak bunching above her bottom. She had to face him now and hear whatever it was he wished to say.

"There are two types of pain, love. One is slight, expected, and leads to intense pleasure. The other is selfish and part of a need to be cruel and harsh. I prefer the former, not the latter."

His words didn't make any sense. Pain was pain, wasn't it? She wrinkled her nose and prepared to argue this, but she never had the chance. He lowered his head and captured her mouth with his. Perdita was frozen in shock. The feel of his soft warm lips moving over hers was strange but increasingly delightful.

She'd never been kissed before but had often imagined how it would feel. She mimicked his mouth and gasped as he licked the seam of her lips with his tongue. The velvety feel of his tongue touching her lips was both sinful and decadent. Her knees went weak beneath her heavy skirts. She grasped his shoulders, frantic not to lose hold of him. The heat between their mouths intensified, and a heady dazed feeling began to slink through her limbs and into her lower belly. She could do this for hours...

His lips wandered from hers down to her throat just above where her cloak covered her shoulders. He placed a kiss there and then suddenly nipped her skin with his teeth. The bite sent a jolt through her, and a fierce, shocking pulse beat between her thighs. She whimpered and tried to push away, not because it hurt, but because the rush of sensations had been too much. She'd never—

"That, my love, is pain mixed with pleasure." Darlington whispered this against the skin of her throat, still holding her fast so she could not escape. Shivers rippled down her spine, and she closed her eyes. This was frightening. *He* was frightening, but a part of her wanted to understand more of what he was showing her.

From the moment she'd first seen him at her mother's garden party a few months before, she'd been intrigued by his mysteries. She wouldn't deny it. Any decent young lady would not have allowed herself to be fascinated by such a notorious rogue, but now more than ever she wondered if perhaps she wasn't as decent as she ought to be.

Darlington slowly released her waist, but the hand that still held her face seemed to burn her skin. He brushed his thumb over her lips, leaving a tingling sensation that trailed from her mouth down to her toes. She raised her eyes to his, her world tilting on its axis as she stared up at him. There was no going back from that kiss. She'd taken a bite of the forbidden apple, and the juices were sweet upon her lips.

"You're still trembling," he observed, his voice was low and gentle, but rather than soothe her, she felt excited by it.

"It is always like that?" she asked, wondering why Mother had never mentioned that lips could meet in such a blaze of fire when she'd discussed the ways men and women could be together.

Darlington touched her lips once more before dropping his hands. "Not always. Too many marriages are built upon the wrong foundations, and passions are rarely taken into account." He turned away from her and walked over to the fire, placing one hand on the mantle as he gazed into the flames.

"If you want to play this game, Miss Darby, it must be played convincingly. Milburn won't accept a mere declaration of our engagement. He knows me too well. He's also not the sort to give up easily." Darlington's face was lit by firelight. For a moment, he looked more like Hades, the Greek god of the underworld, than a mere London rogue. Perdita was entranced by the sight of him. He was a lure she couldn't resist. How many women had come into his room before her and fallen under his spell?

"What did you have in mind?"

"I suppose you recall what befell Alexandra Rockford in my

home? A public display. *That* is what I mean. Milburn will need to see us in a compromising position." He turned to face her. "And that means more than a simple kiss."

Perdita bit her bottom lip. A simple kiss? Not to her. That kiss had been her undoing. She was wise enough to know he had changed her life in a few short minutes.

"If it helps me escape Samuel Milburn, then I agree to do whatever is necessary." She raised her chin, earning a slow smile from him that made her blush.

"What?" she demanded as he continued to smile at her.

"I never would've guessed you would agree. Of all ladies, you seem to be the most..."

Perdita narrowed her eyes. "Most what?"

"Let us say I'm surprised at your defiant streak, that is all."

Perdita stared at him challengingly. "I behave appropriately in public, a dutiful daughter and a well-bred lady, but you have no idea what sort of woman I really am." He truly didn't. She was a lady, well-versed in conversation, a charming hostess, a delight among the *ton*, but that wasn't all she was. There were other, hidden sides of herself she dared not reveal.

Darlington's eyes sparkled with mischief. "Now *that* is most interesting. As your fiancé, I will make it my sacred duty to uncover these hidden facets of your character."

She tilted her head, studying him in return. "How about your services then?" She wanted to keep this matter as businesslike between them as she could manage. He would no doubt rob her of her good sense with his kisses, but if she held fast and reminded them both this was only business and nothing more, then perhaps she might survive this devil's bargain with her heart intact.

"I have one last question before I agree, and I demand honesty in your answer."

She weighed the risk of losing his help against any question he might demand and then nodded. "Ask."

"What hold does Milburn have over you that leaves you in such fear? I do not believe for a moment that your parents would force you to accept a match with him even if he dragged you down with scandal. No, there is something that makes you fear you might have no choice to accept if he pursues you." Darlington played with the cuffs of his right-hand sleeve. "What does he hold over you, Miss Darby?"

It was the one question she didn't want to answer, but she knew she had to.

"In private, he has claimed that he can prove my father was involved in the smuggling of goods into England and evading taxes." She hesitated, hoping she could trust Darlington with such information.

"And is he? Guilty, I mean?"

"No! I mean, that is to say, *he* isn't. But I fear the men he invests with might very well be guilty. I believe Milburn might even be working with them to frame my father, and unfortunately I have no way of stopping them. If I marry him, he says he will destroy the evidence, but if I do not..."

"And you believe that an engagement to me will stop him?"

"It has to," she whispered. "If he no longer desires me, then he has no reason to go through with his threats. And you are one of the most wicked men in London. If he isn't afraid of you and tries to take what is yours, such as a future wife, he would be mad."

The corners of lips twitched. "That is certainly true. I wouldn't hesitate to destroy any who dared take what is mine, especially a woman. Very well, I agree to this scheme, mad though it is." Darlington held out one hand to her. "Shall we shake upon it?" He was quite serious, except for the wicked gleam in his eyes. A gleam that promised every moment with him would be deliciously sinful torture.

Perdita placed her palm in his. "We have an accord."

"Agreed." He turned her hand in his, lifting it to his lips as he kissed her knuckles.

"Good." She hesitated, relishing the feel of his lips upon her bare fingers before she tugged her hand free of his. "My mother is hosting a Christmas party at our estate in Lothbrook. I will see to it that you are invited. Please bring your valet, and have him pack enough clothes to last through Christmas."

Darlington nodded, but when she turned to leave, he caught her arm.

"Yes? Lord Darlington?" She eyed his hand on her arm. He did not release her, not like another man would.

"Given our new intimacy, it would please me to be called Vaughn whenever we are alone."

"Vaughn." She tested the sound of his given name, hating that she liked how smoothly it rolled off her tongue.

"And I expect to be introduced to Lord and Lady Lennox before the end of this year. Will that be possible?"

Perdita nodded. "Yes. I will arrange it as soon as I can."

"Good." He tucked her arm in his. "Let me escort you out."

"Really, my lord—Vaughn. There's no need."

"I need to practice playing the part of a gentleman. I fear I may be a bit rusty."

She remained silent as he led her down the stairs. When he opened the front door, she paused as the bitter wind cut through her. She glanced at him a moment longer before she pulled her cloak hood back up, concealing her features. She rushed to the waiting coach and climbed inside. She chanced one last peek at him through the curtains. He stood there in the doorway without a coat. She remembered the heat of his body pressed to hers and shivered, but not from the cold.

How strange to have made a bargain with Vaughn, Viscount Darlington. They were now bound together, and though they were united in their mission, she felt incredibly alone. She wished she could talk to her dear friend Alexandra, but she was the last person Perdita could confide in when it came to Vaughn.

When Vaughn had kidnapped Alex, it had been a terrifying ordeal, even after Vaughn had revealed he had no intention of harming her. When Alex learned of her supposed engagement to Vaughn, she would no doubt rush to Perdita and try to put a stop to her madness. It was not a meeting Perdita looked forward to, but she and Alex had such different views on how to handle society. Alex had hidden from it while Perdita had embraced it.

Perdita needed Vaughn's dangerous reputation. It was the last shield she had against Samuel Milburn. It was something her dear friend would not understand because she was not the target of Milburn's evil intent. Perdita had sold her soul to a lesser devil to protect herself from a worse one.

She prayed only that their scheme would work, or she was doomed.

2

Vaughn Darlington watched the coach vanish into the wintry night, his smile fading as the distance between him and Perdita Darby grew. He was a tad melancholy after the whirlwind of the last half hour. Part of him was still amused by the little beauty—her tenacity, her courage, even her recklessness in approaching someone with his reputation in his bedchamber. At midnight, no less.

A proposition, she'd said. And what a proposition it had been. The run of bad luck that had burdened him for so long seemed to be taking a turn for the better, and all because of a little country girl with sound intuition when it came to the darker side of Samuel Milburn.

His smile grew grim. She thought his announced interest in her would put off Milburn, but Vaughn knew Milburn better than she did. Whatever intentions Vaughn had for her, as his mistress or his betrothed, her scheme would not likely matter to a man like Milburn. He was a true bastard, a danger to the fairer sex, and would find a way to claim what he thought was rightfully his.

Yet Vaughn hadn't been able to tell her that whatever he did with her would not be enough to stop Milburn. Not on its own.

Vaughn could only hope their little charade would give him a chance to stop whatever Milburn was planning.

He considered the larger problem. Leverage. That was what Milburn had. So long as he held this evidence regarding Miss Darby's father, if it even existed, he would be in a position to pressure and cajole her. First, he would demand she break off her engagement, then bide his time before he held her feet to the fire to accept his own proposal. That sounded like the bastard's style. But without that evidence, his position would crumble.

He would put his butler on it. Craig was far more than he appeared to be, and he had not always been a butler. He had his ways of making men tell the truth. If anyone could get to the bottom of this, it was him.

His thoughts turned back to Perdita and her reaction to the nip he gave her shoulder. While Vaughn was quite notorious for his penchant for pain mixed with pleasure in bed play, he never harmed his bed partners. Milburn, however, had killed his last mistress, or so it was said. The rumors had been murmured in the seediest clubs, and once Vaughn heard he'd been disgusted with the man. Without proof, there wasn't enough to take the case to court. Milburn, as a gentleman, would escape prosecution.

The affair left a sour taste in Vaughn's mouth, which was why he'd agreed to help Perdita. He knew Milburn and his type. The man would stop at nothing until he was married to her, and then the law would do nothing once her new husband revealed his cruel streak.

Perdita was in danger, and the only way to remedy that was to offer her the ultimate protection—his name given in marriage. It was the reason he had taken so long to give her an answer. She had no idea that what she really needed was a true wedding, not a false engagement. And ordinarily, he would have declined.

But something about Perdita had changed his mind. It had happened ever so subtly over the course of their interaction. The way she'd softened in his arms when he'd kissed her. The way she'd challenged him when he'd reminded her of what her reputation would be like at the end of her charade. The way she was a charming and yet innocent country maiden who responded with fire and bravado. She'd intrigued him even as she'd stormed into his bedchamber, where there was no chaperone to save her from his clutches. None of it had been an act. Perdita was a woman worth knowing, a woman with secrets and passions and a mind all her own. *That* was a woman he could marry.

A smile crept back onto his face, and this time it was one of hesitant joy.

Vaughn walked into the drawing room and approached the tray of drinks his butler had set out earlier. He poured himself a glass of brandy before he took a seat in the chair by the fire just starting to turn to embers. He sipped his drink, savoring the flavor as he contemplated the unique opportunity Perdita had presented him with tonight.

It had been so long since he had looked forward to anything. Ever since his parents had died five years past, he'd been mired in debts that were too deep to recover from on his own. No matter what he did, he seemed to be damned. He'd had to close his country estate, let go of his entire staff save for one caretaker, and reduce the staff at his London townhouse.

His only way of getting by had been to win wagers at the clubs, and even that source was running dry. Every man in every major club now knew better than to wager large stakes when they found him across the gaming table. His ability to win should have helped pay off his family's debts, but not even the most gullible lads were foolish enough to stake their fortunes against him now.

He'd become known as the Devil of London in a matter of months. The moniker hadn't upset him as much as he thought it would at first, but it had kept men from playing even a simple game of cards with him. His friends certainly didn't approve of his actions, and in the last few years most had abandoned him.

Of course, he'd done other things, worse things, to drive his friends away. In the fall he had approached White's infamous betting book and found a five-thousand-pound sum wagered for publicly seducing a young woman named Alexandra Rockford, Perdita's close friend.

Kidnapping was not at all a charming prospect to him, unless of course the lady *wished* to be kidnapped. He'd played that particular game more than a few times with delightful results, but kidnapping Alexandra had been...*dreadful*.

He indulged in a moment of self-loathing. The night he had taken Alexandra to his home to fake her ruination for the sake of a wager had left a dark stain. He hated himself far more than he ever had before, and it showed how desperate he had truly become. That loathing had deepened until it left a scar on his heart. One he doubted would ever go away.

When he found Perdita in his doorway tonight, he hadn't expected to feel anything. Yet he had. She'd lowered her hood, and her brown hair had turned a burnished bronze in the lamplight. Her eyes, a gentle shade of brown like topaz stones, turned warm as honey. His blood had burned with desire in a way it hadn't in a long while. If that wasn't reason enough to marry the girl, he wasn't sure what else would be.

He left the drawing room and sought out his butler. He found the older man in his office on the basement of the townhouse.

"Mr. Craig, I have a task for you."

The butler glanced up from the papers on his desk. He gave Vaughn an appraising look. "Am I correct in assuming that this lies outside my usual duties?"

"You are."

Mr. Craig sighed. "I am no longer a young man, my lord."

"This is not for my own selfish desires, Mr. Craig. That young woman you brought to me requires our help. Her very life may depend on it."

Those words seemed to give Mr. Craig new vigor. He rose to his feet like a man twenty years younger. "Name it, my lord."

"A man named Samuel Milburn claims to have evidence that Mr. Reginald Darby has been involved in smuggling and evading taxes. He's using this as a means to pressure Darby's daughter into accepting marriage to him."

Mr. Craig scowled. Though he did not look it, he was at heart a romantic. In fact, Vaughn had caught him reading the works of L. R. Gloucester, a gothic novelist, on more than one occasion. The thought of any man forcing a woman by such means would be anathema to him.

"I want you to look into this. Miss Darby believes her father invested with men who might be working with Milburn. It could be they are trying to lay false evidence that Darby is the one behind the ill deeds. What we need is proof that Milburn is attempting to blackmail the Darby family, or proof of Mr. Darby's innocence. And if at all possible, I want you to put a stop to whoever is causing these problems, if you understand my meaning."

Mr. Craig's grim smile was a reminder of the man he'd once been, a man who'd fought valiantly for his country in the shadows years before.

"Understood."

He rarely spoke of those times, and when he did it was often in an allegorical fashion, but Vaughn had seen on more than one occasion just what Mr. Craig was capable of. And despite his complaints of old age and weariness, it took little to light the old fire under him again.

He left his butler and called for his valet, knowing the fellow would be up late.

"Barnaby!" His voice echoed in the darkened corridor. A few seconds later the man appeared around the edge of the door leading to the servants' quarters.

"My lord?"

"Pack me a valise for at least a week. We're going to Lothbrook in a few days and shall be there for Christmas." He tipped his brandy back and finished it before he headed for the stairs to return to his bedchamber.

Barnaby wrinkled his nose. "Lothbrook again? I'm still scraping the dust out of your trousers from the last visit, my lord." The man muttered this more to himself than to his master. Neither of them cared much for the country. It was so bloody provincial, but if he had to return there to seduce his unknowing bride, then that was where he must go.

He would deal with the details of his travel arrangements in the morning once he had had word from Perdita's parents that he was invited to their estate. With another small smile, he returned to his bedchamber and began to strip down for bed. He always slept in the buff, even in winter. It was a habit that would no doubt shock his little bride-to-be, but he suspected she would shock him right back. He closed his eyes, letting his mind flash images of her as he bent to kiss her, and the memory of it resurrected a smile upon his lips.

Her startled look, then the way she'd melted in his arms. She'd tasted like honey and fire, burning, yet impossibly sweet. He could still feel the velvet of her cloak, crumpled in his hands as he latched on to her. He had wanted to slide his hand up her skirts right then, but that would've been a step too far, no matter how she'd claimed she was not an innocent creature.

She was wanton, he would agree, yet still innocent in so many ways. Introducing Perdita to the mysteries of a man and woman coming together was not a thing to be rushed. Hasty fumblings in the dark would not do. No, she deserved a well-planned, deliciously slow seduction of the body and the mind.

Vaughn sat on the edge of his bed, raking his hands through his hair as he considered his next move. Tomorrow he needed to purchase a ring. He had little money to do so, but he'd find a way. His smile stretched into a broad grin. The invisible forces of fate had seemed determined to stop him from restoring his family's name in the *ton*, and now he had found a way to win against them: marry the *ton*'s darling. Miss Darby was the answer to his prayers. What a shock it would be to them all.

London's sweetest lady mated to its fiercest devil.

PERDITA STOOD BY HER MOTHER'S WRITING DESK IN HER PRIVATE sitting room, her heart racing more than it ought. Her mother sat at her delicate escritoire and was diligently checking the guest list for the party that would occupy their country estate in a few days. Perdita shifted about, her red shawl dropping from her shoulders to hang about her elbows and lower back.

"Perdita dear, you're lingering. You know how much I detest lingering. Either come and speak to me or be off."

Smoothing the skirts of her pale-rose gown, Perdita approached her mother and cleared her throat.

"I should like to add a guest to the list, Mama, if you don't mind. I know we have extra rooms." The estate was an ancient one that, while lacking the pomp of a peerage family with a title, was still a rival to many of the aristocratic homes in the country. It boasted no less than twenty bedrooms, a ballroom, and a music room. Perdita had numerous unpleasant memories of plucking away at a harp during an arranged musicale performance when she debuted two years ago.

Her mother glanced up, wisps of brown hair threaded with silver creeping out from her turban. "Oh? And who do you wish me to invite?"

Perdita straightened herself. "My fiancé."

The quill in her mother's hand seemed to hover a moment in midair before it clattered flat on the writing desk, splattering ink on the corner of the list her mother had been writing.

"Your..."

"Fiancé. Yes."

Her mother's eyes were as large as saucers. "So you accepted Mr. Milburn, then?"

"Er...no. It is someone else."

"What? But who?"

Perdita understood her mother's shock. It had been two long years since her debut, and she had rejected all offers that first year.

The second season she had not received any offers. Rather than become a spinster, she'd cultivated her reputation as a young lady of good character. Debutantes came to her for advice, society mamas sought the name of her modiste, and gentlemen sought her for conversations.

She was well versed to play the role set out for her. Charming and delightful, she was welcome in every London household. The one thing she had *not* done was allow herself to be courted. The men of England had given up, until Samuel Milburn met her a few months ago at a dinner party.

Their encounter had been brief, pointedly cool, at least from Perdita's side. Milburn had taken her cool aloofness in stride and informed her parents the following day of his intentions. Once Perdita learned of this, she'd come up with her desperate plan and had been biding her time until she felt safe enough to go to Vaughn.

"It's Lord Darlington, Mama. He and I have been seeing each other in secret. I know you disapprove of such things, but we wanted to be sure of our affections before we let society pry into our affairs."

Her mother's eyes nearly bulged out of her head. "Darlington? But... Good heavens, what about Milburn? I can't rescind his invitation for Christmas. He was most excited to come shooting with your father."

"I know..." Perdita pretended to consider the dilemma carefully, though she already knew her mind about it. "He must still come. However, we must also extend Lord Darlington an invitation."

Her mother picked up her quill and poised herself to write, but paused. "Are you quite sure, my dear? Lord Darlington is quite wicked, so I hear. I know I teased you in September about pursuing him, but it was only a jest."

"He is a viscount, Mama. His title will further us in society, will it not?"

"It will, but that's no reason to marry a man. If you loved him, that would be one thing, but if you don't, I wouldn't expect you to marry him."

Perdita held her breath, trying to summon the courage to lie to her mother, a thing she had never liked to do and avoided whenever possible.

"I love him, Mama, and I believe with a bit of time I can tame his restless spirit." She gave her mother an imploring look.

"Well, that is entirely possible, even of the worst rogues. I tamed your father, after all."

There was a loud *harrumph* from the doorway. Perdita turned to see her father standing there. He looked dapper in his blue breeches and waistcoat, his gray mustache twitching as he watched them.

"Tame *me?*" her father chortled. "Woman, you didn't tame me."

"I most certainly did!" Her mother stood, moving from her writing desk and to her husband. "You were a terrible rogue in your day, and it was quite the feat to bring you to your senses."

Perdita watched her parents with a blush in her cheeks.

"I only let you believe that." Her father's eyes twinkled as he caught Perdita's mother by her waist and pulled her close, kissing her cheek.

"Heavens, Reginald!" her mother hissed, but she was smiling as she chastised him. "Not here!"

"Very well." Reginald sighed dramatically. "Now, what's all this about taming men?"

"Well." Her mother waved at Perdita. "Your daughter seems to have gotten herself engaged and is only just now telling us."

"Milburn asked you, then?" Her father studied her curiously. His gaze was serious rather than delighted that his daughter had just announced she was to be married.

Perdita shook her head. "Um, no, actually. It was Lord Darlington. You remember him, don't you, Papa? He came to the garden party in September and stayed with us for a short time."

Papa raised one dark brow. "Darlington? You don't say..."

"Yes." Perdita's mother would be too blinded by the joy of

knowing her child was to be married, but her father was a little more levelheaded and might see through things.

"And you want to bring him for Christmas, is that it? Well, bring the lad so I can measure him and see if he is up to snuff. He ought to have come to me first, like that Milburn fellow did." Her father appeared to look stern, but there was a twinkle in his eyes that made Perdita want to laugh. If only she really were engaged. It was surprising to see how happy she had made her parents.

"We were keeping it a secret until we were sure of ourselves." Perdita pleaded with her eyes, hoping her father believed her. She needed Vaughn to come. She'd tried to mention Samuel Milburn's reputation to her father before, but he'd brushed it aside as idle talk. He knew all too well that gossip had been known to ruin lives unjustly and was disinclined to hear any more about it. It was one of the few times she'd ever been furious with him.

"Hmm, well, invite the boy, then." Her father kissed her mother's cheek and left them alone again.

"Perdita dear, I am most happy for you, of course, but are you quite sure Darlington is the one? I mean, you may have offers again from more than one gentleman. I was worried that..." Her mother trailed off, and heavy silence filled the room. It was only a matter of time before the *ton* tired of her and she was left on the shelf to become a spinster. She did not mind, but she knew her parents wished to see her happily married.

"Vaughn is the one for me." She used his given name purposefully, and it had the desired effect.

"Is it truly a love match? You know I only ever wanted a love match for you. That's why I always invite every young man I can find in hopes he might be perfect for you. Milburn seemed so attentive, and everyone spoke well of him. I had hopes that you might feel the same...but if your heart belongs to Lord Darlington, then that's settled, isn't it?"

Perdita clasped her mother's hands and squeezed them. She was a determined matchmaker for sport, but Perdita knew her mother's intentions were pure. She had married Papa for love and only wanted the same for her daughter. As often as her mother could be exasperating, she was also impossibly wonderful. That was why it hurt so much to lie to her.

"Yes. It is a love match. I never thought I'd win the heart of a man like Vaughn, but somehow I did."

"Win his heart?" Her mother chuckled. "You only need to win his mind first. It is he who must win *your* heart." Her mother squeezed her hands in return. "Very well, I shall invite your darling Darlington." She winked at Perdita and walked back to her desk to resume her guest list.

"If you don't mind, Mama, I am to have tea with Lady Lysandra Russell this afternoon at Gunter's."

"Of course." She returned her focus to her list. "Give her mother my regards, and take a footman with you."

"Thank you, Mama. Don't forget to send Darlington's invitation today. I wanted it to come from you so he would feel welcome."

"Consider it done." Her mother pulled a fresh bit of parchment toward her and began to scratch away with her quill, her turbaned head bowed.

Perdita called for Hensley, one of the young footmen, to bring her cloak and summon a coach. It would be too cold for ices, which Gunter's was most famous for. Tea would be preferable. They would also have to meet indoors. Gunter's was a treat when the weather was fine. A lady could arrive in Berkeley Square and remain in her open carriage while the men rushed from Gunter's to bring ices out to waiting customers. Indoors was perfectly fine for her intentions today. She and Lysandra had important things to discuss.

Hensley met her by the door and held out her dark-blue cloak. She slipped it on and took a white mink muff, tucking her hands inside. Then she and Hensley walked to the coach waiting for them.

When they reached Gunter's, Hensley came inside with her but kept his distance so she might enjoy her time alone with her friend. Lysandra Russell was waiting, a tea service in front of her at one of the tables. Her bright-red hair was like a flame that danced in the lamplight of the shop. Lysandra didn't seem to notice the appreciative stares of the men around them. But that was just how Lysa was, her head buried in books, her mind preoccupied with their shared purpose.

"Lysa." Perdita took an empty chair opposite her friend at the small tea table.

"Oh! Perdita, forgive me." Lysa blushed and raised her head from her stack of letters. She tucked the letters into her lap and poured a cup of tea for her friend.

"Thank you." Perdita slipped the muff off her hands and sipped her tea.

Lysa beamed. "Our paper on the astronomical developments of the last few months is ready for publication. I believe we might be accepted this time." Lysa grinned and nodded at the pen name they had chosen to hide their genders: P. L. Bottomsley.

"I've drafted a proper introduction. Officially, we are a gentleman from Tintagel, Cornwall. I've acquired the use of an address there. There's a man named Mikhail Barinov. He's agreed to collect any correspondence and deliver it to London first. I believe this time we shall have our ducks in a row. The Astronomy Society of London *must* publish us."

Perdita couldn't help but smile as well. This was her dream—their observations and scientific discoveries published. As ladies and not learned gentleman scholars, their articles had been continually rejected. And so, a ruse had to be devised. The need for it was maddening.

"Brilliant, Lysa." Perdita took the article and reviewed the neatly written words, checking each page carefully. Then she handed it back to Lysa, who tucked it into a leather folio.

"I will submit it on the morrow with the messenger and let you know once I hear if we've been successful."

"Excellent." Perdita glanced around the shop, her eyes taking in the couples having tea. Gunter's was one of the few places in

London a lady could meet with a gentleman alone and not worry about scandal or ruination. The door opened with a small bell tinkling as a group of men came in from the cold. Perdita recognized one of them, and her heart pitched straight to her feet.

Samuel Milburn was here.

"Lysa, I'm so sorry, but I must leave immediately." She nodded discreetly at Samuel, who was removing his hat and coat.

Lysa's eyes settled on the man as she nodded. "Of course. Good luck."

Perdita waved Hensley over.

"Miss?" Hensley asked, brushing crumbs from his trousers.

"I'd like to leave. Please have the coach brought around at once."

Hensley pulled his coat on and ducked outside. Perdita carefully walked around the edge of the tea shop, weaving between the couples and tables, trying to keep out of Samuel's sight. She pulled her hood up and reached the door just in time to overhear part of his conversation with the other gentlemen.

"You've still not proposed to the Darby chit yet?" one of the men asked.

Samuel chuckled. "Not officially. I'm waiting for Christmas. Women love that sort of romantic drivel. I also need to make sure she's mine. I have to be able to have her before I make my decision. There's enough fire in her that I believe she'd be a pleasure to break. Have to make sure though. She might be one of those weepy virginal debutantes. Can't have that. I want her to fight me before I break her completely."

His companions laughed, one comparing such "sport" with the hunting of a wild animal.

Milburn sneered. "Indeed, except one must be stuffed before it is mounted, while the other must be mounted in order to be stuffed."

The grating sound of their harsh laughter made Perdita nearly toss up her accounts. She couldn't bear to hear another word. She rushed out into the cold, not caring if the biting wind tore at her face. Samuel's threats were unimaginable. How could the *ton* be so blinded by him not to see his evil? Yet she feared that was the sort of darkness lying in his soul. He was a man with no heart, and he cared for nothing except his own needs. She would not become his victim; she would do anything to escape such evil. Vaughn would be her salvation. She trusted him, something which should have been surprising, yet it did not feel so.

Evil and sorrow left very different shadows on a man's face. Evil was a malignant presence that smothered and strangled the goodness around it. But it was different with sorrow. Vaughn's eyes were painted in shadows of pain and loss. It was a shadow that might someday be vanquished by the rays of the sun. She had glimpsed the hope of it in his eyes when she'd kissed him last night, like sunlight streaking through the parted curtains of a mansion that had been shrouded in darkness for eons. It was foolish, she knew, to take pleasure in knowing their kiss might've lessened his sorrows, whatever they were, but she did.

Perdita looked around for Hensley and saw with some relief the coach was already approaching. She could not wait another minute this close to Samuel. He and his companions had confirmed her worst nightmares.

Thank heavens for Vaughn.

Hensley had their driver stop the coach, and he helped her inside. The velvet cushions were cold, but she sighed in relief when Hensley placed a foot warmer at her feet.

"Where to now, miss?" Hensley asked.

"Home, I suppose." She parted the curtains on the opposite side of the square, but then she held up a hand. "Wait. Stay here. I should like to go to that shop. The one just there."

She pointed at the little jewelry shop across the street. She could have sworn she'd seen Vaughn entering it. Had she been dreaming merely because she was thinking of him just now? There was only one way to find out.

❦ 3 ❦

She climbed back out of the coach, heading directly for the row of shops. If it was Vaughn, she needed to tell him what she'd overheard in Gunter's. He had a right to know Samuel's intentions. He might have an idea of how to protect her against the man since Samuel had made it clear he wanted to get her alone.

Hensley closed the coach door behind her and followed her as she passed a milliner's shop and reached the jeweler's. She peered into the windows, which were frosted around the edges from the cold, but she couldn't see Vaughn.

Perhaps he'd gone deeper into the shop. She tugged on the brass door handle. It creaked open, and she slipped inside. The little shop was warm, but a faint musty smell emanated from the shelves where a variety of necklaces hung on stands and both bracelets and rings were displayed in glass cases. It was clear from the designs that these jewelry items were old, not newly fashioned.

Perdita peered around the shop, searching for Vaughn. She paused behind a row of tall shelves, considering the possibility that she'd only seen a gentleman who bore a passing resemblance to him.

A voice came from the other side of the wall of jewels behind which Perdita stood. "My lord, what may I do for you?"

Perdita perked up at the sound and was prepared to seek out the jeweler, but something held her back. She stayed hidden and peered between the dusty shelves, fighting the need to sneeze with one hand. She glimpsed an elderly shopkeeper with a hooked nose and spectacles speaking with a tall man with dark-blond hair. The man stood with his back to her, but Perdita was positive it was Vaughn.

"What can I get for this?" Vaughn held out a pocket watch, a very old but beautiful piece. Its silver cover glinted with light as it swung from a fine chain. The jeweler took it and held it up, leaving Vaughn to shift slightly. His face turned away from the jeweler, offering Perdita a glimpse of his profile and the pain etched in his features.

"Well now, let me take a look." The jeweler paused to push his glasses up the bridge of his nose and studied the watch closely.

"Finely made, with the Darlington family crest... Forty pounds, I should think. Are you quite sure you want to part with it, my lord?" The jeweler eyed the watch and then Vaughn. Perdita held her breath. Hensley shifted behind her, and she threw out a hand, catching his arm and raising her other hand to her lips to indicate silence. She did not want to interrupt whatever Vaughn was doing.

It appeared as though he was selling off his family heirlooms. Given the condition of his home—the lack of furnishings and general disrepair—it shouldn't have surprised her. However, if she was being honest, she didn't want to think of Vaughn as so destitute he was selling such a personal item. Her heart gave a painful twinge as she held her breath, listening.

"Forty? I suppose that's a fair enough price. Is there a ring which I might trade it for?" Vaughn set the pocket watch on the counter between him and the jeweler. His fingers didn't immediately let go of the watch. Perdita's heart gave another painful jerk. He was looking at rings? Why would he wish to sell a watch for a ring?

Then a thought struck her. Was the ring for her?

The jeweler lifted a velvet box onto the counter. "These here are quite lovely." Perdita stood on tiptoe to get a better view. She was thankful the shelves were open for her to peer through.

"This one here, is it a ruby?" Vaughn pointed at a ring. She couldn't see which because his body was blocking her view.

"Yes, a fine ruby. I suppose we could make a fair trade for the watch," the jeweler said.

"Good." Vaughn nudged the watch toward him. "Do you have a box for it?"

"I do." The jeweler disappeared into the back and moments later emerged with a small blue velvet box. He placed the ring inside and handed it back to Vaughn.

"Thank you." Vaughn took the box and tucked it securely into his coat and lifted his hat off the counter.

"Good day, my lord," the jeweler said as Vaughn turned toward the door—and Perdita. Perdita grasped Hensley and propelled him around the opposite end of the shelf, just missing being seen by Vaughn as he left. Once she was sure Vaughn was no longer inside, she and Hensley moved around the shelf and approached the counter where Vaughn had stood. The jeweler was still putting the set of rings back beneath the glass display counter.

"Oh! Good day, miss" the jeweler said. "I didn't realize you'd come in. How may I assist you?" He brushed his hands on his apron and readjusted his glasses with a warm smile.

Perdita noticed Vaughn's watch still sitting on the counter and tried to act slightly interested. "This is a lovely watch. May I see it?" she asked.

The jeweler eyed her quizzically. "The old pocket watch?"

She nodded, chancing one glance at the door. There was no sign of Vaughn returning.

"Of course." The jeweler set the watch down on the counter so Perdita could examine it. It was indeed an old watch, possibly Vaughn's father's or even his grandfather's. How could he bear to part with it? For a ring, no less?

She hadn't thought what it meant to provide evidence to support their story of an engagement. Had Vaughn believed he needed proof such as this? Or was it for a mistress? For some reason, she didn't think so. If he was as destitute as she now believed, he could not afford a mistress. That left her with the sad knowledge that the ring must be for her, and he had sold his watch for it. She had to buy it back. He had sold the watch, one she suspected was dear to him, for a ring she believed he meant to give to her. Therefore, she would make sure he got his watch back when the time was right. Vaughn was a proud man, and she would not endanger his pride by letting him know she'd witnessed this moment.

"How much for it?"

"Pardon, miss?" The jeweler's brows rose.

"How much to buy the watch? I'd like to buy it." She didn't want Vaughn to lose one of the last pieces of his family's past if she could help it.

"Well...I believe fifty pounds is fair."

She met his gaze. "But you traded it for forty."

"Forty-five then," the jeweler countered.

She lifted her chin. "Forty-two."

The jeweler stuck out his chin as well. "Forty-three."

"Agreed." She lifted her reticule onto the counter and counted out the notes. She rarely carried large sums of money, but she had planned to do a bit of shopping today after meeting with Lysandra. She hadn't expected it to be for her false fiancé.

She had the jeweler wrap it for her and then entrusted the box to Hensley.

"We're going home now, miss?" His hesitant tone implied his hope at the thought.

"Not a lover of clandestine meetings or secret missions, Hensley?" she teased. The footman, a man close to her age, blushed to the roots of his hair.

"It isn't that, miss... I just worry about you, is all."

The footman's honest comment caught her off guard.

"Worry about me?" she asked. He was unable to meet her eyes.

"I shouldn't have said that, miss. My apologies." He continued to avoid her gaze, and she didn't force him to speak of it further. Mostly because she was afraid to hear what he would say. There was an infuriating pity that came from servants when they dealt with spinsters, as though even downstairs they felt sorry for the unmarried maids who aged on the shelf.

The thought made her sour. Women had a right to aspire to other positions than simply being a wife and mother, did they not? Yet those were the only positions society valued for them. It wasn't her fault she didn't wish to be seen as a broodmare. The idea filled her with a defiant purpose. Once she and Vaughn were done with this charade and Milburn had lost interest, she would devote herself to seeing her astronomy essays published.

"We have one more stop to make," Perdita announced. "Have the driver take us to Half Moon Street." Then she climbed into the coach and listened for Hensley to give orders to the driver.

She peered eagerly out of the coach window as they reached Lennox House. It was a stunningly built structure that emanated both power and beauty. Her warm breath clouded the glass. She rubbed her gloved hand on the window to remove some of the fog for a better look.

The coach came to a stop, and Perdita instructed Hensley to wait with the driver for her. Depending on how furious her friend Rosalind was at her request, it was possible Perdita would be cast back into the street. A small bout of nerves rose up in her, but she shoved them down. The two were friends, and although she had not had a chance to visit Rosalind since she'd married Lord Lennox and moved into his house, things shouldn't have changed much, or so she hoped.

She rapped the large silver knocker and waited. The butler answered, and she was relieved to be allowed in once he had made the proper inquiries.

The butler directed her to a drawing room. Rosalind was working at a writing desk by the fire.

"Perdita." Rosalind rose once she entered the room. "How are you?" Her voice lilted with a Scottish accent, one she no longer tried to hide as much as she used to. The accent rendered the dark-haired woman utterly charming with a touch of that Highland wildness.

"I am well, and you?"

"Very well." Rosalind's gray eyes twinkled. "Have you come to discuss your investments?"

"Yes, well, possibly. It is a matter of business, but it is also a bit delicate in nature."

Her friend's open smile turned to a frown. "Shall we sit?" Rosalind led her to a dark-red brocade settee and poured a cup of tea from a pot on the table.

"Thank you." Perdita steeled herself for what she had to do. It was not like her to make such requests of friends.

Rosalind seemed to notice her hesitation. "We are friends, Perdita. Ask whatever you came to ask."

"It is a rather long tale, but I shall try to be brief. I'm trying to escape an engagement to Samuel Milburn, whose intentions I do not trust. I do not wish to go into details, but I am under some rather unsavory pressure to accept. I made a bargain with Viscount Darlington to act as my fiancé in order to put Milburn off. But Darlington's price in aiding me is..." She choked on the words, hating to have to speak this way to a friend. "Well, his fortunes have taken a poor turn, and he wishes me to ask for your husband to involve him in his next investment." There. She'd said it, even though it left a bitter taste upon her tongue.

For a long moment, Rosalind didn't speak, her brows furrowed as she studied Perdita carefully. Did she think Perdita was only trying to use her? Was she reconsidering their friendship?

"Darlington, you say?" Rosalind pursed her lips and thought. "I haven't met him, but I've heard of him. Bit of a wild fellow. Are you sure you want to attach yourself to him so publicly?"

Perdita sipped her tea and nodded. "Despite what you may have heard of Samuel Milburn, I assure you that man is a brute. He has every intention of breaking me if he can compromise me into marriage."

"*Break* you?"

"My spirit, and perhaps more."

Rosalind's pensive gaze turned into a scowl. "I haven't heard much about this Milburn fellow, but if he has you frightened, we shan't let him succeed in putting you in a position where you must marry him." She lifted a small bell from her tea tray and rang it. A footman appeared, and Rosalind spoke. "Please tell my husband I wish to speak with him."

The servant bowed and vanished.

"Is there really no way other than to enlist Lord Darlington's help? I'm sure you've heard the rumors about him," Rosalind said.

"I have, but I believe there may be more to him than the rumors give him credit for. When presented with a situation such as I have given him, he wished to help and asked only this favor in return. It's not what I expected of a notorious rogue, but I trust him. Does that sound very strange and foolish?"

"To trust a rogue? That is neither strange nor foolish, if it's the right rogue. I will ask my husband what he knows of Darlington."

"Thank you, Rosalind. I cannot tell you how much I appreciate your help. It's so upsetting to have to ask it of you."

"Nonsense. This is precisely what friends are for." Rosalind covered Perdita's hand and gave it a gentle pat.

Lord Lennox appeared a moment later. He was a tall man with piercing blue eyes and blond hair, not unlike Vaughn, but there was a wild desperation to Vaughn that Lennox did not share. He was calm, relaxed, *settled*. Vaughn had a leaner appearance to him and a grimness to his bearing that gave him a melancholy darkness.

"You summoned me?" While Ashton's tone was cool, his lips were curled in a teasing smile. He came over to Rosalind and pressed a kiss to her hand.

"This is my dear friend, Perdita Darby. She is also a customer of our bank," Rosalind explained. "Perdy, please tell my husband what you told me."

Perdita detailed what she had guessed of Samuel Milburn and his intentions, as well as her scheme with Darlington and the favor required as payment for his services.

"I've met him a few times around London. Not a bad fellow, or so I hear," Lennox mused. "Milburn, on the other hand...well, I've heard about his mistress. The one who fell to her death. An accident, they say, but I'm not sure I believe that."

Perdita nodded.

"So, Darlington is keen to invest with me?" Ashton leaned back in his chair thoughtfully. "He wouldn't be the first, but there are good reasons why I am selective about whom I take into my confidence. Most believe the risks I take are too great, but they simply do not understand my longer plans and fail to see that in the end there is very little risk at all. But I require trust, and not all are willing to give it. I will not have my every action second-guessed. I believe he'd make a good partner. He has a good head on his shoulders, and I understand he was quite successful before his parents passed. The debts they left him with were extraordinary and ruined his own small fortune."

Lennox shared a long glance with Rosalind before he stood and nodded.

"Very well, tell Darlington he may call upon me after the New Year. I shall discuss my next venture with him, and he can decide then if he still wishes to take part."

His words were such a relief that Perdita was overcome with gratitude. "Thank you, Lord Lennox. Truly."

"Any friend of Rosalind's is a friend of mine." He kissed her hand, and with a lingering glance at his wife, which made the lady blush, he left them alone.

"Silly man," Rosalind muttered, though she was smiling.

Perdita had to agree. Lord Lennox was a silly, wonderful man. *Wait until I tell Vaughn. He'll be so pleased.* She had guaranteed not just an introduction, but involvement in Lennox's next venture. Perhaps she would survive Christmas after all.

4

Vaughn felt naked without his pocket watch. It had been a few days since he'd sold it, and he and Barnaby were now headed to Lothbrook. He kept reaching into his coat for the watch, and his hand came back empty.

The piece had belonged to his grandfather, handcrafted by Thomas Mudge himself, and it had been given to him by his own father when he turned sixteen. He'd had it for so long he'd forgotten what it was like not to have it sitting securely in his waistcoat pocket. It was the last thing of any real value he had left to sell.

But obtaining a ring for his future bride had been important. It sat safely in his coat pocket, but he kept checking the box to make sure it hadn't vanished. Between his secret plan to actually seduce her for her fortune and using her to become acquainted with Baron Lennox, he was already indebted to her.

Vaughn was not a man who liked to owe a debt. The ring was his last chance to prove he could offer her something before he ended up owning everything that had once been hers. Even if he had something else left to sell, he couldn't stomach visiting that jeweler's shop again. *Selling my past to secure my future.* He only hoped it would work.

The coach he sat in was stuffed with people like hens in a coop, but a damned public coach was all he could afford. Farmers sat on either side of him, their shoulders pressing into his. The odor of the barnyard was rather too pungent for Vaughn to stomach. He'd taken turns holding his breath and attempting to breathe through his mouth. It helped, but *only* just.

The coach came to a halt at the crossroads, and the driver shouted that they'd reached Lothbrook. Despite the press of bodies, he was chilled to the bone from the icy wind that cut through the coach's cracks. Vaughn surged out of the coach, his boots crunching into a light layer of snow. He stretched his legs, relieved to be away from the crush of the vehicle and its occupants.

The town was covered in snow, the roofs of the shops and houses capped with ice. The skies were dark with wintry clouds that seemed to stretch the darkness across the village and swallow up the meager lights from lamps still sitting in windowsills.

Lord, he missed Lothbrook in the late summer. Even when he'd been here last September, the town had been full of flowers, and the days had seemed endless.

"Oi!" The driver's shout caught Vaughn's attention. He spun in time to see Barnaby rush to catch the valises the driver had unceremoniously dropped to the ground. Vaughn scowled as he and Barnaby collected their cases and walked toward the edge of town.

"What a tosser!" Barnaby muttered as he tramped alongside Vaughn, carrying one of the cases while Vaughn managed the other.

"Agreed," Vaughn said. "But it is the season of forgiveness. And if all goes well, dear Barnaby, we shall never have to suffer travel by public coach again."

"Humph. That's *assuming* you win Miss Darby's heart, my lord. She's a crafty chit, that one," Barnaby noted. Other men might have cuffed a servant for such frankness, but Vaughn had always preferred to employ those with a mind to speak up and share observations. They also tended to be cheaper.

"I think I stand a fair chance. She was quite taken with me the other night." Vaughn puffed out his chest and ignored his valet rolling his eyes. He hadn't imagined Perdita's impassioned reaction to his kiss or his touch. He was an excellent lover and had never mistaken a woman's passion.

The Darby estate was not far, but in the cold...well, it wasn't exactly a pleasant stroll. By the time they set foot on the long stone path that led to the Darbys' country house, Vaughn's feet were frozen, and he couldn't feel his face. The merry candlelight framed in the windows beckoned him forward, and he knocked upon the door. A footman opened the door, bracing himself against the cold.

"Pardon me, my lord, but you are Lord Darlington, correct? Miss Darby has been expecting you and feared you might run late," the young man replied. Damnation, he'd wished to arrive earlier than this. *Bloody public coaches. If we hadn't had to stop every three miles to let off farmers and their damned chickens, we wouldn't have been late.*

"Yes." Vaughn hastened up the steps and gratefully had Barnaby hand them his luggage. Another footman took his hat and coat.

The numerous servants who dashed about the house were all decked out in fine winter livery. They passed several maids on their way up the stairs, and Vaughn swallowed a pang of guilt for his one beleaguered little maid, Pippa, who was responsible for a town-house that should retain at least a dozen more. That would be one of the first things he changed if he could get a successful return on his future investments with Lennox.

"Please, this way. I'll show you to your room. I'm afraid you've missed dinner, but Miss Perdita insisted you have a full tray brought to your room when you arrived."

"Did she now?" He was surprised at her thoughtfulness, but then again, between her and her friend Alexandra, Perdita was the sweeter of the two. Alexandra...now *that* woman had a cornered badger's temper.

Vaughn followed the footman up the stairs, Barnaby trailing behind, muttering about old, cold country houses. They were shown to an elegant chamber, the same one he'd stayed in before when he'd come down for the garden party in September. The large bed looked warm and inviting, as did the fire in the hearth. Thick Aubusson carpets covered the floors, making the room feel cozy.

His own chambers back in London were in a severe state of disrepair, not at all like the dark oak wainscoting here, which contrasted with the dark-green embossed wallpapers with gold ivy patterns. Even the bed hangings, a rich brocade of dark gold, matched the coverlet and sheets.

After the footman left, Barnaby set about putting away his master's clothes in a large wardrobe. By the way his valet sighed wistfully, he knew the young man missed having real furnishings as much as he did.

Barnaby approached the shaving stand, where hot water stood ready in a pristine blue-and-white basin. Clean clothes and face towels were neatly folded next to a bar of expensive milled soap. The valet turned back to him, a little streak of guilt flashing in his brown eyes.

"Perhaps the country isn't as bad as you remember?" Vaughn said with a rueful smile.

"No, my lord." Barnaby's face turned red, and he hastily resumed his work.

Vaughn leaned back against the bed and sighed. Part of him still couldn't believe he was here. But he truly was desperate enough to accept Perdita's offer of a false engagement, because he knew he could seduce her into wanting a real one. Women were quite easy to woo, after all, so long as they weren't in love with another, as Alexandra had been. Of course, should Perdita deny her own desires for him, he would at least still have the meeting with Lennox to help secure his future.

Vaughn straightened as a worried thought streaked through his mind. Was it possible that Perdita already loved another?

Surely if she did, she would have convinced *that* man to participate in this game, not him. With a low growl, Vaughn retrieved the ring and tucked the box into a drawer in one of the night tables by the bed.

He turned at a soft knock upon the bedroom door.

"Enter."

The door opened, and Perdita slipped inside, followed by a footman with a tray.

"Lord Darlington, I wanted to make sure you've been properly seen to. Set the tray on the table, please, Hensley." She gestured to the mahogany fireside table. The footman set the tray down before departing.

Vaughn was momentarily distracted by the sight of the covered dishes. His nose picked up the scents of soup, fresh bread, roast beef, potatoes, and peas. He even glimpsed a berry tart on a small plate. God bless the woman—real food was just what he needed after his long journey.

He forced his thoughts away from the food for a moment, no matter how much his stomach grumbled about it. He approached a fine Chinese lacquer commode in the corner of the room, which contained decanters of brandy and whisky.

"Care for a drink?" he offered, hoping she would sit with him in the two leather chairs facing the fire.

"No, thank you," she replied. Perdita played with her skirts, and the nervous movement almost made him smile. Her dress was blue, with Van Dyke sleeves trimmed with Belgian lace. Her bodice and hem were dusted with silver embroidery, and a lock of her dark hair dangled loose upon the creamy skin of her neck. The woman looked positively edible, like Christmas pudding and a glass of sherry.

"Perdita." He spoke her name, unsure what else to say before he asked the question that was now plaguing him.

She inclined her head. "Vaughn." There was a long silence between them before he approached her.

"There is no other man, is there?" he asked, his heart pounding as he waited for her to reassure him this entire charade wasn't a fool's errand.

Her brows knit in confusion. "Other man?"

"Yes. One you love, who for some reason isn't riding in here on a bloody white charger to save you from Samuel Milburn."

She paled and her fists clenched. A blush replaced the pallor in her cheeks. "No, of course there isn't another. If there was, I would be engaged, not begging someone like you to help me."

He tilted his head. "Someone like *me*? What, pray tell, makes me the fortunate man for this situation?"

Perdita glared at him. "Because... Wait, why are you asking me this *now*? I thought we'd agreed to this..." The look of anger faded to panic, and for some reason that cut into the thick wall around his frozen heart, warming it ever so slightly.

"I did agree," he said. "I merely wish to make sure that I'm not doing this when someone else should be. If there's another who loves you, he should be here. Not me."

Perdita blew out a breath. "No. There's no one. It's why I need you."

Bloody hell, that shouldn't have aroused him, yet it did. The thought of her needing him, even in this way, was enough to fill his head with wicked thoughts that would send her running if she could only read his mind at that moment. He wanted to make her need him in a thousand other ways, until her body could no longer bear the touch of another because only his would satisfy her. He pushed the rush of hungry thoughts aside and focused on their conversation.

"And here I am, minus the white horse, in my rusted armor." He gave her a mocking bow.

She curtseyed elegantly in return. "I suppose that makes me a damsel in a dire state of distress? Good heavens, I'm the heroine of a gothic novel."

"So it would seem." He caught her hand, lifting it to his lips. "I should love to see you fleeing down some darkened corridor, your hair unbound, your body clad only in the flimsiest of nightgowns, clutching a candelabra as you flee from a dark stranger. I would take you into my arms and rescue you. Then, of course, I would make mad passionate love to you so that all worries of dark strangers would be forgotten."

Her pupils widened as he spoke. He took a moment to caress the back of her hand with his fingertips as he watched, drinking in every minute expression of hers.

She seemed torn between laughter and consternation. "*That's* what I am rewarded with? You coming here just to seduce me? I waited a fortnight for you, made sure the cook prepared the best supper fresh for you, and—"

Vaughn didn't let her finish. It had always been his policy to silence a chattering woman the most pleasurable way he knew how. He pulled one arm around her waist and tugged her into his arms. She gasped against his lips, and he couldn't resist smiling.

Lord, she tasted divine. She shivered against him, and he slid one hand through her hair, tugging lightly on the strands. Perdita whimpered and curled an arm around his neck, kissing him back harder.

Seducing her was going to be easy.

He slid his other hand down her body, cupping her backside, then gave it a playful smack. She jolted, and he winced when her teeth sank into his lip.

"Ow!" He pulled back, letting her go as he touched where his lip stung. Perdita steadied herself against the nearest chair, brushing her loosened hair back from her face. He had ruined her coiffure, and she looked as though she'd been thoroughly tumbled in bed. It was a good look for her—soft, vulnerable, and a bit mussed. He licked his sore lip and grinned.

"You don't want a bit of compromise with your engagement? I am ready to offer *all* of my services, not just my reputation." He waggled his eyebrows at her.

"You *struck* me!"

He flashed a crooked smile. "I spanked you, darling. There's quite a difference. Tell me you didn't feel the jolt when I did." He knew she'd deny it, and he was going to enjoy proving her wrong over the next several days.

"I felt nothing!" she snapped.

"Then why are you complaining if you felt nothing?" he teased, twisting her words.

She spun on her heel and headed for the door. "Oh!"

He caught her from behind and pulled her back as he closed the door, trapping her in his arms. "Perdy, wait."

"Do not call me Perdy," she growled and turned to look over her shoulder at him. Their noses brushed, and her eyes flashed with a beautiful fire. It made him hot all over.

"Why not? I know Alexandra calls you that." He smiled as his gaze lowered to her lips. She turned to face him, smacking his chest with her hand.

"Because she is my friend. Friends call me Perdy, but not you." He had to bite back a groan of hunger seeing the fire in her eyes just then. When had a woman's eyes ever been so captivating? He couldn't recall a time before this when he was so fascinated by a woman's gaze.

"We aren't friends," he agreed. "But we are affianced, aren't we?" He caught one of her wrists and brought her hand to his lips, kissing her palm.

"What are you doing?" But she was staring at him as he kissed her palm. Then he began to work kisses up her arm, inch by inch.

"Reminding you"—he paused to kiss her between each set of words—"that we...need to get...more comfortable...with each other...and that means...more of...*this*." He tilted her head up and pressed a slow kiss to her stunned lips.

He could hear the little growl she made and felt it as it rumbled from her chest. There was nothing more delightful than proving a woman wrong about her desires. It wasn't about force, but about slow, thoughtful seduction. Not only of the body, but of the mind and heart as well.

He kissed her for another long moment, waiting until he felt her melting into him, and then he released her. She stood there, eyes glazed with desire, lips swollen, hair delightfully mussed, and her skirts wrinkled where he'd clenched the fabric tight to keep his own frayed control in check.

"I have something for you." He walked to the night table and retrieved the ring. Perdita was pale again, her eyes fixed on the little velvet box.

"Vaughn, you didn't need to—"

"I did and I wanted to. Even if this engagement is false, I would still provide my bride with a token of my affection." He held the box out. He did not kneel, nor did he present it with any fanfare. That simply wasn't the sort of man he was. If she couldn't see what he was offering her and understand the sacrifice he had made, then she wasn't the woman he had thought she was.

She took the box from him, their hands meeting briefly, yet still causing a spark at their touch. He watched her face as she opened the box, memorizing every detail. The way her eyes darkened the moment she spied the ruby ring, the way she tilted her head, the loose curl bouncing against her neck and shoulders, and finally the way her lips parted on a soft gasp.

"Vaughn, no, this is too precious. You must not give me this. Not simply to further a charade." She took a tiny step toward him, the open box held out. He reached up and clasped her hands, closing them over it.

He captured her eyes with his, letting her see how serious he was. "I insist."

"But—"

"No," he responded in a clipped tone. He knew what she intended to say—that he had so little to give as it was—but he *needed* her to have this, even if he could not bring himself to explain why. There were some things a man could not share with his intended bride.

Perdita opened the box again and looked at the ring. "It's very lovely." When she spoke there was a small catch in her voice, and it made his chest clench and his throat tighten.

This is all I can give you. The last of what I have left.

"You like it?" He felt like a fool, begging for scraps of her attention, needing to hear that the sacrifice of his grandfather's pocket watch had not been in vain. She traced the ruby stone and the two small diamonds flanking it, bit her lip, and nodded.

"I do. I don't believe I've ever owned anything so lovely." She paused, and then with a radiant smile at him, she asked, "May I wear it now, or must I wait until Christmas?"

He cleared his throat, that strange tightness still there, making it hard to speak.

"Now is fine, quite fine," he finally managed.

She plucked the ring from the box and slid it on her ring finger.

It was almost a perfect fit, with just a bit of looseness, which could be easily remedied when she visited the jeweler in the village. The ruby gleamed in the firelight.

"Thank you." Perdita stood up on her tiptoes and kissed him. The lingering sweet taste of her felt different from any other kiss. This wasn't one of lust, desire, or anger. This was simply *something else*. It evoked a flutter of strange and unidentifiable emotions in him that he didn't want to think about.

A rose hue accented her cheekbones as she touched her lips. "Eat your dinner before it gets cold, and rest well. Tomorrow the holiday festivities begin in earnest, and I shall need my white knight at my side, rusty armor or no."

Without another word, she was gone, leaving Vaughn to stare after her, his hands twitching with the sense they missed holding her.

5

Perdita lingered in the hallway, watching the coaches pull up outside. Ladies in cloaks and men in greatcoats ascended the steps to the house. Her parents stood ready to greet their guests. Perdita stayed back, slightly distracted, wondering when Vaughn was going to come down. He had ordered a tray for breakfast early that morning, so she'd missed seeing him at the table. After last night, she felt oddly nervous and a bit excited.

Because he's dangerous and the charade you're playing is far too exhilarating. Her inner voice was happy to chastise her for her foolish behavior around Vaughn. But she hadn't forgotten why she was doing this. To save Papa, as well as herself.

She twisted the ruby ring on her finger, even though it felt quite comfortable there. Vaughn had given it to her, not someone else. To think she'd been worried about him buying it for another woman. A hint of a smile escaped her lips, but she wiped it away. This thing between her and Vaughn was nothing more than a cunning deception, and she had to remember that. She would return the ring and his pocket watch once this was all was over. It was the least she could do.

Her mother called to her. "Perdy, dear, come and see to the

guests." She joined her parents with a sigh and a forced air of happiness. A pair of men rode up on horseback, their fine beasts kicking at the fresh snow that had fallen early that morning. She started to smile as they approached, but she halted. Her slippers slid on the snowy steps as she recognized one of the men.

Samuel Milburn had arrived. Fear spiked inside her, and she fought the urge to turn and run.

"Miss Darby." Samuel came up the steps, grinning.

To everyone but her, he appeared to be nothing more than a handsome man with dark hair and dark-brown eyes, with no hint of the real darkness within him. But she knew it was there. She'd heard him herself in Gunter's, laughing with his companions about how he would enjoy breaking her. There was a darkness in his eyes, one that promised pain, not just for her but for her family if she defied him. It was the look of a man who believed he held all the cards and was simply biding his time before collecting his winnings. Knowing what she did about him made Perdita want to run and hide, even though she usually preferred to stand and fight.

She would be damned if she'd let him turn her into property by blackmailing her. However, he was a guest, and she could not prove his evil inclinations to her parents, so she would simply have to be careful during the house party.

That was why Vaughn was here. She hoped his very presence would protect her in ways she could not manage on her own. As much as she hated relying on a man, she felt she could trust him in this matter. And he seemed to know the sort of man Samuel was and thought the man a bastard, just as she did.

"Mr. Milburn, welcome," Perdita said, her tone cool but polite. There was no need to anger him, not if the charade with Vaughn was to succeed. The goal was to simply remove his interest in her, not provide him with reasons to desire retribution.

"Thank you, Miss Darby. I trust you have given thought to what we spoke of when last we met?" He flashed a charming grin that didn't fool her one bit. She did not miss the look of calculation he gave her or the way he eyed her critically from head to toe, the way a man would study a horse he planned to acquire at Tattersall's.

"I have." It was all she would admit to. The time to reveal her engagement had not yet come, and she wouldn't let it slip until Vaughn decided the time was right. He knew how to deal with a man like Milburn.

She stepped back and let him pass, along with his companion. Another coach was arriving, and she was relieved to have an excuse to leave Mr. Milburn to be seen to his room.

Another dozen guests arrived before Perdita was allowed to retire to her room before lunch was served. She decided to stay in her light-green wool gown with red trimming on the sleeves and hem. Most of the ladies would be changing out of their carriage dresses, but since she hadn't traveled, she would do well enough in her day gown.

The entire notion of changing one's dress three or four times a day frustrated her. There were a dozen other things she would prefer to accomplish on any given day, and having to change to suit the time of day or activity was both bothersome and unnecessary. Men didn't have to change clothes so frequently, and she was envious of that freedom.

She chose to visit the library on the second floor on the opposite wing of the house, hoping to catch a glimpse of Vaughn. Most of the guests were staying in the east wing of the house, but she had placed Vaughn on the west side closer to her own chambers.

There was no sign of him in the corridor, however. It was possible he was taking his repose in his bedchamber, or perhaps she had missed him on the stairs. He could be in one of the dozen other rooms in the house now, chatting with the other gentlemen. Or perhaps he had gone riding in the snow. The thought she might not see him was upsetting.

I don't want to miss him...yet I do. Then she shook her head. *I miss his kisses, that is all. I don't know the man well enough to miss him.*

She and Lysandra had discussed on more than one occasion how a man could distract a woman from her academic focuses with their passions. At the time, Perdita had no personal experience to argue with, but now...now she understood completely how a man could so thoroughly disrupt one's thoughts.

Perdita went to one of the bookcases and took out a leather portfolio containing several essays she was working on. She then settled into a little window seat in the library, her latest astronomy paper resting on her lap. She still had revisions to make, but today she wanted to read it for clarity and construction before she sent it on to Lysandra. She raised her legs up in a bent position so that her red satin slippers peeped out from the hem of her skirts, and she rested the pages on her knees.

She wasn't sure how long she'd sat there before she had the distinct impression that someone was watching her. It was far too easy to lose herself in her work, and apparently she hadn't noticed someone enter the library. The hairs on the back of her neck rose, and she tried not to panic, her first concern being that Samuel Milburn had found her alone. She raised her head and glanced about.

A lone figure leaned against the shelf not too far from where she sat in her alcove. When she saw who it was she wasn't afraid, but her heart still jerked into a rushed pace.

"Vaughn!" she hissed. "You startled me!" She set her paper aside as he came over. She tried to stand, but he prevented this by sliding onto the seat beside her.

"You were quite engrossed in whatever you were reading. I didn't wish to intrude upon your thoughts." He gently lifted her feet and stretched her legs over his lap, the position highly scandalous, but the cozy intimacy was so irresistible she didn't protest...much.

"We shouldn't..."

"Nonsense." He moved her skirts so he could place one of his large hands on her left calf.

Perdita jolted. "No, Vaughn..." She grabbed his wrist, and he lifted his face to hers.

"Easy, my sweet, just breathe." His fingers stilled on her leg, and he leaned in to brush his lips over hers. His gentle kiss calmed her, even though a rush of shivers danced along her skin.

"Better?" he asked with a smile against her lips.

She nodded. "Yes. I was just frightened."

"That's what makes passion exciting." He paused to stroke her leg again. "But I will take things as slowly as you wish."

"But I thought you liked control." She said the words softly, even though no one but the books could witness this scandalous moment.

"I do, darling. I adore control. But only once the lady feels safe with me."

"I feel safe with you," she replied truthfully.

"Good. That matters to me greatly." He continued to stroke her calf, and she closed her eyes briefly, relishing his touch.

His fingers were long and elegant but not delicate. Beautiful hands...for a handsome man. Perdita watched in fascination as his hands touched her. The heat of his palms soaked through her white stockings to her skin, and she couldn't stop the wave of heat that followed through her whole body.

A true rogue could conjure up passion like a wizard. He could cast spells that made her forsake rational thought with only a wicked smile and a tender caress from her ankle up to her knee. He let her skirts fall back down over her legs but kept his hand on her skin. There was something seductive about his hand beneath her dress, touching her legs, without being able to see what he was doing. It was as though the excitement of what he *might* do next was greater than what he actually did. She wiggled slightly but made no attempt to flee.

"Now, what were you reading that had you so enraptured?" Vaughn was gazing at her, his blue eyes clear as a summer sky. The sunlight came in through the window, trickling down his golden hair and illuminating the strands until they glowed in a halo about his head. His lips were slightly curved, as though he was lost in a pleasant but possibly scandalous daydream. It was the sort of expression a woman could stare at for hours and wish desperately that it was she the gentleman had upon his mind.

"Oh, I was just..." She tried to tuck the pages of her astronomy essay behind her, but he reached around her body and pulled the essay in front of him to read it.

"Please, don't—"

"Shh. I'm *reading*," he teased as he continued to stroke her left calf in tickling circles with his fingertips, then paused. "Astronomy?" he asked.

"Are you surprised that a woman might have a love of the sciences?"

"Surprised perhaps, but far from displeased. It has been my experience that far too many men lack a proper interest. They learn enough to feign knowledge at their gentlemen's clubs and pass along half-remembered conclusions as if they were their own. It can be quite depressing when one is looking for decent, intelligent conversation."

"And you? Do you have an interest in the sciences?"

"I do, though I admit that I am woefully ignorant of the more detailed elements of the subject of this piece. It seems quite brilliant." His eyes ran the length of the page as though scanning it.

"You think so?" She couldn't resist wanting to preen at his praise.

Vaughn did not answer at first, and his brow was furrowed as he studied the pages. "Do you know the man who wrote this? His observations are quite interesting, though I daresay some of the calculations are over my head."

"Er—yes. I know the man. He's pursuing publication of the piece, once it is ready." She was not going to tell him she was the article's author. He was no doubt the sort of man who believed women did not belong in the sciences.

"I imagine he will have success then. Does he often have you read his work beforehand?"

She nodded. It didn't feel right to conceal anything from him, but this was a part of her life that held no connection to the bargain they'd made, and she would not share this secret with him. She was far too accustomed to men thinking ill of women who had minds of their own, and did not need his ridicule whilst they were trying to keep up their engagement act. "Where were you this morning? I thought you might come down for breakfast."

Vaughn smiled his infuriating cat-in-the-cream grin. "A man ought to have a few mysteries about him." He moved his hand beneath her skirts again, this time even higher, until he touched the soft garter that held the stocking up. He flicked the silk ribbon bows, and another wave of heat rolled through her.

"Would you like me to teach you about passion?" he asked, his voice now velvety soft.

Despite her body's cries of yes, she shook her head. "No, thank you, I'm well versed in it."

He grinned, still toying with the bow of her garter. "Liar. You're afraid to risk it."

"I most certainly am not," she huffed, then curiosity got the better of her. "Risk what, exactly?"

"Falling in love with me, of course." His crooked grin should not have made her heart flutter, but it did.

"I see no danger of that, I assure you." She took the papers from him and climbed off her seat. She set her article on a nearby table and went toward the nearest bookshelf. There were three rows of shelves that were parallel to the door, and she often liked to hide behind the last one to go unseen if someone came to the library looking for her.

Perdita glanced over her shoulder and saw Vaughn following her. He trailed his fingertips along the surface of the walnut reading table. The burgundy waistcoat he wore went well with his dark-tan trousers. Perdita had to jerk her thoughts away from how well-fitted those trousers were.

"So...you say you know of passion, that you are well versed in it, but I assure you, you don't know what it means to be with *me*." He said this softly as he came up behind her. She faced the shelves, hidden from the rest of the library. Vaughn toyed with the flare of her skirts at her lower back, tugging on a red silk ribbon that trailed down her back from the sash at her waist.

"This is not part of our arrangement," she said at last, though less defiantly than she had intended.

"You misunderstand me. What I'm trying to say is that whenever Milburn sees us together, he needs to *believe* we are lovers." He leaned against her from behind, cornering her against the shelf. His lips feathered against her ear, and she shivered. Her womb clenched, and her knees ached.

"He will believe," she replied, though her words trembled.

"I have no doubts that you are a fine actress, but I fear that without some experience you will do no better than a young girl swooning over her first infatuation. Milburn will see it for what it is—drawing attention to itself and utterly unconvincing."

"And what would you suggest?"

"That you let go of your fears and allow me to guide you on a short voyage into those passions, while keeping your greater virtue intact. Only then will you be able to tap into those thoughts in Milburn's presence. Only then will he see in your eyes what you want him to see."

Perdita huffed. "I am sure you would say anything to get under a woman's skirts."

"True, I would. But it does not make my words any less reasonable."

Her eyes narrowed, but she relented. "I have found your kisses a pleasant enough diversion. I doubt whatever it is you have in mind will be much different." She threw out the challenge, and then her heart raced to see what he would do.

"And that, my dear, shows how much you have to learn." The heat of his body pressed against hers made her forget for a moment how to breathe.

"So you would teach me, then?" She kept her tone light, even though she was feeling strangely light-headed.

"Teach you to be wicked? Absolutely," Vaughn said. "When you sit across from me at dinner and I look at you, he will see in your eyes and through the blush of your cheeks that we spent an hour in the library together, doing *this*..." He lifted her skirts, traced his hand up her right leg beneath her petticoats, and touched her *there*.

Perdita gasped, but he covered her mouth with his other hand. Rather than be frightened that he was silencing her, she was excited by the way he took control. She clutched the shelf in front of her, a wet heat pooling between her thighs as he explored her with his fingers.

"He should see that I own you, that I have touched you here and tortured you until you were begging for sweet release." He murmured each wicked thought in her ear, and she struggled to stay standing. She wasn't afraid, not of his muffling her sounds or the gentle but firm exploration of her folds with his fingers. He knew just how to touch her, how to stroke her. She had never known being touched in such a way could feel so...*wild*. The rush of sensations below her waist, the way her nipples hardened against her corset, his warm breath against her neck, all mixed with the press of his body against hers from behind...it was too much.

"Show me your dark side, Perdita," Vaughn whispered, and she felt her body seize and come apart. Stars dotted her vision, and she felt herself falling. Strong arms caught her, lifting her back up.

She realized through the haze of her slowly dissipating climax that he was carrying her away from the bookshelves and back to the window seat. She blinked against the bright sunlight as he set her back down on the window seat's soft cushions. Her head was swimming with a thousand emotions, but most of her felt dazed, shaky, and confused. He had just touched her at the apex of her thighs, and she'd come undone. The sensations, the heated explosion inside her was like nothing she'd ever felt before.

She looked up at him, blinking as she tried to stay calm and not cry. What he'd done had her feeling open and vulnerable. She wanted him to hold her, keep her close while she came down from the steep height her body had climbed. He leaned over and brushed his lips over hers.

"Tonight at dinner, when I look at you, think of this moment, my hands on your bare skin between your pretty thighs. Milburn will see what you wish him to see."

With that he turned and walked away, leaving Perdita bewildered, her body lax yet trembling on a floating cloud of feelings she was too afraid to analyze. Vaughn was a *master* of sin, there was no doubt. She couldn't help but worry that a small part of her might indeed be in danger of falling in love with him.

Perhaps he was truly more dangerous to her than Samuel.

❦

VAUGHN RAPPED HIS KNUCKLES ON THE DOOR TO MR. DARBY'S study.

"Come in."

Vaughn entered and found Darby bent over his desk examining a collection of shells with a magnifying glass. Snow fell outside the bay window behind him, which would leave a fresh layer for any gentleman riding tomorrow.

Vaughn's impression of Darby was that he was a rather studious man, a man invested in the sciences. Just like his daughter, it would seem. He suspected she'd written that essay she'd been reviewing and she had tried to hide the fact from him. But her expression had given her away. Her face had been so open, her eyes so earnest in that moment as she seemed to yearn for his approval.

No doubt she was afraid he would be just like any other man and discount her ideas. But her arguments were sound and her conclusions logical. It was a paper worthy of publication, regardless of who had written it. He would find a way to convince her of that once they were married.

"Ah, Lord Darlington. I've been expecting you." Darby chuckled as he set the magnifying glass down.

"Well, I wasn't sure if...your daughter had informed you."

Vaughn was in uncharted territory here. He'd never expected to be in this situation, yet here he was.

"Your engagement? She mentioned it. I was a little surprised, of course. Perdy tells me almost everything, and she's never mentioned you before, except this past September." Darby studied him with a gentle curiosity. It surprised Vaughn. Most fathers with unmarried daughters would have been chasing a man like him off their estates unless they were desperate. Yet Darby was far more like his daughter than Vaughn might have guessed. He was of a rational mind, just like her.

"I admit we should have come to you at once, but I did not want to trap her into any commitment until she was sure she wished to marry me."

Darby chuckled. "Noble words for one of London's more notorious rogues, or so I hear. You aren't part of that League of Rogues are you?"

Vaughn shook his head. "No, certainly not." The League was not simply some club one could join, though gossip spoke of them as if it was. Investing with Ashton Lennox, one of the League members, was as close as he would get to being part of their number.

"Good, good. So you're here to ask for my permission to marry Perdita?"

He nodded.

"Well, as you know, my daughter has her own heart and mind. My opinion on the matter holds little weight. She will do exactly as she pleases."

"That may be true," Vaughn replied, "but I also believe she values your opinion. I feel duty bound to pass any test you might put me through so that she will feel you accept the match as well."

Darby tilted his head. "Are you aware that another gentleman here at the house has expressed an interest in Perdita's hand?"

"Samuel Milburn? Yes, I'm aware, although he has no idea of our engagement. We were hoping to have you announce our happy news tonight at dinner. We believe it might direct the other fellow to seek another bride." Vaughn knew full well that it would be hard to prevent Milburn from pursuing his blackmail on Perdita, but he secretly hoped that once Milburn saw that Vaughn was in fact going to marry her—assuming he could convince her it was a sound idea—that Milburn would give up.

"I see."

Vaughn waited, but Darby didn't speak further.

"You will make the announcement?" he prompted.

Rather than answer Vaughn, the older man stroked his chin, studying Vaughn as though he were a shell beneath his magnifying glass.

"*Why* do you want to marry my daughter? I'm aware of your financial troubles, but there are many heiresses worth far more that I'm sure you could easily win over. What makes my Perdita of such interest to you?"

That was the test he had been expecting. He had to answer carefully but also honestly. Darby had the look about him of a man who could read a person well. Vaughn reached for a conch shell and examined it.

"What makes this conch shell worth studying more than the rest tucked away on your shelves? The color of this shell and the exquisite pattern of its grooves make it unique among the rest. Perdita isn't like other ladies I've met. She's genuine. She challenges me without fear, and I find that engaging. She's a damned clever creature too. Did you know she's pursuing publication of her scholarly articles on astronomy? She told me she was reading them over for some gentleman, but the handwriting is too clear and neat to belong to a man. I recognized it at once as hers. Her conclusions are brilliant, and I plan to do everything in my power to assist in her pursuits." He smiled at the thought. "Watching her show up those old fellows at the astronomy society would be quite satisfying." Vaughn paused when he realized he'd been gushing over Perdita like a young boy.

Mr. Darby watched him with open amusement. "Glad to see your affections are well placed. But I won't offer my blessings until you *prove* your love. She can marry you or not as she chooses, but know that I have my eye on you, Darlington. Break her heart and I'll bury you in my woods where no one will ever find you."

The threat, though pleasantly delivered, had been unexpected. Darby cared deeply about his daughter. It would have made the older man proud to know his daughter protected him just as fiercely, but as Perdita had made no mention of the blackmail to her father, Vaughn would follow her lead and maintain his silence on the matter.

"Understood."

"Good. Now, why don't you help the other young lads collect the Yule log. We must light it tonight."

"Of course." Vaughn left Darby in the study and asked a passing footman to have his cloak, hat, and gloves brought to him. When he reached the front door, he found a crowd of young men already there, all dressed warmly. They were chatting away and laughing as they readied themselves for the Yule log–gathering party.

"Are you joining them?"

Perdita suddenly appeared at his side. Lord, the woman could be stealthy. Once they were married, he would have to have little bells sewn onto her gown so he could hear her coming.

"I was instructed by your father to assist the others." He took his cloak from the footman who had rushed to him with his outerwear.

"You listened to my father? Goodness, Lord Darlington, whatever reasonable, gentlemanly thing shall you do next? I swear you'll lose your wicked reputation at this rate," she teased him, and he adored the sparkle in her eyes as she did.

"As a *gentleman*"—he emphasized the word—"I would like to invite you to join us."

Her winged brows rose. "Truly? Most men would not think to invite a woman to partake in such a sacred and masculine ritual."

Vaughn glanced at the collection of eager young lads surrounding them and sighed dramatically.

"Miss Darby, please do me the honor of saving me from this hoard of bucks, who will surely drive me to the nearest bottle with their inane antics if I do not have a grounded, sensible creature to accompany me."

She giggled. "In that case, I accept. Let me fetch my cloak and gloves."

He couldn't deny the excitement that fluttered in him at the thought of spending more time with her. When he'd come upon her in the library earlier, she'd stopped him dead. Before, he'd always focused on women most when they were naked in his bed, but there was something different about Perdita. She was fiery, challenging, yet alluring and sweet. He hadn't known a woman could be so complex in personality. He found he rather liked that depth to her.

When he'd spied her in the library window seat, he had known he would find a way to rouse her passions, but he hadn't expected to be so affected by her reactions to him. Holding her in the library, thinking of her secretly penning astronomy essays and defying the conventions of society, then picturing the way she blushed at his exploring hands before trusting him to bring her to climax...something inside him clicked into place.

This plan of a false engagement had begun as a way to climb out of financial ruin, but everything had changed, and that no longer mattered. What mattered now was winning her heart and claiming her as his wife. He knew he'd settle for no other woman. She was a bottomless pool of mysteries, an enchantress who drew him out with her innocent lips and eyes full of secrets. He was quite convinced he could spend years getting to know who Perdita really was.

Vaughn was still picturing how she tasted when he noticed Samuel Milburn staring at him from across the hall. The man was scowling.

Milburn nodded. "Darlington."

Vaughn ignored the sour look he was given and offered a nod

back. Then Milburn came over, dodging the other young men as they bounded about the hall like pups.

"Chasing the skirts of Miss Darby, are we?" he asked.

"Chasing? No. *Caught*." He smiled slowly, watching his meaning sink in for the other man.

"Caught? By that you mean…"

"We are engaged. The announcement is to be made tonight at dinner." Vaughn pulled on his gloves, allowing his usual uncaring manner to be displayed. He didn't want Milburn to see any desperation or urgency. The man must not sense the true purpose of their engagement.

Milburn's cheeks reddened, and his eyes narrowed. "When did you court her? She's been in the country for the last few months, and I know you've been visiting the gaming dens in London."

Milburn was too bloody astute for his own good. Vaughn finished with his gloves and arched a brow. "You can't expect a gentleman to reveal his secrets." Let the bastard make what he could of that.

"I had intentions toward her myself. I'd already spoken to Darby." Milburn's voice turned into a low, warning growl. That would have bothered some gentlemen, especially those who knew of Milburn's cruel and abusive nature. But Vaughn wasn't one of them.

"Sorry to tell you that I got there first, old boy. And you know I have no intention of sharing what's mine with any man." Vaughn slapped the other man on the shoulder. He felt the tension rise between them. They weren't foolish young lads barely out of the schoolroom. They were men, ready to face each other down like stags over territory. Vaughn was more than ready to battle the bastard for Perdita's sake. He'd love a chance to bloody his knuckles on Milburn's face.

Milburn seemed ready to argue further, but Perdita appeared at the top of the stairs, wearing a red cloak with white ermine fur lining the edges. Her dark hair had escaped the loosely pulled up Grecian style, and bright-red ribbons had been threaded into her hair to hold back her locks. She was a perfectly delectable little creature.

And she's all mine.

Vaughn grinned eagerly as she came down the stairs, and he held out his hands to her. She placed her gloved hands in his, allowing him a moment to study her. She had a cloak on, but her gown seemed a bit thin for walking about in the woods.

"Will you be warm enough, darling?" he asked, genuinely concerned. One did not charge about the snowy woods in a fine tea gown.

"Yes. This isn't my best gown, but I didn't want to miss out on the experience simply because I had to change my dress." When her nose wrinkled, it made her adorably sweet, and Vaughn couldn't resist smiling. Damn, since when had such sweetness ever been so fetching to him? His bed partners before had been moody, sensual, and as friendly as cats in heat, but Perdita was nothing like them, and he found that refreshing. She turned as though just now realizing Milburn was standing there next to them.

"Oh, my apologies, Mr. Milburn. Did I interrupt your conversation?" Her wide eyes were filled with innocence, but Vaughn knew she had interrupted them on purpose and was glad for it.

Vaughn answered for him. "No, you did not. We were simply catching up, weren't we, Milburn?" He challenged his rival with one lazy and somewhat contemptuous look.

Milburn's dark eyes burned with a hateful fire, but he couldn't lose his temper in front of the other guests. He stormed off, shoving a few lads out of his way viciously enough to have them grumbling and brushing their coats in displeasure.

"No holiday spirit there," said one.

Vaughn turned to his fiancée. "My, that was exciting. A bit like poking an angry bear." He chuckled and offered Perdita his arm.

It seemed the others had decided they were ready to begin, and the crowd of men suddenly rushed out the front door in a wall of fluttering cloaks and clattering boots. They bounded into the snow like hearty young foxhounds.

Perdita giggled as the men began their wild romp toward the forest that bordered the property. "Heavens, look at them go. You'd think they'd been kept indoors for a week."

"My lady." Vaughn lifted her by the waist and set her down in the snow. Some of the men had already worn down a steadier path ahead of them. It would be much easier on her skirts to walk on packed snow.

Perdita turned her head to hide a blush, then lifted her gown with one hand and began to walk. Vaughn took her other arm, and they moved together into the woods. Due to the heavy snowfall, only a few birds were chattering on trees, and Vaughn couldn't resist the temptation to tease Perdita.

"Look there." He pointed with his free hand toward a blue-and-yellow bird with black markings around its throat and eyes. It clung agilely to a tiny bare branch of a stout little tree.

"Oh, he's lovely." Perdita paused to watch the bird. The branch was thin enough that the bird's weight made it dip and bounce as the creature adjusted its position and fluttered its wings.

"That is a blue tit," he said. "Tits always turn blue in the winter when it's cold. He has a cousin called a great tit, similar markings, but a much bigger chap." He waited, holding his breath to see if she realized the joke he was trying to make, that the tits which turned blue weren't birds...

"I believe you're trying to tease me."

"Whatever do you mean?"

"You know as well as I do that tit has *other* meanings."

"As far as I know it simply refers to a diminutive creature, such as a titmouse or a tomtit. I cannot be responsible for any meanings *your* imagination has come up with."

"Well, nevertheless, you must stop talking about *blue tits*," she whispered in a half-amused, half-scandalized tone.

"I promise to return yours to a lovely shade of pink once we get back inside."

"Vaughn!" she admonished.

"What? You began such talk, but that doesn't mean I cannot

contribute. Yes, I believe a few kisses, a bit of sucking will bring the pink back nicely." He leaned down to murmur the last part, which only made her gasp.

"Stop this," Perdita said, her face already beginning to flush.

"I suppose you don't want to hear me describe chaffinches? They have the most attractive pink breasts."

She looked as if she might punch him, but then she thought better of it. She huffed and walked a few steps ahead before she bent down. Before he realized what she was up to, he caught a face full of snow.

He brushed off the powdery residue from his face, sputtering.

"You will pay for that, my darling." He crouched down and started to collect his own handful of snow in his gloves. When he rose, ready to aim, there was no sign of her.

But he saw a clear track of dainty boot prints in the snow, leading deeper into the woods. With a wolfish grin, he began to stalk his lady, looking for signs of a red cloak within the snowy forest. When he caught his red-hooded lady, she would pay for her mischievous behavior, and they would both enjoy every minute of it.

❊   6   ❊

Perdita wrapped the edges of her cloak tightly about her body to keep it from showing around the base of the large tree she hid behind. Throwing a snowball at Vaughn had been far too great a temptation to resist. She liked to see him ruffled and caught off guard. He seemed more real and a little less like the rogue from a schoolgirl's forbidden daydreams. Not that she minded that side of him, but she longed to see the real Vaughn, not the façade he showed to the rest of the world.

Once she'd thrown that snowball, she knew he would seek revenge, no doubt in a wicked way that would leave her breathless and shaky. So she'd turned tail and fled to make the chase much more rewarding for them both.

She should have chosen her white cloak rather than the red, but she had so loved the contrast of red against the snow.

AND NOW I SHALL PAY FOR IT.

Far ahead of her, she could see the young men in their quest for the perfect Yule log. They needed something large that would burn for twelve days. It wasn't really possible to find a log that large, but men loved to challenge each other over silly things like that.

Perdita turned her focus back to the forest. She closed her eyes, taking in the sounds around her. The chatter of the blue tits and the occasional snap and creak of frozen branches were the only noises she could detect. She opened her eyes, wondering where Vaughn had gone, or if he had moved at all. As she peered around the tree, she almost expected to see him close by, ready to pounce. Nothing. The forest was empty as far back as the path that led to the house.

Where the devil had he gone? She turned back to the woods and screamed. Vaughn had somehow gotten around her! Her heart leapt into her throat at the sudden unexpected sight. He pushed her flat against the tree and clamped one gloved hand over her mouth.

"You left your delectable behind unguarded, sweeting." The *tsk* he gave was gentle and wicked, just as his smile was in that moment. He pressed his body against hers, his hips against her stomach. She'd never felt so small and vulnerable as she did at that moment. It should have scared her. Any young lady in a similar position would have been terrified, but Vaughn holding her captive like a dark winter forest god set fire to her blood.

I am as wicked as he is. The realization was buried beneath a rush of sensations as Vaughn removed his hand from her mouth and kissed her. It was a ruthless sort of kiss, one that marked her, conquered her, and reminded her that she belonged to him—yet not in the way a man like Milburn would. Vaughn didn't own her, and he certainly didn't want to break her. But in this forest, surrounded by the snow and the silence, he owned her very soul for briefest heartbeat of a stolen kiss.

"You are clever," he whispered in her ear. "But not quick enough, I'm afraid. Shall I punish you here?" He swept one hand beneath her cloak to cup her bottom. Her body burned at the touch, even as she wondered what sort of punishment he might inflict.

"Please, Vaughn," she murmured, not sure what she was pleading for. She placed her gloved hands on his shoulders and dug her fingers in, holding on to him. He tilted her head up by placing his fingers under her chin.

"Oh, the things I could do to you..." His eyes raked over her before settling on her lips. "But I believe a kiss is what you deserve." He removed his hand from beneath her chin and bit the tips of his gloved fingers, tugging the leather off his skin. He let the glove fall into the snow beside them.

"Yes, please kiss me." Her gaze fixed on his mouth as she encouraged him. He had the most perfect lips, ones that were soft, warm, and sensual. The kind that drifted along her bare skin and melded with her own lips and seemed to erase the world around them until nothing else existed.

"Lift your skirts," he growled in a dark and demanding tone.

She shivered and whispered back, "What? Why?"

Vaughn arched a brow in a way that she was coming to recognize—that she was treading on dangerous ground by questioning him. A lady who asked him to explain his seductions might end up with more than she expected. Vaughn had mentioned spanking once before. The idea had startled her at first, but his idea of a love pat was not one of cruelty or abuse but of pleasure. The thrill of thinking of him smacking his hand lightly on her bottom was undeniably erotic, and she wanted to experience it.

"Lift them now and ask me to kiss you, darling." His voice was now low and smooth. "If you do it properly, I'll reward you. Fail and I will punish your darling little bottom. I don't care if I must bend you over my lap in the snow for all to see."

Her heart hammered while she glanced around, afraid someone would see them. "But..."

His hand caught her chin, making her focus on him again. "No one will see us, darling. The men are too far off." He swung his cloak over her left side, shielding her from anyone who might see them from that direction. "Now, raise your skirts and ask me for a kiss. And when you do, you will call me *my lord*."

The confident set of his body as he moved back, giving her room to raise her skirts, was almost as infuriating as it was exciting. Perdita clutched her skirts and hiked them up, revealing her underpinnings. The cold air hit her legs and made her shiver.

"Please kiss me..." She hesitated, and her lashes lowered for a moment, but only a moment. "My lord."

"Impertinent little creature. But that will do, for now." His condescending tone made her bristle.

But she didn't have time to reply. He swooped down on her, capturing her mouth in his. She nearly dropped her skirts, but his bare hand was suddenly between her thighs. He didn't slip his fingers into her, not like he had in the library. He only touched the sensitive nub at the top of her mound. He pressed on it, then moved the pad of his finger in small circles over it.

She shivered and tried to wriggle away. It was too sensitive, made worse in the outdoor chill, but he gripped her throat with his other hand—not squeezing but holding her still in a gentle but possessive grip. She was a prisoner of his delicious torment. Arching her back, Perdita knew she had to surrender to him, and in that moment she *wanted* to.

His tongue traced the fullness of her lips as she kissed him back hungrily. His mouth was urgent, exploring and demanding. It was everything she loved about him.

The realization sent a jolt of sensations down her body to meet his fingertips between her thighs. She wanted to belong to him, to be the only woman who ever knew his dark side, one that matched her own.

We are twin souls curled around one another, always straining for that next kiss, that next lingering caress stolen at the right moment.

Her body shook as pleasure rolled through her. She leaned back against the tree, Vaughn's cloak shielding her as the ripples of pleasure continued to flow through her. He teased her a few seconds more before he withdrew his hand and let her skirts fall back into place. He pulled his lips away from hers. They were close in body, but in that moment, she felt there was no distance between them at all. They could have been one being, one beating heart and soul.

When Vaughn's lips curved into a smile this time, there was no wickedness to it, only a boyish delight. Her heart turned over at the sight. The cool intensity of his gaze was gone. She was seeing that secret part of him she'd longed for. It was as though she'd wandered into an old attic and come upon a portrait covered in old curtains. She'd pulled away the faded fabric, and as the dust cleared, sunlight from a high window illuminated the hidden face painted in oil just for her.

It was her own private moment, one she would never have to share with the rest of the world. A piece of him that belonged to her, if only at this moment in her memory. The dreamy intimacy of it held them both spellbound.

Vaughn leaned in slowly this time, and his next kiss was sweet, soft, yet deep. His lips lingered and coaxed hers into a slow, playful dance that seemed to go on forever. She twined her arms around him, caressing the back of his neck, making him tremble when she reached a sensitive spot where his neck met his shoulders.

"What in the blazes are you doing to me?" he murmured. The confusion in his voice was soft and sweet, making her smile against his mouth.

"*Me?* It is *you* who has me bewitched," she responded.

"Then we are both under some sort of spell." He brushed his gloved hand over her cheek before he dropped his cloak from her body and bent to pick up his discarded glove. She had to let go of him, and her arms felt empty without him.

Vaughn cleared his throat. "We should catch up with the others before we are missed." He put his glove back on and then held out his hand to her. She took it, and they began the long walk into the woods to find the other men.

The rest of the party was deep into the woods by the time they found them. They had discovered a log they all agreed would be perfect as the Yule log.

"Ho there, Darlington. Care to give the beast a good whack? We're just about through." One of the young men held up a sizable ax and pointed its blade at the fallen log.

"I suppose." Vaughn removed his cloak and tossed it at the young man before he claimed the ax.

Perdita stepped back, as did the others, giving Vaughn room enough to swing.

He wielded the ax as though he'd been a woodsman to some ancient medieval queen. The silver blade arced through the air and sank into the wood with a heavy *thunk!* The trunk broke in four hard swings, and he moved four feet down its length to separate it again from the ragged base next to the stump.

"Is that enough, do you think?" he asked.

"I believe so," one of the men replied. Four others bent to lift the Yule log and begin the burdensome process of carrying it home. Vaughn went to retrieve his cloak, and another young man engaged him in conversation.

Perdita wished to join him, but such an intrusion might seem rude.

"So, you and Darlington are engaged?" Milburn's cold voice made Perdita jolt. He caught her from behind by the arm, squeezing hard, and she was rooted to the ground with him holding her in front of him, her arm twisted behind her back. If he twisted it much farther, it would break. Pain radiated up from her elbow, and she bit her bottom lip to keep from crying out.

"Unhand me. You're hurting me," she hissed.

Milburn ignored her. "I spent *four months* playing friends with that old fool you call your father, and now you accept another man in your bed? I will not stand for this. Don't forget what I told you. I can turn over my evidence to the magistrate anytime I wish. If I do, he'll be facing imprisonment or worse."

Perdita's tongue seemed to swell, and her throat choked with fear. "I haven't forgotten."

"Then I suggest you come to your senses and tell Darlington to break it off. Otherwise, your father will pay for your stubbornness."

Milburn's threat was so different from Vaughn's. Vaughn had punished her with kisses and with pleasure. Milburn was a coward and a cruel beast who simply wanted to control her every action. Despite her fear, rage came roaring to the surface. She had to fight him. If he won now, like this, she'd never be free.

"Unhand me now or I will scream. Then you will be forced to explain to these gentlemen here what you were doing." She spun to face him, her hood falling off her head. "You may frighten every other woman in London, but *not* me."

She jerked her arm free of his startled grasp, and then she leaned close. "I could not break my engagement with him even if I wished to." It was a lie, but she hoped Milburn would believe it. "Lord Darlington won't give me up, not for anything. If you harm me or my family, you will face his wrath. Never forget that," she hissed. "Speak to me like that again, and I will have you chased off my property by the dogs until your feet are sore and blistered." She kept a steady stare at him, the way one would at a dangerous animal, before she turned and strode off.

POLITENESS BE DAMNED—SHE WAS GOING TO JOIN VAUGHN. HER

temper had only just covered the swell of fear inside her at Milburn's actions. To grab her and threaten her like that? He was bolder in his intentions than she ever could've guessed, and far more dangerous than she'd wanted to believe.

She had hoped her false engagement to Vaughn would deter him. That clearly wasn't the case. She hadn't overestimated Vaughn, but she *had* underestimated Milburn. He wasn't afraid to use his supposed evidence to destroy her father. What was she going to do? She tried to convince herself that his actions were only because the wound to his pride was still fresh. Perhaps in time he would lose interest. This plan had to work, or else everything would fall apart.

Vaughn turned at her approach, his mask of cool aloofness on his handsome face.

"Miss Darby." He bent his head in polite greeting, and the other gentleman did the same. "Is everything all right?"

She painted a false smile on her lips. "Yes." She knew if she told Vaughn what had happened, he might use the ax he still held to chop Milburn into pieces. As appealing as the idea was right then, she couldn't allow that to happen.

"Are you cold? I offer myself as an escort back to the house." He provided his arm gallantly in front of the other men.

She nodded and slipped her arm through his. "Thank you." He handed the ax back to the others, and they started to walk back. Milburn was nowhere to be seen at first, but then she spied him a dozen yards away, talking to his companion. It didn't reassure her. She had a terrible feeling that Samuel Milburn was not going to back down.

❦   7   ❦

Vaughn lounged against the wall at the back of the large drawing room which was already full of gentlemen in their evening clothes. He did not feel like joining in their conversations at the moment. The ladies had been coming down in pairs for the last hour before dinner, but there was no sign of Perdita.

He didn't like it. She wasn't the sort of woman who took overly long preparing herself for dinner. Guilt gnawed at him. He worried that what he'd done in the woods had been a step too far. She had been pale and withdrawn on the journey back, and he hadn't been able to coax her out of her thoughts, even to tell him more about her love of science. He'd even teased her about the names of constellations, pronouncing them wrong, but she hadn't corrected him.

The distant look in her eyes had eaten away at his confidence. He'd never worried about his actions with a woman before, but with Perdita *everything* he did mattered.

Did I push too much? Demand something she couldn't give? Most gently bred ladies did not enjoy his particular flavor of passion—the commands, the obedience, the edge of pain blurring into pleasure. It was why he never seduced innocents and kept his activities restricted to widows and mistresses who shared his hungers.

When he'd kissed Perdita today in the woods, she'd surrendered *so sweetly* and had turned his world on its axis, shifting everything like tumbling sands in an hourglass. He was still unsettled at how perfect she was, how much it had tested his self-control not to take her there and then. But perhaps he had seen only what he wanted to see. Perhaps she had been afraid of him and not truly interested in him.

Was he so starved for a woman's touch that he'd misread her? Was she even now hiding from him because she was too ashamed of what had happened, afraid he would do it again? He couldn't bear the thought. He wouldn't forgive himself if it turned out he'd had it all wrong. But before he could seek her out to apologize, the door opened at the far end of the room and Perdita appeared.

She wore a ruby-red silk gown with a flounced hem trimmed in white lace, as though snowflakes had been caught on the lush fabric. Her bodice was embroidered with tiny flowers, and puffed sleeves clung to her elegantly sloping shoulders. A few loose dark curls bounced and caressed her creamy skin. Skin that he longed to taste. The woman was a vision of loveliness, and he feared he had ruined any chance of marrying her.

He held his breath, pacing around the room's edge toward her, watching her as she spoke to other guests. He studied every tilt of her head, every move, trying to figure out what was going on in her head. His blood burned at the thought of her, but fear held him back. At last he decided to speak to her. Perhaps her tone toward him would reveal more.

Perdita's father stepped in between him and his goal. "Darlington."

He met the older man's amused face with smothered frustration. He needed to speak to Perdita, to ask if she was all right. The last person he wanted to speak to was her father, a man who would most likely shoot him if he knew what Vaughn had been up to with his daughter.

"Yes?"

"I have spoken to Perdita, and she's agreed that making the announcement tonight will be fine. I thought I would make a toast during dinner. Does that suit you?"

"You spoke to her?" Vaughn hung on that single fact, his heart racing. "When?"

Darby tilted his head. "After you returned with the Yule log. I trust things haven't changed since we spoke this afternoon?"

"No, certainly not. I am just glad to hear she spoke to you." It gave him a glimmer of hope that perhaps she had enjoyed their time in the woods and that he hadn't frightened her off. Still, she could just as easily be continuing with her plans to dissuade Milburn's pursuit.

"She did." Darby's eyes held a twinkle. "I admit, I didn't believe it until she told me how fond she was of you. I won't deny my daughter her heart's desire, but"—he leaned in close to Vaughn —"my threat about burying you still stands. You'd best not break her heart, or they will never find you."

Vaughan nodded slowly in understanding.

"Good." Darby smacked his shoulder with an open palm and stepped out of his way.

Perdita was alone now, watching him. He could feel the eyes of the room, particularly those of the ladies, tracking him as he and Perdita met. They would whisper behind their fans about this meeting, speculate on every look, every smile or word shared between them. He couldn't stop them, nor would he try. That was the entire point of this charade—for people to talk, to notice that they were together, and for word of it to reach Milburn over and over until he lost hope of his pursuit.

For a moment, neither of them spoke. She opened her lips, and he found himself afraid of what she might say. He rushed to speak before her. "About today...in the woods." He looked for any sign of horror at the reminder of that moment. "I didn't... I shouldn't have made you do that."

Perdita's lips parted even farther, and her eyes widened. "But..."

She leaned in closer. "I *liked* what we did." She frowned. "Did it not satisfy you?" She raised a gloved hand to her lips, her cheeks pinkening with a sudden blush.

"No!" He reached out to grasp her other hand. "That is to say," he clarified at her wounded expression, "I did enjoy it. Too much. I feared I'd frightened you, that you'd seen my black heart and it was too much for you." He faltered when he realized he was confessing to such wild things. Things that no man should say to a woman. He sounded like Vaughn's friend Ambrose. That fool had rushed headlong into love for Perdita's friend and never looked back. Vaughn had no intention of falling in love, even with his future wife. He'd always wished to have an affection for his wife, because it would make a marriage happier, but love was too dangerous, too volatile an emotion. He never wanted to risk his black heart for love.

Rather than rush to reassure him or deny that she had been afraid, Perdita raised her chin. Her warm brown eyes seemed to glow with some mixture of amusement and elation.

"Vaughn, if you had tried to do anything to me that I did not wish, I wouldn't have let you." Her lips curved into a ghost of a smile, and the wit and confidence he'd feared had left her was back.

Still, he could not resist asking. "But when we came back, you were so quiet. I was worried—"

"The infamous rogue worries over me?" She was still smiling, but for a brief instant, he saw that shadow in her eyes. Then it was gone. "I admit my thoughts were elsewhere," she said. "But it had nothing to do with you or what transpired between us."

The flood of relief at her words was surprising. He hadn't known until that moment just how much he needed her to tell him she was all right.

"Now, I'm afraid we shan't be sitting close at dinner. Mother has spread us out in the seating arrangements." Her nose wrinkled as she showed her clear distaste for this arrangement.

"She didn't put you near..." He gave a slight jerk of his head toward Millburn.

"No, thank heavens." Perdita's eyes brightened again. "After dinner, I thought we might talk. We must prepare for him seeing us together, correct? One in private?" Her gaze dropped to his lips, and he could guess what she was truly thinking. The excited gleam in her eyes was impossible to miss. The little minx clearly missed him and all the wicked things he could do. *And to think I was concerned she didn't enjoy it.*

She bit her lip. "Oh dear, you're grinning again."

"Hmm?" He realized she was right, but he couldn't stop.

"You worry me when you look like that. Like a wolf looking at a rather plump rabbit."

His smile widened. "I do like my rabbits plump." He offered her a playful smirk and won a heated blush from her.

The door to the drawing room opened, and dinner was announced. Vaughn tucked her arm in his with a chuckle.

He leaned down to whisper in her ear. "Remember our time in the library. Whenever I drink from my goblet of wine, I shall be thinking about how you taste." He felt a shiver ripple through her. *That* would keep her occupied this evening, because he planned to drink a lot of wine.

The couples convened in the dining room, their voices bouncing through the corridors. Darby House seemed to always be a place of life and delight, no matter the time of year. The gold lamplight glowing on the shimmering evening gowns painted a pretty picture amidst the fine furnishings. There was a lively elegance to it all that spoke of money spent, but spent well. It was nothing like his parents and how they would have run the home.

When his older brother, Edward, had died, the loss had broken his parents' spirits. They had never been deeply in love as a married couple, but they had shared a love for their eldest son that bound them together in grief. Vaughn hadn't been given much thought before his brother's death, and after his passing he became only a forced interest. His father had retreated to his club, and the debts soon began to mount, while his mother withered away day by day, sometimes spending hours in Edward's room, clutching a miniature portrait to her breast.

The servants moved like ghosts in the gloomy, quiet house, and Vaughn had no strength in him to fight his parents' plans to turn their home into a mausoleum for their dead son. Instead, he'd obtained a bachelor's residence on Jermyn Street and stayed there until they died. It had left him with a bittersweet ache for the beauty and the warmth he felt here at Darby House. His desire to secretly win Perdita's hand was growing, but he now doubted his ability to give her a warm and happy life she deserved. He hadn't been raised by sensible, loving parents like she had, and he wouldn't know the first thing about making a life like that for her.

"Now *you* are frowning," Perdita teased, mimicking his scowl.

He couldn't resist a gentle laugh. "I am. Deep thoughts always make me frown." He buried his dark thoughts and added in a low whisper, "I think we should meet tonight. The library after midnight?"

"Agreed," she answered back, just as quietly.

They entered the dining room, and there was no more opportunity to speak privately. Vaughn escorted Perdita to her seat at the far end of the table before he walked back to his own. He was seated near Perdita's mother.

Damnation. He couldn't see Perdita's face, the various decorations on the table blocked his view. A large stuffed pheasant's colorful feathers flared out as though it was ready to take flight. Vaughn could just see the curve of Perdita's neck through the dip of the back of the bird's wings.

Dinner wasn't going to be as enjoyable as he had hoped. He looked toward the elderly gentleman who sat to his left. He had a better view of Perdita.

He nudged the older fellow. "Excuse me. Would you mind trading places with me?"

The old man's face turned ruddy as his eyes darted quickly to Mrs. Darby and back to him. "Trade places?" he blustered. "Good

God, man, the lady of the house is right there beside you. The sanctity of a lady's table seating is the cornerstone of our empire!" He announced this so loudly it drew surprised gazes from the ladies and gentlemen nearby. Even Perdita was staring at him, worry creasing her brow.

Vaughn rubbed a hand over his face and sighed. *Cornerstone of the empire? For God's sake.* There was nothing like public mortification in the middle of a Christmas dinner to shame even a hardened rogue like himself. He was half tempted to find the nearest Christmas pudding and shove his face into it to avoid the stares. The elderly man was still watching him.

"What the devil would make you demand to swap seats, young man?"

Vaughn almost choked. *Young man?* He hadn't been called that in years. Hadn't *felt* like that in years. He was twenty-seven, not some boy fresh out of school. He cleared his throat.

"I merely hoped to have a better view of a certain young lady." Damn, why did he feel flushed all of a sudden?

"A lady, you say?" The old man lowered his voice and leaned in conspiratorially. "Empire be damned." He poked Vaughn. "Out of your chair, boy."

Vaughn glanced toward Mrs. Darby, seeking her approval.

"I'll allow it," Mrs. Darby said. She smiled a knowing little smile before she turned to the guest on her other side to engage him in conversation.

Vaughn hastily exited his chair and switched with the old man. When he sat down, he glanced toward Perdita. She raised one hand to cover her mouth, no doubt hiding a smile. Even from across the vast distance of the dinner table he could see that darling twinkle in her eyes, and it made him feel...*giddy*. He grinned, feeling like a damned fool, but oddly, he didn't mind. Vaughn reached for his glass of wine and took a sip. Perdita blushed, and he chuckled. Perfect.

"Nice to see young love," the old man commented. "Everyone seems to assume that when you're my age we forget what it's like to be young. You'd better hold on to her, my boy." The older man's tone turned wistful, and he tugged on his cravat.

"Oh, I'm not in love. I barely know her."

"Balderdash. Love doesn't require you *knowing* everything about her. Sometimes love is part of the mystery. Especially for men. Women will always have their secrets, the little twinkles in their eyes, the hidden smiles that make us wonder just what it is they are thinking about. My Arabella is still quite the mystery, and we've been married fifty years." He nodded toward an older woman who sat close to Perdita. Her loveliness hadn't faded with time, and Vaughn could still see the attraction.

Vaughn was tempted to argue that it wasn't really possible to love someone you didn't know, but Mr. Darby stood up with a glass in his hand, drawing everyone's attention.

"Thank you for joining my family for Christmas. It's so lovely to have guests during the holidays. It warms my heart to have my house full of people." His thanks were followed by a murmur of agreement by the guests. "And tonight, I have some wonderful news. I'm delighted to share with you all that my daughter, Perdita, and Lord Darlington are engaged. I would like to propose a toast— to Lord Darlington and my daughter, Perdita."

The guests echoed his toast and drank to it. Perdita sipped her wine, her head down, but she was red-faced. Vaughn was tempted to do the same. Everyone at the long table stared at them as the news settled in. It was one thing to be invited to Darby House for a party, but to be announced as Perdita's intended was going to cause ripples in the various social circles. He'd expected that, of course, even counted on it, but watching it occur before his eyes in a roomful of people was both embarrassing and fascinating. He wasn't sure what he ought to do, so he resorted to his usual behavior and flashed a cool smile at the curious faces turned his way.

"And finally, to remind you all," Darby said, clearing his throat, "tomorrow night, we shall have the ball." This second announce- ment did the considerate job of distracting the ladies, who all murmured in delight at the coming dance. Many of the young men in attendance grinned eagerly, and the dinner began.

Vaughn paid little attention to much else over the next two hours. His focus was on Perdita. He loved to watch her. There was something enchanting about the way her eyes lit up as she talked. She was an animated creature, but there was no falseness about her, no shallow vapidity like far too many ladies her age tended to display. She was both genuine and honest. Her words were always well chosen and truthful.

A gentleman beside her made her laugh, and Vaughn grinned at the sound. A pang of jealousy followed. He wanted to be the man who made her laugh like that.

"Someone's not happy you won the fair lady," the old man on his left muttered. His words dragged Vaughn's attention away from Perdita.

"What do you mean?"

The man nodded down the table. "That fellow at the far end. He looks quite put out. Did you steal his sweetheart, I wonder?"

Of course it was Samuel Milburn who was glowering at him, his black eyes filled with rage, his mouth a thin line. Vaughn had been so focused on Perdita that he'd forgotten the whole reason he was here: to save her from that bastard.

"Actually, I didn't steal her. I rescued her," Vaughn responded truthfully.

"Did you, now?" The old man chuckled before he took a sip of his soup.

"I did," Vaughn affirmed, his focus still on Milburn. That man would bear watching over the next few days. He was the sort of man who would seek revenge if his plans were foiled—which meant his threatened blackmail might yet come into play. He only hoped Mr. Craig was making some progress on that front.

Vaughn spent the remainder of the meal dividing his attention between his dinner companions. The man on his left, Mr. Chatwin, was the one who had graciously switched places with him.

After dinner, the ladies returned to the drawing room while the men proceeded to the billiard room for port and cigars. Vaughn didn't really wish to play, nor did he wish to smoke and converse with anyone. He was careful to slip out of the room once the others were sufficiently distracted.

A cold voice disrupted his walk down the hall. "I know what you're doing." Vaughn froze next to a marble bust of a noble lady and turned to see Milburn closing the door of the billiard room behind him.

He forced himself to relax, even though every muscle inside him was ready for a fight. "What, pray tell, is that?"

"You and that little fool. She thinks she can outsmart me by bringing you here. But I'm no fool. We both know you really don't want to marry her. So what is she giving you? Sharing her bed wouldn't be enough. It must be something else. Is she paying you? Whoring out for your services? I know you are desperate enough, but I still can't believe you'd be such a *pathetic* man." Milburn *tsked* snidely. "How far the Darlington name has fallen."

Vaughn's hands curled into fists at his sides, but there was no point in bashing the man's head, even if it would feel bloody good. He drew in a slow, calming breath.

"You are mistaken. I am going to marry her, and I'm not desperate. It seems to me *you* are the desperate one. Are you angry she refused you? Maybe you shouldn't have shoved your last mistress out a window. Or maybe it's because you attempted to blackmail her. That tends to dampen any romantic notions a lady might have for a man. Unlike you, I don't hurt women."

"Oh, but you do." Milburn countered, his voice quiet but clear in the hall. "We both know what kind of man you are. Does she know what you need? How you find your pleasure? Someone should warn the poor girl." Milburn's grin was so arrogant Vaughn actually took a step forward, ready to raise his hand against him.

Milburn opened the billiard room door. A couple of heads turned their way, wondering who was about to enter.

"Careful, Darlington. I wouldn't want to see you thrown out of the house for brawling. Then no one would be there to comfort Miss Darby. Oh wait, *I* would. Go ahead, throw a punch."

With a low growl, Vaughn lowered his fist and forced a smile.

"You're hardly deserving of such attention. If you were any more beneath my notice, I'd have to check the bottom of my boot heel to find you." Before he could let Milburn antagonize him further, he went upstairs to his room.

It was going to be a long wait until midnight. He would have to distract himself from thoughts of making Milburn bleed, instead picturing how he would enjoy spending time with Perdita beneath the kissing boughs in the hidden alcove of the library.

$$\text{❧} \quad 8 \quad \text{❧}$$

Perdita waited for her lady's maid to lay out her nightgown.

"Beth, would you be upset if I called you after midnight to undress me?"

Beth, a sweet girl with reddish-brown hair, glanced at her in surprise.

"Miss?" Beth never asked direct questions, but Perdita knew this was her maid's way of inquiring.

"You remember what I told you about Milburn?" Perdita had confessed her fears a few weeks before.

"I do." Beth took one of Perdita's dresses and smoothed out the wrinkles before carrying it to the tall armoire.

"Well, I am to have a secret rendezvous with Lord Darlington tonight."

"Miss..." Beth's tone was full of reprimand. Her maid could say so much with one word.

"I know you don't approve, but he is the only chance I see of escaping Milburn's interest. We're going to arrange for him to see us somehow. I hope that will dissuade him."

Beth gave a huff of disagreement.

Perdita placed her hands on her hips. "What is it?"

"Miss, there's no reason a man would want a secret rendezvous with you. Not unless he has a specific desire in mind."

"Beth, he doesn't *want* me, not in that way. Men like Darlington are excellent at playing the role of seducer, but that's all it is. Playacting. I paid my price to him by arranging a meeting with Lord Lennox after the New Year. That is all Darlington truly wants."

Her maid gave another disgruntled sound. "You are one of the sweetest and loveliest ladies I know, miss. He'd either be blind or a fool not to want you, and his eyesight seems to be just fine. I'm only asking you to take care. That's all."

"I promise." Perdita knew Vaughn had enjoyed their time in the library and the woods, but she knew men like him. He could have his pick of ladies who knew what to do to please a man, and she could not possibly be interesting enough for him. Vaughn would have no designs upon her, not in the way her maid feared. She was a virgin, and he'd made it abundantly clear upon their first meeting that he didn't seduce "innocents," as he'd called them, yet he had said he might make an exception for her.

"I shall wait up for you," Beth said, clearly unconvinced.

"Go on to bed. If I need you, I'll come and wake you."

Her maid frowned. "You shouldn't have to come fetch me in the servants' quarters, miss."

"Stop worrying." Perdita shoved her out the door. "Go on to bed now."

When her servant was gone, she waited in her room, trying to pass the time until the appointed hour. She tried to read a book, but she couldn't focus. Finally, she left for the library ten minutes before midnight. She was nervous and excited, but it was only because she was engaging in her second midnight rendezvous, *not* because she was excited to see Vaughn again.

When she reached the library, she ducked inside and began to pace, her slippers wearing paths in the carpet by the fire. At the sound of the door opening she turned, an eager smile upon her lips which quickly faded when she saw who it was.

"Finally, we have a moment alone," said Samuel Milburn.

Perdita was afraid to move. Afraid to breathe. All she could think was that he'd once thrown a woman out a window and that she could meet the same dreadful end.

For a long moment, they simply stared at each other, like a cat watching a mouse frozen with fear. Then he walked toward her. Perdita was torn between the desire to run and to hold her ground. This was her house, by God. Who was he to menace her in it? And by the dark look in his eyes she sensed running would only make things worse—and things were already very bad indeed.

Her heart pounded inside her chest, but she tried to remain outwardly calm.

"Darlington will be here in a few minutes. It would be wise of you to leave." She took two slow, careful steps to place a tall armchair between herself and Milburn. The crackling fire and the ticking of the old clock above the marble mantle were strangely loud in the tense silence of the room.

Milburn wore no coat, and made a show of rolling the sleeves of his shirt up. It was intimidating, not that Perdita could explain why. If Vaughn had done the same action, she would not have been afraid but rather excited.

"When I am done with you, he won't care. He certainly won't *want* you any longer." It was her only warning. Milburn lunged for her, and Perdita, too terrified to scream, simply acted. She shoved the chair at him. It wasn't as heavy as it looked and it toppled over, striking him in the knees. He crumpled onto it with a violent shout.

Perdita raised her skirts and ran for the door. But something snatched her ankle, and she fell. When she tried to scramble to her feet, she was pulled back to the ground. Pain shot up her right leg. She kicked out instinctively, again and again.

"Stop that, you little bit—" The hoarse curse turned into a grunt of pain as her foot connected with Milburn's face.

She had only a few precious seconds of freedom, but her palms, slick with sweat, found no purchase on the wooden floor.

"*Help!*" she screamed, but a heavy weight came down on top of her, crushing her into the floor. Air rushed out of her lungs, and a hand dug into her hair, lifted her head up, then shoved it hard on the ground. Her forehead struck the wood floor, dazing her.

"Little bitch. How *dare* you," Milburn growled, his body pinning hers down. His other hand slid toward her skirts, dragging them up.

Perdita's head throbbed in pain, and she couldn't breathe and couldn't move.

The library door was only ten feet away, but it might as well have been ten miles. Her eyes blurred with tears as the horror of what was happening sank in. She dug her nails into the wood, the scraping sound an undertone beneath Milburn's growl as he jerked her skirts higher and panted.

The creak of the library door opening did not stop him, if he had noticed it at all, but Perdita raised her head at the sound, praying someone, *anyone* would see.

"Help—" She tried to shout again, but her lungs were crushed and her vision was tunneling. She couldn't breathe.

There was a distant roar, as though coming deep from a well beneath layers of water, far away. The crushing pressure on her chest vanished, and her ears filled with the harsh, violent sounds of men shouting and furniture crashing.

She crawled toward a bookcase, using the wood to support her as she took shelter, guarding her head as she gasped for breath, her eyes closed. When the sounds stopped and she opened her eyes, she saw Vaughn had hold of Milburn's shirt with one hand and was shaking the unconscious ruddy-faced bastard. When he seemed satisfied the other man was out cold, he dropped him onto the floor, then turned to her. His eyes were hard as diamonds, sharp and burning. His knuckles were covered in blood.

Perdita's lips quivered, and a sob escaped her. His gaze softened, and he rushed over to her, lifting her into his arms.

"My darling, my darling." He buried his face in her hair as he carried her out of the room. He walked hastily down the corridor and back up the stairs. "Which way is your room?" he asked.

"The last one on the left." She tucked her face against his throat, her body still shaking. He carried her to her bedchamber and set her down on her bed, then touched her face, lifting it so he could see her eyes. The anger had returned.

"There is something I must attend to. I will fetch your maid at once."

"No!" she said with a gasp. "I mean, please, do not wake her. She would only worry and ask questions that I'm not ready to answer."

"Are you sure?" Vaughn hesitated at the door. "Will you be all right to be left alone for a few minutes?"

She nodded. She didn't want Beth witnessing her shame and fear. She only wanted Vaughn. He made her feel safe.

"Good. I will return shortly." He placed a kiss upon her brow and left.

Perdita sat there on the edge of the bed and looked down. She was missing one slipper, her gown had been ripped in several places, and her forehead throbbed. She extended her ankle and whimpered at the sharp twist of pain she felt. A minute later, the door opened and her father came in, Vaughn behind him.

"Perdy?" Her father rushed to her side, hugging her. After he was certain she was in no immediate danger, he nodded at Vaughn. "Come. We'll take care of this right now."

She didn't know what they were talking about and was too distraught to ask.

They both left her alone again. When they returned, her mother was with them, and both Vaughn's and her father's boots were covered in fresh snow.

"Papa..." Perdita whispered.

"You're safe now," her father growled. Perdita exhaled, relief sweeping through her, but it didn't erase her humiliation or the pain she was in. Her mother came to her, hugging her fiercely, a stark look of fury and fear in her eyes that filled Perdita with guilt.

But then she remembered Milburn's threats. By tossing him out of the house, Vaughn and her father had given Milburn the excuse he needed to carry out his threats. Her father would soon be exposed for a crime Perdita was certain he was not guilty of. She covered her stomach with her hand as she endured a wave of nausea.

"Perdy, dear, are you all right?" her mother demanded. Then she spun on Vaughn. "What happened to her? What did you do?"

"Mama, please!" Perdita gasped. "He saved me from Milburn."

"What? Milburn? But that's not possible."

"I'm afraid it is," her father said. "Darlington and I just threw the bastard out into the snow."

"That is all?" Her mother's voice rose. "Reginald, you need to go out and find that man and shoot him. Do you understand me?"

"As much as I adore your thirst for vengeance, my dear, we cannot shoot a man in the back. Not even the local magistrate would allow that."

"Then shoot him in the front! The local magistrate be damned!" her mother snarled like a protective wolf.

"Darby, she needs a doctor. Can you send a lad to ride to the village? I'd go, but I will not leave her here alone." Vaughn approached the bed and gingerly cupped her cheek, trying to offer her a reassuring smile, but he faltered.

"Perdita..." For some reason that tenderness, *his* tenderness broke her last bit of strength that had kept up her composure. She burst into tears, slid away from her mother, and reached for him. He curled his arms around her body, delicately at first, before his hold tightened. The warmth of his chest and his dark masculine scent mixed with a hint of winter chill that clung to his clothes soothed her.

She knew her parents were speaking, but she didn't want to face them. Not yet. "Vaughn, make them go to bed, please. I don't want them to stay up and worry. I need to be alone."

He cleared his throat. "I understand, sweetheart." He let go of her and walked over to where her anxious parents stood. Perdita turned away and lay upon her bed, her face buried in the blankets.

"Leave her alone? With you? Absolutely not!" Perdita's mother hissed and came over to her by the bed so that Perdita couldn't avoid her gaze.

"Mama, I wish to be left alone. But I would feel safer if Lord Darlington remained with me."

"But..." Her mother struggled for words. "We have guests. It isn't..."

Perdita sat up and grasped her mother's hands. "I don't care one whit about scandal right now. He saved me from a man who deserves far worse from them. Let them wag their tongues about Milburn's actions, not Vaughn's."

Her mother's lip quivered, and she stared at Perdita for a long moment before she nodded. "Very well. You are engaged, after all..." Then she turned to Vaughn. "If you do anything..." Fury flashed in her mother's eyes.

"I won't." Vaughn's tone was completely serious. Perdita lay back down and closed her eyes, wishing for the humiliation and pain of this moment to end.

She heard the door close. The candles by the bed were snuffed out except for one, which remained close to her side of the bed.

"They are gone. If you decide at any moment that you wish them to return, I will fetch them at once. They will bring the doctor when he arrives, and you will see him for your injuries. I insist upon that." Vaughn's voice was firmer now. The natural command in his tone was a comfort. But she was afraid of his tenderness, afraid it came from a place of pity and not affection.

The tears coating her cheeks dried and made her skin tingle. Affection? She wanted Vaughn's affection? When had that become a concern?

"Perdita?" She flinched when he touched her shoulder. He moved his hand, and she immediately missed him.

She sniffed. "Vaughn, please don't pull away. I'm still rather jumpy after..." She couldn't face the awful horror of what almost happened. He stood beside the bed, his eyes glowing and his hair falling over them. His hands were still bloodied, and she realized his skin was broken in a few places.

She sat up and reached for his hands, catching them before he could pull them away. "You're hurt."

"It's only a scratch or two." He pulled his hands away from hers and walked over to the washbasin, dipping his hands into the water.

"Damn, it's cold," he muttered, and wiped his hands on the spare cloth beside the basin. When he turned to face her again, his grim expression made her stomach clench in anxious knots.

"What happened tonight with Milburn..." He paused, and she knew with dreadful certainty what he was going to say. So she decided to beat him to it.

"I understand. Milburn cannot possibly expect to take my hand now. You've done more than I asked. You are free to return to London. I will have my father announce the breaking of the engagement tomorrow."

He quirked one brow. "That is not what I was going to say." He took a step toward her, then halted as if rethinking his closeness.

"You weren't?" A silly girl's hope flooded through her. The bargain was over, and he had no reason to stay, even though she wanted him to.

"I was going to say that given everything that has happened, I think it's best if we see this through to its end." He looked down at his boots, his voice strangely quiet. "I brought a special license with me."

She wasn't sure what he meant, and her head was aching something fierce. "Vaughn, please, say what you mean." She touched her forehead. The spot where she'd hit the floor was still tender.

"We ought to marry. As soon as possible. Perhaps Christmas Day? That would give you tomorrow, Christmas Eve, to plan a small ceremony at the local church."

Perdita was speechless. Marriage? Was he serious? She had only just admitted to herself that she liked him.

"I know this is sudden and unexpected, but I believe it is a good solution. Milburn won't stop, until you're properly protected as the wife of a peer. Only then will you be safe. I fear, however, that it won't stop him from hurting your father with his supposed evidence, but we shall weather the scandal together. I am no stranger to those." There it was, her safety, his only reason for proposing a hasty marriage. Not because of love or even infatuation, but a simple desire to protect her.

Some ladies would find that chivalrous act enough reason to say yes, but not her. Whenever she had contemplated marriage, it had always been with one thought in mind—to marry for love. A great, all-consuming, passionate love whose flame would challenge even the stars.

"Shall I tell your parents you agree?" he asked.

The silence in the room grew until she felt once again she couldn't breathe.

"No."

He stared at her, his gaze inscrutable, before he began to chuckle wryly.

"You find it amusing that I've rejected you?" She sniffled, tears burning her eyes. She would not cry—*she would not*.

"I think it is, yes. I suppose it's because I mistakenly believed that you bore some *tendre* for me. You don't, do you?"

"I..." She *did* care about him, but that wasn't why she'd refused him. It was because *he* didn't care about her, not in the way she wanted. Her hesitation lit his eyes with a soft fire that left her speechless.

"So, you do care. How curious. What, pray tell, is holding you back then?" He eased down on the bed beside her. He looked so inviting, so charming at that moment, with his hair ruffled and his coat gone. She wanted nothing more than to crawl onto his lap and cover his face with kisses and forget the world outside the room. But she couldn't, he didn't care about her.

"Perdita, we can be honest with each other, can't we?" he asked, cupping her chin gently and turning her face toward his. A tear trailed down her cheek. He caught the bit of moisture delicately with his finger, the way one would catch a dewdrop from a flower's petal.

"You don't...you don't love me. And I understand. This was an arrangement meant to solve both our problems. But you go too far. I could never marry a man unless he loved me. Loved me madly. Loved me to distraction. I deserve a great love. Even you deserve that. We cannot marry simply to afford me protection from Milburn. It is not reason enough."

Vaughn brushed the pad of his thumb over her cheek, his eyes a pair of dark sapphires.

"I do not know if I'm capable of love, but I care for you more than I have for any other woman. And that is no idle boast. When I'm with you, things seem sharper, clearer." He seemed to struggle with his words. "It was as though I was in a listless, hazy dream. When I first kissed you in London, I woke up, clear as a bell ringing in my ears. Everything seems more real, more true when I'm with you." He closed his eyes and shook his head. Then he leaned forward and pressed his forehead to hers, holding her face in his hands.

"I don't know *how* to love, if I am honest. But I don't want to stop this. It was always a charade for you, but it never was for me. I *always* wished to marry you."

She stared at him, pulling her face away from his, but only to see his expression more clearly. "What?"

"Yes. The night you came to my townhouse, I decided then that I wished to marry you."

"But..." How could he have made that decision then? It didn't seem possible.

"Take this chance with me," Vaughn said. "Say you will marry me. We need only the vicar at the church and a gown for you. I even have my wedding clothes ready. They're a tad old, I'm afraid, as I couldn't afford a new set." His face reddened at the confession.

Perdita's heart raced wildly again. Could she do this? Marry him on a leap of faith that he *might* one day love her?

"Answer one question."

"Ask it." He continued to stroke her cheek, the gesture sweet and soothing. How unlike the cold rake she'd believed him to be. Perhaps he could surprise her one day with love. He made her want to believe anything was possible.

She watched him carefully. "*Why* do you care for me? What makes me different from any other young heiress you could marry to satisfy your debts?"

Vaughn didn't pull away, but he didn't respond immediately, either. She searched his eyes for any hint of deception but saw only a flicker of hope. "I have had plenty of chances to marry others. Even a reputation such as mine does not scare away the most determined mothers with marriageable daughters or those looking for a tie to a title. Accepting your offer to participate in a false engagement, however, was never about your fortune. If you recall, my terms were to be introduced to Lennox in order to make my own fortune."

Perdita nodded. She couldn't forget or ignore that truth.

"That would have been enough for me. But I've been intrigued by you since I met you at the garden party in September. You had this cleverness about you, and when I learned that you write astronomy articles, well..."

"You know about that?" Her heart leapt into her throat.

"Of course, I do. The penmanship on the draft you showed me is very feminine, but I suspect you would alter that when you felt it was ready to present. I adore that you write, that you think, that you defy the role society has set for you. Do you have any idea how refreshing that is in a woman? I quite love that about you."

"Would you demand I stop if we married?" she asked quietly, hope and fear warring inside her.

"Stop? Heavens no. I'd encourage it. I've never wanted a normal life, let alone a normal wife. I want a woman who will not shy from trouble, who defies convention, who loves it when I tell her to be good in bed and trusts me to teach her about passion.

You've always been the answer for me, Perdita. Don't you see? I could marry no one else *but* you."

He smiled then, that boyish smile she'd seen in the woods, the one that made her chest tighten and her head feel faint.

"You promise our marriage would be one that would not trap us both? I cannot agree to being trapped in a gilded cage."

"Nor could I. If there's one thing I'm certain of, its that marrying you would be thrilling." He dropped his gaze to her lips, still smiling. "What's it to be?" he asked. "Give this rogue a proper chance? I swear I shall make an excellent husband once I'm reformed, and I quite welcome the challenge."

Perdita sniffed and smiled shyly. "This may be madness, but perhaps for once I should embrace it. I accept." She leaned in the same moment he did, and they kissed. It was a gentle kiss that burned slow and hot, despite the tender brush of lips and the tentative touch of hands upon skin.

When they finally parted, Vaughn carefully touched her forehead with his long, elegant fingers, scowling.

"I wanted to kill that man for what he did to you. I wanted to wring his bloody neck. I was so afraid..."

"I was too, but when I saw you come in the door, I knew you would save me." She crawled into his lap, and he wrapped his arms around her, holding her close.

"I never want you to feel that you need to be saved. But I vow to protect you, to always be there for you, sweetheart." His gently spoken promise made her heart flutter wildly. For the Devil of London to utter such words, it had to be a spell born of magic, the magic of love she hoped for...someday.

At that moment the doctor knocked upon the door. Vaughn reluctantly set her down. She felt his hesitation to let her go. It made her feel warm all over.

"Come in," she called.

Dr. Williams was a middle-aged man with a black bag, and his coat was dusted with snow. Perdita's parents were behind him, both looking anxious.

"Could everyone wait outside, please?" the doctor asked. "You too, lad."

Vaughn didn't leave the bed until she nodded at him. He joined her parents outside, and the doctor set his bag down on the table by the bed.

"There now. Let's take a look at your head first, Miss Darby."

~ 9 ~

Vaughn wore a path in the Persian rugs covering the floor of the hallway, barely aware that Perdita's parents were watching his every step. On either side of him, paintings of happy lovers seemed to mock him with their innocence.

Mr. Darby fixed him with a formidable gaze. "Darlington, I sense there's more to tonight's events than Milburn suddenly accosting my daughter. I believe you know what's happening, and you had better tell me."

Vaughn took in a deep breath. He stopped pacing. Just beyond her parents, Vaughn could see heavy drapes drawn over the windows to keep out the cold. He stared at them for a long moment, focusing his thoughts before he finally spoke.

"How much do either of you know about Samuel Milburn?"

"Oh, not much," Perdita's mother said, her brows knitting. "He's well set up, and the *ton* seems to approve of him. The society pages paint him as a generous and eligible bachelor. I had no reason to know he was..." She didn't continue, but her eyes blurred with tears.

"I admit I didn't do much asking," said Perdita's father. "I figured if Perdita told me she was interested in him, then I would start asking questions." Darby suddenly paled. "She mentioned... Oh God, she said something about him having a cruel streak, but I didn't listen."

Vaughn crossed his arms over his chest. "Let me tell you what sort of man he is, then. Milburn is a brute and a coward. He killed one of his mistresses, though no one can prove it wasn't an accident. But he bragged about it in the gambling hells. He likes to hurt ladies, force them to his will, break them in ways I will not speak of. That is what he tried to do tonight to your daughter. And he was trying to force your daughter into marriage by threatening you."

"Me?" Mr. Darby looked as if an assassin might pop out at any moment.

"He claims to have documents that prove you have been involved in smuggling goods into the country and he threatened to take that proof to the local magistrate."

Mrs. Darby covered her mouth, her complexion paling. Perdita's father put an arm around her shoulders.

"Breathe, Minerva. Just breathe." He patted her shoulder, keeping a tight hold as he met Vaughn's gaze. "That's utter nonsense. I haven't been involved in any such..." Darby struggled for words.

Vaughn nodded. "I believe you. We think he is working with your investment partners, arranging for you to take the blame for their illegal acts. Perdita feared Milburn and his evidence so much she came to me at my home in London and beseeched me to enter into a false engagement with her. As you may know, I have a somewhat unscrupulous reputation in certain circles. She hoped that an engagement to me would scare Milburn off. Unfortunately, our charade only made the bastard furious enough to attack her. In his twisted mind, he already owned her."

Neither Mr. nor Mrs. Darby spoke for several seconds.

"But... Are you saying you *aren't* going to marry her then?" Mrs. Darby finally asked.

"Far from it. A true affection has grown between us, and she has agreed to proceed with the wedding without false pretenses. Milburn won't dare come after her if I'm there to protect her."

"Why does he want to hurt her? I still don't understand," Mrs. Darby said. "Why didn't he simply blackmail my husband directly? We have plenty of money. He could have demanded we pay him off. Why go after our daughter?"

"Why indeed? That is why I believe the evidence to be false. You would not pay a man off for fabricating a lie."

Mr. Darby nodded at this. "I wouldn't pay him a half penny for such a thing."

"But how could your daughter possibly ask if such a scandalous accusation was true or not? And what if you denied it and she had doubt? That fear is what Milburn preyed on. Sometimes the thought of a misdeed can hold more power than the proof."

Darby shared a knowing look with Vaughn before he continued.

"But it goes beyond that. Do you know the sort of man who buys a spirited horse because he likes to break the beast? He takes pleasure in destroying its spirit and ruining it until it's a mindless, frightened scrap of horseflesh."

Mrs. Darby nodded. Everyone knew that kind of man, a man who would kick a helpless pup or slap a woman for raising her eyes at him. Cruelty was the shield of many cowards.

"He's such a man?" she asked Vaughn. "He saw my daughter's spirit and fire, and he wanted to crush it?"

Vaughn sighed and nodded. "If we can save Perdita from him, then all we need to worry about is Milburn's supposed proof. Even if it is fabricated, he may intend to harm your good name."

Darby clenched his fists. "We can handle that. I'm not so foolish as my partners believe."

"And you, Lord Darlington?" Mrs. Darby asked. "Are you the sort of man to hurt a woman like my daughter?"

"I would sooner end my own life. Perdita's fire and spirit draw me to her. I feel alive in ways I haven't felt in years. It would be an honor to take such a woman as my wife. That is why I offered to marry her. And it's why she accepted. We wish to marry on Christmas Day. I already have the special license and hoped you could both help us arrange the ceremony." A flutter of nerves bubbled up inside him as he waited to see how her parents would react to this.

Mrs. Darby sputtered. "But...that's the day after tomorrow."

"It is, but I see no reason to delay, only to make haste."

Mr. and Mrs. Darby glanced at each other.

"You haven't given us...*reason* to rush this, have you?" Darby asked.

Vaughn shook his head. "My concerns are regarding Milburn only. We've not gone so far in our passions for there to be cause for worry." He admitted this bluntly, smiling a little. "It would seem she draws out the gentleman in me."

"Good. Or I might've tossed you out in the snow as well," Perdita's father replied.

The door to the bedchamber opened. The doctor came out, closing his bag. The silver clasps clicked into place, and he faced them all, his face etched with worry.

"How is she, Henry?" Mr. Darby asked.

"A little shaken up. Her headache was fairly strong. I've given her a bit of a sleeping draught and bound her ankle to keep it from being turned again. She doesn't wish to sleep alone, and she is still anxious. I was told she was attacked?"

"Yes," Darby said. "The gentleman guilty of that act has been cast out of this house."

"Good. She did not say if..." The doctor flushed. "How far the attack went."

Vaughn understood what he wasn't saying. "I stopped him before he could harm her in that fashion."

The doctor's shoulders sagged with relief. "Good. You are Lord Darlington, I take it?" Vaughn nodded. "She wishes to see you again. I asked if she wished to have her maid sent for, but she has declined. She only wants Lord Darlington."

"Thank you." Vaughn walked past him to enter Perdita's bedchamber, but he paused in the doorway, staring at her father.

"I will stay the night with her. On my honor, my intentions are pure."

Darby stared at him and nodded. "Very well." He held his hand out to the doctor. "Let me see you to a room upstairs, unless you wish to ride home."

"Thank you. I think I will stay the night." The doctor followed Perdita's father down the hall. Only Perdita's mother lingered.

"Tell me you will love her," she said earnestly. "After hearing what might have become of my daughter, I need to hear it."

"I've never been in love, madam," he replied solemnly. "But if there was ever someone worthy of my heart, it is she. Although I doubt I'm worthy of hers."

For a moment, he saw Perdita clearly in her mother's face. Had he really thought she was once a silly woman? Now he saw her as her daughter and husband did. A caring mother, a loving wife, a woman who wanted what was best for her child.

"That's not exactly the answer I wished to hear."

"I know," he replied with a soft smile. "But you deserve the truth."

"Do you really believe I'll let you go in there with my daughter and spend the night after admitting you do not love her?" the lady challenged.

Vaughn paused with his hand on the door latch. "I admit to not feeling love; that does not mean I feel nothing. I am fond of her, so much so that I would pledge myself to her protection even if her heart belonged to another. She is frightened and ashamed of what happened to her, afraid that Milburn will come for her. I've seen women in her condition. They jump at every shadow. Even if you stayed with her and locked the door, she would not feel truly safe. I, on the other hand, will sit in a chair with a pistol aimed at the door all night if that is what is required."

Mrs. Darby studied him hard, but at last she relented. "Very well. But if you hurt her…"

"Yes, I know. Your husband has mentioned my being buried where none shall find me on more than one occasion." Vaughn offered her a wry smile before he slipped into the room and closed the door behind him.

He wished he could have said he loved Perdita, but he still didn't know what being in love was like. He'd loved his brother, Edward. The love for a brother was a fierce love, a love that had rough edges and a toughness about it. Love for a woman was...well, it had to be different. He sensed that truth in his bones. It wasn't lust, and it wasn't friendship. What was it?

I want to love her. I want so badly what Gareth and Ambrose have found with their wives.

But the truth was he was afraid his heart was so hardened by his life that it could never soften enough to open up for another soul.

He studied her room before he faced her. He had been far too focused on her to notice anything before.

A telescope stood close to a set of French windows that opened onto a balcony. His little secret scientist and her tools. Half a dozen pillows were on the bed or chairs, and when he studied one more closely, he noticed the needlework showed familiar shapes. Constellations. The stich work wasn't flawless by any means, and he suspected that she spent her time better by penning essays than practicing with a needle and thread. Rather than a dainty escritoire, she had a large desk covered in charts and writings.

Perdita lay on the bed, her eyes half-open, still glassy from the sleeping draught the doctor had given her. Around her, the bed hangings of a soft rose silk brocade with leafy patterns made her look like a princess half-asleep in her bed.

"Vaughn, you will stay, won't you? I'm afraid of even the shadows."

He came over to the bed and brushed the hair back from her cheek. "I'm going to stay. We should get you changed. Can you sit up?"

She struggled to sit up, and he knelt at her feet and removed her remaining slipper. Then he slid his hands up her skirts, removing her stockings. She placed her hands on his shoulders to keep her balance when she stood. He stroked her legs gently, and then he had her turn to face the bedpost. She did so without question while he unfastened the buttons down the back of her gown. And then it fell to the floor. Then she tugged her petticoats down, revealing a perfect set of hips and rounded behind.

"Almost done," he promised, eyeing her stays. He took care to unlace them gently and not tug too hard so she didn't lose her breath. Then they too fell to the ground. She stepped out of them, wearing only the loose chemise that came down to her knees. Vaughn pulled back the bedclothes and urged her to get under the covers. She sighed and curled up against her pillow, her hair falling in loose tumbles over it. He plucked the pins out of her hair one by one, then gently massaged her scalp to make sure there were no pins left.

Perdita sighed. "For the Devil of London, you have turned out to be quite an angel."

"Am I?" he asked. The Devil of London. That nickname had always amused him. Given his choice of bed play, added to his reputation at the gambling tables, the *ton* had awarded him the unfortunate moniker.

"Yes." She reached behind her to catch his arm and pulled him into the bed. "Lie with me."

It was a command. Her eyes locked with his, and even though her gaze was soft and a little distant from the draught she'd taken, he saw the glint of determination to get her way.

He wasn't about to ignore it. He removed his boots and slipped in the bed behind her. He curled one arm around her waist, tucking her against him.

"Don't I scare you? You should be afraid of all men after what happened." He wasn't sure why he asked it, knowing the answer could be crushing.

She was quiet, her breathing slow. She wasn't afraid of him.

"Not all men are the same. And not all men saved me. Milburn is a monster. You...? You are my white knight."

"I am no white knight, as much as I wish I could be. I'm afraid my armor is tarnished rather than shining."

Perdita stroked his cheek with delicate fingertips, her eyes grave. "A knight in shining armor is a man whose metal has never been tested. And you have proven more than once just how strong your *mettle* is."

Her words made his heart clench tight and she didn't miss his play on metal and mettle. How could she know just the thing to say that made him feel both cut open and exposed, yet unafraid? Vaughn closed his eyes and sighed before he spoke again. "What can I do? Tell me and I will do *anything* for you."

"Are you sure? You might not like what I ask."

Vaughn expected some vow of vengeance against Milburn— which he would be happy to oblige. "Anything."

"Then I wish to *know* you."

That caught Vaughn short, and he wasn't sure he was prepared for it. "Know me?"

"If we are to be married, I wish to know everything about you. I wish to know the man, not just the persona he woos women with." She rolled over in his arms, and he could see her face, accented by winter moonlight.

His heart pounded. Would she even *like* such a man? One who was simply a person to her and not doing and saying the things he knew she wanted to hear? "What do you want to know about me?"

"Tell me something wonderful. Something that you cling to when the shadows threaten to drown you." She put one hand to his jaw, her fingers exploring along his skin. Her touch burned in a wonderful way that made his heart skip.

"Something wonderful..." He would say this moment, but she was searching for his past. Something that revealed the true Vaughn to her. He swallowed thickly, knowing the memory he would share with her.

"I had a brother, Edward, who was older than me by five years."

"I didn't know you had a brother." Her eyes, dark in the room, seemed to channel the thin glow of the moonlight from the window, like two pools frosted with ice, yet her gaze wasn't cold. It made him feel warm to have such intensity focused on him.

"Edward was...well, perfect, and I mean that in the best way. He was intelligent, amusing, generous—he was simply the *best*. Our parents were drawn to him, as the eldest and the favored. But I didn't hate him or the long shadow his life cast over mine. Far from it—he made me happy to be me, just Vaughn, Edward's little brother. We would go riding in the late summer, just the two of us, racing through the glens. He *always* let me win. Even when my gelding threw a shoe once, he stopped his horse, walked back to me, and announced I had beaten him. That was exactly the sort of man he was. And I could never measure up to that." His voice caught on the last few words, and he didn't speak for a moment.

Perdita's fingers stilled on his throat, and he felt her tremble. "What happened to him?"

Vaughn tried to smile. "Let's leave it at that. You asked for something wonderful, after all."

"I asked to know everything about you. Good and bad. What happened?"

Vaughn's throat felt like he had swallowed shards of glass. "He went riding alone one day. I was only sixteen at the time. I was away at Eton, and he was tending to the estate. He was thrown from his horse and died from the fall."

He shut his eyes, holding Perdita close, clinging to her as pain that he'd buried long ago clawed its way up. He remembered receiving the letter at his rooms in Eton. His mother's spidery handwriting on the parchment was blotted with tears as she'd informed him Edward had died. His heart, whatever had still been open to life and love, had turned to stone that day.

"You loved him dearly," she said.

"I did." He dared not open his eyes, because the treacherous tears would cling to his lashes.

"That means you *can* love, Vaughn. It means that someday you might even love *me*." She brushed one finger over his lips, as though memorizing the shape and the feel of them.

A strange tremor ran through Vaughn. He thought back on each kiss he'd stolen from her, how she'd returned that fire, but it had always seemed like something *more* in a way he couldn't describe. To hear her speak of love, of hoping that someday he would love her, he realized then that she was telling him that *she* loved him. It was frightening and exciting, and he didn't know what to do except hold on to her and breathe as emotions ran riotously through him.

In that moment, he knew that if he lost Perdita, he would never recover, never come back from such devastation.

"Sleep now. I am here to watch over you." He kissed her brow, and she tucked herself tighter against him. All would be well. He had to believe that.

❧ 10 ❧

Perdita did not wake until midday. The bed was empty, but the imprint where Vaughn had lain was still warm to the touch. She had been so tired after taking the sleeping draught, but she hadn't forgotten what he'd told her about his brother, about loving and losing him. She had seen the pain in his eyes and heard the catch in his voice. Her viscount's heart was not made of stone or even ice. It was there, beating and bleeding, just like her own.

She climbed out of bed, wincing at the stiffness of her muscles. It was going be a long day, and tonight was the supper and the ball, which meant she'd have little time for rest. She lifted her head when her maid came in.

Beth came over and gave her a gentle hug. "My lady. I was told about last night by your mother. I am so sorry! Why didn't you send for me?"

"It's all right, Beth." She patted Beth's back before she released her. "I didn't wish to wake you, and honestly...I wanted to be left alone after what happened." She wouldn't admit to Beth that she'd been ashamed of being attacked and that she'd felt foolish.

Her maid stared at her before she spoke, as though she understood Perdita's feelings. "I do wish you had sent for me. I wouldn't have..." Beth struggled for words. "You're *my* lady, and I would have done anything to help you." The maid hugged her again. Perdita's eyes pricked with tears as she patted the girl's back.

"Thank you, Beth." For a long moment, neither of them spoke, but when Beth straightened, Perdita had banished her fear and was acting as normal as possible.

"I've been given strict orders that you are to remain off your feet, miss, except for dinner. And you are not allowed under *any* circumstances to dance."

"But—"

"Not one step." Beth began to lay out a fresh dress and slippers. It was a white gown.

"Please, not that one. Surely I can at least choose what I wear."

Beth gave her a challenging stare. "And just *which* gown did you expect to wear?"

"I was hoping to wear my blue gown, the one with the white roses on the bodice and sleeves. I wish to wear a new gown, and it will help me stand out among the other ladies who will likely wear white, red, or green to celebrate Christmas Eve."

"Very well, the blue one. But no dancing," Beth commanded.

Perdita rolled her eyes and let her maid help her get dressed. She discovered a small purple bruise on her face that she would to try to hide with her hair. It would be difficult, though. She hoped no one would notice.

An hour later, she was walking to the kitchens, hoping to steal a few biscuits. She'd had no appetite early this morning, but now she was feeling more like herself at last and was a bit peckish. She was shocked to see Vaughn join her at the stairs leading down to the kitchen.

"How are you?" he asked. He put one hand on the small of her back. Despite the layers of fabric between them, she could feel the heat of his palm through it all.

She ducked her head, embarrassed to face him with the bruise so visible on her face. "Well enough."

Vaughn stopped at the bottom of the stairs and cupped her chin, lifting her face up to face his.

"Damn," he cursed softly. "It looked less dark earlier this morning before I left."

This morning. So he had left just before she'd woken and kept his promise to stay the night with her.

"It is fine. I'm just afraid to let any of the guests see. Scandal and gossip travel so fast."

"That it does." He touched her hips with his hands, the hold gentle but firm. "Why don't we meet in the library in one hour? I have a plan."

"I was going to fetch something to eat."

"I will take care of it. Now go rest and meet me in the alcove. One hour."

"All right." She lifted her skirts to go back upstairs, but he captured her arm, halting her so that he could steal a deep kiss, and then he released her. Breathless, she stood there for a moment, her body hot enough that she wanted to run out into the snow to cool herself. Then he headed down the corridor to the kitchens, and she went back up to her chamber, wondering what he had planned.

She had her answer an hour later when she tiptoed into the library. She gasped.

Vaughn stood on the edge of the window seat, seeing to the hanging of a large kissing bough. At his feet on the floor was a large blanket with plates of food and a pitcher of lemonade with two glasses. Several books were in a neat stack by the blankets and pillows arranged against the wall. He'd created a picnic for just the two of them.

What man would take such time and effort to produce a lovely little scene such as this? It was utterly charming. She sniffed as her eyes burned. The blow to her head made her feel quite silly. It did not escape her notice that he had taken a room she loved, a room where something terrible had happened, and made it feel like a safe place again. And to think he believed he wasn't a gentleman...

He still had his back to her, and she admired the lean lines of his legs and the firmness of his backside in his dark-blue trousers. He was not wearing knee britches, but he would change later when he went to the ball...without her. She was going to miss dancing with him, miss dancing in general until her ankle healed and the doctor thought she could chance a quadrille or two.

"You've outdone yourself," she said as she reached the picnic blanket.

Vaughn flashed a brilliant smile as he climbed down from the window seat. They both stood beneath the kissing bough now. Outside the snow glittered on the lawns, painting a pretty winter picture that made her heart leap.

He nodded at the bit of greenery that would no doubt lead to something very wicked. "Care to put it to use?"

"I think that's a wonderful idea." She stood up on tiptoe to curl her arms around his neck. At the same moment he lifted her up by the waist and kissed her. His lips were soft yet gentle as he explored her mouth. Perdita gave in to the exquisite taste of him and the heat of his body. He made her forget her worries. Surely that made him perfect.

When their lips parted, he stared at her in wonder.

"What is it?"

"You." He brushed the backs of his knuckles over her cheek. "Even after what Milburn tried to do to you, you can stand here and kiss me. You're astonishing."

A flutter of panic rose in her at his words. Did he think her wanton or unaffected by last night?

"Whatever you are thinking, stop," he said. "What I meant is that few women would be as brave as you to even be alone with a man after what happened."

She lowered her gaze to the floor. "What happened to me... That doesn't make me weak. It doesn't make me less."

"Yes," he agreed. "You are strong. You always have been."

She raised her gaze to his, hoping she would see no condemnation in his eyes.

"And that strength makes you astonishing." He feathered his lips over hers in a light, sweet, tender kiss that made her knees weak. For a man who claimed he could not love, he could kiss like one who loved more than the most romantic of poets.

"Would you like to sit down? We may have our picnic, even if it is a little bit late." Vaughn helped her down on the blanket and began to serve the cold cuts and the fruit he'd brought up from the kitchen.

"Vaughn, when we are married, are we to move into your town-house?" she asked. It was strange to think she was to be married so soon, to the Devil of London, no less. It was equally strange to think that the *ton* had favored Milburn as a gentleman and condemned Vaughn in the same breath, yet society couldn't have been more wrong about both men.

At least my devil is really an angel in disguise.

"We could, unless you wish to move to a different residence." He answered carefully, his words measured. "I've had to close up the country estate." He didn't say it, but she knew what he wasn't saying. That he wouldn't use her money to reopen the estate unless she allowed him to use her money for such a purpose.

She took a drink of her lemonade and looked at him.

"Last night when you spoke of Edward, I sensed you were unhappy. I want you—*us*—to be happy. What if we used some of my dowry to open up your country home? If we are able to fill your tenant farms again, we could have some success at creating a sustainable estate. I admit, I prefer the country to London and would enjoy living in the house where you grew up, if you wish." For them and the children she hoped would come. She had never been interested in children before, but when she looked at Vaughn and pictured children with his golden hair and blue eyes...she wanted them desperately.

"If you don't mind, I would like that. But I assure you, once my investments with Lennox bear fruit, I will restore the money we used to your accounts. People will talk, of course, when we move to the estate. They'll say my marrying you was only to improve my family's name and my circumstances." Heavy regret layered his tone, and it softened her heart even further.

"Let them talk." She met his gaze. "It is nothing we haven't heard said of a hundred others. You and I know the truth of what lies between us."

She pushed her plate off the blanket and held out a hand to him. The afternoon sun from the window bathed them both as they sat next to each other on the floor by the window seat.

Vaughn placed his hand in hers, and she pulled gently on his arm. He raised his brows in a silent question. She grinned. There was one thing she wanted more than anything right now. Him. She knew he would have to be tempted after everything that had happened, and she would do whatever she must to convince her gentlemanly rogue to claim what was his. She wanted to erase the bad memories here and cover them with new ones. But more than that, she wanted to be with Vaughn. Not because she wanted to get over Milburn's attack, but because she'd wanted Vaughn before, before all this had happened.

I will not let Milburn take my happiness or my passions from me. I can love and make love without his specter haunting me.

"Tomorrow we are to be married. You have been the perfect gentleman, but I don't want a gentleman right now. I want you, my dangerous rogue, to do what you do best. *Seduce me.*"

His blue eyes darkened, and he crawled over to her as she lay back on the blanket.

"Are you sure? After..." He hesitated, afraid to say the word.

"What Milburn tried to do will not define me, and it hasn't changed how I feel about you."

His lips twitched in a wicked fashion. "Anyone could come in and see us," he warned as he leaned over her prone body.

"They could. But everyone is busy preparing for the dance tonight. Since I'm not allowed to dance, I would much rather be here with you right now, like this."

His wolfish grin made her heart skip. "A wicked lady for a wicked lord I do believe we are *perfectly* matched." He unbut-

toned his waistcoat as she helped him remove his shirt. She flattened her palms over the smooth, sculpted planes of his chest and
the corded muscle of his stomach. She clenched her thighs
together as a wave of heat rolled through her lower body.

"I WANT TO STRIP YOU OUT OF THAT GOWN, BUT WE CANNOT

risk it." He lowered himself on top of her. She tucked her skirts up, and he settled between her parted thighs. He stroked one hand down her right leg, playing with the ribbons of her garter. Then he slid his hand between their bodies, touching her between her thighs. She jolted at the press of his fingers. She was so aroused, so ready for more, that she tensed against the slight intrusion.

"It will hurt a little," he warned. His eyes blazed with a fire that echoed her own body, and she nodded.

"I know, but I want you." She lifted her hips in encouragement, and he began to kiss her lips and her throat before she felt him fumble with his trousers and shift above her. Something hot and hard nudged at her entrance. She tightened her legs on his hips, trying to draw him closer.

"I am ready," she whispered against his mouth.

Vaughn thrust. In one blinding moment of pain, she welcomed him into her body, and he stilled above her, his breathing hard.

"That's it, darling. Breathe with me." He kissed her gently as he began to rock inside her.

The pain blurred into something different, something sharp, yet not painful. It was a building pleasure. He moved his hips, pulling in and out of her more quickly. The sensation was almost too much to bear. Her breasts ached as they pushed tightly against her bodice.

"Vaughn, it's happening again." Her body burned all over like it was kissed with fire. His lips captured hers, his arms braced on either side of her shoulders. He rose above her, all muscle and power. Yet there was no fear, only pleasure as it ripped through her. She cried out against him and he joined her, harshly cursing as they both went limp.

Every muscle that ached from last night's ordeal was now relaxed. She couldn't have imagined that making love would be so calming once it was done.

"How do you feel, darling?" Vaughn asked, his blue eyes touching upon her face as he searched her gaze.

She sighed and lifted her head, kissing him. "Wonderful."

"Just imagine how much better it will be on a bed, when I can take hours exploring you, my mouth and hands touching secret places on your body."

"Hours?" Lord, she couldn't fathom that.

"*Hours*," he repeated in a low whisper. "And it will make you so exhausted you won't be able to leave our bed."

Our bed. Those two simple words wrapped her heart in a cocoon of warmth.

"We could stay here," she whispered. "Forget dinner and the ball. Let's stay right here." She ran her hands up his arms, relishing the way his muscles felt beneath her fingers. The sunlight created a wild halo of gold as it hit his hair, and she ran her fingers through the burnished strands. The ruby stone of her ring gleamed a dark blood red, like a pulsing heart.

"Is that what you desire, to hide away? Not that you need any excuse after what you've endured. We've plenty of books, but we shall need more food. I'll get dressed and go down to the kitchens, shall I?"

"Yes, please."

He pulled away from her, and they both straightened their clothes. She helped him button his waistcoat, and then he left her alone. She settled into a window seat, her body languid. She could stay here just like this for an age, watching the sun glint off the snow in the gardens. Fresh snow. They'd had more early this morning.

She studied the snow, then leaned carefully against the glass to get a better look. There were footprints...leading right up to the windows of the house one floor below. None of the servants would be outside, not so close to the house. But who would be prowling about in the snow, peering into windows? Only one name came to mind.

Milburn.

He was still here. She would have to tell Vaughn.

Perdita stared at the steps leading down to the coach that would carry her to the small church in Lothbrook. She couldn't ignore the flutter in her belly. In a few hours she would be wife to the Devil of London.

"I cannot believe you are getting married!" Her best friend, Alexandra Worthing, stood next to her, a puzzled look on her beautiful face. "Nor can I believe *who* you are marrying."

Once the rest of society heard the news, she knew she would be flooded with letters from all of her friends and acquaintances, desperate to hear how such a match came about. It would be exhausting to tell everyone.

For a brief moment, she considered reaching out to Lady Society, the infamous mystery woman who penned gossip columns in the *Quizzing Glass Gazette*. That might be a way to tell London the story in a way that would allow Perdita to enjoy her honeymoon without an endless deluge of inquiries.

"I know. But it feels right," Perdita answered. She shifted her bouquet and finally addressed the unspoken tension between her and her friend. "Are you angry with me? For marrying Darlington?

I know after what he did, kidnapping you, that you must despise him..."

Perdita swallowed whatever else she had planned to say. In some ways, Alexandra probably viewed Vaughn the way Perdita viewed Milburn, though Vaughn had never planned on forcing himself on Alex. It had all been for show to win a wager. But she felt she was betraying Alex somehow by marrying him, and the thought was breaking her heart.

"I..." Alex glanced down at her boots. "I am surprised, I admit. I didn't think he would be good enough for you. I'm still not convinced he is, but if you love him and he loves you..."

"He does," Perdita said, though she wasn't sure it was true, at least not yet.

"Then that is all that really matters, not what I think of him." Alex tightened her cloak and held out her hands to Perdita in a way they'd always done as girls. It was a sign of friendship, a sign of trust. Perdita grasped her hands, the bouquet caught between them as they stared at each other.

"It is your wedding day," Alex said with a broad smile. "And our husbands are good friends. Today is a happy day."

"It is," Perdita agreed. "Darlington and I are so happy you came."

"Of course! I had a letter from your mother the moment you told her of your engagement. I'm only sorry we weren't here sooner. Worthing would have helped Darlington drag that bastard out into the snow and drawn his cork!"

"Alex!" Perdita tried not to laugh at her friend's bloodthirsty words.

Alex pointed one booted foot in a ladylike way. "He deserves far worse," she grumbled.

"Yes, he does." For the tenth time that day, she glanced around but saw only her footmen and the coach. It didn't take away the sense she was being watched. She'd told Vaughn yesterday of her fears that Milburn hadn't returned to London. He had vowed to keep a vigil on her at all times, and it was only with her insistence that he even agreed to leave her to go to the church first.

"Come on, Perdy, we mustn't delay." Alex took her arm, and they walked down to the coach and climbed in. Her father came out of the house and joined them, grinning.

"Nothing like a Christmas wedding, eh?" he asked.

Perdita smiled back. What a wonderful day to be married.

❧

VAUGHN FELT THE WEIGHT OF HIS PISTOL TUCKED SECURELY into a pocket of his cloak as he walked up the steps of the small gray stone church. Greenery hung over the doorway and covered many of the pews that lined the aisle leading to the altar. Many of the villagers of Lothbrook were waiting in the pews, wearing their finest Christmas clothing. Everyone had come, it seemed, to witness the wedding.

My wedding. He smiled a little as he removed his cloak, careful to keep the pistol secure as he handed it to his valet, who took it to the front row near the altar and set it down. It was his only protection in case Milburn decided to show up. After Perdita confessed she'd seen footprints outside of the house alongside the windows, he feared Milburn was still somewhere in the village waiting for them.

He'd tried to calm her concerns, but the truth was Perdita was more correct in her fears than she knew.

His butler, Mr. Craig, had arrived the day before with news. Mr. Craig had used his cunning and his contacts from days before to track down Darby's investment partners. After making some inquiries down by the docks, he ransacked their offices during the night and found a couple of hidden ledgers, dating back to several years prior to Darby's involvement. No doubt whatever falsified documents Milburn possessed had used these as their template, with the dates changed accordingly.

Craig had taken the documents to the local magistrate, and the investment partners involved had been taken into custody for further review. Milburn no longer held any power over Perdita, fabricated or not, and the scandal that had broken over London would inevitably ensnare the vile man and ruin his reputation as well. Milburn would be out for blood.

"Stop fidgeting," Ambrose muttered in his ear. "Don't want the bride-to-be to notice you're afraid."

Vaughn swallowed a laugh. When his best friend, Ambrose, had arrived with his new wife, it had been a blessing that Vaughn had never expected. He had almost destroyed their friendship by kidnapping Alex to win a wager. For his friend to be here today, on his wedding day... A thousand words were on the tip of Vaughn's tongue, but he was too ashamed to speak any of them.

"All will be well," Ambrose said, as though he could read the pain and regret in Vaughn's heart.

"Thank you," he whispered. Ambrose nodded, smiling.

The vicar, in his Christmas vestments, waited beside Vaughn. They both stared at the door, listening for the rattle of a coach on the cobblestones, the one carrying his bride-to-be.

"Worried she'll run?" The vicar, a man in his early twenties, chuckled. "Don't be. I've known Miss Darby since I was a lad. There's nothing that will stop her when she wants something. And from what I hear, she wants *you*." The man's eyes twinkled, and Vaughn relaxed.

She did indeed want him, just as he wanted her. The previous evening, he and Perdita had spent hours in the library, reading to each other and making love. It was worth the risk of being discovered to show her how proficient he could be. And she had been perfect. *Wonderfully perfect.*

And now he would join his life to hers before God. For the first time, he understood the strange condition his friend Ambrose had fallen prey to.

Love—love brought on by sheer joy. He never would've imagined he would feel this way. Not after the heartbreak of his brother's death.

The doors opened, and Perdita came into the church wearing a white silk gown. It was simple but elegant, just as she was. She bit her lip as she walked toward him, and he realized she was trying to hide a smile. Mr. Darby led her to him and kissed her cheek before he took his place in the front pew.

The vicar began the ceremony, and Vaughn struggled to hear the words of the vows and sacraments. All he could think about was how he'd bared his soul to this woman beside him and how she had worked her way into his heart with her cleverness and sweetness. His life was now divided into life before her and life with her.

At last he was given permission to kiss her, something he did without hesitation. She giggled against his lips, and they moved to the vestry to sign the register. Then he took his cloak from his valet and she took hers from her maid, and they prepared to meet their guests on the steps of the church.

Mr. Craig stood close by, his cool eyes and weathered face taking in the quaint scene of the Christmas town. Vaughn nodded at him. The older man appeared haughty and aloof to most, but to Vaughn he was a trusted ally, and he was glad Mr. Craig had been able to attend the wedding.

"Are you ready to go?" Perdita asked, eyes bright with mischief.

"I am. Quite ready, that is, to get you flat on your back on a bed." He whispered this so that none of the guests around them could hear.

"Wicked man!" she chastised, but her cheeks had already flushed. He couldn't help but notice how her breasts pressed against the bodice of her gown as she inhaled. Soon he would be exploring every bit of her body with intimate pleasure.

Vaughn was so lost in thoughts of his honeymoon and the coming feast he was distracted as they left the little church. People gathered around them, shaking hands and congratulating. It wasn't until the crowd thinned Vaughn realized something terrible was unfolding.

Samuel Milburn stood in the cobblestone street, disheveled and wild. He stared at them on the steps.

"You've ruined everything!" Milburn shouted and raised his arm. Light glinted off the pistol as he took aim at Perdita.

Vaughn never understood what his father had meant when he'd spoken of a soldier's instincts until that moment. He acted without thought and stepped in front of his wife. The pistol fired, and Vaughn grunted as the bullet struck.

Pain, sharp at first, then dulling to a heavy ache, but he found himself unable to even utter a curse. Around him everyone was screaming, yet Vaughn kept Perdita pressed safely behind him, even as he stumbled and fell. He struggled to pull his weapon from his cloak as Milburn produced a second pistol.

Mr. Craig stepped forward, pressing Vaughn behind him. "Pardon me, my lord," he growled and raised his own pistol, firing at Milburn.

The man fell to his knees and landed facedown in the snow, a red pool of blood seeping into the snow around him on either side, his weapon cocked and still gripped in his hand. For a second no one moved. Then Mr. Craig tucked his empty pistol into his coat and turned back to Vaughn.

"Terribly sorry, sir. But your wound would have hampered your aim."

"Good man." Vaughn chuckled and then winced. "Good man." He'd always been glad his butler had a very particular set of skills, and today those skills had saved him and his wife.

His butler nodded solemnly.

Perdita fell to her knees next to him. "Vaughn."

"I'm all right, darling. Would you mind fetching the doctor?" He kept his voice calm because she was crying and clinging to him. The chaos outside the church had calmed only a little, but he didn't focus on any of that. He kept his gaze on Perdita and hers was on him.

"And to think you were worried I didn't love you," he teased.

Her eyes filled with tears. "Vaughn." She clutched him fiercely. "Please don't joke about that."

He managed to wrap one arm around her as he righted himself. Only then did he dare to look at his wound. It wasn't deep. He'd been hit in the shoulder, the bullet passing through muscle alone. It was really more of a graze.

"Is it bad?" Perdita asked, holding herself close to him.

"No, not at all. Lucky for us, I'm damned hard to kill."

Perdita stared at him, blinking rapidly as tears formed in her eyes, and Vaughn knew she was upset at his teasing.

The doctor arrived a few minutes later. His residence, thankfully, was not far from the church. Vaughn and Perdita went back inside while his wound was tended. They sat in the last pew, where Vaughn removed his cloak, waistcoat, and shirt.

"Damn, it's bloody cold in here," Vaughn muttered as the doctor cleaned his wound.

"Lucky, that's what you are," Dr. Williams said. "Mostly a graze. I'll bind it up, and you must take care to keep the bandage fresh. No vigorous activity for a few days, I'm afraid." The doctor shot Vaughn a pointed look and then said to Perdita, "I understand young love and the passion of newlyweds, but none of that, you hear? Not for three or four days."

"Like hell," Vaughn growled.

Perdita squeezed his arm. "If he says we mustn't, then we won't. But I shall make up for it. Once we can." Her cheeks pinked in a delightful blush.

"I'll hold you to that promise, darling." He had a few delicious ideas of what he'd do once he was mended.

She smiled back, her eyes sparkling with tears. "Good."

Dr. Williams grunted as he bandaged Vaughn's wound. By the time they were ready to leave the church, they found Perdita's father waiting outside. Milburn's body had been removed from the street.

"Your butler has called for the magistrate, Vaughn. I doubt there will be any further questions. Everyone saw what happened."

"Thank heavens." Perdita rested her head against Vaughn's shoulder. The gesture made his stomach flutter with a quiet sort of thrill, one that lingered and made him feel dizzy.

Mrs. Darby smiled warmly at him. "Let's get you both home."

Home. Home with Perdita and her family. *They are my family now.* With a little grin, he walked with his bride down to the waiting coach, ignoring the twinge of pain in his shoulder. He was not alone. Not anymore.

❧

THREE LONG DAYS LATER, PERDITA FOUND HERSELF SITTING ON the edge of her bed, holding a small box, wearing nothing but her shift. Nerves danced in her chest and belly. She couldn't help it. Tonight she was going to give Vaughn his Christmas gift, albeit a few days late, and she prayed he would not be upset with her.

Many men would not react well to having matters of pride exposed. But in the last few days so much had changed between them. Since they could not make love, they had lain in each other's arms and whispered in the dark about their hopes, their dreams, and their lives before.

It astonished her to realize it was indeed possible to love a man who'd been a stranger to her so recently. Yes, lust had been there, but after everything they'd shared, love had crept up on her, silent as a thief, and now she truly loved him. She knew he loved her too. If stepping between her and Milburn's pistol hadn't been enough, the last three days had proven it. The gentle smiles, the way he listened, the way they'd lain together, their heads close and limbs entwined. Hearts beating as one.

She sat up straighter when her bedchamber door opened.

Vaughn walked in, flashing her a wicked grin that made her laugh.

"Three days, as ordered. And now you're mine. *All mine.*" He started toward the bed, but she held up a hand.

"Wait."

He stopped, his eyes questioning hers. She looked at the little box and thought of what it contained.

Please understand why I must give it back to you.

"What is that?" he asked.

"A Christmas present, long overdue." She raised it up, and he slowly took it from her. He was so beautiful, the way only a man could be while wearing nothing save his buckskin breeches and a dark-blue silk vest. Vaughn opened the box, his eyes locked on the gift.

It was, of course, the pocket watch she'd bought back from the jeweler.

"I..." His voice broke as he took the watch from the box. The silver glinted in the light. "How..." He gave his head a little shake. "This was my grandfather's. I had to sell it."

"You promise not to be angry with me?" she asked.

"I promise." His eyes blazed, though not with anger.

"I saw you, that day at the jeweler's. I didn't mean to see what I did. But once I realized you might be buying me a ring, I couldn't let you give up something I could tell was dear to you."

"All this time you've kept it?"

"I was afraid you would be angry with me for buying it back, but I couldn't leave it there. It belongs to you. You're not upset, are you?"

His thumb brushed over the silver lid of the watch before he set it on the table by her washbasin. He unbuttoned his waistcoat methodically, then removed his shirt. He loosened the placket of his trousers, but didn't remove them.

"Vaughn..."

"Remove your shift," he commanded. His voice was low and dark. His eyes, however, promised that wicked, forbidden fantasies would be fulfilled. She stood uneasily in the wake of his intense gaze. "*Now.*"

She rushed to remove her shift. He plucked it from her hands the moment it was free of her. He folded it and set it on the armchair by her vanity table.

"When we sleep, you will remove your shift. I like to be beside you skin to skin," he murmured as he reached up to trail a finger along her collarbone.

Perdita shivered and moved to cover her breasts, but his dark gaze stopped her.

"In this room, I am in control," he reminded her. She nodded, her body heating. She would never let him control her outside of bed, but in bed she would willingly succumb. She craved his commands, his control. It was both thrilling and exciting.

"Lie back for me, darling."

She did so, trying to lift her head to see him as he retrieved his neckcloth from his shirt.

"What—"

He hushed her as he came back to the bed. He took her wrists and bound them together with the cloth. Then he raised her hands above her head and tied them to one of the bedposts.

Perdita's heart raced. She struggled against the restraints but couldn't get free.

"Here, alone, we can indulge our dark sides," he said, a smile curving his lips at the corners. "Do you trust me?"

"Yes." She did trust him. The bandage around his shoulder reminded her that this man would give his life for her.

"Good." He climbed onto the bed, caging her body as he kissed her. His lips moved expertly over hers. Then he traced a burning path down to her bare breasts. Perdita sucked in air as his lips fastened around one nipple. It was an overpowering sensation to feel his hot mouth on her breasts, sucking. He nipped the tender bud, a whisper of pain blending in with the pleasure before he moved to her other breast. He moved lower and lower down her body. Her thighs clenched together, but he shoved them apart.

"You're such a pretty pink," he whispered against her mound before he kissed her inner thighs. She opened her mouth to speak, but he silenced her with another of his wicked looks.

"You're mine, sweeting. To play with, to taste. You may only say 'my lord' or make sounds of pleasure. Understand?"

She gave a jerky nod and then gasped in shock as he licked her down there. The unexpected burst of sensations had her whimpering, her thighs shaking. His tongue continued playing with her folds and caressing her before he closed his lips around her throbbing bud. Then he sucked on that bundle of nerves, and she screamed in shock at the hard rush of pleasure that exploded through her.

"That's it," he coaxed gently as she drifted down from the exquisite high.

"My lord..." She panted softly, barely able to think past those two words.

"Yes?"

She had closed her eyes, but she could hear the smile in his voice. "You are the most wicked man in London. Nay, in England."

His chuckle surprised her.

"Well, you *did* marry the Devil of London." He rolled her onto her stomach. Then, without warning, he smacked her arse with his hand. The blow was not hard, but it made her squeak in surprise. He did it twice more, then stroked his palm soothingly over her bottom. It felt wonderful on the slightly stinging skin. Then she was turned on her back once more as he leaned over her.

"Too much?" he asked.

"No, my lord."

"Good." He pressed a heated kiss to her lips before he settled on his knees between her parted thighs. Then he lifted her hips, bringing her close to his lap but lifting her up enough that she could see her body. He tugged his trousers down, and his erection jutted toward her.

"Watch while I claim you," he ordered. There was a growl in his voice, a hint of the animal just beneath his skin that made her shiver in anticipation. He guided his shaft into her.

"Bloody Christ, you're tight." He pushed deeper and deeper

into her. She watched in aroused fascination as they joined completely.

He began to thrust into her until they both made soft sounds at the back of their throats as their bodies joined over and over again. "Don't look away. Don't shut your eyes." The muscles of his chest and arms bunched as he pumped into her, and she couldn't look away, even if she wanted to. Her dark god of the underworld was owning her, body and soul. When their eyes met, she saw in that blinding instant as they came apart at the same time that she owned him too.

Hours later, Perdita lay on top of Vaughn, her legs now tangled with his, their bodies damp, and his slowly measured breathing, that of a man almost asleep, was comforting.

"It wasn't too much?" he asked.

She lifted her face to rest her chin on his chest. "No. It was perfect."

The boyish grin she adored was back. He toyed with a lock of her hair, spooling it around one of his fingers.

"A man could get spoiled having you for a wife."

"Indeed. I am wonderful," she agreed, biting back a smile.

"Cheeky little chit." He slapped her buttocks with his free hand, and she hissed. He had shown her his dark desires tonight, and she had discovered that hers matched his.

This beautiful, mysterious man loves me. He excites me. He makes me feel alive.

She kissed his chest and laid her head back down.

"Tell me we shall always be like this."

"It will always be like this. Except for, of course, when the children are old enough to sneak out of the nursery to find us. It will be even more fun evading the scamps to get a moment alone." He laughed, the rich sound rumbling deep from his chest.

"You want children?"

"More than anything, except for you."

She held on to him even tighter. "I'm glad of that."

He nuzzled her cheek and placed a kiss on her temple. "Are you truly happy to be my wife?"

She lifted her head again. "Infinitely so. And you? Are you happy to be my husband?"

His eyes were serious. "I am. There is something indescribable about the joy of sharing myself with you, of letting you into my heart. It was frightening at first, but now I can't imagine a day without you."

"So you love me?" She tried to sound teasing, but she had to hear the words from him.

"I do. I love you to distraction, to the depths of my soul and beyond."

"I love you too. My white knight." She brushed a hand over his chest. She'd come to realize that a man in perfect shining armor was a man who'd never been tested. Vaughn, in his tarnished armor, had proven how strong his mettle truly was more than once, and he loved her in ways she'd never dreamed of.

She slid up a few inches to kiss him, knowing that she had found love at last. It was on his lips, on his tongue, and in the way he held her. She knew snow was falling outside tonight and whispered a silent prayer of thanks for the gift of loving someone who loved her in return. It was the sort of miracle she had long given up hope on ever having.

Christmas, after all, was a season for hope, for miracles, for faith, and for love unending.

You've just read the 3rd book in the Seduction series. The other books in the series are, book 1 *The Duelist's*

Seduction, book 2 *The Rakehell's Seduction*. Turn the page to start reading book 4 in the Seduction series *The Gentleman's Seduction*!

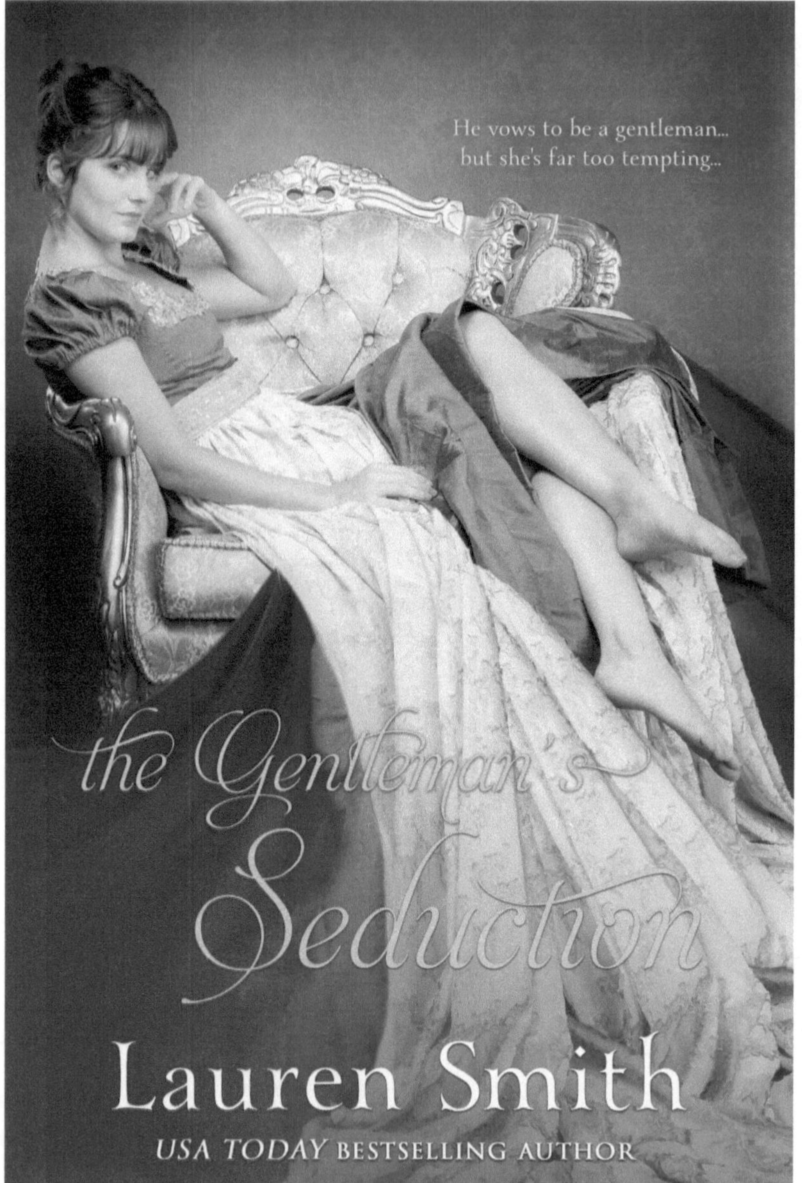
He vows to be a gentleman...
but she's far too tempting...
the Gentleman's
Seduction
Lauren Smith
USA TODAY BESTSELLING AUTHOR

THE GENTLEMAN'S SEDUCTION

THE SEDUCTION SERIES BOOK 4

PROLOGUE

London, December 5, 1814

"Please, you cannot do this!" The hoarse pleading echoed in the silence of the hall.

Seventeen-year-old Martin Banks hid in the shadows, watching his father plead for mercy with Edwin Hartwell in the foyer of their small townhouse on Gracechurch Street. Edwin's tall stature, broad shoulders, and cold face cast fear into Martin's young heart. His twin sister, Helen, clutched his arm as they peered around the curtain's edge from their hidden vantage point.

"I can and I will." Edwin's face was hard as he stared at William Banks. "You owe me ten thousand pounds, and I'm calling in that debt. If you cannot pay, you shall be out within the week."

"Out?" Their mother, a lovely woman with a delicate constitution, leaned heavily against the banister for support. She should have been resting upstairs, not facing this brute next to her husband. Martin wanted to go to her, but he was frozen with a childish fear. If his father was afraid of Edwin, then Martin knew he had no chance to stand against him.

"Yes, madam." Edwin's reply was cold enough to ice over the river Thames.

"Oh, please, you can't. What about the children?" She held a hand out beseechingly to Edwin, but he shrugged off her touch and stepped back.

"If you had cared at all about your children, you would not have made such a risky investment. I loaned you the money, and I am owed my due."

Martin's throat tightened, and he curled his hands in fists so tightly that his nails dug into his palms hard enough to draw blood.

"I'll get you the money," William said, rushing to reassure Edwin.

"You may try, but none of the banks will extend you credit."

"They might," his father argued. "I have not fallen completely out of favor with them."

"We shall see. If not, you will be cast out in seven days." Edwin set his hat on his head, and the butler opened the door for him. As the man stepped out into the night, Martin stared at the his back, burning the sight into his memory forever.

Edwin Hartwell, the man who ruined their family.

"William, what shall we do? If the banks won't help us..." his mother began.

"I still have friends at Drummonds. I'll go there first thing tomorrow."

"Please, I'm so worried. It is so close to Christmas. What if we cannot afford another place to live?" His mother hugged his father, and Martin's heart swelled with hope. Surely his father would be able to do something. He had to; they needed a home to live in.

"Everything will be all right, Mary. You'll see. There's bound to be some rooms somewhere, even if we must move to a less respectable area of town." His father let her go, and she brushed away a tear, her hands trembling.

"Go upstairs and rest. You've had too much to worry about today." William's eyes were dark with concern. Martin was worried too. In the last few days, his mother had grown weaker than she ever had been before.

She started for the stairs but suddenly collapsed. Her body crumpled to the floor.

"Mary!" his father shouted and rushed to her side, cradling her in his arms.

"Mother!" Martin fled the shadows and joined him, Helen right behind him.

His mother lay like a fallen angel in his father's embrace, her lashes fluttering like the frantic wings of a butterfly trying to stay aloft in the midst of a storm. Her ashen face, pale lips, and cloudy eyes warned Martin of a truth he had never wished to see—that one's parents were not invincible.

"Fetch the doctor!" William shouted.

Martin grabbed his coat from an anxious footman and ran into the street, calling for a hackney. The doctor they knew lived only a few streets away, but Martin feared even that short distance would be too far. He'd seen his mother's face, pale and her limbs going slack. He had seen death.

Edwin Hartwell had stolen more than Martin's home—he'd taken his mother's life, and someday Edwin would pay.

CHAPTER 1

London, December 10, 1825

Martin Banks despised Christmas. He sat in his armchair at his club, Brooks's, and listened to the men around him discussing the balls and winter festivities to be held over the next few weeks leading up to the holiday. He unfolded his copy of the *Morning Post*, trying to focus on the articles and block out the stories of the men around him as they shared memories of snow forts, figgy puddings, and quests for a Yule log.

Nonsense. Foolish, sentimental nonsense.

At the age of twenty-eight, he was past his reckless youth but not old enough to look back fondly upon it either. Men his age were celebrating the holiday with new brides or new children. But not Martin. He had taken careful steps to *avoid* marriage, which had been easy in his early twenties. After his mother died, his father had lost his will to live, and their lives had fallen into shambles.

By age twenty, he and his twin sister, Helen, were orphans and had moved to Bath to seek employment, him as a clerk and she as a governess. They'd both failed to achieve those respective goals. Fortunately, Helen had married, and her husband had given Martin financial support while he'd worked his way into the world of investments. Without much money at hand earlier on, the young ladies of Bath had ignored him despite his fair looks. Not that he cared. It hadn't been until a few years later when he'd earned his fortune that women looked upon him with eyes toward marriage, and by then he'd lost his desire to marry.

I won't make the same mistakes my father did. A man who doesn't love anything can't lose anything.

For the past eight years, he'd worked toward establishing himself as a smart investor. Unlike his father, he had far more luck and had amassed quite the fortune. Now ladies looked at him with open interest, which he happily ignored. He didn't need a wife, but if he was honest with himself, he needed a new mistress. His bachelor residence was a bit lonely at times. He knew many men wouldn't set their mistresses up in their own residences and would simply visit them. Martin had preferred the closeness of his companions much more than he cared for society's rules. Since he did little entertaining it didn't matter overmuch that his mistresses usually lived in his town house.

It had been a while since he'd had a mistress under his roof. Martin didn't like that he was having fits of the blue devils more frequently. At times, the only cure was to visit his twin sister, Helen. Her two young children, his niece and nephew, gave him no end of joy.

"Banks, you devil, where have you been hiding these days?" A familiar jovial voice broke through Martin's grim thoughts. A ruddy-cheeked man with a ready smile stared down at him over the top of his newspaper.

"Rodney!" Martin grinned and folded the paper and set it aside. "Join me, would you?" There were plenty of men Martin could claim as friends, but Rodney was closer to a brother.

"Just for a bit. I have to escort my wife to Bond Street. The children need presents, you know." Rodney's delight was evident by the warmth with which he said this and the way his eyes glinted with fatherly pride. A twinge of pain in Martin's chest surprised him, but he buried the pain with another smile.

"I haven't seen you in months," Martin said. "Did you take the course of action I suggested on the annuities?"

Rodney nodded and took a seat close to Martin, glancing around the room at the other men.

"I certainly did. Paid off handsomely. Still is, in fact." Rodney slapped his thigh and leaned back in his chair.

"Good. Glad to hear it." Martin had known Rodney for eight years. When they'd first met, the man had been a bit of a gambler, but he'd outgrown the habit and settled down, prosperously.

"And you? Tell me, are you still seeing that opera singer? She was most enchanting."

Martin chuckled. "Stella and I parted ways four months ago. I didn't mind her upkeep, but we had both tired of each other. Once the spark is gone, it's gone," Martin said with a sigh. "Still, she is doing well in Paris, I hear."

"Why don't you come out with me tonight? I've got an invitation to meet with some gentlemen at the Argyll Rooms. They're having a ball of sorts, and a few tables of faro and whist will be set up, I imagine."

"I don't know. Who are you meeting with?"

"Lord Pentwith, Mr. Smythebrooke, and a few others. Come, Martin, have a little fun this evening."

Martin stroked his chin thoughtfully. "Perhaps I shall." He could always leave early if the evening bored him.

"Splendid. Meet you at the Argyll Rooms at nine tonight." Rodney rose from his chair and gave Martin a congenial thump on the back as he departed.

Folding his paper, Martin decided it was time to go. He waved at one of the reading room attendants, and the boy fetched his hat and coat. As he left the club, he inhaled the crisp, cold winter air and looked skyward at the purple skies and the setting sun, which softened the harshness of the city at twilight. In a few hours he would be at the Argyll Rooms, and he would likely have a chance to make the acquaintance of a few lovely ladies looking to secure a protector and benefactor. It was a role he would be happy to fill for an enterprising young beauty who might catch his eye.

By the time he reached his residence on Park Lane, he was eagerly looking forward to meeting up with Rodney again. The townhouse had cost him thirty-three thousand pounds, but he had embellished it with renovations and furnishings for another hundred thousand pounds, so now it was quite an attractive home. Any woman he met tonight would be quite enthusiastic to share it with him for a time. The front door opened as he carefully wiped his boots on the boot scraper to rid them of the ice from the pavements.

"Welcome home, sir." Mr. Harris, his butler, collected his hat and coat, passing them to the first footman.

"Evening, Harris. Please notify Mrs. Wilson I shall be out tonight and won't need supper."

"Of course, sir. Should I have your coach ready at a certain time?"

"Half past eight would be sufficient." He glanced about the Palladian-style home with its grand white marble staircase, envisioning a beautiful young lady ascending the stairs, ready to be taken to his bed.

Damn, it had been too bloody long since he had a woman around his home. It would be good to have a new mistress, someone to warm his bed and keep him company in the evenings over a glass of sherry. He had missed that, certainly. Martin climbed the stairs to the primary floor and entered his chambers. His valet, Will Byrd, was tending to the collection of snuffboxes in a glass case. Martin never used snuff, but he liked to collect the beautifully painted boxes. There was something about the tiny painted porcelain scenes that fascinated and amazed him.

"Evening, Byrd," he greeted. His valet nodded and murmured a polite reply.

"I'll be going out tonight. Draw me a bath and set out evening clothes suitable for the Argyll Rooms."

"Yes, sir. Oh, a letter came for you earlier this evening, sir." Byrd passed him a letter, which he took. He plucked a silver letter opener from his escritoire and sliced the wax seal open. He recognized his sister's handwriting at once.

MARTIN,

I hope this letter finds you well. The children have been begging for news about when you will visit again. Four months is far too long to go without seeing you. Gareth and I thought it would be lovely if you came to visit over Christmas. I know you don't like the holidays, but it would delight the children and me too if you came to stay with us. Please say you'll consider it.

Yours,
Helen

"OH, HELEN." HE FOLDED THE LETTER AND SET IT DOWN ON HIS desk. Despite his vow to never love anyone or anything, Helen was the one exception. She was his twin, someone he'd shared their mother's womb with. That was an unbreakable bond. He had his friends, like Rodney, and acquaintances. But if those friendships were stolen tomorrow, it would not break him, not like losing someone he loved like Helen, Gareth or the children.

"Very well. You want me home for Christmas, then I will come home." No doubt she had plans to introduce him to more simpering young ladies from Bath, but he didn't want his sister to play matchmaker. He would not let the holidays melt the ice around his heart.

Nothing could do that.

CHAPTER 2

Martin entered the Argyll Rooms on the east side of Regent Street and glanced around the hall. Frescoes were painted on the walls to represent Corinthian pillars. Grecian lamps illuminated his path as he passed through the elegant crimson folding doors and into the festivities. The men and women around him were boisterous. The sounds of their gaiety bounced off the walls, creating such a din he could barely hear himself think.

Martin paused as he reached the main staircase. The green cloth beneath his feet was covered with a Turkish patterns. He'd always enjoyed the elegance of the Argyll Rooms, and tonight was no different. But rather than take in the sights, he searched the crowd for Rodney. The jovial crowd and the excitement of the night's pleasures around him started to affect him. A smile curved his lips, and he hummed a little to the strains of a familiar song from an orchestra playing in the main hall.

Then his heart stopped and his world tilted on its axis.

There, at the entrance to the Turkish Room, was a man he had not seen since he was seventeen. He felt as though he were suddenly plunging from a great height. The man he loathed more than anything in the world was there—Edwin Hartwell. In all these years, they had never crossed paths at a club, ball, or dinner before, but he would never ever forget that face.

Hartwell wasn't one for society unless he was sniffing out a business opportunity, yet there he was, speaking to a group of gentlemen. A cold rage frosted Martin's insides as he started toward the man. His fingers itched with the urge to grab him, slam him against the wall, and strangle the breath from his body.

Hartwell was speaking earnestly to a man Martin didn't know. They soon disappeared into the Turkish Room, and Martin followed. The room was a novelty. The elegant blue carpets and blue drapes were accented with Ottoman sofas spaced throughout the room. Beneath the beautifully painted ceilings, an eagle made of gold clasped a thunderbolt in its claws. A massive chandelier hung below the eagle. Between the sofas were card tables neatly arranged and games already underway. Hazard tables were surrounded by gentlemen, most of them dressed like dandified peacocks, prancing about as they tossed dice. Games of E.O., faro, whist, and even rouge et noir were all being played. Hartwell stood near the rouge et noir table.

Martin lingered a few tables away, studying the man who had destroyed his family. Hartwell had been an impressively tall man with dark hair and a hard twist to his mouth all those years ago. A nightmarish figure to a young lad.

Now the man's hair was streaked with gray, his shoulders were a little stooped, and his face was lined with a weariness born of strife. The cold nobility he'd once carried about him like a shield had decayed into a struggle to survive. The cut of his coat was loose, as though he'd shrunken a little, and the fabric was noticeably threadbare. Hartwell wasn't doing well.

Martin's pulse began to race. He felt like a hound who had caught the scent of a fox on the air and was ready for blood.

A group of men abandoned the rouge et noir table. Hartwell leaned in to place a wager on a red diamond compartment, his face desperate. The dealer laid out two rows of cards and stopped when the cards reached thirty-one or more on the black side of the table. Then he did the same for the red side. There players who'd wagered on black cheered and collected the winnings. Hartwell's face fell, and he turned away from the table. He moved on to a game of whist and took an empty seat. Martin made his move, claiming the seat beside him. He waited to see Edwin's look of dread, or anger, of anything.

"Evening," Hartwell murmured.

The man doesn't even recognize me.

After killing his mother and casting them out into the cold, Martin wasn't even a passing thought for him. For a second the thought burned like fire in his chest, but then he realized he could use this to his advantage. He could play against the man and win. Desperate men, like the lad he had once been, never played well. When a man had something to lose, he was edgy and less focused.

A man sat down opposite him, one who would be his partner, and another man sat down opposite Hartwell. The game began. As the cards were dealt, thirteen to each man, Martin held his breath and watched his partner closely for hints and signals. They soon accumulated points in their favor.

"Wagers, please," the dealer asked the men. Martin produced several hundred-pound notes, and the table went still. After a minute, the other two men added matching sums, and then they looked at Hartwell. The older man bit his lip and looked directly at Martin.

"Would you accept a vowel?"

Martin slowly smiled, as the opportunity he'd waited for had arrived.

"I would indeed." He nodded in approval to the dealer, and the other men did the same. The vowel, as it was called, was nothing more than an IOU.

That was exactly what he wanted, to have Hartwell indebted to him.

The dealer delivered a hand of cards to each man, and the amount increased again as more wagers were placed. More points were awarded to Martin and his partner. By the time the pool was over a thousand pounds, Hartwell's hands were visibly shaking. When the final card was revealed, Hartwell's face drained of color and he folded his cards down on the table.

"I'm sorry," he muttered. "I cannot play."

The men at the table went still, and the dealer declared Martin and his partner victorious.

"I'll pay you for your half of this man's vowels," Martin said to his partner as they rose from the table. The man glanced at Hartwell's ashen face and nodded. Hartwell's partner sighed and paid his dues, while Martin reimbursed his own partner for his portion of Hartwell's debt outright.

"Thank you, Mr...." Hartwell tilted his head at Martin.

"Martin Banks."

"Banks? Have we met before?" The older man's eyes searched his, seeking a memory, but unable to find it.

Martin fixed him with a chilly gaze. "Yes. We have. I will pay a call upon you tomorrow evening, and we will discuss your debt then."

"Banks?" It was clear Edwin was still struggling to make the connection. Martin would let him worry about it overnight.

His blood was pounding against his eardrums as he fought to control himself.

"You should be worried about how I shall collect your debt."

I have him where I want him. Killing him now wouldn't do any good.

Hartwell staggered, knocking his chair over. "Please, I can find a way to pay you..."

"Please!" Hartwell grabbed his sleeve.

Martin stared at his hand, and Hartwell hastily released him. "As I said, I will call upon you tomorrow evening," he repeated. "We will discuss the payment terms then." Martin walked away, his hands shaking as he tried to calm himself.

Soon he would have his revenge.

Lavinia Hartwell was perched on a window seat facing Duke Street with a book in one hand and a cup of tea in the other. She was lost in the pages of a sensational Gothic novel, *Lady Leticia and the Dark Duke* by L. R. Gloucester.

Lavinia, or Livvy as she preferred to be called, found these two characters particularly compelling. There was something delightful about a darkly handsome man who played a reluctant hero and a young lady who fought bravely to save herself from a dastardly villain. Her life was not so interesting as what happened between the pages of the novel she held.

At eighteen, she'd only just experienced her first season and hadn't met a gentleman who reminded her of the dark duke in her book. There were plenty of pleasant men, of course, and far too many rakes. There was also the occasional rogue, but none had turned her head. It was a bit foolish, she knew, but she was hoping to fall madly in love with a man the way Leticia had. Her mother had cautioned her that most of the matches made in England wouldn't be love matches. It was the way of things.

Still, I wish for one.

She looked up from her book and peered out through the heavy old curtains of the window seat she sat in. The darkened streets outside the window were now illuminated with a few flickering gas lamps, lending an eerie feel to the streetscape. Livvy closed her book and finished her tea. Just as she left her seat, she heard her father's shout in the hall.

"Elizabeth! He's here!" Edwin's voice boomed loudly enough that the library door rattled.

Livvy rushed from the library and paused at the top of the stairs. Her father was having a heated discussion with her mother near the foyer. Livvy strained to listen.

"Edwin, how could you let him come here?" Elizabeth snapped. "Last night you promised you would do well at the Argyll Rooms, but you lost everything we have. I don't want that man in my home!" Her mother's face was pale, and she was twisting a handkerchief wildly in her hands, wrecking the fragile lace.

Lost everything? The words didn't have any meaning at first. Livvy tried to make them fit into her mind in a way that made sense.

"He owns *everything*, Elizabeth. He must be allowed in. I will beg him for clemency." Her father nodded at the butler. "Show him into the drawing room, Howell."

Howell, their butler, hastily opened the door to allow entry to this harbinger of doom.

Livvy ducked down behind the banister, struck with the sudden need to hide. Her father and mother's conversation still haunted her. Her father had gambled away all their possessions at the Argyll Rooms last night? Icy dread gripped her, squeezing the breath from her lungs.

Everything was to be taken away. *My home, my clothes…my books?*

Any chance she had of making a good match this season was ruined. Her father was a mere gentleman, though her mother was the daughter of a duke, which made Livvy granddaughter to a duke and therefore most attractive. Though her grandfather's title could not pass through her, the family's connections to members of the peerage were always welcome. But the scandal around becoming destitute would tarnish even that.

Her grandfather, the Duke of Sussex, was a wonderful and well-liked man. Why hadn't her parents gone to him for help? He'd let her mother marry for love. Surely he would not refuse to help her if she faced money troubles? Livvy bit her lip hard. Perhaps her mother's pride might be the problem.

Howell opened the door, and Livvy peered from her hiding place in the shadows as a man entered her house. His gold-blond hair was striking, and his features were those of a fallen angel or a Byronic hero.

"This way, Mr. Banks. My master will see you shortly." Howell escorted the man into the drawing room. Livvy looked for her parents, but they had stepped into her father's study.

After a moment, her father appeared and just as quickly disappeared into the drawing room. Howell stood with his back to the door like a sentry. Livvy abandoned her hiding place and rushed down the stairs. When Howell saw her, she held a finger to her lips. He nodded and stepped aside for her. She pressed her ear to the door, listening to the voices.

"As I said last evening, Mr. Hartwell, I now have a debt of four thousand pounds with your name on the vowels. I want you and your wife to vacate this home by tomorrow, and I will sell it by Christmas to discharge the debt you owe me. I understand this house is still partially owned by Drummonds?"

"Yes." Her father's reply was soft, broken.

"I will buy out the bank's interest and sell the house then," Banks said, his words calm and even. Without emotion.

Livvy knew she had to intervene. Surely this man had some shred of decency and mercy within him. She flung open the drawing room door and burst inside.

"Please!" she exclaimed as she faced the man who stood by the fireplace. He was taller than she'd realized, so much that he dwarfed her when she approached him. His piercing blue eyes glow in the firelight.

"Please," she repeated more softly, her heart now hammering. "Give my father time to pay back what he owes. It's almost Christmas..." She feared her plea fell on deaf ears as Banks continued to stare at her. His broad shoulders and fine clothes spoke of his wealth. He didn't need their money, surely. She felt very young and foolish standing before him in a gown that was two years old, the hem let out twice and the color faded from too much wear. It hadn't bothered her before, but now? Now she felt very silly when facing a handsome, well-dressed man like Mr. Banks.

His eyes lingered upon her, sweeping from her face down to her slippers and back up, and she swore she could almost feel invisible hands touching her.

"Hartwell, who is this *enchanting* creature?" His lips, once pursed in a tight line, now softened into a slow, seductive smile.

"This is my daughter, Lavinia."

"Livvy," she corrected automatically, and a wave of heat enveloped her face.

"Daughter…" Banks murmured the word as he rested one hand on the marble fireplace. "This quite changes things."

Hope blossomed inside her, and she started to smile.

"Then you will give me time to pay you back?" Her father stepped close to her as he spoke to Mr. Banks, putting one hand on her shoulder.

Banks's gaze settled on her, then slid to her father. "No."

"But—"

Livvy was cut off as he continued. "I have decided to accept another form of repayment allowing you to keep your house."

Her father's fingers dug into her shoulder. "No. Anything but that," he growled. "Take the house."

"Anything but what?" Livvy demanded. She couldn't understand why her father was upset.

"You, my dear," Banks said smugly. "He means anything but *you*."

She tried to battle her bewilderment. "Me? But how can I repay you?" Did he mean that if she were to marry soon she could convince her husband to pay her father's debt?

"Delightfully innocent. How charming." Banks's tone was laced with sardonic amusement that made her bristle.

"Take the house, Banks. You cannot have her. She has marriage prospects and a good life ahead of her." Her father stepped between her and Banks.

Banks drummed his fingers on the mantel and faced the fire once again. "I could wreck those prospects. My reach is wider than you realize."

"Yes, I'm now aware. You're William Banks's son, aren't you?" her father asked.

"At last you make the connection."

Livvy didn't understand, she glanced between them, confused.

"Who is William Banks?" For a moment she thought neither her father or Mr. Banks would answer her.

"He was a man who owed your father money. Your father cast us out of our home. My mother died that night, just minutes after he left us ruined. He took her from me, and now justice has seen fit to give me the chance to return the favor and take something from him, which would be you, my dear."

His words left her stunned and she her gaze darted between her father who looked stricken with grief, and the cold, impassionate man, Mr. Banks. Livvy studied his handsome profile, and only then did she understand what he suggested. He wanted *her*, not any money from a future husband. And there was only one reason a man in his situation would want her when it was clear he did not intend to marry her.

She buried her fear as best she could and composed her features. "If you take me, will you consider my father's debts fully paid?" she asked. Her body shook as she came to grips with what she was considering: to give herself to this man to save her family.

"Livvy, you will not." Her father looked down at her, fear and anger in his eyes. She pushed past him to stand face-to-face with Mr. Banks.

"Well?" she asked.

He crossed his arms over his chest, scowling a little. "Yes. You in exchange for the entire debt." His stare burned into her with such intensity that she shivered with dread.

She cleared her throat. "What are your conditions?"

He stroked his chin, seeming to ponder the question, but she sensed he already had an answer. "You will be mine for as long as it takes me to tire of you."

Icy tendrils curled around her, paralyzing her. How long would it take for him to grow bored and let her go home?

"No," her father snapped. "She isn't going with you. Livvy, go into my study and stay with your mother."

She wished she could obey her father. More than anything else in the world, she wanted to run from this horror she was agreeing to. But she was no longer a child. She could not hide behind her mother's skirts and allow her family and home to be ruined. Her parents had sacrificed much for her over the years. It was her duty to return that devotion.

"No, Father," she said quietly, then looked Mr. Banks in the eyes. Her blood pounded so hard in her ears she could barely hear her own voice. "I agree to your terms."

CHAPTER 3

"Livvy, I won't let you do this." Her father gripped her by the shoulders and gave her a little shake.

"Papa, I *have* to do this. I cannot let you and Mama be tossed into the street. It is within my power to save you." She glanced toward Mr. Banks and saw him smirking, as though her family dilemma was somehow amusing to him.

"The lady has made her choice, Hartwell. She comes with me. Tonight."

"T-tonight?" She choked on the word.

"Yes, tonight."

His cool reply made her dizzy. "I'm not ready. I can't—"

"Tonight," he repeated. "You may pack a valise, but bring no more than a few dresses. You won't need them. I will provide you with suitable clothing for the position of my mistress. And you will not be given a separate house. You will share my home with me so I may have you at my beck and call."

"Banks, you bastard!" Her father lunged, his fists raised. Mr. Banks looked equally ready to strike her father.

Livvy leapt between them, placing a hand on her father's chest and one on Banks to keep them apart. "No! Mr. Banks, may I please speak to my father alone?"

He lowered his fists and tugged on his waistcoat to straighten it.

"Yes. I will return to my coach outside. Join me when you are ready."

"I will be out shortly." She promised, meeting his cold blue eyes. He accepted with a swift nod, then left the room.

"Livvy..." Her father's voice softened. He curled his hands around her shoulders and drew her into a fierce embrace. "You mustn't go."

She hugged him back, but her mind was made up.

"I have to, Papa. He will take our home away. I know you and Mama have been saving these last few years, but it hasn't been enough, has it? We lost most of our servants ages ago, and we can barely afford new clothes and—"

"I know." Her father cut her off, but not harshly. Sorrow and regret dimmed the light in his eyes. "But this is my fault. I should be punished, not you. I made a mistake many years ago. I took away his home. His father owed me about eight thousand pounds, and I..." He choked on the words. "I was desperate. I had my own debts to pay, so I evicted them. He must have been just a lad then, seventeen or eighteen."

"You...you did this to him?" Horror gripped her heart, and she couldn't meet his gaze.

"Yes. I was wrong to do it, but it's too late to make amends. That man outside will *never* forgive me. You must not go with him. He will be cruel. He could—" Edwin didn't finish.

"I think his cruelty is not of the physical kind, Papa." It was a hunch, perhaps a silly hope, but there was something about Mr. Banks that seemed to suggest he would have more of a cutting tongue than a brutal fist. And a tongue was something she could deal with.

"Papa, you have taken care of me all these years. Let me help you now." She kissed his cheek and then fled the drawing room before he could stop her.

She rushed upstairs, trying to think of everything she must pack. When she got to her room, she took a valise from the closet and began filling it with stockings, chemises, three dresses, a small hand mirror, hairpins, black boots, and a pair of slippers. It would have to be enough. Then she carried her case downstairs and paused as she passed the library.

A book! She must take one. It would be her only ally, her only way to escape. She picked up the book she'd been reading, *Lady Leticia and the Dark Duke*, and carefully tucked it into her traveling case. Then she made her way to the front door.

Her father appeared in the doorway of the drawing room, his eyes misty and his face pale. She set her case down and gave him one last embrace.

"I will be all right, Papa. I will write to you once I'm settled."

"Don't go. Stay," he pleaded again and cupped her face in his hand. She patted his hand once before she blinked away tears and stepped back.

"Tell Mama not to worry." Then she dashed down the steps to the waiting coach.

A handsome young man caught her traveling case which he secured to the back of the coach before he opened the door and assisted her inside. She took a seat opposite Banks. He watched her with hooded eyes. She could just make him out in the dim light.

"So your father gave you up after all, eh? I always knew he was a coward." His sneering words cut her heart even deeper. Without thinking, she leaned forward and slapped him.

"It was my choice to go with you. You will not speak of my father like that ever again. *You* are the coward, blackmailing him like that."

Banks touched his cheek, glaring at her. "Your father drove my mother to her death. I will say what I damn well please about him."

His mother was dead? She bit her lip, unsure of what to say. She didn't want to accept that her father had done something like that.

They were both silent for a long moment before he spoke, more softly this time.

"While you're with me, we shall not speak of him."

"Thank you." She didn't feel as though she had won a battle, but it made her brave enough to try to negotiate their situation further.

"I came with you by my own free will, and I wish to settle the terms of our arrangement."

Mr. Banks leaned forward slightly. "The terms have been settled, but I will hear what you have to say."

"You shall not tell anyone that I am staying with you. I need to save what little face I can if I am to make a marriage after this...interlude is over." She paused, and when he did not interrupt she continued. "I know it is impossible not to be seen out in society, but I would ask that you do not parade me about like a prized pony. And if we are to go out in society, I will need some decent clothes. What I have brought with me will not suffice. I do not require anything expensive, merely serviceable, and only a few at that." Her threadbare garments would draw far more attention than the man she would be accompanying. In some ways, an impoverished woman was worse than a fallen one. Men saw two very different kinds of desperation within those women. One could be preyed upon to mutual benefit, the other not as much.

"Anything else?" Mr. Banks asked.

"I ask that you not imprison me each day in the townhouse. I should like the freedom to go out, have fresh air, and not be trapped in a bedchamber all day." She would not be treated like a bed toy for his pleasure. She needed to have some small measure of freedom or she would go mad.

"That isn't unreasonable."

"And my last request, after we part ways, we shall never seek each other out again. I want no reminders of our days together. Nor, should I think, will you."

Martin held out his held to her. "Easy enough terms to live with. I accept."

She shook his hand, relieved. The situation was more tolerable now that she had regained some measure of control of her life. He didn't immediately release her hand and she was disturbed about how warm his hand was and how well their palms fit together. Finally, she pulled her hand away first and he let go.

"I will see you settled tonight. Tomorrow I will buy you some clothes that are more appropriate to your new position."

As his mistress... Livvy closed her eyes, her heart racing. When she opened them, he was watching her again. She shifted restlessly.

"You should know that I have no plans to force you to share my bed."

This took her by surprise. "But I thought...?"

"Yes, you are to be my *mistress*, but there is more to such a relationship than the bedchamber. And quite frankly, I have no interest in an unwilling partner. I find the notion...unpalatable."

Livvy didn't know what to say, but before she could get too comfortable, he grinned at her wolfishly.

"But..." His eyes fixed on her mouth. "I'm quite certain you will succumb to my charms in time. I have never left a lover unsatis-fied." The smug way he said this made her bite her tongue to avoid saying what she really felt. There was *nothing* he could do that would convince her to like him, let alone bed him, no matter how attractive he was. This was a business transaction. If he chose to take the high road and not force himself upon her, then she would think better of him when this nightmare was over. Nothing more.

The coach stopped at a townhouse on Park Lane. Mr. Banks exited the coach first and held out a hand for her. She raised her chin in defiance and braced herself on the door of the coach.

He huffed in open displeasure. "Don't be silly." He gripped her by the waist and pulled her out. She gasped as he easily lifted her up and set her back on the ground. She trembled as their bodies pressed flush against one another. She'd never been this close to a strange man before. It was thrilling and exciting, yet she didn't *want* to be close to him. He was a wretched man, albeit a handsome one.

She inwardly chided herself for letting his looks distract her. There were no excuses for his behavior. Still, she couldn't forget what he'd said her father had done. She loved her father, despite knowing he'd tossed this man into the streets and led his mother to an early death.

If I can forgive my father, perhaps I can learn to at least tolerate this man. Her body was more than willing to tolerate him. She felt like a silly girl barely out of the schoolroom, ready to swoon over his handsome looks, and she despised that part of herself that was so inexplicably drawn to him.

"Please, let me go." She only added the word *please* to appear more complacent. He might have gotten her to agree to be his mistress, but she would not be fearful.

Banks held her a few long seconds more and then released her. He turned to face the house and walked up the steps. A butler opened the door for him, and the two men talked briefly, the butler casting a look her way before Martin went inside without so much as a backward glance toward her. A footman came down the steps and took her valise, then rushed back inside.

Livvy stared up at the fine Palladian façade of the place she would be staying for however long Banks wanted her.

I hope he tires of me sooner rather than later. If he did, she could go home. Home to her own life, even though it would be tarnished by scandal once London learned she'd gone from innocent debutante to a fallen woman. She didn't want to think about the scandal that would come if anyone learned she lived with him at his residence rather than be tucked away in a love nest in another part of London.

She lifted her skirts and walked up the steps into her new home. Her throat tightened, and she tried not to cry. She would not give him the satisfaction of seeing any weakness. As she entered the house, she came face-to-face with a genial-looking man named Mr. Harris, who introduced himself as the butler.

"If you need anything, you need only notify me or Mrs. Wilson, the housekeeper," he said. "The master has informed me that you will require a lady's maid. Mellie, one of our best upstairs maids, will attend you."

"Thank you." She glanced around the entryway, but Mr. Banks was already gone. She relaxed a little. Perhaps he would leave her alone tonight. She could only hope so. She had no interest in seeing his "charms" tonight.

"May I escort you to your chambers, Miss Hartwell?"

"Yes, thank you." She followed the butler to the second floor. He opened the door to the first room at the top of the stairs. Livvy's breath caught in her throat. The room was decorated in an Egyptian style. The bed frame had hieroglyphics carved into the mahogany wood, and hand-painted motifs of water lilies and lotus flowers covered the walls. The vanity table had sphinxes for legs and sat close to a large bay window. Rich blue muslin curtains hung over the bed from the canopy, and a matching coverlet was embroidered with lions, serpents, sphinxes, and crocodiles.

"Oh my..." She breathed out the words, stunned by the exquisite furnishings and the extravagant decorations. Anyone who slept in this room would dream she was Cleopatra awaiting a visit from her lover Julius Caesar. For a brief instant, her mind was filled with images of her lying upon the bed in scandalous Egyptian dress and a man standing above her, removing a bronze chest plate to reveal an equally chiseled chest—a man who looked like Banks. Flushing with heat from the burst of erotic imagination, she turned away from Mr. Harris.

"Is the room suitable?" he asked.

"Yes." She cleared her throat. "Quite sufficient."

"There's a bell cord by the bed. Please ring if you need anything." Harris's eyes were warm and kind, and a hint of pity lingered there as though he knew she was not there because she wished to be. She couldn't help but wonder if she wasn't the first woman he'd blackmailed to stay here.

"Thank you, Mr. Harris. Would it be too much trouble to ask for some tea and biscuits? I'm famished."

"Of course." He bowed and waited for the footman to enter before he departed. The young man set her valise on the bed.

"Shall I unpack for you, miss or do you wish to wait for a maid?" he offered politely.

"Oh no, I can see to it. But thank you." She didn't want him to see her torn and mended stockings or the faded fabrics of her dresses. Shame squeezed her throat. If she had to wear her modest clothes, he and the rest of the house would see how unfit she was to be in a house such as this, but she wanted to delay that moment as long as possible.

"Very well. Good night, miss." The footman left her alone, and she opened her traveling case. The sight of her book was welcome.

She picked it up and clutched it to her chest. "My only friend."

"Your only friend?" She whirled to face Mr. Banks, who now stood in the doorway, leaning against the jamb. The lamps from the hall outside her room silhouetted him. It intensified his dominating air, and she shivered, stepping backward. She bumped into the bed behind her and froze when she realized she could not retreat without climbing onto the bed.

"You say your only friend is a book? How dreadful." He pushed away from the door. He could not have been watching her for long, but he had overheard her whisper to herself. "It must be some book to be clutched so protectively against your bosom. Let me see it."

He held out his hand. For a moment Livvy feared he would rip it from her and cast it into the fireplace.

"I won't take it from you. You deserve some comforts while you are here. I have an extensive library down the hall at your disposal." He held out his hand. "May I?"

With a shaky breath, Livvy handed him the novel. He examined the spine and gave a low chuckle.

"A Gothic novel? You know, I've never read one of these. I always thought them to be rather silly."

"They aren't silly," Livvy argued, then stopped herself.

I shouldn't speak back to him. The last thing I need is to anger him. She could see from his build that he could easily hurt her if he grew angry, yet she sensed he wouldn't use his body against hers, but rather this words.

Eyes fixed on her, his lips formed a firm line before he spoke. "I won't hurt you, Miss Hartwell, if that is what you fear. Feel free to speak your mind. I have never liked quiet church mice for my mistresses."

Livvy was many things, and while she was not a chattery creature, she was not a church mouse either. "Perhaps you should read it, Mr. Banks. A Gothic novel can be thrilling, and this author is excellent."

He flipped the book open and read a paragraph before closing it. "Ah, but if I take this and read it, you will lose your only friend. Why don't I show you to the library? You may choose another book to keep you company while I borrow this one."

Livvy's throat tightened as she followed him. The library, which was actually a bedchamber converted to a world of stories, was only three doors down from her chamber and far bigger than she expected. Floor-to-ceiling shelves filled the walls, each one stuffed with books. A pair of chairs and a reading table sat close to a fireplace. It was a cozy and inviting room. She moved immediately to the shelves and searched the titles until she found a book that she had read once before: *Northanger Abbey* by Jane Austen. It was a satire on Gothic novels, but tonight she found herself very much in need of the comfort of the young heroine, Catherine Moreland.

Banks joined her at the shelf, the heat of his body close to hers. "What have you chosen?" he asked.

She tensed, expecting him to touch her. When didn't she turned around and faced him.

Why did he have to be so handsome?

"Well?" he asked more softly. His eyes lowered to her lips, and she hastily raised the book between them like a shield. He took it from her, examining it.

"Austen? Not a bad choice." He gave the book back to her.

"Austen is a wonderful writer," she argued, finding his praise of her far too faint.

He leaned one shoulder against the shelf beside her, his smile widening. "I agree."

Livvy slipped away, not at all liking that her body flushed with heat whenever she was so close to him.

"May I retire for the night?" she asked, not looking at him.

"Come here first."

Heart hammering, she returned to stand before him. Banks lifted his hand to cup her chin.

"I shall steal one goodnight kiss from you. If you do not like it, you're welcome to slap me. I won't be angry with you, I promise." He curled his other arm around her waist, pulling her into him so their bodies pressed close together.

She closed her eyes and felt his lips cover hers. His warm, rich scent teased her nose. She'd never been kissed and didn't know what to expect, but it felt...pleasant. More than pleasant. The light coaxing of his mouth on hers made her chest tighten and her heart flutter with a strange excitement. When his tongue traced the seam of her lips, she gasped in surprise. He used that to his advantage and slipped his tongue inside her mouth. A shocking flash of heat shot through her, and it felt as though the earth itself trembled with her. Her knees buckled, and he held her.

The book in her hand dropped to the floor, and she clutched his shirt. A feeling she only barely understood pulsed within her. His tender kiss turned harder, just enough that she could feel the power of being trapped in his arms. She didn't mind it, not even as he kissed her ruthlessly. There was a dreamlike feel to this moment, and she didn't want to return to reality to face the fact that she'd enjoyed kissing the man who'd blackmailed her into being his mistress right before Christmas.

Their lips broke apart. A shiver rippled through her, but it wasn't from fear. How could he kiss her like that and make her yearn for more? She wanted to hate him and his touch, but she didn't.

Banks cupped her face in his palms. "You taste so sweet and innocent. It makes me ache," he said in a low, silken voice that made her senses stir to life.

"I..." But she didn't know what to say.

"Yes. We shall do very well together." He bent, retrieved her book, and placed it in her hands. "Now, off to bed before I change my mind."

Livvy turned and fled the library, racing back to her room. She jolted at the sight of a maid with a tray by her bed.

"Didn't mean to startle you, miss," the maid said in a Scottish accent. She had beautiful red hair with curly tendrils escaping her bun, and merry blue eyes. She had a tray of food that she set on the table close to Livvy.

"It's quite all right. I simply wasn't expecting anyone. You took me by surprise." She set the book on the bed and eyed the tray of food. Her stomach rumbled loud enough that the maid heard it.

She giggled. "I thought you might be hungry, miss. I brought soup, a bit of meat, cheese, and some wine. I'll just unpack for you."

"Thank you, um..."

"Mellie."

"I am Lavinia, but please, call me Livvy."

The maid blushed. "Well, I can't, the master would be furious, Miss..."

"Hartwell. I would like you to call me Livvy when it's just the two of us. I desperately need a friend." Livvy held out one hand to Mellie. The maid seemed to be close to her in age and would be a welcome ally under the circumstances.

"Only when we are alone, Miss. I don't want to be dismissed for too much familiarity," Mellie whispered, leaning in conspiratorially. Then she grasped Livvy's hand and gave it a gentle squeeze before letting go.

"Now, let me help you undress. Then you can settle into bed and eat." Mellie held up the single nightgown that Livvy had packed and brought with her.

Livvy sighed in relief as the maid helped her undress. "Thank you."

Once she was dressed in her nightgown, she peeled back the sheets and climbed into bed. Mellie handed her the tray and put her book next to her.

"I'll see you in the morning, Miss...er...Livvy." Mellie grinned as she corrected herself. She left, closing the door behind her.

Livvy began to nibble on the cheese and cold cuts, then sipped her wine. She'd never eaten in bed before, at least not at night. There was something wonderfully indulgent about it. She reflected on how her father and mother were able to keep their house running, but she knew they were struggling. The year before, her father had invested their money in the silver mines in Cornwall, and the mining had recently been deemed a failure. Their income from the mines had shrunk with each passing month and would stop. Livvy hadn't blamed her father, but she felt shaken now to be at a palatial home like this, enjoying dinner in bed while her parents could not.

But I am paying the price for it.

The delicious food turned bitter, but she finished it nonetheless and set the tray on the table close to the bed. She wasn't so silly as to deny herself sustenance as she recalled her true purpose here. She reached for her book, turning to the first page, and settled in to read. It was important she find a way to distract herself from thinking about Banks...and the sinful way he kissed her.

CHAPTER 4

Martin sat in a chair in the library, turning the pages of the book Lavinia had brought with her, but his mind was miles away. What on earth had possessed him to bring her home? Yes, he'd kept his other mistresses here, which he knew was unusual, but the daughter of his worst enemy? He should have kept her far away, some little cottage all alone to suffer. But she was lovely, and fiery, and...he didn't want to let her out of his sight.

He'd wanted to destroy Hartwell, throw him out on his ear. But when Lavinia, a daughter he had not known existed, had rushed into the room, his heart had stopped in his chest. When he saw her pale creamy skin, hazel eyes that looked like chocolate coated with honey, and those pale pink lips parted in surprise, he had been lost. Lost in fantasies of kissing those lips, touching her skin and seeing those eyes flash with heat and desire as she lay beneath him in bed. Taking her away from Hartwell had been too bloody easy. And he knew with a cold-blooded delight that he wouldn't even have to lay a finger on her to hurt Hartwell. The man would be beside himself with fear and worry, and that was enough for Martin.

The man was pathetic to let such a young girl fight his battles for him. Martin sobered suddenly as the past came flooding back. Helen, his twin, had once bravely defended him, had even fought a duel against her future husband to save Martin's life. He'd been only twenty-one, just a foolish lad, but he had made too many mistakes.

A man should fight his own battles. If Hartwell was too much of a coward to do so, then Martin would continue to use Lavinia as payment. He had no intention of harming the girl, of course. She was sweet-tempered, and yet there was a fire in her eyes that he didn't want to see extinguished.

He wished he could woo her into his bed. The villainous role he'd acted at Hartwell's home was not the man he really was. He had come to his senses enough to remember that, even though she presented a temptation most men wouldn't be able to resist. The kiss they'd shared tonight had proven she would respond to him. She hadn't stood there unfeeling, nor had she fought him off. She had kissed him back. Was she living out some wicked fantasy with him that was inspired by one of her Gothic novels? If so, perhaps he could work it to his advantage.

His body hardened at the thought of where those future kisses would lead. He was an excellent lover, and while most men might say that only to boast, Martin knew it to be true. He'd spent years learning the art of seduction, of pleasing a woman before himself. There was an immense satisfaction in knowing that he could make any woman desire him and that he alone could fulfill their needs.

I will show Lavinia just how wonderful it can be.

He set the book down and rose from his chair. He had promised he would leave her alone tonight, but it wouldn't hurt to make sure she had settled in, would it? He exited the library and made his way to her room. He could see a light on beneath her door, but he had sent her to bed three hours ago. Was she still awake? He tested the handle and found the door unlocked. He eased it open and peered into the bedchamber. A few candles were still burning low. Tiptoeing into the room, he blew out one candle, then stoked the fire and added several more logs. He couldn't forget how cold Hartwell's house had been, and he didn't want Lavinia to be cold tonight.

He moved to the bed, where the last candle was still lit on a table beside the bed. Lavinia was fast asleep, her book still open to the third page. Martin carefully extracted the book from her hands, set it on the table, and gazed down at her. She looked so innocent, her hair unbound, her face softened in the shadows. Had he been that innocent at her age?

It seemed like a lifetime separated him from Lavinia, rather than ten years. Yet he knew she wasn't a child. She was a grown woman, one he now hungered for. Yet rather than feel a desire to awaken her, a strange protective urge filled him. He couldn't help but think what he would do had he been in her place, had he been able to offer himself in some way if he'd known it would have saved his mother's life. He would have done exactly as Lavinia had. He tucked the bedclothes up to her chin, wanting to make sure she stayed warm enough. Then he brushed a stray lock of hair from her cheek before he bent, blew the candle out, and left her to sleep.

As he returned to his own bedchamber and allowed his valet to undress him, he gazed at himself in the mirror. A frown was upon his lips, one that had been there for ages. The fear he'd seen in Lavinia's eyes had left him unsettled.

"Byrd," he said as his valet undid the buttons on his cuffs.

"Yes, sir?" the man replied, head bent as he focused on his task.

"Do you find me imposing?"

Byrd glanced at him. "Imposing, sir?"

"Do I frighten you?"

Byrd tilted his head, his lips parted as he hesitated.

"Come now, Byrd. I'm not angry." He paused, not wanting to sound like he cared overmuch, but just enough. "I was thinking of Miss Hartwell. I don't wish to scare her now that she's here."

"Ah." Byrd relaxed and stepped back as he gave Martin room to pull his shirt over his head.

"I think you can be a little intimidating, sir, but it is likely because you are used to dealing with businessmen who would cut your throat if you weren't careful. Even your other female guests were used to you and your manners. But Miss Hartwell... Well, she's a proper lady, isn't she?"

"Yes. She is." Byrd was right. Opera singers, socialites, and courtesans knew how to behave around men, but Lavinia was not part of that world. She had never been alone with a man, let alone been kissed. If he was going to get her in his bed, his seduction would have to be slow and careful.

Byrd spoke again. "Might I make a suggestion?"

Martin nodded.

"Well, ladies, no matter their station, like gifts. Flowers, jewels, sweets, gowns. And they like to be courted. Take her riding, take her to the opera or a play. Ladies like a bit of fun."

Byrd was right, damn him. Lavinia was not her father, and the fact that she had made herself a sacrificial lamb for his debts didn't mean she deserved to be treated harshly. It was not as though he'd ever intended to treat her badly, but he hadn't given much thought to what he would do with her.

"Thank you, Byrd. That is good advice." He offered his valet a smile. "I believe I can see to the rest this evening. You may go."

Byrd collected Martin's boots and left him alone. Martin stripped out of his trousers and removed his stockings before he climbed into bed. He blew out his candle and lay on his back, arms folded behind his head as he gazed up at the ceiling of his canopy bed.

Lavinia's visage preyed on his mind. He would never forget the bravery she demonstrated in coming to her father's aid.

She has captivated me. It was a dangerous thing to admit. But he would tire of her as he had all the rest and would send her home soon enough, he was sure. As sleep finally overtook him, he was plagued with dreams, or rather nightmares, ones that played over and over in his mind. Hartwell destroying his life, his mother collapsing, his father broken and defeated. And Martin, doing the same to Lavinia.

Am I no better than her father? But he couldn't send her home. The die was cast. He had kissed her and had tasted her sweet passion like the petals of a rose in spring. Even if it made him a villain, he would have more.

You are mine, Lavinia. You simply don't know it yet.

ॐ

LIVVY SLEPT WITHOUT DREAMS, WITHOUT WORRIES. WHEN dawn arrived, Mellie pulled back the window curtains, and Livvy remembered all the events of the night before.

"Did you sleep well, Livvy?" the maid asked as she bustled about the room and started selecting clothes for Livvy to wear.

"I... Yes." She couldn't believe it, but it was true. Here in this beautiful bed, she had slept without a care. How was that even possible?

"Do you wish to bathe this morning or this evening?"

"Er... This evening." Livvy stretched and sighed before she pushed the covers back and slipped out of bed. The maid helped her change into a lilac muslin day gown and white slippers.

"What about your hair, miss? I know quite a few styles." Mellie's eyes twinkled in the reflection from the mirror on the vanity table.

"I would love something fashionable. How are the ladies wearing it?" She had only been to a few balls since her come out and had been so distracted by the dances she hadn't had time to focus on the hairstyles of others.

"A few curls at the front on each side and an elaborate chignon in the back." Mellie picked up the silver hairbrush from the night-stand and began to comb Livvy's hair. When she was finished, she held the mirror out to Livvy who examined the results.

"Oh, it's splendid! Thank you!" She carefully set the hand mirror back on the table.

"Breakfast should be ready now if you wish to eat," said Mellie. "I'd be happy to show you to the dining room."

Livvy followed her downstairs and was directed into an elegant dining room. The robin's-egg blue walls and white wainscoting gave the room an airy feel that was accented by the large table set for breakfast.

Chafing dishes kept food hot on a nearby sideboard, including slices of ham, capers, and eggs. Toast and a pot of hot water for tea were also available. Livvy was so distracted by all this that she did not immediately notice Banks seated at the table.

She froze when she turned and saw him. An empty plate was on the table in front of him and a cup of tea close at hand as he perused the paper.

"Come in and eat." It was a command, but his tone was gentle. When he didn't immediately look at her, she relaxed and took a spare plate from the sideboard.

Once she was seated with her breakfast, she took a peek at what he was reading, the financial section of the *Morning Post*. He noticed she was watching him after a moment and laid down his paper to stare at her in return.

"You are engaged in business?" she asked softly.

"I am." He angled his body her way, and his gaze made her feel unsettled, though not in an entirely unpleasant way.

"Do you invest in the funds?"

At this he tilted his head, seeming somewhat surprised. "It is where I make most of my fortune. Are you familiar with it?"

She nibbled on a piece of toast and nodded. "My father prefers to invest in businesses, but I rather think funds are safer. I tried to convince him to invest in some India bonds and annuities last year. He didn't, but my instincts were correct. The bonds I suggested had a reliable return on investment of 4.8 percent."

"That was very sound advice," Banks agreed, his blue eyes still on hers. "What did he invest in?"

She sighed. "Silver. It's such an unreliable market, and the odds of it doing well at this time are slim." She lifted her tea cup up, taking in the enticing aroma of the tea.

Banks's lips twitched in a hint of a smile. "Again, you are right."

"And that surprises you, does it?" she asked. She'd met enough young debutantes in the past year to know that her knowledge of business was not typical among the young ladies.

"Yes, but it also delights me. I believe I shall enjoy our conversations. My past mistresses were educated in other ways—music, literature, and art. And while these things were pleasing, they weren't enough to stimulate me."

She cringed at the word *mistress*. She was reluctantly here for that purpose, but she would never like how it made her feel. She wanted to be loved by a man, not used. Whatever happened between them, she would not let him change her into something she didn't want to be. She was in control of how quickly their intimacy would progress, if at all.

"Could we not use the word *mistress*?" she asked.

He closed his paper and leaned back in his chair. "I would be happy to call you whatever you like, but that does not change the fact that you are here to serve me in that capacity."

Livvy drew a deep breath, trying to steady her nerves and calm the flare of temper. But she had nothing to say in her own defense. He was right. She had agreed to come here to be...*his*.

"If I called you my companion, would that suit you?" It was as though he'd read her mind. Heat flooded her face, and he smirked a little, but strangely the expression didn't seem cruel but rather boyishly teasing. It put her at ease more than she expected.

"I think *companion* would be agreeable, if you still agree that I shan't be forced into your bed."

"The choice is and will always be yours, but I believe you will be tempted." His intense, smoldering gaze made her tense, not because she was afraid of him, but because she feared she would indeed be tempted.

"What...?" She paused, deciding to change the subject. "What do you have planned for today? Am I to remain here and wait for you?"

"*We* have plans to go shopping. Those rags you are wearing aren't suitable in the slightest, and you have no proper winter clothes. I know you see me as a bastard, but I am not cruel. You may have fine clothes, jewels, whatever your heart desires."

Except my freedom.

He remained with her as she finished her breakfast, once more opening his paper to read. When he finished a section of the paper, he glanced at her.

"Would you care to...?" He waved at the paper. "I have the *Morning Post* every day, but I would be happy to procure any other paper you would wish to read. I understand many ladies prefer the *Quizzing Glass Gazette*."

"The *Post* is quite fine." She collected the paper and took some time to peruse it. Over the next half hour, they took turns sharing the paper, passing a tray of toast, and even smiling at each other when they both reached for the butter at the same moment. It was as though they'd shared a breakfasts many times, enjoying an amiable silence the way a happily married couple would. She finished, and a footman cleared away their plates.

Mr. Banks rose. "Fetch your cloak, and we will head to Bond Street."

"Mr. Banks, I—"

"Martin, please. I insist on that, Lavinia." He held the dining room door open for her as they departed. If he wished to be more familiar by name, then she did as well.

"Very well, but please don't call me Lavinia."

His dark-gold brows rose in response. "No?"

"It's the name my parents use when they're cross with me. I prefer Livvy."

"Livvy." He smiled. "I like that much better. I had a great-aunt on my mother's side name Lavinia. She was quite an old battle-ax."

"What a dreadful thing to say," she gasped, but Martin only laughed.

"Trust me, she would see it as a compliment. If the Vikings of old were to ever invade England again, my great-aunt would be there to stop them single-handed." He mimicked swinging a battle-ax, and his boyish expression of mischief was so unexpected that Livvy giggled. For a moment she completely forgot that he had effectively purchased her the way one would a horse. Her laughter died, and his grin faded.

"Sir, the coach is ready," Mr. Harris announced.

"Go get your cloak." He waved at the stairs, but she had anticipated him and was already on her way. She returned, cloak in hand and he helped her put it on.

"Thank you," Livvy said, blushing before she followed Martin as they exited the house. His coach was painted blue and black, something she hadn't noticed last night. Martin held out a hand, and she pressed her palm in his so he could help her into. Once they were seated, he took a cane that was tucked into the corner of his seat and rapped it on the roof of the coach. Their driver jerked the horses into motion.

"You're truly going to buy me a new wardrobe?"

"Yes. It was one of your conditions, as I recall. I am a man of honor, despite what you might think." Martin's gaze was focused on the street outside the window, but she had the sense he was assuring her once again that he would not force her to do anything, in bed or out, while she was with him. For a brief moment she wondered if perhaps he was not altogether a villain like she believed, but was perhaps a good man trying desperately to be bad because he felt he needed vengeance.

"Thank you," she said softly.

"My pleasure. I believe in a fair exchange, and your requests were quite reasonable."

As much as she didn't want to admit it, she would be happy to add a few new dresses, perhaps a thicker cloak, and stockings that weren't so threadbare.

She and Martin didn't speak for the rest of the ride. She had questions, but she didn't ask a single one. When they reached

Bond Street, Martin helped her out of the coach and gave instructions to the driver to return in three hours. Then he offered her his arm. Livvy slipped her hand around his sleeve, walking carefully on the icy sidewalk. The chilly wind made her wince, but she knew that they would soon be inside.

"Here we are." Martin stopped at an expensive-looking modiste's shop with a name she recognized.

"Mrs. Benson is a fine dressmaker. Too fine for me!" she protested. A few shoppers passing by stared at Livvy. Martin merely pursed his lips and opened the door for her. A blush flamed her face, but she entered the shop and he followed behind her.

The interior of the shop was cozy, warm, and illuminated with dozens of lamps, which accented the bolts of expensive silks and colorful muslins. A lovely woman in a dark-blue dress emerged from the back room and smiled when she saw them.

"Mr. Banks! What a pleasure to see you again."

Martin's grim expression faded at the dressmaker's genuine smile.

"Mrs. Benson, it has been too long." There was an intimate familiarity in his gaze, not one of love, but of friendship. The woman turned her attention to Livvy.

"And who is this young lady?"

"Miss Hartwell." He did not elaborate further, but Livvy swallowed a wave of shame as she faced the modiste.

"I see." Mrs. Benson's tone wasn't disapproving, but crisp, as though she was already thinking of the gowns Livvy would need. "The usual, Mr. Banks? Or perhaps a little something special?" Mrs. Benson walked in a circle around Livvy, eyeing her critically the way an artist would a blank canvas.

Martin stroked his chin. "Perhaps something special is in order. She's not...like the others."

Livvy closed her eyes for a moment, holding her tongue. Was that meant to be an insult or a compliment? She honestly didn't wish to know.

"She certainly isn't," Mrs. Benson muttered as she came back to face Livvy, and her sudden but small smile was hidden from Martin, who stood behind her. "She's lovely and innocent, and I imagine she's sweet. The others were...not so much." Mrs. Benson waved a hand at Martin. "Have a seat and let me find a few ready-made gowns that will suit her. Then, after we set her up with the necessities, we can plan a few custom gowns."

"Excellent." Martin passed by Livvy to sit in a chair by a trio of mirrors and a small raised platform. She knew she would soon be standing on the short dais, feeling Martin's eyes roam over her body as he dressed her to his satisfaction.

"This way." Mrs. Benson motioned for her to go behind a changing screen. She soon returned with several gowns of various colors.

"Let's try a few of these. And I will get your measurements for the rest of the gowns."

Livvy picked up the first gown on top of the pile Mrs. Benson had set before her. She sighed heavily. It was a lovely blue silk gown the color of a summer sky. She couldn't help but swoon at the expensive clothes. There was nothing lovelier in the world than to feel the sweet slide of silk upon one's skin or to twirl before a mirror as her netting overskirts sparkled in the candle-light. Every woman liked to feel beautiful, and Livvy was no different. The dresses here were far above those she would have chosen for herself. Expensive, finely made. She would even be able to keep them...as payment for being Martin's kept woman.

The dreamy smile on her lips wilted. How was she going to get through this with her pride intact?

CHAPTER 5

Martin leaned back in the chair, sipping the tea the shopgirl had brought him. He had sat in this chair on more than one occasion, watching his mistresses try on gowns, flashing saucy grins or batting their lashes, hoping for extra boots or kid gloves. He had smiled back and given in, buying the lady whatever she desired.

Mrs. Benson was right. This was different.

Livvy was innocent and sweet, but not a woman easily pushed. He liked that. He'd never been attracted to women who bowed and scraped in deference to men.

His gaze turned to the changing screen when a flash of movement caught his eye. Mrs. Benson emerged, smiling broadly as she waved a coaxing hand at Livvy. As she exited the shield of the screen and stepped out onto the platform in front of the mirrors, his breath caught. His pulse quickened in longing as he stared at the beautiful gown that clung to the gentle curve of her hips and breasts. She ducked her head shyly at his continued stare, but he didn't care. He wished to take his fill, sate himself on the sight of her.

"The gown is perfect for her in length and needs no adjustments," Mrs. Benson said, pointing out the elements of the gown. The orange ribbon around her waist accented the light blue gown and put her breasts on display. The fabric was watered silk, and it accented Livvy's contours to their advantage.

"What do you think, Livvy? Do you like it?" Martin asked.

She blinked as though startled by his asking her. "Why—yes. I do love the colors," she admitted with a blush. Her alabaster skin warmed to the most delicious pink, and he wondered if the rest of her would blush as prettily as she lay beneath him writhing in pleasure.

"Mrs. Benson, we shall take it. What else do you have? She will need several gowns to start and a cloak, boots, gloves, slippers, extra chemises, and stockings, I imagine. As well as the usual nightclothes."

Mrs. Benson nodded. "We have several nightgowns I think will be ideal." She walked over to a counter and removed a box, lifting the lid and unfolding the tissue paper to lift up a diaphanous nightgown. The material was so sheer that Livvy gasped. Martin chuckled. The look of scandalized fright on her was comical. She knew he would see every bit of her beneath the thin fabric but she would come to love it. Once she allowed him to teach her the joys he had to offer, she would be excited to wear it.

"And this?" Mrs. Benson set the nightgown aside and retrieved a dark-blue and gold embroidered cloak, with ermine trim around the hood. She wrapped it around Livvy and tested the hood.

Martin nodded. "Yes, it's perfect." He reached up to caress the fur of the hood, and Livvy tried to turn away, her cheeks now a dark rouge.

"You look exquisite," he said. "You shouldn't hide, not from me."

The fire that suddenly blazed in her eyes surprised him. "You need not remind me that I belong to you."

He frowned. "I meant only that you should enjoy these clothes. Do not shy away from them, just because I happen to be looking at you." Despite their unusual circumstances, he wanted her to embrace her own passions and pride herself in her beauty, because she was beautiful.

"What else do you require? A few ball gowns, a riding habit?" he asked.

"Mr. Banks, I have some fashion plates from the *Lady's Magazine* if you would like to see them," said Mrs. Benson.

"Yes, thank you." He guided Livvy off the platform, and they joined the dressmaker at the counter to peruse the plates. At first Livvy held her tongue, but Martin continued to nudge her with questions, and soon she was excitedly discussing cuts of fabric, trimmings, and a variety of dresses: morning, walking, opera, evening gowns. He'd forgotten how many kinds of gowns a woman needed. The expense didn't matter; he simply found the amount of effort involved staggering.

"Mr. Banks, what do you think?" Livvy pointed at an evening gown plate. It was colored, done by Mrs. Benson no doubt to entice customers. "She says it can be made in any color. Bishops blue, or even Devonshire brown?"

"Devonshire brown," he replied. The rich brown color held a reddish tint which would accent the color of her dark hair and warm hazel eyes. He couldn't help but think of the last time he'd been here, with Stella, the opera singer. She would whisper suggestive comments in his ear about how lovely it would be for him to strip her of her new gown.

He shrugged off the memory and focused on Livvy and the sweet, hopeful way she eyed the dresses. There was no pretense of flirtation, no coy seduction involved. She was open and honest in her emotions, even the negative ones. And right now she stared at the Devonshire brown gown with such longing that it made him wish to give her the world on a silver platter.

"Excellent choice, Mr. Banks, most excellent," the modiste said. "That's it. We have you all settled for clothes."

Martin was disappointed that they were done. He would have much preferred to stay there and watch Livvy try on a dozen more dresses, perhaps even show him silk stockings and... He stopped his train of thought before his arousal went beyond a point which he could control.

I am not a monster. I am a gentleman, and she is my companion. She will not be touched unless she asks me to touch her.

Livvy thanked the woman and went to a display of reticules. Martin watched with amusement as she opened several, studying them closely, and then turned to face him, one clutched to her breast, but she blushed when she seemed to realize that she'd been about to ask him to buy it.

"Bring it over." He smiled, and his heart gave a strange little flip when she joined him and added the dark-green reticule to the pile.

"Thank you," she said shyly.

"You're welcome," he replied. He despised her father, but as long as Livvy stayed with him, her happiness mattered. A happy woman out of bed usually meant a playful, affectionate lover *in* bed.

"I'll have the remaining gowns delivered late next week." Mrs. Benson and her shopgirl packed up the gowns and other items in beautiful colored boxes. Martin summoned his coach to have the items loaded inside. He insisted on the cloak remaining unpacked, and he placed it around Livvy's shoulders. Then he thanked Mrs. Benson and stepped out into the street.

"Where should we go now?" Livvy asked.

"I think I know just the place." He helped her into the coach, but he did not share their destination.

"Piccadilly, please," he said to the driver before he joined her in the coach.

The coach dropped them off at number 187 Piccadilly in front of a shop named Hatchard's. Livvy looked up at the store windows and realized where he had brought her. Her lovely eyes brightened with tears.

"Books?" she breathed, a delicate smile flitting about her lips.

"My library, while extensive, is lacking in books that entertain. I thought you could help me add to my collection. Are you up to the challenge?" After last night, he had a feeling that books would cheer her up.

She nodded enthusiastically and practically sprinted to the door. Again, his heart gave a strange flutter as he saw the joy on her face. He followed her inside and paused to take in the clublike atmosphere of the shop. There was a fireplace with the day's papers spread out for reading. Benches lined the walls for servants to wait upon their masters and mistresses. The shop was warm and inviting, and quite a few people had stepped inside to escape London's bitter winter. Livvy was already plucking titles from the shelves, and she returned to him with a stack nearly up to her chin.

"Set them down. Let's have a look." He gestured to the two chairs by the fire, and he moved the papers out of the way. Livvy placed the books down and picked up the top novel, handing it to him.

"Roche's *The Discarded Son?*"

"It's a horror tale; I thought you might prefer that to Gothic novels."

He chuckled. "No *Mysteries of Udolpho,* eh?" He had heard of Mrs. Radcliffe's Gothic novels many times, but he'd never read them.

She bit her lip. "No, not unless you want that."

"What's next?" He chose another book. "*The Mutual Attachment?*"

"Oh that's…" She tried to take it from him, but he kept it out of her reach.

"A romantic novel?" he asked as he flipped through the pages.

"Yes. I thought it might be for me."

"Then we must purchase it, of course." He picked up the next book, which he realized was actually a trio of slender volumes bound in leather and trimmed in gilt.

"*Glenarvon.*" She whispered the title, clearly scandalized, judging from the red flush of her cheeks.

He chuckled again, stroking the spine of the first volume. "Lady Caroline Lamb's thinly disguised tell-all. The titular fellow is

Lord Byron, I hear. She thought it would resurrect her dead social life, but it has had the opposite effect."

"Yes, quite true. But I've always longed to read them." She collected the rest of the books, and he took them from her.

"Allow me. Please, take another look and make sure there aren't any others that you wish for me to purchase."

"These are plenty."

He quirked a brow. "Are you sure? I don't mind and can easily afford more."

She bit her lip in a way that filled him with a desire to take her in his arms, but he resisted. "Go on," he encouraged and shooed her away.

She returned to the shelves, her head tilted at an angle to better read the spines. Martin carried the chosen books to a bookshop clerk, who began wrapping them and tabulating the prices. By the time Livvy returned with a second stack of books, the clerk's eyes were round with delighted surprise. Martin summoned his coach again and had the books carefully loaded into a trunk at the back of the conveyance.

"Where are we off to next?" Livvy asked, her spirits certainly brightening a bit.

"We still need to visit a shoemaker and a milliner. Then I must run an errand while you remain at the house."

Her smile wilted a little, but she didn't argue. He couldn't tell her about his secret errand. If he could take her, he would have, but ladies did not visit Tattersall's horse auction house.

I will buy her the most beautiful mare in London, and she will ride beside me with pride in Hyde Park.

Two hours later, he deposited Livvy back at his house. It took three footmen to carry the massive hatboxes, dress boxes, shoeboxes, and the packages of books inside. Once the carriage was emptied, he instructed his coachman where next to go.

The auctioneering yard at Tattersall's consisted of many stables, loose boxes, and an enclosure for watching the paces of thoroughbreds put up for sale. Martin walked past the enclosure, noticing a bust of King George IV in the cupola in the center. Despite the cold weather, there were quite a few men watching the horses in the pacing enclosure.

"Banks!" someone called out.

Martin turned to see a familiar face. "Lord Sheridan!" He clasped Cedric Sheridan's hand. The viscount grinned and pointed toward the enclosure.

"Here for a piece of horseflesh? I have one to sell if you are."

"I am, actually." Martin followed Cedric's pointing hand. There was a dappled gray mare with a black mane and black stockings that was proudly prancing around.

"She's stunning," Banks said. He and Cedric leaned over the edge of the paddock to get a better look at the mares. "How much are you asking for her?"

Cedric whistled, and the groom leading the mare around brought her to them. Martin reached out and brushed a hand over the mare's nose. She blinked at him, her dark brown eyes assessing him, but she wasn't unfriendly.

"I'm thinking a thousand guineas."

"What's her breeding history?"

Cedric smiled and patted her neck. "She was sired by a thoroughbred and born from one of my pure Arabian mares. I can provide a pedigree."

"How old is she?"

"Three years," Cedric replied.

Martin studied her teeth and legs, watching the groom with her hooves. She was a patient beast and took sugar cubes from Cedric eagerly. There was a delightful ladylike quality to her that reminded him of Livvy.

"A thousand guineas?"

"Yes. You have her in mind for someone?" Cedric grinned. "I thought you and your mistress separated. Went to France, I hear?"

"She did. I have a new companion. This mare would be perfect for her. A thousand guineas is a bit steep, but she looks to be worth it." He held out his hand, and Cedric shook on the offer.

They made arrangements to have the mare brought to the house tomorrow morning.

Livvy was going to love this horse. And maybe then she would love him.

The thought came out of nowhere, and he quickly shoved it aside. He didn't want her love. He was quite fine without that. Besides, he could never love the daughter of the man who destroyed his life all those years ago. He couldn't deny he felt a certain pleasure knowing he was nice and gentlemanly to her while her father and mother were likely panicking.

He was still lost in thoughts of the past as he left the auctioneering yard and returned to his coach.

"Home, sir?" the driver asked.

"Yes—wait, not yet. Take me to Oxford Street. I need to visit a jewelers."

"Yes, sir." Martin climbed into the coach and gazed out the window as the coach jerked forward.

The London winter was beautiful when snow coated the tops of the houses and merry light illuminated the windows of the houses in the fashionable parts of town. He knew how harsh it could be too. After Hartwell had evicted his family, they had been forced to rent a tiny two-bedroom living space. They'd lived in near squalor for months. They had buried his mother, and for an entire year, he, his father, and Helen had been in mourning.

Martin closed his eyes, still feeling the biting chill of the air as he remembered standing at his mother's grave, watching the freshly dug dirt covered with falling snow. The pain in his chest had nearly choked him. Despair dwelled in the crumbling ruins of his soul. He felt like the sun would never shine again, and yet...

Something had changed. The moment Livvy had burst into the drawing room, he'd felt it. The soft stirrings of sunlight upon his battered soul. He didn't want to admit that she'd raised such feelings in him, but she did.

It would be unfair to ignore how much she makes me feel, wouldn't it?

He did not want to think about how it would be when she left.

When the coach stopped at his favorite jewelers, he went inside, examining the glass cases of various necklaces, brooches, and earrings.

An elderly man with a kind smile greeted him. "Mr. Banks."

"How are you, Harold?" He shook the man's hand. He had known Harold Garland for several years now.

"I'm well, thanks to you. The bonds you recommended have been doing well."

"Glad to hear it." Martin always loved to hear when his advice was heeded by a friend and that it had paid off.

"What are you looking for today?"

Martin studied the jewelry laid out in front of him, frowning a little.

"Pearls, I think." He could picture pearls around Livvy's neck and how they would accent her lovely skin.

"Pearls, let me see..." Harold bent down and brought up a case and set it on the counter.

"*coque de perle* earrings?" He removed two earrings and set them on a velvet cloth on the counter. The earrings were large, with oval-shaped pearls forming a sort of delicate cluster that dangled from the posts.

"*Coque de perle*?" Martin had never heard that term before.

"It is French. They are cut from East Indian nautilus shells similar to pearls. It's actually a shell rather than a regular pearl. But they look just like pearls. More unique, you see, and quite popular in France at the moment."

Martin held up the earrings, marveling at the beautiful gold backings and their relative light weight. It would look stunning, yet not too extravagant, nor would they be too heavy on Livvy's ears.

"And this to complement?" Harold held up a single strand of lustrous pearls held together by a gold clasp. "Elegant, refined, but exquisite in taste."

Martin lifted the pearl necklace, brushing his thumb over the rounded pearls, feeling the silky textures.

"Yes, I shall take them."

"Excellent. I'll box them up for you and put them on your account." Harold quickly took the jewels and velvet pouches and placed them in sleek black boxes.

"The lady is very lucky," he said, handing them over.

"She is." Martin chuckled, but he also felt lucky to have such a sweet woman who belonged only to him. He left the jewelers with a spring in his step. Tonight they would have a quiet dinner together, and then he would begin his seduction. Slow as he needed to be until she was begging to be taken to bed. For the first time in months, he couldn't stop smiling.

CHAPTER 6

Livvy was curled up in a chair in the library reading *Glenarvon* and enjoying every deliciously scandalous page when she heard Martin return. She couldn't help but wonder what other errands he had seen to after he had taken her back to the townhouse. She closed her book and left her chair, creeping up to the library door. It was only open a crack, and she could hear Martin speaking.

"Everything go well this afternoon?" Harris inquired.

"Yes, perfect. I've an excellent mare at my disposal now, and a bit of jewelry should ease her temper a bit."

Livvy winced. He truly thought so little of her that he would liken her to a broodmare? And jewelry was supposed to appease her? She balled her fists.

"Where is she, by the way?" Martin asked.

Sparking mad, Livvy shoved the library door open and eyed Martin coldly.

"You're broodmare is right here."

Martin blinked and then burst out laughing. He couldn't even *pretend* to be embarrassed for being caught saying such things? She almost slapped him.

He walked up to her and cupped her chin, still smiling. She tried to pull away.

"*You* weren't the mare I was referring to. I bought a horse for you and had every intention of making it a surprise until I saw how upset you were just now."

"You bought me a horse?" Embarrassment blossomed across her face. She'd been almost shouting at him while his butler was still present, ready to rail about how perfectly dreadful he was. Shame dug its claws into her, and she wanted to vanish somewhere until the feeling passed.

"Yes, I bought one from a friend. Viscount Sheridan has been breeding Arabians with thoroughbreds. The mare is...well, I will let you see her tomorrow, and you may share your thoughts then."

"I... I'm sorry. My outburst was misguided and inexcusable—"

He pressed a finger to her lips. "You need not apologize. I'm quite deserving of your anger and suspicion given how we met and..."

Though she did not say it, she knew he was thinking about how she *belonged* to him. It only added to her already conflicted feelings.

Martin removed a pocket watch from his waistcoat and examined the time.

"An hour until dinner Why don't you change and meet me in the dining room at seven?" His blue eyes were soft and kind, too kind. She wanted to hate him, and yet she couldn't.

She nodded and rushed up the stairs. Shame still prickled beneath her skin. Mellie was in the hallway carrying some of Livvy's new clothes, freshly pressed.

"Time for dinner, miss?" the lady's maid asked.

"Yes." She followed Mellie to her bedchamber and sat down to wait for the maid to display her options. There was the Devonshire brown evening gown, a cream gown with gold gauze overlay, and a capuchin dark-orange gown. Livvy and Mellie examined all the outfits.

"You're in tonight for dinner, so perhaps the Devonshire brown? It's a simple cut but a stunning color," Mellie suggested.

"I think you're right." She turned her back, allowing Mellie to unfasten the gown for her, and Mellie offered her fresh stockings and dark-gold slippers.

"May I dispose of these?" The maid lifted the thrice-mended stockings.

"Yes, I have more than enough pairs now." Martin had bought her a dozen pairs of stockings. It was far too much money to spend, but she had to admit she liked the idea of enjoying a little luxury.

She put on the stockings and tightened the ribbons, then put on her new petticoats, chemise, and stays before Mellie assisted her with the gown. The sleeves were long down to her wrists and puffed out at the shoulders like mutton legs, but she liked the flexibility of the brown satin gown. There was a reddish hue to it under a certain light that made the gown glow with color.

"Your hair?" Mellie finished putting up the back of her gown and led her to the vanity table. "I was thinking a chignon on the back and curls at the front and sides."

"That sounds lovely." Livvy missed having an accomplished hairdresser at her disposal. Their single maid had been adequate, but the styles she was most comfortable with were severely outdated. She'd also been forced to spend most of her time cleaning and couldn't attend to Livvy or her mother as much as they might have wished.

Mellie selected a mother-of-pearl comb Martin had purchased this afternoon. The comb ran through her hair, and for a moment neither woman spoke.

"Have you worked for Mr. Banks for very long?" Livvy finally asked.

The maid stroked her hair again. "Two years. He's a fair and kind master, if that's what you're asking. Never takes liberties, if you know what I mean."

"I do." Livvy cringed. She may be innocent, but she knew that female servants were often at the mercy of their masters.

"What... What were his other mistresses like?"

Mellie giggled. "I'm surprised you're only asking now. I would've asked last night." Her open honesty made Livvy smile.

"I was a bit overwhelmed last night. I still am, to be honest, but I'm starting to understand what it means to be here...like this."

The maid set the brush aside and began binding back her hair to style it.

"Most of them were fancy birds, but none so sweet as you. He usually has opera singers or ballet dancers or courtesans. You're the first real genteel lady to be here."

That surprised her little. She had wondered if Martin had blackmailed other ladies before, but it didn't sound like it.

"Has he ever had a woman come here for..." She couldn't find a way to pleasantly say what she meant.

"For?" Mellie asked.

"Um... Well, I'm here because my father owes Mr. Banks money."

Her maid gaped at her. "What?"

"Yes. I agreed to satisfy my father's debt—ouch!" She winced when Mellie tugged part of her hair.

"I'm so sorry, miss. I was thinking of how I wanted to strangle him and pulled too hard." Mellie's face reddened with embarrassment.

"It's all right," Livvy assured her. "I wanted to strangle him too at first."

"He's never brought anyone else here for a reason like that. I thought he was a better man than that. Not that I ever said that to you, miss."

"No, I understand your feelings," Livvy muttered. "So, I am to be unique then. I cannot say whether that's good or bad."

"Perhaps good?" Mellie suggested. "He's been different around you."

"Different how?"

"Well, it's only been a day, but I'd say he's behaving…softer, more uncertain. Like a boy meeting a girl, not a man of eight and twenty." Mellie continued to work with her hair until the style was complete. Lovely ringlets bounced on her cheeks, framing her face. "It's a pity you have no jewelry. The gown would look lovely with some earbobs and a necklace."

Livvy placed a hand to her bare throat, trying to picture it with jewels.

"It's fine. I'm sure he won't notice." Mellie placed white flowers about each cluster of curls. The delicate floral scent would make a person think of gardens in the spring.

"Where did you find these flowers?" It was winter, and she didn't think the maid would've gone to a florist.

"The master has little hothouse at the back."

Hothouse? She loved flowers and decided she would ask him to show her tonight after dinner.

"There we are," Mellie declared with a smile. "You're ready."

Livvy stood and glanced about for her shawl, the dark-gold one that matched most of her new gowns, and headed for the door. Martin was waiting at the base of the stairs. She held her breath when he glanced up and noticed her. He leaned against the banister, his physique well framed in buff trousers and a dark-blue waistcoat. She licked her lips as she descended the stairs toward him.

There was an untamed masculine pride that radiated off him. From the moment she had first seen him, he'd made her want to act reckless and daring. Some secret part of her that she didn't normally listen to imagined him kissing her, sliding those strong hands along her body and promising to do all the dark, delicious things that men did in her Gothic novels. She was a candlewick and he was a flame. What would happen between them would be inevitable, and she didn't wish to deny her body's own desires.

In that moment she made a decision. If her reputation or prospects did end up damaged, it would happen regardless of what did or did not happen within these walls. Therefore, she was free to choose whether or not anything did happen. She was here to be his companion, and he was a beautiful man. She *wanted* to enjoy her nights in his bed, and if she embraced the passion that his gaze promised, she might find some pleasure in it. Her mother had told her that women could enjoy the marriage bed if their partner was skilled. By the way Martin was watching her, she guessed he might be a talented lover indeed.

I will put my trust in him tonight. If he can give me pleasure, then perhaps my time here will be enjoyable.

"You look lovely," he said as she reached him. "But something is missing." His gaze slipped over her critically. "Ah yes..." He removed a black velvet pouch from behind his back and handed it to her. She took it, confused, and poured the contents into her hands. A pearl necklace and a pair of extravagant earrings fell into her palm.

"Oh!" she exclaimed. "I can't—"

"Put them on. I wish to see them." He gestured to a tall mirror that hung in the hall. She approached it, and he draped the necklace around her neck. Then she slipped the earbobs on. The effect was outstanding. The pearls on her skin accented the brown silk of the dress. He brushed his fingers along her neck. She wanted to sigh at how good it felt to be touched like that. He pressed ever so slightly into her body from behind in a way that made her skin flush all over as she imagined their bodies pressed together as one breathing being. He was hard, she was soft, yet together they would feel perfect. The thought was so terribly wicked and delightful that she knew it would take ages before she would cease blushing.

"You must take care to wear them often. Pearls are living things. They need to breathe, to be worn." Martin's soft, seductive voice made her tremble.

"They're lovely." She touched the beaded pearls at her collarbone, taking in the naturally silky feel of them. She'd never given a thought to pearls as living things before, but in a way it made sense. There was magic to the idea that those tiny glistening pearls would need sunlight and air as much as she did, and it made her love them all the more.

"My mother was never one for diamonds or any other jewels, but pearls were different," said Mr. Banks. "She was fascinated by the idea that a simple clam could take a grain of sand, something so common and insignificant, and turn it into one of the most beautiful things on earth."

Livvy was lost in his voice as he spoke. Her heart tore for him at the thought of losing his mother so young. He'd been a year younger than she was now. She could not imagine losing a parent, how it could break one's heart.

But he survived, because he's strong. Maybe being cold and heartless on the outside is what kept him safe? She had seen that infinite tenderness in his eyes for brief moments when he thought she could not see it. She'd seen the same in her father's eyes when he looked upon her and her mother.

But I do see. There is goodness in you, and I won't let the bad beginning between us, or our circumstances, ruin another moment of our time together.

She knew that a lesser man in his position would have taken advantage of her long before now. Yet Martin had not.

"Are you ready for dinner?" Martin's gaze met hers in the reflection of the mirror.

She turned to face him, smiling a little shyly. "Yes." She'd never dined alone with a man before.

"Good. My chef is most anxious to serve us some exquisite dishes of his own design. He's French, and he knows his way about a kitchen."

"You have a chef?" Livvy slipped her arm through his as he led her into the dining room. She couldn't believe he'd hired a French chef. Only the truly wealthy did that.

"I do. He's quite worth the extra expense."

Martin's dining room was lovely. Livvy took in the cherrywood paneling of the bottom half of the room and the dark bottle-green painted walls above the paneling. The dark-gray marble fireplace was the focus of the room, with a massive gilded mirror that reflected the light from the windows. Oriental rugs covered the floors, and a cherrywood table was set for dinner. A place was set at the head of the table and another close beside. It didn't proclaim extravagance too loudly, but it did show the level of luxury Martin was accustomed to.

She pointed at a group of four portraits. "Who are they?"

One she was sure she recognized as a young Martin. His blue eyes were brave and yet kind in the oil painting. That was the man she imagined he'd once been. A man she would have fallen hopelessly in love with had they met under different circumstances.

His eyes softened as he studied the portraits, as though he were seeing his parents again in the flesh, not through layers of oil.

"They are my family. My parents, myself, and my twin, Helen."

"Twin? You have a sister?"

He blushed a little, the height and color in his cheeks oddly charming. "Er... Yes. She lives near Bath."

"Is she married?" Livvy knew she ought not pry, but she wanted to know more about him and his life.

"She is, to a man named Gareth Fairfax. They have two children, a little boy and a little girl." He smiled as he pulled out a chair for her to sit. He then took his own seat, and a footman brought in a tray with two bowls of leek soup.

"Do you visit them often?" she asked before she tasted the soup. It was delicious. Normally she found leek soup a bit dull, but Martin's chef had done something remarkable with it. Was that coriander she smelled?

"Not often enough. I find..." He paused and cleared his throat. "I tend to focus my time here in London, visiting the banks, watching my investments."

"Sounds rather...productive."

Mr. Banks smirked. "You mean dull."

"Well, as stimulating as finances can be, it does sound like your experiences of living life are...limited?" She knew that probably upset him, but the truth was he had sounded bored saying it. He had a fortune, and he had a family, so he ought to be out in the world, living a life full of memories and adventures.

Martin chuckled. "Do they now? I think you're right. I spent so many years attempting to ensure I had money and security, that I didn't stop to ever actually enjoy myself."

Livvy tilted her head, studying him. Was he being facetious?

Wade the footman came in, and the soup was cleared away. The servants next presented plates of goose, French beans, lobster, and a basket of pastries with a side dish of braised ham.

Martin sipped his wine, watching her as she tasted the goose. "If you had wealth and freedom, what would you do?"

"Me?" She was surprised he cared, but she daintily wiped her mouth with a napkin as he nodded for her to speak further. "Well, I suppose I would go to the opera, to the ballet, to plays. I would travel the world. I've always longed to see India."

"That is quite a lot."

She shrugged. "Life should be about experiences. If you stop and let yourself grow cold to the world around you, then you aren't truly living." She knew it was the wine that was freeing her tongue, but she couldn't seem to stop. "My father has been badly off these last few years, and while I know there are many people worse off, I can't help but feel sad not to have a chance to be out in the world among people. For years we have lived as poor as church mice, and my only escape has been through books. It's why they are so important to me." She finally stopped herself from continuing any further. "I'm sorry. I should not have spoken so...so—"

"Honestly?" Martin leaned back in his chair, his fingers stroking his chin as he studied her.

"Yes. *Honestly* is a nice word for my prattling on."

"You fascinate me," he said, his voice silky and low.

"Fascinate?" she repeated, her heart beating fast suddenly. She quickly focused on her meal, hoping he would change the subject. "I think you are exaggerating."

He leaned forward and finally began to eat his own food. "What is it about India that interests you?"

"I've read several books about it. The colors, the warmth and the exotic feel of it draws me. But also the culture. I want to see places that are very different from England. I want to taste curry upon my tongue and watch the natives ride elephants and the women dance with golden bangles on the hems of their gowns and around their wrists." She blushed, and went silent to monopolizing their dinner discussion. They were silent a moment longer before he spoke, his tone suddenly eager.

"I could take you to India."

Their eyes met, and her heart skipped a beat as something unspoken seemed to pass between them. A lighthearted hope mixed with a heated desire to please each other.

"I have a few friends stationed there, you see. An army captain I know has often reminded me that I owe him a visit. We could go if you like." He seemed to realize he'd been too hopeful, and his expression shuttered a little, as though he tried to put some distance between them. Still, she wanted to know if he truly meant that.

"You would take me to India?" He couldn't be serious. India was so far away, and they were... Well, she wasn't sure how to define their relationship except to say that she was his companion. Possibly his mistress. Did men take their mistresses to India? She almost giggled, damn the wine.

"I've never been, but I too have heard of its allure, and your desire has renewed my own interest in visiting. After the winter passes, we can book passage."

After the winter passes? He planned to keep her past the holidays?

"Finish your dinner." His words, gently spoken, broke through her scattered thoughts. She quickly finished her meal, her hands trembling.

"Tell the chef we'll take the ices in my bedchamber—that is, if Miss Hartwell wishes to," Martin told the footman before he began clearing plates away from the table. He looked to Livvy expectantly, and she knew she could say no, but she wanted to say yes.

"That sounds like a wonderful idea, Mr. Banks."

Martin rose and approached her chair, holding his hand out to her.

If you do this, there will be no going back.

She placed her palm in his, sealing her fate.

CHAPTER 7

Martin curled his fingers around Livvy's hand as they left the dining room. Just the simple act of touching her, even innocently, sent flutters of excitement through him. Damn, he was as nervous as a green lad. He had seen the warmth and desire in her eyes, and it emboldened him. Yet he had given his word. And truth be told, he grew more and more reluctant to suggest such intimacy in light of her reasons for being here. God, what had he been thinking to take a woman in lieu of a debt? And yet she intrigued him in ways he could not fully describe. If only they had met under better circumstances.

But if she wished it, he would give her a world of pleasure. He would worship her body for hours until she fell into an exhausted sleep. The thought was so inviting and so arousing that he had trouble controlling his body's natural excitement.

The grandfather clock in the hall chimed the late hour, the soft metallic dings breaking the easy silence between them as they ascended the stairs to his bedchamber.

Steering her toward his bedchamber, he couldn't help but pull her closer. The brush of her skirts against his legs was so distractingly soft, and the tilt of her head and the momentary question in her eyes was like the quiet stirrings of a fire in the early morning hours.

He stopped at the door to his rooms and turned toward her, offering his most reassuring smile. He lifted her hand to his lips, brushing the backs of her fingers as their eyes met and held. She gave a little nod of agreement, and then he turned the door handle and pushed his door open.

The footman had lit the lamps, and the fire in his bedchamber felt cozy and inviting. Like Livvy's room, it was in an Egyptian style with sphinxes, lotus leaves, and gold painted wood accents. He'd often wondered if he'd gone too far in his designs, but he rather liked the exotic feel to the two bedchambers.

He'd been to Egypt once, only for a brief period of time, but the place had left a lingering hunger for hot, sultry nights, gauzy curtains of bright colors, and the whisper of rushes by the Nile. He'd done his best to bring that feeling home. His bed was large, the frame sturdy and the bedclothes expensive, the dark-red colors creating a more masculine tone than the soft blues of her room.

"It's like my chamber," she exclaimed, smiling at him.

"You like it? I felt a little silly indulging in this much decoration, but I think it is rather magnificent."

"It *is* magnificent! I adore Egyptian decorations." She reached out to touch the red silk hanging around his bed before she turned to face him. She leaned back against the bedpost and tilted her face up to meet his gaze. Only a foot separated them, and he could see the fan of her dark lashes as she looked up at him. His body tightened with arousal, but he didn't want to rush this moment.

"I've been to Egypt," he announced, then felt foolish for bragging. But her eyes widened.

"You have?"

"Yes, it was simply incredible." He could barely put into words what it was like, but he wanted to try. "The air is warm and dry there all the time, and there's always a scent of some sweet flower in the air that reminded me of honeysuckle. I think it was the lotus flowers. I loved the colors and the food with its wild spices. Coming back home seemed so bland." He reached up to brush his fingers along her cheek, and she leaned into the touch.

"Did you visit the temples? Or the pyramids?"

He nodded eagerly. "Karnak was perhaps my favorite, but the pyramids were impressive. It was a bit like standing before the gates of the Egyptian gods, seeing structures so immense one could not imagine how mere mortals ever built them."

"I wish I could see the world as you have." She sighed softly, and it made his heart sink. He knew how she felt: trapped, impoverished, destined never to leave London. It was the fate of most people to never set foot on a path that would take them far and away to places full of adventure.

"I promise you that I will take you somewhere. India, Egypt... choose and we will go."

She eyed him incredulously. He leaned in a little, cupping her face, his gaze torn between her lips and her eyes.

"You shouldn't make promises you don't intend to keep," she whispered, her tone broken. It made his chest ache.

"If I make any promise worth keeping, it is that one. I will take you wherever you wish to go." He burned the vow deep inside his heart. He would give her a chance to be free from the hard life of London, even if only for a little while. She seemed to believe him and reached up to place a hand on his shoulder.

"You make me want to believe in a life of beauty and passion." Her eyes dropped to half-mast and focused on his lips.

"You make me feel the same way." That damned fluttering started up in his chest again, and they shared a small smile between them, one full of nervous excitement. He couldn't help what he blurted out next.

"I want you," he said, and swallowed his foolish excitement. Why did she make him feel like such a young man? He wasn't a lad of eighteen anymore.

"I think perhaps...that I want you too." She reached up, touching his waistcoat. Her fingers glided over the blue silk, and he tried to ignore the hunger inside that was shouting at him to grab and kiss her.

"You think? You are not sure?" He caught a glimpse of her white teeth as she bit her bottom lip.

"I've never done this before. I'm not entirely certain I know what *wanting* someone is like."

Her innocent confession made him groan softly. He covered the hand that lay on his chest, stroking the back of her hand down to her delicate wrist.

"How does it feel when I touch you?" he asked, stroking her skin.

"It makes me shiver."

"Shiver good, or shiver bad?" Martin watched her eyes as he trailed his fingers down her arm to her elbow. Her lashes fluttered.

"Good," she answered. "Very good."

"And this?" He leaned in, tilting her face away so he could press his lips to the sensitive spot just behind her right ear. She clutched his shoulders, suddenly gasping as he flipped the tip of his tongue along her skin. If there was one thing he knew aside from how to build a fortune, it was where to kiss a woman to make her body hum to life.

"Good," she panted. "*Very good.*" She didn't push him away, and when he made as though to step back, she clung to him harder.

"Livvy, whatever happens between us... I don't want you to do it because you have to. You understand?" Martin had no idea why he suddenly wanted to play the hero. They both knew he owned her due to her father's debt, but she was still free to tell him no...or preferably yes.

Her eyes were clouded with confusion. "But you brought me here for..."

"I know I did, but I'm not a monster. My bringing you here was because of your father and the pain he caused me. You are not him, and I don't wish to hurt you. While I insist upon your company, I will make no demands upon your body, now or ever. But...if you want me, want to share my bed, all you need do is tell me."

Their bodies pressed together, heat building between them as she considered his words and her own feelings. He could see her desire to be with him at war with her need to prove that she did indeed have that power. Her eyes raised to his, and he saw a bold look in them that gave him hope.

"I wish to be here...with you." A heavy blush stained her cheeks, and he felt almost giddy with a rush of joy at her words.

She started to speak again, but a footman knocked and entered with a tray of lemon-flavored ices. Martin took the tray and thanked the servant before he closed the door.

"Please, I insist." He handed her a small bowl and a dainty dessert spoon. She accepted them and leaned back against his bedpost again, tasting the ice.

"You may sit on the bed. It won't invite me to ravage you," he teased. But it did give him terribly wicked ideas about he how he would ravage her if given the opportunity.

Livvy perched on the edge of the bed, and he joined her. They ate in silence, and when she was finished, he took her bowl and set it on the night table beside the bed.

"I want to thank you for today," Livvy said. "For the clothes, the jewels, the horse." She reached up to touch the pearls as she spoke.

"You don't need to thank me," he assured her. "I was merely holding up my end of the terms we agreed upon." He didn't like to think about buying her affections. It had never bothered him before, but his previous mistresses had come to him of their own free will. With Livvy it was different. "I fear I started this thing between us badly," he admitted.

"Some would say irreparably," she replied, but her tone was colored with a light amusement. "I should hate you, but well, I think you aren't so terrible now." She was speaking more clearly now, less afraid of him and their situation than before.

"Not so terrible?" he echoed, his pride a little bruised.

She met his gaze, her bravery clear in her eyes. "I need more time."

"More time?" Then all was not lost. She hadn't said she wished to be left alone completely. Livvy was beginning to trust him and to trust that he wouldn't hurt her or take away her power of choice.

"Yes. But..." Her face flushed. "You may kiss me good night." Her lips curved in a hesitant smile. He could see she was acting very courageous.

"One kiss, then," he said, and leaned over to cup her face in his palm. Her eyes shimmered with the candlelight, and he felt his entire body focus on her lips. He fought to control the dizzying currents racing through him.

One kiss... I must make it count.

Their lips met in a press of velvet heat, making desire sing in his veins. He explored her mouth, taking his time, tracing her lips with his tongue. It felt like they were sharing intimate whispers as they both breathed in unison. How could kissing Livvy feel like such ecstasy? How could he become drunk on her taste? His tired soul seemed to shiver back to life the longer he kissed her.

Livvy quivered as he let his lips turn rougher. He wanted her to taste his hunger, to feel his need pulsing between them. He wanted to break his promise of one kiss and show her that her hunger matched his own. His senses reeled as he finally broke their mouths apart. She was clutching him again, her need for more shining her eyes.

"One kiss good night. Well delivered, I trust." He nuzzled her cheek before she slid off the bed and backed away.

"Yes, it was. Until tomorrow."

She retreated to the door and stepped into the corridor, but his heart was still pounding long after she'd gone. His body was tightly wound, and he knew it would be hard to relax after having Livvy so close to being in his bed.

He settled back on his bed and blew out a frustrated breath. Never in his life had a woman tied him up in such knots.

I may have made a grave mistake in bringing her here.

❧

LIVVY PRESSED HER FINGERS TO HER LIPS, SMILING AT THE memory of his kiss. Had she really asked him to kiss her good night?

I did.

And it had been wonderful. *Too* wonderful. Yet he'd kept his promise, and nothing had happened beyond that kiss. She shouldn't have asked him to keep it to just one kiss. Yet there was a small rational bit of her that was glad she'd managed to buy some time to calm things down between them. If she acted foolishly and rushed headlong into things with Mr. Banks, it would break her heart.

She entered her bedchamber and was relieved to see Mellie laying out a thin, lacy nightgown.

"How was dinner?" the maid asked.

"Lovely. More lovely than I expected," Livvy admitted.

"I hope the master was on his best behavior?"

"Good enough, I would say," she giggled. He'd nearly convinced her to toss all good reason aside and stay in his bed tonight. She knew she would at some point do just that, but she wanted to see how strong she was, and more importantly to see if he kept his promise of letting her choose how fast their relationship would progress.

Mellie twirled a finger in the air. "Let me unbutton you."

She offered the maid her back, and Mellie started unbuttoning her gown.

"As long as you are enjoying your time here, that is all that matters."

Livvy bit her lip, thinking it over. She was enjoying it. Yes, she and Martin hadn't had the best beginning, and yes, she was here to pay her father's debt...but she felt less restricted than she'd expected. Less a prisoner and more a guest. Perhaps her situation wouldn't be so terrible? The gown dropped from her, and she waited for Mellie to undo her stays.

"He said he is taking me riding tomorrow," she added, then relaxed as the tight stays loosened.

"That will be wonderful. He loves to ride, even in the winter. He usually goes alone, mind you, so it will be quite a treat for him to have a lovely lady to escort."

"He didn't ride with…his other mistresses?"

"Oh no!" Mellie chuckled. "He only took them in his carriage. Riding is something he enjoys to do alone."

Well that was something. She didn't like to think that she was like all those other women who had come before her, and she especially didn't want to be treated like them.

Once she was in her nightgown, she removed the pearl earrings and necklace and placed them carefully in the hands of the lady's maid.

Mellie sighed. "So lovely."

"Aren't they?" She waited for her to undo the pins in her hair. The two girls giggled as Mellie combed her hair out. Then Livvy climbed into bed, and Mellie added two more logs to the fireplace before she slipped into the corridor and left Livvy to sleep.

Livvy blew out the last candle by her bed. Then she puffed her pillow, nestled into the covers, and closed her eyes. It was no good. She couldn't stop herself reliving that kiss and how wonderful it felt. The thought of it still plagued her. She was falling too quickly into Martin's seduction. No self-respecting lady would let that happen. Yet she had.

What if it was all one elaborate deception? What if he wasn't the man she'd hoped he was, the kind, sweet, seductive man she was starting to care about?

CHAPTER 8

Hyde Park in the winter was truly magnificent. The ice glittered from the tips of the bare branches like crystals hanging from chandeliers. Livvy marveled at the sight from the back of her new horse, a dappled gray mare that was utter perfection. The mare's black nose and four dark socks along with the mix of shadowy gray spotted coloring was exquisite and unique. The horse was sturdy like a thoroughbred, yet her legs were more slender and curved like an Arabian.

"Well then? How do you like her?" Martin asked as he maneuvered his own dark-gray gelding close to hers.

"She's wonderful. Wherever did you find her?" Livvy asked. She kept a careful eye on the other riders in the park, since the ice was still slick upon the ground and she feared their horses might slip and collide with another horse and rider.

"She was bred by an acquaintance of mine, Viscount Sheridan. I mentioned him before. He and the Duchess of Essex have developed a successful breeding arrangement in the last three years, siring three excellent foals. The duchess has excellent thoroughbreds, and Sheridan has Arabians. I met with Sheridan at Tattersall's and thought she would be perfect for you."

Livvy patted the horse's neck and looked at Martin. He seemed every bit the fine gentleman in his tan breeches, green waistcoat, and dark-blue greatcoat. When their gazes met, she flushed with the memory of his kiss last night.

"Thank you," she said quickly.

A glint of amusement lit his blue eyes. "You are most welcome. How does your riding habit fit?" He assessed her outfit with a critical eye.

"Fine." She blushed and glanced away. She would never get used to having Martin look at her like that...like he owned her. There was no cruelty in his gaze, but there was possessiveness, just not the way she wanted. She wanted—yes, *wanted*—him to look at her with the possessiveness of a man passionately in love. In the Gothic novels she cherished, the heroes were always a little callous in the beginning and would later transform into gentlemen in love.

She knew that once Martin sent her home, she would never have that chance again. She would be lost to good society, damaged goods. She would be lucky if she could hide away from the world, but most likely she would have to seek out another protector.

Protector. What a handsome word for a man who would use her for his own pleasure. It would be nothing more than a business transaction.

My body for his money.

Her stomach rolled fitfully, and she raised her chin, staring straight ahead.

"Livvy, what's wrong?" Martin asked.

"Nothing is wrong." She sniffed. Damnation. She would not cry, not in front of him.

"Livvy..." Martin reached over and grasped the reins of her horse, pulling them to a stop. She had to look at him now.

"'Tis the cold air making my nose run," she lied.

For a long moment he stared at her, then sighed heavily and let go of the reins, and they started moving again. They completed a circle of the park, and Livvy suddenly noticed several pieces of paper scattered on the ground. Something was printed on them.

"What are those, Mr. Banks?" She pointed to the ground.

"I'll have a look." He slid off his horse and knelt, picking up a pamphlet. Then he read aloud.

"*Notice, whereas you J. Frost have by force and violence taken possession of the River Thames, I hereby give you warning to quit immediately. Signed A. Thaw. Printed by S. Warner on the ice.*" He turned the paper up toward her, suddenly grinning. "By God, they must be having a frost fair!"

"What's that?"

Mr. Banks mounted his horse, still grinning. "You must've been a child during the last one in 1814. The Thames froze over so completely that the city of London hosted a fair on the ice. Quite the event. I went with my family just a few days before..." His joy faded.

"Before?"

"Before... It is nothing." Martin gazed at the pamphlet for a long moment, and Livvy feared she knew what he meant to say. *Before your father took everything away from me.*

"May we go? I would love to see the frost fair."

"I think perhaps we can," he said. Part of his smile returned as he tucked the paper in his waistcoat.

They moved their horses forward, exiting Hyde Park. It wasn't until they were back at Mr. Banks's house that Livvy spoke again.

"I'm sorry," she said as their eyes met.

"Sorry? For what?" He dismounted and then came over to her. He reached both hands up to her. She leaned down and placed her hand on his shoulders as he caught her by the waist. As he carried her down, their bodies slid against one another and her breath hitched.

"I know what you meant to say earlier. I'm sorry my father caused you so much pain." Those words had weighed on her, and she knew she had to speak them, even if he wasn't willing or ready to listen. His blue eyes softened, but his expression was hard to read.

"You have nothing to apologize for. The sins of the father

should not be passed on to the children." He brushed a lock of her hair back with one gloved hand. "Now, come inside so you can warm up. If you wish to attend the festival, you'll need a sturdy dress and your new cloak."

He led her inside and ordered the footmen to bring them a light luncheon to be served in his study and her bedchamber.

"May I dine with you in your study, Mr. Banks?" Livvy followed him after she'd given her riding gloves and hat to Mellie, who met them at the foot of the stairs.

He seemed genuinely surprised. "You wish to dine in my study?"

"Well, yes, if you would let me. If you don't want me to intrude—"

"No, that's quite fine," he replied, and waited for her to follow him. "And please, call me Martin."

Livvy had to admit she was quite curious as to what his study would look like. Men did not often allow women in their private sanctums. She'd only been inside her father's study once or twice.

Martin stopped at a door at the end of the corridor and stepped back after he pushed it open. She entered ahead of him, glancing about. The walls were a soft forest-green, and the light paneled wood at the base of the room gave it a distinguished look. The desk was large, but not overly elaborate. It was functional. He had several shelves with books, packets of documents, and the occasional decorative bit of art. The rest of his home was clearly designed to impress, yet here, in this private space, she caught a glimpse of who Martin really was. A man focused on business. She shivered, wondering if that applied to everything in his life.

Am I nothing more than a business transaction to him?

He took a seat at his desk, focusing on a stack of unopened letters. She hastily plucked a book from the shelves and seated herself on one of the two comfortable armchairs facing his desk. She opened the book, turning a few pages before she peeped up at him.

Whatever he was reading was making him frown. Suddenly

overcome with an impish desire, she scooted to the edge of the chair and rested her elbows on the edge of his desk. She stared at him. He still kept his gaze on the letters, using a letter opener to slice a wax seal apart as he worked.

Livvy mimicked his deep frown, exaggerating the expression to the point of comedy. Still he did not notice. What would it take to get him to smile, she wondered, or at the least notice her?

A truly wicked thought struck her. She stuck out her tongue and pulled down her cheeks to widen her eyes a little and then wiggled her nose. The movement finally caught Martin's attention as he saw her, then dropped the stack of letters he'd been rifling through all over the ground and on his desk, knocking over his quill and ink bottle.

"Bloody hell!" he growled, rushing to grasp the bottle and turn it back upright.

"I'm sorry!" she gasped. "I only wanted to make you laugh."

He raised an eyebrow in challenge. "Oh? Well you ruined the letters. I have half a mind to put you over my knee and spank you."

She was the one frowning now. "You wouldn't. I'm a grown woman, not a child."

"A grown woman does not make such silly faces!"

"Oh, you are impossible."

Martin was on her instantly, catching her wrist and tugging her around his desk. She squeaked as he bent her over his lap and gave her bottom a hard smack, which didn't hurt in the slightest because of all her skirts and petticoats, but she didn't want him to know that.

"How *dare* you!" He gave her another few smacks, though lighter than the first, despite her kicking protests. Her pride was bruised by the time he let her get up, but he didn't let her leave He simply pulled her across his lap so that she sat on him, and his hands settled on her waist as she he gazed at her and then suddenly grinned and chuckled.

"Try and make that face again," he dared her. There was a sensual light in his eyes. She clutched his shoulders then, her eyes dropping to his lips. His hands on her waist tightened as though in silent encouragement.

He wants me to kiss him, to make the first move.

She wanted that too. She had coaxed a grin from him, and he'd even laughed a little. Her skin warmed at the thought. His smile was purely male as she closed the distance between their faces. Livvy knew she had been pulled in by the raw power of her attraction to him, but she couldn't stop herself from pressing her lips to his. Raw need met pure desire as it grew into a deep, open-mouthed kiss. He coiled a hand in her hair at the base of her neck. The lust he drew forth in her was timeless and potent. She feared he was ruining her for all other men.

But it didn't matter. Well it did, but she knew it *wouldn't* matter once he was done with her. No other man would take her except as a mistress. Her dreams of a marriage and children were gone. Sorrow gripped her heart, and she broke her lips from his. He stared at her, his eyes still glazed with lust.

"I...suddenly don't feel all that well. I think I will return to my chambers after all."

She slid off his lap and hastily retreated toward the door.

"Livvy? Livvy, wait, I'm sorry!" Martin rushed after her, but when he caught up to her at the door, sliding one arm around her waist, she put a steadying hand on his chest.

"Did I...? Was I too rough? I was only playing. I didn't mean to —" He struggled for words, his face pale.

"It isn't that," she whispered, her face flushing. "I liked how playful you were, but..." He looked so concerned and inviting, but she had to keep her distance.

If I don't, I'll do something terribly foolish like fall in love with the man who bought me for a debt.

She would despise herself if she fell that low...and her heart would be shattered.

"What is it?" Martin cupped her chin, and the touch was so warm that she leaned into it a little. She couldn't tell him the truth. He wouldn't understand.

"Female troubles," she said, hoping he would believe her. She placed her palm on her abdomen.

"Oh? Oh! Is there anything I can do?"

"No, I just need to lie down and rest."

"I see. Very well, I'll have your food sent up to you." His fingertips dropped from her chin to her waist, and he gave her a gentle squeeze. "I confess I don't know much about..." He blushed again. "But please, if there is anything... A hot bath, perhaps? Something I may do to help?"

"I promise, I'm well. I need to rest... *Alone*."

She thought it was possible that he looked wounded at her response.

"Of course. Do whatever you need to be comfortable." He let go and stepped back. Livvy felt the distance between them, a chasm that made her heart ache. But she welcomed such pain, if it kept her heart safe.

"Rest well. If you feel well enough, we may try to attend the fair later this afternoon."

She nodded and left his study. By the time she reached her chamber, she felt numb and cold inside. Mellie helped her into a comfortable dressing gown so she could rest on the bed. A footman brought her food a short while later, but she barely ate. Mellie lingered by the armoire, hanging up her riding habit, her worried eyes drifting over to Livvy.

"Miss...are you all right?" she asked.

"I..." Livvy closed her eyes a moment and then met the maid's gaze. "I'm afraid."

Mellie the tilted her head slightly. "Afraid of what?"

"Of falling in love with him." The maid closed the armoire and came over to perch on the edge of the bed.

"Why are you afraid of that?"

"Because..." She plucked the dark-blue fabric of the expensive dressing gown Martin had bought her. It was lovely, like everything in this house, like everything he'd bought for her.

"Because...?" Mellie prompted.

"He won't care about me, not in the same way. I'm just a dalliance that he will turn out once he tires of me. I don't want to love someone like that. Love is special. It has meaning. But what he feels for me will never be love."

Mellie's blue eyes glinted with amusement. "I think you might be wrong."

"I'm not. You don't know him, you don't know how much he despises my father. That much hatred in his heart will erase any love he might ever have for me. I'm worried this is all temporary, that when he's done with me he'll turn cold and callous and—" She choked on the last word as she saw Martin standing in the doorway. From the look on his face, she could tell he'd heard every word.

"Martin—" She started to rise, but he turned and vanished from the doorway. She struggled to get off the bed, nearly tripping in her haste to wrap her dressing gown close, but she could not reach him in time. He slammed the door to his chambers, and she heard the lock bolt slide into place.

"Martin, please, let me explain," she cried at the door. She heard no sound, no hint of breathing, no shuffle of boots. Simply silence, a sound so thick it threatened to smother her.

Two footmen lingered at the top of the stairs, watching her. She ducked her head and rushed back to her room, flinging herself onto her bed and burying her face in the pillows. Her heart was aching, and she could feel the sobs coming. Mellie patted her back gently before left and Livvy heard the door to her bedroom close.

Livvy blinked away the tears, feeling them soak the pillow. She hadn't meant for him to hear what she said. She wasn't even sure if she meant any of it. He hadn't been cold or callous, except that first night he brought her home. He'd been warm and comforting ever since.

If she'd hurt him, she would be the callous one. She knew that she didn't have to feel guilty, but it didn't change the fact that she did. He'd shown her kindness, and he hadn't pushed her, hadn't forced her to share his bed. He had let her be in control, and she'd repaid that with cruel words.

She stilled as she came to a realization. *I want him. There's no sense in fighting my own desires.*

If she gave herself to him as she longed to do, love may possibly follow. She would have to take a chance. But how?

CHAPTER 9

Martin waited a quarter of an hour before he slipped out of his bedroom and summoned his butler. Harris met him in the hallway, smiling.

"What are the plans for you and Miss Hartwell this evening? Raphael is most interested to try some new recipes."

"I'm sorry, Harris, but you will have to tell Raphael I'll be having my dinner out tonight. I'm going to stay at my club for dinner instead. I may not return this evening."

Harris's eyes widened. "Oh? And what of Miss Hartwell?"

"She shall remain here. You may serve her meals in her chamber. She is not to go out, nor to have anyone come to call. Is that understood?"

"Yes, yes of course, sir." Harris waved a footman over to him. "Shall we have your coach brought round?"

"Yes. I'll be in my study. Fetch me when it arrives." He left the hall and entered his study, scowling at the sight of his desk. The ink spill had been cleaned, his letters fixed, and yet he could still feel Livvy in his arms as he kissed her, could still see the impish grin on her face as she teased him. She'd been fiery and warm and adorable, but something had changed.

She called me cold and callous.

The words still clung to him like sharp briars, prickling him sharply. He hadn't thought he'd been harsh, at least not today or the day before. How was he to know? He left his heart buried so deep that it was entirely possible she was mistaking his need to be distant as being cold and cruel.

But he couldn't, *wouldn't* change, not even for her. He was not about to develop feelings for the daughter of the man who'd killed his mother and destroyed his life. That simply could not happen. He would enjoy Livvy's company, and more if she allowed it, but to develop romantic notions for her? No. She was the last woman on earth he could fall for. And she would never fall in love with him either. The sense of obligation because of her father's debt would always hang between them.

Even if he somehow found a way around his hatred for her father, his twin sister would see it as a betrayal. And he had to protect Helen. He'd failed to once before and had almost lost her. He could not fail her again. He wasn't sure how long he sat in his chair with his thoughts a decade in the past, before he realized his footman stood in the doorway, hat and coat in hand.

"Your coach is ready, sir."

"Thank you." Martin rose and donned his coat. He strode to the front door and, with a nod to Harris, left the townhouse.

Martin settled into his coach and closed his eyes as the vehicle rocked forward. He could spend the night at Brooks's and give himself some space, perhaps. It would be good for the both of them. He would protect himself, and Livvy would learn that her words and actions would have consequences. Just as her father's actions had consequences.

When he reached Brooks's at number 60 on St. James's Street, he felt as if he'd aged a dozen years. This morning when they had gone riding, he felt like the day had ended well and Livvy was willing to share his bed. He had not planned on being driven to his club in a black mood. He noted the flurry of excitement in the gaming halls as he entered. The club was well known for its high stakes. Fortunes would be made by some and lost by others. He lingered only a moment in the doorway, watching the young bucks cast their fates with the cards. He wondered who the high flyers would be tonight. A young lad, one of many who served at Brooks's, collected his hat and coat.

"May I do anything else for you, sir?" the lad asked.

"See if there's a room open tonight. If there is, reserve it for me. My account is under the name Martin Banks."

"I'll see to it, sir." The boy rushed off. Martin left the main corridor and headed for the meeting rooms, but he froze when he heard Hartwell's name being bandied about.

"Hartwell owes you two thousand?" the man asked his companion.

Martin hesitated, lingering in the shadows as he listened to the two gentlemen standing at the end of the hall by the gaming room they'd been in moments before.

"He does, and I have half a mind to collect in another way." The second man laughed. He was perhaps Martin's age or a few years older, but there was a cruel twist to his lips.

"What do you mean to do, Stamford?" the first man asked.

Lord Stamford? Martin inwardly cringed. The man was rumored to be a bounder who had little respect for women and animals.

"Hartwell has a daughter. A ripe little peach, or so I hear. If he wants to avoid debtor's prison, he can give her to me. I heard another fellow bought her off him not too long ago for a debt. Shouldn't be too hard to do the same, assuming that other man hasn't worn out her usefulness." Stamford laughed cruelly.

Martin's stomach turned violently. This man was a dark mirror image of himself. He'd taken Livvy just as this man planned to. He was no better than Stamford, except that he would let Livvy come to his bed, rather than force her. But that gave him no comfort in this moment. He swallowed hard, tasting bile as he tried not to think about how he and this wretched man were alike.

"Been a while since you had a bit of muslin, eh?" the first gentleman said with a snicker.

"Not that long, but I need a good chit to shove on her back for a few hours each day, and a sweet little creature like that..." Stamford groaned in delight, and his friend laughed.

Martin's vision colored red as he stormed toward the two men. He lunged at Stamford and slammed him against the wall. Hitting him felt good, cathartic in a way Martin didn't want to think about.

"How dare you speak like that!" he shouted.

"What the devil are you talking about?" Stamford curled his hands in fury and then punched Martin in the face.

He took the blow hard, grunting as his left eye was struck. He let go of Stamford for just a moment.

"You touch Miss Hartwell and I will kill you." He couldn't take back what he'd done to Livvy by taking her away from her home, but he could save her from a man like this.

Stamford puffed up. "Oh? You fancy her as well?" He started to straighten his waistcoat, but Martin lunged for him again.

"Hold on!" The first man stepped between them, slapping a palm to each of their chests.

"We can settle this matter."

"Can we?" Stamford laughed darkly. The smug look on his face made Martin feel wild and reckless.

"I'd be happy to settle this on the field," Martin growled.

Stamford answered with a jackal's grin. "As would I, Mr...."

"Banks. Martin Banks."

"You're the fellow who bought the little chit." Stamford grinned evilly.

"And I'm going to be the fellow who shoots you," Martin warned darkly.

"Wait, Banks? I've heard of you!" the first man said. "You're quite the fortune maker, I hear."

Martin knew Stamford's companion was doing his best to ease the obvious tension, but Martin didn't care.

"Littleton Field. Tomorrow at dawn."

"Agreed. Tomorrow." Stamford jerked his head in a nod. He and his companion beat a hasty retreat into the gambling rooms.

Martin stormed in the reading rooms and threw himself into the nearest chair. He sat there, stewing over the encounter with Stamford for some time before someone handed him a glass of brandy.

"You look as though you may need this, old boy." Rodney Bennett chuckled as he took a chair beside Martin.

"I suppose I do." He accepted the brandy and took a long gulp, ignoring the fiery burn of the liquid in his throat.

"Let me guess. You and Stamford are dueling tomorrow?" Rodney asked.

"How on earth would you know that?" Martin grumbled.

"He's boasting in the gaming rooms about it. Arrogant bastard."

Martin winced as he felt his eye already starting to swell. He'd be lucky if he had good enough vision in his right eye to fire a pistol. "You'll be needing a second, then?" Rodney's tone was light and far too normal. But then again, he'd been through all this before. The last time had been several years ago when Martin had lost the last of his then meager funds to a man named Gareth Fairfax. Gareth had challenged him to a duel, and Rodney had been his second.

Only I never fought that duel. Helen did in my place.

And Gareth had fallen in love with her, the brave woman who'd fought a duel disguised as her twin brother. If she knew he was facing another duel, she would strangle him. But he had to do it, to protect Livvy, because he was the damned monster who'd put her in this situation to begin with.

"Martin, what's the matter, old boy?" Rodney leaned forward, worry lines etching his face.

"Have you ever had the sudden realization that a course of action you took was incorrect and it may have caused more harm than you intended?"

Rodney's lips tilted down in a frown. "Not sure I follow."

"I challenged Stamford to a duel over him wanting to buy a woman to satisfy the debts of the woman's father."

"That was noble of you." His friend grinned.

"It wasn't." Martin sighed, and the sound was world-weary, which was exactly how he felt.

"What do you mean?"

"Because I already bought the girl a few days ago for a debt owed by her father. I'm no better than Stamford."

Rodney paled. "You *bought* a woman?"

Martin nodded. His stomach was still coiled in tight knots. "I bought her companionship, though now I believe there is little difference."

"But...how?"

"It was the night we went to the Argyll Rooms. The girl's father and I have a history, one of a personal nature and enmity on my part. I saw him losing, and I took advantage. In the end, he owed me a vast sum, far more than he could pay, and I went to his house, planning to toss him out. And then I saw her. She was lovely and brave and... She offered herself to me. I accepted. I took her home that night."

"Good God, man!" Rodney's face was red with anger. "Send her home!"

"I would, but..." *I can't.* Martin drew in a breath. "If I do, I fear Stamford will show up on her father's doorstep, demanding the same. I fear others will hear of it and seek similar satisfaction. What have I done?" He buried his face in his hands, pressing the heels of his hands so hard into his eyes that he saw stars.

"But you haven't...?" Rodney cleared his throat.

"No. She has nothing to fear from me. If she wants me, all she needs to need to do is ask, but I won't force her."

His friend nodded. "Good. I'd call you out myself, friend or not, if you did something like that to any woman."

"That's because you're a good man." Martin said dryly. "Far better than me."

"Well, I don't know about that." Rodney laughed before he

grew serious again. "So tomorrow you duel Stamford. Where and when?"

"Littleton Field at dawn."

"Then I'll be there," Rodney declared. "Do you plan to sleep here tonight?"

Martin nodded. He couldn't imagine himself going home under these circumstances.

"Then get some rest and have someone look at that eye. It's likely to swell and compromise your vision tomorrow."

"Thank you." Martin slapped Rodney's shoulder as the other man rose from his chair and headed out. He would no doubt be going home to his wife and children, and for the first time Martin envied him. For a brief second he dared to imagine Livvy was at home, waiting up for him with a babe in the nursery and her smile ready and warm when she saw him.

That is a life you will never have. Certainly not with her.

The thought turned his heart cold, and he reached for the brandy. It would be his only companion on a cold night like this.

⚜

LIVVY STARED AT THE CLOCK ON THE MANTEL IN HER CHAMBERS. It was nearly midnight. She couldn't sleep. Not after how she'd seen Martin hurt at her words. It was her fault she had driven him away. Mellie had said that he left for his club and would not be back tonight. The staff had been given orders to keep her in her room, but she had a suspicion none of them would enforce it. She tiptoed out of her chambers, wrapping the dressing gown tight around her to keep warm. Thankfully Martin's townhouse wasn't as drafty as her own home had become.

She reached his bedchambers. The door was unlocked, and she slipped inside. His valet was there, polishing a set of his boots. He startled when he saw her and blushed.

"Sorry. I didn't mean to disturb you." She backed toward the door.

"It's all right, miss. I'm finished. I usually take the boots down-stairs, but with the master out..." The valet brushed the polishing rag over the tip of the boot, then put the boots in the armoire against the wall on the far corner.

"Thank you." She leaned forward against the beautiful bed, watching the valet tidy up.

"Do you need anything, Miss Hartwell? Before I go?" he asked.

"Oh... No thank you." She glanced toward the fireplace, which was beginning to run low. "Except perhaps more logs. I could feed the fire myself, if you don't mind."

"Not at all." The valet bowed. "I'll have a footman bring some up shortly."

After he left, she wandered about the room, examined the fine porcelain washing basin, the shaving razor, the sandalwood scent in a small bottle. She raised her nose and inhaled. The scent brought back memories, *vivid* ones of Martin holding her close, kissing her in a hard but pleasing way. She'd never imagined kisses could be so passionate, wonderful, frightening.

And I drove him away. Did it matter that he'd bought her? Shouldn't it only matter what she felt? She felt good when he kissed her, good when their breaths mingled and their bodies pressed flush against one another. Maybe that was all that mattered.

Pride—*her* pride—shouldn't matter, not anymore. The damage was done. She was no longer innocent by society's standards. Shouldn't she at least enjoy the sins she would be ruined for anyway?

She would risk falling for him, but perhaps that was inevitable. She was already drawn to him, and it was not simple carnal fascina-tion, but something else. The haunted look in his eyes when he spoke of his family and the early death of his mother, the hints of the reluctant amusement in those mysterious blue eyes, the tenderness of his lips and hunger of his hands created an insepa-rable tangle of emotions for her. She could not view him as just one thing. He was not the cold and callous man she'd mentioned in speaking to Mellie. He was anything but that.

Livvy climbed into his large bed and stared into the depths of the dwindling fire, her mind lost in a chaotic swirl of thoughts.

Do I risk it? Do I dare give myself over, heart and soul, and pray the glimpses I've seen of a good man are real? That a man like him could learn to love me?

Hope was all she had to cling to in the darkness. Hope that she would find the answers, and hope that once dawn was here, Martin would come home to her.

CHAPTER 10

Martin studied the pistol in his hand, feeling the weight of the metal and the polished wood grip, which was cold in his palm. All around him the field was quiet, the predawn sky lit in a pale purple light. The coach that brought Stamford and his second, the man from the night before, Stephen Albright, had only just arrived to present him with his choice of pistol.

"What you think? Does it shoot fair, you suppose?" Rodney whispered next to Martin.

"Devil if I know. I rarely handle the damn things."

"What?" Rodney hissed. "Bloody hell, man, do you even know how to shoot?"

"Of course I do." He knew how to shoot well on a pheasant hunt with a rifle, but that wasn't the same as firing a dueling pistol.

"Are you satisfied with the weapon, Mr. Banks?" Mr. Albright inquired. He shot a nervous glance at Stamford, who was glaring at them.

"I suppose," Martin replied. He'd woken that morning with a headache and a sense of dread, and it wasn't until the servant had come to serve him a brief breakfast that he remembered he was to face Stamford on the field in less than two hours.

"There is one last chance to reconcile," Rodney interjected. "Mr. Stamford, I believe you made unpleasant and ungentlemanly comments toward a young lady last evening. Do you withdraw such comments?" Rodney placed himself slightly in front of Martin, acting as an emissary. In that moment Martin saw how good a friend the other man was. Over the years Rodney had always stood by him and by Helen.

Helen... He couldn't believe his twin sister had faced this same trial, had taken his place against Gareth all those years before, disguised as Martin, while he lay unconscious in a broom cupboard after she'd knocked him out.

He briefly closed his eyes, picturing her that day, willing to face death for him. He'd never been worthy of the people in his life who loved him. All he had done was let them down over and over again. If he died today, Livvy wouldn't miss him—she would be grateful he was gone. Her debt would be paid, and she would go home...only to have a man like Stamford come and claim her in the same way. Fury rose in him like a violent storm, wind lashing the inside of his mind and heart. He could not allow such a thing.

"I do not withdraw my comments," Stamford declared. His aristocratic features were defined by the cruelty which shadowed his eyes.

"Very well," Rodney sighed. "Backs together, and each man must count to twenty paces. Then turn and face each other."

Martin and Stamford approached one another. It took a fair amount of self-control to not toss the pistol to the ground and tackle him into the earth and throttle him. He drew in deep breaths and turned his back. Stamford did the same. Then they began to step away, counting their paces. When he reached twenty, he turned, facing his opponent. Albright and Rodney stood to the left, some yards away from the line of fire.

"Pistols may be raised," Rodney announced.

Martin adjusted his stance. The meadow grass coated in ice was slick and uncomfortable beneath the soles of his boots. Then he carefully raised his arm. His fingers trembled slightly, and with one eye almost swollen shut, he felt like this was a very bad idea now, but he could not let Stamford just walk away, not after what he said he'd do to Livvy.

Stamford raised his arm.

"On the count of three, you may fire." Rodney's voice rang out over the frozen field.

"One..."

Martin licked his dry lips and adjusted his grip on the pistol.

"Two..."

Stamford's lips suddenly curved in a devil-may-care grin.

"Three—"

Crack!

Martin jerked sideways. Pain knifed through his upper arm. He cursed but kept his pistol up.

"Banks! You've been hit?" Rodney shouted.

"Grazed," he grunted. "I think." He looked at Stamford, who was staring at him, his face ashen.

"It is your shot, Banks. You may fire at will," Rodney said. Both he and Albright watched in worry.

"Well!" Stamford almost shrieked. "Get it over with!" He stamped his foot like a petulant child, but even at this distance Martin couldn't mistake the stark fear on the man's face as he tried to stand sideways to reduce his chances of a lethal shot.

He stared at Stamford, his gun raised. "Sell me the note Hartwell owes you and I won't put a bullet through your black heart."

"What?" Stamford shuddered.

"Don't make me repeat myself," Martin warned, his voice low and calm. How he managed that when his own arm hurt like the devil he didn't know. Hot blood trickled down his arm beneath his coat, but he ignored it.

"Why do you want it?" Stamford asked.

Martin continued to hold his pistol steady. "That's my business. Do you agree to sell me the note?"

Stamford frowned, still eyeing the gun. "Do I have a choice?" Martin growled. "Fine, the note is yours."

"Good," Martin said. "I'll have the funds delivered later today."

Stamford exhaled in relief, his shoulders drooping. Martin raised the pistol into the air above the other man's head and fired.

"Bloody hell!" Stamford snarled, leaping back.

For some reason Martin found that all too amusing, and he burst out laughing. The world spun a little, and he grunted as he fell to his knees. Blood dripped down onto the snow. So much blood...

"Banks." Rodney was at his side at once. He grabbed his good arm, hoisting him up. "Come on. We need to get you to a doctor."

Martin stumbled across the field, letting Rodney guide him into the waiting coach. He fell onto his seat and closed his eyes.

He must have lost consciousness, because when he came to, a doctor was crouched in front of him and they were outside a townhouse he didn't recognize.

"Mr. Banks, glad to have you back with us," the doctor announced. Martin shivered, and he realized he was bare-chested. The cold air permeated the coach, and he cursed softly.

Damnation, he felt weak.

Rodney's face suddenly appeared in the doorway of the coach. "A decent wound, eh?"

"A decent wound?" Martin asked. "Is there such a thing? Ouch!" he yelped as the doctor cinched the white bandage around his arm.

"Well, you know, something romantic for the ladies to swoon over. My Anna would gush without end if I were shot defending her honor." Rodney prattled on with a good-natured grin. Behind him the streets were bathed in morning light.

"Bennett, where are we?" If anyone saw him being tended for a wound from an illegal duel, he could be in trouble.

"On Duke Street. I brought you to Dr. Phillips. He's one of the best."

"Thank you, Dr. Phillips." Martin tried to smile at the man. "What's the damage?"

Dr. Phillips smiled a little, but he remained focused on the wound as he finished bandaging it.

"A flesh wound with some minor muscle injury. You will need to take care. I want to see you in a few days to see how you're healing. Mr. Bennett has given me your card. I shall call upon you, if that's all right?"

"Yes, that's quite fine," Martin said.

"Good." The doctor helped him put his shirt and waistcoat back on. The garments were bloodstained, and his valet would be cursing him once he got home.

"You need me to go home with you?" Rodney asked as the doctor packed up his black bag.

"No, that's all right. I'm sure Anna is missing you. I'll send you a message if I need you."

Rodney's eyes deepened with concern, but he nodded and started to pull his head from the coach door.

"Bennett!" Martin called out.

His friend turned back to him. "Yes?"

"Thank you. For today...and for the day you stood by Helen all those years ago. I never understood what she faced, not really. This morning..." He shuddered and carefully favored his bad arm. "What I mean to say is, you're a good friend. I don't deserve you."

Rodney grinned cheekily. "You certainly don't. Anna and I will be in London for the holidays if you wish to attend the dinner at our house."

"Thank you." Martin watched Rodney cross the street and hail a passing hackney. He leaned out of the door and told his coachman to take him home. He'd barely slept at the club, and the brandy he'd drunk the night before along with a swollen eye and wounded arm were now taking their toll on him. As soon as he got home, he was going straight to bed. He would not think about Livvy until later in the day when he'd had a chance to rest and think.

When he reached his home, the coach driver helped him out of the vehicle and up to the door.

"Thank you, Jim." He nodded to the coachman before entering. Harris was exiting the door to the servants' quarters and froze when he saw Martin.

"Sir?" Harris gasped. "What happened?"

He waved Harris off when the butler came over to him. "I will explain later, but I'm all right."

"Can I get you anything?"

"No, not now. I think I just need to sleep for a few hours." He started up the stairs, his feet dragging. He felt as weak as a pup. When he got to his room, he sighed against the door as he turned the latch. He was suddenly very weary. If he could just make it to his bed, everything would be all right.

The door swung open, and he started toward his bed. But the moment his eyes touched upon his bed, he stumbled. It wasn't empty. Livvy was lying there, beneath his sheets, asleep. Her dark hair rippled out across the pillow. She looked so sweet, so innocent and lovely it made his heart ache.

I should go to another room, but I'm too bloody tired. Martin fumbled with his waistcoat and shirt, wincing as he removed them. When he collapsed onto the bed beside Livvy, darkness closed in around him almost instantly.

L ivvy curled into the warm, hard object that lay beside her. It was like sleeping close to a roaring fire while it snowed outside. She sighed and rubbed her cheek against whatever it was.

I must be dreaming. It felt simply wonderful. It slowly occurred to her that there was no way her father could have afforded extra logs for the fireplace in her room.

She jolted awake and stared at the still form lying in bed beside her. She wasn't in her room at home. She was in Martin's bedchamber.

"Martin?" she whispered tentatively, touching his back. He lay on his stomach, one arm underneath his pillow, his face turned her way. His face was pale, and a slight frown creased his brow, as if whatever he was dreaming bothered him. When had he come back? She had crawled into his bed around midnight and had been quite certain he would not return. Yet it was barely past seven if the clock on the fireplace mantel was correct.

She started to slide out of bed, but Martin rolled onto his side and curled an arm around her waist. She gasped as she saw a thick white bandage around his upper arm. That same arm now gripped her in the way a child would a beloved stuffed toy. And one of his eyes was puffy and dark. She winced. What had happened to him while he was away?

"Martin?" She spoke his name a little louder, and he shifted, muttering something about finding a good horse. *He must be dreaming.* Livvy carefully tried to pry herself away from him. The soft skin of his arm was tempered with the hard and heavy weight of his muscles. For a moment she found herself looking at those muscles in fascination. Then she chastised herself and focused on lifting his arm. Her attempts only made him curl tighter around her.

"Martin!" she growled.

"Hmm?" The drowsy murmur made her temper flare. She really needed to use a chamber pot soon. She pressed her palm tightly on the wrapped wound, knowing it would hurt, but she had to get his attention somehow.

Martin hissed and released her waist immediately, then rolled up into a sitting position, clutching his wounded arm to his chest.

"What the devil?"

"I'm sorry! I didn't mean to hurt you." She pushed back the covers of his bed and tried to help him, but she didn't know how.

He growled like an irritable badger and got out of bed. "It's fine." He turned his back on her as he stalked over to his wash-basin and splashed his face with cold water. He scraped the cloth over his chin and cheeks, drying his skin.

"What happened to you?" She slipped out of the bed and came up behind him, trying not to let the sight of his muscled back distract her.

"I don't wish to discuss it. What the devil are you doing in my room?" His cold tone made her step back. "A man could get the wrong idea about a woman in his bed. You say that I'm cold, that I'm callous? You don't know a thing about me. I vowed not to touch you without your permission, but when you're touching me, how do you expect me to respond?"

"Well...I didn't intend... But you can't blame me for what

happens while I sleep!" she snapped back, feeling a strange flush inside her as she verbally sparred with him.

"Then you shouldn't have been in my bed in the first place. A man is liable to wander between his own sheets, and if he finds a soft, feminine body to hold, well, you can't be mad at me for that." He lips were twitching as though he was fighting between a frown a smile, and for some reason that set her off even more, wanting to provoke him into doing something utterly dangerous, like share another kiss.

"Can't I?" she challenged, and he acted just as she hoped he would and took the bait.

He spun around and circled his arm around her waist, holding her captive at the same moment she almost threw herself at him. His kiss bordered on cruel, the savagery of it startling her, and she couldn't help but surrender as her body betrayed her by melting into him. She dug her nails into his shoulders, wanting to get closer, needing the fury of their argument to blend into the heat of his kiss.

She shouldn't like his anger or his rage, but something about it was deeply sensual and aroused her. He tightened his arms around her, lifting her up until her feet left the ground and she was carried to the bed. Livvy gasped as she was dropped onto the sheets. He stood over her, panting as he gazed down at her like a warrior ready to claim a captured princess.

She really had to stop reading Gothic novels. Her fantasies were starting to affect her rational mind.

"Still think it's safe enough to stay in my bed? I'm the monster who bought you, Livvy, never forget that. You despise me, you made that much clear. I considered sending you home, but another man, one even worse than me, would surely collect you for debts as I have. So here you shall stay until I deem it safe to return you to your parents." He glanced away, a tic working in his jaw. "If I find you in my bed again, I won't restrain myself. So if you want to be bedded, you know where to be. Otherwise, stay out of my room."

Livvy scrambled off the bed and rushed to escape. His foul

mood shocked her, but it was clear that whatever had happened last night had changed things. She had been wrong to say those things about him, and now it seemed he was determined to make them come true.

She retreated to the refuge of her own chamber, where Mellie was laying out one of her new dresses. It was a lovely pale-blue gown with golden flowers stitched on the bodice and a light-gold netting dropped over the skirts. She'd never worn such a fine gown before, and guilt suddenly formed a knot in her stomach.

"Everything all right, miss?" Mellie asked.

"Yes." Her reply was a little too quick, a little too tremulous even at that single word.

"The master is home now. Did you see him?" the maid asked, her brows knit with worry.

"I—yes." She headed toward the dressing room to make use of the chamber pot. "He was injured last night, but I'm not sure how. He was most boorish toward me and wouldn't share any details."

The maid stayed in the bedroom, giving her a moment to attend to her needs. When she returned, she was ready for Mellie to help her into her new gown.

"There. Now, go and have some breakfast." Mellie shooed her out of the room, and she resigned herself to the fate of being alone all day. It wasn't that she minded being alone, but this was different. The tension between her and Martin seem to fill the house with an invisible knot of ill omens, and she didn't like it. She prepared a plate of food in the dining room and sat in a chair looking out a window facing the gardens.

It was not as though anyone would care that she wasn't at the table. Martin wouldn't be down anytime soon. She balanced the plate on her thighs and nibbled on a poached egg while she examined the frozen rosebushes that touched the edges of the window-panes. The frost turned the heavy green leaves to pale seafoam, and crystals of ice in exquisite shapes painted the glass. She'd always liked ice and snow. Yes, the cold could be a dreadful thing, but winter itself was beautiful. She reached out to the window, gently tracing the patterns of frost on the glass. She smiled, dreaming of simpler times.

"What are you doing?" Martin demanded from behind her. She jumped, nearly toppling her breakfast off her lap.

"Oh!" She steadied the porcelain plate and relaxed. "I was looking at the frost." She gestured toward the frosted windowpane.

"Frost?" he repeated darkly. "Why the devil do you care about frost?"

She bit her tongue. She'd provoked him by being cruel-tongued first. She would not make matters worse. She focused on her response instead.

"Frost is beautiful."

"Why is it women are so focused on beauty?" He turned his back on her to lift up a lid of a chafing dish and inhaled deeply.

"I'm not focused on beauty for beauty's sake," she argued, trying not to bristle.

"Oh?"

"Yes. I love studying beauty, particularly in nature. Frost is beautiful because of its symmetry. It's the same with snowflakes."

"Symmetry?" He turned to face her, a full plate in his hands as he joined her at the window. He seemed less upset now and more intrigued.

"Yes." She pointed to the edge of the frost. "Examine the edge, where the frost begins to form. There is a recursive self-similarity. I read about it in a book of mathematics. A seventeenth-century philosopher and mathematician named Gottfried Leibniz discussed recursive self-similarity. He proposed the idea that such repeating patterns he discussed in objects in nature were close to geometry, yet no one has been able to properly link those fractional components, as he called him, to geometry. Most mathematicians put up resistance to such theories, simply because they are afraid to dive deeply into the unknown. But I find it fascinating."

"You have a mathematical mind?"

"No." She laughed wryly. "But I do have a mind that focuses on concepts. I can see the patterns, recognize them, but I've no way to explain them with equations or formulas."

"Philosopher, then," Martin concluded. His lips twitched, and her heart gave a jolt. He wasn't angry now. Could she take a chance and apologize? Yes. She could.

"I didn't mean what I said."

Martin didn't speak, and for a moment she feared he hadn't heard her.

"You're entitled to your opinion of me, even if isn't completely true," he finally said.

He was still looking at the frost, not her, and she hesitantly put a hand on his where it rested on his knee.

"My opinion was wrong. You bought me out of anger, and that anger is only a small part of who you are. There are other parts, better ones, that make you the man you are."

"I'm not a good man, Livvy."

She studied him closely. "You are, but I believe it's been a long time since you let yourself see that part of yourself."

He frowned at her, but it wasn't an expression of anger. It was more as if she had begun to pull at a thread that held up the mask he was trying to hide behind. She would tug it down completely one day, and he would see that he was a better man than he thought.

"Finish your breakfast," said Mr. Banks, then he paused briefly before continuing. "We could go to the frost fair if you feel up to it?"

"Yes!" she exclaimed. "Oh, that would be lovely." She dug into the remains of her breakfast, and he did the same. She tried to contain her excitement, but she was bursting with relief and joy. They'd made amends, and it seemed the awful distance between them had almost completely faded. When she looked at him now, she saw a man with a vulnerable heart just like hers, one hungry for affection and acceptance.

"Fetch your cloak," he said with a gentle smile as they exited the dining room together.

"I'll just be a moment."

She rushed upstairs to retrieve her cloak and muff and put on her sturdiest black boots. By the time she got back down the stairs, he was waiting by the front door, hat in hand and wearing his black greatcoat, an image of masculine beauty. She blushed, trying to hide her face as she slipped her hands into her ermine muff and joined him.

"My coach will take us to the Thames."

Martin led her down the steps to his coach, and they climbed inside. They sat beside one another this time rather than across. Their new closeness was far more intimate than she'd expected, and her skin flushed each time his knee brushed hers. She couldn't help but imagine what it would be like soon when they...and how their bodies would...

Lord, I have to stop imagining going to bed with this man or my face will stay as red as a cherry all day.

She shivered a little, and he noticed.

"Are you cold?" He reached around her and placed an arm over her shoulders, pulling her into his side. It was such a simple thing for him to do, and yet it was torture for her because she could breathe in his leather-and-sandalwood scent, and she wanted to crawl onto his lap and get even closer.

"Yes, I was," she lied. If she confessed to the nature of her thoughts, he might just kiss her, and then they may never get to the frost fair.

The closer the coach got to the Thames, the more she leaned toward the vehicle's window because she could hear the crowds. When they reached the river, she stepped out onto the embankment with a gasp. The river was truly frozen over, and for nearly two miles on the ice, a town had been constructed. Wooden huts, vast canvas tents, and all other manner of stalls had been hastily constructed. Thousands of people were on the ice, and the noise of it, the cacophony of the impromptu village, was startling.

"Quite the thing, eh?" Martin asked with a chuckle. He gave her his arm, and she looped hers through his as they began to walk down the slope to the river's edge. Her boots slid and she gasped, her heart jumping into her throat as she lost her footing. Strong arms banded around her waist, and she was caught safely by Martin, their bodies pressed close together. Even through the layers of fabric she could feel the heat from his body, and it made her delightfully dizzy.

She tentatively stepped out onto the ice and held her breath. When the ice beneath her feet didn't shatter, she let the air out of her lungs in relief. She was walking on the Thames!

"What's that?" she asked, pointing to a massive slab of stone at the river's edge. Words were carved on it.

Martin read the inscription:

Behold the liquid Thames now frozen o'er
That lately Ships of mighty Burthen bore.
The Watermen for want of Rowing Boats
Make use of Booths to get their Pence & Groat
Here you may see Beef Roasted on a spit.
And for your Money you may taste a bit.
There you may print your Name, tho' cannot write,
Cause num'd with Cold: 'Tis done with great Delight.
And lay it by, that Ages yet to come
May see what Things upon the Ice were done.

"It's from the last fair in 1814," he added. He kept an arm around her waist, holding her as they walked carefully over the slick ice to a strip of sand that formed a pathway toward the small town built upon the river.

A group of men stood at the edge of the ice city, and the leader held up a hand to Martin. They were dressed a little rough and a tad dingy.

"Ten shillings for you and the lady." The man held out a box with a slot in the top to collect coins.

"Of course. Here you are. Which stalls have the best cider and beer?" Martin asked as he paid the man, and the group stepped back to allow Livvy and Martin to pass.

The man in charge of the money smiled and pointed at a stand in the middle of the first row of set up shops. "That'd be O'Malley's Pub. Decent fellow, even if he is Irish. Best beer on the Thames."

"Thank you." Martin nodded at the men as they passed.

"Why did you pay them?" Livvy asked with a glance back at the men who were still guarding the entrance to the frost fair.

"Those are watermen. They usually make a living transporting people up and down the Thames, and they help the lightermen who move the goods. When the river freezes over, they lose the ability to make a living. They are in charge of the fair. All these traders here you see have paid to build stalls." Martin pointed as they walked down the sand-and-ice avenue. Leather makers, jewelers, and even temporary pubs were all there on the ice. They were getting close to Blackfriars Bridge when a monstrous gray shape appeared at the edge of the bank of the river.

"What's that?" Livvy pointed at the shape. As they got closer, she almost laughed as she recognized it, although she was convinced she had to be dreaming.

"An elephant! It must have come from the zoo. My God, look at it." A boyish look of wonder and delight shone upon his face, and Livvy's heart skipped a beat. This was the Martin she wanted to be with, the man who made her feel like she still had a future to be courted and loved and destined for a happy life.

"Come on. They're going to have it walk upon the ice!" Martin tugged her by the hand as they raced like children for the elephant and the crowd watching it. The huge, beautiful creature was marching proudly over the ice. An Indian man in colorful clothing was smiling and encouraging the elephant to keep walking. It was one of the most magnificent things Livvy had ever seen. Her eyes burned with tears as she watched the elephant lift its trunk and touch its handler's shoulder with affection.

"Could we get closer?" Livvy asked Martin.

"I suppose so. This way." He led her toward the crowd until they were only half a dozen feet away.

"Sir!" Martin called out to the man leading the elephant.

The man turned their way, smiling a little he patted the elephant's trunk. "Yes?"

"May we come closer? My..." Martin glanced at her. "My wife would like to see your magnificent beast up close."

"Would she?" The man's smile broadened. "Come, come, madam." He waved Livvy closer.

She approached, spellbound by the leathery gray-skinned creature. It gazed down at her, ears flopping slowly as it raised its trunk in an inquisitive way and swayed slightly on its feet.

"May I touch it?" she asked the man.

"Yes, yes, please." The man held out his hand to Livvy, and she came closer, only a foot away from the elephant. The elephant's trunk touched her cloaked shoulder, and she reached up, removing her gloves so she could touch it. The skin was leathery like it appeared, yet it was also softer than she expected and covered with fine hairs. She laughed in delight when she shook the trunk the way she would someone's hand in greeting.

"Oh look, Martin!" she called out. He was watching her from a few feet away. "Come and touch him. He's wonderful."

Martin shook his head. "I think I'm close enough. I saw one of these in Africa during my time in Egypt. They aren't native to Egypt, but some gentleman of my acquaintance had insisted on them being brought there. There was one bull elephant, gigantic fellow, and he grew angry at being dragged through the sands and stomped on a man, crushing him to death."

Livvy eyed the gentle giant beside her and sighed. "Martin, I can see his eyes. They're so noble and full of peace. He won't hurt you." Livvy patted the elephant, and he flapped his ears slowly as if in agreement.

"He's an awfully big fellow and—" Martin hedged.

"Martin, if you come over here right now, I will come to you tonight." She made her tone quiet but very clear.

His eyes widened. "What, tonight?"

"Yes." She'd made the decision earlier that day when she'd seen him at breakfast. She wanted to find the man she laughed with, shopped with, swapped books with.

"If I touch an elephant..." He cleared his throat. "Then..."

"Yes," she repeated. "Now stop being so frightened."

Martin approached her and the beast, eyeing the elephant nervously.

"Elephants are gentle," the Indian handler assured him.

"My experience tells me otherwise," Martin muttered. He put an arm around Livvy's waist, and with the other hand, he touched the elephant's trunk. He tensed when the elephant swayed again and made a soft trumpetlike sound.

"Take off your glove," Livvy encouraged. When he did, the elephant lightly tapped his shoulder. The Indian man handed him a peach.

"Give him this."

Martin accepted the peach and held it up. The elephant deftly plucked the fruit from his palm, lifted it to its mouth, and ate it in seemingly one bite.

"Isn't he the grandest thing you've ever seen?" Livvy pressed her cheek to Martin's shoulder. She'd made him conquer his fear, and she was glad. He had done it for her.

"He certainly is." Martin patted the elephant's front leg, and then he and Livvy stepped back to allow the handler to take charge of the elephant. Martin paid the handler a few coins for his patience.

"Shall we go have a drink?" Martin offered.

"Yes, please." Livvy waved goodbye to the handler as they pushed back into the crowd. When they found a pub on the ice, Martin order two pints of ale and handed her one.

"Drink it slowly," he cautioned.

She sipped and made a face. The bitter taste was not to her liking. She much preferred wine or sherry.

"Not for you, eh?" He chuckled. "I'll drink it then." He waved one of the barmen down. "A glass of wine for the lady."

Martin carried his two pints to a small table, and Livvy sat beside him. They drank in pleasant silence while watching the crowds and the games being played out on the ice. The frost fair was truly amazing.

"Can you believe this hasn't happened since 1814? There have been times where part of the river has frozen, but never so much that it was safe enough to walk on."

She leaned against him. "Why doesn't it happen more often?"

"It has to do with the speed of the river flow and the depth. Shallow rivers freeze more frequently. The king has been improving the waterways by deepening the river. It won't freeze easily now."

"What a pity," she sighed. "I find this quite magical."

"As do I, but magic always fades in the wake of progress."

They both fell into a quiet silence as they finished their drinks and observed the fair around them. Livvy wanted it to last for hours. She noticed a large dancing area where a group of men were playing a few violins and people were twirling to a jig.

"May we dance?" She'd always loved dancing, loved the way it felt to fly in the arms of a handsome partner. She had attended only two balls this year, but each one had been breathtaking.

"I suppose we could." Martin finished his second pint and stood. He offered a gloved hand, and she accepted.

When they reached the dancing area, they found the ice covered with a layer of sand, just as the walkways had been.

"Be careful," he cautioned as they joined the other couples queueing up in a line to dance. The musicians started up a lively tune, and the couples facing each other took turns dancing down the row, then they all broke apart to dance in pairs of wide circles. Livvy giggled as she and Martin twirled about, doing their best not to slip on the ice.

After three dances, Livvy was flushed and panting, her corset sitting a little too tight.

"Let's rest for a bit." Martin led her away from the dancers and walked down a row of impromptu shops. They paused at a stall selling canes.

"Oh, these are lovely, Martin. Do you have a cane?"

"No, but I don't have need of one." She was aware of that, but a man with a cane was, well, *distinguished*.

"I think you would look very dashing with one," she said as she went to the shopkeeper who lingered close by, a hopeful gleam in his eyes.

"Dashing? Trying to make me the hero one of your Gothic novels?" he teased. She grinned cheekily.

"Perhaps. I admit, I do love a darkly handsome man with a brooding face who brandishes a cane."

He rolled his eyes. "Well, I'm far from darkly handsome." He pointed to the golden hair that shone in the bright winter light.

"Agreed. More of a fallen angel, perhaps."

"Angel? Bah!" he harrumphed good-naturedly.

"What is a devil but a fallen angel?" Livvy countered. "But I'm serious. I think you should have a cane. Look at this one." She chose a dark cherrywood one. The handle had a curved elk horn on it. The antler had been carved to bear a noble wolf's head.

"Well now, that is a fine one." Martin studied the cane and then Livvy. She hoped he would buy it. It would indeed fit her private Gothic fantasies all too well.

"All right. How much?" he asked the shopkeeper.

"Twenty shillings."

"Here you are." Martin paid the man and took the cane, using it to balance as he and Livvy crossed a slick patch of ice as they continued down the row of shops, until it was time to go home.

Darkness was creeping over the edge of the buildings by the time they arrived back at the townhouse.

"Why don't you rest a bit? We have a few hours before dinner."

"I think I will, thank you." She stood up on her tiptoes and kissed him soundly on the lips before she dashed away. It felt all too easy to be with him, and tonight she would keep her promise. She would go to his room and...

She blushed even thinking about it.

But a promise is a promise, and she wanted to fulfill this one very much.

CHAPTER 12

Martin took his time dressing for dinner. He couldn't shake the flutter of nerves he felt as Byrd finished folding his cravat.

"Everything all right, sir?" his valet inquired.

"Yes, of course, why do you ask?"

"Well...you're fidgeting." Byrd chuckled. "Most unusual for you, sir."

"I..." Martin swallowed, embarrassed at being so transparent. "I admit I'm a little nervous."

"Perhaps you are falling for Miss Hartwell?" Byrd asked as he finished with the cravat and stepped back to check his work.

Martin nearly growled. He didn't *love* the daughter of the man he'd sworn to hate. He could admit he liked her, was attracted to her, but falling in love?

"It's not love, it's an infatuation at best, but it does seem to have me in knots." He studied his appearance critically in the mirror. His bottle-green waistcoat with silver threading made the silk shimmer, and his buckskin trousers looked very smart. Would Livvy approve? She had called him a fallen angel. Did that mean she found him appealing, or simply a presentable devil? He knew he was favorable in looks, but to have a lady say it to him was a different matter.

"You look fine," Byrd assured him. "Your source of *infatuation* will approve too," the valet added with a smug little smile.

It hadn't escaped Martin's notice that his staff had already taken to Livvy. He liked her too. She was witty, intelligent, and quite amusing, among other things.

"I won't need you after dinner, understood? The evening is yours." The valet nodded, understanding but knowing better than to pry.

He didn't bother with an outer coat tonight and headed down to dinner. Livvy was already there, standing by the fire, rubbing her hands. She wore the red silk gown he'd bought her, the one with the deliciously low-cut bodice. Black netting studded with tiny crystals layered over her skirts, letting the provocative red peek through the wide panel at the front of her gown. It wasn't an overly elaborate dress, but it had the desired effect on him. All he could do was picture sliding his hands up beneath the red silk, watching the firelight glint off the hundreds of crystals sewn into the black netting of her skirts.

He tamped down the flood of heat that ran through his body. It would not be at all attractive or comfortable to sit through three courses while his shaft was erect.

Steady, old boy, he silently commanded himself.

"You look lovely," he said as he joined Livvy by the fireplace.

"Thank you." She smiled at him, and his knees buckled treacherously. Why was he allowing this woman to have such an effect on him?

"Er, shall we have dinner?" He waved at the table.

"Yes, thank you."

Martin pulled back the chair closest to his at the end of the table, and she slid gracefully into it. He'd always marveled at how ladies could move so silently and gracefully. Livvy was no exception. He brushed the tips of his fingers over the back of her neck, delighting in the little shiver he felt. Then he sat down and waved for the footman to bring the first course.

It was turtle soup, one of his favorite dishes. Livvy seemed to enjoy it as well, and by the way she was smiling a little he knew she was thinking of something.

"What is it?" he asked, leaning toward her.

"I cannot believe we are...that I said I would..." A blush tinged her cheeks. "I cannot believe I did that."

Martin swallowed a curse. Was she trying to back out? If so, he'd be sleeping tonight with the bluest balls of any man in history. But he'd vowed to let her set the pace, and he would keep his word.

"Do you wish to change your mind? I would not demand..."

"No!" She giggled, but her face was flushed. "No. I mean, I want to, but I admit to being frighteningly nervous."

"Oh. Yes, I see." He cleared his throat. "Because you've never—"

"Yes."

"Well, it's much better if you're not hungry." He reached for his wine glass and drank deeply. His own nerves were edgy. It felt like he was also a virgin facing their first night together.

"I believe I am too nervous to eat," she admitted quietly, and set her spoon down.

"What... What can I do?" he asked.

"Could we do it quickly?" she asked.

"Quickly?" The word tasted foul on his tongue. One did not make love quickly, especially not with a virgin.

"No, I'm sorry. That didn't come out right. If we got started soon it might...ease my fears." She pushed her chair back from the table and stood, holding out one hand to him. He stared at her hand for a moment, wondering if she was serious.

She was...completely serious. *Good Lord.*

Mystified, he took her at her word, and they both abandoned their dinner. She paused when they reached the top of the stairs.

"Your bed or mine?" she asked.

"Mine," he replied, his voice a little gruff as he fought to control his growing arousal. He had to keep from frightening her with his lust. As they entered the room, he closed the door behind them. When he turned back to her, he saw panic flashing in her gaze.

"Livvy, you don't have to do this," Martin assured her. He didn't want to force her to do anything she didn't want to do. She leaned back against the post at the end of his bed and looked up at him through her dark lashes.

"I want to, but would you kiss me first?" she asked.

He nodded mutely and approached her. Her lovely hazel eyes glittered in the firelight, and he studied his reflection in her gaze, hoping he could make this night wonderful for her. She put a hand on his chest and slowly lowered it to his stomach. Her exploring touch made his abdomen clench. He caught her wrist gently and lifted her hands to his lips, placing a soft kiss on her palm before he used his other hand to tilt her head back.

Lust burned inside him, but he clung to his frayed control. His fingers yearned to touch her, his mouth to taste her, his body to press into hers and merge into a single breathing, sated being. Yet he knew that once he and Livvy came together, it would be infinitely better than it had been with any other woman.

Pleasure pulsed in his veins as he slowly lowered his lips to hers. Her lips were plump and all too kissable. He could have nibbled and kissed them for days. He let his mouth tell her what he couldn't find the words to say.

I'm falling in love. He'd tried to fool himself into believing it was only infatuation, but this went far beyond that. There was no denying now what he felt.

His kiss was long and leisurely, taking every moment to enjoy exploring her. But after he felt her panting, he sensed she was ready for the rest of what tonight would bring.

He gently turned her so he could unfasten her gown and let it drop to the floor. Then he unlaced her stays, and she let her petticoats fall to the floor. When she was down to her chemise and stockings, he lifted her up so she sat on the edge of his bed. Then he raised one of her feet and reached up her thigh to loosen her stocking ribbons. He toyed with the silk ribbons, and she gasped when his fingers wandered upward. Then he rolled each stocking off and dropped them to the floor.

Their gazes locked, and he couldn't help but notice the pulse at her throat as he touched her neck with his fingers. She trembled as they gazed at one another. He could have let his touch linger on her forever, taking his time to explore her, but there was an anticipation in her eyes that electrified the moment even further.

"What about you?" She reached for his waistcoat.

"All in good time." He lifted off her chemise, and she trembled as she lay gloriously naked upon his bed. She looked like a sacrifice to the pagan god of lust. He may not be a god, but he was going to enjoy taking her as a sweet sacrifice.

"Mr. Banks—" She tried to cover her breasts, but he caught her wrists in one of his hands and pushed her onto her back. Then he pinned her wrists above her head in the soft bedding.

"One of these days, you'll trust me enough to call me Martin all of the time and not just some of the time."

"One of these days," she agreed, relaxing a little.

"Let me show you pleasure, Livvy. Close your eyes and just feel."

She did as he asked, and he lay beside her, nuzzling her neck, licking and kissing the sensitive spot behind her ear and along her collarbone. He moved his focus down to her breasts. She whimpered and jolted as he sucked one nipple into his mouth, making it turn a soft red that pleased him. Her skin was like velvet, soft and sweet and he covered her with kisses. Lord, the woman's breasts were utter perfection. He couldn't wait to bury his head against their pillowy softness after he was done making her scream in pleasure. He released her wrists and slid his free hand down her belly and over her mound. He parted the dark thatch of curls that defined the lips of her sex. They were wet and hot as he explored her with stroking fingertips. She bucked her hips when he slid one finger inside her.

"My, you're tight."

"Tight?" she gasped, her eyes flashing open. "Is that bad?"

He chuckled. "No. It's quite good. But it's going take me a little while before I can enter you. Do you understand?"

"I... Yes. I think so," she whispered, a fresh blush staining her cheeks.

He pushed a second finger inside her, thrusting them in a slow, sensual rhythm as he started kissing her again. He kept her on her toes, surprising her with soft and hard kisses. All the while he played with her, letting her feel the tight penetration of his fingers before he felt she was ready.

She was panting and dreamy-eyed as she watched him climb off the bed and strip out of his clothes. Then he rejoined her on the bed and parted her thighs as he eased down on top of her. Livvy tensed and her breath grew ragged as he guided his shaft to her entrance.

"Try to relax. It won't be like this after the first time." He pushed in, and she gritted her teeth, pain showing in her lovely eyes.

This was not going to work.

Martin nuzzled her throat and captured her lips in a deep, searing kiss. She relaxed and he thrust in hard and fast. He felt her maidenhead tear, and she whimpered against his lips, but he kept still, giving her time to relax and adjust to him. He poured himself into the delicious task of distracting her with kisses and eased himself to give her a chance to recover. Her hands moved into his hair, tangling in the strands and clasping him closer to her.

He'd always wanted passion from his lovers, but this was different. Livvy was sweet, innocent, yet passionate in a way he'd never expected. Her hands didn't caress with the cool, seductive slide of his last mistress. She clutched, gripped, clawed, moaned, and wriggled, letting her body and her desires dictate her actions. He sucked on her tongue, letting her taste his hunger as he finally began to move his hips. He withdrew from her and then slid slowly back in. She gripped him tight as a fist, and he almost blacked out from the exquisite pleasure of it all. It took a minute to work his way back inside. The hot wet heat of her center welcomed him by his third thrust.

"Does it still hurt?" he whispered.

"No—no," she answered and gasped as he tilted his hips and penetrated her at a new steeper angle.

"Thank God," he moaned and rammed himself home, driven by hard and primal need. He'd never been one for gentle lovemaking, at least not once he had properly sated a woman. He was trying to be slower, gentler.

Livvy dug her nails into his back, and he hissed out of breath. "Faster."

Martin let go of his threadbare control and possessed her body, driven like a hungering beast seeking the pleasure of her climax and his own. She lifted her hips, taking him deeper. He thrust hard, then shallow, then slow, then fast, never letting her find a rhythm. He liked the glint of delighted and aroused shock in her eyes each time he took her with another surprising move.

Without warning, she came apart beneath him and called out his name. She went limp beneath him, and he pistoned even harder until his body ached, demanding one more push, and then he came. A rough shout escaped him as he melted into her. He should have withdrawn, or used a French letter, but he had become lost in this woman and in this moment. He stayed there, lying on her, feeling her channel squeeze him with rippling aftershocks. His release had been pure bliss, and he couldn't deny that everything about this woman in this moment had felt *right*.

He looked down at her, and she gazed up at him, cheeks flushed and eyes bright. "How do you feel?"

"Like I'm going to perish." She paused and then added, "Perish in the most exquisite way."

"You're not hurt?" He had to be completely sure.

"No." She shifted beneath him, wincing. "Well, perhaps a little sore, but I don't mind."

"Stay right there," he commanded and carefully withdrew from her. He retrieved a cloth from beside his washbasin and returned to the bed. They both blanched at the streaks of blood on her thighs as he wiped her clean, which extended to his own shaft as well. He cleaned himself, and when he turned around she was already burrowed deep beneath the blankets, still naked.

"Is it all right if I stay? Or should I sleep in my own chamber?"

The thought of her leaving made him want to growl and block her escape. "You are *exactly* where I wish you to be."

A delighted smile flashed across her lips. "Good, because my legs are as unstable as a newborn foal's, and I'm not sure I could've walked back to my room."

"I'd be more than happy to carry you anywhere, but right now I want you here." He climbed under the covers, tucked her body against his, and sighed in contentment. He'd never felt so calm and at peace in his entire life. She tangled her legs in his and gazed up at him with half-lidded eyes.

"I should hate you," she murmured. His heart sank, but then she continued. "I should, but I don't. I like you...far too much." Her confusion stunned him, but before he could say anything, her lashes fanned down and she sank into an exhausted sleep. Martin held her tight, afraid she might slip away like a phantasm after uttering the words he'd been too afraid to hope to hear.

She likes me, far too much. And I like her far too much. What was he to do?

He couldn't keep her, even though he wished to. He'd vowed never to love, never to care except when it came to his sister. Helen was the only one he could safely let into his heart.

Martin brushed a lock of hair from her face and smiled as he watched her sleep. Would she dream of him? From her content and relaxed expression, he hoped she would, because he knew he would dream of her. Dangerous, wonderful, tempting dreams that made his chest tighten with an emotion he never thought he'd feel again after his parents died.

Hope.

CHAPTER 13

Livvy wasn't sure how long she slept, but she woke to a possessive yet gentle hand caressing her hip and felt a little kiss upon her lips. She opened her eyes, noticed Martin's own eyes were closed, and she let him continue to kiss her. It was still dark outside, and she ought to go back to sleep, but she was amused at Martin kissing her.

Was he dreaming? It seemed like it. A blend of warmth and lust filled her despite her soreness. She *wanted* Martin to be inside her again. The first time had been a little frightening, but once the pain had passed, she'd given in to her urges, overcome by the power that her desires gave her. She stretched a leg over his lower body, hoping to convey her interest. He made a soft sound of delight as he cupped her bottom and gave it a light smack. She giggled and wiggled over him, kissing him more heatedly.

He opened his eyes as their lips briefly broke apart. "Do you wish to learn how to ride a man?" he asked. His eyes burned like blue diamonds lit by firelight.

"Is that...how is that possible?" She raked her nails down his chest, and he hissed out a groan.

"Let me show you." He shifted her so that she lay fully on top of him. "Hips up, darling." He tapped her hips with his hands, then reached between their bodies and gripped his shaft. It stood at attention, and she finally understood. She could ease down on top of it and—he thrust up into her, pulling her hips down, and she squeaked in surprise. The new position made her feel *impaled* upon him, so much so that for a moment she struggled to breathe.

"Oh Lord," she panted, shifting a little as he filled every inch of her.

"Still sore?" he asked.

"A little, but it's not bad." She laid her palms flat on his chest and leaned forward to steal a kiss. He gripped her backside and lifted her up, then pulled her down again, showing her the rhythm to set. She sat back, arching her back to find the most comfortable angle, and he gazed up at her, her breasts bouncing as she rose up to ride him.

It really is a bit like riding. The thought was so scandalous that she knew later she would be blushing violently.

"That's it," he encouraged in a low growl. His hands moved from around her breasts, pinching the hard nipples and rolling them between his fingers.

She hissed and rocked on him faster and harder, desperate for that surge of blinding pleasure that only he could give her. When he lowered one hand to stroke his thumb over her tight bundle of nerves, she came hard, and his gruff shout told her he'd come as well. Passion burst between them, and Livvy felt tears blur her eyes as she sank down on top of him. Their skin shimmered with perspiration, and he slowly ran his hands up and down her back. She laid her head on his chest, feeling the steady beat of his heart.

"It's after midnight. Are you hungry?" he asked.

"I am. May we get something to eat?" She slid off him, hating to separate their bodies, but they needed to be able to move.

"Yes. Stay here. I'll fetch something." Martin slid out of the bed and retrieved his dressing gown. He wrapped it tight, and with a wicked grin he exited the bedchamber.

Livvy lay back on the bed, watching the shadows cast by the

firelight. Her fantasies of being Cleopatra had certainly come to life. She bit her lip and hid a smile. A few minutes later, Martin returned and set a tray beside her. Then he stoked the flames and added a few logs to the fire.

She sat up and pulled the sheets up to her collarbone, waiting for him to join her. He let his dressing gown drop, and she had a chance yet again to admire his lean, strong body. Once he was in bed, he set the tray between them and gestured at the food.

"Please, eat."

She picked up a bit of cheese and a few slices of apple, and he did the same. They ate in silence, and for a moment she was able to forget *why* she was there. She was not Martin's mistress, nor was he the man who'd purchased her in lieu of her father's massive debt. She was just herself, in bed with a man she loved. *Loved.* The word was there, easy upon her lips. She was in love with him and had known from the start it was a risk.

"I wish it could always be like this," she said softly. Martin stilled as he reached for another piece of cheese.

"So do I," he finally replied.

"But it can't, can it?"

He didn't respond right away. "I don't think so. Even though I might wish differently."

She swallowed her last bit of food, her appetite waning now. "Because of my father?"

"I can never forgive him for what he did. I watched my mother's heart give out. You can't possibly know what that was like. In only a few years, Helen and I were completely on our own."

Livvy wanted him to share more of his life with her, even if only by conversation. She shifted closer to Martin, and he set the tray on the table beside him. "I should like to hear more about her."

"She's wonderful. I truly mean that. I know plenty of men who find their sisters tiring, boring, or costly. But Helen is…splendid. She's the smarter of the two of us and the braver as well. She fought a duel for me once, when I was young and foolish."

"She did what? A *duel*?"

Martin chuckled. "I was in Bath, gambling, doing everything I could to try to increase our fortune, but I lost it all. A man named Gareth Fairfax was furious when he discovered I had no means to pay my debt back. He challenged me to a duel, but when Helen found out, she locked me in a room and went in my place. She dressed in my clothes and hid her hair. It was quite the thing, or so I was told."

"What happened?" She covered his arm with a hand and tucked herself against his side.

"She and Garrett dueled, she grazed him and revealed she was a woman, and he took her home as a way to pay off my debts."

Livvy stiffened. "Like you did with me?"

"Yes," he sighed. "Believe me, the similarity between that situation and ours is not lost on me. But I gave you a choice. Helen had less of one."

"So she went home with him," Livvy prompted.

"They fell in love, if you can believe it. They've been married for seven years and have two children."

Livvy rested her head on Martin shoulder, wondering why she and Martin couldn't be so lucky, but she knew the truth. Her father's actions all those years ago would forever hang over their heads and keep them apart.

"Does she live in London?"

Martin shook his head. "She lives closer to Bath. But she and Garrett have a townhouse, and they sometimes visit."

"Oh..." Livvy tried to fight off a wave of disappointment. She knew she couldn't ever meet Helen, she was a mistress. Men didn't introduce their mistresses to their family.

"I'm sorry. We haven't done much socially since you have been here. I could write her, see if she wishes to come. I had planned on visiting her for Christmas, but..."

But they both weren't sure if she would still be with him for the holidays. Livvy ignored the pang that thought created in her chest and focused on the present moment.

"But she can't meet me...I'm not..."

"You're a fine young woman. You're not like the others. Helen is more...open in her thoughts than most ladies. She wouldn't cast judgement upon you, not when the sins are mine. I think she might come."

Livvy tried to calm her excitement and kissed his cheek. "That would be wonderful!"

Martin hugged her back, then slipped out of bed to stoke the fire once more and blow out the remaining candles. Then he rejoined her in bed, and they settled into sleep. Livvy curled herself around Martin, wishing she didn't have to think about the day they went their separate ways. Her heart would surely break when they did.

⁂

THE NEXT TWO WEEKS PASSED IN A BLUR FOR LIVVY. SHE AND Martin were locked in a dream of passion and delight. They went riding in the morning and went out during the day. At night he made love to her until they collapsed, exhausted, in each other's arms. In all the ways but one, they seemed to be living a full life together. Only a shadow of how they'd met lingered now, but it was enough that she could not forget for one minute that she wasn't Martin's wife, but his mistress.

Livvy lingered in the door of the library and eyed the empty settee. Martin was due to meet her here for a light luncheon before they headed out for the day. She stared at the couch, and an impish idea filled her. If she was being honest, she'd been inspired by a scene in one of her favorite novels and wanted to see if Martin would like it.

She removed her slippers and stockings, then lifted her blue-and-gold silk skirt out of the way as she sat crossways on the couch. Leaning her back against one armrest, she tossed her legs over the opposite arm in a scandalous pose that exposed her legs up to her thighs. Then she crossed one leg over the other at one knee and waited. After a few minutes, she heard Martin whistling softly down the corridor.

"Livvy?" he called out.

"In the library!" She covered her mouth to stifle a giggle. She couldn't wait to see his face when he walked inside.

The door cracked open, and he peered around the frame. "Livvy, I—" He froze, his lips parted as he gazed down at her. Then his shock transformed in raw lust as he closed the door behind him, locking it. Livvy gripped her skirts, moving them higher still as he stepped toward her.

"Playing a game?" His voice was low, with a dangerous edge to it.

"I thought I might, if you wish to play too." She batted her lashes and then did something she hadn't planned on. She slid her hand between her thighs, parting her undergarments, then pushed her finger in her own slick channel.

Martin sank to his knees with a groan in front of the settee. Livvy watched him through hooded eyes as she continued to stroke herself, and finally he couldn't seem to stand waiting another moment. He pulled her to face with him on the couch and spread her legs wide, tossing her skirts up to her hips. Then he tore at the delicate underclothes until he found his way to her. He put his mouth to her folds, his hot breath fanning over the most sensitive parts of her. His clever tongue set off a blinding heat inside her as he explored her.

Livvy panted, throwing her head back as he lashed inside her over and over again. The sensation made her dizzy with heated delight. She writhed against him, and he caught her hips, holding her still.

"Behave, little hellion, or I'll bend you over the nearest table and fuck the fight out of you."

His dark, delicious tone only made her white-hot with need.

"Don't promise something like that..." She dug her fingers into his golden hair. "Unless you intend to follow through."

He sheathed his tongue inside her, and she arched her back,

crying out at the flood of pleasure. She was so close, so deliciously close.

He got to his feet and pulled her away from the settee. Before she could react, he bent her over the reading table and tossed her skirts up to her hips from behind. He unfastened his trousers, his thick shaft filling her, pushing deep into her.

Livvy moaned, pressing her cheek against the table, glad to feel the cool wood, because everything inside her was on fire. She opened her legs wider to receive him. As he claimed her, she completely forgot who she was. She had become a primal creature, driven by a savage need to be filled by the man behind her. She was mad for him, mad to be possessed by him, never wanting him to stop.

Martin's energy dominated her as he gripped her hips and drove into her over and over. This...*this* was the delicious danger that drew her in like a moth to the flame. He could burn her up with his body, yet she came back wanting more.

When she came, she cried out his name. Seconds later, he forcefully uttered hers before collapsing on top of her.

"Are you all right?" he murmured, and kissed the nape of her neck.

"I'm quite..." She drew in a deep breath. "Wonderful. You?"

"Wonderful as well." He chuckled and nipped her earlobe tenderly before he stood and withdrew from her. He used a handkerchief to clean them before she tugged her skirts back into place and then tried to walk. She made it two shaky steps before she collapsed in Martin's arms, laughing. He scooped her up and carried her over to the settee and sat down, settling her across his lap. They remained like that, chuckling together while they both recovered their breath.

"You never cease to amaze me," he said with a soft, sunny smile that filled her with warmth.

She trailed a finger along the folds of his cravat. "I hope that's a good thing."

"It is a most excellent thing."

He nuzzled her before kissing her softly, slowly, so delicately that it felt like she was caught up in the most wonderful of daydreams. She never wanted it to end.

"Livvy, I—"

Whatever Martin was about to say, she would never know. A knock on the library door interrupted them.

"Sir, you have visitors," Harris called out from behind the closed door.

"Visitors? Who is it?"

"Your sister and her husband...and the children, of course."

"Good God." Martin hastily set her off his lap and collected her stockings and slippers, his face ruddy. His jerky movements of getting his trousers back up underscored his anxiety.

"Helen is here?" Livvy almost tore her stockings as she pulled them on.

"Yes. Why don't you go to your bedchamber while I see to my sister and this mess?"

Livvy tried to ignore the fact that she'd been called a "mess." She fled to her bedchamber and slammed the door, resting her back against it. Martin was right. The situation was a mess. She could not be introduced as his mistress to his sister and her family. It would be scandalous, and no doubt his sister would see it as an insult. She had been a fool to think she could ever meet his family.

I must wait until they leave. She ignored the burning tears in her eyes. She'd been so foolish to ever talk of meeting his family. It had never been a possibility.

I am his kept woman, not his wife.

CHAPTER 14

Martin checked his cravat once more in the mirror in the hall and scrubbed his hands through his hair, trying to tame the wildness from where Livvy had tugged on the strands in the midst of their passion. Then he entered into the drawing room and faced his twin sister.

Helen stood by the fireplace. She was only a few inches shorter than him and bore the same blonde hair and handsome features he did, though hers were reflective of her feminine beauty. In her arms she held Delilah, her two-year-old daughter, and beside her stood Gareth, her husband. He held the hand of their five-year-old son, Jeremy, who whooped with delight when he finally saw Martin.

"Uncle Martin?" Jeremy tore free of his father's hand and rushed toward him. It was a tradition between the two of them. Jeremy would fling himself at Martin, and Martin would catch him. He wound his arms around the little boy. He had his mother's bright blue eyes, but his dark brown hair was that of his father. Delilah, on the other hand, favored her mother completely.

"I say, old boy," Martin said, jiggling the child in his arms, "you must've grown a dozen inches since I last saw you. Won't be long now before you're taller than me!"

Jeremy grinned and wrapped his arms around Martin's neck, hugging him fiercely. Martin's breath caught in his throat. There was a magic to be found in the embrace of a child. It was pure love, pure trust. He had missed his family more than he wished to admit. When he set the child down he saw Helen's eyes glint with tears, but she was smiling. Martin nodded at his brother-in-law.

"How are things, Gareth?"

"Quite good. I've heard the same for you. So much so that you've been too busy to visit us." There was a hint of censure in Gareth's tone, but he was right. Martin avoided visiting at times because seeing them so happy when he could not be himself felt like torture.

"We *both* want you to visit more," Gareth quickly added. Since Martin had lived with them for a few years as he got back on his feet, he and Gareth had formed a deep friendship, one he'd neglected as of late.

"I will visit more often," he promised. "I had plans to come for Christmas."

"Had?" Helen came over, shifting Delilah in her arms. The child was drowsy and rested her head on Helen's shoulder, her eyes half-closed. Martin brushed a knuckle over her soft cheek, and the toddler sighed happily.

"Well..." He'd had every intention of coming until he'd brought Livvy home, but he couldn't leave her alone and certainly could not take her with him.

"Is it because you're engaged?" Helen asked. Her gaze searched his, and a frown deepened her expression.

"Engaged?" He choked on the word.

"Yes, I have been getting letters all week from friends who said you've been spotted touring the city and taking morning rides with an enchanting woman. Who is she?" Now Helen's face was so full of hope that he couldn't avoid telling her the truth.

"She's not my fiancée. Perhaps you had better sit down, sister." He gestured to the nearest settee and glanced at Gareth. "Why don't you show the children to the hothouse? Jeremy might enjoy the new Venus flytrap I recently acquired. Harris can show you which one it is."

Gareth nodded and collected Delilah from Helen. Then he and Jeremy left the drawing room.

Helen eased down onto the couch, eyeing him with concern. "Martin, what is it? Just tell me."

"I have been seeing a woman, but she is my companion, not my fiancée."

Helen's gaze narrowed. "Do you mean mistress? You have had mistresses before, but you've never been seen out in society with them to the point that the *ton* is talking about it."

He cleared his throat. "This one is...different."

"Different how?" Helen patted the settee, and he finally sat down beside her.

"She's wonderful. Sweet, fiery, intelligent. She makes me feel..." He glanced away, unable to say that Livvy filled him with dreams of love in the future, dreams he was too afraid to embrace because he only ever lost the things he loved.

"And you cannot marry her?"

"If I did, I would never be able to get past her family. Nor would you."

His sister frowned, puzzled. She reached out to grasp one of his hands in the way she'd done a thousand times when it had been just the two of them against the world.

"Who is she?"

He could see she had some inkling of the truth but needed to hear him say it.

"She is Hartwell's daughter."

Helen jerked her hand away, and even though he expected it, it still stung.

"Hartwell has a daughter?"

"Yes. She's nothing like him. I—"

"How the devil did you become involved with Hartwell's daughter?" Helen asked, her tone a little shaky.

"I saw him at the Argyll Rooms a few weeks ago, and I wanted to take from him what he took from me. I won a large debt off him that I knew he could not pay, then went to collect. I had every intention of throwing him out into the street, just as he did to us, but then I saw Livvy and—"

"Livvy. That's her name?"

"Yes. I saw her and it was as though I was struck by lightning. My breath was knocked from my lungs. When she offered to trade herself for her father's debt, I couldn't say no."

"Martin..." Helen looked away, unable to face him. "You shouldn't have done that."

"I know. Believe me, Helen, I know just how wretched a thing it was to do, but I adore her and I can't let her go."

"No," Helen said firmly. "You *can* let her go. Either do the honorable thing and take her as your wife or send her home. Life as a man's mistress will never be enough for her, and if she is as smart and lovely as you say, she deserves a better life than the one you are condemning her to. If you care about her at all, you cannot do this to her."

She was right. Life as a mistress would take its toll on Livvy. At some point it would extinguish the fire in her that he loved so much.

"Send her home after we leave. Then join us for Christmas."

Martin swallowed hard, but it felt like he couldn't breathe. Send Livvy home? He didn't want to. But his sister was right.

"You must do it, Martin. For her sake. If you care about her at all, you will do what's best for her."

"Yes," he agreed quietly. There was an awful stillness inside him when he thought of being alone in this house once more. No more laughter. No more sweet moments in the dark in his bed. No more shared breakfasts and reading together in the library.

Helen stood and smiled sadly. "I'll find Gareth and the children and we'll leave you. Please do come, once you can. We want to spend Christmas with you."

"I will come," he promised.

"Good." Helen embraced him, and then she left to find her family in the hothouse.

Martin wasn't sure how long he remained in the drawing room thinking, but at last he went to find Livvy. It was best to make a quick break. Send her home now before he could dream up a dozen excuses to keep her there with him.

He found Livvy in her room, curled up on the bed. *Northanger Abbey* was in her hands. But he could see that she wasn't reading because her eyes weren't moving from the first page.

"Livvy." He spoke her name, dread forming a dark pit in the stomach. Was this the last time he would see her? The last time he might speak her name?

"Martin, what's the matter?" She closed the book and slipped off the bed, coming toward him.

He had to be strong. He couldn't let her know how much he didn't want to do this. If she saw a crack in his shell and she felt about him the way he did her, then she might refuse to leave. And living as his mistress would only crush her spirit over time.

"Livvy, you must be ready to leave in an hour. A maid will pack your things." The words cut him like knives.

"What?" She reached out a hand to touch him, but he stepped back.

If she dares to touch me now...

"I have decided to forgive your father his debt and free you from your obligations. You're going home. I wouldn't want you to miss the holidays with your family." He spun and left the room, closing the door to put some space between them. When she didn't come after him, that hurt more than he expected. Maybe she didn't feel the same about him after all. He found Harris downstairs and motioned for the butler to join him in his study.

"Miss Hartwell is to go home in an hour. Please have a maid pack her up and summon the carriage."

Harris's eyes widened. "Leaving? Sir, may I have leave to speak frankly?"

Martin nodded, though he had a suspicion that he knew what his butler would say.

"Everyone on the staff adores Miss Hartwell, and I suspect you might as well. Must you send her away?"

Martin was quiet a long moment before he answered. Harris had been with him many years, and his loyalty and confidence were beyond reproach. The man deserved the truth, at least part of it.

"I care too much for her, Harris. That's exactly why she must go. The longer she stays here, the more I destroy her future. I've already ruined the poor girl, but I can't change that. However, if I send her home, she still might be able to find a husband." He knew the chances were unlikely, if word about her arrangement with him had spread as far as he feared, but there were men out there willing to take a pretty bride even if she wasn't a virgin.

"I..." Harris cleared his throat and continued. "I don't suppose marriage is possible?"

"No," he answered. "Her father and I have a dark history, and it is not something I could ever overcome. Not even for her."

"Ahhh..." Harris's disappointment was obvious, but he spoke no further on the matter, for which Martin was relieved. Her departure was going to hurt all of them.

"I will see to it that Miss Hartwell is packed." The man turned to leave.

"Harris. Make sure she takes all of her clothes, and see to it her horse is transferred to her family's stables." He paused a moment, wondering what else he could possibly do, aside from the impossible. "And she is to take all the books she wants."

"Yes. Of course, sir."

Martin sank into a study chair as Harris left, trying to ignore the battle of emotions raging inside him. It felt as though his world was coming down around him. There was a stillness inside him, one that felt like frozen despair, heavy as lead. He feared it would drown him.

I fell in love with her. The daughter of my most hated enemy.

Misery the likes of which he'd never experienced before took hold of him. He'd believed he'd become dead to pain since his parents died, but he'd been so damnably wrong. It was as though a gray light of gloom cast its deathless shadow over him. Martin covered his face with his hands, pressing hard against his eyes lest any tears betray the rending of his heart.

CHAPTER 15

Livvy didn't speak as Mellie silently packed her valise with her new clothes, nor did she speak when her books were packed in a trunk. Words simply wouldn't come. It felt more like a funeral than a farewell she was experiencing.

When it came time to leave, Mellie made no effort to hide her tears. As Livvy walked down the stairs and accepted her cloak from a waiting footman, she whispered a thank-you to him. His face was downcast as he said goodbye, clearly upset. She understood how he felt. In the last few weeks she'd come to view this townhouse as her home and her life with Martin as her future. When she got to the coach waiting for her outside, she pulled her hood up to hide her face.

I will not cry, I will not.

To her credit, she kept her vow, not even as the coach pulled up in front of her father's townhouse. She went inside, no longer caring about her valises or trunks. Her father rushed out of the study and froze when he saw her. It had been almost a month since she'd left, but he looked somehow ancient.

"Livvy? You're back."

She nodded stiffly.

Her father rushed to embrace her. "You never should've gone."

"We would've lost our home, Papa."

He gazed down at her, his eyes full of conflicting emotions. "I know, but you aren't the one who should have taken that burden upon your shoulders." He rubbed her arms, his face lined with worry. "Did he hurt you?"

Now she could feel them, the burn of treacherous tears. "No, Papa. He was kind. More than kind." She waved at their only servant, who was carrying in the valises and the trunk. "But he sent me home, and so here I am."

"Why don't you go upstairs and rest? We'll have dinner in a few hours." Her father gave her another gentle hug, as though she was incredibly fragile.

"Thank you, Papa." She headed up to her room and closed the door, then threw herself on the bed and buried her face in the bedding. Hot tears came, but she made no sound. She was numb.

Why had he sent her away? They'd been so happy, so wonderfully happy. What had gone wrong? It must've been something to do with his sister and her visit. Perhaps Helen had learned that Livvy was living with Martin as his mistress and demanded he send her away once she learned who her father was? Martin and his sister were twins, and those bonds ran deep. He would do anything for his twin.

Including send me away.

It was for the best, she knew. She could not have stayed with Martin for long. She would've felt caged in like a bird, no friends, no social acceptance. She would be limited to a world of shadows and midnight Cyprian balls with other kept women. At least this way she might in time have a quiet life as a spinster with a few understanding ladies who would still call her friend after word of her ruination had been replaced by other scandals.

Livvy drifted to sleep for a while, dreaming fitfully of the elephant on the icy Thames and shared kisses in his library. She awoke to the sound of arguing outside her room. She jerked up, trying to clear her head of the fog of sleep as she listened to the voices.

"Where is she?" a man's cold voice demanded.

"You will not take her, do you hear?" Her father's shout was desperate.

"I will. You owe me, Hartwell, and she's the payment I want. I know you've whored her out before. Now you can give her to me."

The door handle rattled as someone tried to open it, but Livvy had locked it when she retired, not wishing to be disturbed.

"Open this door at once, Miss Hartwell!" the man shouted.

"No, Livvy, don't!" Her father's warning was cut short. She heard him grunt and a heavy thud as he fell to the floor.

"Papa!" she shouted, pressing herself against the door.

"Miss Hartwell, you will come out at once or else I will permanently damage your father."

"You wouldn't dare!"

"Wouldn't I? Your father owes me, and I assure you, given my position, the courts will side with me, even if I were to kill him by *accident*."

Livvy's heart sank. She drew in a deep breath before she opened the door.

A tall, dark-haired man stood inches away from her. The second he saw an opening, he shoved the door hard. She stumbled back, wincing as her chest burned with pain from the impact. The man was on her in an instant, grabbing one of her arms and jerking her to her feet.

"You're coming with me. Now," he growled, and she was dragged from the room. Her father was an unconscious heap on the floor.

"Who are you?" She tugged on the man's arm.

"Lord Stamford."

Livvy shuddered as recognition struck her. She'd heard about him, a vile brute of a viscount, well known for escaping the consequences of his actions.

"You will pay for your father's debt on your back."

Livvy swallowed hard, barely able to breathe. "Please, let me go." She knew begging would be of no use, but what other options did she have?

"Know your place, woman, and you will find the time passes easier." He pulled her through the entryway and outside. She was thankful she hadn't yet taken off her cloak or else she would have been freezing. Stamford shoved her into a waiting coach, and she cowered in the corner as far away from him as she could. She had to think of a way to escape.

He sat back, a cruel smile stretching his lips. She couldn't help but see how different he was from Martin, despite the odd similarities of the situation. A pang of longing stung her heart. She would have given anything to be back in his arms.

"Why did you take me?" she asked Stamford. "Are you so desperate for a mistress that you must leverage debts to obtain one?"

Stamford smirked. "You have a tongue on you. Take care that you do not accidentally bite it off."

Livvy gritted her teeth.

"I have taken you because some bastard named Banks challenged me to a duel over you, and I wish to punish him."

"Martin fought over me?"

"I shot him, but only grazed him." Stamford clenched his hands into fists on his thighs. "By all rights I won that duel, and I will not be made a fool by him or any other man."

Livvy suddenly remembered Martin returning the morning after she'd hurt him with her careless words. He had been wounded, but he'd refused to tell her how.

"You'd better be a damned good lay. Your life may depend on it if I am in a foul mood." Stamford's deadly calm as he delivered the threat nearly paralyzed her.

Don't let him frighten you. You must find a way to escape.

She wanted to crawl into a tight ball to escape the fear growing inside her, but she couldn't. She had to be brave.

The coach stopped. He got out first and snapped his fingers

impatiently. She rushed out after him, and he grabbed her arm, shoving her up the steps. She nearly tripped, and he snarled a curse at her but made no attempt to help.

She followed him inside his townhouse and glanced around. The decor was far too bold, as though he wanted to beat visitors over the head with his strength and fortune, but with no sense of place or purpose. The Persian rugs clashed with the Grecian lamps and Turkish Ottoman sofas. It was so very different from the refined elegance of Martin's home.

"Baird!" Stamford bellowed at the haggard-looking butler.

"Yes, my lord?" Baird glanced at her and hastily looked away.

"Take this woman upstairs to my bedchamber. I want her stripped and bathed. She is to wait for me there." Without another word, Stamford walked away.

Livvy and the butler exchanged glances. "This way...Miss..."

"Hartwell. Livvy Hartwell." She raised her chin, desperate to hide her fear.

"Miss Hartwell." Baird's eyes were apologetic as he waved for her to follow him. She lifted her skirts and followed him upstairs. When the butler showed her to his master's room, he kept his eyes downcast.

"A maid will be up shortly to assist you. A footman will fill the tub."

Livvy swallowed her response. It would do neither of them any good to tell him she wasn't going to strip and bathe. She waited for him to close the door, and then she turned the key in the lock after she heard his footsteps recede.

Stamford may prey on other women, but he would not prey on her. She faced the room and noticed a heavy writing desk. She dragged it across the room and wedged it against the door as best she could. Then she rested a brief moment, her stays pressing tight against her ribs, making it hard to breathe.

There was a wide window behind her, and it gave her a sudden idea. She rushed to the window, opening it wide. She dug through the armoire until she found extra bed linens. She worked to knot the sheets together, then dropped one end of the makeshift rope down the side of the house. It worked for Lady Leticia in a Gothic novel, so it just might work for her. Of course, she wouldn't use it the way Leticia did, but it would serve a purpose all the same.

She tied the other end to a metal pole at the base of the windows used to hold back the curtains. She feared there was no way her rope would carry her, but if she could *trick* Stamford into believing she had escaped, it would give her time to slip away while Stamford's focus was elsewhere. She slipped under the bed to wait and prayed her plan would work.

CHAPTER 16

Martin gazed unseeing at the snow falling outside his study window. Stacks of letters lay unanswered, their words left unread. His cup of tea, hot only a short time ago, was now tepid. The room was icy despite the fire some kind footman had lit for him during his distraction.

His happiness, what little of it he'd claimed in the last few days, was gone. It was like losing his mother and his home all over again. If he didn't know better, he might have sworn his black heart was broken clean through. If it was, it would never heal.

My Livvy is gone. Gone because I was too much of a coward to fight for her. Regret weighed so heavily upon him that it was hard to draw in a breath without his chest aching.

He knew his servants would be worried, and his clients' letters needed answering, but Martin couldn't find the strength or desire to care about anything at the moment.

His thoughts were miles away, on Livvy and how she'd been so brave to touch the elephant at the frost fair. How she had made him do it as well and face his fear. She'd brought out the best in him over and over.

And yet I was afraid of what she made me feel.

He rubbed his eyes, suddenly very weary.

"Sir?" Harris's voice came through the closed door.

He turned away from the window. "Yes?"

"I hate to disturb you, sir, but Mr. Hartwell is here."

"I will not see him," Martin growled.

"Sir." Harris's voice was louder now and more insistent. "He's been badly beaten. He told me he needs your help. Someone named Stamford has kidnapped Miss Hartwell."

"What?" Martin leapt out of his chair so fast he knocked it over. He opened his door and faced Harris. The butler nodded toward the front door. Edwin Hartwell stood just inside the doorway, hat in hand, his face swollen around one eye.

"Livvy's been taken? What the devil happened?" Martin demanded.

"She'd only been home a few hours. She was sleeping and *he* showed up, demanding to take her for a debt. It seems word of your arrangement with her has spread around town." Edwin's face darkened.

"A debt? I paid him for that debt. He has no right to her. Why didn't you stop him?" Martin wanted to blacken Edwin's other eye.

Edwin stared at him, his face stony. "I refused his demands, and the bastard hit me hard. When I awoke, they were gone. I would've done anything to protect her."

"You didn't protect her from *me*!" Martin snapped. "How was I any different than Stamford?" He hated the truth of those words, but he couldn't deny them either.

Hartwell looked at the floor. "My shame for not standing up for her more with you is what drove me to stand up to Stamford. But you are not the same kind of man as him. I saw the clothes and books you sent back with her. I saw her face when she talked about you. My daughter loves you, and I think perhaps you might love her as well. Whatever you feel for me, hatred, loathing, I am sure I deserve in full measure. You must understand that everything I did was to protect my own family. I was not lining my pockets with your family's money—I was keeping my own family in our home. It doesn't erase the villainy of my actions toward you, but what I did, it was for Livvy. If you at all care for her, you must help her now. Please, I'm begging you." Edwin's eyes were full of desperation. "What I did to you was beyond despicable, but please don't let Livvy suffer for my sins. I fear what Stamford will do with her."

Martin cringed inside. He shared that fear. The man was dangerous. "Harris, have my coach brought round at once."

"I have a hackney already waiting," Edwin said. "I'd hoped you would come with me."

"Then let us make haste." Martin didn't bother to fetch a coat. He was on fire with a building rage. If Livvy was harmed in any way, he would *kill* Stamford.

❧

LIVVY LISTENED TO THE POUNDING ON THE BEDROOM DOOR.

"You little—*aargh*!"

The door broke open with a thud, and the desk blocking it shifted a few inches. Another thud and the desk shifted yet again. Each time the wooden legs scraped harshly on the floor, the sound made her ears hurt. She covered them with her hands and watched the desk shudder and slide inch by inch as Stamford threw himself at the door. Then he had space to squeeze through and stomped around the room. Livvy watched his boots as he paused at the window.

"Think she can get far? We'll see," he growled and left the room. Livvy held her breath. After several moments, she slid out from under the bed and tiptoed toward the desk and open doorway. She heard Stamford's distant yelling from below on the first floor. There weren't any servants about as she quickly rushed down the stairs and headed for the front door. If she could just get to the street...

Pain ripped through her skull as she was yanked backward by her hair.

"Think yourself a crafty bit of muslin, do you?" Stamford's deadly purr pushed her to fight. She reached up and clawed his cheek, drawing blood. He hissed and released her, only to strike her with a closed fist. It caught her cheekbone, driving agony through her. Her knees buckled, and she fell at his feet. Stamford kicked her in the stomach, and she curled up on one side, gasping for breath. He began to lift his foot again, and she curled into a tighter ball. A rap on the door made Stamford back away. He stared down at her.

"One bloody sound out of you and you won't live to regret it," he warned.

Livvy cowered in the shadows behind the door, and Stamford opened it.

"What are you—"

The scuffle and sounds of a fight made Livvy close her eyes at first. Then she opened them to see Stamford staggering back. A second later Martin, her avenging angel, advanced on Stamford, his fists raised.

"Where is she?" Martin demanded.

"I'm here!" Livvy choked out.

Stamford took advantage of the distraction to lunge at Martin, tackling him to the ground. Stamford seemed ready to drive Martin's skull into the floor when someone else suddenly knocked Stamford off of him.

"This is for my daughter!" Her father had mounted Stamford and was punching him over and over. Livvy watched in horror while Stamford groaned and writhed, her father attacking him like a wild animal. Martin gripped her father by the shoulders and dragged him off as Martin said something in her father's ear. Only then did he get off Stamford, though he kicked the man in the ribs and then dusted himself off before he was done with him. He looked up and saw her.

"Livvy!"

"I'm here." Livvy used the wall to stand up, though her legs were still shaky.

"Thank God." Her father embraced her. "Did he hurt you?"

"Yes, but not as much as you hurt him, I think." She winced as her ribs screamed in protest. Fire lit her father's eyes as Martin put a steady hand on his shoulder.

"Take her to the coach," Martin said. "I'll handle this."

She followed her father outside but turned to see Martin as he stood above Stamford, his hands curled tight at his sides. He looked at her a moment, then, without expression, closed the door. It was for the best. She didn't want to see whatever he might do, even though Stamford deserved it. The coach swayed as she and her father climbed inside. She sank back against the cushions, breathing hard. Her father watched her anxiously.

"Why did you bring Mr. Banks?" she asked quietly. After everything she'd just gone through, her body felt like it was on fire. She wanted to cry. She wanted to go back in and punch Stamford herself. She wanted Martin to come back and hold her. The conflicting desires were almost too much to bear. She clasped her hands in her lap to conceal their trembling.

"Why? Because it's obvious the man is in love with you."

"You are mistaken." *He wouldn't have sent me away if he was.*

"When I told him Stamford took you, he was enraged..."

"He's a gentleman. I am sure he came to my aid for only that reason."

Her father stared at her as if she were mad. "Trust me. I know that look. It is the look I carry for you and your mother. That love I have for you both made me do things I now regret to keep you safe and happy. I see the same look in his eyes. That man adores you."

Martin finally entered the coach and wiped his bloody knuckles on his trousers. He glanced away from Livvy when he caught her watching. For a second it was as though her father wasn't in the coach with them at all. They were alone, just the two of them, and that was all that mattered.

"I shall see you both home," Martin finally said, tugging his gaze away from her.

Livvy recoiled at the cold response and tasted bitter disappointment on her tongue, but she forced herself to speak.

"Thank you for coming to my aid, Mr. Banks."

Martin nodded stiffly and looked out the window. Livvy looked to Martin, praying for some sign that he was hurting as much as she was. But he didn't even spare her a glance. He kept his focus on the window opposite her.

When the coach reached her home, she motioned for her father to leave, but he shook his head. "Let me have a moment with Mr. Banks."

She left the coach and headed inside. Livvy put a hand to her mouth as she turned away, swallowing a fresh wave of pain inside her heart. Was it possible for a heart to break a second time? Because she was quite certain it had shattered again.

❧

"TELL ME YOU DON'T LOVE HER," EDWIN SAID.

More than you can ever know. More than I ever dare admit to anyone.

"I..." The words were there on the tip of Martin's tongue, but they wouldn't come. It wasn't easy to admit his feelings to a man who had taken so much from him.

"I know you and I will never be friends, and the barest cordiality will exist between us, but please do not let my sins destroy your future with her, if that is what you desire. I can make no excuses for the wrongs I've committed against your family. I can only say that I was fighting to prevent my own family from being ousted from our home. I made regrettable decisions to protect Livvy and her mother, but I don't regret trying to protect them. I know you understand that, if nothing else. If you love her, don't let the past ruin that." Edwin's eyes held no cruelty, no mockery, no evidence of the man he'd been over a decade ago. Was it possible the man really had changed?

"I will think on it," Martin said finally, but even as Edwin exited the coach, Martin knew how he truly felt. After seeing

Livvy bruised and hurt, his rage filled him with a blinding need to protect her.

I cannot live without her. If that means forgiving her father in some small way, I shall do it. She was worth keeping, worth protecting. Worth loving at any cost.

He rapped the ceiling of the carriage with his cane. The cane she had convinced him to buy at the frost fair.

There was much to do.

CHAPTER 17

He didn't come for me.

Livvy sat in the drawing room, a book clutched in her hands, the words unread. The embers were dying in the fire, and outside the snow was falling thick in the early morning. It'd been a full week since she'd been rescued from Viscount Stamford, and it felt as though she'd been trapped here. All she could do was replay that moment when Martin came to her rescue. But then he'd let her go home with her father, and she knew then that she would never see him again. She'd carried hope within her that he might come and whisk her away to be married. But he hadn't. He'd cared for her, but it wasn't enough for him to come back.

She put the book aside. It had been like that for days, a listless wandering of her thoughts, a lack of desire to even rise from her bed most mornings. Food seemed to lack taste, and the world seemed grayer than it used to be. Life itself had become pale. She knew she suffered from a broken heart. It hurt enough that it might kill her, and yes, she knew that sounded terribly dramatic, like something from one of her Gothic novels, but it was true. Frighteningly true.

"Livvy, dear?" Her mother's voice disturbed her from the dark gloom of her thoughts.

"Yes?"

"I've had a new gown made for you. I would love to see how it fits."

It sounded like a dreadful way to spend her time, but what else was she to do? She joined her mother upstairs in her bedroom. A large white box sat on the bed, and upstairs maid Sally was waiting to assist.

Her mother nodded at the box. "Well, go on and have a look."

"Mama, I don't need a new gown. I have plenty from—" She didn't finish. She noticed her mother's threadbare purple gown and wished her mother had bought herself a gown instead.

"Please, Livvy." Her mother sounded oddly desperate.

She sighed and opened the box. Inside was a stunning rose-colored gown of expensive watered silk. It was too fine for a day gown, it looked more suited for an evening gown, but the décolletage was higher. She pulled the gown from the box and held it up, spinning a little in front of the mirror, fascinated and a little confused. How could she afford this? She caught sight of her mother's watery smile in the mirror.

"Mama, what's the matter?"

Her mother wiped tears from her cheeks. "I am just picturing how lovely you will be in it. Please, put it on." She motioned for the maid to help Livvy change.

Once Livvy was finally dressed, her mother took her gently by the elbow.

"Your father and I would like you to meet someone." Livvy's stomach knotted with nerves as she followed her mother downstairs. Her father wore his best black coat, holding up her new cloak.

"Papa, who are we meeting?" she asked. Her parents were acting far too strangely. It was creating a ball of tension inside her.

"Someone I hope you will be happy to see," he said. He kissed her forehead, and the three of them climbed into a hired hackney outside. Livvy studied her parents apprehensively, trying not to think of who she would be happy to see. *Please let it not be some suitor Mama met over tea.*

There was only one man who would make her happy, and she was too afraid to hope it would be him.

Martin.

Her heart gave a jolt with hope, but it couldn't be. He had let her go. Now more than ever, she felt a kinship with Lady Leticia from her favorite Gothic novel. She'd been cast out by the duke and sent home for her own safety, and the duke had whispered in her ear, "My time in the sun has ended, and now I must face the winter of my life without you." Lady Leticia had of course returned and rescued the duke from his treacherous younger brother, and the danger had passed. It would not be the same for Livvy, and she knew that. There was no happy ending waiting for her. The coach stopped, and Livvy peered out through the windows, shivering as a slight chill seeped through the window of the coach. They had arrived at St. George's Church.

"Papa?" She looked to her father, but he was smiling, expressing a blend of joy and melancholy. He got out of the coach and then helped her and her mother out. Together they walked up the steps to the church. Her father ushered her mother inside, but he and Livvy remained on the steps a moment longer.

"Papa, what is happening?" Livvy demanded, her heart racing wildly.

He brushed his knuckles down her cheek the way he used to do when she was a little girl.

"You gave yourself to save our family, Livvy. That was..." His voice roughened. "That was once my job. But I failed you, my darling child, in more ways than you know. But now I can make it right."

"There's nothing to make right."

"There is *everything* to make right. You deserve the life I've always dreamed to give you. And now I can."

He moved toward the heavy wooden doors of the church and

opened them, then offered her his arm. Livvy struggled to breathe as she entered St. George's, her eyes darting over the beautiful interior of the church. It was empty and quiet except for her mother and three men who stood at the front by the altar. A clergyman, a dark-haired man with a gentle smile, and one other man with golden hair that was illuminated by the morning sunlight like the halo of a fallen angel. Her angel.

"Martin!" she gasped. Those blue eyes she'd once thought were so cold now shone like the surface of a summer lake reflecting the bluest sky. She looked to her father, and he was wiping at his face, brushing away his tears.

"Yes," her father said with a chuckle. "His friend, Mr. Bennett, agreed to be an extra witness."

"But he didn't come back for me," she whispered, her heart so fragile and so full of hope. She feared to believe what she was seeing.

"He wanted to more than anything, but he had to make things perfect for you before he did." Her father gestured to her new dress. "He's done so much for us, all of us, Livvy. As long as you love him, I will do whatever I can to win back his trust and respect."

Livvy bit her lip hard enough that she almost drew blood.

"I do love him." *So much it hurts.*

Her father chuckled. "Then let's make a husband out of the boy."

When she reached Martin, his eyes searched hers, worry lines creasing his eyes and mouth.

"This doesn't have to happen if you don't want to," he said quietly.

"Do you love me?" she asked. That was the only thing that mattered to her.

"Yes. More than is wise, more than any man should love anything or anyone. I love you to distraction, I love you to—" She flung herself at him, kissing him, her heart ready to burst. Only when the clergyman cleared his throat did she remember that she was in the church and her actions were highly inappropriate. But from the smile on the clergyman's face, he did not mind *too* much.

She beamed up at Martin, and the soft sweet fire in his eyes promised her a lifetime of moments like this. He lowered his head to hers and pressed their foreheads together. She felt in that moment they were the only two people existing in the world. It was true. He wanted her for now and forever. The world seemed to come back to life around her. Color and joy found its place again.

"You know," Martin began with a low chuckle, "I think I finally know what to call you."

"Oh?" She tilted her head, studying him.

"Not mistress, not lover, not companion...I was thinking...*wife*."

"Is that your way of proposing? It's a bit late—I'm already here," she teased, trying not to laugh.

"Then I'd say it was successful, as long as you agree, *wife?*" he asked, his lips curving into a grin that was full of mischief.

"I suppose I could live with that." She winked at him.

"Hellion," he said teasingly.

"*Your* hellion," she replied. Together they faced the clergyman, side by side.

Some futures could be broken over the turn of cards, while others won by those very same wagers. Livvy had bet her heart on loving Martin—and she had won.

Christmas at the Fairfax house was magic. Martin could not deny it. He had spent so many years avoiding the cheer of the yuletide season but that was impossible now. He watched Livvy chase his nephew across the snow covered grass, throwing snowballs at one another. He laughed when she slid and fell on her bottom in the snow and Jeremy pounced on her. They both rolled, laughing in delight.

"She's wonderful, Martin. Just as you said." Helen spoke from beside him. She held her daughter in her arms and the toddler was playing with a lock of Helen's blonde hair.

"I didn't ever think…" His throat constricted. "That I would be able to forgive what happened to our parents, what happened to us."

Helen smiled and waved a hand to him. "Let me show you something." She took him to a small patch of frozen bushes by the window the library. A single rosebush it somehow withstood the winter, possibly because the afternoon sun reflected off the windows heated the air around the glass.

"You see that?" Helen pointed to the bush where blue roses grew. He'd never seen blue roses before.

"Do you remember what our mother used to tell us? About the legend of the blue rose?"

He smiled and nodded. "She said it can only grow when two enemies fell in love."

Helen shifted her daughter in her arms and smile as she saw Gareth join in with Livvy and Jeremy to play in the snow.

"We both married people we thought we could not and yet....those marriages have been the greatest gift of all."

Martin had to agree. The moment Livvy had said yes in St. George's, his life had transformed into an eternal spring. As long as he had her, there would always be blue roses blooming, even in winter.

Livvy finally abandoned her snowy games and rushed over to him. Her youthful exuberance reminded him he was not as old as he felt once. He could be young with her, recapture that magic in every laugh, every smile, every kiss. He caught her by the waist, holding her close. She smelled of the wintry woods and flowers, an enticing blend.

"Are you happy?" he whispered against her lips. His heart quickened his as she smiled up at him. She brought warmth to his heart, like a blazing fire in the deepest winter. He wasn't a man of poetry or romance so he told her with his lips with his words could not.

"I don't think there's a single word that could fully express my happiness. The emotion is far too big." A glint of a tear shown her hazel eyes and in that moment he knew he was truly and completely devoted to her. Everything good, everything noble and pure in this world started in the curve of her lips and continued in the shine of her eyes as she looked at him with tenderness. He had not forgotten how he felt that first moment when he beheld her, and now he felt no different. She made him breathless, delighted, surprised and full of joy. Livvy was every dream he'd been too afraid to hope for.

"And you?" she asked. "Are you happy?"

He placed one of her gloved hands to his chest just above his heart and he managed a nod. He was too full of emotion to speak. She seemed to understand and stood up on her tiptoes. The breeze tugged playfully on her dark curls and he twirled a lock around his fingers just before their lips met. The kiss was barely a whisper at first, a quiet promise of the years of passion ahead of them. But it turned harder, burning like the sun on his face after a long cloudless day.

"There are no words... But there are kisses," he vowed. Kisses to build the rest of their lives upon and to entwine their hearts like the stems of blue roses, blooming against all odds.

THANK YOU SO MUCH FOR READING THE 4TH BOOK IN THE Seduction Series, *The Gentleman's Seduction*!

Stay tuned for the next book *The Captain's Seduction* coming soon! You'll travel to India for a new love story!

Turn the page to start reading *His Wicked Seduction*, another steamy Christmas story!

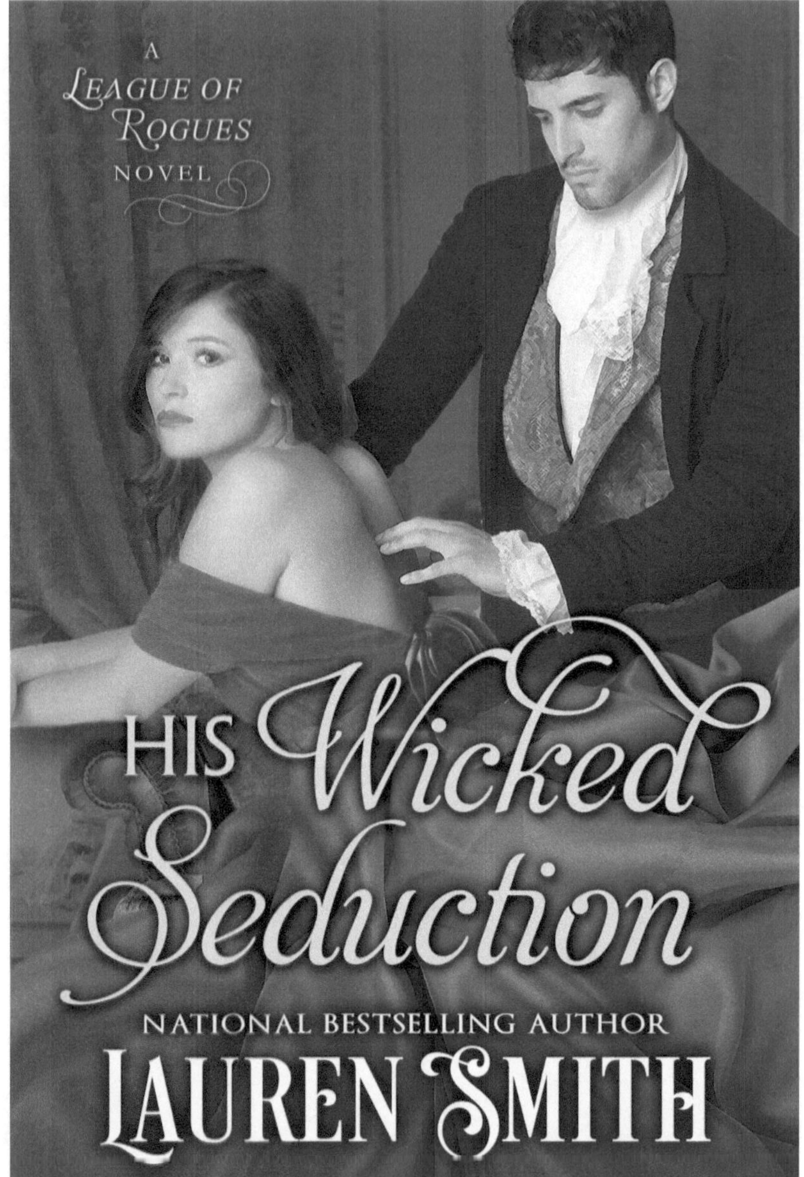
A LEAGUE OF ROGUES NOVEL
HIS Wicked Seduction
NATIONAL BESTSELLING AUTHOR
LAUREN SMITH

HIS WICKED SEDUCTION

THE LEAGUE OF ROGUES BOOK 2

CHAPTER 1

League Rule Number 2:
One must never seduce another member's sister. Should this rule
be broken, the member whose sister was seduced has the right to
demand satisfaction.

Excerpt from *The Quizzing Glass Gazette*, September 30,
1820, The Lady Society Column:

*Lady Society has turned her eye this week to one of
London's most notorious paramours, the Marquess of Rochester. Member of
the infamous League of Rogues, the marquess is rumored by ladies of the ton
as a fiery-haired devil capable of shocking delights behind closed doors.*

*It has come to Lady Society's attention that no lady has held Rochester's
interest for long. Does he secretly pine for someone of good breeding and
good sense, perhaps?*

*Lady Society would like to learn the answer to this most fascinating
question. Perhaps Rochester indulges himself to ease the pangs of unrequited*

love for some mystery woman. Should one hazard a guess as to the unlucky —or perhaps lucky—maiden who has stolen our dark marquess's heart?

LONDON, DECEMBER 1820

She is going to be the death of me.

"Lucien! You're not even listening to me, are you? I'm in desperate need of a new valet and you've been woolgathering rather than offering suggestions. I daresay you have enough for a decent coat and a pair of mittens by now."

Lucien Russell, the Marquess of Rochester, looked to his friend Charles. They were walking down Bond Street, Lucien keeping careful watch over one particular lady without her knowledge and Charles simply enjoying the chance for an outing. The street was surprisingly crowded for so early in the day and during such foul wintry weather.

"Admit it," Charles prodded.

Lucien fought to focus on his friend. "Sorry?"

The Earl of Lonsdale fixed him with a stern glare which, given that his usual manner tended towards jovial, was a little alarming.

"Where is your head? You've been out of sorts all morning."

Lucien grunted. He had no intention of explaining himself. His thoughts were sinful ones, ones that would lead him straight to a fiery spot in Hell, assuming one wasn't already reserved for him. All because of one woman: Horatia Sheridan.

She was halfway up Bond Street on the opposite side of the road, a beacon of beauty standing out from the women around her. A footman dressed in the Sheridan livery trailed diligently behind her with a large box in his arms. A new dress, if Lucien had to hazard a guess. She should not be out traipsing about on snow-covered walkways, not with these carriages rumbling past, casting muddy slush all over. It frustrated him to think she was risking a chill for the sake of shopping. It frustrated him more that he was so concerned about it.

"I know you think I'm a half-wit on most days, but—"

"Only most?" Lucien couldn't resist the verbal jab.

Charles grinned. "As I was saying, it's a bit obvious our leisurely stroll is merely a ruse. I've noticed we've stopped several times, matching the pattern of a certain lady of our acquaintance across the street."

So Charles had been watchful after all. Lucien shouldn't have been surprised. He hadn't done his best to conceal his interest in Horatia Sheridan. It was too hard to fight the natural pull of his gaze whenever she was near. She was twenty years old, yet she carried herself with the natural grace of a mature and educated queen. Not many women could achieve such a feat. For as long as he'd known her, she'd been that way.

He'd been a young man in his twenties when he met her, and she'd been all of fourteen. She'd been like a little sister to him. Even then, she'd struck him as more mentally and emotionally mature than most women in their later years. There was something about her eyes, the way her doe-brown pools held a man rooted to the spot with intelligence—and in these last few months, attraction...

"You'd best stop staring," Charles intoned quietly. "People are starting to notice."

"She shouldn't be out in this weather. Her brother would have a fit." Lucien tugged his leather gloves tighter, hoping to erase the lingering effects of the chill wind that slid between his coat sleeves and gloves.

Charles burst out into a laugh, one loud enough to draw the attention of nearby onlookers. "Cedric loves her and little Audrey, but you and I both know that does not stop either of them from doing just as they please."

There was far too much truth in that. Lucien and Charles had known Cedric, Viscount Sheridan for many years, bonded during one dark night at university. The memory of when he, Charles, Cedric and two others, Godric and Ashton, had first met always unsettled him. Still, what had happened had forged an unbreakable bond between the five of them. Later, London, or at least the society pages, had dubbed them The League of Rogues.

The League. How amusing it all was…except for one thing. The night they'd formed their alliance each of the five men had been marked by the Devil himself. A man by the name of Hugo Waverly, a fellow student at Cambridge, had sworn vengeance on them.

And sometimes Lucien wondered if they didn't deserve it.

Lucien shook off the heavy thoughts. He was drawn to the vision of Horatia pausing to admire a shop window displaying an array of poke bonnets nestled on stands. Her beleaguered footman stood by her elbow, juggling the box in his arms. He nodded smartly as Horatia pointed out a particular bonnet. Lucien was tempted to venture forth and speak with her, possibly lure her into an alley in order to have just a moment alone with her. Even if he only spoke with her, he feared the intimacy of that conversation would get him a bullet through his heart if her brother ever found out.

Charles had walked a few feet ahead, then stopped and turned to kick a pile of snow into the street. "If this is how you mean to spend the day then consider me gone. I could be at Jackson's Salon right now, or better yet, savoring the favors of the fine ladies at the Midnight Garden."

Lucien knew he'd put Charles out of sorts asking him to come today, but he'd had a peculiar feeling since he'd risen this morning, as though someone was walking over his grave. Ever since Hugo Waverly had returned to London, he had been keeping on eye on Cedric's sisters, particularly Horatia. Waverly had a way of creating collateral damage and Lucien would do anything to keep these innocent ladies safe. But she mustn't know he was watching over her. He'd spent the last six years being outwardly cold to her, praying she'd stop gazing at him in that sweet, loving way of hers.

It was cruel of him, yes, but if he did not create some distance, he'd have had her on her back beneath him. She was too good a woman for that, and he was far too wicked to be worthy of her.

Rather like a demon falling for an angel. He longed for her in ways he'd never craved for other women, and he could never have her.

The reason was simple. His public reputation did not do justice to the true depth of his debauchery. A man like him could and should never be with a woman like Horatia. She was beauty, intelligence and strength, and he would corrupt her with just one night in his arms.

Within the *ton*, there was scandal and then there was *scandal*. For a certain class of woman, being seen with the wrong man in the wrong place could be enough to ruin her reputation and damage her prospects. These fair creatures deserved nothing but the utmost in courtesy and propriety.

For others, the widows still longing for love, those who had no interest in husbands but did from time to time seek companionship, and that rare lovely breed of woman who had both the wealth and position to afford to not give a toss about what society thought, there was Lucien. He seduced them all, taught them to open themselves up to their deepest desires and needs, and seek satisfaction. Not once had a woman complained or been dissatisfied after he had departed from her bed. But there was only one bed he sought now, and it was one he should never be invited into.

He glanced about and noticed a familiar coach among the other carriages on the street. Much of the street's traffic had been moving steadily and quicker than the people on foot, but not that coach. There was nothing unusual about it; the rider was covered with a scarf like all the others, to keep out the chill, yet each time he and Charles had crossed a street, the coach had shadowed them.

"Charles, do think we're being followed?"

Charles brushed off some snow from his gloved hands when it dropped onto him from a nearby shop's eave. "What? What on earth for?"

"I don't know. That carriage. It has been with us for quite a few streets."

"Lucien, we're in a popular part of London. No doubt someone is shopping and ordering their carriage to keep close."

"Hmm," was all he said before he turned his attention back to Horatia and her footman. One of her spare gloves fell out of her cloak and onto the ground, going unnoticed by both her and her servant. Lucien debated briefly whether or not he should interfere and alert her to the fact that he and Charles had been following her. When she continued to walk ahead, leaving her glove behind, he made his decision.

Lucien caught up with his friend still ahead of him on the street. "I'll not keep you. Horatia's dropped a glove and I wish to return it to her."

"Plagued by a bit of chivalry, eh? Go on then, I want to stop here a moment." He pointed to a bookshop.

"Very good. Catch me up when you're ready."

Lucien dodged through the traffic on the road and was halfway across the street when pandemonium struck.

Bond Street was turned on its head as screams tore through the air. The coach that had been shadowing him raced down the road in Lucien's direction. Yet, rather than trying to halt the team, the driver whipped the horses, urging them directly at Lucien.

He was too far across the street to turn back; he had to get to safety and get others out of the way. Horatia! She could be trampled when it passed her. Lucien's heart shot into his throat as he ran. The driver whipped the horses again, as if sensing Lucien's determination to escape.

"Horatia!" Lucien bellowed at the top of his lungs. "Out of the way!"

He'd never forget the look on her face. The way her confused expression changed into unadulterated joy at seeing him, then to terror as she realized the curricle was headed straight for them.

Lucien crossed the street moments before the horses reached him. He tackled Horatia, knocking her to the ground in an alley between the shops. The curricle's wheels sliced through the snow and slush inches from his boots, soaking them with icy water.

For a long moment, Lucien couldn't move. She was alive. He'd made it. The curricle hadn't run either of them over…

Then his body seemed to realize it had a woman under it. A woman with the finest curves God had ever made to tempt a man. Her bonnet was askew, revealing long lustrous curls of deep chestnut hair. Her dark eyes, so innocent, fixed on his face in wonder.

"My lord…" she murmured in a daze. Her gloved hands rested on his chest, holding him at bay. He felt the tremble of her hands all the way to his bones, and his body responded with interest.

"What in blazes?" Charles rushed into the alley, gray eyes alight with fury. "Did you see who was driving that curricle?" Charles paused and took in the scene before him with a smile. "Horatia, love, how are you? Not too bruised I hope?" Charles had never in his life bothered with titles or propriety. Neither did Lucien for that matter. So it didn't surprise Lucien that his friend treated Horatia as he did.

"Oh Charles!" she exclaimed. She seemed to realize only now she was on her back in an alley just off Bond Street, with a street full of curious people peering in and Lucien on top of her.

Lucien gritted his teeth. "Oh Charles!" she'd said, but Lucien was always "My lord." It grated his nerves that she didn't offer such intimacy to him. It was his own damned fault. He pushed her away at every opportunity, just to keep himself from tugging her into the nearest alcove and kissing her. Something about her seemed to render him into the most barbaric state possible. He had little else on his mind other than how she'd taste, how she'd moan and sigh if he could just get his hands on her.

"Lucien…" Horatia stammered. His name on her lips was more erotic than a lover's sated sigh. "What on earth just happened?"

"I fear someone just tried to run me over, and you were, unfortunately, in the way," he explained, worried by the dazed expression swallowing her dark eyes.

"I say, Lucien, you might want to get off the girl, she's turning blue," Charles teased. "Besides, stay on top of her any longer and people are bound to talk. Wouldn't want to end up married just for saving her life, would you?"

Horatia was red-faced and Lucien wasn't sure if it was from lack of air or because she lay beneath him near a public street in such a compromising position. He rolled off her and got to his feet. Charles handed Lucien his hat and he set it back in place. He brushed off the snow from his clothes with one hand while offering the other hand to Horatia.

Her hesitation struck him like a blow. Finally her gloved hand settled into his and he helped her up, tugging just enough so that she stumbled into his arms. He couldn't resist smiling down at her.

If he leaned down just a few inches, he could kiss her, part her lips... For a moment, he lost himself in the dream of how she would taste. She stared up at him, unblinking with those damned lovely eyes that warmed until they were fiery with echoed desire. It would be so easy to—

"Ahem." The footman held out the box with a most pitiful expression on his face. "My lady..." he croaked as he showed her the package. It was soaked clean through, just as Horatia and Lucien now were.

She tugged free of Lucien's arms. "Oh dear!"

The spell he'd cast over her was broken as she rushed over, taking the box from the footman. "Oh dear, oh dear." The glitter of tears were sharp in her eyes when she turned to face him.

"My dress. It's ruined."

Tears for a gown? The behavior was more suited to her younger sister, Audrey. The loveable little chit was obsessed with fashion. Horatia, however, had always been quieter, and more academic in nature.

"Can't you buy another?" Charles asked.

"No... I cannot ask Cedric to spend any more than he has."

Ahh, there she was. The Horatia he knew was frugal to a fault. Cedric was as rich as Croesus but Horatia would never let him spoil her.

"Oh..." Charles replied, a little confused. He was a spendthrift, that was no secret.

Lucien took the box from the footman, eyeing it critically.

"It might be salvageable. We'll escort you home and you can have your lady's maid see to it."

Horatia glanced uncertainly between Charles and Lucien. "I'm not putting you out of your way? Peter and I are fine to go home on our own, aren't we, Peter?" She shot a determined look at her footman, who nodded hastily.

"We'll be fine, my lords."

"Nonsense," Lucien said. "You've had a shock and are soaking wet. We're escorting you home. End of discussion." He gripped her elbow with one hand and shoved the package back at Peter.

They must have presented an odd spectacle. Lucien and Charles flanking either side of the drenched Horatia like guards, with her footman following close behind carrying a sodden box in his hands.

Lucien ignored the curious stares and simply enjoyed the relief at being able to see Horatia home without another life-threatening incident.

When they reached the Sheridan residence, Horatia slid her drenched cloak off her shoulders and excused herself as she fled upstairs with the package. Lucien lingered in the hall, watching the flutter of her wet skirts, wishing he could follow her to her chambers and slip into the hot water of the bath she was no doubt going to take. The thought of Horatia, naked in a bath was only slightly less tempting than the dream he'd had the night before about her. She haunted his thoughts all too often of late.

"Shall we wait for Cedric?" Charles asked, joining him at the foot of the stairs.

"He isn't in?"

Charles shook his head. "The butler said he is looking for Horatia as it were."

Searching for his sister? What on earth for?

"We should wait," Lucien suggested. "Come, let's get some brandy."

His friend grinned. "Now that is more the activity I had in mind when we set out this morning."

They followed a footman to the morning room to wait for Cedric's return.

Charles settled into a large brocaded armchair, crossing an ankle over his knee. "Lucien, do you think Horatia will be all right?"

"I suppose..."

"Given her past, I mean," Charles explained. "With her parents and the coach accident. You were there. Do you think this will bring back the memories?"

Lucien shuddered. That was the day Cedric had lost his parents. They'd been traveling through town when two men had decided to race their curricles through the streets. Horatia, only fourteen, had been in the coach with her parents. The crash had been dreadful. Screaming horses with broken legs, several people who'd been too close wounded by the wreck. One young man dead, another terribly injured. Cedric and Horatia's parents hadn't survived the impact of the coach when it had rolled.

Horatia had been stuck in the coach with the bodies of her parents, unable to get out, dazed from the shock. She hadn't even screamed for help. When Lucien had reached the scene, he climbed up the carriage's side and opened the door. He called her name and she'd looked up at him, eyes full of terror. He'd pulled her out of the coach and into his arms. His stomach roiled at the memory of her body shaking violently against his.

"She's strong. She'll be fine." Lucien's words were more an assurance to himself than to Charles. He had to believe she'd not be too upset after this morning.

Thinking of her distraught left a hollow feeling in his chest. Despite his intention to ignore her as much as possible and pretend she didn't exist, she had possessed his every waking thought for the past few months. He knew exactly who to blame for this. The Duchess of Essex, formerly Miss Emily Parr.

His friend, Godric, the Duke of Essex, had kidnapped Miss Parr earlier that fall. The scheme hadn't gone at all as planned and Godric had found himself leg-shackled in matrimony a few months ago.

Lucien found himself smiling, which should have unnerved him, given that the hallowed state of matrimony was one he feared more than death. But damned if he wasn't a tiny bit jealous of Godric's easy happiness with Emily. The two were quite opposite in nature, and yet they were a love match.

The events after the kidnapping had thrown Lucien into Horatia's world again. All the effort he'd put into tactfully dodging dinner parties and balls were for naught. The League was so fond of Emily that not one of them could resist coming when she called. Cedric called it the "lapdog" effect—they'd been turned from perfectly dangerous rakehells of the worst sort to perfectly behaved gentleman in the presence of the Duchess of Essex. If only Emily and Horatia hadn't become such close friends, Lucien might have avoided her with more ease.

That Horatia was still unmarried at the age of twenty surprised him. How was it no other man had wanted to bed a creature with doe-brown eyes and such curves that were made for holding? Or spend an entire day planning jokes just to win one rich laugh from her soft lips? Knowing Cedric, however, there were probably several young bucks in the *ton* running scared at the thought of approaching him for permission to court his sister.

Lucien had tried to slake his thirst for Horatia between the thighs of other women, but it was no use. Only the previous night he'd attempted to bed a woman and found he wasn't aroused enough to perform. If word of that got out, he'd become a laughing stock. The irony of his rakehell reputation being damaged by an innocent woman was not lost on him. At this moment he dreaded his friend's arrival, considering the dream he'd had the previous night.

Horatia had been stripped of every scrap of clothing, all laid out before him, ankles and wrists bound to his bedposts by red silk. Perspiration slicked her skin as he moved up her body to nuzzle her perfect nipples. She arched into him, rubbing her sex against him, searing him with the wicked heat of her arousal. He thrust his tongue into her mouth, tasting her, and cupped her luscious bottom, raising it for the best angle of a powerful thrust. The dream had dissipated into mist, leaving him with an erection hard enough to pound a hole in the wall.

It would be a miracle if he could school his features and hide his guilt from Cedric after dreaming of doing such things with the man's sister.

Lucien glanced at the clock on the mantle. It was now nearly noon. Cedric should have been here by now.

There was a serpentine crawling sensation beneath his skin that unsettled him. He'd had this feeling before, just before a storm was about to break. Worry knotted inside him, twisting his stomach until he could scarcely breathe. Dark clouds were on the horizon.

Charles frowned and leaned forward in his chair, concern weighing down the corners of his mouth. "Are you feeling all right?"

One deep breath. Two. The iron dread in his chest eased. "I've been better, I suppose. I just..." Lucien hesitated.

Charles reached for the decanter of brandy and poured Lucien another glass. "What is it?"

Lucien opened his mouth, but the door to the room crashed open, Cedric framed the doorway like an avenging angel, or a demon. He strode inside holding a note in one hand, knuckles white as he gripped his silver lion-headed cane in the other.

"What's the matter, Cedric?"

Cedric's rage was all too apparent. "That bastard!"

There was a moment of silence as Lucien shared a worried glance with Charles.

Charles stood and walked over to the cigar box on the side

table against the far wall. "You'll have to be a bit more specific; there are a lot of bastards about." He ran the cigar underneath his nose. "Some are even in this room."

Lucien rose and paced towards the window overlooking the street front. He spied a comical scene of an overdressed dandy prancing about with a quizzing glass, examining various ladies' dresses as they passed by him. The man seemed to feel Lucien's gaze and raised his head. A cold chill swept through Lucien. Something about the man and his flat, cold eyes fired Lucien's nerves to life, leaving him unsettled. Had he seen the man before? A sense of foreboding raked his spine. The man turned away and disappeared through a door a few houses down opposite Cedric's townhouse.

Lucien forced his attention back to his friends. "So who is this bastard?"

Cedric threw himself into a red and gold brocaded chair and rapped the tip of his cane on his right boot. "Who do you think?"

Lucien's heart froze. "Waverly."

Cedric nodded.

"That isn't news to us. Someone tried to run Lucien over on Bond Street. Horatia happened to be nearby. Fortunately Lucien got her out of harm's way." Charles explained the morning's incident to Cedric, who spoke not a word as he listened. They all knew what Waverly was capable of. What was perhaps more worrisome was the man's complete lack of honor. He had no qualms about attacking his enemies from behind or, it would seem, their loved ones.

Lucien crossed his arms over his chest and leaned against the wall facing Cedric. Beneath the man's fury, lines of worry stretched thin near his eyes.

"Is my sister all right?" he asked.

Lucien nodded. "She's as well as could be expected. I was able to get her out of the way, but she is terribly upset." Thankfully, only the gown had perished by Waverly's villainy. He tamped down on the urge to find the fiend and throttle him with his bare hands. Lucien knew that Horatia wouldn't appreciate him murdering a man on her behalf. His passions tended to rule him more than they ought to.

Regardless of the fact that she wasn't his, he could at least keep her safe. Horatia had to be protected at all costs.

"Cedric," Charles interrupted Lucien's thoughts. "Why did you go out looking for Horatia?"

Cedric's faced darkened again. "I was heading off to join Ashton and Godric at Tattersalls when one of my footmen found this letter tucked beneath the door knocker."

He held out the scrap of parchment in his hand.

With trepidation, Lucien took the note and read it. Charles stood behind him, bending to read over his shoulder. The note was on thick expensive paper. A black scrawling hand, unfamiliar to him, clearly not Waverly's, layered the surface of the note with sinister certainty.

Lucien read the words aloud for Charles to hear. "'Carriage accidents are a terrible thing, aren't they?'"

Lucien handed the note to Cedric who pocketed it. "It doesn't look like Waverly's handwriting. Are we sure it's him?"

Cedric shrugged. "Who else would dare to remind me of such a horrific event?"

"If it is the past he's referring to," said Lucien, "perhaps the timing here was deliberate."

Charles walked back around and threw himself into a chair, scowling. "He's threatened us before, but nothing has come of it. What's changed?" The earl's eyes glimmered like mercury, bright and ever shifting.

"Hell if I know." Cedric caressed the silver lion's head of his cane. "He's spent the past few years abroad. Now he's returned and renewing his threats."

Lucien wondered if his body had somehow known that something was set in motion. He could almost hear the clock gears ticking, but it was damned hard to know how to protect those he loved if he couldn't see from which direction the threat would come.

Cedric rose, rubbing his face with a hand. "Bad news aside, I would like to extend a dinner invitation to you both tonight—and I realize it is last minute, but Audrey is determined to see the entire League." He glanced between his friends hopefully.

Charles grinned. "You know I'm always eager to see your sisters!"

Cedric arched a brow. "Not too eager, I trust."

It was a damned nuisance. Every fiber of Lucien's being demanded he break the League's second rule. He didn't want his lust directing him into a situation where he would be facing Cedric on a field at dawn or something equally ridiculous. With any other woman he would have bedded her and moved on. This was impossible with Horatia. Just thinking about her heated his blood and sent a throbbing ache straight to his loins. He shifted uncomfortably and adjusted his breeches.

"What about you, Lucien?" Cedric fixed a powerful stare at him. "Don't you dare give me any excuses."

Lucien had told Cedric ages ago that he didn't feel comfortable around Horatia. He'd said it was because she'd ruined an engagement proposal he'd made to an heiress years before. But it was a half-truth if anything. Horatia had been there, and the proposal had gone sour when Horatia dumped a bucket of water over his intended's head. But his need to avoid Horatia now had everything to do with wanting to take her to the nearest bed and... He shook his head, clearing it of such thoughts.

He began to protest. "Cedric, you know I—"

"Come now. You aren't afraid of my sisters, are you?"

Damn. There was no way he'd get out of it this time. "I'll come."

"Wonderful! I'll expect you at seven!" Cedric declared with satisfaction.

"Wonderful," Lucien echoed dully. How was he going to survive this?

Horatia pressed two slim fingers to her temples as the bouncing form of her younger sister flitted past, distracting her from her latest book. It was not the way a young lady ought to behave, but trying to stop Audrey was like trying to command a storm. Horatia attempted to concentrate on the words, but between Audrey's chaotic squirming and memories of this morning's incident, she couldn't. The remnants of her fear tasted bitter in her mouth. She despised herself for being so weak as to let such anxieties rule her. One minute she'd been enjoying a walk, and the next there were horses screaming, curricle wheels spinning and icy cold water soaking her to the bone as she hit the pavement.

It was like her childhood all over again. Death had struck out at her without warning, and like last time, she'd been spared. But the event had awakened old fears. As before, Lucien had saved her life. He would never know how alive she'd felt when he'd knocked her back into the snow in the alley or how her heart had thrashed like a wild bird against her ribcage. His hard body above hers, pressing down onto her—he'd been so close she'd glimpsed shards of green embedded in the brown of his eyes like a dark forest beckoning her. Any fear she might have had at being trampled was swept away by the confusing wave of heat she'd felt when Lucien shifted above her, their hips and chests pressed together. Surely she'd nearly been compromised. If someone of note had seen Lucien on top of her it would have been scandalous.

She would never forget Lucien's face or his fierce, protective response. But that protectiveness was no match for her brother's, who'd rushed upstairs to check on her as soon as he'd heard. He had shown them a letter containing a vague threat about carriage accidents. Cedric was ready to pack the pair off to France and change their names to protect them. It had taken every ounce of diplomacy she possessed to convince him that she and Audrey were safer here.

"Oh Horatia, cheer up! Cedric said we will have a dinner party tonight with the League!" Her cinnamon eyes were intent upon her older sister's face. Audrey mistook Horatia's brooding for unhappiness and not the concern that it was.

"Audrey—cease that infernal bouncing." Horatia's tone was sharper than she intended. She bowed her head, fingers pressing deeper into her temples as her frayed nerves sparked with pain. She looked up to see the smile on Audrey's face drop. "And stop calling them the League. You sound like that dreadful Lady Society in the Quizzing Glass."

"I'm sorry, Horatia, I just ..." Audrey stammered, a pinprick of a tear in the corner of her eye. "With all that's happened today, I just wanted to cheer you up." She turned and slipped from the room, her energetic bounce gone.

Horatia started to go after her. "Audrey, wait—" Horatia stopped and sank back onto her chaise, her head still aching.

A moment later her lady's maid, Ursula, strode in. "What's all this now? That poor girl looked ready to weep for a week." Ursula was in her early forties, a plump but attractive woman with a threading of gray in her blond hair. She'd been with the Sheridan family for ten years and was the closest thing to a motherly figure Horatia had.

"She was acting like a child, so I snapped at her. I tried to apologize." Horatia only partially defended herself. She was at fault here, not Audrey. Her temper should never cause harm to others.

"And what put you in such an indelicate mood I wonder? I know the accident must have frightened you, but Lord Rochester was there and you're no worse for wear, are you?" Ursula went to the tall armoire and started searching for a gown to dress Horatia in this evening.

It was one of the many things about Ursula that Horatia admired—her ability to treat situations and problems with a cool rational mind, rather than an emotional one. Now that she'd determined Horatia had mistreated Audrey out of her own bad temper, she would no doubt discern what had upset Horatia, then decide upon a course of advice to give.

"No, you're right. I'm fine. A bit rattled, but it could have been worse," Horatia said.

In truth she was panicked about Lucien coming to dinner tonight. When she'd encountered the Marquess of Rochester this morning, well...it had been explosive. His touch, his gaze, his warm breath on her cheeks, all of it had lit a fire in the pit of her belly that refused to go out. If only they could have remained so close...

She couldn't help but dream about where it might have led. Would he have dared to kiss her? *Of course he would*, her inner voice replied, *he's a rake*. Had they been alone, he might have taken advantage of the situation and by God she would have let him.

It was a blessing he normally seemed determined to avoid her. Yet she couldn't help wanting to see him now, to catch his scent when he stood close to her, or the brush of their hands at breakfast when they both reached for the eggs.

As irrational as it was, she even craved the hungry way he looked at her with those smoldering eyes, lust simmering just below their hazel surface. Her heart slammed against her ribs and her palms slickened with sweat.

Ursula pulled out a violet colored gown with dark Parma slippers for Horatia to wear. "Your new Christmas gown was ruined after all, I'm afraid. No woman could be in a good mood after that sort of tragedy." Ursula's tone was half teasing. The other half was sarcastic.

"Yes, it is a pity about the gown."

The gown was a loss, but she could live with it. It was the sort of everyday drama one was prepared for. What she hadn't been prepared for was Lucien. Horatia had dug her fingers into his chest and stared up at him, oblivious to the cold of the ground. His gaze had been wild. It terrified her, to see the sudden change in his demeanor. It was a side of him she'd never seen.

She'd been forced to face the truth that there were things about him she didn't know. Secrets and passions ruled him. Is that why the men in the League were so close? Did they share something she couldn't understand? Was that why Lucien kept his distance? Maybe he wasn't in control of his passions. Maybe that's why he avoided her.

But I'm not the sort of woman who would test a man's control. Her inner voice chided her for being so foolish as to think she'd present a temptation for Lucien. She was no seductress. All he needed to do was crook one long finger and she'd come running. Pathetic, but true. It was a mercy she didn't seem to be worth the effort to seduce.

She let Ursula dress her. When she had finished, Horatia walked out of her room and towards the stairs. A black and white cat strolled into view, its yellow eyes wide and a dead mouse hanging limp between its teeth.

"Muff! You know better than to bring your presents inside!"

She darted after the cat. Muff ran down the stairs and past the main door into an unused parlor. The cat slipped between the marble fireplace and the fire grate, vanishing from sight, along with its prize.

"Oh honestly," Horatia growled as she pulled back the grate.

Muff had disappeared up into the fireplace, possibly even the chimney. The dinner guests would be here soon and she couldn't risk getting covered in soot. Luckily no servants would light the fire in this room tonight. Hopefully the cat would have enough sense to vacate the chimney before morning.

Muff was one of a pair of cats residing at the Sheridan town-house on Curzon Street. The other cat, Mittens, was a black female. Cedric had bought them for Audrey as a Christmas present when she'd been a child. She'd also been given a pair of mittens and a muff, and had naturally named her cats the same. But that was the sort of thing Audrey would do back then.

The felines were quite ancient now. Horatia dreaded the day she'd find one or both of them passed away. They were her faithful companions, guardians of the library, defenders of the kitchen.

Horatia was more reserved and subdued than Audrey. She had few friends and often spent her days reading or riding. The cats would join her in a window seat or a chair and curl their tails around their bodies, purring with unconditional love. Being around them she forgot her troubles, forgot that she desired a man who was nothing but cold to her.

The front door knocker rapped. Audrey flew past the open study door, her face beaming with excitement. It seemed her sister had recovered from her scolding. Horatia hesitated before joining her in the hall. She knew Lucien would be there, and as always, she was torn between wanting to see him and dreading his callous disregard of her. Taking a deep breath, she went out to meet her guests.

Her eyes always found Lucien first. Among the group of handsome men standing in the hall, he alone enraptured her. With dark red hair just long enough to curl above his collar and burning hazel eyes, he was temptation personified. Horatia would happily fall at his feet and offer her body, heart and soul to him as tribute. But he'd reject her, just as he always did.

Lucien's gaze fixed on her while the rest of the crowd headed towards the drawing room. He remained still, tracking her every breath, every move. The gleam in his eyes startled her as a flash of heat went from her breasts down between her legs. Her face flushed. Lucien answered with a cold smile, as though he knew exactly what he'd done to her.

Lucien offered her his arm, and she hesitated only a moment before crossing the hall and dropping her fingers onto his sleeve. He tucked her arm more firmly in his, the warmth of his fingers burning her skin. She glanced about, wondering if anyone would notice, but no eyes looked her way. Unable to resist, she leaned into him, settling her arm in the crook of his, relishing the warmth where their bodies touched.

"Shall we?" Lucien's voice was soft and dark. A tone more suited for the bedroom than the hall.

Her throat went dry, but she managed a shaky nod.

AFTER DINNER LUCIEN AND THE OTHER MEN OPTED TO PLAY whist, but he couldn't focus on the cards. The ladies in the far corner of the room had his attention. Ursula, one of the Sheridan girls' lady's maid sat in a chair, reading from a thick tome, oblivious to her young charges. Horatia and Audrey sat on either side of Emily, the young Duchess of Essex. Emily and Horatia were clad in shimmering gowns, while Audrey's was a light pink muslin. Their heads bent close as they whispered, making him think of three fairies who escaped from the court of Queen Mab in *Romeo and Juliet*. Occasionally one shot a glance at the men before returning to their secretive conversation.

Lucien would have paid anything to be a fly nestled on the wall close to them—to better see Horatia's lips part and form each word, just as much as he'd love to have those lips wrapped around his aching shaft, sucking him to sweet oblivion.

Christ. Lucien forced his gaze away from her.

"What do you suppose they're talking about?" Charles asked him.

It seemed he wasn't the only one dying of curiosity.

"God, I wish I knew," he admitted truthfully, just as Audrey broke into a fit of giggles.

Charles waggled his fingers at Audrey and blew her a kiss. Audrey blushed and quickly turned her back on them.

"You ought not to encourage her, Charles. She's young and impressionable." Lucien remembered all too well the perils of having a lovesick child follow him about.

"What is there to encourage? The little sprite hasn't the least bit of interest in me." Charles smiled wryly. He leaned back in his chair in a picture of relaxed ease.

"What? Are you sure? I always thought maybe she..." Lucien trailed off when he noticed Audrey's head turn in a very definite direction, and it wasn't towards Charles.

"Oh dear," Lucien kept his voice low. Audrey clearly had eyes for Godric's half-brother, Jonathan.

"Oh dear, indeed. We best watch out for fireworks. Cedric will rip Jonathan to pieces." The smug look on Charles's face nearly made Lucien laugh.

"You *want* him to get caught, don't you?"

Charles yawned. "This month has been a dead bore as you well know. After Tisdale gave his notice I just haven't been out as much unless it's with you. Watching Cedric chase Jonathan about town over Audrey's honor would certainly entertain me."

Lucien's humor fizzled. If Cedric ever found out that he wanted Horatia—in ways that would bring a blush to a courtesan's cheeks—Lucien was a dead man.

When the men finished their game of whist and downed the last of the brandy, they decided the evening was at last over.

"That's enough for me." Godric turned towards the ladies. "Come along, Em. Time to depart."

Emily didn't spare her husband a glance. She had one hand on Horatia's shoulder and another on Audrey's while she spoke to the pair of them in a huddle. None of the men really bothered trying to figure out what women whispered about. Lucien guessed it would always remain one of life's mysteries, like why a woman needed countless bonnets when they were such ugly and useless things. It was a damned nuisance trying to untie yards of unnecessary ribbons in order to touch a woman's hair while he was kissing her.

"That's an unholy alliance if I ever saw one," Cedric noted.

The Sheridan sisters were trouble enough, but adding Emily was like a lit match near a very large powder keg.

"I'd best collect my wife before she causes trouble," Godric replied.

Lucien didn't miss Godric's pleased tone as he had said 'wife.'

Godric stood, then walked quietly over and plucked her away from the group, scooping her up into his arms.

"Godric!" Emily kicked her feet in outrage. "Put me down at once!"

"I don't think so, my dear. It's time I put you to bed." Godric bent his head low so his face was inches from hers.

"Oh if you must." She tried to sound reluctant, but there was a breathless quality to her voice that fooled no one. For a moment, Lucien was struck with a sharp sense of envy. If Horatia weren't related to his friend, he would have been carrying her out the door in the same fashion, to find the nearest bed.

"Good night, everyone!" Godric called over his shoulder as he and Emily left the drawing room.

Cedric shook his head, but his eyes glinted with merriment. "By the way they act I swear you'd never know they were married."

"They are indeed fortunate," Ashton said. "To be so in love that marriage is a blessing rather than a burden."

"Perhaps we ought to leave as well?" Jonathan cast a nervous glance in Audrey's direction, who stared right at him mischievously. He had been staying at Ashton's townhouse to give the newlyweds some time to themselves before he moved in with them. Godric had settled an unentailed estate upon Jonathan, but had put it in trust until his brother was ready to settle down and run the property himself. Until that time, Jonathan would live with Godric and his new wife.

"After you, Jonathan." Ashton inclined his head to Lucien, Charles and Cedric, and bid the Sheridan ladies good night before departing with Jonathan.

Cedric looked hopefully at his remaining companions.

"You are both welcome to stay the night."

Charles agreed at once. "I'll send word to my valet."

Lucien, however, was reluctant.

Cedric's eager smile faltered. "I'll understand if you wish to decline, Lucien, but I do hope you will stay. After receiving that letter about coach accidents, it would be good to have a few of us keeping watch."

His friend looked so earnest that Lucien didn't have the heart to desert him. "Very well, then."

"Excellent," Charles and Cedric chimed in unison.

Lucien felt as though he'd made a grave error in judgment and would soon pay dearly for it. Still he would rather be here protecting Horatia. She was safer with her brother, himself and Charles keeping watch. Then again, she wasn't protected from every threat. Lucien felt the desire to slip into her bedroom tonight and crawl into her bed, pinning her beneath him and...

Damnation. Being in the same house with Horatia for an entire night was both his greatest temptation and his worst nightmare.

CHAPTER 3

Horatia still hadn't changed into her nightclothes. Restlessness had her up well past midnight. Knowing Lucien was somewhere in the house was unsettling, and she worried about that blasted cat. Muff should have been curled up on the extra pillow in her bed, but he was conspicuously absent. There was a chance a passing footman or maid had closed the grates around the fireplace and he hadn't been able to get back down.

Unwilling to let him stay in the cold chimney all night, Horatia abandoned her room and went in search of the cat. She tried to think of all of the other places he could be, and not the one place she wished *she* could be at that moment. In Lucien's arms.

It had been months since he'd last spent the night, and her brother was delighted to have him and Charles there. If not for the League, Cedric would have been exceedingly lonely. She knew he loved her and Audrey, but he'd always longed for brothers. It was hard to miss the way he brightened whenever his friends came over for dinner, or how he looked forward to afternoons at his gentlemen's club, Berkley's. Perhaps it was because he could relax around them, and not have to play guardian.

After their parents died, Cedric had taken on a great amount of responsibility, not only to care for and raise her and Audrey, but matters of business and peerage as well. It was good he had such friends to ease his burdens and the pressures of family.

She slipped down the stairs to the ground floor and passed by the drawing room, where cigar smoke scented the air and muted laughter echoed against the partially open door.

At least someone was having a good evening. Irritation rippled beneath Horatia's skin. Lucien seemed to enjoy torturing her. Between his heated looks and cool smiles he was driving her mad. It was frustrating to not know how to act around him, whether to be warm or to keep her distance.

One of the men said something and Lucien's rich laugh teased her ears. Her insides shook with longing. She wanted to make him laugh like that, to be the center of his focus.

A small dark shadow flitted across the hall and dashed through the library door.

"Muff!" Horatia hissed, hoping to both summon and chastise the rebellious feline. Given the nature of cats however, she knew it was a fool's errand.

Horatia entered the library, lit a candle and started searching under couches and behind chairs. She almost missed the soft click as someone came in behind her and shut the door. The flame of the candle in her hand sputtered as she turned.

Lucien stood not five feet from her, watching her with hooded eyes. The aroma of brandy quickly reached her. The candlelight threw flickering shadows across his handsome face, highlighting a small scar near his brow.

In a few slow strides he towered over her. Horatia was suddenly very aware of his masculinity—the breadth of his shoulders, his height, and that the top of her head barely reached his shoulders. She knew herself to be tall, but next to Lucien she felt small, delicate and vulnerable. It was strange, but she liked feeling so helpless around him. Filled with longing, she barely stopped herself from reaching for him. He was too handsome, too virile. Whenever he was near he reduced her to a wild, wanton creature that would do anything for the chance to know pleasure in his arms.

"Horatia." Her name rolled off his lips like a fine dessert, sweet and decadent. "You ought to be in bed."

The wicked way he said "bed" made her lightheaded.

"I couldn't sleep."

He leaned forward, his body close to hers as he blew out the candle in her hand. The sudden darkness around them made her catch her breath. A beam of moonlight broke through, lighting their faces. The smoke curled and danced up between them. Lucien's smile offered her a world of knowledge about pleasure.

"There's a lovely little remedy for sleep that I always employ. Do you want to know what it is?" His low voice set her skin on fire.

I shouldn't answer. I know what he's going to say. "What is it?" *Blast!*

The faint moonlight from the tall library windows lit his face as he leaned even closer to her.

He grinned down at her like a Cheshire cat. "I find the nearest beautiful woman, slip into her bed and wrap myself around her." His warm brandy-tinged breath fanned her face. Tingles of awareness spiked through her body and she stifled a gasp.

He raised a hand, drawing one elegant finger along her cheekbone. "Your face is warm. Have I made you blush? I'd like to make other parts of you blush as well." Lucien took the candle holder from her and set it on a shelf.

Horatia's knees shook. She stepped back and her head collided with the bookshelf behind her. Lucien closed the distance between them and braced his hands on either side of her face. His lips were inches from hers.

"Shall I kiss you, Horatia? I find you hard to resist when you look up at me with those dark eyes. They are begging me to kiss you. Did you know that?" His voice was a soft growl that made her breasts heavy and her nipples harden.

Incapable of speech, Horatia managed to shake her head. She wanted to throw her arms about his neck and drag his mouth to hers. She ached to run her hands through his dark red hair. Endless nights had been spent imagining what this moment would be like, when he'd be close enough to touch, to kiss.

Something deep inside her tore in anguish. He wasn't meant for her. Everyone knew he took only experienced, beautiful women to his bed. Lucien would never really consider her that way. She was acceptably attractive, but no diamond of the first water. With nothing to offer Lucien, he must be teasing her the way any rake did an innocent. He was the serpent, offering her carnal knowledge. Everything she wanted and couldn't have. It was an awful thing to be in love with such a devil.

Lucien moved his lips to her ear, using a finger to trace a loose pattern along her collarbone, down her chest and towards the valley between her breasts.

She inhaled, her breasts thrusting upward. "You've been drinking, my lord," she said. When he teased a finger below the fabric of her bodice, brushing a tight nipple, she gasped.

The grin he gave her was one of pure sin. "I certainly have…"

Horatia reached up and tore his hands away from her bodice. She tried to knock his other arm out of her way to leave. "How dare you!"

Lucien grabbed hold of her, dragged her back against the bookcase and trapped her with his body. He fisted a hand through the loose coils of her hair, dragging her head back. Her eyes rose to meet his. A hunger churned in his gaze, swirling in eddies of changing colors.

"Tell me to let go of you," he begged in a ragged whisper. "Tell me."

She stared at him, unable to voice a protest.

"Christ. I'm not a saint, woman. I can't… Oh to hell with it."

The warmth of his breath tickled her lips before he devoured her neck in a slow languid kiss. Pools of wet heat built up between her legs and his tongue flicked out against her skin as he tasted her. She moaned. Lucien slid his hand down over her bottom, catching her in his grasp, jerking her hard against his stiff shaft.

Her legs shook against him, loose and unprotesting as he parted them with his thigh. He dragged her up the length of his leg so her toes barely touched the ground. The movement sent shock-waves of excitement through her and made her inhale sharply. Her hands fell to his shoulders, seeking to hold on to him. His lips found hers again and her palms skated up his neck into his hair, the strands whispering over her skin. She dug her fingers in and tugged on his hair. He growled deep in his throat and kissed her harder.

Saying no to him was the furthest thing from her mind. There was nothing beyond this moment—his kiss, the sliding touch of his palms, his fingers digging possessively into her flesh, cupping her bottom until a staccato rhythm throbbed deep inside her. It beat against his hard, muscular thigh, flooding her with awareness. She tried to rock against him, to create more friction. Anything to get closer to him, to satisfy her need for something she didn't fully understand.

"My God, you were made for sin," Lucien groaned as he tried to move his other hand deeper into the confines of her bodice.

She was made for sin? Was she nothing more than a body he'd like to bed? A temptation to release his needs upon? The words lit a flame under Horatia. She clawed his chest and sank her teeth into his shoulder to get free. Lucien jerked back with a low curse, letting her feet hit the floor again.

Undaunted, he said, "Careful with that temper of yours, my dear," and moved in to kiss her again.

Under other circumstances she might have melted in his arms. But he'd gone too far. Horatia brought her knee up into his groin.

Silence filled the room. For a moment Horatia wondered if it had made him a statue. At last a moan, several octaves higher than before, escaped his lips as he staggered back a couple of steps, then sank to his knees.

"Damn you, woman!"

"Serves you right, you...you horse's arse!" She covered her mouth, shocked at her own language.

Despite Lucien's pained groan, he chuckled.

"Touché, my sweet. Touché." He tried to reach for her again but Horatia bolted to the door.

"Damnable creature. I was going to apologize," Lucien muttered to himself as he hobbled over to a chair and collapsed.

The numbing affect of his brandy had worn off and guilt was wrapped around him like a death shroud. He'd been an absolute bastard. He should have known better than to drink when she was near. There had to be a way to make up for his lack of judgment.

He wracked his mind for some idea, some way to make amends. He'd apologize of course, but women were masters of holding guilt in trust and collecting interest on it. A trinket perhaps? A lovely bauble she could wear with a new gown... A gown! He'd buy her a new Christmas gown, one to replace the one that had been ruined.

Horatia never spoiled herself, other than to buy an expensive gown each December. The rest of the year she wore her usual silk garments, fashionable but rather understated. It was only during the holidays that she seemed unable to resist the allure of an enchanting dress. He wished he could have seen her gown this year before it had been ruined.

He would buy her something new, something with a precariously low but still socially acceptable neckline, made from bright red silk, his favorite color and fabric. Even now he could imagine how it would feel under the light pressure of his hands as he caressed her, explored her. His loins tightened with lust and the pain of his recent injury inflamed all over again. He was being duly punished for his rash actions.

Upstairs in her bedchamber, Horatia panted, her face

flushed. She trembled with a mixture of longing and regret. Even when the man was a merciless rake she still wanted him. That was part of the allure she supposed, that threat of his passion manifesting itself in an explosive kiss, a demanding caress of covered places. Sleep would be impossible now.

Where was Ursula? Had she already retired? Her lady's maid never failed to stay up late to help her undress. But Horatia was too exhausted to worry about that. She wanted to sleep and didn't want to wake the house looking for her maid.

A light scratch at the door had her turning in relief.

"Oh Ursula, I hoped—"

Yet it wasn't her maid. Lucien leaned against the doorjamb. He looked less foxed than before, which surprisingly didn't comfort her at all.

She tilted her chin up. "What do you want, Lucien? Haven't you done enough damage for one night?"

"I'm sorry, Horatia. I was indeed a horse's arse." He smiled a little.

"Well then, since we are in agreement, you may leave. I have things to see to. Besides, if Cedric found you here—"

"Things? What could you possibly have to do after midnight? Off to a secret rendezvous with a lover, I suppose?"

The very idea was ridiculous. She would never look at another man when he was all she'd ever wanted. It made little rational sense to love a man who had no real interest in her, yet here she was. When she'd been younger, Lucien had been exceedingly kind to her. He'd been the one to rescue her from her parents' coach.

Unwanted memories whispered at the corners of her heart, slicing her soul deep. Her parents lying broken and lifeless around her like marionettes with their strings cut. Their eyes, open yet seeing nothing, heads at awkward, unnatural angles. The coach on its side, massive splinters of wood embedded in bodies. People screaming. Then a burst of light as the coach door crashed open above her and she glimpsed a halo of fiery hair and warm hazel eyes. "Come now, sweetheart, reach for me.

There's a good girl. Take my hands, Horatia, and I'll keep you safe."

Safe. It was all she'd ever wanted, and for a short time, he'd kept his promise. But when she'd ruined his proposal to a woman, he began to keep his distance. It only became worse when she'd had her come out two years ago. He'd taken one look at her when she'd entered Almack's assembly rooms and strode away, leaving her feeling utterly alone in a ballroom of familiar faces. Where he'd been only distant before, he'd now become cold. Her heart was cursed. But she could dream about what might be, so long as he remained unmarried. It was pitiful that she had only her dreams to look forward to, and even worse to love and desire a man who would never truly see her.

"Please leave." She tugged at the back of her gown, exhausted.

Her struggles didn't escape his notice. "Having a bit of trouble?"

Before she could protest he shut the door and rotated her so her back faced him, then proceeded to unlace her gown.

She tried to pull away. If anyone found them there'd be the devil to pay. "You shouldn't be in here, let alone helping me undress!"

He swatted her bottom and she gasped, shocked yet aroused at the same time. "Do you want out of this gown or not?"

She jerked free of him and he lifted his hands in surrender. "Fine! Sleep all night in that. I don't care."

He was nearly to the door when she spoke. Her voice small, tentative and unsure. "Lucien."

He hesitated, hand at the doorknob.

Slowly, she offered her back to him. It amazed her she could still trust him after what he'd done in the library.

Lucien resumed his work of freeing her from the gown. She knew his reputation, knew he'd been with scores of women. While that bothered her, she couldn't help but notice his fingers were clumsier than she expected.

"Shouldn't a rake be practiced at this sort of thing?"

Lucien answered with a growl of irritation, his fingers tugging at the knotted laces.

"Who trussed you up like this? These knots look to be the work of an expert seaman." With a final tug the bodice hung free about her, then he loosened her stays. Horatia's heart quickened as she crossed her arms over her breasts, hiding them. She'd been so focused on undressing she only now realized Lucien was in her bedchamber and she was half-naked. Never before had she been so vulnerable.

A harsh breath hissed through his teeth. His hands moved up to her neck, falling on the grooves between her shoulders and throat. She repressed a shiver of fear and delight. Would he kiss her again? Would he dare do more than that? Her body and soul screamed for more, begged to be held by him.

God, I am a glutton for punishment.

Lucien cleared his throat and awkwardly stammered, "I'm... I'm sorry about what happened earlier. I was not myself."

Horatia's heart thrashed. She turned to look at him over her shoulder. His eyes were fixed on the column of her throat, but his expression was unreadable.

"You are forgiven." She ought to have said she never wanted him to do something like that, but deep within her she knew she wanted him to lose control and kiss her like that again.

If only he hadn't been so cold, so ruthless when he kissed her, as though she was nothing more than another conquest in a long line of women begging for one ounce of his affection.

❦

LUCIEN'S BLOOD THUNDERED IN HIS EARS AS HIS SELF-CONTROL waned. Horatia stood still as a statue, her breath faint as if she waited for him to act further. He shut his eyes, banishing the image of her naked beneath him until he could summon the strength to remove his hands from her and step back.

"Thank you," she breathed.

"You're welcome." He wanted to drag her into his arms and plunder her mouth with his, but the moment had passed. He snagged the reins of his remaining control and left her alone.

Lucien exited Horatia's bedchamber and hurried back to his own.

He questioned his sanity for touching her, kissing her, wanting her. He was a stout defender of the League's 'no seduction of sisters' rule. How many times had he threatened Charles upon pain of death to stay away from his own sister?

If Cedric ever found out I kissed her, and helped her undress… Lucien cringed. Men had killed over smaller slights to their sisters' honor. Cedric? He was a God-fearing man, but put in that position it would be wise to fear Cedric more than God.

Lucien had the door halfway closed when Charles burst inside.

"What the hell are you doing?" Charles shut the door, grabbed Lucien by his shirt, and shoved him backward. Lucien stumbled and hit the bed behind him.

"Care to explain why I just saw you coming out of Horatia's room?"

"It isn't what you think. We weren't—"

"Do not lie to me. You're worse at that than you are at whist." Charles's gray eyes were fathomless. "You weren't in there long enough for anything serious, but you *were* in there. I want to know why."

"I insulted her earlier this evening. I had to apologize."

"And you couldn't do that in the bloody hallway?"

Lucien folded his arms over his chest and glared back. "I didn't want her to slam the door in my face, so I went in after her. You know how women are. They hold grudges of biblical proportions if you don't apologize immediately. I've had enough upset mistresses to know when I need to beg forgiveness for the sake of peace."

"So you're treating Horatia like one of your kept women?" Charles arched a brow.

"Believe me, Horatia is the last woman on earth I would willingly seduce." The lie was heavy and bitter on his tongue. He'd started to seduce her mere moments ago. But he wasn't thinking straight. The damned brandy had him tied in knots. Reminding him of when he'd tangled his fingers in her stays. God he wanted to go right back to her room and shred her clothes from her body and take her to bed.

"There is no rule against being friends with a man's sister. Cedric would never shoot you over that. But you've been cold to her these last few years. Is friendship beyond your grasp?" Charles crossed his arms over his chest.

Lucien sighed heavily and leaned back on his bed. It was time to resurrect the old lie. Charles couldn't be trusted with the truth, it would be the same as telling Cedric.

"Do you remember, years ago, when I was courting Miss Melanie Burns?"

"Of course..." Charles voice trailed off.

Melanie Burns, one of the wealthiest, prettiest heiresses had nearly married Lucien. Instead, after Horatia's interference, she had refused his proposal and a month later was engaged to none other than Hugo Waverly. Rather than be truly angry with Horatia, he'd been thankful. She'd saved him from marriage to a woman who ended up his enemy's wife. For the next four years he'd been cordial, but maintained some distance. Then there had been her coming out when she turned eighteen. He'd never forget the first night she went to Almack's. Her hair had been artfully styled, her dress more elegant than her usual day gowns. She'd been utterly captivating that night and the only thing he could do was run. Put distance between them before he did something foolish. Resurrecting the proposal incident had been the only straw he could grasp as a reason to stay away from her. If he couldn't get his hands on her, he couldn't kiss her, couldn't make love to her, couldn't love her. It was for the best, though of late, it was working less and less.

"Are you saying Horatia had something to do with Melanie Burns?"

"Yes," Lucien answered flatly.

"How? She was a child back then."

"Horatia was with Cedric at my estate in Kent on a visit. Melanie Burns was there. I was in the middle of proposing when Horatia dumped a bucket of pond water over our heads from the gazebo roof. Melanie was humiliated, her dress was ruined and the little imp, Horatia, dared to laugh at her. No matter how much I apologized later, Melanie refused to marry me."

"Then she married Waverly. If he's more her type, you ought to thank Horatia, not punish her."

"There's more to it. Horatia professed her love for me. She was only fourteen," Lucien growled.

"A child's infatuation. That's no reason to be cruel," Charles replied softly.

"I told Horatia I would never love her. That she meant nothing to me."

A epiphany struck Charles's face. "You broke her heart."

"I couldn't help it. I was so much older than she. Now she's grown and I don't want her setting her cap at me. I'm not attracted to her and never will be." Lucien prayed with every fiber of his black-hearted soul that he sounded truthful.

Charles was silent for a long moment.

"Ash once told me that between love and hate there is a fine line. Sometimes you can cross it without even realizing it."

"You can't seriously be suggesting that I love Horatia! You know the sort of woman I need. She's too prim and proper for my tastes. I don't feel anything at all for her—certainly not *love*." A bitter taste filled Lucien's mouth at such a denial. He felt too much for her, and although it couldn't be love, it was stronger than lust and therefore more dangerous.

Charles frowned, his gray eyes surprisingly tinged with sadness.

"Are you so adamant to avoid her because of the second League Rule? Have you learned nothing from Godric and Emily?"

"Wouldn't you avoid a woman if it meant your friend might seek satisfaction against you? Charles, you know me. You know how I am with women. I couldn't stay around her for much longer and not desire more than friendship, and anything beyond that could end very badly. I don't have to remind you how protective Cedric is of his sisters. He's always taken Rule Two very seriously."

"You really cannot control yourself around her? Your only solution is to be cold and cruel in order to avoid temptation?" His friend seemed baffled, but then, Charles was the sort of man who was never tempted by forbidden things—he dove headlong into them.

"Unfortunately, that's exactly what I'm saying. The more I'm around her, the more I want to be with her. We both know I'm not the marrying type, so any time spent with her would have one conclusion and no one would like the result."

Charles raked a hand through his hair. "You're a fool, and you're hurting Horatia because of it. I can't stand to stay here, not when I'm tempted to box your ears."

"Charles." Lucien put a hand on his friend's shoulder as he turned to leave, but Charles shrugged free as he turned to leave.

"Good night, Lucien."

Lucien stared at the door as it closed. A lump worked in his throat. Was Charles right? Had he been keeping his distance from Horatia to avoid more than bedding her?

Lucien loved women, but he didn't *fall* in love with them. It wasn't in his nature, and the women he'd had understood this. Horatia deserved a man who could be loyal. He could never have her, not as a lover or a wife. Cedric would never give him permission, and in any case there was the League's second rule. Still, the thought of having her, calling her his very own...

Why did it make his heart hurt so, knowing it could never be?

CHAPTER 4

When Lucien came down to breakfast late the next morning, he noticed both Horatia and Charles were missing.

"Where is Charles?" he asked, stopping himself short from asking about Horatia as well.

Cedric glanced up from his plate. "He's taken Horatia riding in Hyde Park to exercise my Arabians."

"Oh?" A stab of jealousy lanced through him like a hot poker. The idea of Horatia with someone else—especially Charles—made his vision turn crimson.

Audrey was quieter than usual. Her youthful gaiety, which so often amused him when he was over, seemed to be absent.

Cedric seemed to have noticed it as well. "I say, what's gotten into you, my dear? First Horatia is in a fit of the blue-devils, and now you are quite Friday-faced."

It was no secret that Cedric didn't like to see his sisters unhappy. It was something Lucien understood all too well. He had a sister of his own, and seeing her upset always set his teeth on edge.

"I wished to go shopping today, but Horatia went riding and you've business to attend to at Lloyd's, so I'm stranded here alone."

Audrey moped the way only a pretty young woman could, with her Cupid's bow lips plumped into a pout. When this reaction garnered no attention, she added a theatrical sniffle. Her eyes were glistening with diamond bright tears. It was always entertaining to watch Audrey try to work her magic on her elder brother when she wanted something.

Lucien immediately found a solution to dry her eyes. "With your brother's permission, I'd be happy to escort you. I have a few errands to run myself and would be delighted to have your expertise on the latest fashions."

All signs of tears vanished as Audrey looked expectantly at her brother. Cedric gave her a nod. "Very well, but take your maid with you."

Audrey dashed off to her room to retrieve her reticule, bonnet and cloak. When she returned she curled her arms about her brother's neck and kissed his cheek. Lucien stifled a laugh at the bemused look on Cedric's face.

"Anything to keep you in good spirits." He patted Audrey's back and gently pushed her away. She left the room like a puppy with boundless energy.

Ahh to be that young again, Lucien thought.

Once they were alone again Cedric asked, "You're sure you don't mind escorting her?"

Lucien grinned. "Not at all. I do need her advice on a few things. The child does know her fashion." She was a clever girl, but she filled that brain of hers with far too much fluff on the types of gowns and the styles of bonnets. Then again, he shouldn't be wishing her intelligence was put to use elsewhere. Lord knows the little chit might end up a brilliant political hostess or married to a member of the House of Lords. He wouldn't give her credit for anything less and the very idea of her having any influence over a man in politics was terrifying.

"Very well then, I shall see you both later." Cedric drained his coffee, set the cup down and reached for his cane resting against the table's edge. Cedric never let the cane out of his sight. A reminder of vigilance, perhaps. He paused at the door's edge. "Remember to be on your guard, my friend."

Once Audrey was ready to leave, Lucien ordered one of Cedric's carriages to take them to Bond Street. With Lucien as an escort, Audrey would be free of the ogling of the charming Bond Street Beaux. They knew better than to stare at any woman in Lucien's company. He viewed them with no small measure of condescension, like the harmless popinjays they were. The real danger for Audrey was being seen in public with someone like him. Rumors could spread like wildfire, and the press only fanned the flames.

Audrey flitted about on his arm, oohing and ahhing over every colorful window display they passed until she finally chose a fashionable modiste maker. Her lady's maid, Gillian, a quiet girl around Audrey's age dressed in a gray cotton gown, followed behind.

"Madame Ella is the best dressmaker in London," she said. "She made that lovely gown of Horatia's, the one that wretched driver destroyed."

It seemed fortune favored Lucien today. This was exactly the place he needed to be to buy Horatia a new gown.

He kept his tone soft to prevent being overheard. "Audrey, would you be interested in helping me with a special favor?"

She grinned at him. "Oh I suppose, but I shall demand a favor from you someday."

He had said nothing to give away his intent, yet she seemed to know she had him exactly where she wanted him. Were she a man, Audrey would have been a magnificent politician.

He tried to act casual. "As long as it is within the confines of the law and your brother won't challenge me to a duel, then you shall have it."

"Excellent. We have an agreement." Her brown eyes twinkled with devilry, and he knew he'd come to regret this day. "What is it you need help with?"

"I'd like to replace your sister's ruined gown, but I don't wish to buy the exact same one she had before. I want something better. Something red perhaps..." His voice trailed off as Audrey's lips parted in shock.

"You want to buy Horatia a gown?"

"Er...yes." He held his breath, waiting for Audrey to reveal her knowledge of his secrets. Thankfully, she didn't.

Her expression changed from surprise to one of calculation. Her shrewd gaze was fixed on him, as if she knew something about him that even he did not. It was most unsettling.

"Very well. Red you say? Silk perhaps?" she suggested with a smile that was beyond any hint of innocence.

She couldn't know about his visits to the infamous Midnight Garden, or the games he'd played there, restraining women with red silk ties so he could take his time bringing them to screaming climaxes. He paid quite a handsome sum to keep his interests private. Yet the girl seemed to hint that she knew more than she should about him.

"Red is an excellent color on her, I agree. I haven't the faintest idea why she doesn't wear it more often." Audrey turned and went to embrace the stately, mature woman who had appeared near the back of the shop. "Madame Ella!"

"Miss Audrey! I'm so glad you're back. I kept those York Town gloves, the fawn colored ones you were so admiring a few days ago." Madame Ella brushed a loose coil of dark hair back from her face and retrieved a small glove-sized box. Audrey barely repressed a squeal.

Madame Ella curtseyed when she saw Lucien hovering in the doorway. "Good morning, my lord."

Lucien inclined his head and came over. He'd met her once before, a few years back when he'd come with his mother and Lysandra, his sister, to buy her wardrobe for her first Season. It seemed Madame Ella had an excellent memory.

Audrey took charge and commanded Madame Ella's attention. "We are here to order a new gown for my sister."

Madame Ella's brows knit in concern. "She was not pleased with my creation?"

"On the contrary. She loved it, but it met with an unfortunate fate." Audrey explained the previous day's events.

"I see. So what did you have in mind, Miss Sheridan?"

"A green ball gown with a red satin over dress. Embroider the gown's sleeves with holly designs, trim the hem with a flounce of white Belgian lace. And a green satin wrapping under her bosom." Audrey looked over at Lucien, measuring him intently before she added, "Also, trim the décolletage with sprigs of faux mistletoe."

Both Lucien and Madame Ella raised their eyes at this last request.

"Mistletoe?" Lucien asked Audrey in a hushed tone.

Audrey giggled.

"Don't you see, Lucien? She'll look so lovely in this dress, wrapped up like a beautiful Christmas present." Audrey wiggled her eyebrows suggestively.

"And they say I'm wicked," Lucien said to himself.

If the image Audrey had created in his head was even close to reality, Horatia would be a Christmas present worth unwrapping. With that mistletoe nestled against her breasts, he would be tempted to kiss every inch of her bosom to honor the tradition properly.

"Would she wear such a gown?" Lucien asked Audrey. He wouldn't mind the cost of the garment, but if Horatia refused to wear it, it would be an unspeakable crime against the gown, its maker, and Lucien's very ungentlemanly thoughts at that moment.

"She would wear it, if you asked her to," Audrey replied, her attention now fixed on the gloves she'd taken from the box. She rubbed one of them against her cheek, gave a sigh of pleasure and set them back in the box.

"And what do you mean by that?" Lucien felt breathless as he awaited her response. Just what did she know?

Audrey shrugged. "She values your opinion. If you gave the gown to her and asked her to wear it then she would."

Her answer seemed so resolute that Lucien couldn't help but believe her.

"Then you have our order, Madame Ella. Just as Miss Audrey requested."

"It will be my pleasure, my lord. Miss Audrey has the finest taste."

Lucien patted Audrey's soft hand. "Indeed she does."

He instructed the modiste to send the bill for the gown and gloves to him. As they left the shop, he pulled Audrey aside, her maid staying discreetly a few feet away.

"You mustn't let Cedric know I bought the gown. Do you understand? Lie if you must, say you purchased it."

"Why should I—"

Lucien shushed her. "I can't buy a woman a gift such as that and not have the entire *ton* thinking she's my mistress, your brother included. Think of the consequences." When her eyes widened and she gave a curt little nod, he knew she understood. Her sister's reputation was paramount.

⚜

HORATIA CLUNG TO HER DARK BLUE VELVET CLOAK, PULLING THE ermine lined hood tighter against her face. Charles slapped the ribbons over the backs of the pair of horses, urging them to speed up. They were headed towards Bond Street, where no doubt Audrey had dragged Lucien to do some shopping since Cedric would be busy with other matters.

"Why are you in a hurry, Charles?" She leaned back in the carriage and glanced over her shoulder to check on Ursula, who rode in the back. "We barely rode at all in the park before you insisted we return them to the stables."

When Charles shot a look her way she saw his gray eyes were oddly turbulent, mirroring the stormy winter clouds above their heads. "I just remembered I need to take Audrey to see Avery. He's back in London, you know. I'd be in trouble if I didn't take her out on the Town for the afternoon with him. He does so adore your sister. You are welcome to come." He glanced her way again.

Horatia shook her head. She didn't feel the least bit sociable at the moment.

"You needn't drop me off at home. Ursula and I can hire a hackney to get back."

He scoffed as though affronted at leaving her alone. "Nonsense. I see Lucien up ahead. He's with your sister. I'll have him escort you home." The words came out in an oddly strained manner, as though he was torn on the matter. "You don't mind if I leave you with Lucien?"

"No, I do not. He will see me home safely, just as he's always done." Why she added the last part she wasn't sure, but she felt it necessary to reassure Charles.

Horatia put a gloved hand on his arm. He didn't even seem to notice. "Charles, are you unwell?"

He tensed. "No, I'm well enough. There's much to give me worry these days. Don't fret on my behalf."

She stared at him for a long moment, wondering if she ought to inquire further as to the nature of his distress. Charles was always close-lipped when it came to such things. Her brother always claimed Charles couldn't keep a secret, but Horatia knew better. When it came to matters of the heart, the Earl of Lonsdale could remain silent forever. She turned her attention to the streets again.

When they rolled up next to Lucien and Audrey, Charles called and waved them closer. He then got down to help Ursula off the carriage.

"Lucien, I need you to take Horatia home. Audrey and I have a lunch engagement with Avery, don't we?" He slanted a look at Audrey.

She blinked once before remembrance flashed across her face. "Oh yes!"

Before Lucien could protest, Horatia and her maid Ursula were dumped into his care as Audrey and her maid Gillian usurped her sister's spot on the curricle, and Charles tore off down the street.

"Did Charles just leave you behind so he could take your sister and my brother out for the afternoon?" Lucien asked in almost a stupefied tone.

"It would seem so." Horatia was just as mystified. She blushed when she realized she'd been leaning into him as they watched the curricle drive off. With great reluctance she pushed away, not missing the way his hand lingered at the small of her back, as though he wished to keep her close. A little pang pinched her heart.

Lucien hailed his waiting carriage to take him, Horatia and her maid back to Curzon Street. He helped Horatia inside allowing her the seat facing forward. The carriage leapt into motion before Lucien had properly seated himself and was flung back onto Horatia. She cried out, more from surprise than any pain. He scrambled off her, apologizing profusely.

"Are you quite sure you are all right?" he pressed.

"I'm fine, my lord." She made her tone cool, determined to erase the memory of last night's bruising kiss and fiery touch. "You simply startled me. I'm not nearly as delicate as you seem to believe."

When he grimaced she suspected he was recalling his encounter with her knee. The thought did not displease her.

"Did you have a pleasant time with Audrey?" she asked after an awkward silence.

"Yes, she convinced me to buy her Christmas present early this year."

"How kind of you," Horatia replied, thinking back on her own gifts from him.

Every year Lucien bought her a book, which she secretly treasured with all her heart, despite her knowing he only did it not to show favoritism with Audrey. Her sister was everyone's favorite. Normally this didn't bother Horatia, but with Lucien it struck her deep in the chest. His hazel eyes were fixed on her now, as though he could read her thoughts.

"I bought your gift as well, but it shan't be ready for at least a few days. Madame Ella assured me it would be done in less than a week."

"Madame Ella?" Horatia's heartbeat skittered.

"I thought perhaps you would like a gown, since your other one was ruined."

"You bought me...a gown?" Her entire body tensed at the thought of wearing something he'd given her. It lit her blood on fire with excitement.

"Would you prefer to have another novel? I could cancel the order—"

"No!" Hope filled her so tightly she had trouble breathing. "A gown would be lovely. However, I hope you had the good sense not to tell my brother."

"Perish the thought." He flashed that all too appealing rakehell grin. "Your sister and I designed this confection especially for you this Christmas season and it would be a shame for it to go unworn."

Horatia bit her lip as excitement bubbled up within her. It was scandalous for him to buy her a gown, but she was secretly delighted. It meant he was thinking about her.

The coach pulled up in front of Sheridan House and Lucien got out. He came around to her side of the coach and had the approaching footman assist Ursula down while Lucien helped Horatia down. Ursula and the footman disappeared inside, leaving Lucien and Horatia alone for a moment.

She offered her hand but he ignored it and moved forward to catch her by the waist, lowering her to the ground. Heat rushed through her in a violent wave as he let her slide down the length of his body. When he set her down, she raised her eyes to his face.

"The ice is fresh. I wouldn't want you to fall," he said.

A passing carriage's wheel dipped into a slushy puddle nearby, casting an icy spray. Lucien dragged Horatia into his embrace and shielded her from the splash with his body. He winced as the icy water soaked his clothes.

He was wet. Again. Why her own body shivered against his,

she wasn't sure. Droplets of water dewed on his eyelashes and hung from the wet lock of hair that fell into his eyes. She stared at him, fascinated at the way the jewel-like drops clung to his dark, long lashes.

"Blast. I must have offended the gods of carriages in some past life." He gazed down at her, a wild wolf-like expression, both wintry and fierce filling his eyes. His passion could be her undoing if she let him. His lips were faintly blue and trembled. She ached to warm them with hers. A ridiculous notion, but damned if she didn't want to taste him again, just one...little...

"I should go," Lucien whispered.

"Stay."

"I shouldn't." His warm breath fanned her face and heated her blood.

"At least come in and have your coat dried by the fire."

I have only ever wanted to care for you, Lucien. Just let me care for you.

"Perhaps that is wise. I've no interest in getting a chill from wet clothes. Carriage gods be damned." Lucien made no move to step back from her as she turned, staying caged by him as they reached the door. His breath tickled her neck and she shivered from something other than the cold. The door swung open as the butler and a footman helped them both inside. A sigh escaped her as reality intruded on her once again and she was forced to step away from Lucien. Why did they always have to move apart?

❦

ONCE INSIDE, HORATIA TOOK HIM TO THE MORNING ROOM TO warm up, but to their surprise the fire was unlit. Lucien peeled off his wet wool overcoat and looked at the cold fireplace with a raised eyebrow. For a moment she just stared at him. He glanced down, wondering what she was looking at. His shirt clung to his arms, highlighting his forearms and biceps. When he looked back to her, she'd gone wide-eyed and scarlet. Horatia hastily darted past him to the fireplace and pulled back the grate. He bit the inside of his lip to keep from grinning. She'd liked what she'd seen, he was sure of it.

A low and angry echoing sound announced either the presence of a ghost, or a cat up the chimney. "*Mreooww.*"

"Muff!" Horatia got down on her hands and knees and peered up the chimney. "Come down right now!" She reached up into the sooty confines of the fireplace.

Horatia's backside was on full display to him as she tried in vain to coax down the stubborn feline. The icy chill he still felt dissipated beneath the heat that swept through him. How would her hips feel between his hands? How would his name sound as it was moaned from those lips? Lucien shook his head, trying to erase those images and, more importantly, discourage an enthusiastic response in his loins.

"Here, let me see if I can get him." Lucien knelt beside her. With the advantage of his longer arms, he could reach the crevice in which the renegade feline had lodged himself. "I see him. The question is whether I can reach him. You might want to shield your eyes, my sweet." The endearment fell off his lips without thinking. He reached up, grabbed the cat by the scruff of his neck and dragged him down. Lucien coughed as he dislodged a wave of soot and it rained down around him and Horatia. They both fell back out of the fireplace and onto the floor.

Muff hissed and lunged into Horatia's arms in his bid to flee. He dug his claws into her arms before propelling himself away, leaving a sooty trail of paw prints out of the drawing room. Horatia sneezed and tried to rise. Lucien caught her wrists but his hands came away bloody as he helped her to stand. Her forearms had been sliced by Muff's not-so-tender escape.

Horatia, covered in soot and clutching her bleeding arms, looked absolutely miserable. Something in Lucien's chest tightened. She was so brave; she hadn't made a squeak of pain. If it had been him he would have bellowed like a wounded bear. Not her though, not Horatia. She bit her bottom lip, blinked away the moisture in her eyes and all he wanted was to drag her into his arms and kiss her senseless.

"Come now, let's get that taken care of." He wrapped an arm about her shoulders and led her out into the hall and up the stairs to her bedchamber. He instructed a passing footman to bring warm water, some bandages and have the fire lit in Horatia's room, assuming the blasted cat hadn't gotten there first.

A few moments later, Cedric's housekeeper, a matronly woman with graying hair at the temples, entered the room carrying water and bandages.

"Here we are…" She winced at the sight of Horatia's injuries. "Oh my poor dear!"

"Thank you, Mrs. Stanwick. Could you bring us some hot tea?" Horatia asked.

The housekeeper's lips parted in surprise. "I shouldn't leave you alone…"

"It will only be for a minute. Leave the door open if you must." Lucien's tone was less a suggestion and more a command.

"Very well, my lord, I'll be back shortly." Mrs. Stanwick set the bandages and hot water on the side table and went to fetch tea.

"You don't have to stay. I can see to it," Horatia said.

"Nonsense. I always took care of you when you were young, didn't I?" The words were out before he could take them back. The baffled look on her face, highlighted by her rounded eyes, made her seem so young. She was nothing like his usual women. He liked them fine-boned and full-figured. Horatia had ample curves and a lovely face, but she lacked that edge of cool passion that all of his conquests had.

Lucien pushed her to sit on her bed while he took the cloth towels from the footman. The footman started a fire while Lucien cleaned his hands of soot. The newly lit fire crackled and snapped over the logs. It warmed his back, putting him in a strangely gentle mood.

Her bottom lip shook a second before she opened her mouth.

"Shh…" He wetted a towel and cleaned Horatia's hands of the

soot and wiped the dried blood away. After applying some salve to the cuts, he wound the bandages snugly around her arms. Then he then toweled off his face, as did Horatia. Lucien noticed she missed a few spots.

"What?" she asked when she caught him staring.

"Hold still." He captured her chin and tilted her head back.

Her knees broke apart, allowing him to step closer to her. He brushed the moist edge of his towel over the tip of her little upturned nose, resisting the sudden urge to kiss it. He wiped away a patch of soot, just above her collarbone. Horatia seemed to be holding her breath.

When he finished, he dropped the towel and placed his hands on her skin. He traced her bottom lip with the pad of his right thumb, feeling its fullness. Horatia's lips closed around his thumb as she kissed it. The warm wet caress of her tongue made his entire body tighten. Mesmerized, he pulled his thumb away and leaned down, closing the distance between her lips and his.

He coaxed her lips apart with an exploring tongue. Lucien's hands curled around her hips, holding her still as he pressed himself into the cradle of her body.

The barrier of their clothes didn't seem to matter. Horatia made a little sound of satisfaction as her tongue moved with his. For a brief moment he could forget she was innocent and everything he couldn't have. She was just another beautiful woman that he was going to reveal a new world of dark passions to. Her throaty purrs drove him to the edge. He slid his hands down her outer thighs, coiling up her skirts and petticoats, relishing the satiny skin beneath his fingertips.

Horatia gasped out and jerked back. Their mouths separated with a soft pop.

Reality crashed down. He stumbled back and tried to gather his wits.

Horatia blinked, her brown eyes warm and sleepy. Her pink tongue flitted out to lick her lips and he all but dragged her back into his arms.

She batted her lashes. "I'm sorry... You just startled me."

"No. It is better this way. We can't... This never happened. Do you hear me?"

"But..." Horatia touched her lips, her eyes drawn up to his face, unable to look away.

Lucien had to put distance between them, and not just physical. "Listen to me, Horatia. I'm a hot-blooded rake, I got carried away. You should not have encouraged me."

Her eyes flashed with barely hidden fire. "Encourage *you*? I did nothing of the sort."

"You licked your lips and gazed at me with longing. It makes a man unable to resist you. It was clear you desired a kiss and I felt compelled to oblige."

"You kissed me out of *pity*?" She looked torn between hurt and anger.

He hesitated, but only a moment. "Yes."

Horatia's voice shook and her eyes darkened with tears. "Pl... please leave."

"Happily." He left her room, slamming the door.

⸎

CAN'T THAT MAN EVER SHUT MY DOOR NORMALLY?
Horatia buried her face in her pillows and took several deep breaths, but it did no good. She fought the urge to cry, but tears still ran down her cheeks. It was then that Mittens sauntered out from under the bed, jumped up and nestled against Horatia's stomach, purring.

There was something comforting about the animal's unconditional love. Only after stroking the cat's satiny fur did she finally calm down, but it was a long while before she could look rationally at the problem.

Over the years she'd heard whispers from maids and footmen about his sort. And of course, her brother's warnings always rang inside her head. *Never trust men, Horatia. If someone asks to show you the garden at a ball, run and find me. You don't want to end up with someone like Lucien. They'll steal your innocence, break your heart and ruin any chance of a decent marriage. Word gets around and for us, reputation is everything."*

Lucien didn't want an innocent woman. He wanted a wild and wanton creature in his bed. If she were to ever catch his attention it would require something drastic. After today, she was positive that he had some small attraction to her. If she could just get close enough to him to make him act on it... But she couldn't get close to him. Most of the time he seemed to have enough sense to stay away from her. If only there was a way she could trick that stubborn marquess into seeing her as a woman, not his friend's sister.

Horatia's eyes fell to the open drawer of her vanity table. A silver loo mask lay in the drawer, a piece from a masquerade earlier that year. It spawned an idea. She needed to be someone else, the type of woman he would seek out.

But how to go about it? It would have to be in a location far away from her brother's watchful eye. Someplace dark, perhaps at night so she would have less of a chance of being seen. If she could interact with Lucien in a place where she could wear a mask, he might not know it was her. The risk was high that he would recognize her after talking to her, but if she had it her way there wouldn't be much talking.

All she needed was a chance to convince him that she was worthy of his attention. She wanted to be the seductress he made her feel like. Perhaps if she proved she was passionate, he would offer for her.

I'm such a peahen. The bitter thought struck her like a hard slap. Lucien wouldn't offer for her. He'd use her and then move on. Then again, he'd come close to marriage once. Why not once again? And a tiny voice in her head whispered that ruination at Lucien's hands would be worth it. Even if she spent the rest of her life as a lonely old spinster, one night with him outweighed a lifetime with someone she had no feelings for.

Forcing herself to focus on her idea, she evaluated her choices of clandestine meeting spots. This plan had all the earmarks of one of Audrey's schemes. Audrey! That was it. The moment her sister returned, Horatia would consult her. She wouldn't tell her what she intended to do, but she could solicit advice on how to bribe a footman from Lucien's household to divulge the Marquess's nightly activities and the places where he could be found.

For the first time in days, Horatia smiled with glee.

CHAPTER 5

Lucien entered his townhouse on Half Moon Street in a rage, his jaw clenched and aching. Today had been a disaster. He'd let himself lose control, get too close, and he'd enjoyed every minute of it.

If it hadn't been for those warm brown eyes of hers, pleading for his kisses...

The door to the servants' quarters opened and his valet, Felix, emerged with a stack of freshly pressed white shirts in his arms.

"Felix, I'm going out tonight. Ready my things."

The valet nodded and hurried to Lucien's room. Lucien's hands twitched, feeling the urge to break something. He stormed into the drawing room and grabbed the first thing within reach, an expensive oriental vase. He arced his arm and—

"I say, Lucien, you all right?"

He spied his brother, Lawrence, a few feet behind him in the open doorway. Except for the fact he was five years younger, he was a mirror image of Lucien. Anger still boiling deep inside him like a dormant volcano, Lucien now aimed the vase at his meddlesome brother.

Lawrence stepped back, hands raised in surrender. "If you

break that, mother will be most upset. She spent a fortune getting that back from Shanghai for you. To hear her tell it, she hired an entire caravan of elephants like Hannibal for part of the journey."

With a snarl, he set the vase back down on the cherrywood side table and glowered at his smirking brother.

"I thought you were in France."

His brother gave a casual shrug. "I came back with Avery."

"Have you obtained lodgings?"

"Not as of yet."

"Then you must stay here," Lucien replied, but his heart wasn't in the gesture. He wasn't in the mood to entertain, not even his family. Was it so bad to want some peace and quiet to sort out the messy tangle of emotions that plagued him?

His brother flicked an invisible speck of dust off his coat sleeve. "I'm only here for a few days and I wouldn't dare to impose, especially since you seem to be having rather heated issues with your décor." Lawrence was well known for his sarcasm. Lucien had had words, and more than words with him over such remarks when they'd been younger.

"Just because we are no longer children doesn't mean I won't box your ears."

"You could try."

Lucien swung his fist good-naturedly at his brother, who danced back a step. They laughed, and Lucien found his anger deflated. God bless Lawrence.

"If you don't wish to stay the night, what brings you here?" Lucien asked. "I thought perhaps you'd go straight to mother." A terrible thought occurred to him. "She isn't here is she?"

Lucien half-expected the formidable Lady Rochester to explode out of a closet. His mother had on more than one occasion hidden herself to eavesdrop on her offspring, only to reveal her presence suddenly and scare the bloody hell out of her children. Linus, Lucien's youngest brother, refused to shut the closet doors in his bedchamber for that very reason.

She did so out of love of course. It was even a family joke. She'd been so besotted with their father that she'd insisted on naming every child with a name starting with L for love. Therefore they'd been named Lucien, Lawrence, Linus and Lysandra. Avery had been the only exception to their mother's naming scheme. He looked just like their father and so bore the same name as him. The other Russells favored their mother in looks.

"Mother's in Kent," Lawrence said. "She sent word to you that she wanted to spend Christmas at home. Did you not get the letter?" Lawrence seemed genuinely surprised, since Lucien was the best of the Russell brood when it came to correspondence.

"I've been a bit preoccupied of late." It was an understatement, a grand one at that. His study was littered with unopened letters, his mother's latest one no doubt among the clutter on his desk. Lucien stroked his jaw with his thumb and forefinger. "Does mother expect me to come visit her?"

"Lord, no. Not that she wouldn't mind, but I think she's happiest when left alone to torment Linus and Lysandra." Lawrence chuckled. "They're both with her now, God help them."

"What about Cambridge? Surely Linus has finished by now." A thread of guilt wound through his chest, knotting around his ribs. Had he been so consumed with his own affairs that he'd lost track of his siblings' lives?

Lawrence gave another shrug. "Only a short while ago."

"If you are leaving in a few days, you must dine with me tonight." Lucien's desire to be left alone had changed, and he hoped his brother would agree. Lawrence would be a welcome distraction and keep him from dwelling on hopeless desires.

Lawrence smiled deviously. "Actually, I have scheduled an evening at the Midnight Garden. You are welcome to join me. Madame Chanson does miss your patronage."

The Midnight Garden was a discreet club, full of hidden scandals and romantic trysts. The most public secret in London. Madame Chanson tailored it to the needs of any individual, man or woman wealthy enough to pay for membership. She brought in the most beautiful ladies, hired only the most handsome men, and the decadence of the surroundings promised sinful pleasures of all kinds. She'd also acquired the good will and patronage of those necessary to keep it open.

Lucien had, until recently, been a frequent guest of the Garden. But since he had been thrown into Horatia Sheridan's life once more, and he'd not returned in search of pleasure. The one time he had ended in disappointment on all sides.

Perhaps that is what I need—a naughty tumble to erase the memory of Horatia from my mind. Lucien scraped a palm over his jaw before nodding. "I believe I shall. I've been too melancholy of late and my spirits need lifting."

His brother laughed. "As do other parts of you, I suspect."

Lucien ignored him. "What time is your engagement?"

"Nine o'clock. You'll need a mask. Madame Chanson is in a masquerade mood this month and she's requiring all her patrons to wear them. Rumor has it a delegation from Italy has arrived, and it's for their benefit."

Lucien frowned. Did he still have a mask? Surely he did. He had gone to many of those parties at Vauxhall during the Season and a number of them had required masks.

"I'd best go find one." He started towards the stairs.

"I shall meet you at the Garden then, around nine," Lawrence called out.

"Felix!" Lucien called out.

The valet popped his head into Lucien's bedchamber. "My lord?"

"Change of plans. Set out my finest black breeches, black hessians and a black silk shirt. Also, do I still have a black domino mask?"

Felix's eyebrows rose. "Are we dressing you for a specific occasion, my lord? I was under the impression that abductions were not among your interests." The valet's eyes were cool, but Lucien caught the glimmer of amusement there.

Lucien sometimes forgot that what were considered secrets upstairs were sometimes common knowledge downstairs. No doubt he referred to Miss Emily Parr's adventure some months before.

"Abductions, when done properly, can turn out quite satisfactory. But fear not, Felix, tonight I'm off to the Garden. Madame Chanson requested all guests to wear masks."

"Ah. The Italians are back, no doubt. Well, you are in luck, my lord. I kept a nice half-face mask that you wore last year. It should look splendid with your chosen outfit this evening." Felix went to one of the dressers and dug through its contents until he found the mask. He set it down on a side table and slipped into the dressing room to fetch Lucien's evening clothes.

Lucien left his bedchamber for the small washroom where he had a tub. He pulled the bell cord to signal to the servants below that he wished to bathe. It would be a while before the bath was ready so he had a footman fetch some letters from his study to read.

Once ready he sunk low into the tub of hot water and let the tension ease out of him. Being around Horatia always wound him up into knots. He splashed his face and scrubbed at his skin, trying to remove the memory of her body against his. Soot still clung to his hair, and he washed it thoroughly as well, wanting nothing left to remind him of how close he'd come to losing his sanity.

The more time he spent around her the closer he came to acting on those base desires that would betray his principles, ruin her reputation and incite her brother's wrath. Yet the idea of coming to her and teaching her how to embrace her passions was too tempting. It was this that held the thrill for him.

He did not spend his days counting conquests like other men, but rather he prided himself on helping women conquer their own souls and bodies by accepting their needs and learning fulfillment in bed. Passion was a thing meant to be shared between a man and a woman, and he'd never liked the idea of a woman simply lying limp beneath him. Sex was a mutual exploration, a gift shared, not something stolen or taken by another. So while his reputation as a rake was forever assured, one would receive quite a different opinion about him from his women. To them he was a liberator, no matter how brief their time together.

After his bath, Felix helped him dress, and Lucien was out the door. A footman hailed a black cab so his presence would not be noted when he arrived. The Garden was not a place where the insignia of the Marquess of Rochester should be seen. Lucien kept his mask on, checking the ribbon as his hackney pulled up front of the stucco townhouse that was the facade for the Midnight Garden.

A footman hurried down to meet him and bowed his head respectfully. "My lord." The footman did not know his true identity, but all men and women in the Garden were greeted as lord and lady. If nothing else, it was good for business.

"Is Madame in?" Lucien asked the footman, following him up the steps. The young man nodded and opened the door for Lucien.

Day or night, the Midnight Garden was always dimly lit. It carried the ambience of a midnight rendezvous. Gilded wall sconces lined the entry way and halls splitting off to various rooms, of which there were at least twenty between the three floors. The walls were a deep burgundy with gold trim and the furniture was richly brocaded. Everything was selected to offer decadence and sensuality to the patrons who paid to enjoy their desires here.

For a good many years, Lucien had haunted these halls, seeking bedmates that would not fear him or his desires, and would trust him to master the pleasures of their bodies. Someday he hoped to find someone he could trust in return, but so far he had not. Since Emily Parr's abduction he'd been reluctant to return to his old habits. He wanted to find a connection between himself and his bedmate. The brief, wild couplings, or the slow pleasure of seducing a woman into being bound was not the same as savoring a woman he truly cared about. After his frustrating encounters with Horatia, however, he was desperate for relief.

Madame Chanson, a curvaceous woman in her late forties emerged from a nearby room with a woman Lucien recognized. Evangeline Mirabeau, the Duke of Essex's former mistress. Her eyes fixed on him, and he knew she recognized him as well. She gave him a cool nod. After her indirect help against a threat to Godric a few months ago, he had found a new, albeit limited appreciation for the French woman.

"My lord, you've returned! I had feared you would not, given that Lady Society has deemed you smitten and leaving your ways behind you. It gladdens my heart to see you return." Her voice was low and rich, a sultry voice that reminded him of his nights here. Her pale blond hair and gray eyes, which always seemed half-closed, made her appear as though she'd just woken up from a night of devilish bed sport.

"Madame Chanson, it is a pleasure to see you again. Do not believe everything you read. Lady Society is often wrong." He smiled at her and she winked. She had no trouble recognizing him with the mask on, his height and the rare color of his hair was a giveaway to those that knew him.

"You are in trouble with me, my lord." She teased him with an affection born of years of friendship. "I do not like that you have been absent so long."

"Perhaps later you might exact your punishment on me." He gave her his most rakish grin, one that made even the experienced Madame blush.

"Perhaps I shall," she replied. Madame Chanson never slept with the customers who came to her house, but she'd made an exception for Lucien. She'd all but begged him on more than one occasion, and he'd happily obliged.

Once a rake, always a rake.

"I heard that my brother has engaged a room this evening?"

"Oh yes, of course. Shall I escort you to his chamber?"

"Yes, thank you."

Lucien followed her down the corridor towards one of the finer rooms, one that had a terrace where a person could open the French windows to the gardens below. Lawrence must have paid a great deal for the privilege. Madame Chanson rapped lightly on the door.

At the sound of Lawrence's muffled reply to enter, she opened the door. Lawrence was seated on a loveseat feeding grapes to a buxom young woman. Both were wearing masks.

"Brother," Lawrence said.

"Brother," Lucien replied in amusement.

The young woman straightened in Lawrence's arms. "My lord." The young woman greeted him with sly smile.

Lawrence chuckled. "Feel free to join us." He cupped the woman's right breast with a smile and she gasped in mock shock. "There are plenty of grapes."

Lucien turned to Madame Chanson. "Do you have anyone new who might interest me?"

She hesitated a moment. "Why yes...a young lady came here tonight, not half an hour earlier. A Lady of Quality, one might say. I offered her the services of my best men, but she wished for me to arrange a rendezvous with a man of equal social status. I told her there were several such gentlemen visiting the house, and if I could arrange it, she would spend the night with one of them. I did not mention names, but I did hint that you would be arriving soon. She seemed greatly interested when I described you. I know I should not have presumed to offer your company to her, my lord..."

Intriguing. It wasn't unheard of for married women to seek out pleasures when their own marriage beds grew cold. He had little interest in a jaded woman tonight. A young lady of quality though...one who was new to the atmosphere of the Garden was certainly of interest to him. "An innocent?"

Madame Chanson nodded. "I believe so. She hides it well, but I see the innocence in her eyes. I know such women aren't to your usual taste..."

Ordinarily the Madame would have been right. Innocent women had never been of interest before, and there was always the risk of them reading too much into their first encounter. But the masks meant this woman knew what she was seeking, and that put his mind at ease. He wanted someone soft and sweet, someone who reminded him of what he was denied. He could close his eyes and see Horatia, feel her body beneath his...

"I'm feeling adventurous, Madame. Please send her to me. Do not tell her my name."

"Of course." Madame Chanson curtseyed and swept out the door in a swish of purple silk.

Lawrence had resumed feeding grapes to his companion. Lucien removed his coat and waistcoat, flinging them over the nearest chair before reaching for the decanter of brandy on a side table. He had no problem being in the same room with his younger brother while the man seduced his current plaything. Lucien was even open to sharing, but tonight he needed a drink and his own woman. There was nothing more relaxing than to have a woman to hold and kiss when one's frustrations had been out of control. Unlike others, Lucien didn't take out his temper with boxing or drinking. He preferred a good woman and a sturdy bed. He often felt the world would be a better place if more men agreed.

There was a knock on the door.

"Enter."

When it opened, Lucien almost dropped his brandy. The young woman in the doorway wore a silver mask, but even at this distance he recognized her.

Horatia.

He'd spent too many nights picturing her seduction to forget even one inch of her form. He was relieved his mask concealed his identity.

What on earth was the silly creature doing here? It was full of wolves who'd pounce on her, just like he wanted to...

Madame Chanson's words came back to him. The young lady was interested in him when he'd been described to her. Had she come here, looking for a man like him to satisfy her own frustrated desires? Or had she been even more clever and discovered he was coming here tonight? Lucien found himself grinning. No matter her reasons, Lucien was going to show her just how foolish she was. He would make her regret this decision, and he would enjoy embarrassing her in the process.

Her evening gown of shimmering white silk had an over dress of silver netting. The bodice, cut low in a wide U, was made in a gauzy georgette that was pleated and tucked. The gown had short sleeves of the same fabric that seemed to increase the effect of her décolleté. The skirt, a silk in the same color, began just under her breasts. Though slightly pleated it skimmed her figure as she moved. In short, she was an utter vision and his body responded. She turned when the door shut behind her, startled, displaying the low neckline on the back of her gown.

"Please, come in," he purred, coming to her and taking her by the arm.

She gazed up at him, and he saw the flicker of recognition in her brown eyes beneath her silver mask. She knew it was him. Lucien glanced over at his brother who was far too occupied with his own woman to recognize Lucien's prey.

"I believe I may have been directed to the wrong room," she said, her chest rising and falling as she attempted to pull free of his hold.

Lucien tugged her up against the length of his body. "Nonsense, my little dove. Come, sit with me." Lucien pulled her onto his lap in the nearest chair. She all but squeaked in terror.

This shall be so much fun. He pulled her tight to his body, letting her feel every inch of his body that touched hers. She was rigid in his arms, but he'd soon change that.

"Frightened?" he asked in a low whisper only she could hear.

To his surprise, she gave a jerky little nod. "A little."

He couldn't resist smiling. "Sometimes a little fear with someone you trust can be a good thing."

Before she could argue, he tipped her chin up with one finger, exposing her neck with his touch. She swallowed hard, and he could see the pulse beating in her throat just as he bent his head and covered her neck with slow, soft kisses.

HORATIA COULD BARELY BREATHE, LET ALONE THINK. NO DOUBT because her plan had worked and yet completely backfired at the same time. An hour ago, she had located the mysterious Midnight Garden. It cost her a pretty penny to pay one of Lucien's footman to tell her where the Garden was and learn that he would be there this evening. She'd arrived by hackney and paid Madame Chanson to secure her place as Lucien's chosen lady for the evening. She'd had to explain to Madame Chanson that her desire was only to spend the evening with Lucien. The Midnight Garden's owner had eyed her shrewdly and assured her that she would be with Lucien this night and no other. That had given Horatia some sense of calm.

She'd had the foresight not to give away her identity to the Madame, but she had not thought beyond that. Having no experience, Horatia was quite unprepared for Lucien's maddeningly quick seduction. She found herself on Lucien's lap, mere feet from his brother Lawrence, who she easily recognized despite his mask, as he entertained another woman.

"Why so tense, my dove?" Lucien's large hands massaged her shoulders, pleasure emanating from the force of his fingers rubbing her tight muscles. Horatia felt the heavy temptation to relax into that touch, to melt into him. It would be so simple to surrender. It was what she wanted after all.

"Are you scaring her, Lucien?" Lawrence teased between mouthfuls of grapes.

"Perhaps I am." Lucien cupped Horatia's chin, keeping her gaze level with his. "Are you still frightened?"

Despite the seriousness of his question there was a lift in the corners of his mouth that told Horatia he was barely containing his laughter.

"I am not used to having an audience, my lord," she managed to say, casting a nervous glance in Lawrence's direction. A treacherous blush rose in her face, only half-hidden by her silver mask.

Lawrence sat up a little straighter before leaning in their direction. "Tell me, brother, how on earth do you manage to bed the most naively charming women? She blushes like a bride!" He lost interest in his own woman and pushed her away when she leaned against him possessively.

Lucien's fingers slid down Horatia's back and dug into her hips, holding her still over his lap as he studied her.

"Would you prefer my brother to me? I daresay he would take you if you find me too frightening." Lucien's voice was like melted chocolate and just as sinful. Horatia looked between the two men, so alike in their black clothes, masks and dark red hair.

"I would prefer you, and you alone, my lord," Horatia said. She saw the gleam of triumph in his eyes and wanted to slap him for his presumption.

Lucien clamped a firm hand around the back of her neck and urged her forward to meet his lips. He rewarded her with a deep thrust of his tongue, playing with hers in a sensual, suggestive rhythm that had her panting for breath when his lips moved to her neck and down towards her collarbone.

"Do you have another room, brother? Or must I convince you to take a turn in the gardens with your lady?" Lucien seemed to have no qualms about turning his younger brother out.

Lawrence inclined his head to the right towards a gilded door. "There's a bedchamber through that door."

Without looking at his brother, Lucien continued to explore the sloping indentations of Horatia's neck and collarbone with his lips and tongue. "Then take your woman and go there."

With a sigh Lawrence got to his feet and tugged his companion up to follow.

"Leave the grapes," Lucien added as Lawrence reached for the plate of fruit, leaving him to complain about whose money had paid for the room in the first place.

Horatia shifted restlessly as he returned to torturing her with his mouth. Her hands settled on his broad shoulders as she watched Lawrence and his woman leave the room and shut the door behind them.

"Now, shall we get comfortable?" Lucien slid her off his lap, leaving her in the chair while he stood before her, legs braced apart as he removed his shirt and tossed it aside. When his hands fell to the fastenings of his breeches, Horatia's heart leapt into her throat. He smiled and reached out to hold her chin, tilting her head back to look up at him again.

"There's that charming blush. I find it lovely, but I wonder...do you blush from modesty or inexperience? Surely you suffer from neither of these, in your line of work?"

How *dare* he? Lucien knew full well her story was that she'd asked for someone of equal social status and here he was accusing her of... Horatia shot to her feet, unfortunately bringing herself closer to him than was wise. Any response she might have made was silenced by Lucien's mouth on hers. He caught her wrists, twisted them behind her body to hold them captive against the small of her back. He freed one hand to smooth down the silver netting of her gown over the swell of her bottom and then pulled her sharply against him.

"Feel how much I want you?" he murmured against her.

The better question, Horatia decided, was how could she *not* feel him? The bulge of him against her pelvis made her body respond with a sharp ache between her legs. Lucien released her and moved over to the loveseat his brother had vacated. He lifted up the plate of grapes and sat.

"Join me," he said, patting the empty space next to him.

"But," she began. She was regretting her brazen plan more with each passing minute. Surely there was a more rational way to get him to come around to liking her. Then again, perhaps not.

"Now." His command was not sharp, but did promise punishment if she refused him.

She darted onto the love seat, smoothing her gown with fidgeting hands. The gown's bodice clung to her breasts, making it harder to breathe. She'd had it made a few years ago, before her figure had filled out. It was the only dress she knew Lucien had never seen on her. Horatia had never been so aware of her body as she was now. The bodice clutched her breasts, her nipples rubbed against the fabric and the juncture between her thighs felt damp and tingly. He scowled at the obvious distance between them.

"Closer," he growled.

She shuffled over.

He didn't seem satisfied however until she'd come so close that her left hip was pressed snugly against his right. He wound an arm about her waist, jerking her even closer before releasing her. The warmth of his bare skin was impossibly delicious against the thin silk of her gown. The muscles of his bare chest were sharp and angular, carved and beautiful, like corded ropes of steel bound by a soft layer of skin.

"Do you like what you see?" Lucien teased.

Horatia was not sure if it was safe to answer that. Her gaze wandered over his body, imagining how it would feel to be in his arms again. She licked her lips, noticing his eyes fix on her tongue. He took a grape from the plate and slipped it into his mouth, then held up a second piece to hers. Horatia just blinked, unnerved by such an intimacy as being fed by him.

"Open for me," he coaxed.

His voice made her insides burn. It held an entirely different meaning than offering her mouth up to take a grape.

He had no idea who she was, and he was seducing her like a normal woman, not someone he avoided. She would risk her virtue if only to let Lucien rob her of her sanity with his passion. Foolish as her actions were, her need for him was far greater.

She took the grape from his fingers with her lips, moaning at the sweet flavor. But she barely had time to swallow before Lucien leaned forward and captured her mouth with his. The kiss began sweet, soft, teasing, but the sugary taste went straight to her head. A little noise of pleasure escaped her.

The plate of grapes toppled to the floor. Lucien gripped her hips and tugged her down to lie beneath him on the settee. With one expert hand, he rucked up her skirts and pushed her knees apart so he could slide into the welcoming cradle of her thighs. One of his palms stroked the outside of her leg, playing with the ribbons on her stocking. He deepened the kiss, covering her body with his and grinding his hips against hers in a slow rhythm. His tongue met with no resistance when it slipped between her lips. He tasted like an intoxicating glass of sherry on an empty stomach. But the couch was far too narrow for what their melding bodies needed.

Horatia laughed as Lucien tried to get his body better situated and almost fell off. He grinned and pressed himself down hard against her, once more trying to assert dominance over her. This time his one knee did slip off, causing him to roll to the ground.

"Blast it! We need a bed," he growled.

He ripped himself away from her then tugged her up onto her feet. The moment her body was free of his weight, some semblance of sanity returned, and Horatia fought his dominating grip on her body.

"Don't fly off yet, little dove." He purred like a cat luring a plump sparrow too close to the ground. "I've not had enough of your taste."

Horatia stumbled back but was saved by Lucien's firm grip on her wrist as he dragged her to the nearby bed.

"Lie down," he said, pointing.

Horatia balked, her feet tripping beneath her as she stepped back. "What?"

Lucien's response was to take her and put her there himself. She was still reeling from the shock of him tossing her onto the bed when he pulled out several long strips of red silk from his pocket. He caught her right hand and quickly anchored it to the bedpost. Horatia struggled to free herself but it wouldn't budge. Lucien tugged her other wrist towards the far bedpost and secured it as well.

Horatia had only enough slack in her bonds to strain a few inches off the bed. Panic set in, her breathing rapid and shallow. What was he planning? Should she tell him who she was? He would surely stop if he knew, and then she'd be safe. Unloved, but safe. It was almost as if he could read her thoughts as he laid his palm on her cheek and turned her face towards him.

"Do you trust me?" His eyes were dark and his voice rough, but in that moment she was spellbound. "I need your complete trust. I will bring you only pleasure, no pain." His face held passion but beneath that was nothing but a desperate need for her to trust him. And she did.

Still, Horatia's quick breaths would not ease. She struggled to stay focused on his face and not the fact that she was bound to a bed. Never before had she felt so helpless, so exposed. It was a risk like no other, to trust him now, like this.

"If I trust you, will you take care of me? I haven't..." She couldn't finish that sentence.

Understanding softened the intensity of the eyes behind his mask. "I promise you will be cared for. If anything hurts, tell me at once. Do you understand?"

"Yes, my lord." How desperately she longed to breathe his name but she couldn't reveal herself and ruin the magic of this night.

"When we are done tonight, you will be well educated in the ways of passion," Lucien assured her, and with that he moved forward to undress her.

CHAPTER 6

Lucien began with her silver slippers, sliding them off and setting them on the floor. His palms slid up the length of her calves and along her thighs to unfasten her stockings and unhook her garters. He removed her stockings with ease and kissed the sensitive skin behind each ankle. He could feel every tremble, every shiver as his hands explored her body.

He forced himself to focus solely on Horatia and not his own arousal. Her pleasure had to come before his because he could not have her fully. He would push her to her limits, but he would not take her innocence. Not in the way that mattered for dowries and weddings at any rate.

Kneeling between her parted legs, he coaxed her to bend her knees up and widen. He needed to have her open for his tasting. He slowly slid his hands under her gown up to her hips and assessed her undergarments. Usually women in the Garden did not bother with much in the way of underclothes, but Horatia had enough petticoats on underneath to decorate a castle's battlements.

"A little overdressed for the occasion, aren't we?"

Horatia blushed. "I'm wearing what a proper lady should…"

"A proper lady? I have no interest in that. Not tonight, my dear. These petticoats must go." He slid off the bed and retrieved the small paring knife from the loveseat and returned to her. Her eyes widened and her chest began to rise and fall with frightened breaths. Her gaze narrowed in on the knife.

"Are you..." she began.

"I'm not going to hurt you. I don't wish to remove your gown, so I am going to cut the petticoats open." He brushed a hand along her waist. With quick precision, he split her petticoats up the middle until they fell open onto either side, but he didn't remove them. He dug his hands into the fabric and ripped them a little higher. Finally she was bare to his gaze, her gown pooling around her hips in a shimmering haze.

Lucien settled his hands at the top of her raised knees, gazing down at her sex. She was wet, swollen, and perfect. He enjoyed looking upon a woman's body, but never had there been such a strange sense of euphoria accompanying it. It made him hurt deep in his chest, to know she wanted him like this. This was perhaps the only time he could be with her, and he would savor every moment of pleasure he intended to give her, no matter how it agonized him later.

He began a slow trail of kisses along her inner left thigh. Her breasts jerked up against her bodice. He almost smiled, enjoying the jolt of panic he'd caused. She knew he wouldn't hurt her, yet she was excited and anxious as to what he might do. That was where the pleasure in bondage lay. He could do wonderful things to her and she had to accept it, couldn't rush it or demand it, merely accept it as it came. Though begging was always welcomed.

"What are you doing?" The bravado of her question weakened against the trembling of her voice.

"Why, you surprise me! Have you never been tasted?" He knew the answer full well, but he enjoyed the game of ignorance they played.

"T-tasted?" She jerked beneath his grasp, trying to dislodge his hands now holding her spread open beneath him.

In answer, he flicked out his tongue against the sensitive skin mere inches from her core. She trembled and tried again to push him away, but his shoulders were level with her knees, stopping her.

"But you can't!"

He used his hands to open her folds and took his first sweet lick. A strangled cry of shock ripped from Horatia and her head flung back. Her hands fisted in the sheets at the corners of the bed. Lucien licked again, swirled his tongue, her taste like a drug to his senses. The pain in his loins only intensified with the sensual moan of encouragement from Horatia.

"Again?" he asked, his warm breath teasing her inner thigh.

"Yes." Her hesitant reply was tinged with a need neither could deny.

He bent his head again, this time determined not to stop for any reason. He began to lick her, tonguing her sensitive spots, sucking on the swollen bundle of nerves until Horatia was shifting restlessly beneath him.

"I feel...I feel unwell," she said.

Startled, Lucien paused and looked up. Her eyes were closed and the silver sparkles of her mask glinted like a smattering of stars across her nose and cheeks as she panted for breath. A woman undone and on the verge of ecstasy. Never had he seen anything more beautiful.

"Does it hurt?" he asked, concerned.

"There's a...tightness in my stomach. It feels as though my heartbeat is there and not in my chest," she confessed.

She was so innocent she did not even recognize the arousal she felt.

"That's not sickness, my dear, but desire. It will not make you unwell. Be brave and I will show you how wonderful it can be." Lucien felt her muscles go taut beneath his hands. He would have to coax her into relaxing. He slid up her body, settled his hips into the cradle of her legs and kissed his way up from the swell of her breasts to her mouth. After a deep, rich kiss she melted again, once more languid in his arms.

"There now. Feeling better?" He breathed in her ear as he licked it and then nipped the lobe softly.

"Yes," she admitted, her hips rising into his.

"Good girl." Lucien slid one finger deep into her wetness. She tensed again.

"Relax." He distracted her with the play of his tongue in her mouth and began a gentle rhythm with his finger. She settled into it beautifully. Her tongue became more demanding and he smiled against her lips while working a second finger into her tight sheath. Her hips tilted in response and her back arched, pressing her body tighter to his. Lucien increased his rhythm, enjoying Horatia's quickening breath as she began that delicious climb towards satisfaction.

THE HEAVY AND SHARP ACHE IN HORATIA'S WOMB BUILT ALL over again. She was dying, her body burning, exploding, building up to a terrifying moment. She was climbing higher, her breath faint, her heart racing, her vision spinning out of control. She couldn't remember who or where she was. The only thing that kept her grounded was the red-haired devil on top of her. The fallen angel with the black mask who seduced her into delicious sin.

"So close. I can feel you trying to hold me inside you." He bit down on the skin between her shoulder and neck. His fingers plunged into her, faster, harder, unforgiving in their pace. It was more than Horatia could bear. Her last shreds of control slipped away and she cried out as she fell off a cliff and into nothing but a weightless sensation. Pure thrill. Why couldn't she hold Lucien, cling to him, to save herself by anchoring her life on those broad shoulders above her? Instead she was perishing beneath him. But maybe that was his intent all along. She was dying in splashes of pain and pleasure as a tingling heat spread through her wilting body.

❧❧❧

For a brief moment Lucien almost believed he'd killed the woman with pleasure. Horatia had shaken so violently, had cried out so loudly, he'd regretted every action that led to it. He'd seen the fear in her soft brown eyes, yet he'd felt no rush of pleasure at having caused it. Instead, he'd been too frantic to free himself from his pants and sate his own aching pleasure with his free hand.

He shouted something unintelligible as he came and had to fight with all his might not to collapse on top of her as she finished coming. Somewhere along their journey he'd bitten her neck, the reddening bruise evidence of his possession. It sent a wave of primal pride through him, quickly replaced with worry as Horatia's eyelashes fluttered open. Their chocolate depths were hazy with the aftermath of their passion.

"I'm not dead?"

He tried to stifle a laugh before he kissed her quivering lips. Never before had he kissed to ease a woman's fears. He'd never had to. All of the women he'd been with before had been unafraid of him and were willing to explore their passions. Horatia was so new to this side of herself and to lovemaking that it must have frightened her. He didn't want her to be afraid, only excited. It was strange to yearn so deeply to please her, to comfort her, yet it felt so right. He could no sooner deny that the sun rose in the east than he could deny Horatia the comfort she so desperately needed after her first climax.

"Perhaps a little. The French call that *la petite mort* for a reason. But I assure you, you are very much alive," he said between comforting kisses.

Horatia let out a long sigh of relief rather than contentment.

She looked like she had a thousand questions to ask him but not one made it past her lips.

"Still feeling unwell?" he asked after he'd removed his hand from between her legs and fixed his breeches.

"No. Quite the opposite in fact."

Lucien almost smiled but instead he reached around her to unfasten her hands from the bedposts, suddenly worried she might have hurt herself in her struggles. He checked her wrists, searching for bruises, but there weren't any.

An odd flutter blossomed within him. She had been the first woman to truly trust him like this, to surrender her body to his full control. The one woman he could never possess was the first woman he'd ever felt uninhibited with, completely and totally free with. Others had agreed to be bound, but none had reacted as Horatia had, as though the surrender to him was an act of pleasure for her as well. Her need to trust, his need to be trusted. She was a perfect match to him. Fate was a cruel and punishing mistress, Lucien decided.

"Did you find pleasure too?" The silver half-mask did little to hide the red blush over her face.

"Yes," he answered, offering her a smile.

She took stock of her destroyed petticoats bunched above her waist and raised her eyes to his.

"What am I supposed to do? I can't very well leave here with them like this." The torn under clothes hung loose and visible from beneath her gown.

Lucien studied her gown and then waved at her legs. "Lift your skirts, quickly, love. I'm going to cut as much of them off of you as I can to free up your skirts."

Horatia gripped her gown and hoisted it up as Lucien grabbed the knife, taking care to cut away parts of the ruined petticoats that hung too low. It was a messy fix, but surely she wouldn't be seen by anyone who would recognize her.

Once finished, he set the knife down and caught her hand.

"Care to take a stroll in the gardens? I know it may be cold, but

I promise to keep you warm." Lucien didn't know why he was offering. It was far too romantic and would send the wrong message. He'd done what he'd meant to do, but in the hopes it would scare her away from him. Instead, she was *glowing* —damn her!

❦

HORATIA PULLED HER STOCKINGS BACK ON AND THEN HER slippers while Lucien dressed. They proceeded out through the terrace door, stepping over patches of snow that had settled in clumps along the cobblestone walkway. Above them, the night sky was clear of clouds and the luminescent stars glittered. It never ceased to amaze Horatia how beautiful the sky was in winter. In the summer, one could see the countless stars, but the glow was fickle and undefined. Winter stars burned with a crystalline sharpness in the thick velvet sky. They reminded her of herself, stalwart in the light of eternal solitude. Horatia was pulled from her inner musings when she realized Lucien's attention was fixed upon her.

"Do you like the stars?" he asked, twining a lazy arm about her hips and tucking her into his side. She blushed. The simple gesture sent ripples of pleasure through her. At that moment being with him seemed so unlike her tortured dreams or the harsh reality of their strained relationship. His black mask melded with the night sky so well that only his hazel eyes and his seductive smile shone through the darkness.

"I adore the stars in winter. They seem brighter somehow. Stronger, yet so very alone." She traced the constellations above in her mind.

"Have you ever studied them?" he asked, his gaze flicking from her to the heavens above.

"Oh yes. Astronomy is one of my guilty pleasures. Aud... that is to say, my little sister often made me feel quite silly for loving them, but she doesn't understand. Studying the stars is like studying the expanse of forever. I feel that when I look at the sky I am gazing into the mirror of creation and seeing the divine patterns that were formed long before I existed, and will continue to exist long after I am gone. It is humbling."

"But beautiful." Lucien's tone was so smooth that she shivered. Did he understand what she meant? Too often she'd been told by irritated suitors she tended to converse philosophically. It was perhaps why she'd been relegated to the shelf on the Marriage Mart, but she didn't care. Such opinions didn't matter, and those who held them were not worth her interest.

He grinned rakishly. "Would you be willing to tutor me, oh lovely stargazer?"

She returned his grin with a teasing smile. "I thought I was your little dove?"

He tugged her towards him so that her back was pressed against his chest. He nuzzled her neck, his lips dancing against her skin.

"You've quite surprised me tonight. I had not expected a scholarly philosopher. I find I like the depth of your mind. A change in your term of endearment was certainly required. Henceforth, you are my lovely stargazer."

"A bit romantic, but I shan't complain." She turned her head back towards his, letting him steal a deep kiss before she added, "Shan't complain at all."

She knew she was entirely a romantic creature. Lucien had helped make her so through those novels he gave her every Christmas. Each one was a love story.

"Well then, guide me through the heavens."

Horatia reached up a hand to point to the sky. "Do you see the trio of stars in a row?" She pointed just over the city's rooftops. "Just there?"

"Yes," he whispered, his breath warming her neck.

"That is Orion's belt. And the far northeastern star is his sword."

"Beautiful," he replied. She turned herself around in his arms to agree with him, but her nose brushed against his. He wasn't looking at the stars at all.

"You, my lord, are not looking."

"I am. I see the stars in your eyes."

The words were too wonderful, too perfect. Horatia, starved for his love, drank them in, knowing how foolish she was to do so. She'd waited half of her life for Lucien to see her as a woman, and even if he thought her to be a high paid doxy, it didn't matter. She could pretend he knew the truth, that he knew it was her. His arms tightened about her waist as she moved towards him for a kiss. Horatia was ready to indulge in her new guilty pleasure, Lucien's lips, but a pair of voices nearby startled her.

"Did you hear that?"

"Hear what?" Lucien's mouth grazed her neck, distracting her as they dragged along her silky skin.

She elbowed him as the faint cold breeze in the garden carried the echo of the voices again. "That!"

Lucien stilled against her back. "I recognize one of the voices. Come this way. Do not make a sound." He took her hand and led her through the maze of hedges until they were much closer to those speaking. Horatia did not recognize either man but their words cut her to the bone.

"I expect the Sheridan problem to be dealt with in a timely fashion." The man's voice was refined, but cold.

Dealt with? Horatia's mouth opened but Lucien clamped a hand over her lips.

"Aye sir, of course," the other man said, as though they were discussing a routine chore. "Everything is arranged, all that's lacking is opportunity. That requires patience. Fortunately, I have no lack of that commodity."

"Good. I appreciate a man who understands these things. There must be no mistakes. I have a bank draft here for the first part owed to you."

The second man growled low. "I told you no bank drafts. Coin only. My business cannot be traced back to either of us."

"I assure you this is not from that kind of account." The gentleman huffed as it became clear that was besides the point. "Very well. I see caution is also something you don't lack. I don't have enough in coin on me tonight. Let us meet back here tomorrow morning; the garden will be empty of tonight's visitors and no one will have arrived for the evening's activities that early."

"I shall be waiting. And the rest of the payment?"

"Not a penny until the conditions are met, and there is dirt falling upon a grave."

CHAPTER 7

Audrey Sheridan was alone with Lord Lonsdale at last. Lady Lonsdale, Charles's mother, had turned in for the evening, thinking Audrey had already returned home. But Audrey had returned under the guise of forgetting a glove, and she'd beseeched Charles to let her stay a while longer. It gave her more time to accomplish her mission. Namely, becoming compromised so that she might finally be married. It was a risk however, because she had no real interest in Charles.

She wished to marry Jonathan, the Duke of Essex's younger half-brother. But since finding a moment alone with him was next to impossible she had to settle on a more cunning strategy. If she managed to get Charles to compromise her, then she might convince her brother that she must marry soon. He'd never let her marry Charles, of that she was certain. Her plan was to persuade him Jonathan was a safer choice.

Audrey had even spoken to Emily about her plan, hoping she would know how to help. She was quite knowledgeable when it came to outwitting her brother and his dashing League of Rogues. But Emily had warned her it carried too much uncertainty and risk, and asked her to wait. She planned to bring up the subject with their mutual friend Ashton, believing him to have the best chance of reasoning with Cedric.

However, Audrey was not a patient person. Horatia had inherited that trait, and Audrey envied her for it. No man ever coddled her or treated her like a babe still clinging to her mother's skirts. Men treated Horatia with respect. If Audrey could get married, then perhaps people would have to take her seriously as well.

"Did you find what you were looking for?" Charles's rich voice broke through her determined thoughts as he sat down next to her on the couch.

"Yes. I dropped my glove near the couch." They were settled in Charles's drawing room, completely alone. He hadn't even been suspicious when she'd asked to stay a while longer after finding her "missing" glove. The time had come for her to reveal her hand and see what level of mischief she could achieve.

Charles lounged on the red velvet cushions, his golden hair tousled as though he'd just woken from a pleasant nap. Audrey felt her pulse leap, though more with excitement and guilt than attraction. But she was a Sheridan. She took pleasure in the thrill of the game. This was no exception.

Audrey rose from her chair, and smoothed her rose-colored muslin gown, trying to keep her hands from shaking. She knew she looked fetching tonight. She prayed it was enough to seduce Charles. Her russet brown hair hung loose in a Grecian fashion, wound with periwinkle blue ribbons. Despite her efforts, her hands continued to shake as she approached the loveseat. He looked at her curiously.

"What's wrong, love? You've been awfully quiet this evening. You haven't even tried to tell me about the latest fashions from Paris."

Audrey held in a sigh. She was about to make him very angry, and she was already regretting it.

"Surely *you* don't care what styles of gown are most in fashion?" She wrinkled her nose as she slid into the seat next to him and gave him a coy smile.

Charles chuckled, but it was a hesitant sound, as though he'd sensed something had changed. "Right, er, well, it was good to see Avery again, wasn't it?"

Charles swallowed hard when Audrey moved several inches closer. He put his right hand down, as though hoping it would act as a barrier between their bodies. Audrey glanced down at it, then brushed a fingertip along the back of his hand in a sensual pattern. He jumped and yanked his hand back.

"Audrey," he warned when she scooted over the last few inches, now pressed right against him. She could feel the heat of his body radiating from his dark blue waistcoat and tan breeches.

"Shh, my love. Not another word." She leaned into his body, lips puckered.

Charles went rigid, then thrust out his hands, as though trying to ward off an evil spirit. His eyes were alight with panic and Audrey giggled, guiltily, enjoying the look of terror on the rake's face. This was the infamous scoundrel Charles Humphrey, the Earl of Lonsdale, and he was frightened of *her*? She ducked under his arms and hopped onto his lap, twining her arms about his neck.

He squawked like a startled goose and fell off the love seat. Audrey, with a death grip on his neck, fell flat on top of him. He grunted beneath her and tried to shake her off.

"Kiss me, Charles." Audrey captured his surprised mouth.

His struggling slowed. Audrey didn't know the first thing about kissing, but it didn't seem to be as romantic as she'd expected. Charles lay closed lipped beneath her, gray eyes glaring up at her. She blinked, released his lips and moved back a few inches.

"Are you quite done accosting me?" he asked.

Audrey frowned and forced her lips over his again, but still he refused to cooperate. She sighed, sat up and scowled. "You're supposed to at least kiss me back. I have no idea if I've done enough to be properly compromised." Audrey crossed her arms over her chest.

Charles leapt up so fast that Audrey toppled off his lap. He scrambled to his feet and moved behind the loveseat, as though the furniture would barricade him from her. She suspected this was the first time in his life he was the one trying to avoid unwanted advances.

"Properly compromised?" he snapped. "Audrey, what in God's name are you playing at?"

"I want to be married. I want to be happy. That's what I'm thinking." She smoothed her skirts and climbed back onto the love seat. He stumbled as he beat a hasty retreat from her outstretched arms. He bolted for the door, but Audrey was fleet of foot and threw herself at the door just as it opened, slamming herself against him and the door at the same time.

Charles stared down at her, blinking rapidly. "Have you taken leave of your senses, woman?"

"Certainly not! I know exactly what I'm doing." She tip-toed her fingers up his chest and he frantically, almost girlishly, swatted her hand away as though it were a fly he was trying to swat off.

"Audrey...you do not want to do this." He suddenly picked her up by the waist and bodily set her aside so he could beat a hasty retreat away from her.

"Get back here!" she said and dove for him.

He spun, trying to avoid her, and tripped over the arm of a couch. With a little *oomph!* he landed on his back on the couch and she climbed onto him. "Now touch me. That's what you're supposed to do next."

"Good God, Audrey! You are a genteel lady! You should not be doing this!"

"If it will get me married, I will do whatever I must!" She tried to lean down and kiss him.

"I'm certainly not going to marry you. It's out of the question. Your brother—"

She giggled. "Oh I have no interest in marrying *you*. That would be ridiculous."

Charles ignored the barb to his honor. "Then why try to seduce me?"

"Because when I tell Cedric you compromised me, he'll see sense and let me marry."

"After he shoots me!"

"Oh it wouldn't come to that. At that point he'll just be relieved I've settled down with someone other than you."

"First you try to seduce me, then you tell me I'm not a marriageable option, then you suggest that anyone is a better option? You are not exactly winning my support, Audrey."

"Honestly! Charles, we both know your reputation and... What are you doing?" He caught her by the upper arms and in a quick move, flipped her beneath him on the couch.

"I ought to teach you a lesson," he growled. "If I'm not an option, then what is all of this nonsense about?" He pinned her against the cushions and he leaned over her, glaring.

"You're the last person Cedric would let me marry. He knows your reputation better than anyone. I will be able to suggest someone preferable, and he'll agree so I won't have to marry you."

"You're forgetting one detail. Your brother is one of my closest friends. He might believe me when I say you were the one seducing me." His hands on her arms were tight, but he didn't hurt her.

"He would never believe that *I* tried to kiss you," Audrey replied haughtily. "I'm the darling innocent child. You're the seasoned rake."

"You are too clever for your own damn good," Charles said darkly. "But I remind you—your brother would shoot me dead. Is that what you want?"

"A bluff. He would never shoot his friend," she insisted. "He just says that to scare away the weak and unworthy, like a test set up by a Greek god. The problem is, like those gods he makes them all but impossible to pass."

"If that is what you truly believe, then you really are a child. Your brother wouldn't hesitate to kill me if he thought I'd touched you inappropriately."

Surely Charles wasn't serious. Cedric would never do that...at least not to his friends. Audrey's eyes welled up. No one understood her frustration, especially her brother. Not one of her desired would-be suitors cared to seek her out after Cedric scared them off. It wasn't fair that she was relegated to the back of the room when it came to the attentions of men. How was she supposed to get married if no man would dare look at her?

She wanted not the marriage so much as the man. She hated hearing the other girls speak of their beaux. While other girls her age were ignorant of the ways of men and women, Audrey had paid close attention to Emily and Godric, and she wanted what they had. She wanted to be desired and loved. Cedric had given her all the love a brother could but it was not enough. Audrey had yearnings, both physical and emotional, which she no longer had the desire to resist. Marriage was the best solution, and Jonathan was the one man she wanted desperately. She would do anything to claim him.

Audrey had even sought advice from a source she trusted to be frank with her on such matters. Evangeline Mirabeau, the Duke of Essex's former mistress, was reputed to be one of the most desired ladies in London. She had agreed to meet Audrey for tea once a week over the last few months. She was an invaluable font of information and surprisingly, the two had become good friends. There was a fearlessness to her that Audrey admired and tried to emulate. Recently, Evangeline had tried to teach her the art of seduction so she might win over Jonathan. But first she needed to start with Charles.

Audrey needed to move this evening along to achieve her goal. Picturing in detail the tearing of her favorite gown, she managed to make herself cry. A lovely theatrical stream of tears ran down her cheeks.

"Don't you dare!" Charles barked. "Don't even think—"

Audrey blinked, causing more tears to flow.

"Bloody hell," Charles groaned. "Audrey love, you know I didn't mean to... That is to say..." Charles's words died on his lips.

"I just want to get married!" Audrey wailed and tugged free of his hands. She threw herself against the back of the loveseat and buried her face in the crook of her elbow, a scheme that had worked countless times on her brother.

Charles sat down next to her, patting her back awkwardly. "There, there, love. It will all work out. You'll see."

"You don't understand! Cedric frightens away all my suitors. No man wants to offer for me now. Even my dowry has ceased to draw the braver gentlemen to our door."

"And your solution was to compromise yourself? Audrey, that's not the most intelligent thing for you to do nor is it the healthiest for me. Why didn't you speak to Cedric about this?"

"And have him yell at me? Declare outright that no man is good enough? I'm desperate Charles. I have needs and urges..."

"Er...I don't believe you need enlighten me any further on those, and perhaps you ought to never tell your brother such a thing. Ever."

"Oh it is *so* much easier for men. You can run out and find a mistress and—"

Charles cut her off. "Yes, it is easier for us. I don't envy you your position in life."

He seemed to understand. He was a rake for a reason. He understood women better than most, and he had to know they desired pleasure just as much as men. It was undeniably unfair that they had less freedom, at least the unmarried ladies.

Audrey had never believed that women were lesser creatures or deserved to be restricted. Something deep in her soul cried out at the injustice enforced by the church, by the courts, even by the newspapers. Not that she could explain that to most men. They had countless reasons for why women weren't their equals and each made Audrey want to scream in outrage. Her single outlet into that world was one she had to keep a secret, even from Cedric. Even from Horatia. But it gave her a voice where before she had none.

Yet if she were married, she could do so much more. She could change herself, and no longer simply be a protected sibling.

Perhaps she could work for changes for other women. Deep down, it was what mattered most to her. Having the right to do as she wished, and seeing such a right given to others.

"So what was your plan? Have me compromise you and then convince Cedric to marry you off quickly?"

"I know how he thinks. Besides, I had Emily speak to Ashton, and she said he promised to speak to Cedric about seeing to my marriage. He was supposed to recommend Jonathan as a suitable match. This night was simply meant to speed matters along."

Charles smiled. "I suspected you liked him."

"Oh I do, very much! But he doesn't notice me."

"He does, love, he does. I assure you."

"Really?"

"Actually," Charles snickered, "you frighten him quite out of his mind."

Audrey jabbed him in the ribs. "That's not making me feel any better."

"If you want Jonathan, we will have to go about this carefully. Where your brother is concerned that's always sound advice. As far as Jonathan goes, you ought to do to him what you did to me tonight. Men like aggressive women. Corner him, kiss him, make him know that you want him." There was perhaps a glint of mischief in Charles's eyes, but it did match with Evangeline's advice

"Does that mean you're going to help me?" She widened her eyes, giving him her best doe-eyed look, one that melted any man into a puddle at her feet.

"Of course. However, if this starts to turn bad, you must promise not to let that overprotective brother of yours shoot me. I rather enjoy being alive."

"What are you going to do?" Audrey asked.

"I'm going to take you home tonight and it's going to look like you've been compromised. So much so that he'll no doubt want to kill me."

Audrey blushed when she caught his meaning.

"And how will we achieve that?"

Charles took her by the hand and pulled her to her feet.

"You'll see."

⊷❧⊷

CHARLES HAD A CARRIAGE SUMMONED AND WITHIN A FEW minutes he, Audrey and her lady's maid, Gillian, were trundling along in the dark cobblestone roads towards Curzon Street.

"Come over here by me. We've got to fix your clothes and hair." Charles patted the empty space on his side of the carriage.

"Miss!" Gillian gasped and grabbed Audrey's arm to stop her. "You mustn't!" Gillian had been left in the coach during Audrey's adventure indoors, and a good thing too.

"Do stop being such a peahen, Gillian. Don't you want me to get married? I'd much rather be a lady of my own house. Think of it! You could be a lady's maid to the lady of a house. Wouldn't that be better?" Audrey prayed Gillian would have some sense of ambition.

Gillian bit her lower lip. "I will keep quiet, Miss Audrey. But only because I know marriage would make you happy." She turned to face Charles. "You will not kiss her, nor anything else I do not approve of."

"Where were you a quarter of an hour ago?" Charles muttered.

A smile crept across Audrey's lips. Her maid, normally shy, was showing a rare bit of courage and she thoroughly approved.

When Audrey took the seat next to him, he immediately cupped her face, then spread his fingers outward into her hair, mussing it up. He artistically pulled a few tendrils and wisps free here and there before nodding to himself in satisfaction.

Audrey glanced down at her gown. "What about my clothes?"

Charles frowned. "My dear, I'm going to have to go one step further. It will require your consent of course."

"Oh?"

"Yes. Your hair is mused, but the clothes...well, and your lips of course."

"What about my lips?" Audrey touched her mouth, not understanding his meaning.

"You need to bite them hard to ensure the authentic appearance."

She did as instructed and bit her lower lip and pinched her cheeks for extra color. Charles began to crush her gown around her knees, wrinkling it. He tugged one of her sleeves down over her shoulder. Charles caught her chin and examined her carefully just as the carriage rolled to a stop.

"That should do it," he said with an approving smile.

Audrey raised a trembling hand to her lips. They felt swollen, plump and then she understood what Charles had meant. She looked properly compromised, and she certainly felt compromised.

"What do you think, Gillian?" asked Charles.

"I think I'd have slapped you had I seen her come home looking like that."

"Perfect!" said Audrey.

"Ready to play your part?" Charles's amused countenance turned to one of annoyance as he assumed the false air of an angry rake as the carriage came to a stop.

"Just one more detail, I think." She ripped her gown near the shoulder, letting one strap fall off her shoulder.

Audrey donned her own mask of rage and let him drag her out of the carriage and up to her brother's door. She fought off a giggle as Charles beat on the door with a closed fist. Charles would be lucky if Cedric didn't shoot him after all.

CHAPTER 8

Alone in his study, Cedric slumped in a chair, legs stretched out in front of the fire. The embers crackled and spat, reflecting his mood. He had much on his mind, the safety of his sisters at the forefront. In one hand he loosely twirled his silver lion's head cane. It was an old habit, one that used to irritate his mother, God rest her soul.

The clock on the mantelpiece ticked in the heavy silence. The sound grated on his ears. He hated an empty house, truly hated it. Since his parents had died, it had just been him and his sisters. Often that was enough. But tonight he was alone and the dark thoughts that engulfed him were almost overwhelming. He shuddered, wracked with an uneasy sensation that something was wrong.

The cane fell from his fingers, thumping on the carpet below. He propped his elbows on his knees and buried his face in his hands. Was it possible that his life was slowly unraveling? Audrey had her first come out this year during the Little Season in London, and far too many suitors had tramped through his door throughout October and November. Thankfully he had managed to frighten all of them off.

Audrey had wept quite piteously for weeks after her last suitor had fled when Cedric threatened to pull a pistol on him. If the dandy couldn't stand up to a simple threat then he was not worthy of his sister's time. Audrey needed a real man, not one who would spout drivel at family dinners and holiday gatherings. And children! He wouldn't let Audrey bear the offspring of a spineless sapskull. That would happen over his dead body.

Then there was Horatia. How could he ignore that prickly problem? He wouldn't mind in the least that she remain under his roof and never marry, but he knew that was selfish, and sensed a deep unhappiness in her. If only he knew what could be done to make her happy. He'd seen brief moments of excitement flicker in her eyes ever since Godric's wedding, but he wasn't quite sure what had caused them.

The door to his study opened. The butler stepped through, sighted Cedric and addressed him.

"You have a visitor, my lord."

"Oh? Who is it?" he asked, getting to his feet. Perhaps the evening was looking up?

"Lord Lennox, my lord."

"Show him in."

Cedric grinned as Ashton strolled in. His friend was a welcome sight.

"Ash, you devil. What brings you here?" Cedric clasped his hand in warm greeting. Even though it had been only a day since they'd last met, it felt like ages. Melancholy often had that effect on him.

"I thought I might enjoy the evening with you. Jonathan is having dinner with Emily and Godric."

"And Horatia," Cedric added. His sister had told him she'd made plans to dine at Essex House.

"Oh? He did not mention..." Ashton's brows drew together. "He must have forgotten."

"It was last minute as I understand it. Care for a brandy?"

"Yes, thank you." Ashton shrugged out of his dark blue coat. Had Audrey been here, she would have oohed and ahhed over the silver waistcoat's finely embroidered pattern of birds in gold thread. A fleet of swallows, if Cedric was any judge. While Charles was the most interested in fashion among their number, Ashton was always elegant and presentable. Cedric, on the other hand, tended to put on whatever his valet laid out for the day. He didn't give much thought to his appearance beyond that, much to his valet's horror. The poor man likely wished he had a master more appreciative in the time and care taken to set his wardrobe to rights, but Cedric couldn't find it in himself to care.

Cedric poured him a drink and the two men took chairs near the fire.

"And where is young Audrey this evening?" Ashton inquired.

"She is dining at Charles's."

"Oh?" The single syllable held such heavy innuendo that Cedric blinked and watched his friend more closely. He was up to something.

"She's gone to his home for dinners before," Cedric pointed out.

"She's not a little girl anymore, Cedric. She's a young lady out in society. A dinner with Charles without a proper chaperone is tempting ruination." Ashton's heavy tone was full of warning.

Cedric bristled at the implication.

"She went to dine there at the Countess of Lonsdale's invitation and took her lady's maid with her." Charles's mother should have shielded Audrey from any impropriety, but he supposed including a chaperone would have been one step better. One could never be too careful.

"On a related subject." Ashton waited until Cedric glanced up. "It just so happens I've been meaning to speak to you about Audrey."

Cedric raised a brow as he sipped his brandy. The warm burn in his throat soothed him. "What on earth about?"

"I believe you should see her settled soon."

Cedric knew what Ashton meant, but feigned ignorance to buy him a moment to secure his temper.

"Settled?"

"Married." The word echoed like canon fire.

Cedric set his brandy aside to scowl at his friend. "Not that my sisters are any concern of yours, but why?"

"I've been speaking to Emily and—"

"Oh Lord," Cedric muttered. Would their suffering at the hands of that meddlesome Duchess never cease? As much as he adored Emily, she could drive him mad.

"Emily has a far better grasp of these matters than you or I, Cedric." Ashton moved to the edge of his chair, propping his hands on his knees. "And she has become one of Audrey's confidantes. Emily came to me, if that puts you in a more amiable mood. For my part I had no intention of bringing up such a delicate subject with you, but she insisted only I could do it."

"Did she now?" Cedric allowed his sarcasm to show.

"Yes, she did. She believes you are less likely to draw a pistol on me than the others for suggesting something as shocking as marriage." Ashton was no stranger to sarcasm either.

"Are you offering yourself in this discussion?" Cedric asked carefully, his fingers tightening around his glass.

"Of course not. Audrey's a darling woman, but I've no interest in settling down with someone like her."

"Too good for my sister, Lennox?" Cedric slammed his drink down on the side table between their chairs.

Ashton gave him a rueful smile. "You know my shipping line requires my constant attention and frequent voyages, and she is a lady who belongs in London if there ever was one. It would be most unfair to a sweet young bride. And you, my friend, are trying to make this about me, rather than her."

"Fine, fine. But you aren't telling me this without having a suggestion at hand, are you." It wasn't a question. Ashton would have thought this discussion through long before and come up with options.

"I had thought that Jonathan would make a suitable match. He's not too much older than she is. Eighteen and twenty-four is not so great a distance."

Cedric nearly spat out his brandy, which would have most certainly ruined the carpets. "Jonathan?" he sputtered. "You can't be serious!"

"I'm quite serious. You don't have any objection to him because of his background?"

The question was insulting. Cedric had never paid heed to titles and didn't care one whit about Jonathan's background. "No, of course not."

"Then what has upset you? He needs an easier way into society. Marriage to Audrey would secure his place very nicely."

"Secure his place? My sister is not a rung on a bloody social ladder!" he bellowed.

"I'm not saying that she is, so you may stop that infernal shouting." Ashton kept his cool as always. "Listen, Cedric. Audrey is very taken with Jonathan. She told Emily she has a mind to set her cap for him. Why not let her? Jonathan is a good sort."

"He's a St. Laurent." Surely Ashton knew better than to suggest Audrey marry a rakehell. She needed a good, loyal man who could handle her when her temper flared and more importantly, wouldn't seek the beds of other women. Surely there had to be one man in England that was a more appropriate match.

Ashton nodded. "Granted, Godric had a few rough years to be sure. But he's happy with Emily, and he's loyal to her. You know that."

"But who's to say Jonathan will be the same?"

"I've spent quite a lot of time with him lately, and he has taken his new life very seriously. He's no innocent, of course. As you said, he's a St. Laurent. But he is no longer actively pursuing women, not like we were at his age. If he married Audrey, I believe he would settle into the married life without any fuss."

"And here I thought you genuinely wished to see me tonight." Cedric narrowed his eyes. "No, instead you beat down my door to discuss Audrey's suitors and marriage! This might as well be a business meeting. Fancy the rising trend in salted pork? Or should I invest in Mr. Stephenson's new railway scheme in Stockton?"

"What's really troubling you, Cedric?"

"There is nothing troubling me." His grumbled response made him sound like a wounded bear, but he didn't care.

Ashton leaned back in his chair as though settling in. "You are a terrible liar." Why that enraged Cedric, he couldn't say, he only had the sudden urge to blacken one of Ashton's eyes.

"And you are a terrible friend."

Ashton's eyes widening was the only indication of his surprise. "Perhaps you're right. I came here to discuss Audrey's future and I had no thought as to how that would affect you."

Cedric was increasingly uncomfortable. He knew his friend was right but, damn the man, he felt terrible for not having better composure.

"Would you like me to leave?" Ashton asked.

Cedric looked back to the fire. The tense silence became suffocating. Ashton rose from his chair.

"I'll see myself out." He nodded in farewell.

Only when Ashton reached the drawing room door did Cedric call out to him. "You haven't finished your brandy."

Ashton looked back at the lonely glass on the table. "It would be rude of me to leave it half full, I suppose."

"Impossibly rude." Cedric gave the barest hint of a smile. Ashton returned and made a great scene of sitting deep into his chair, as though he would not be leaving anytime soon.

"Now, since I'm not done with my drink, there is plenty of time for us to talk."

It took Cedric a few moments to properly gather his thoughts.

"I'm failing as a brother, Ash. Horatia is dreadfully unhappy, Audrey is distressed over my boorish treatment of her would-be suitors and the truth is that I'm doing everything within my power to not end up here alone." There was the crux of the problem. He didn't want to be left with an empty house, no family, just silence and servants. He feared it like nothing else in the world, save losing those he loved.

"Let us take one problem at a time, shall we? Firstly, you won't be alone. The League is constantly infiltrating your life, and on occasion your home, for our nefarious purposes." The twinkle in Ashton's eyes was a comfort beyond words. "Just because your sisters may someday leave does not plunge you into eternal solitude. You know you may call on any of us at any time should you feel the least bit melancholy. Now, as to Audrey, you know my opinion on the matter. Marry her off to a good man soon, and if it is Jonathan, you'll see her quite often. She loves you far too much to abandon you for any husband. Hasn't our policy always been the more the merrier?"

Cedric grumbled. "Dash it all. I hate how bloody sensible you are. I sound like some mulish fop who fears losing control over something he never actually had control of."

"You're not a fop. Mulish absolutely, but a fop? Never."

"You're very lucky that I like you. Otherwise I would be tempted to point a pistol at you after all."

Ash grinned. "Yes, yes. Now, about Horatia. What is making her unhappy?"

"That's just it. I have no idea."

"Not one?" Ashton seemed surprised.

"She mopes about, sighing and her eyes often seem red as though she's been crying. And then there was this morning with Charles."

"Charles again?" Ashton mused.

"He offered to take her riding, something she usually loves but at first she declined. It was only when I mentioned that Lucien and Audrey would be down soon for breakfast that she couldn't seem to leave fast enough."

"It seems you already have the answer to her unhappiness."

"I do?" What the devil was Ash playing at?

"Of course. Horatia has no problem with her sister, does she?"

Cedric swirled his brandy glass, considering the morning's odd turn of events. "Well, no, other than the usual sisterly squabbles."

"And the only other person you mentioned was?" Ashton prompted.

"Lucien? But why would she…" Cedric didn't want to consider what that meant.

"That is what we must discover," Ashton said.

"But Lucien barely notices her."

"Perhaps that is the problem. No one likes to be ignored, especially on purpose."

"But she's gotten along fine with it for years. It has only been since September when Emily first came here that Horatia started showing signs of unhappiness."

Ashton's eyes narrowed. "How very curious."

"Not really. Lucien blames her for ruining his match to Melanie Burns all those years ago."

This caught the fair-haired baron completely off guard. "Pardon?"

Cedric explained the long buried secret of that day in the gardens when he'd taken his sisters to Lucien's estate in Kent.

"She said she loved him? Perhaps that's it. She still does," Ashton suggested.

"How could she love someone who won't spare a moment's thought for her?" His sister was smarter than that. She wouldn't pin her hopes on such a man. Horatia was sensible, not a fool.

Ashton sighed. "Aren't you familiar with the term 'unrequited love?'"

"This isn't a joke, Ash."

"I'm not speaking in jest. It's probable that Horatia is still in love with Lucien. She has seen too much of him lately and has suffered his cold manner and it has made her upset."

"If that is the case then it is my fault. I've been pushing him to stay here more often and I haven't cared to think about his feelings in the matter, or hers it would seem."

"Do not punish yourself. There is every chance that Lucien sees Horatia as some form of temptation and treating her coldly is a way of keeping his distance."

"What on earth do you mean?"

Ashton took a sip of his brandy. "We have our rules, remember, and Lucien has a sister. He understands the brotherly instinct to protect those under his charge. It is possible that he fears Horatia will someday be a target, however unintentional, of his natural charm." Ashton stroked his jaw. "Therefore he is cold to her, in hopes her declaration of love from years ago never resurfaces."

"I don't follow. Are you saying he *desires* my sister?" The idea of Lucien even thinking of Horatia as he would any other woman made Cedric's blood boil. He refused to believe it.

The other man merely smiled.

"Never mind, Cedric. We won't worry any more about it tonight." Ashton took another sip of his drink.

A sudden pounding on the front door alerted both men to the world outside their thoughts.

"Now who the devil could that be?" Cedric muttered. He and Ash abandoned their brandy and headed into the hall where a tired footman was already moving to open the door.

Charles stormed in, dragging a disheveled, swollen-lipped and upset Audrey. Cedric, unusually observant about his sister tonight, immediately assessed the clearly dangerous situation. Someone had been kissing his sister, kissing her hard enough to give her that singularly bee-stung plumpness to her lips. Furthermore, she was upset, though not as though she meant to cry. No, she was livid, like a spitting mad cat.

"What on earth?" Cedric began.

"Sheridan!" Charles snapped as he shoved Audrey deeper into the hallway as the footman shut the door.

"Charles?" Cedric replied in shock.

"You have to do something about your sister! Marry her to the first oaf in Hyde Park if you must, but for God's sake, get her married!" After Charles's violent outburst the hall became deathly silent.

"Oh dear," Ashton said. This would not end well.

CHAPTER 9

"Not a penny until the conditions are met, and there is dirt falling upon a grave."

Horatia's heart shot into her throat as she struggled to listen to the low voice on the other side of the garden hedge.

"Oh my God," Horatia hissed at the same time that Lucien growled, "That bastard!"

Lucien pulled Horatia by the hand back through the hedges and once more into their room.

"We have to leave now," he said in a tone rough.

"I can see myself home." She couldn't keep her voice from shaking.

"No chance of that, Horatia. I'm taking you to Godric's."

Horatia froze.

"How...how long have you known?" Her hands flew to her mask, still firmly in place.

"How long have I known what?" Lucien asked as he grabbed his overcoat and cloaked it around her shoulders.

"How long have you known it was me?" She fought to remain

calm, despite the wild gallop of her heart, and clutched his coat tighter around her.

"Since you walked in the door."

Horatia's stomach pitched straight towards her feet.

"What we did...that was..." She had no words to say anything more. "And you knew!" Her tone came out more accusatory than she intended. She had meant to seduce *him* after all.

"Tonight was a lesson for you to be careful around men," Lucien replied. "A lady of your standing shouldn't be here. What would Cedric think if he found out?"

"What about the garden? The stars? Was it all a lie?" Horatia's lower lip shook, but the anger she wished she could summon did not appear. She was bruised and hurting inside. Why was it whenever Lucien was around to wound her she lost the urge to fight? Was it because she cared so much about him that she didn't want to quarrel?

"Everything that happened tonight was a lie. Deep down you knew that. I gave you what you sought while retaining your virtue, at least in the most literal sense. Others would not be so considerate. I was playing along for your benefit."

"My benefit? Don't you dare cheapen what happened between us!" Horatia winced at the shrillness of her own voice. Her right hand raised as though to slap Lucien. "I won't let you!"

"Go ahead, my dear. Strike me for my villainous ways and my dastardly schemes. But we have more serious matters to attend to." Lucien waited patiently for her to slap him but Horatia, tears stinging her eyes, merely shook her head and took a step back.

"Even though you deserve it, I could never willingly hurt you." She turned away from him. This only seemed to infuriate him, however. He chased her to the door, grabbed her shoulders and spun her around.

"I don't want you to feel anything for me," he hissed. "Not love, not pity, not even kindness. Do you understand?"

Horatia managed a sad smile. "I understand. But it doesn't change how I feel." Her words seemed to light a fire within him.

He pressed hard against her, hands raking up and down her body. Lucien forced his mouth down over hers, scorching her with the violence of his kiss. Horatia melted into him, knowing he hated her for it. He cupped her bottom, jerked her tighter into him, demanding with his aggression that she scream and fight him off. It was as though he ached to wound her but nothing could compare to his betrayal of her heart.

"Fight me, damn you!" he snarled. "Strike me. Hate me." But Horatia offered only soft lips and yielding caresses until he pulled away.

She raised her chin, unafraid and determined to prove it to him. "I won't. You're trying to frighten me on purpose. It won't work. You'd never hurt me."

The growl at the back of his throat was wild and warning her to stay away.

Glowering, he moved her aside so he could open the door, then pulled her along by the wrist until they were leaving the Midnight Garden's townhouse. Lucien called for the footman near the main door to summon a hackney.

When the coach rolled up, Lucien shoved her inside and instructed the driver to go to Half Moon Street. He didn't apologize. Didn't say a single word. He tore off his mask and when he caught her staring, he leaned over and ripped off her mask as well, then tossed both onto the floor. She kept her eyes on him.

"Stop looking at me!" Lucien shouted. Horatia flinched, but did not look away. "Did you hear me?"

"I suspect all of London heard you." Her tone was surprisingly cool. She was rather proud of herself, standing up to him so.

"Then do as I say."

"I may care for you, but that doesn't mean I have to obey you. Especially when you are being so rude. It's not as though we're married."

"Heaven forbid I ever suffer that fate."

Despite his cruel words Horatia could not do as he asked. She was unable to look away from the depths of his hazel eyes. He had no idea just how alive she was when he touched her. Even his roughness made her burn with desire. She longed to fight back, to match his passion, but until he loved her in return, she could not give in to that side of herself. There would be no turning back if she ever showed him the darker side of her nature—the secret, forbidden desires she longed to fulfill in his arms. It was better if he never know how truly alike they were.

They managed the rest of the coach ride in silence. When they reached Essex House, Lucien ordered her to stay put. She did obey this time, but only because she needed a moment to herself, to get control of her emotions.

Once Lucien left the carriage, the tears started. She sniffed and wiped her eyes, trying to swallow the painful lump in her throat. Tonight had been such a wonderful dream, until Lucien had ruined it. The pig-headed fool. How could he have faked such sweet emotions? Would he never again call her his lovely stargazer? Had that too been a lie?

God, I'm the one who's a fool.

She admitted twice tonight that she cared for him only to have him scorn her for it. Horatia wasn't a child anymore, but it seemed clear that Lucien still thought her to be the enemy. She wasn't even worthy of a second chance.

Her mind flashed back to that moment on the bed, when he'd driven her to a height of pleasure and comforted her as she experienced the frightening spiral of sensations. How was she supposed to reconcile that sweet, seductive man with the overbearing tyrant he'd become when his mask was off? He could be as different as light and dark and the constant switching back and forth was driving her mad.

Horatia hastily wiped her face as she heard a number of voices approach. She moved over to allow Emily, Jonathan, Godric and Lucien into the coach. It was a tight fit, the three gentleman all pressed on one side, allowing the ladies to have the opposite bench.

"Ouch, Jonathan, that's my knee!" Lucien hissed.

"Isn't this cozy?" Jonathan laughed. Godric grunted as Lucien jabbed an elbow into his ribs when trying to settle back into the seat.

Horatia found herself reluctantly smiling as the three grown men squirmed against each other like fidgety schoolboys.

"Are you going to tell us what this is about, Lucien?" Godric asked once the coach started moving again, this time towards Curzon Street.

"I shall explain once we're at Cedric's. It will be best if I tell everyone at once. That way if anyone has questions, I won't have to repeat myself." His eyes warned Horatia to say nothing.

"Very well," Godric grumbled, trying again to settle in and looking more than a little surly.

Emily leaned over to Horatia and asked in a low whisper, "Where were you tonight? I thought you were coming to dinner?"

"It's a long story, one I can only share when we're alone. But would you cover for me? If Cedric asks, could you say I was at dinner with you?"

"Absolutely," Emily assured her. "I'll let the others know."

"What are you two whispering about?" Godric watched the pair of them curiously.

"Probably the overthrow of Parliament," Lucien said sourly.

"Don't be silly. That was weeks ago. We've moved on to Europe now," Emily replied with a dark grin.

Godric snorted. "Clearly you have too much free time on your hands, darling. I shall have to correct that once we return home." He flashed his wife a grin that Emily returned with interest.

"Now what are you *really* up to?" he asked.

"It is none of your concern, darling." Emily now dared to smile sweetly at her husband who frowned.

"You are my concern."

"Of course, darling." She agreed as though they'd had this discussion many times before.

"Emily." Godric crossed his arms over his chest.

"It doesn't concern me. Therefore it is none of your concern either."

When he started to protest, she kicked him in the shin with the tip of her boot.

"Ow!" He gasped in indignation more than pain.

"Oh I'm dreadfully sorry, did that hurt? How clumsy of me! This coach is awfully crowded."

"You will pay for that, my dear."

"And I expect I shall quite enjoy it." For a brief second, Horatia worried the newly married couple would forget that there were three other people in the carriage and engage in public displays of affection.

Horatia envied the love that so clearly bound Godric and Emily. Would she ever have that? The odds didn't appear to be in her favor.

When the coach arrived at Cedric's townhouse, Lucien leaped out and dashed up the steps. Godric followed, helping his wife down. Jonathan was next but waited patiently to assist Horatia. She noted the pair of masks lying on the carriage floor and picked them up, one black and one silver. She bit her bottom lip. Tonight the last of her childhood dreams had been crushed. Never again would she entertain such foolish thoughts of love and happiness. She wished she had the strength to cast away the masks, but her fingers wouldn't let go of them. She exited the coach, taking Jonathan's offered hand for support.

"Thank you," she whispered.

"You are most welcome," he replied, a smile of genuine affection on his handsome face.

Jonathan was a true gentleman, and it was a pity Audrey was so infatuated with him. Horatia ought to have fallen in love with a man like him. At least then she would be respected. Perhaps not loved, but she was going to have to accept that. She was doomed to never love again.

"It seems we are not the first to arrive," Jonathan observed as he joined her in the open doorway.

They were met by an unpleasant sight. Ashton had his arms about Audrey's waist, holding her back. Cedric was throttling Charles against the wall, his feet off the ground and poor Charles's face was a rather disconcerting shade of purple.

"What the devil?" Jonathan blurted out. Godric had already rushed to pull Cedric off of Charles.

"What in God's name is going on?" Lucien demanded.

Audrey delivered a sharp elbow into Ashton's ribs as she fought to free herself. When Audrey tried to deliver another such blow, Ashton spun her delicately into Jonathan's unsuspecting embrace.

"Hold her, man!" Ashton ordered. "And watch the elbows, they're like fire pokers!" Jonathan's arms locked about Audrey's waist, holding her captive. Now that Ashton was free, he sighed and rubbed a hand over his ribs.

"It seems Charles compromised Audrey this evening," Ashton said, finally answering Godric and Lucien's questions.

"What?" Emily's head whipped towards Ashton in disbelief.

Godric finally succeeded in wrenching Cedric away, and Charles collapsed to his hands and knees, wheezing.

"Cedric, we don't have time for this," Lucien cut in. "Something important has happened. Don't give me that look, it's more important that your sister's honor."

"What could be more important than that?"

"The safety of yourself and everyone you hold dear."

"What on earth are you talking about? You don't mean that note on my door, do you? I thought we'd agreed they were more idle threats?"

"I will be happy to explain, but we ought to send the women upstairs. There is much to discuss, and I haven't the time to deal with feminine hysterics," Lucien said.

His callous remark drew an arched brow from Emily and a glare from Audrey.

Godric came over, prepared for his wife to fight him. "I quite agree. It is a matter that cannot be shared with the ladies."

Emily held up a hand. "We will retire upstairs as you so politely requested. I would rather be in the company of hysterical women than ridiculous men. Ladies?" Emily indicated for Audrey and Horatia to follow her. Horatia was the first up the stairs, but Audrey still had to free herself from Jonathan.

"Let go!" she growled.

He looked down at her, holding her in his arms, as though surprised she was still there. Audrey stomped on his toes and he jumped back with a shout. She huffed and stalked up after Emily and her sister. Cedric trailed them all the way to Horatia's room and once inside he locked the the door. Audrey shouted vile curses no lady and few sailors should have known, some of it in French, ending with a hearty kick to the door. Unfortunately, her slippers were not the most effective weapons and she let out a yelp of pain. She hopped madly back and forth, clutching her bruised toes.

"Why on earth did you let them lock us away?" Audrey whined.

"Because you haven't been subjected to the indignities I have when those men downstairs don't get their way. It is most unpleasant to be manhandled, and far more undignified than this." Emily smoothed her midnight blue velvet skirts and sat down on Horatia's bed, looking at her expectantly. "Besides, I believe Horatia knows exactly what is going on."

Audrey looked to her sister as she limped over and joined Emily on the bed. "Well?"

Horatia sighed. "Very well. But you must not say a word until I'm finished. No, Audrey, not even a peep."

Audrey, whose lips had already opened up, stopped and clamped back shut.

After a brief narration of the night's events, heavily edited for propriety's sake, Horatia waited for either of her companions to speak. Worry shaded Emily's eyes, turning them a deeper shade of purple. Audrey just blinked, gaped and blinked again.

"This is more serious than I thought. There is a death threat out on your brother?"

Horatia nodded. "Lucien seems to know who is behind it, but

he cannot understand why the men were discussing it in such a place."

"The Midnight Gardens are renowned for secrecy," Emily said. "Everyone seeks it and so nobody listens upon another's private matters.

Horatia pursed her lips a moment. "There is another possibility. Maybe they wanted to be overheard?"

"But why?" Audrey asked. "What advantage would that give them? We know Cedric is in danger now and we can protect him."

Horatia met Emily's gaze, reading the other woman's thoughts. "Audrey, remember when Cedric took you shooting once? He had a groundskeeper swat at the underbrush to shake the pheasants out of their hiding places. Perhaps they are shaking the bushes and waiting for them all to fly out."

Audrey paled. "Oh dear, then that would mean he has some plan in place and likely knows how Cedric and the other men will react."

"Exactly," Emily said. "Since they will not recognize the trap, nor will they know how to escape it even if we warn them, it may be left up to us to protect them from themselves."

For a long moment none of the ladies spoke as they contemplated the dangerous task ahead.

"You really are in love with Lucien?" Emily asked, mercifully changing the subject.

The rush of heat to Horatia's face betrayed any denials she might have made. "I am. It's a stupid, foolish thing to love someone like him, but I can't help it."

Emily laughed, the sound delicate, but her eyes were sharp. "I fell in love with Godric the same way. I was convinced the entire time it was bound to end in disaster and heartbreak, yet it didn't."

Biting her lower lip, Horatia considered this. "Godric loves you, though. Lucien doesn't love me. I think he doesn't even really like me at all."

Emily snorted, though not inelegantly. "I think there's a fair chance he may fall in love with you. I have learned a few things about these men. Lucien wouldn't have kissed you if he hadn't wanted to. Not only that, but I've seen signs of possessiveness and jealousy where you're concerned, not disgust."

Horatia's heart fluttered in excitement though she tried to hide it. "You have?"

"Oh yes. He glowers at any man who kisses your hand, and always escorts you into dinner whenever we dine together."

They were fair points, but they didn't exactly prove Lucien's undying love.

"Now, let's return to this assassination business. We know Waverly wants the League dead, and it seems now they mean to start with your brother. I'm sure Lucien was upset."

"I don't know that it was Waverly," Horatia said. "Lucien said he recognized the voice, but didn't say whose it was."

"Waverly is the only man I know that seems to come up in their conversations when they speak of enemies," Emily said.

"No wonder they sent us upstairs," Horatia mused. "No doubt those foolish men are making plans to go to war and want to keep us out of harm's way. It is a thoughtful gesture."

"Thoughtful?" Audrey objected. "They want to ruin our fun."

"I'd hardly call such a threat fun," said Emily. "But keeping us out, no matter how well intended, is a mistake."

"Well, we ought to formulate our own plan then," Horatia declared. "We are capable of far more than they give us credit." If her brother's life really was in danger, she wasn't about to let the men handle it alone. She would protect her brother on her terms.

"That is an excellent idea!" Audrey jumped to her feet as though they were planning a party.

Emily was already deep in thought. "It is. But first, I'd like to know why Cedric was trying to do away with Charles. This is the worst possible time for the League to be divided, and I can't help but remember our last conversation, Audrey."

Audrey flushed. "I...I know you said you would talk to Ashton about Jonathan, but I was having trouble waiting."

A laugh escaped from Horatia. "You always were too impulsive."

Emily pursed her lips as if bracing herself for disaster. "Audrey, what exactly did you do?"

"I convinced Charles to help me."

Horatia narrowed her eyes. "Help you *how?*"

"He may have introduced me to the finer points of kissing," Audrey confessed.

"Audrey!" Horatia gasped. Would her sister never learn that actions had consequences? Admittedly she wasn't one to talk, given her own night's events, but she knew Lucien would never be forced to marry her. Audrey and Charles might end up engaged if Audrey wasn't more careful.

"It was an intriguing experience, given that I have no real attraction to Charles."

"Audrey, you didn't let him kiss you?" Emily pressed. No wonder Cedric had been murderous. "I warned you about—"

"Nothing happened, except that I kissed him. He didn't even kiss me back. To get this way—" she gestured to her disheveled appearance "—he fixed my clothes and hair and told me to bite my lips a bit. I wanted Cedric to think that I'd been compromised. I'd hoped he might allow me to marry Jonathan instead..."

Horatia sucked in a breath at her sister's brash behavior. *Am I the only sane Sheridan in the family?* As soon as the question passed her mind she stifled a groan of embarrassment. She was no better than Audrey, really.

"And he did it to help you?" Emily sounded dubious.

"Oh yes." Audrey nodded. "But he took some convincing. He was quite angry with me, especially after I accosted him in his own drawing room. The poor man hid behind a couch to escape me."

It was simply too amusing an image, Charles scrambling over furniture to escape the kisses of a pretty debutante. Horatia had to bite down on her fist to still her urge to laugh outright.

Emily was not so restrained. "I would have given the world to see that!" she said, gasping for air, laughing.

Horatia was wiping tears from her eyes. Audrey was back to her old self, imitating Charles's fall off the couch when she'd kissed him. She made a theatrical squawk and toppled to the floor with a thud. By now Horatia was laughing so hard she could scarcely breathe.

ONE FLOOR BELOW, LUCIEN AND THE OTHER MEMBERS OF THE League gazed up at the drawing room's ceiling. Arms crossed over his chest, he raised a brow as they listened to the strange noises from above.

There was a loud shriek, a thud, and hoots of unrestrained laughter.

"What the deuce is going on up there?" Charles asked.

"Probably jumping on the beds," Cedric grumbled.

"They're no longer children," said Lucien. "Someone should tell them."

"Do you suppose it was wise to leave them alone up there?" Godric asked. His head was tilted like a dog hearing strange sounds.

"They're fine." Now that he'd caught them up on more relevant events, Lucien had to bring them back to the point of the meeting. Lives were in danger. "Now, what are we going to do about this threat?"

"Waverly won't succeed," Cedric said with confidence. "We can defend ourselves."

"Nevertheless," said Godric, "it would be unwise if one of us wasn't keeping an eye on you and your sisters. Even if Waverly intends to kill you, they might get harmed in the crossfire."

"I don't intend to let them leave the house," said Cedric. "If they absolutely must, they'll have an escort."

"We mustn't forget how easily the defenses here were breached in the fall," Ashton reminded the others. "That was a close call with the man who stole Emily. This is a house, not a fortress."

Lucien vowed never to feel that helpless protecting Horatia.

But Cedric could not be pulled so easily from his previous source of rage. "Before we discuss Horatia, I need to defend Audrey from that damned bloody cur," Cedric shot a finger at Charles, "who seduced her in a bloody coach!"

"I did not seduce her, Cedric." Charles raised his hands in defense in case Cedric lunged at him again. "I warned you she ought to marry soon. You're lucky she came to me first. Another man might have actually taken advantage of her."

"Are you saying you didn't touch her?" Cedric demanded.

"Touch? Yes, but I didn't kiss her. She asked for my assistance to make her look compromised."

"Look compromised? You *bastard*!" Cedric looked ready to go after Charles again. "Women have been ruined for such a thing as a lustful glance, and you go and muss up my sister? What if word got out to the Quizzing Glass of her appearance? Then she would never find a suitor."

Ashton stepped between the two of them, throwing up a hand to prevent Cedric from advancing.

"Come now, gentlemen." Ashton's steely tone stopped the two men. "Do we need to solve this in a ring?"

"I wouldn't recommend that," Godric said with a wry grin. "But if it does come to it, I'll stake ten pounds on Charles."

Both Cedric and Charles shared cautious looks with one another before declining, perhaps in part because none of the others would take that bet. Ashton dropped his hand when he seemed satisfied that Cedric would not resume trying to kill Charles. Lucien gave a sigh of relief. He had no desire to jump between his friends. Charles was a champion boxer and Lucien didn't want a blackened eye simply because he'd try to impose peace. If Ashton wished to risk his face, that was entirely up to him.

Jonathan, who had lingered at the edge of the group, suddenly spoke up. "Is this how all of your League meetings go? Perhaps we might focus ourselves back on the real problem and the importance of protecting the ladies."

Ashton turned to Cedric, his voice hard. "Quite right, Jonathan. Back to the matter at hand. I think it would be best, Cedric, if you take Horatia and Audrey away from London, at least until the rest of us sort this out."

"You want me to turn tail and run?" Cedric looked shocked and outraged at the very idea.

"You know I would never ask that of you." Ashton's voice was softer now. "But for your sisters' sake, yes. You'd grab them and run to the ends of the earth if it would protect them. We all know this."

The fierce resistance in Cedric wavered against the persuasive power of Ashton's reasonable request.

Cedric slumped. "Where would you have me go then?"

Godric chimed in. "Some place Waverly would not immediately think to look for you."

Lucien's heartbeat kicked up as he realized the perfect place to keep Horatia safe. "How about my estate in Kent? You could take your sisters there and stay until the New Year. My mother is in residence along with Lysandra and Linus, so you'd be properly entertained." He didn't need to add that, should Hugo's men make discreet enquiries as to where they might have gone, Lucien's estate would be the last name on their lists.

Getting the Sheridan sisters out of London seemed like a very good plan. Anything to get them out of the line of danger, and Horatia away from him. Two birds with one stone, so they say.

"That's an excellent idea," Ashton agreed. "The rest of us can remain here and attempt to sort this mess out. Lucien, you'll accompany Cedric and his sisters, of course."

"What?" Lucien sputtered. That was the worst idea in the history of the world. Put *him* in his estate with Horatia where he knew every nook and cranny he could secret her away to? Damnation! "I could be of more use dealing with Hugo's men," he countered.

"It is your estate," Ashton reminded him in a firm tone. "And you were also the first one targeted in these attacks. You will escort Cedric and his sisters. Hopefully this issue will be resolved before Christmas. If not, then you will be with your family for the holidays."

That did not make the situation any more appealing. Lucien fought the urge to stamp his feet like a boy in a temper tantrum. Jonathan shared a sympathetic look with him, as though he seemed to know just what being around Horatia would do to him. Was that how Jonathan felt around Audrey; did he have an interest in the younger Sheridan woman, the way she did in him?

Here he was trying to do the decent thing and stay away from temptation, and Ashton was practically handing Horatia to him on a silver platter. He needed her to be safe—not just from the Waverly but from himself. Having her so close to his bed at home was the opposite of safe.

What other choice did he have though?

"Fine," Lucien said with poor grace. "I will go with Cedric."

He didn't want to spend hours in a coach with Horatia, and he certainly did not want to be stuck at his estate with her over the holidays. It was worse knowing that his mother would be there. She had an irritating way of meddling in his affairs, and he feared she would interfere with Horatia. His mother had a soft spot for the Sheridans, Horatia in particular. Letting his mother near Horatia would be more trouble than he wanted to deal with.

"When should we leave?" Cedric asked Ashton.

"As soon as possible. Do you think your sisters could be ready by first light?"

Cedric barked out a harsh laugh. "First light tomorrow? Absolutely not. You must at least give Audrey a day to pack or the little devil will harass me about it all the way to Kent."

"A day then, but I want the lot of you packed and in your carriages before the sun rises." Ashton was deadly serious. "Godric and I will go tomorrow morning to the Midnight Garden and see if we can't catch the two men from last night at their arranged time.

I'd like to see for myself if there is any proof it was Waverly. We need to know what we're up against."

"Now that's all settled," Cedric growled, "would all of you mind getting the hell out of my house?"

"Capital idea," Godric said. His eyes then drifted to the ceiling.

"It's awfully quiet up there," Jonathan observed.

"Too quiet," Lucien agreed. Suddenly anxious, the six men proceeded out of the drawing room and up the stairs towards Horatia's room. The door was still locked. Lucien leaned against the wood and listened. Not a sound came from within.

CHAPTER 10

"Do you hear them?" Charles asked.

Cedric held a finger to his lips.

Lucien strained to hear even the smallest rustle or creak, but heard nothing. Cautiously, Cedric unlocked and opened the door. The bedchamber was empty. The windows were closed and latched and there was no sign of the women.

"Ash?" Godric said in a low whisper. Ashton nodded and proceeded inside, his sharp gaze leaving nothing unseen. There was no evidence the women had hidden themselves. No sign of hasty departure. They had simply vanished.

"Where the bloody hell is my wife?" Godric yelled into the aether.

As if in response, a footman came up the stairs and handed Cedric a slip of paper. Dumbfounded, Cedric opened it and read it aloud.

My Dear Gentlemen,

We await you in the dining room. Please do not join us until you have decided upon a course of action regarding the threat to Lord Sheridan. We will be more than delighted to offer our opinions on the matter, but in truth, we suspect you do not wish to hear our thoughts. It is a failing of the male species, and we shan't hold it against you. In the future, however, it would be advisable not to lock us in a room. We simply cannot resist a challenge, something you should have learned by now. Intelligent women are not to be trifled with.

Fondest Regards,
~The Society of Rebellious Ladies~

"FONDEST REGARDS?" LUCIEN SCOFFED.

A puzzled Jonathan added, "Society of Rebellious Ladies?"

"Lord help us!" Ashton groaned as he ran a hand through his hair. "They've named themselves."

"I'll wager a hundred pounds that Emily's behind this. Having a laugh at our expense," Charles said in all seriousness.

"Let's go and see how rebellious they are when we're done with them." Cedric rolled up the sleeves of his white lawn shirt as he and the others stalked down the stairs to the dining room. They found it empty. The footman reappeared and Cedric wondered if perhaps the man had never left. At the servant's polite cough he handed Cedric a second note.

"Another damn note? What are they playing at?" He practically tore the paper in half while opening it. Again he read it aloud.

DID YOU HONESTLY BELIEVE WE'D DISPLAY OUR CUNNING IN SO simple a fashion? Surely you underestimated us. It is quite unfair of you to assume we could not baffle you for at least a few minutes. Perhaps you should look for us in the place where we ought to have been and not the place you put us.

Best Wishes,
~The Society of Rebellious Ladies~

. . .

"I am going to kill her," Cedric said. It didn't seem to matter which of the three rebellious ladies he meant.

The League of Rogues headed back to the drawing room. Cedric flung the door open. Emily was sitting before the fire, an embroidery frame raised as she pricked the cloth with a fine pointed needle. Audrey was perusing one of her many fashion magazines, eyes fixed on the illustrated plates, oblivious to any disruption.

Horatia had positioned herself on the window seat near a candle, so she could read her novel. Even at this distance Lucien could see the title, *Lady Eustace and the Merry Marquess*, the novel he'd purchased for her last Christmas. For some reason, the idea she would mock him with his own gift was damned funny. He had the sudden urge to laugh, especially when he saw a soft blush work its way up through her. He'd picked that particular book just to shock her, knowing it was quite explicit in parts since he'd read it himself the previous year.

"Ahem," Cedric cleared his throat. Three sets of feminine eyes fixed on him, each reflecting only mild curiosity.

Emily smiled. "Oh there you are."

"Are you finished with your little meeting?" Audrey asked, setting down her magazine and smiling up at her brother.

The way she'd said "little meeting" left Lucien with no doubt they were having fun at their expense, or perhaps it was her biting her bottom lip to prevent her laughter that gave her away. Regardless, Cedric's sisters had challenged the men and they were in no mood to play games. Especially Cedric.

"You." Cedric pointed to Audrey. "Bed, now!" His accusing finger then swept towards Emily. "Since when do you embroider? I distinctly recall you telling me once that such a thing was a complete and utter waste of time."

"Considering your rather callous behavior tonight in leaving us out of your decisions, I decided to renew the rather useless habit," Emily replied as though speaking of the weather. She politely held up the embroidery hoop, which was festooned with flowers around a simple phrase every single man in the room could read, *Never Challenge a Woman*. Lucien could only imagine how she must have embroidered that in so short a time.

"We left you out of it because this matter doesn't concern any of you ladies. Besides, it is a delicate and dangerous situation," Cedric said.

"Hmm," Emily responded, the feminine sound came out strangely condescending. "Perhaps we ladies are keeping you out of a dangerous situation and haven't bothered to inform you of our intentions. If you insist on keeping us in the dark, we will persist in our efforts to keep all of you alive regardless of your belief that we are incapable females."

Godric frowned. "No one said you were incapable. You know we don't think that, Emily."

Horatia came to Emily's defense. "She's right. You keep secrets from us that will only divide us and put us all at risk. You will explain yourself, Cedric. I will not leave this house until you tell me what you and the others have planned."

"Fine, tomorrow morning, I'll tell you, but not tonight. It's late and everyone needs their rest," her brother shot back.

"Nonsense, you can tell us right now," Emily insisted.

"Godric, collect your wife and take her home before I use her as a pincushion," Cedric threatened.

Godric, who tried to hide an appreciative smirk, seemed to find his wife's besting of the men most amusing. At Cedric's impatient tone, however, he jumped into action.

"Come along, Em. I believe you've made your point for now." He picked up the embroidered frame and tossed it on a nearby empty chair. He then wrapped an arm about her waist to pull her to him, planting a kiss on her brow.

"You wouldn't let him use me as pincushion would you, darling?" she asked, twining her arm through his after he released her.

"Never, my dear. He's just annoyed that he can't figure how you got out of Horatia's room when he locked you in, or come here undetected."

Emily cast an arrogant glance at Cedric's direction. "And he never will."

"But you'll tell me, won't you?" Godric looked down at his wife in adoration.

"Perhaps, if you entice me enough."

"Are you asking me to seduce you?"

"What else would I be asking?" Emily laughed.

"Oh for the love of all that is holy! Take her away Godric," Cedric pleaded. Shows of such tender teasing always seemed to distress him.

"He's right, Emily, we ought to go home." He tucked her into his side as he escorted her from the room.

"I should be going as well." Ashton bowed to the others and departed in Godric and Emily's wake.

"Jonathan, would you be so kind as to return Audrey upstairs? She seems not to have heard me when I told her to go to bed," Cedric said.

Jonathan tried to argue. "Under the circumstances, tonight I would prefer not to, what with your reaction to Charles—"

"Unlike Charles, you have a sense of honor. I trust you enough to escort her upstairs."

Charles and Lucien watched the scene unfold with no small amount of amusement. Cedric seemed oblivious to the position he was putting Jonathan in. Lucien opened his mouth to say something, but thought better of it when he noticed Cedric's scowl.

"And you!" Cedric finally turned his wrath to Horatia but found himself unable to do anything with it. "Well, er, I'll get back to you." He turned to Charles and without warning, punched him square in the eye.

"That is for compromising my sister, you scoundrel. I hope it blackens well and warns women against straying from their moral compasses in your presence, at least for a sennight."

Charles groaned and clutched his face. "I was helping Audrey.

If you don't understand that, then I will take my leave and see you again when your temper has cooled." He mockingly bowed to them and departed. Without another word Cedric left the drawing room, slamming the door behind him.

Audrey watched the two remaining men, Lucien and Jonathan, as they stood at the opposite end of the drawing room. Jonathan eyed Audrey with hesitation, then looked to Lucien, who shrugged indifferently. She bit her lip, trying not to smile. Watching him squirm was more than a little amusing.

"Miss Audrey, would you please accompany me upstairs? I should like to—" but Audrey cut him off.

"No, I don't think I shall," she declared. All of the men had been so boorish this evening she wasn't about to give ground, not even for him.

She reached for her fashion magazine again. Jonathan's eyes narrowed. She feigned a yawn, noting the way his nostrils flared and his fists clenched. There was a wicked pleasure to be found in getting under his skin. She knew he only wanted to cement his role in the League and she was making that difficult.

"She needs a firm hand, Jonathan. Show her who's in charge," Lucien encouraged as he leaned back against the wall, grinning.

Jonathan grimaced and walked over to Audrey's chair.

"Miss Audrey." This time his tone was clearly a warning. "You will come with me at once."

With a lift of her chin, Audrey declared war. "You wouldn't *dare* touch me, not after what my brother did to Charles." Secretly she hoped he would be daring enough. The thrill of making him work for her attention left her heart beating madly.

"Audrey, don't encourage him," Horatia cut in. Clearly she saw the storm brewing. Her sister abandoned her book and made to stand, but Lucien pushed away from the wall, blocking her.

Horatia dropped back down into her seat as she met Audrey's gaze and gave a warning shake of her head.

"I would dare to touch you, and more, you rebellious little chit," Jonathan said. Before she had time to properly react, he scooped her up into his arms.

She kicked and squirmed. He was ruining the way she'd planned their encounter. It wasn't supposed to go this way. She wanted to be seduced! When her struggles proved futile, she retaliated in a way that worked against small children and unruly pets.

She rolled her magazine into a tube and started whacking him over the head while screaming, "Have at it, you fiend!" Despite the assault, Jonathan never flinched, even when she walloped him soundly between the eyes.

He glared down at her with such a level of irritation that sparks seemed to fly. "Fiend, am I?"

Jonathan marched out of the room with her in his arms and carried her up the stairs. When he reached her bedroom, he nearly kicked the door down. Audrey abandoned the magazine and resumed her struggles.

Lord he is strong, she thought with a sudden pang of desire. Being overwhelmed like this was something she hadn't counted on, nor had she expected to enjoy it so much. Perhaps there was something to be said about being manhandled. What if he lost control of himself and ripped her clothes off? She gasped at the dizzy excitement that overtook her.

He started towards her bed, and suddenly she was airborne. The horrid man had thrown her! She hit the mattress with a startled squeak and rolled right off the other side, landing on the floor with a painful thud.

"Ouch!" she gasped, her left hip smarting. She'd fallen to the floor twice already, a third time was not helping. She tried to get up and a small whimper escaped her lips. No doubt she'd bruised something this time. In an instant Jonathan was there, taking her once more into his arms and setting her more gently back down on her rose-colored bedspread.

"I'm so sorry, Miss Audrey. I got carried away, I didn't mean to..."A heavy blush of mortification spread across Jonathan's face. A lock of his sandy blond hair fell across his forehead and Audrey reached up to brush it back. He flinched from her touch, but Audrey was too entranced by the closeness of his lips.

Those countless conversations she'd had with some of the more open maids hadn't been forgotten. They'd enlightened her to many of the secret intimacies between a man and a woman. The way tongues could touch, the way a man's body would harden, even how a man and woman could kiss each other below the waist to increase pleasure. Audrey had absorbed their tales with fascination, and the hunger for her own experiences had only grown stronger.

But it wasn't until she'd met with Evangeline Mirabeau that she'd learned more specifically how to entice a man to bed her. The ways to coax him to respond, to lure him with lust...

Like a starving woman eyeing a plate of food, she curled her fingers into his cravat and tugged down. His startled mouth collided with hers and she licked the seam of his mouth with her tongue, trying to get him to part his lips. He resisted only a moment before he groaned against her and mounted her on the bed. His hands pushed her dress up past her knees and she spread her legs open beneath him.

He knew how to kiss and she was learning quickly. His lips and tongue danced feverishly against hers with a wild abandon she'd only dreamt about before.

"You taste so sweet," he said as he trailed kisses along her jaw towards her ear.

Audrey was caught in a thunderstorm of panic, pleasure and fascination all coursing through her body at once. More, she needed more now! She released his cravat and slid her hands down his neck, across his shoulders and under his waistcoat, then began to peel it off his shoulders. Never stopping in his kiss, he threw the jacket off and pinned her beneath him again.

One of his calloused palms stroked her thigh, a worker's hands she realized, and for some reason that pleased her. He did not merely exist, he lived, and that set fire to her blood and filled her with a strange recklessness. She wanted to be with him, to live the way he did, and experience things with him. This was no idle gentleman, but a man who earned his living, just as she wished to earn hers.

A pang of hunger streaked through to the juncture between her thighs. She tensed, startled at the frightening feeling of losing control of her body's reactions. Jonathan pressed himself deeply against her at the same moment, as though knowing how she would react. Audrey moaned and arched her body upwards as her hands roamed his tightly muscled body. He hadn't lived a life of leisure; he was corded steel layered with primal sensuality. A rough nibble of her lower lip, a grind of his pelvis against her core and she melted into him completely. One of her hands strayed below his waist, seeking the bulge in his trousers that he fervently pushed against her. He groaned helplessly. They were a symphony of ancient instincts, exotic sensations and thrilling sounds in a perfect moment that should have gone on forever. But it didn't.

Recalling what Evangeline had said to do, she moved one of her hands down to his groin and rubbed at the hard shaft pressing against the front of his trousers. He hissed against her lips, then almost snarled as he took her mouth hungrily. She tried to curl her fingers around as much of his covered length as possible and squeezed. She'd been told it was the best way to stimulate a man's interest so she made sure to squeeze as hard as she could.

Something seemed to shift a little in her hands, like Chinese baoding balls.

Jonathan gasped. His face had become a silent scream. But that face wasn't supposed to come until later, was it? Quickly she realized it was not a look of pleasure. Quite the opposite.

Jonathan ripped himself away from Audrey and dove for his jacket. Without a backward glance he sprinted from the room. Truth be told it was more of a bowlegged hobble. Audrey lay still on her bed for a long moment, struggling for breath, trying to ease the heavy panting and the disappointment she now felt. She'd come so close. What went wrong? One thing was clear however—kissing Charles had certainly not felt like that.

⚜

THE DRAWING ROOM WAS FILLED WITH CANDLELIGHT, FIRELIGHT and two people who should not have been in the same room. Horatia, not willing to concede defeat, had curled up in her window seat again, her silver gown tucked up around her slippers, knees nestled under her chin. She clutched her novel, *Lady Eustace and the Merry Marquess*, trying to focus on its pages and not the real life marquess sitting by the fire. In the short span of time between Jonathan's battle of wills with Audrey, and Jonathan's hasty departure soon after, Horatia and Lucien found themselves in a battle of their own. Though Lucien's gaze was on the fireplace's vermillion flames, she could sense his attention on her—as though his thoughts had become physical and caressed her skin, making her burn with awareness she wanted to ignore but couldn't.

"How do you find your novel? Amusing? Trite? Impossibly lurid?" The cold silence of the room succumbed to the surprising warmth in his voice.

She shouldn't have answered, but couldn't help it. "It may not be a literary masterpiece, but..."

"But?" Lucien turned in his chair, propping an elbow on the armrest and resting his chin in his palm, looking genuinely interested in what she had to say.

"Well, it is just that Lady Eustace is a most irritating heroine." Horatia idly flipped through the pages she'd already read before chancing a look back in his direction.

"I agree. Eustace is an inferior example of a female character. She lacks all the great qualities that would attract a man."

"And what, pray tell, would those qualities be?" Horatia closed the volume and eyed him curiously.

"Cunning, cleverness, intelligence," Lucien said.

"You don't prefer women to be sweet, demure and obedient?"

"Such a woman would be a dreadful bore. Perhaps a woman could be sweet, but if she was demure and obedient as well that would deprive a man of all the joys of a complex woman, and a woman ought to be complex. Simple things and simple people are quite overrated. Now let us return to this book. Surely the plot entices you to keep reading, despite Lady Eustace's disappointing lack of complexity?"

"Admittedly, it does. Eustace keeps finding herself in the most absurd predicaments. For example, on page fourteen, she gets locked in a tower. A tower! What woman is insipid enough to trust herself to a man's whims like that at the start of the story?"

"It is foolish to get locked in a tower, but as to trusting in a man...given certain circumstances, it can be most thrilling. Wouldn't you agree?"

His eyes were like honey, but his words had reminded her of the sting that often followed such sweetness.

"Thrilling, yes, but not ultimately satisfying, given that trust seems to end in betrayal." She returned to the book, trying to focus on Lady Eustace's mad flight from the marquess's castle in the dead of night. What rubbish! Yet the Merry Marquess's character also kept her attention, probably more than it should, rather like the very real marquess who sat only feet from her.

"Not ultimately satisfying? I seem to recall your screams of pleasure as my fingers—"

"Stop!" she hissed, slamming her book shut. "Or do you forget how that ended?"

He grinned devilishly. "You'll have to make me."

"Oh? Now who's the child?"

Lucien shut his eyes and licked his lips. "I can still taste you. Even though it's been hours, I can't help but wonder if my memory is doing you justice. Would you shiver beneath me? Moan my name in helpless pleasu—"

Lady Eustace and the Merry Marquess had its revenge by catching Lucien right in the face. He cursed, clutching his nose and shot a dark look at Horatia who still sat in the small window seat overlooking the back garden, eyes now fixed on the ceiling. Lucien got up from his chair and started towards her, a predatory gleam in his eyes.

"What are you doing?" Horatia flattened herself against the cold windowpane, hands braced behind her on the chilly glass.

"I think it's time I taught you a lesson, and since there's nothing else you can throw, this seems like the perfect opportunity." He strolled right up to the window seat, hands on his hips.

Horatia raised her chin. "Just being in the same room with you is punishment enough." She crossed her arms over her chest in what was meant to be an imposing pose, but it only seemed to draw his eyes down to her breasts.

"Being with me is a punishment?"

Horatia wondered if she'd said the wrong thing.

"I suppose the better question is why do you see me as a punishment if you claim to love me? And don't deny it. Even now your pupils are dilated and your breath is quickening."

He was right, the arrogant rogue. Her heartbeat was fast and her breath unsteady.

"Do you still desire me even after all that I've done?" He leaned down and cupped her face, brushing his lips teasingly over hers. Horatia swayed towards him, wanting more than that torturously brief contact between their lips.

"Why?" he repeated, his tone low as he nibbled her lower lip.

Horatia refused to answer. He knew full well why. He trapped her back against the window, the frosty glass burning her shoulder blades. His hands slid up her outer thighs, baring her legs to his touch and pooling her silver skirts around her waist. Lucien thrust one knee and then the other between hers as he knelt on the seat, caging her against the window. He spread her legs so he could lift her up against him and made her straddle his lap. Her knees clutched at his hips, molding her to him.

"You didn't answer my question."

"What question?" she asked in a pleasure-filled daze. She felt his body fill with silent laughter and for some reason that angered her, bringing a wave of clarity with it. Horatia leaned back and balled her fist, striking in the general region of Lucien's stomach. In a whoosh of air he doubled over and they both fell from the window seat. Horatia heard her gown rip as she fell off to Lucien's side. He lay on his back, one hand clutching the wounded area.

"Good God!" he howled. "I'm fairly certain you just obliterated my insides. Did your brother teach you to punch like that? Perhaps Charles was in more trouble than I thought; I should have taken up Godric's wager."

"It serves you right for being such an insufferable tease. You're lucky I admire your face so much or I'd claw your eyes out." Her own eyes narrowed as she scrambled to her knees, glaring at him.

"Getting to be quite the harpy in your old age, aren't you?" Lucien laughed.

"Harpy? *Old?*" Horatia's voice was embarrassingly shrill and she clenched her fists, ready to punch him again.

"You've had what? Three seasons? You're practically ancient, my dear. You even have the cats to play the part." Lucien looked to the drawing room door where Muff sat idly licking a white-tipped paw. The cat paused when he caught the two humans fixed on him.

"*Mrreow?*"

Unable to help herself, Horatia laughed. This clearly annoyed Muff and he walked off, his black bottlebrush tail waving like a feather plume. Horatia regained control of herself and got up to retrieve poor Lady Eustace from her spot on the floor. Several pages were bent, like broken wings. Horatia's throat tightened. She'd worked so hard to keep her books in good condition, especially the ones Lucien had given her. Why did the man always have to tie her in such knots?

❧❦❧

LUCIEN PROPPED HIMSELF UP ON HIS ELBOWS ON THE FLOOR, legs crossed at the ankles, watching her through hooded eyes. He'd enjoyed rousing her, but the resigned hurt in her eyes now made him uncomfortable. She was trying to bend back the pages of the novel and her lack of success was distressing her.

"It's just a book. You can buy a new one."

Her brown eyes misted over. "It wouldn't be the same."

"Don't tell me that you've grown impossibly fond of Lady Eustace in the last few minutes." He was trying to tease her but she wasn't smiling.

"It's not Lady Eustace I'm fond of."

Horatia got to her feet, not seeming to notice the rip in her gown near the shoulder. The silver fabric sagged off her left shoulder, exposing part of the creamy mound of her breast. Lucien silently begged for the gown to drop farther. Would her nipple be a soft peach, or a sweet berry red? He ached to know its taste, to explore that nipple with his mouth, his tongue. Would she like to be laved, bitten or sucked on? All of these questions suddenly seemed vital. He had to know the answers. Lucien whimpered in protest when Horatia tugged the ripped sleeve back up, hiding that taunting bosom from him.

"If you'll excuse me." She made to leave but he lunged to his feet and caught the back of her gown, stopping her dead in her tracks. She reached behind her and gripped the wrist that held her gown, digging her nails into his skin. He didn't even flinch at the pain.

"Release me."

"Answer my question." He found himself grinning, knowing she would break. He wouldn't let her leave otherwise.

"You know the answer," she replied, releasing his wrist and crossing her arms. She turned her face away from him.

"You're no fun tonight," Lucien muttered.

"Since when do you ever want me to be fun, or even want me to *have* fun? As I seem to recall, your life's mission is to rip my heart and soul out and crush them under your boot heels. And congratulations Lucien, you've succeeded. Bravo. Now please let me go, so when I start to cry I may do so in peace. Please, save me the humiliation of breaking down in your presence."

Lucien would not have believed she was close to crying, her tone was too strong. But the almost invisible quake in her pale pink lips spoke volumes.

"I promise to let you go if you answer my question directly." He lowered his voice, speaking more gently. "Do you still desire me after everything I've done to you?"

"What do you think?" Horatia blinked back the shimmer of tears in her eyes. "I feel like a mouse being toyed with by a cat. You're worse than Muff. You bat at me with your paws, claw me, excite and thrill me with your wild antics, but it is all a game to you. You seduce me because you're bored. You derive pleasure from giving me hope of returned affections, then lay ruin to my dreams. I'm begging you, Lucien. Either kill me now or leave me alone forever, but for God's sake stop this infernal dance. I am in agony every minute of every hour of every day, fearing what you'll do to my heart next. Put me out of my misery and be done with it."

Lucien was stunned. Never had he thought she would be so honest over something so private. Her warm brown eyes blinded him. The pain in her voice cut through him, leaving scars he justly deserved. She was right, he'd gone out of his way to ignore her these last few years, only to tease her when he couldn't stand to stay away, and what use had that been?

Why did he persist in torturing Horatia? In treating her so callously he'd taken a grim satisfaction from his ability to control his desire for her, though that had become more and more difficult as of late. Slowly he loosened his grip on her dress. A moment passed as neither of them moved and then Horatia, clutching her book like a shield, fled from the room and up the stairs. Lucien shut his eyes at the distant sound of her door closing.

Something had changed tonight. He wasn't sure what, but he felt it deep in his bones. It was as though he'd been set on a course and turning back now was impossible. What was more he didn't want to. The only thing he knew was that his life's mission, as Horatia had called it, had changed.

Starting tomorrow he'd never again pester or tease Horatia, or be cold to her for that matter. He would maintain a polite but hopefully warm distance from her. And once this dreadful business with Waverly was over he would start looking for a wife. If Godric could settle down, then Lucien could too. It just couldn't be with Horatia.

Cedric would never condone that marriage. If Lucien were in his place, he wouldn't have allowed it either. Cedric had seen him sleep with two women at once, and knew Lucien had done things in bed even some of the League shied away from. Stupidly, he'd boasted of such conquests and the cunning methods of seduction he'd used.

No, Cedric would never allow his sister to marry a man like him. Nor would Lucien find a woman who would rouse his passions, but then he'd always known he'd be doomed to a loveless marriage. He'd find some quiet unobtrusive girl, marry her quickly and be done with it. If Horatia saw him married, then she'd be able to move on herself. *And the past will be truly buried,* he thought.

A sleek, furry, black body appeared in the drawing room doorway. Muff had returned. Lucien, too weary to go and summon a hackney to return to Half Moon Street, decided to stay here, warm by the fire, still burning with the memory of Horatia's form against his. He walked over to the couch against the wall, puffed a few pillows and threw himself down on it. The fire crackled, the only light in the room after he'd extinguished the candles. Muff gave an odd little chirp and pounced on Lucien's chest.

Lucien, like Cedric, was a lover of all animals and he scratched the wizened cat behind the ears. The responding purr was loud but soothing. As sleep started to close in on him, he wondered if he could spend the rest of his days as a bachelor, with nothing but a cat like Muff for company. Or perhaps he would spend his days at the Midnight Garden, whose ladies were always eager to make his dreams come true.

It wasn't ladies he dreamed about however, but one teary-eyed beauty in a torn silver gown. A Cinderella whose Prince Charming had not danced with her at the ball, nor kissed her before the clock struck midnight. In the dark moonlit palace of his dreams, he held a lone silver satin slipper and wept, for what he did not know.

The next morning, Horatia donned a morning dress of twilled French silk in a dark rosy pink and went down the main stairs. The house was quiet, which meant that Cedric and Audrey were still asleep. Her normally soft steps became tiptoes as she trod through the house. She passed by the drawing room, paused in puzzlement and retreated back a few feet to gaze discreetly through the open doorway.

In the far corner, Lucien was stretched out on his back, asleep on the daybed. Muff, the little feline devil, was stretched out on his back across Lucien's stomach, one paw raised in the air, tail twitching at the very tip. Lucien had one hand flat over the cat's belly, his fingers surprisingly graceful as they caressed him. It was the sort of caress a person made half-asleep, or half-awake.

Horatia felt an ache rise in her as she watched. She would never know if Lucien would stroke her this way in bed. Only then did it occur to Horatia that Lucien hadn't left last night. A flash of remorse shot through her. She'd been a horrible hostess. A room should have been prepared and a bed turned down for him. Lucien should not have suffered the discomforts of a daybed.

Horatia took a tentative step inside, but Muff shifted upon

seeing her and began to purr. Fearing she'd wake Lucien, she retreated to the breakfast room where a hot meal was already awaiting her. The coffee was fresh and the rich scent danced out into the hall. Horatia, preferring tea, saw to preparing herself a warm cup with plenty of sugar. She'd only started to bite into her toast when a sleepy-eyed Lucien joined her.

Even as he yawned and ran a hand through his tousled red hair he was a god among mortals. He gave her a surprisingly sheepish smile which would have sent her straight to the floor had she not already been seated. It reflected a bashfulness for having done something devilishly intimate the night before. Horatia's breath caught as he tugged his rumpled waistcoat down and tried to straighten his cravat. Was this how his mistresses saw him after a night of passion? If they had they would have insisted on getting him straight back into bed. At least that's what she would have wanted. The thought made her blush but Lucien didn't seem to notice.

"Morning," he said, taking a chair opposite her.

"Good morning," she managed to reply. It had startled her, this change, this lack of cold hostility or casual flirting. What was he playing at?

"Is the coffee still hot?" he asked.

"Yes, it's been freshly brewed." She leaned forward to pour him a cup.

"Wonderful. Two sugars, please," he asked when she started to slide the cup and saucer over.

She hastily dropped two cubes into his cup. Odd, she always thought he'd take it black and strong.

Lucien noticed her puzzled look and grinned.

"I can never stomach the stuff unless it is sweet. It has been noted, according to my brother Lawrence, as one of my greatest faults."

Horatia giggled, despite her intention to remain stoic.

"Then perhaps you should know that I once saw Lawrence put *three* sugars into his tea one afternoon last spring." She relayed this in a conspiratorial whisper. "He tries to do so when no one is looking."

"That cur! Tea I can drink straight, and the little weasel dares to needle me? Oh the things I endure!" he bemoaned theatrically, clutching his chest. "I will get even with him the next time I face him in the boxing ring." Lucien threw this out with dramatic flare.

Horatia winced at the image of Lucien striking his younger brother in the nose hard enough to draw blood. But men often did the most foolish things. Her own brother was clear proof of that.

"I trust you slept well?" Lucien changed the topic of conversation.

"Yes, well enough, but oh…you should have had the servants prepare a room for you, Lucien. To sleep on that daybed must have been wretchedly uncomfortable." She could feel her face warm as she spoke. It was a clear admission of her failure as a hostess. Thank goodness her mother wasn't alive to witness it.

He shrugged and sampled his coffee. "Nonsense, it was fine. A bit stiff, but nothing less than I deserved. Which brings me to the point I must speak to you about."

Horatia shook her head as she tried to stop him from saying anything that would ruin such a pleasant beginning to the day.

He held up a hand and any protests she had died on her lips. "Now hear me out, Horatia. What happened last night, everything I said, I apologize unreservedly. I was childish and cruel. I have no reason to ignore you or be so cold. So please accept my apologies and tell me you agree that we should let bygones be bygones."

He reached across the breakfast table, offering one of his hands. Before Horatia could stop herself she was sliding her fingers into his firm grasp.

"Friends?" he asked. This simple connection was more intimate to her than any kiss he'd given her before. It was a touch he'd offered out of friendship with good intentions, not because he was toying with her—and it scared her. It reminded her that she would always want more, but this she would take happily.

"Friends," she agreed.

"Excellent," he said. He eyed the newspaper lying near her elbow. "Is that the *Morning Post?*"

"Yes, would you like it?" She slid the paper over.

Lucien loved the news. Whether he was actually concerned with the latest political or social gossip, or merely using it as a shield at breakfast, she wasn't sure, but it was a habit he'd had as long as she'd known him. Horatia watched him take the paper and whip it up, hiding him from the world. She understood that need better than anyone. Every year she used his Christmas presents, the books he gave her, as a refuge of sorts. She'd spent more than one afternoon tucked away in the library reading, rather than join Audrey and Cedric on a tour of Hyde Park. It was easier to hide than to face the realities of the world. She didn't want to be husband hunting, not when she was already in love with a man.

"Care for toast?" she offered, pushing a tray in his direction. His paper wall wilted over his fingertips, allowing him to peer over the pages to eye the tray.

"Sounds lovely." He reached for the tray and after retrieving a piece he returned to his paper. Horatia blinked. Was it possible they were actually getting along? Unfortunately, her quiet reflection of this question was disrupted when Audrey and Cedric arrived in breakfast room, squabbling like children.

"A day? A single day? Cedric, I can't be ready by then! That's barely enough time for my maid to pack my hats, let alone my entire wardrobe! Must we go so soon?"

"I'm sorry. I'll ask the lurking assassins in the shadows to give you more time to prepare, shall I?"

"Don't be so dramatic," said Audrey. "It doesn't suit you."

"What's in a day?" Horatia asked politely, hoping to quell Audrey's rising temper. Her younger sister spun on her, seeking an ally.

"Tell him, Horatia. Tell him that one day to pack for Kent is not nearly enough time."

"Lucien, help a man out and tell her that she need not bring *every* article of clothing with her?" Cedric begged as he threw himself into the seat next to his friend.

"Why are we going to Kent?" Horatia asked. There was only one place in Kent she'd ever been to, and surely Cedric wasn't sending them there. Not after what she'd done the last time. She had been a child, but the embarrassment pulled at her as if it had been yesterday.

Lucien stirred a spoon in his coffee, raised it to his lips and met her gaze over the top of the rim. "You, Audrey and Cedric have been invited to join my family for the Christmas holidays. We leave for my estate tomorrow, before first light."

"See! No time at all!" Audrey punctuated her complaint with a glare at Lucien, who had abandoned his paper and was smiling rather too sweetly back at her.

Horatia knew that look well. Her little sister had better watch out, or Lucien would trick her into doing something she didn't want to do.

"Surely we would be an unnecessary burden, especially during the holidays." Horatia gave a pleading look at her brother, seeking his support.

"Sorry, Horatia, but Ashton has given me orders."

"Do you always let him dictate your life?" Audrey snapped.

Cedric didn't answer, but Lucien did.

"Your brother listens to reason from his friends when your safety may well depend on our guidance. I would not become too upset, ladies. My mother will insist on taking you to town shopping until you have more clothes than your trunks can carry. Wouldn't that be nice?" Lucien was nothing if not a charmer.

Audrey flounced into the chair beside Horatia and sighed. "I suppose I can endure that. I do so love Lady Rochester. She reads *La Belle Assemblée* you know."

Lucien smiled and Horatia's heart turned over. Everyone who knew Lady Rochester was privy to her obsessions, fashion being among them.

"Hmm...indeed," he murmured as he sipped his coffee.

Audrey started a lengthy discussion on the various modes of neck cloths and the proper styles for an evening out. The men responded with low grunts of agreement whenever she seemed to pause and wait for their attention. Not that she seemed to care what their response was, nor did they. Had she asked for a thousand pounds and a new horse they no doubt would have agreed as well, strictly to keep up appearances that they were listening to her talk.

Horatia finished her breakfast and quietly slipped out of the room, something she found easy to do whenever Audrey discussed fashion. Horatia would be packed and ready to leave in a mere two hours. But there was nothing she could do about the flutter in her stomach as she realized the four of them would be squashed most uncomfortably in a carriage for several long hours. Despite Lucien's new desire to be civil to her she still carried a deep-seated uneasiness inside. He had to be up to something, and she dreaded what he might have in store for her.

Something wasn't right. Ashton shifted uncomfortably in his knee-high black boots. The actual gardens behind the Midnight Garden were chilly and his breath puffed out in small pale clouds as he waited in a concealed area of tall shrubbery to see where the two men from last night might rendezvous.

Lucien had been positive that he'd heard Waverly's voice as the one giving orders to the hired assassin. But it was easy to let prejudices color a man's memory. Ever since the League had confronted Waverly that night by the River Cam, when he'd attempted to drown Charles, Waverly had transformed from mere mortal to bogeyman. An innocent man had perished during their struggle and enmity had been born. It was only a matter of time before someone would pay for the life lost that night.

Ashton knew it was nonsense to lay the blame for every misfortunate at Waverly's door, but the man did seem to have a knack for spreading pain and trouble. Ashton had done his best to remain detached from such thoughts. Still, if Lucien had heard correctly, then Waverly was finally trying to make good on his threat.

Ashton could still hear Waverly's cruel shout from the shore opposite them after they fished Charles out from the river. "You'll pay! Each and every one you! Not one of you rogues will know peace or a long life! Do you hear me? You are all damned!" Their enemy had been clutching the body of the man who'd died. It was a sight Ashton couldn't erase from his mind, nor the guilt lurking behind it. Perhaps he was right. Perhaps they were damned.

It was Charles who suffered the worst. He still sometimes woke in a fit of screams, unable to recognize a soul around him and crying out about the water filling his lungs. When they happened to be under the same roof for a night, Ashton was adept at quieting Charles and doing it so quickly that he never woke up anyone else. It was why the poor man always slept so late.

Godric joined him, crouching down, his boots crunching in the snow. "I don't like it, Ash. This place is far too quiet." The two of them had arrived first thing in the morning to see if anyone had witnessed Waverly or if any evidence existed that could lead to the man or his hirelings. So far, they'd come up with nothing, not that Ashton expected differently. Most of last night's visitors had crept away by coach or foot in the early hours before dawn to return to their daily lives.

"I don't either. It's too bold, too much of a coincidence that Lucien overheard them." Ashton knelt into a low squat, balancing on the balls of his feet as he traced a gloved fingertip over the indentions made by a boot. A pattern of prints had led away from the meeting spot last night just through the area where he and Godric now waited and hid.

"Do you think he has another target in mind?" Godric asked.

"You mean have us scrambling to protect Cedric, when it is another of us he plans to kill?" Ashton raised a brow. "It is certainly possible. I wish I knew how to better protect us. If we scattered it would diminish our strength in numbers, but we'd be harder to find. If we kept ourselves together, it's easier for him to focus his resources. Either way we will be in danger."

"Sometimes it is a pity we have a standard of morals. I for one would love to put that sniveling piece of filth in his grave." Godric's eyes were sharp as jade daggers.

"If I didn't have some concern for the state of my immortal soul, I would have ended his life back in Cambridge," Ashton agreed solemnly.

Godric placed a hand on his shoulder.

"Our souls were stained enough that night, and we had to rescue Charles from a watery death. If we had it to do over again, I would still let Waverly escape. I'd choose Charles's life over Waverly's death every time," Godric said.

"It's not a choice I regret, but Waverly is a menace. Something has to be done."

"Agreed." Godric rubbed his gloved hands together to warm them.

"It is half past ten now," said Ashton, examining his pocket watch. "We should send word to Lucien before he and Cedric leave. I think that the rest of us should remain in London, but keep in close contact. I want everyone to report in to your townhouse Godric, every night by ten o'clock. I don't want anyone getting hurt by not paying attention."

"I'll have Jonathan move in with Emily and me so you won't have to worry about him," Godric suggested.

"He's fine where he is. I'd actually prefer to keep him under my roof. He has excellent instincts. I think I'll have Charles move in for the holidays as well. I'll keep them both with me until this is over, and we can continue our investigation here."

"Then we'll only have to defend against Waverly on three fronts."

Godric and Ashton started walking back through the hedgerows when a man in a cloak and cap exited the nearest door, heading straight towards them. They ducked behind a tall cluster of trees as the man strode past them, cloak unfurling behind him like a black flag. He walked directly to the spot just beyond where Ashton and Godric had been moments before and seemed to be waiting, most impatiently.

"Do you think that's one of the men?" Godric nodded at their suspect.

"I think it highly likely," Ashton whispered. "Stay here and watch the door to the Garden's house. I shall endeavor to get a closer look at our mystery fellow."

Ashton used the cover of more bushes to conceal himself as he crept along the nearest path created by the shrubs. Through the thick foliage he could make out the fluttering of the man's cape as he paced back and forth. There wasn't a clear enough view through the bushes for him to get a glimpse of the man so he had to chance raising his head or peering around the last bush when the path ended. He opted for peering around rather than over the bush.

A fallen twig snapped beneath his boot and the sound drew the pacing man up short. He spun, and their eyes met. Not long, but long enough for Ashton to see cold caution change to decisive action. The man drew a pistol from his cloak and fired. The shot rang out like a crack of thunder and a spike of fire surged through Ashton. He cursed and clutched his left arm. When he pulled his hand away, his black leather glove gleamed with the sheen of blood.

"Ash!" Godric ran in his direction, glancing about for signs of the shooter, but the man had vanished. He hadn't returned to the Garden house, nor had he gone in any direction they could see.

"Should we go after him?" Godric asked. "I didn't see which way he went."

"Nor did I. Must have had an escape route planned."

"Clever bastard," Godric said. "Why did he shoot at you?"

Ash shrugged, wincing. "He saw me peer around the edge of the bush and reacted. I think he fired because he recognized me."

"Good thing he missed."

Ashton stumbled and gripped Godric by the sleeve for support. "He...he didn't actually." Blood began to flow freely down his left arm. The pair quickly ducked back inside the Midnight Garden.

"What? Ash, you're bleeding! Hell man, why didn't you tell me you'd been shot?" Godric's face turned white as marble.

"Pardon me if my mind is a bit fogged with pain at the moment," Ashton replied sarcastically. "Hurts like the very devil too. Do you mind if we get out of here before I lose any more blood?"

"Right, of course. Come on." His friend gripped him by his good arm and helped him over to the door leading back into the Garden's house.

The owner of the Midnight Garden, Madame Chanson ran over to them. "Did I hear a gunshot?" she asked in a panic.

"Yes. It seems the man we were looking for didn't wish to be found."

"Should I contact the Bow Street Runners?"

"He's already long gone, I'm afraid, and there's your anonymity to consider. Could you summon my carriage immediately? And have a doctor sent to my residence quickly." Godric gripped Ashton's right arm firmly to keep his wounded friend on his feet. As he spoke, he removed his cravat and tied a makeshift tourniquet.

Godric's carriage pulled up and he helped Ashton inside. The bullet, whatever sinister path it had taken, had left a nasty wound in Ashton's arm.

"My home isn't far, we can wait for the doctor there. Emily can fuss over you until then."

"You'd subject me to your wife's fussing?" Ashton gave a pained chuckle as he clamped his right hand over his wound.

"Of course I would."

"Have I wronged you somehow? Why would you let Emily tend to me? I might lose my entire arm in her desire to play nursemaid."

"I fear more what Emily would do to me if she's not allowed to help."

Ashton groaned in pain and his vision blurred. Godric shouted for the coachman to go faster.

"Stay awake, Ash," Godric barked as Ashton gave in to the temptation to close his eyes for a moment.

"Trying to," Ashton muttered. "In all of the times we've gotten into scrapes, I've never been shot. You hear of soldiers speak of it with some degree of pride and bravado. The experience, I've decided, is highly overrated." His frowned down at his bound arm. "Perhaps you ought to distract me?"

"That I can do. So I spent all of last night trying to seduce my wife into telling me how she and her companions escaped their room last night and into the drawing room without us seeing them. But despite my best efforts, she disclosed nothing. What are your theories?"

Ashton gritted his teeth, trying to formulate an answer.

"I would say that they convinced one of the servants to let them out and they snuck down to the dining room while we were still in the drawing room. Once we went upstairs they moved once again and waited there for us."

"That is what I assumed as well. Though I still cannot figure out how Emily embroidered that phrase *Never Challenge a Woman* so quickly. I know she hasn't been doing any needlepoint." Ashton smiled but his expression changed into a wince as the carriage rolled to a stop at Essex House. A footman was at the carriage door. He opened it and helped Godric take Ashton out and up to the house door.

"Thank you, Timmons. We're expecting a doctor. Have him brought in immediately."

Godric threw Ashton's good arm around his shoulders and helped his friend get inside.

Emily was waiting at the top of the stairs and with a panicked cry she rushed down to help them.

"What happened to him?" she asked.

Godric motioned for her to open the door to the drawing room. Emily did, then called for a maid to bring some water and cloths.

"Lay him on the couch, Godric." Emily indicated a blue and gold brocaded bit of furniture. She hastened to help Ashton sit down. He took a deep shaky breath that made Godric and Emily share a look of concern.

"We've sent for a doctor," Godric told her.

"That's all well and good, if he doesn't bleed out before then,"

Emily snapped.

Godric took hold of Ashton's shoulders and looked his friend in the eye.

"Do you plan on bleeding out, Ash?" he asked, partially in jest. Ash shook his head in a wobbly sort of way.

"No, Your Grace." He chuckled. The blood loss was making him feel a little silly, not because he was losing much of it, but because the sight of blood sometimes made him lightheaded. Besides, his friend bickering with his wife was far too amusing.

"See? He'll be fine, darling." Godric wrapped an arm around her shoulders and tucked her into his side.

"Don't you *darling* me, Godric. If he dares to die in my drawing room, I'll revive him only to kill him again myself!" Emily helped remove the old binding on his arm and then peeled off Ashton's coat. "Followed shortly by yourself."

The maid returned with cloths and a bowl of water. Emily made short work of removing Ashton's shirt, then used a thick strip of cloth to make a fresh tourniquet. Godric helped her, taking note of the wound's condition.

"Looks like it went clean through. No bone damage that I can see," Godric said, but Emily was too busy cooing to Ashton as she placed a wet cloth to his forehead.

Ashton stared up at her, admiring the way she tended to him. Godric was a lucky man. He couldn't help but wonder if he'd ever be so lucky. He'd always viewed relationships with the intent of what he might gain in the way of business and it had won him many partnerships in bed, but never love. Perhaps he was becoming a sentimental fool.

It's just the blood loss, nothing more. A man faces death and he starts thinking all sorts of wild things.

"How did this happen?" Emily asked.

"Ash and I were at the Midnight Garden, hoping to catch the men Lucien overheard last night. They said they would meet there this morning. The hired man caught sight of Ash spying on him and shot him before fleeing. We didn't even have a chance to give chase."

"Did you see who it was?" Emily stroked Ashton's pale blond hair back from his face. He leaned in to her gentle touch with a soft sigh.

"No one I recognized, though the reverse may not be true."

Emily shut her eyes. "Do you still believe Waverly is behind this?"

He nodded. "Many dislike us, a few despise us, but only Waverly has ever proclaimed to want us dead."

EMILY WAS SILENT A LONG TIME. SHE SAT DOWN NEXT TO Ashton, keeping the cool cloth to his head.

Ashton held an important part in Emily's heart. He'd championed her cause to Godric, and had been the first to see that she and Godric were in love with each other. Without his cool head and warm heart, the pair might never have believed enough in their love for each other.

Ashton began to close his eyes and Emily slapped him forcefully across the cheek.

"Don't you dare fall asleep, Ashton!"

His stunned gaze at the assault seemed to amuse Godric. It took quite a lot to shock Ashton.

"You slapped me?" he asked, shocked by Emily's behavior.

"And I'll do it again if you shut your eyes," Emily threatened.

Ashton had the gall to let out a hoarse chuckle. "Now I know how Charles must feel on a daily basis. Still, I'm sure the benefits more than compensate for it."

Despite her concern, Emily smiled. No doubt if Ashton had enough energy to tease her, he wasn't dead yet.

A footman appeared at the drawing room door, informing them they had a visitor.

"That will be the doctor." Emily guessed as she jumped up and ran towards the door. But it wasn't. It was Anne Chessely, Baron Chessely's daughter and one of Emily's closest friends.

"Anne?" Emily said in disappointment.

The crestfallen look on Anne's face wasn't hard to miss, even from where Godric stood. "Should I go? I would not wish to intrude." Anne chewed her bottom lip, looking doubtful as Emily ushered her inside.

"No, please come in. I was just expecting someone else." Emily attempted to hide the truth, but Anne was too clever by half.

"Was that blood outside in the snow on the steps? I see it here too." Anne pointed to a trail of droplets leading towards the drawing room.

"Er, what?"

"That *is* blood." Anne abandoned her muff and bent down to dip a finger into the nearest splotch. Her gloved fingertip came back bright red.

"Emily, you didn't *kill* Godric did you? I mean, I'm sure you had a good reason, but it's foolish to leave a blood trail." Anne's gaze swept the hall, seeking the truth.

"Murder? Heavens no, Anne. Wherever do you come up with such nonsense?" Emily tried to lead her away to another room, but Anne, who was fairly strong for a woman, pulled free and opened the drawing room door.

Emily froze behind her, fearing Anne would faint as she took in the scene of Godric tending to a half-naked Ashton. A bloody shirt lay on the ground near his feet.

"Oh my…" Anne exhaled in shock.

Ashton turned his head in her direction, bright blue eyes now dim with pain.

"Miss Chessely, I do beg your pardon for my lack of proper attire. As you can see I was shot this morning. Hurts something dreadful," Ashton finished in a breathless apology. "So, if you don't mind, some privacy would be appreciated."

"Forgive me, Lord Lennox, it is I who intruded." Anne backed up so quickly that she trod over Emily's toes. Emily squeaked and jumped out of the way.

"Sorry," Anne muttered as she retreated into the hall, away from Ashton and all that blood. "What happened to Lord Lennox? Did he fight in a duel?" she asked in a scandalized whisper.

"Don't be silly. He's too levelheaded for that. No, this is a much longer story I'm afraid. Would you care to come to the morning room for some tea?" Emily offered.

"If it's not too much trouble."

Just then the footman, Timmons, came in through the front door, with a doctor in tow. The two men went straight to the drawing room and shut the door. Emily breathed a sigh of relief.

"That was who I was expecting when you came," Emily explained as she and Anne entered the morning room. "I'm sure the wound isn't that serious. At least it didn't appear to be once Godric got it cleaned up." She glanced back at the way the doctor had gone. The blood had panicked her, but now she was sure Ashton would be fine. If he had the breath enough to tease her and speak to Anne, the man was not ready for the next world yet. Didn't Lady Society in her articles always say that no bullet could kill a rogue?

A maid brought them a tray of tea and Emily quickly narrated the disturbing events of the previous night as well as this morning's close call with Ashton. Emily always felt free to speak with Anne, especially in matters concerning her husband and the League.

It had been Anne who had first told her, or rather warned her, about the League of Rogues. Anne was acquainted with Cedric and knew about the others only through reputation since she and the League both avoided the social events of the season like the plague.

Cedric had courted Anne briefly, the year before Emily's abduction. He'd had no success in seducing her and sadly had abandoned the endeavor entirely. Emily thought it a pity, but Anne didn't want to marry. She was content to live with her father and breed Thoroughbred horses for racing. She kept her fortune and her land this way, but she was also lonely. At least, Emily suspected she was.

"So, where are the other rogues?" Anne asked as she sipped her tea.

"Charles, Jonathan, Ashton and Godric are all still in London. But Cedric and Lucien are on their way to Lucien's estate in Kent. But you must tell no one of this."

A flicker of emotion passed over Anne's face so briefly that Emily thought she might have imagined it. Was it possible that Anne felt something for Cedric after all? She'd never indicated anything but mild irritation at his attempts to woo her. But the moment he'd stopped calling on her, Anne had started showing up at the Essex doorstep with surprising frequency. Anne never asked after Cedric, at least not directly, but she did ask where the other League members were each time she came over.

"Will you and your father be spending the holidays in London?" Emily asked.

"Yes. I wish we weren't though. The snow is much prettier in the country this time of year and I usually like to take a ride on Christmas morning."

Emily sighed wistfully. "That sounds lovely. It is a pity that Cedric will be in Kent. I might have persuaded him to take us out on the town in his curricle with his pair of Arabian mares."

At the mention of Cedric's Arabians, Anne's eyes brightened.

"Is it true that he won them in a wager from a sheikh?"

"Has he not told you the story himself?" Emily was genuinely surprised. She knew that part of Cedric's purpose in courting Anne was to achieve his desire of breeding his mares with Anne's stallions.

"I'd only heard the rumors from the papers." Anne looked put out at this.

"When you next see him, I'll have him tell you. I could never do the story justice." That was certainly the truth. At the time Cedric had told her the story, she'd been fairly distracted by

Godric and the rest of the League, what with being their prisoner at the time.

"If we weren't so worried for his safety right now, I would insist you and I go to Kent. But as it is, Godric is one minute away from locking me in a blasted tower for my own safety."

"I imagine Lord Sheridan was not fond of going to Kent?" Anne asked astutely.

Emily nodded. She was surprised Cedric hadn't fought harder to stay in London, at least by Godric's account. Cedric was incredibly brave and it must have killed him to turn his back on a fight, especially where Waverly was involved.

When the ladies had finished their tea, Anne rose and started for the door.

"Anne, would you and your father like to come to dinner this evening? I know it's short notice. I promise to have my hall cleaned of blood by then," Emily jested.

Her friend smiled and gave a little nod. "My father and I would be delighted. See you tonight."

Anne departed and Emily turned her attention back towards the drawing room. She squared her shoulders and walked in, eager to check on Ashton and her husband.

CHAPTER 13

The Russell family estate in northern Kent, four miles east of the village of Hexby, was in an uproar. Jane, the Marchioness of Rochester, was on the verge of strangling her second youngest child, one Linus Winston Russell. Despite her own knowledge that she had birthed that troublesome boy twenty-one years before, sometimes she swore he hadn't matured past the age of eight.

The young man in question was balanced precariously on a rickety ladder in the entryway of Rochester Hall. He held a sprig of what Lady Rochester feared was mistletoe. That child was in for a thrashing when she got hold of him. She'd found his handiwork all over the house. Every single doorway, window, and alcove was adorned with that dreaded poisonous plant. The chaos and impropriety that would ensue from his little prank could bring down the very stones of Rochester Hall.

Lord knew, her brood were wicked enough that they didn't need the help of mistletoe. It was in their blood, and sadly, not a trait taken from her husband's side.

Linus, having a full head of red hair like all of her children, was at the moment wiping a sheen of sweat off his brow before he resumed reaching for the upper doorjamb to affix the mistletoe. The forest green waistcoat and buff breeches he wore were well tailored to him—the body of a man, her baby boy no longer.

Lady Rochester blinked back a rebellious tear. How had her child grown up so fast? Hadn't it been yesterday that he'd put a frog in Lysandra's bed and tacks on Lucien's study chair? It had to be the holidays bringing up all this silly emotion. She stormed down the stairs to deal with her youngest's antics.

"Linus Winston Bartholomew Russell!" She bellowed the name in such an imperious tone that Linus dropped the mistletoe with a cry of alarm and scrambled to steady himself on the now wobbling ladder.

"Mama?" He hesitantly turned to face her as she glared up at him from the ground, her foot tapping with anger.

"Get down here at once," she barked.

Linus practically fell off the ladder, his boots smacking loudly on the marble floor.

"Just what do you think you're up to?" she demanded.

"Nothing." He tried to nonchalantly kick the mistletoe under a cabinet with a booted toe. As if she wouldn't notice!

Lady Rochester grabbed him by the ear. She was two seconds away from hauling him up to the old nursery when the knocker on the front door clanked four times. Linus grinned at his apparent reprieve and tugged free of his mother's hold.

"I'm not done with you yet. There *will* be a reckoning." She gave him one of her death glares before her face transformed into a heartwarming smile suitable for guests. She waved off the butler, who was advancing towards the entryway. "I'll answer it, Mr. Jenkins." She opened the door to find a welcome surprise. Her eldest child, Lucien, was there as well as his close friend, Viscount Sheridan, and his two sisters.

"Mother!" Lucien greeted her warmly, bending down to kiss her cheek.

"Lucien, my dear boy, so wonderful to see you. But it would have been more wonderful if you had sent me a note in advance.

Especially if you were bringing guests." This last bit was delivered in a low warning tone.

Lucien lowered his head. "We apologize for the short notice, Mother, but it was important to come straight away." Lucien offered Horatia his arm to escort her inside and Cedric did the same for Audrey.

"Oh?" Lady Rochester's eyes narrowed.

"It's a long story, Mother, but I will explain later. May we have some tea? The trip was devilishly long and tiresome."

"Yes, of course. Right this way. Lovely to see you all, Lord Sheridan, Miss Sheridan, and Miss Audrey." Lady Rochester let Cedric kiss her hand before she embraced the two girls warmly. Then she led them to the nearest parlor where a strapping young footman awaited her orders—Gordon, if she remembered correctly. One of the recent replacements she'd had to acquire.

"Tea and scones if you please, Gordon," she said.

The servant nodded and departed to see to her wishes.

Lady Rochester caught sight of her youngest trying to sneak past the open doorway of the salon unseen. "Linus!" He froze mid-step, shoulders hunched in resignation before he sighed and came back into the parlor. She fixed Linus with a look that promised misery if he tried to escape again. "Greet our guests."

"Good afternoon," he replied, bowing towards Cedric and his sisters.

Lady Rochester did not miss Audrey's look as she tried to fight the urge to laugh. Linus and Audrey were quite good friends, as good as men and women could be without the complications of their genders getting in the way. Perhaps co-conspirators was a more apt description. Still, they were now at that age where it would be unwise to leave them alone together.

Lucien sat back in the chair he'd chosen, perfectly at ease. Lady Rochester watched as the eldest of her brood of hellions interacted with the youngest.

"How are you, Lucien?" Linus asked.

"Well. And you? How was Cambridge?"

"Fine. But I am glad to be through with it," Linus admitted.

"I'll bet." Cedric sniggered. It wasn't a secret that he'd loved everything about school, apart from the schooling.

Gordon returned with a tea tray and Linus moved to sit down next to Audrey on the loveseat. With no small amusement, Lady Rochester studied their interaction out of the corner of her eye, whilst they believed everyone else was looking away and talking. Audrey prodded him with a sharp little elbow. He eyed the offending weapon, and the second the opportunity presented itself, he pinched her arm in retaliation. Audrey let out a strangled little sound that came out somewhere between an *eek* and *ouch*.

She blushed and held her teacup in defense. "The tea is rather hot."

"Really?" Lady Rochester eyed the teapot, trying not to laugh at the mischievousness of youth. "Now Lord Sheridan, may I offer you rooms at the Hall through the New Year? It would be lovely to have you all here to celebrate Christmas. The house will be happily full, you see. I've just invited the Cavendishes to come from Brighton."

"We'd be delighted to stay, Lady Rochester," Cedric answered.

"The Cavendishes will be coming?" Audrey asked excitedly.

The Cavendishes were old family friends of both the Russells and the Sheridans. It wasn't too hard to guess what Audrey was excited about. Eligible men were always exciting for a young lady.

"The entire family will be here. I'm hoping that Mrs. Cavendish and I might manage to marry off one of our children before either of us dies." She threw the statement out with inner glee, waiting for the fireworks to begin.

"Mother!" Lucien choked on the scone he'd been eating.

"Oh don't give me that horrified look, Lucien. I quite gave up on you years ago. But perhaps I can convince Lysandra to set her cap for Gregory Cavendish. He's quite a handsome young man, and well-inlaid you know."

Linus watched her in terror. "Mama, just because he's a bang-up cove, doesn't mean Lysa will have him, or even that he'll have her." Linus seemed most insistent on defending his sister, probably because he believed there was no worse fate than marriage.

"A bang-up cove? Where do you learn such language?" Lady Rochester sighed and looked up, imploring the heavens to explain why she'd been burdened with such obstinate offspring.

Linus grinned and reached for a scone. They both knew vexing her was one of the true joys of his life.

He piped up as he swallowed the last of his scone. "Lord Sheridan, may I escort Miss Audrey outside? I'm sure she would like some fresh air after the long carriage ride here."

"Not without a chaperone," Lady Rochester intoned.

"But Mama," Linus whined.

Audrey put a hand on his arm indicating him to shush.

"My sister shall chaperone us. Won't you, Horatia?"

"Yes, of course," Horatia replied.

"If I'm not worried, Lady Rochester, then you shouldn't be," Cedric reassured her.

"I suppose that is safe enough."

"Come on then," Linus offered his arm to Audrey. Horatia followed the pair out of the salon and into the hall. Linus and Audrey immediately bent their heads together, whispering now that they were out of sight of Lady Rochester.

Horatia groaned as she heard Audrey giggle wickedly. Linus must have had a scheme afoot and he was determined to rope Audrey into it. Knowing Linus as she did, which unfortunately was quite well, Horatia guessed it would be a prank of some sort. From time to time Linus and Audrey shot looks over their shoulders at her, as though worried she might be eavesdropping on their plotting.

Horatia raised her hands in surrender. "As long as I am not the victim of whatever you're planning, I won't spoil your fun."

"I make no promises," said Linus. The rascal was one year her senior in age, but not nearly as mature. It was why he'd always taken more to Audrey. Horatia couldn't even begin to count how many afternoons she and Lysandra had been the target of pranks from this unholy alliance.

"Linus, where is Lysa?" Horatia asked. She'd rather seek out her friend than linger in their presence. Her role of chaperone was nonsense, everyone but Lady Rochester seemed to know that.

"Last I saw, she was in the library." With that, he and Audrey darted up the stairs and vanished from view.

Horatia found herself alone in the massive entryway of Rochester Hall. It was a beautiful Georgian country house with sandy stones on the outside and marble within. She admired the tapestries on the walls depicting various scenes of pastoral bliss. Gazing at the scenes, she lost track of time, remembering the last time she'd been here. The memory was still so fresh that she felt it emerge from the gloom of her memory and envelop her fully.

CHAPTER 14

ochester Hall, Kent, 1815

It was a perfect day in May with the heady scent of blooming flowers filling the gardens. Horatia was idly picking her way through the maze of tall hedges as she searched for Linus and Audrey. At fourteen, she was too old to enjoy hide and seek but she still humored the other children. She had counted to one hundred and was now having a devilishly hard time finding the others on the vast grounds of Lord Rochester's estate. *Lord Rochester*, she sighed aloud at the thought of his name. He was twenty-six years old, her brother's close friend and unbelievably handsome.

She also knew Lucien was a rake; she'd heard that whispered in the servants' hall among other places. At first she'd thought it odd that the Marquess had been likened to a gardening tool, but after listening to her brother talk to his friends, she'd learned a rake had another meaning with no botanical connection whatsoever. After a bit of pleading with one of the laundry maids at their townhouse in London, she'd learned what a rake in this particular context meant.

From that moment on she'd been hopelessly entranced by the

marquess. At fourteen she knew she was too young for him, but her heart didn't seem to care about age. She'd nearly squealed with joy when Cedric had come home the day before and told her they'd be visiting Lucien at his estate for the weekend.

Unfortunately, when they arrived, Horatia learned that a beautiful young heiress named Melanie Burns was also visiting. It was with no small amount of indignation that Horatia had been ushered by an elderly maid to the nursery—*of all places!*—while Cedric, Lucien, Lady Rochester and Miss Burns took tea that morning. By the afternoon, Lysandra was practicing her embroidery and the other children, Linus, Audrey and herself had been sent outdoors to play in the gardens while the weather was still fair. Horatia heaved a sigh but it was cut short when a pair of large hands clamped down over her eyes.

"Guess who?" a rich voice asked in a soft playful chuckle. Horatia's heart stopped for a moment, then fluttered like a hummingbird.

"Lord Rochester?" She knew it was him. She could be blind for a thousand years and know that voice, and his scent of sandalwood and pine. Being near him reminded her of Christmas somehow, even in the spring.

"How on earth did you know it was me, you little hoyden?" Normally being called that would not have pleased her, but when he released her to tug her brown curls, watching them bounce as she gazed up at him, what he called her hardly seemed to matter. Her head tilted back. He was so gloriously tall, like Achilles from *The Iliad*. With deep red hair and warm hazel eyes, he was a god, or very close to it.

Horatia felt her body twist inside in ways she didn't understand. With anyone else this onslaught of physical sensations would have scared her senseless, but with Lucien it did not. Whenever she was with him she trusted him, adored him, and nothing could rip that trust away, not even the awakening of the woman in her.

"Are you enjoying the sun, little Horatia?" He reached down

and ruffled a hand through her hair, the price she paid for refusing to wear one of those dreadful bonnets.

"Yes, the weather is lovely," she answered in what she hoped was a mature tone. She even dared to raise her chin defensively, but Lucien laughed as though he saw right through her.

"I spend all day talking about business, politics, and other dull topics with adults, don't you dare grow up on me." He grinned and reached for her hand. She gave it to him without hesitation. "Now, let us take a turn about the garden and speak of anything else. What do you say to that?"

"Only if you promise to tell me of your wicked conquests," Horatia said boldly, with a glint in her eyes.

Lucien's grip on her hand tightened and he jerked her to a stop. He looked down at her in shock.

"And just what do you know of my wicked conquests?" he demanded, a little on edge.

"Not much I'm afraid. No one tells me anything." Horatia worried her lower lip with her teeth, afraid her boldness had gotten her in trouble.

"And it will stay that way," he replied as he resumed their walk.

"Then what shall we talk about?" Horatia almost had to skip to keep up with him. As they rounded the corner of the nearest hedge, Lucien froze. Miss Burns was sitting on a stone bench, hands folded on her lap. She was complete to a shade, her gown a lovely blue that favored her pale blond hair and brown eyes. Horatia swallowed down a wave of jealously, knowing she would never grow up to be as beautiful. Her own chin was too sharp, her nose too pert; she had none of those classic features that Miss Burns displayed from beneath her bonnet.

"Pardon the intrusion, Miss Burns," Lucien said, smiling at the young woman. It made Horatia's chest ache. Something felt wrong. It felt...it felt hard to breathe.

"My lord, how nice to see you." Miss Burns smiled back. Lucien's grip on Horatia's little hand loosened.

An overwhelming sense of dread flooded through her. Her instincts screamed that this wasn't right.

"Er, you ought to go on ahead, Horatia. I'm sure the other children are looking for you." He released her hand and gave her a brotherly pat on the head, sealing her fate. He might as well have slapped her, for all the pain his disinterested dismissal gave her.

"Yes, do go off and play," Miss Burns said before turning her wide smile back to Lucien who joined her on the bench.

Horatia felt as though a rug had been pulled out from under her. Lucien was no longer paying any attention to her, however. He reached over and put his hand on one of Miss Burns's, the pad of his thumb stroking her wrist slowly. Miss Burns blushed and giggled.

Horatia fled.

Another moment of that and she was certain she would die.

She ran so frantically that she didn't watch where she was going and crashed into Lady Rochester. The lovely matron caught Horatia's chin and turned her face up.

"Whatever is the matter, dear?" she asked.

Horatia was nearly on the verge of tears. "It's nothing," she gasped, trying to breathe.

"It is most certainly not that. Now tell me what's upset you. It must be something serious if a well-possessed young lady such as you is distressed." Lady Rochester had always been so kind to her and Audrey. It was as though she knew she couldn't replace Horatia's mother but had tried to anyway, and Horatia loved her for that.

"It is Miss Burns. I cannot stand her. And he *likes* her!" There didn't seem to be any clearer way to put it.

"By he, you mean Lucien?" Lady Rochester asked.

Horatia managed a shaky nod. "He's with her right now. They were holding hands."

Lady Rochester's eyebrows rose. "Are they? Oh dear. Well, we can't have that."

"What?" Horatia hadn't expected that from Lady Rochester. Miss Burns was her guest after all.

"We cannot allow Lucien to get involved with her sort. That will not do."

"Her sort?" Horatia repeated dumbly. Was she secretly from a common background? Or worse, French?

Lady Rochester sighed and took Horatia's hand.

"Miss Burns is pretty, wealthy and accomplished, but she's not a good woman. I am friends with her mother, but her? I do not want her as my daughter-in-law. She despises children. I once saw her twist Linus's arm to get him to behave. There is discipline and there is abuse and being a good parent is knowing the difference. I shudder to think what my grandchildren would suffer at her hands. That is why we must stop them."

"We're going to stop them?" Horatia asked, hope rising in her chest.

"Of course we are. My son is too blinded by Miss Burns's charms to know the needs of his heart."

"How?" Horatia was serious now. Lucien was the need of her heart and she would do anything to protect him from such a horrible woman.

"I don't know. We'll have to think of something. Now dry your eyes, there's a good girl, and go find the others. I am sure that Linus and Audrey are up to no good. I expect you to prevent any mischief they have planned." Lady Rochester smiled at her, always treating her like the adult she wished she was.

Horatia once more entered the gardens and avoided the path that would lead her back to where Lucien and Miss Burns were sitting. Eventually she came upon a white painted gazebo adorned with a rose covered trellis on one side. Marring the scene of bliss was a little boy near her age and half her maturity. Linus. He was climbing up the trellis with a large metal pail of water. It sloshed as he scrambled up to the gazebo roof and out of sight. Audrey was at the bottom of the trellis waiting for him to return. Her white apron was covered in dirt and her cheeks were rosy as she watched the champion of mischief climb back down.

"Linus, what are you doing?" Horatia demanded.

Linus laughed. "We're going to drop these pails of water on the next person who comes into the gazebo." His tone was haughty as he showed off the second bucket he held.

"You will not. Your mother told me to put a stop to whatever mischief you were up to. Now get back up there and take that other bucket down." Horatia stamped her foot.

"No. You do it," he challenged. "Unless you're scared."

"Fine. I will." Horatia stormed past him and started up the trellis. "Both of you, back to the house." She slipped a few times, getting cuts and scrapes on her hands where thorns bit into her skin. She was nearly to the top when she heard voices. Linus and Audrey stuck their tongues out and ran off, abandoning her to whoever was coming her way. She would get in trouble for climbing up here, even if she was trying to foil Linus's sinister plot. Better to hide. She scaled the last few inches onto the roof. The pail of water was near the hole in the middle of the roof. Horatia saw Lucien and Miss Burns approach the gazebo and come fully inside until they were in its center directly below her. Horatia held her breath, afraid to move in case they heard her.

"Miss Burns, may I ask something?" Lucien began.

"Yes," Miss Burns's melodious voice answered back. Horatia watched the scene unfold with a mixture of horror and revulsion.

"We've known each other for two months and I've grown fond of our times together. As improper as it is to ask you without first speaking to your father, would you consider marrying me?"

Horatia knew Lucien must have been giving Miss Burns one of his most handsome smiles.

"You wish to marry me?" was Miss Burns's not-so surprised reply.

Horatia thrust a fist into her mouth to keep from screaming. He couldn't marry her, he just couldn't! He had to be stopped from making a mistake. Horatia grabbed the pail of water and tipped it over. The water sluiced down in a messy waterfall over Miss Burns's head. Then, unable to stop herself, she dropped the bucket down the hole as well. By God or the devil's grace it landed on her perfectly, fitting her like a medieval helmet.

"Bloody hell!" Lucien hollered as Miss Burns let out a harpy-like shriek that reverberated through the metal.

Unable to stop, Horatia giggled. Miss Burns pulled the bucket off only to trip down the stairs and fall face first into a flowerbed. With another shriek of rage she tore off back into the gardens. Lucien ran a few steps as though to pursue her but then looked up, his eyes meeting Horatia's through the slats on the gazebo roof.

"Horatia Sheridan, get down here this instant!" He stormed out of the gazebo.

Horatia climbed back down from the roof, her body quaking with fear. When she was within reach of him, Lucien gripped her by the waist and wrenched her from the trellis. Horatia felt more thorns tear into her but she dared not make a sound, not even one of pain.

"What did you do that for?" he snarled, hazel eyes blazing.

His tone terrified her and she gulped. "I…" She fisted her hands in her skirts and stepped away from him.

"Spit it out!"

He would never harm her, not physically, but the idea of him being angry at her made her heart jerk against her ribs.

"You can't marry her," she begged.

"What?" Lucien looked angry and confused.

"She's awful. You can't marry her. You can't."

"Whom I marry is my business and mine alone. Do you understand? It is none of your concern."

"But I love you." She had never spoken that thought aloud before, never even knew that she felt it that strongly. But once she said the words, she knew they were true. At fourteen, Horatia had fallen in love with Lucien.

The words silenced Lucien, but not for long. "You don't know the first thing about love. You're a child," he spat.

She looked up at him with pain in her eyes, humiliation bleeding through her, enhancing the splintering of her heart. She put a hand to her mouth to silence her cry of agony, both of body and soul.

"I...I'm sorry," she said. Tears blurred her vision and pain laced her every movement.

Lucien wasn't looking at her, he was looking straight ahead. Miss Burns had returned to the gazebo and had seen everything. She flashed them both a hateful glare and turned away.

Lucien cursed under his breath. "Do not bother to apologize. What you've done today can never be forgiven."

He turned on his heel and chased after Miss Burns.

Horatia sat on the gazebo floor for several long minutes, trembling. Something deep inside her chest seemed to break, and it was only after she finally remembered to breathe that she realized it must have been her heart.

CHAPTER 15

Horatia hated how that memory always managed to choke her at the worst times. She blinked and turned at the sound of a polite cough. Lucien was leaning against the wall a few feet away, watching her.

"Are you all right?" he asked, pushing away from the wall and coming towards her.

"I'm fine."

Lucien frowned and cupped her chin in one hand, turning her to face him.

"I can always tell when you lie," he said, as if the knowledge of this surprised him.

"Yes. I hate that." She needed to get away from him. She needed room to breathe.

He dogged her steps as she left and picked a room at random to try and hide from him. She shut the door and slid the lock into place, relaxing when he tried the knob and couldn't get inside. Leaning back against the door, she listened to him walk away. Her heartbeat slowed in her chest.

Suddenly one of the study bookshelves swung open. Lucien emerged and eased the bookshelf back into its place, grinning.

Horatia gaped. Rochester Hall had secret passageways? How had she not known about them? She truly ought to have been nosier as a child.

"Why do you hate that I can read you so easily?" he asked.

Horatia studied the room with a slight frown. This was Lucien's study. His scent filled the air and a messy pile of letters littered his large desk. She couldn't have picked a worse room to try and escape from him. He was everywhere. And she would not be able to hide from him anywhere on the estate. There were likely passageways all through the house connecting all the rooms.

"Lucien, could you please just leave me alone? You've made your peace with me, and I with you. Can we not leave it at that?" She turned her back to him but he chuckled, coming closer.

"My dear Horatia, I fear you and I are England and France. We quarrel and battle and therein lies the pleasure of our relationship." He brushed back a loose curl that had draped over her shoulder. She flinched, though not from displeasure. Even the barest hint of heat from him was something she could not endure for much longer without wanting to turn in his arms and beg for a kiss.

"I am tired of battling with you, Lucien. It has caused me nothing but grief." She moved towards the window behind his desk, looking over the snow covered gardens. The flowers were all withered and sheathed in ice, and it struck her how much she sympathized with those flowers. Her heart felt much the same, withered and frozen. But Lucien wouldn't let her alone. He was right there behind her, warmth emanating off him in sweet waves, heating her back.

"Then I will leave you, but only if you allow me to honor tradition first. I've heard it is bad luck to ignore such things." His breath fanned her neck, sending shivers of anticipation through her. Who would have thought the word *tradition* could be so seductive? Horatia whirled around to face him, her nose brushing his as she hadn't realized how close he was.

"Tradition?" she asked.

Lucien's eyes flicked up to something over their heads. A sprig of mistletoe, pinned to the wood above the large window.

"But if someone were to come in and see us..." she trailed off as she focused on his lips.

"This is my study. No one will disturb us. Besides, you locked the door." He reached up to brush his knuckles across her cheek, and then his fingertips danced down to her neck where they wrapped around the back of her head. He massaged her scalp in slow tender movements as he pulled her closer. When she was flush against the length of his body, his other hand banded securely about her waist. She moaned and he caught the sound with his lips, plundering her with a possessive tongue.

"I've wanted to do this all day," he said between languid kisses.

"You have?" she asked faintly, leaning more into him than was wise or proper.

"God yes!" The hand about her waist dropped to her bottom and clenched her tight, pushing her against the evidence of his desire. "Have I told you how good you taste?" he murmured, brushing against her lips in a teasing fashion. Horatia shook her head the slightest inch. "You taste heavenly, yet sinful." He licked his way to her left ear, pulling the lobe between his teeth.

Horatia's knees buckled. She clutched his upper arms to keep from collapsing like a rag doll. Lord, the things he could do to weaken her! Hadn't she only just resolved that morning to move on?

"Lucien," she gasped.

"Lucien, yes or Lucien, stop?" He flicked a fingertip over the hardened nub on her right breast through the silk of her gown.

"More," was all she could manage.

With a growl of desire he backed her up into the corner between his bookshelves and the wall. He dipped a hand down to her skirts, rucking them up to grip one of her thighs. With a swift stroke he bared her leg and had it wrapped around his hip so he could push closer into the welcoming cradle of her body. Her head fell back, allowing him access to the underside of her chin and her neck. He devoured her skin with kisses like a starving man.

The closeness of their bodies was both startling and enchanting. Horatia lost herself to Lucien's seduction. How could she have ever wanted him to leave her alone? For one single kiss she'd walk through fire, for a heated glance she'd brave her darkest nightmares. All Horatia could think beyond more, more, was that she would do anything for him. Even after all these years that hadn't changed—so how could she have convinced herself otherwise?

❦

LUCIEN COULDN'T STOP HIMSELF. HER HANDS FISTED IN HIS HAIR and her silken mouth welcomed his tongue with a reckless intensity he'd never experienced from any woman before. He'd had countless lovers and mistresses, but none had so completely abandoned their control as Horatia did. She did not lose herself. She was still Horatia, from the soft brown waves of her chestnut hair to the tips of her blue slippers. But when she kissed him, she threw caution, morals and hesitancy to the wind in a way that had him desperate to possess her.

He'd always prided himself on his own self-control. Of course, lately he seemed to have little of it and Horatia had been testing what remained to its limit. He wanted to sink so deep into her that he'd never leave, wanted to lose himself in her eyes and drown in the symphony of her breathless cries. He'd thought of nothing else the entire carriage ride to Kent. Each time a curl of her hair was jostled by the bumpy road, he'd watched with envy as it caressed the tops of her breasts. When she'd fallen asleep, her lips had softened into a cupid's bow. Usually she kept those lips pursed into a tight line around him. The things he wanted those lips to do made him groan helplessly as he pushed himself even harder against her.

Through the haze of his desire, Lucien was suddenly aware of a voice calling his name, and it wasn't Horatia. It was like a pail of cold water dropped on his head, followed by the pail. It was Cedric, outside the study door.

"Lucien, you devil! Where'd you run off to?" With regret he stepped back from Horatia, holding a finger to his lips to indicate silence.

"Quick, under my desk," Lucien said in a hoarse whisper.

⁂

HORATIA TOOK REFUGE UNDER THE DESK, NEVER MORE thankful it was a large bulky beast and not a spindly-legged dainty creation. Tucking her skirts under her, she curled up just as Lucien unlocked the door before moving around to the front of the desk, to block the small bit of open space between desk and floor. Horatia held her breath as her brother opened the study door and entered.

"There you are! I thought perhaps we'd have a game of billiards to pass the time before dinner. What do you say?" Cedric offered hopefully.

Horatia heard Lucien clear his throat. "Uh, yes. Excellent. You go on. I'll be there directly. I just have a letter I need to see to first."

"Are you all right, Lucien? You look a bit flustered."

"Of course. It's a natural reaction to my mother's rantings about marriage, no matter who her current target might be."

Cedric laughed. "That I can well understand. I shall wait for you in the billiard room." She heard the door click shut.

Lucien exhaled a long slow breath. Horatia echoed it with one of her own. She didn't want to think about what would have happened had Cedric found the door unlocked. Lucien helped her out from underneath the desk. He held her still as he inspected her with a critical eye. Then his hands moved to her hair, tucking stray wisps back into place and securing pins.

"Better," he said as he worked.

"Have you had much practice at this?" She regretted the words the moment they left her.

Lucien raised one brow. "Do you wish for me to deny it?"

She could never ask him to deny what he was. She loved all of him, even the wicked parts. "No."

"There. I think that should do." He stepped back to examine her, cool and distant once again. These mood swings of his were impossibly frustrating.

"You can use the secret passage. It opens up down the hall. I apologize. I ought not to have done this to you. You don't deserve to be manhandled in my home. I promise it won't happen again." Before Horatia could find it in her to reply, he was gone.

"That's a promise I wish you hadn't made," she told the empty study.

Horatia waited in Lucien's study and found herself gazing at the bookshelves. There was one section, near the window that caught her eye. Six books were placed neatly in a row, and each title was familiar to her. Among them was *Lady Eustace and the Merry Marquess*. These particular six titles were a matching set of the books she'd received the last six Christmas holidays. Curious, Horatia crooked an index finger into *Lady Eustace's* spine and pulled the volume off the shelf. She opened it, finding an inscription on the title page that read "Gave to Horatia Sheridan, 1819." He was documenting his gifts to her? To what end?

She examined the other five books, finding similar notations inside, and each book looked well read. Horatia had the most astonishing vision of Lucien reading each book as she did, as if to try and see what she would experience in each book. It was a decidedly happy thought, to know he took great pains to connect with her, even in such an indirect fashion. The sting of his promise to not repeat his seduction lessened in light of these small treasures.

When Horatia finally left Lucien's study she did not find herself alone in the hallway. Lady Rochester was exiting the chamber across the hall.

"Horatia." She waved for Horatia to come to her. Horatia swallowed uncomfortably as she approached Lucien's mother.

"You're blushing, my dear," Lady Rochester observed. "You needn't worry that I shall press you as to the reason why. I suspect that my son is involved."

"Linus?"

Lady Rochester shot her a look that seemed to ask what genus and species of fool Horatia took her for.

"We both know that you've loved Lucien since you were a child. Let us not deceive ourselves in this any longer. Now, come this way. You and I are going to have a little talk."

"But..."

"Don't protest, Horatia. I'm an old woman and I'm used to getting my way."

Horatia tried not to show her incredulity. Lady Rochester may have been in her fifties but she seemed anything but old. She followed Lady Rochester to a room a few doors away to a small, personal chamber of Lady Rochester's.

"Have a seat, Horatia. For heaven's sake, try not to look so ill. I do not mean to bite you." Lady Rochester seated herself in a pale blue chaise across from her.

"So you are still in love with my son." Horatia didn't reply. "Do you wish to win him?"

"I think it is fair to say that I shall never have any chance of winning him."

Lady Rochester smacked her armrest with surprising force. "Nonsense. He's perfectly susceptible to being won over by the likes of you."

"The likes of me?" Horatia did not particularly like the sound of that, given the context of their conversation.

"You are smart, beautiful and a challenge to him. He may not realize it, but he won't be satisfied until he's had you. Am I correct in assuming he has not fully claimed you?"

Horatia felt her head spin, she who never once had the inclination to swoon in her life. "I'm sorry, Lady Rochester, but your question—"

"Oh come now, Horatia. We are women of the world. Society would have you believe otherwise but these topics should be discussed, and frequently. I have never encouraged my children to hide their curiosity or enjoyment regarding the act of lovemaking. Hang polite society and their close-minded nonsensical propriety. A little more boldness and a lot more candor on such matters, and people would have a far easier time of match-making."

Lady Rochester's faint hint of a smile reminded Horatia of Lucien. He favored his mother in looks and characteristics.

"So he hasn't compromised you then. Fully I mean?"

"No, Lady Rochester, we haven't..." she finally managed to say.

"That will make this much easier for us."

"What will?" Horatia found herself asking.

"He's not yet had you. He clearly desires you. If we use that lure of forbidden fruit to our advantage, and I may yet have a wedding before I reach my grave."

"I don't wish to trap him into a marriage. He would despise me. I would not do even one thing to incur his wrath again."

This statement had a great effect on Lady Rochester. "What have you done to incur his wrath before?"

Horatia laughed bitterly. "I'd imagined the whole house knew. You really do not know why Lucien has been cold to me these past six years?" Lady Rochester shook her head. "You recall the last time I was here, when I was fourteen?"

"Naturally. I often wondered why you and Audrey did not return when Cedric came to visit after that. But then your brother always was a tad overprotective, and I've seen fathers and brothers do similar misguided things in the name of good intentions. "

"The day that you found me in the gardens distraught by Lucien and Miss Burns, I found Linus placing a pail of water on top of the gazebo and went up to take it down. But Lucien chose that moment to take Miss Burns into the gazebo to propose marriage. I acted rashly, childishly, and dumped the bucket over her head. She ran away and Lucien yelled at me. I told him I loved him and he laughed in my face. He blames me for Miss Burns's refusal to marry him and I have suffered every moment since. That is why I cannot win him."

Through the entire explanation Lady Rochester was still and quiet, but by the end of the tale she was uncommonly pale.

"Lady Rochester, are you well?"

"My dear, it was me. God in heaven, it was me," Lady Rochester said.

"What do you mean? What was you?"

"When Miss Burns came into the house, wet and furious, Linus and Audrey saw her. My boy teased her by waving an empty bucket and I assumed he had dumped the water on her. Then I saw her strike my son. I told her then in no uncertain terms that she was to leave Rochester Hall immediately. I said that if Lucien were to continue to court her or propose to her, and if she did not refuse him, I would destroy her, and I left her with no doubt that I could do so. I had no idea my idiot offspring would connect you and her departure in such a foolish fashion."

Horatia didn't know what to say. For the past seven years she had believed herself solely responsible for what had transpired that awful day. The view of her world tilted on its axis like a wobbly globe and she couldn't help but wonder if she was one awful spin away from careening off her stand.

Lady Rochester came over to Horatia and wrapped her arms around her shoulders. "I will make it right. I'd had such high hopes you'd marry one of my sons and I'll be damned if I just sit back and not correct my mistakes. You and I will show Lucien how wonderful you are and I promise he will come to his senses. Then I might have grandchildren to dote upon in my old age."

Horatia blinked black tears. Lady Rochester had said this with such conviction that for a moment Horatia completely and totally believed she could do exactly that.

"Now, let us dry our eyes and find your sister. I'm sure what we all need is a good outing. To Hexby, perhaps. There is a decent modiste's shop and a talented milliner that I'm sure your sister will approve of."

Lady Rochester escorted Horatia into the main hall and insisted she wait there until Audrey could be located. Quite alone now, Horatia had a moment to compose herself. She listened to the distant sounds of Lucien and Cedric laughing as they played their game. It was so good to hear them both enjoying themselves.

CHAPTER 16

In a private room of the gentleman's club Boodle's, Sir Hugo Waverly lounged in a chair, swirling a glass of brandy as he listened to the report from Daniel Shefford. Shefford had been his man for years now. Loyal, highly skilled, and one who would do anything he asked for king, country, or his more... personal whims. Shefford stood in front of Waverly, calmly narrating the events that transpired the morning before last when Lord Lennox had narrowly escaped death.

"I managed to track down the man you sent me to meet at the Garden. He said Lord Lennox was waiting in the Garden. He suspected it was because you had been overheard last night. Our man there confirmed that Rochester was at the Garden last night. It seems a likely scenario."

"Rochester was there?" Hugo frowned. Was there no place in London he could find refuge from those damned rogues? How was he supposed to conduct his business without tripping over one of those men?

"And what did he do when he saw Lennox?"

"He took a shot at him. I was told by the Madame of the Garden, acting as a concerned friend of Lennox, that he was shot in the arm. It did not appear to be fatal, but it was no scratch either."

It was fortunate that Lennox had suffered only a minor wound. It was only a matter of time before Lennox and his friends were rotting corpses in the ground. But not before the proper time.

Shefford crossed his arms over his chest. "I returned to my station outside the Sheridan house. It seems the Sheridans have left London, and my source there informed me that their destination was Rochester Hall in Kent."

"Lord Rochester was awarded the honor of playing nursemaid to Sheridan's sisters? How amusing. I daresay that makes things much easier, having the League divided. Did one of your men secure a position?" Waverly asked.

Shefford nodded.

Two months ago, Shefford had acquired five men to infiltrate the League's ranks. Most had already done so and were already feeding him valuable information, and unless told otherwise, that was all they would do. One, however, had so far only been able to find employment at the gentleman's club they frequented, but that particular person had unique potential and, unlike the others, just the right amount of desperation. "Excellent. Now I should like for you to send a message to Sheridan and Lonsdale. I think it is time we leave them both a little gift."

"Do you wish to send this message to Lonsdale's house on Curzon Street?"

"Yes. I'm sure that fool Lennox is watching the Sheridan townhouse carefully, since it is close to his own. I want you to get inside both houses and do what you do best."

Everything was falling into place. In time, the center of the League would be destroyed and their power disbursed to weaker men and less unified heirs. Then? Then the rest would be easy.

"I will deliver an appropriate message, sir. Will that be all?"

"Yes, on that matter. We still have more serious matters to discuss." Waverly returned his attention to his drink.

Killing the League would be easy, though he could never do so in haste without risking exposure. But haste was not his goal. He had more pressing concerns, such as protecting England, it was how he had earned his knighthood. Running spy rings across the continent was no easy feat. Even one of Rochester's brothers was involved in the various tentacles of his operations. The irony of this was not lost on him.

It was what truly mattered to Waverly, protecting the things he cared about. The League had taken so much from him. Two lives were gone because of them. He considered them a threat to himself and therefore a threat to England.

Normally a threat to the nation would be dealt with swiftly and mercilessly. But that was not his intention here. These men deserved...special attention. He knew it was a weakness to indulge in such melodrama and subterfuge. Worse, it was reckless. But then, such risks made life worth living. They were a vice, but one that had sustained him, gave him purpose. A tree of hatred grew inside his heart and would soon bear bitter fruit.

He turned his attention back to Shefford. "Now, where are we on the Spanish matter? It's been almost a month since Panama declared its independence. We need to know what repercussions this will have across Europe. I want men in every court and noble household we can reach. If Spain wishes to go to war to reclaim Panama, we might have an opportunity to pry loose Spain's grasp on their other colonies and destroy their strongholds."

"Of course." Shefford changed topics effortlessly, but Waverly was barely listening. Already his mind had returned to thought of the League and his plans for them.

❦

CEDRIC BENT OVER THE BILLIARD TABLE AND AIMED AT A BALL. "Tell me the truth, Lucien."

"About?" Lucien lounged back against the table's edge, arms crossed.

"Are you quite all right with Horatia being here? I know I have been pushing you to accept her into your life again, but I can stop. I had hoped enough time had passed and perhaps we might put this all behind us." Cedric pursed his lips as he took the shot. He pocketed the green and grinned. Cedric was competitive and excelled at nearly all games and sports.

"You have every right to push me. I'm being obstinate and foolish." After everything they'd been through, resisting Cedric's sister was not going to break them apart, not if he could help it.

"I am relieved to hear you say that," Cedric admitted.

Neither man spoke, both lost in thought. Lucien was visited by the awful memory of the day when Cedric's parents died.

Lucien knew that Cedric had been watching over Audrey at the Sheridan townhouse on Curzon Street when a footman had come running. Cedric once told him that everything seemed to slow from that moment on. The footman was flushed and sputtered about a carriage accident and finally blurted out, "Dead, sir. Both Lord and Lady Sheridan are dead. Your sister suffered a broken arm, but is alive. Lord Rochester was nearby and helped in rescuing your sister."

Lucien would never forget that moment when he'd brought Horatia home after the accident. Cedric had taken two steps towards the door and his legs gave out, sinking to his knees. Lucien had seen to Horatia's care then went back to the accident to see to the care of the bodies.

The bodies...no longer were they Lord and Lady Sheridan. He couldn't allow himself to think of them as such. Not until later.

When Lucien had returned, he found Cedric sitting in the drawing room on a brocaded couch, a favorite place of Lady Sheridan's when she used to embroider or read. He held a tiny, ten-year-old Audrey in his arms. She'd said nothing, would say nothing to anyone for a full three months after. The light in her little brown eyes had dimmed so much that they'd feared daily she might slip away.

He would never forget holding Horatia in his arms. She cradled her broken arm, which had been splinted and bandaged. She cuddled up to him, and would not let go of him until Cedric began to whisper to her softly to comfort her. Horatia had never told him from that day to this what had happened in the carriage before or after the accident. Some memories should never be remembered, and Lucien hadn't pushed her.

Cedric had been lost himself, so young to become the head of his household. He knew nothing of raising children, and poor, sweet Horatia had abandoned her childhood the day after her parents' funeral to help Cedric raise Audrey. Lucien had been at Cedric's side, helping him get his father's estate in order and taking over the title and the responsibilities. No one else save his sisters had ever witnessed his grief. He'd borne it well to his other friends, but Lucien had seen Cedric cry as though he were a boy barely out of leading strings. That bond, that strength of their friendship had to withstand everything. If it couldn't... He would not entertain such dark notions.

Lucien's thoughts returned to the present, though not to the game. "Horatia has grown up these past few years."

"She's not the child she once was," Cedric agreed. "Not for a long time now." The melancholy note in his voice made the air in the room heavier.

"She's certainly not. Old enough to consider marriage. Has no one asked for her?" Lucien attempted the casual question and lined up and took his shot, sinking a red.

Cedric's head shook. "No. There were a few at first, but she has that quiet way about her, you know. Most men find the idea of a woman with her own thoughts off-putting. They didn't continue to court her. I didn't have to scare them off as I do with Audrey's. I know too many men who prefer agreeable chatterboxes for wives. What about you? I know you haven't asked for a woman since Melanie Burns. Have you given up?" Cedric abandoned his cue and turned his full attention to Lucien.

Lucien cleared his throat. "You know... After September..."

"After Emily Parr, you mean?" Cedric supplied with a low

amused chuckle. "We should mark a new calendar with that date—Before Christ, Anno Domini, and now After Emily Parr."

"Quite. But after watching Emily and Godric fall in love, I realized that I had never loved Melanie. We simply played our parts exceedingly well. The charmed and the charming. I think I loved the idea of being in love with her. Does that make any sense?"

Cedric laughed, fixing his brown eyes on Lucien, eyes that reminded him so much of Horatia just then. It was more than familial resemblance alone. Both Cedric and his sister often smiled with their eyes, it was in their natures.

"All too much sense. You were besotted with an ideal, a woman raised on a pedestal. One can worship women on pedestals, but those women can never love one back the same way. A flesh and blood woman on the other hand is another matter entirely, or so I'm told." Cedric's wry chuckle spoke volumes.

Lucien nodded. "Once I realized that, it occurred to me that perhaps I ought to be more thankful to Horatia for her timely interference."

Cedric grinned. "That is perhaps quite the most intelligent thing I've heard you say."

The two men finished their game in companionable silence. It was one of the things Lucien liked best about Cedric. He was not a man who over-talked. Charles was prone to narrating fantastical tales, Ashton always waxed the philosophical. But Godric and Cedric were more often quiet, either lost in whatever game was being played, or consumed by thoughts of their own. Lucien valued that, the gentle support of good friends. One did not need to be wining and wenching to enjoy oneself. Those days were long past and he was glad. He was grateful to have such good friends.

A commotion from the hall alerted them to the presence of others.

"It seems the shopping party has returned," said Lucien. "I daresay we should make ourselves scarce." But before either man could scamper to a more hidden location, Audrey came barging in, with a disgruntled Linus in tow.

"Cedric! You must correct Linus and tell him that my new bonnet is fetching. He says it looks like a poorly constructed bale of hay." Audrey pointed to her rather broad brimmed hat that used a most peculiar style of thatch work.

"I believe my exact words were 'a hastily gathered haystack.'" Linus grinned at Audrey's flabbergasted expression, but his amusement was short lived. Audrey grabbed the pool cue from Lucien's hands and jabbed the fat handle into Linus's ribs, causing him to double over.

"And that is my *cue* to leave." Lucien chuckled and slipped out, leaving Cedric to handle his sister and Linus.

"That's awfully rotten of you, Russell, to abandon me to death by billiard cue!" Cedric called out as he dodged the stick Audrey swung around, attempting to impale Linus with the pointy end.

Lucien expected to find Horatia somewhere in the hall, but it was his mother who was lying in wait for him. She looked more dangerous than a cobra nestled in a basket.

"I should like a private word with you, Lucien."

Her tone did not bode well. It was too close to the one she used to lure him into a false sense of security before he was paddled as a child. He was well beyond his paddling years, but should his mother entertain such thoughts again he would most assuredly escape out the nearest window or door before she could get her hands on him.

He'd often wondered if perhaps there was some secret pamphlet that a mother received upon the birth of her first child that bore instructions on how to instill fear in one's child with only a look. If there was, his mother had been a quick study. Perhaps she had written the latest edition.

"Lucien, don't dally. Attend me now." His mother proceeded to her personal rooms. She seated herself and waited for him to follow suit. He did so, reluctantly eyeing the door he'd foolishly shut behind him.

"What is it, Mother?" A nervous churning settled over him as he recognized the determined look on her face.

"It has come to my attention that I've made a grave error. One that has had unseen ramifications for the past several years."

Lucien was dumbfounded. His mother was admitting to a mistake? Surely cows were hurtling over the moon and pigs were discovering the luxury of wings. He eyed his mother cautiously, waiting for her to continue.

"On the day that you proposed to Miss Burns—"

Lucien was on his feet, not wanting to hear his mother say another word.

"On that day." Those were the words she said. The tone, however, said, "Sit down."

Lucien glared at her and returned to his chair.

"I encountered Miss Burns after the accident in the gazebo. Linus saw her and began to tease her with an empty bucket. She struck him, Lucien. She struck your brother, and it was not the first time she'd done this. I informed her that she was to refuse to marry you or I would make sure she would regret it. She was unkind to those beneath her and especially cruel to children. I would not tolerate such a match, nor such a woman to bear my grandchildren. I am telling you this now because I've only just discovered that you've blamed an innocent party all these years."

Lucien felt as if he'd been shot as her words sank in. *You've blamed an innocent party all these years.* Miss Burns had rejected him, told him if he couldn't stand up to a mere child to defend her, then he wasn't a man worth marriage. He'd been furious at the time, but he'd seen the truth of Miss Burns's character later when she'd married Waverly.

He couldn't tell his mother that Miss Burns barely mattered anymore. He dared not confess it was a convenient excuse to keep him away from temptation, though one that had become ineffective as of late. The pain his mother's words struck was entirely his own fault. He'd only just begun to try to undo the wrongs he'd done to Horatia and to have his mother throw his sins back in his face was worse than he could have imaged.

"I can see that you need some time to come to terms with what

I've said." She got up. "I will leave you now. But Lucien, do not postpone your apology to her."

Lucien looked up at his mother. "What could I ever do to make right seven years of coldness?"

Lady Rochester's eyes were softer and more motherly than he'd seen in years.

"A kind word to begin with. Despite your attempts to drive her away, she has clung to the memory of your kindness like a piece of driftwood in a storm. The fight has worn her down, but some tenderness will ease her suffering and strengthen her faith in you again."

Lucien realized, not for the first time in his life, that his mother was well and truly wise. For all her obsessions over the latest fashions and horrifying attempts to marry off her children, she was a woman of great understanding and intelligence.

"Thank you, Mother," he whispered.

Lady Rochester inclined her head, put a soft hand on his cheek and then left him alone. Lucien collapsed back into his chair. What was he to do? Where was he to start? But before he could ponder his course of action he was arrested by a distracting and ludicrous sight out the nearest window overlooking the expansive gardens.

"What in God's name?" he muttered and stepped closer to the window.

CHAPTER 17

The afternoon seemed to stretch for hours. Linley's back ached from hiding in the mews outside Jackson's Salon. The dark suit he wore was borrowed and slightly too big, as were the waistcoat and breeches. The entire ensemble was nearly threadbare and didn't keep out the chill of the winter wind. With each gust, he hastily gripped the edges of his white-powdered wig on his head, keeping it secure.

He prayed that the man he was sent to watch would appear soon. His fingers were turning blue and his blood was like ice in his veins. His quarry, the Earl of Lonsdale, a skilled boxer, could spend hours in the salon. There was no telling when Linley would get a chance to escape the cold and seek shelter inside. He rubbed his hands together, attempting to generate warmth. It didn't help.

A sudden wave of exhaustion swept through him. He didn't want to be here. His master had made him come here. Sir Hugo Waverly. A true bastard if there ever was one. Tom tried not to think about it but failed.

He was the man who'd taken advantage of him... and stolen something precious from him. Stolen everything, really. Including his freedom.

The month following his master's assault, Waverly's wife had dismissed him without references. That alone had threatened his future and now he had someone who depended on him. But Hugo could always make it worse. It had been easy for his master to take advantage of his desperation and force him into this job. This new identity. This new life of shadows and subterfuge.

My poor baby girl. He thought with aching sorrow of Katherine, the child he cared for. His Kate was the most important thing in Tom's life. Waverly had threatened to take her away, and Lord only knew what he would do with her...

Unless he gained the confidence of the Earl of Lonsdale and infiltrated his household. Tom sensed something darker and more horrifying was afoot but he was helpless to stop whatever his master had planned. His orders were simple, though far from easy—get hired by Lonsdale to replace the valet who'd recently left his employ and regularly report back to Waverly.

Tom didn't want to lie to anyone, and certainly not the earl. After a week of discreet surveillance, he'd learned enough about Lonsdale not to want to betray him. He was a rake but not a cad. He was a man who would offer a hand in aid of those who needed it. Tom had seen him more than once toss several coins to paupers as he passed and never had a harsh word for others, even when men deep in their cups tried to start arguments. But to save little Kate, Tom would have to damn himself and do wrong by one good man for the sake of a bad one.

❧

THE BIZARRE SIGHT OF AUDREY AND LINUS CHASING A STRAY goat dressed in a lady's spencer was one Lucien could not draw his eyes away from. The garment, once a lovely shade of baby blue, was now torn in several places and beginning to fray at the edges.

Lucien watched from the window as Audrey screamed bloody murder. She dove at the goat and fell to the frozen ground as it bolted away. Linus had taken up a garden hoe and was charging at the animal but a shout halted his blow. Horatia arrived, hastily dressed for the cold, and urged Linus to back away from the angry goat.

Lucien chuckled at the bleating creature whose wild eyes promised retribution on anyone who dared accost it further.

Horatia bent over and held out a carrot, coaxing the stubborn thing to eye her less viciously. It took a few cautious steps closer, then nibbled the carrot. When Horatia set the vegetable down the goat did not pay any attention to her as she casually extracted the spencer from it. She then returned the ruined garment to a distraught Audrey.

Lucien held his breath from his vantage point, enjoying the sight. Horatia's hair was a bit windblown and her cheeks flushed with the thrill of the chase. Horatia's womanly body with ample curves was made for passionate lovemaking and wicked fantasies. She was, in truth, the woman he'd always wanted, always needed. Even in light of his mother's revelations, it could never happen.

She was Cedric's sister, and the League had rules.

Lucien couldn't trust himself with her. He wanted to make love to her by candlelight, to better see the shadows playing across the curves of her body. He enjoyed restraining a woman and rousing her to peaks of pleasure. Never to hurt, no. But he loved to have power over a woman, and more importantly, her trust. He could learn every sensitive place and dark desire she harbored so he might fulfill it. He never once left a woman unsatisfied after a night tied to his bed, and he refused to enjoy himself until his lover had first been fully sated.

Now, this finely honed talent would go to waste. The one woman he longed for was the one woman he could never have. He wanted to be with her in ways he'd never been with other women, to show her a side of himself he'd always held back from others. Perhaps Horatia's allure was derived from her unattainability. Forbidden fruit. He could only pray she was safe from him, so long as he exercised that damned self-control that had frayed at the edges lately.

Lucien tore himself away from the window as he heard Audrey's shrill voice echoing in the main hall.

"I swear, Linus, you are the worst sort of man! How could you put my best spencer on a goat?"

"I thought the little fellow looked chilly."

"It already has a coat. What more does it need?"

"'Tis the season of giving. You should be thankful I exercised my goodwill to ensure the goat's warmth."

"The season of giving? I'll give you something!"

There was a thump and a responding shout of pain.

"What in God's name did you put in that...rocks?" Linus bellowed.

Lucien came out of his mother's room in time for Audrey to dodge around behind him, using him as a shield from Linus's revenge.

"Save me, Lucien!" Audrey begged, her little hands fluttered about his shoulders, along with a rather heavy reticule.

"Hand her over, Lucien. It's high time I took my hand to her backside." Linus sounded positively medieval as he glared at the woman.

"You ruined her spencer on that goat, Linus, and I'm sure it was an expensive one." Lucien crossed his arms and glared back at his youngest brother, lucky to have the advantage of age, since Linus equaled him in height.

"That jacket was six weeks' worth of pin money I shall never get back," Audrey said. "Perhaps I ought to have it from your quarterly allowance?" Audrey smiled impishly.

Linus reddened. "Why you..." He took a step forward but Lucien halted him with a firm palm.

"I think that is an excellent idea. You shall pay back the full amount of the spencer, won't you, Linus?"

Linus growled but gave a curt nod and stalked off.

"Oh and Linus," Lucien called after him. "You have one week, or I shall pay her myself and deduct it from your allowance,"

Audrey clapped her hands and danced about Lucien. "Oh you

are such a dear! My champion!" Audrey stood up on tiptoe to kiss his cheek before she dashed off, no doubt to further incite his brother and cause more trouble. So be it.

"That was awfully kind of you." Horatia's voice gave Lucien a start. She'd been hidden near the door to the back garden.

"It is only fair. Linus is over twenty now. He ought to be growing up. The years for pranks are over, but he seems determined to learn this the hard way. I can't understand why he still acts like a child. Mother coddles him too much, I suppose."

"Audrey's provocation doesn't help matters," Horatia added. "They played too often together as children to really adjust to their more mature roles in life. It's one of the reasons I never worry about my lack of diligence as their chaperone." Horatia confessed this with a small little smile.

Lucien's chest tightened as a wave of guilt struck him. An awkward silence settled between the pair. Horatia's warm smile wavered and then wilted as the silence lengthened.

"Pardon me," Lucien said gruffly and turned to leave. He couldn't bear to be near her anymore. Caught between deserved guilt and wicked desire, he was damned if he claimed her and damned if he didn't.

Lucien called for the footman, Gordon, to send a message to the stables that he wanted his horse then went in search of his greatcoat and riding gloves. A ride would do him good. Cold air and solitude would cool his ardor and give him time to think. Thankfully, Horatia did not follow him.

A groom brought Lucien's stallion to the hall steps. The beast twitched its tale. Lucien nodded to Gordon and then mounted up. He trotted from the main yard and crossed the snowy meadow to the east of the hall. His horse plodded along on the icy snow, carefully treading until the snow became thicker. Then Lucien coaxed it into picking up the pace. Then wind whipped through his coat as he cantered through the meadow.

Gray clouds formed a thick winter wall, leaving the land ahead of him a shadowy world between intermittent snowfalls. There was something beautiful about the desolation of Kent in winter, especially this year. More often than not, snow was rare, but this year the grounds were covered with it. The decay of life lay inches below the snow, unobserved. That world held secrets, like the moment before a swimmer breaks the surface for breath, the seeds in the ground waited to breathe, to reveal themselves. Lucien felt much the same, waiting to breathe, waiting to break free.

He remembered the multitude of kisses he'd stolen from Horatia, both in anger and desire. Now, without anger to fuel his emotional blindness, he could see the truth. It wasn't merely desire, nor lust for forbidden fruit, it was something more. Something secret lay hidden beneath the flames of his passion.

I shouldn't, but... He watched his breath blossom in a pale cloud as he examined his confusing thoughts about his feelings for Horatia.

Lucien's horse had slowed to a complete stop now, something the beast had never done before without encouragement.

How odd.

He dug his heels into the horse's side to give it a kick of encouragement. The horse whipped its head around violently. Lucien kicked again, and this time the horse bucked and whinnied. Lucien clung to the reins as he sought to keep himself in the saddle. The horse reacted even more fiercely and this time Lucien was unprepared. He was flung from the horse, his arms tangled in the reins as he landed with a crunch on the icy ground. Pain exploded through his head and body. His vision spun in slow circles, then started to fade...

CHAPTER 18

Seeing Ashton wounded had shaken the very foundations of Charles's existence. He needed to restore some sense of order to his world, to reassert his strength and defense. He stood in the ring of Jackson's Salon practicing his boxing technique. Sweat gleamed on his forehead and dampened his hair.

He fought like a man possessed. Punch after punch, opponent after opponent, and still he battled on, ignoring his aching muscles. As he punched and ducked, all he saw was Ashton. Pale from blood loss, resting in Essex House as he recovered from his injury. The doctor had assured everyone there was little to worry about and that Ashton would recover control of his arm in time.

Many of the men in the best circles enjoyed to play at boxing, but not Charles. He took the art seriously. A pugilistic match was his way of fighting back against his fears and insecurities.

Conquer the ring and you conquer your demons.

Today, he sported a blackened eye, one he'd deserved but not gotten in the ring. Charles grinned as he withstood the ribbing by the other gentlemen at Jackson's. They'd all assumed he finally lost a fight and he was not about to tell them the real reason.

His current opponent was a man named Everard Ralph, a

young pup compared to Charles, eager to test his mettle against Jackson's unofficial reigning champion. The two traded blows for a good twenty minutes before Ralph began to weaken.

"Had enough?" Charles asked. His usually light tone was on edge.

Ralph stumbled back a step as Charles pressed his advantage.

"Enough, Lonsdale, enough!" Ralph gasped as he dodged another jab from Charles. "Lord, you fought like the devil himself today."

He was a decent enough fellow with the sort of grin that made virginal maidens swoon and widows leave their calling cards in his coat pockets. He had nothing on Charles though. Charles had been a rakehell since the age of seventeen and the more blackened his reputation became, the more women seemed to "stray" across his path. However, the game was beginning to change.

It was one thing to abduct a girl like Emily Parr and revel in the delight of such a devilish scheme. But it was another thing altogether to get into his carriage after a night of carousing and find a lady waiting inside to be compromised by him. That was not how the game ought to be played. He was supposed to give chase and the lady to flee, but for the past couple of years he felt as though he was the one fleeing.

Matchmaking mothers schemed when he entered ballrooms and seemed to hear wedding bells when his name was announced at Almack's. Despite his notorious reputation, he was always able to obtain vouchers to the club's assembly rooms, probably because the risk of allowing him entrance was worth the opportunity for someone to catch him.

When Charles had relayed this unfortunate turn of events to Ashton, the man had said in his usual wise way, "Perhaps a bit of respectability and restraint would dim your allure to the unmarried ladies." At the time, Charles had scoffed. "Ash, you and I both know I am capable of many things, but respectability and restraint are not among them." To which Ashton had pointed out, "It has done wonders for Godric. Look at him and Emily."

Charles had huffed and stalked away.

"Thank you for the match, Lonsdale. It proved most instructive." Ralph offered a hand to Charles. Charles shook it before leaving the ring and retrieving his towel. He wiped his face and contemplated the poor state of his clothes. His valet had just left his service to marry a maid from a neighboring household. Charles liked to be immaculately dressed and would need a new valet quickly. It was just one more problem on a growing list.

He needed a drink. Now. With this in mind, he headed for his gentleman's club, Berkley's. None of his friends would be there tonight, which was a blessing. He was not fit for company. He was in a foul mood and would soon drink enough to reach a state of oblivion for the rest of the evening. He could also ask around to see if anyone knew of a valet looking for a new position.

In half an hour, he was sitting alone in a private room, glass in hand, listening to the fire crackle in the hearth. Voices outside in the halls sounded merry, so contrary to his own spirits. The door to the room opened as a servant entered. There were many young men and errand boys employed by Berkley's. Charles rarely interacted with them, unless he was determined to get deep into his cups and he needed them to keep the brandy coming.

"Afternoon, my lord. Care for another decanter?" the lad asked. He was small for his age, with light hair hidden by a cap, and blue eyes. His features were perhaps a little too delicate, his frame a bit odd in places, all the signs of awkward youth. He'd grow into his body like all men did. Funny, he'd never given much thought to the servants here before. Something about this boy however, grabbed his attention.

"Have I finished the first already?" Charles seemed surprised. He looked to the side table where the tray of brandy and extra glasses were. Sure enough it was empty. The lad brought the second to Charles and topped his glass with the warm amber liquid.

"Thank you." Charles hastily tipped the glass back and downed its contents.

The boy's eyes went wide with shock.

Charles merely chuckled. "Ever had brandy?" he asked.

The boy shook his head, a lock of hair escaping from his powdered wig to fall across his eyes. Just then, something melancholy stirred inside Charles like twisting shadows. Had he ever been that young? If he had, he couldn't remember when.

"How old are you?" Charles asked the boy.

"Twenty, my lord."

"Twenty? That's a lie if I ever heard one. You're far too—scrawny." Charles knew he was a little too drunk to curtail his tongue. The boy's eyes narrowed.

Charles raised his hands in defense. "My apologies, lad. I'm determined to get foxed and you are the victim of my being two out of three sheets to the wind. Come, sit. I trust they have no need of you downstairs for a while." Charles pointed to an empty chair by the fire. He hadn't thought he'd wanted someone to keep him company, but the young man looked as though he could use a rest. His eyes were shadowed with dark circles from lack of sleep. Charles could give the lad a rest and ease his sudden desire for companionship tonight.

"Oh I couldn't, my lord!" the boy protested. "It's against the rules."

Charles dug into his pocket, retrieved a handful of shillings and held them out.

"I'm a member of this club. As such the rules bend when I need them to. I request that you see to my needs. One of those needs is that you sit and keep me company."

The boy heaved a sigh and took the offered shillings with a grateful smile. It seemed he was in bad need of coin. He knew a man's pride could keep him from taking charity.

"What's your name?"

The boy hesitated. "Linley, my lord. Tom Linley."

"Tell me, have you worked here long?"

Linley shook his head. "Only a few months. I used to work as a valet, but haven't been able to find new employment. My old Master would not give me a reference."

"Oh?" Charles sat up a little. "Why's that?"

Linley scowled. "He and I did not see eye to eye on the upkeep of his wardrobe. Clothes are there to help define a man's character, and my master did not respect the importance of that."

This young man had ideas akin to Charles's own mind. A proper wardrobe was crucial for a man to make a powerful impression upon society. This lad could well be the answer to his valet problem.

"Do you like your employment at Berkley's? Be honest. I shan't tell the club owners what you say." As he waited for the boy to answer, he was seized by a strange desperation to save this lad. Why he couldn't say. Perhaps he wanted to pass on the kindness his own friends had shown him. Linley was in sore need of someone to look after him. It wasn't hard to deduce that the lad's father was out of the picture and there didn't seem to be any brothers.

"It isn't wise to trust a man deep in his cups," the boy said warily.

"Ha! Never have truer words been spoken!" Charles laughed and spied a smirk from the lad. "Now, I am drunk enough to consider offering you a position, but sober enough to swear on my father's grave my intentions are good and I won't forget my promises in the morning. Would that interest you? I would pay double whatever you are getting paid now."

"But my lord, you do not know how much I'm currently paid!" the boy exclaimed, eyes widening to the size of saucers.

"Believe me, Linley, whatever you are receiving here, it is nothing compared to what I'd pay for a decent servant. I have need of someone to attend to me while I'm about town. For me a valet is more than a personal attendant."

"Surely you possess footmen for such duties?" Linley inquired.

"I do, but their duties keep them homebound. They're hard working, but not much fun to be around. There's only so much professionalism I can stand. I'd rather hire a scamp like you to entertain me." Charles had noticed Linley's articulated speech and controlled grace, something that only came from a person raised in a good environment. "You seem to be educated enough to provide amusing conversation."

"I am the son of the lady's maid to the Dowager Countess of Haverton," Linley supplied.

"Haverton? I know the earl, he's a good man. Now, what say you, Linley? Care to take on the job?" A delightful buzz was warming his veins as he mellowed. Linley was already proving a useful distraction.

"Before I agree...permit a question, my lord."

"Go on."

Linley fidgeted in his chair. "I am not the sort of man who would agree to—well I wouldn't allow you to *use* me." The young man's face flushed as he sought the words to clarify his meaning. "I mean, I have no interest in men and will not allow you to...to use me for physical sport. If that is your intention, then I must respectfully decline."

"What? Don't be ridiculous," Charles laughed. His sexual interests had always been towards women and he was amused by the man's assumptions. "I know I have a certain scandalous reputation, but it isn't for that. Mr. Linley, the truth is you remind me of myself when I was younger. Scared, alone and in need of a friend." He paused, shocked at how the truth came so easily. "I offer only a position and some companionship. Nothing else. Have I passed your test?"

Linley studied him before he replied. "I should like to know exactly how much I'd be paid and where I would expect to lodge. Also, I have a problem." Linley's brows furrowed. He paused to draw a slow breath. "I am the sole caretaker of my young sister, a babe only one year old. I must have a means to care for her as well."

Charles contemplated this news with a surprising level of seriousness. He did want the lad to work for him, and a baby seemed to be part of the terms. There was certainly room at Charles's house.

"Very well." He lightly smacked his hands on his thighs and stood up. "I should like you to start right away. No sense in you staying here a moment longer. I will speak with the management to secure your release on good terms. You may accompany me to dinner tonight at the St. Laurent house. Afterwards we can see about moving you into my townhouse and finding a nursemaid for your sister. I daresay my housekeeper would be up to the challenge whilst you see to your duties with me. Her own child just left for school and I fear she's becoming lonely." Charles set his glass of brandy down. "I am willing to offer thirty-five pounds a year as your salary. What say you to that?"

Linley's eyes grew round as he mouthed the words back in wonderment.

"May I take your befuddled reaction as an acceptance?"

Linley nodded mutely.

"Excellent. Have a drink of brandy, in celebration of your new employment." Charles handed Linley his glass and Linley took a small sip, sputtering almost immediately. Charles laughed and slapped Linley on the back as the boy coughed.

"Haven't much experience with liquor?" he asked.

Linley's face drained of color. "Only to receive the beatings of those too deep in their cups."

Charles's chest tightened. He despised those who used drink as an excuse to unleash their demons on others.

"If you don't mind my asking, sir, how did you come by that shiner?" Linley asked quietly.

"This?" Charles touched his purple eye. "I got this after I aided a friend of the female persuasion."

"Someone tried to harm you when you helped a young lady?" Linley looked doubtful.

Well, if this young man was going to be his valet, it would be best if Linley understood what kind of adventures—or rather misadventures—he could expect to see in his service.

"The lady was a sister of my close friend." He paused, uncertain of how to explain what sounded like terrible behavior. "She wishes to marry someone, but her brother is being a bit of an arse, if you will. So she asked me to make it look like she'd been compromised so that her brother would be willing to discuss her marriage to this other fellow."

"Oh?" Curiosity gleamed in Linley's eyes. "Did she succeed?"

"Somewhat. Her brother has agreed to discuss marriage, once he's done with some, er...business." Charles found himself limiting his comments. One could never be too careful. Waverly had a vast reach in the London underworld and Charles knew better than the others how low he would stoop to achieve his evil ends.

"That is fortunate, for the lady I mean," said Linley. "She is lucky her brother is so kind and understanding."

"I wouldn't go that far. I got this after all." He pointed again to his eye. "But it will all work out in the end. I trust in that."

The resigned look the boy had entering the room earlier was now gone. Charles felt a warmth in his chest that seemed to spread through his body and it had nothing to do with the brandy. Helping the boy had made him feel good in a way he hadn't felt in ages. It reminded him of how the other members of the League once saved him.

Linley cleared his throat. "Thank you for the opportunity, my lord."

"Think nothing of it, lad."

Linley made an odd little noise before trying another sip of his brandy. It seemed to go down easier this time. Charles took in the companionable silence as he waited for Linley to finish off his glass.

"Well, we'd best be off if I'm to dine at Essex's tonight. First, we'll see to your employer, then I shall need to return home to change."

Horatia stared at Lucien's riderless horse as it galloped around the side of the house and found its way back to the stables. Even as fast as it was moving, it seemed to be favoring its left foreleg. The reins hung limply in front of it.

Where was Lucien? She ran to snatch her cloak and left through a side door close to the stables. She dashed outside and took hold of the horse's reins. The horse fixed her with a baleful stare. It was then that Horatia saw the trickle of blood near the back of the saddle. She loosened the girth and raised the saddle with trembling fingers.

A sprig of barberry was embedded into the horse's skin, the thorns causing a painful wound on the animal. If Lucien had sat back too hard he would have forced the thorns deeper. Horatia gazed out towards the field. Where was Lucien? Perhaps the horse had escaped him when he'd returned.

She brought the horse to the stables where a groom took the reins.

"He had some barberry tucked under his saddle," she informed him.

"What?" The groom looked mortified. He removed the horse's saddle to inspect the damage. "Blast, the thorns must have caught on the saddle blanket somehow. Did his lordship find this?"

"No. I thought Lucien was here. Did he not return?"

When the groom shook his head, Horatia felt her heart leap into her throat. She ran to the nearest occupied stall where a stout horse was feeding contentedly. She pulled out a loose bridle and quickly fixed it before dragging it from its stall.

"I'll saddle him quickly. Allow me to go with you." The groom hastily threw a blanket and saddle over the horse's back and strapped him in. "You'll need help if he's had an accident."

Horatia shook her head. "No. If he's had an accident I need you to get the doctor from Hexby immediately. We can't waste any time." She raised a hand when he started to protest. "You'll be able to ride faster to the village to get the doctor."

"Very well." The groom frowned but did as she asked.

Once mounted, she guided the house out of the stables and looked along the ground for hoof prints. Only one set of tracks led away from the hall. Horatia followed them, urging the horse to gallop. Its heavy large hooves pounded through the snow steadily.

Lucien, where are you?

After what seemed like acres of endless white, Horatia spotted a dark shape in the distance. As she drew closer she realized with horror that it was Lucien's body.

"Oh God!" she gasped. "Faster, damn you!" she shouted at the draft horse and it increased its pace.

When she was within a few yards she slid from the saddle and ran to Lucien. He was face down in the snow, cloak wrapped about him. Horatia rolled him onto his back and paled when she saw the bloody gash above his forehead. His eyes were closed and his pale lips parted.

She couldn't lose him now, not after everything that had passed between them. Memories flashed across her eyes—the way he'd twist his lips up in a wicked smile, the brush of his lips against hers, the sweetly whispered words he'd spoken to her when they'd shared the room at the Midnight Garden.

"Lucien!" She bent her ear to his lips, praying to feel the warmth of his breath. It was there, but barely. Horatia put her palms on either side of his cheek, letting her warmth seep into his cold skin. Once her hands grew too cold she dragged his body into her lap and held him close, rubbing him, praying her body heat would have some effect. After what felt like an eternity, Lucien's dark lashes fluttered. When his hazel eyes focused at last, it was not on her face but on her bosom, which was mere inches from him. He managed a weak smile.

"Heaven looks quite lovely from this angle." The smile changed into a playful leer, even as Horatia's eyes narrowed.

"I'll ignore that because you are alive." She cupped his cheek and pressed her trembling lips to his forehead in a thankful kiss. She could have wept with relief, but she pushed the tears back. He wasn't out of the woods yet. She needed to get him back to the house and have the doctor see to him.

"Scared you, did I?" Lucien teased but still she couldn't stop shaking. "More than I'd care to admit. What happened?"

"Not sure, I was riding and suddenly my horse threw me."

"There were thorns under the saddle blanket digging into your horse."

"Thorns?" Lucien struggled to sit up.

"They must have snagged on the blanket as it was being saddled." Horatia allowed him to pull away as he unwound his cloak and tried to stand. He wobbled so unsteadily that she threw one of his arms over her shoulders to support him as she led him to the horse.

"Can you mount him?" she asked.

"I'd rather mount you," he said with a grin. His gaze seemed to grow unfocused again.

Horatia gripped the horse's neck and mane as she pulled herself up in the saddle.

"This is not the time nor the place, you fool." Horatia pinched his arm, bringing him back to reality. "Now, focus! Can you get up or not?"

"Hold him steady and I shall find out." Lucien managed to swing himself up. He immediately slumped against her back, his head falling on her shoulder.

"Stay conscious, Lucien. Hold on to me." He wrapped his arms about her waist and she urged the horse back to Rochester Hall.

It seemed to take ages to reach the house. There were a few more moments when Lucien threatened to slip away into unconsciousness. Horatia knew little in the way of medicine, but she'd been told she should not allow him to fall asleep with a head wound.

"Stay awake!"

"I'm trying." His frustrated voice vibrated against her ear. "You're too damned warm. I just want to hold you and fall asleep..." His words softened into a drowsy murmur.

"What would keep you awake?" she hissed. "If I could turn around I'd happily slap you—" His hands slid up from her waist to her breasts, cupping them and then gently kneading them. Horatia arched in shock, though not without pleasure.

"Now this is keeping me very awake."

"Take your hands off of me!"

He squeezed her breasts and chuckled, then shifted even closer to her from behind. She felt a distinctive prod against her backside.

She glanced up at the skies. Even in grave bodily danger the man was a cad. "Fine. If it helps you stay awake...but I swear to God, Lucien, the second we're in sight of the house, move your hands, unless you want my brother to see!"

That comment had him drop his hands straight back to her waist, but he stayed awake the rest of the journey home. The sting of disappointment that he hadn't tried to push her further surprised her. Did she want him to just walk all over her and force her to admit she wanted, no, craved his touch? Yes. She loved it when he did that.

When she drew the horse up by the main doors she was relieved to see a carriage and a separate pair of horses had beaten them there. The two riders she recognized at once.

"Avery, Lawrence, help!" The two younger Russell brothers leapt from their horses and ran to her.

"What happened?" Avery reached up to help her down. She let him catch her waist and drop her gently to her feet.

"His horse threw him. I found him out in the meadow a good deal away." Horatia pointed to Lucien who slumped immediately without her body for support. "He was unconscious, and he has a nasty head wound. Before I left I sent the head groom for the doctor in Hexby."

"Well done, Miss Sheridan. Come on, Lucien. This way, towards me." Lawrence coaxed his drowsy elder brother down from the horse.

Avery seemed reluctant to release Horatia. "And you, are you all right?"

"I'm fine, really. Help Lawrence."

The brothers carried Lucien inside like he'd staggered home drunk from a tavern. Horatia handed the bridle to a groom, then took off after them.

The entry hall of Rochester Hall was full of people. Lady Rochester had apparently been in the midst of welcoming the Cavendishes, who had arrived at the same time as Lawrence and Avery.

"Get out of the bloody way! Wounded man coming through!" Avery bellowed as he and Lawrence carried their brother through the crowd towards the stairs leading to Lucien's bedchamber.

Lady Rochester started to follow them but Lucien shook his head. "I'm fine, Mother. Please, stay with the guests. Horatia will see to me and send you up when I'm settled." His tone, while breathless, brooked no argument.

"I'll be up to see you soon, my dear," she promised him.

Horatia tried to follow after Avery and Lawrence, but Lady Rochester grabbed her arm, demanding answers. In a breathless rush she explained the events in an attempt to calm the crowd at large. Strangely, the act soothed her for the moment as well.

"He looks well," Sir John Cavendish said. "Don't fret. If he's walking and talking he'll be fine. I suffered worse during the war."

Sir John Cavendish and his wife Marie were old family friends of the Sheridans and Russells. Until Sir John had moved his family to Brighton four years ago, the three families had often spent the holidays together.

His calm words drew a trembling nod from Horatia. He was right. Sir John was always right. She'd never met a more level-headed man.

"Sir John, how lovely to see you again." Horatia greeted him with real warmth and embraced the lovely and Rubenesque Marie. The Cavendishes had two children, Gregory and Lucinda with them. Lucinda was Horatia's age with blond hair and blue eyes. She was a more feminine version of her impossibly attractive brother Gregory, who had been schoolmates with Avery at Eton and Cambridge, being only year apart in age.

"Excuse me, I must go and see how Lucien is." Horatia managed to slip away from everyone and dash up the stairs.

Lucien's door was open and he was lying in his bed stripped of his wet clothes. His eyes were closed and his chest bare with the blankets pulled up only to his waist. His muscles were smooth and sculpted and for a second her mind blanked before reality crashed in. Three pairs of eyes studied her and Horatia felt her face heat up.

"I..." she stammered.

Lucien stirred. "Horatia?" His voice was hoarse.

"Yes?"

Lawrence stood back, allowing Lucien's seeking gaze to find her.

"Come in, please. I wish to speak with you. Alone." He shot pointed looks at both of his brothers.

The two exchanged a look of disapproval, hesitating until finally Lawrence gestured towards the door that he and Avery should leave. Lawrence, still frowning, made a grand show of leaving the door ajar. Lucien in turn scowled comically at the open door.

"If only he knew he was mere inches from you at the Midnight Garden," Lucien chuckled dryly. "I daresay he'd faint if he knew he'd offered to ravish you there."

Horatia blushed, even as a smile pulled at her lips. The memory of that night should have been painful, embarrassing, but it wasn't. There was a part of her that relished it. Perhaps that was the price of falling in love with Lucien. His wickedness was rubbing off on her.

"How do you feel?" Horatia lifted her skirt a bit so she could sit on the edge of the bed. She leaned over and stroked his hair back to better examine his wound. It had been cleaned and looked more likely to bruise than to develop an infection like she'd feared.

Lucien shut his eyes and rubbed his thumb and forefinger over his closed lids. "I think I'll live."

As she tried to pull her hand away, he caught it, kissing the inside of her palm. He glanced up at her, his hazel eyes dark and warm. "I have you to thank. If not for you I might still be out in the meadow. Who knows what might have happened?"

Horatia shuddered at the sudden sense of dread she felt overtake her. Unable to control herself, she threw her arms about his chest and buried her face in the crook of his neck, trembling. She wondered how she could hurt so much over losing him when he'd never belonged to her. It seemed that loving someone that was never hers made her fear losing him all the greater. Losing Lucien to death would have been worse that losing him to another woman.

His arms settled around her body, pulling her closer, keeping her against him when he should have been pushing her away. When she'd mastered herself again, she bravely raised her head, her nose brushing his cheek. His arms around her chest tightened, and his breath hitched.

"You should thank God I'm weak as a newborn kitten, my dear. Otherwise I'd be thanking you properly for saving my life, and that blasted door would be bolted shut," Lucien murmured as he placed a soft, lingering kiss on her jaw.

Horatia's blood heated at the images his words created. An all too familiar ache started within her. She tore herself away when his hands moved to her breasts.

"No," was all she said. She cleared her throat and wiped the remains of tears from her eyes, then smoothed her skirts and left for the open door. She paused in the hallway and turned back to him.

"I wish you a speedy recovery, my lord." She dipped into a curtsy, something she'd never done to him before and left. The absence of his arms around her already made her hurt with longing, but she dared not linger.

CHAPTER 19

Dinner at Rochester Hall was always a grand affair, which was just the way Jane liked it. There was something wonderful about having her children and friends gathered around her table, eating, drinking and talking. The table in the formal dining room sat thirty people when all the leaves were inserted, but tonight it was perfect for accommodating the more intimate party of thirteen.

The doctor had come and gone, assuring Jane her son was well enough to dine with them if he wished and that he'd only suffered a minor concussion. With instructions to rest for the next few days, he'd exhibited the stubbornness he'd inherited from his father and come down for dinner. Jane snuck a glance at him, still concerned about the pallor of his complexion.

She had arranged the seating so that the younger children were all paired together. Cedric and Horatia sat across from each other by the head of the table on either side of Lucien. Lucinda and Linus were next, and on down the line were Avery, Lawrence, Audrey, Gregory, Lysandra and finally John, Marie and herself.

She'd noticed a great many things throughout the evening and wasn't sure whether she ought to worry about how the close quarters of the three families over the holidays would affect everyone. Linus kept sneaking glances at Lucinda across the table. For her part, Lucinda politely attempted to include him in her conversation with Cedric, but Linus would only spit out a quick reply and look away, anything to make it look as though he had no real interest in the girl.

Jane wasn't fooled, but she was worried. Although he was one and twenty, Linus was still young enough to act rashly. His interest in Lucinda Cavendish, if acted upon, could force both of them to the altar, and for Linus she feared that would be too soon. As much as she desired at least one of her brood to marry, he was not ready, and no one desired a marriage due to scandal. He was still immature, and it would drive his wife positively mad if he married now.

It wasn't surprising to see Linus intrigued by a woman. He was a Russell after all, and had her passionate blood in him. However, the most interesting development of the evening was Lysandra. Jane's only daughter had always seemed like a miraculous anomaly after so many troublesome boys, yet Lysandra managed to be just as vexing as her siblings. The girl had no interest in fashion and spent far too much time in the library. Not that books weren't a healthy pursuit for a woman. It was important to be intelligent. She saw it as a woman's duty to be smarter than most men, but a woman could not marry books, nor could books give Jane the grandchildren she longed for.

There was nothing so important at a particular point in a person's life than seeing their children grow, marry and bear their own children. Grandchildren were a special treat, and Jane was envious of her friends who had them. She longed to hold a sleeping baby in her arms once again, and breathe in the clean sweet scent of its skin and whisper sweet lullabies. She would see all of her children married and producing children if it was the last thing on earth she ever accomplished.

As dinner progressed, Jane saw something new in her daughter. There was a flush in her cheeks, a brightness to her eyes and a startled look as though Lysandra had woken from a dream of pale pastels to see the world in its true vibrancy at last. Only the desire of the heart could form that new sight. And the way Gregory Cavendish threw back his wine with reckless abandon told Jane everything she needed to know. Lysandra was officially a Russell if she was wreaking such havoc on the dashing young man with mere glances. He would be an excellent match for her daughter.

Jane resisted the urge to preen at the knowledge that she and her friend Marie would soon be family after their children had married. It was only a matter of time.

However, whatever had happened between the pair—and something had, she sensed—it had not gone as planned. One could never take back a kiss that was given, or perhaps stolen as the case might be. Jane only prayed that her daughter's hot-blooded actions had not been too bold. It would be most unacceptable to have to marry her daughter for reasons that would be obvious in a few months time. For her sons to marry under such circumstances was almost expected of them. Not one of them had even a smidgeon of self-control, but Lysandra ought to be stronger. She was a woman after all.

As an array of desserts was brought out, Jane turned her attention to Lucien and Horatia. They were speaking amongst themselves and Jane hated that she couldn't hear a single word.

It was so obvious that Horatia loved him. What would it take for Lucien to realize the same? No other woman could hold such a depth of emotion, nor handle his tempers the way Horatia did. The woman ought to be awarded sainthood for her bravery in loving such a man.

I must not interfere...well, not too much.

Tonight there would be dancing and playing on the pianoforte, and Jane would rally allies for her mission of pushing Horatia into Lucien's arms.

Once dinner had ended, she stood and addressed her guests.

"I thought we might all move to the ballroom for the remainder of the evening and have a bit of music and dancing."

This suggestion was met with approval and the group moved together towards the ballroom. Jane intercepted her three younger sons, trapping them in the dining room alone with her once the others had gone.

"Mama, what are you on about?" Linus asked, forgetting that she still owed him a tongue lashing for his mischief earlier that day.

"Sit down, all of you." She'd spent twenty years perfecting that tone of voice and Avery, Lawrence and Linus all but dove for the nearest chairs. Once seated she began to pace back and forth, knowing full well she was behaving like a commander of His Majesty's armed forces.

"I have decided that tonight you three must seduce Horatia," she announced.

Avery blanched, Lawrence frowned, and Linus, who'd been balancing on the back two legs of his chair, fell over with a crash.

"What?" Lawrence started to rise.

"Did I say you could stand?"

Lawrence promptly dropped back down.

"Have you gone mad, Mother?" Linus asked, righting his chair and sitting back down. "Shall I send for Dr. Lambert in Hexby?"

"Good heavens, no." She laughed. "I am sane as ever and plan to be here as long as I must to see that all of my children are happily married so you might as well get accustomed to my presence."

"Is that what this is about?" Lawrence crossed his arms in such a way that he suddenly reminded her of her late husband. He was the gentlest man there ever was, but he could certainly appear as cross as the devil himself when he wanted, a trait Lawrence had inherited. "You wish for one of us to marry so you've gone and selected Horatia in the hope that one of us will like her?" The disapproval in his tone was as clear as cannon fire.

"Don't be foolish. She's in love with Lucien."

"Then why have us seduce her?" Linus asked. "It seems to me you should have cornered your firstborn for this." He leaned back in his chair, forgetting his accident not one minute ago, a placating grin stretching his lips as though he were humoring a small child. Jane was on the verge of exasperation. Had none of them inherited her wits or cunning?

"I swear, by the way you three act, I might have dropped you on your heads when you were babes. If Lucien sees you all vying for Horatia's attentions, he will become jealous and act on his feelings for her. He needs encouragement and sibling rivalry in this house has never been in short supply. I believe it is time we put such energies to good use."

"Clever," said Avery, who had been quiet so far in all this.

Linus huffed. "Who says Lucien has feelings for her? I thought after Miss Burns and the gazebo disaster he did not favor her at all." His irritable tone was probably the result of guilt since he had caused the aptly named disaster.

"Miss Burns left that day because of something I said to her, Linus. I have only recently informed Lucien of the truth. He has changed his opinion of Horatia for the better, I believe."

"A change of opinion does not herald wedding bells, Mother," Lawrence said.

"He cares for her, and he desires her," Jane insisted. Lawrence and Linus grumbled in disbelief.

Avery sat up in his chair. "Actually, I believe mother may be right in this. I am more than ready to believe Lucien feels something for Horatia."

His brothers whipped their heads in his direction.

"And how do you know that?" Lawrence asked.

Avery grinned. "Remember that night you met Lucien at the Midnight Garden, Lawrence?"

Jane let out a horrified gasp but Avery ignored her.

"How the devil do you know where I was?" Lawrence asked.

Avery continued to smile. "Do you recall the woman in the silver gown and mask Lucien was so interested in?"

"Of course," Lawrence answered. "She was quite beautiful. There was a charming naiveté about her that—oh God."

Avery's smile deepened. "Yes, that woman was Horatia. She paid Madame Chanson to send her to Lucien that evening."

Jane gave a little cry and half-fainted into a chair. She peeped up at her son from beneath her lashes. None of them were paying attention to her. Instead they were more interested in Avery's source of information. Did they not even realize what their wild, reckless behavior was doing to her nerves? Well, if they were going to act like devils, then by God, she'd make them use their devilish talents to suit her ends.

❦

LAWRENCE FELT READY TO TOSS HIS ACCOUNTS. HE REMEMBERED every detail of that night and his jealousy when Lucien had offered to let the woman, Horatia, choose him over his brother. Lawrence had all but shoved his own woman off his lap, in the hopes of taking Lucien's prize. A woman he'd never once thought of romantically. It was hard to accept.

"Are you telling me that the woman I practically begged to steal from my brother that night, the one he shamelessly seduced in front of me was..."

"Indeed," Avery said. "But I must return us to the point of this revelation. Lucien knew it was her the entire night. He was very clear in declaring his desire for her and she for him."

His mother had roused herself to sit up from her theatrical swoon and was once more engaged in the conversation. "Did he... did they... Horatia told me they hadn't..."

"No, not at all," Avery reassured her. "Well, not fully." He then made twiddling motions with his fingers.

Linus got up and held out his arms, expecting their mother to faint for real this time.

His mother screeched. "Dear Lord, I've raised a pack of libertines and hedonists! Indulging in passion is one thing, but this?"

Lawrence ignored his mother's exclamations regarding the

damnation of her sons' souls and focused instead on his younger brother.

"Avery, how did you come by this knowledge? You weren't at the Garden that night."

"I have my sources," Avery replied cryptically. It wasn't even the first time he'd made that comment to them.

"You and your bloody sources. One of these days you will get yourself into trouble," Lawrence warned him. "The war is over. Don't you think your line of work ought to end too?"

"Wars never end," said Avery. "Only the battlefields and objectives change."

Avery's missions to the continent were a well-kept family secret, highlighted by the fact that they knew so little of it. It was dangerous work, and he didn't want Avery bringing danger and trouble to the family's front door.

"Lucien and Horatia must marry," his mother said. "At this point my conscience won't allow otherwise. 'Not fully' indeed…"

Lawrence pondered this. "Do you really suppose he'll want her more simply because of jealousy?" They were not boys anymore, no longer fighting over toy soldiers in the gardens. Women were a serious business.

"Knowing the three of you, if you do your best to tempt her to passion, he will notice and respond."

"Not with bullets I hope," Avery mused. "To be called out by my own brother…that would be highly embarrassing."

"Don't worry, Avery," Linus sniggered. "I shall attend your funeral. It will be a lovely service. I'll have the headstone read, 'Here lies Avery Russell—Stealer of Hearts and Secrets.' I'm sure you'll have at least a few people who will mourn your loss."

"Hush, pup!" Avery snapped.

Lawrence stretched out his legs and crossed them at the ankles. "I'd be more concerned about Cedric." There would be no avoiding him. Lawrence knew how protective the man was of his sisters. "He'll be bound to see our amorous overtures to his sister. Imagine his reaction."

"Leave him to me," his mother said.

Lawrence supposed she would enlist Audrey's help to keep Cedric distracted. God save them all if it didn't work.

Jane waited until she had her sons' full attention once again and gestured for Avery to speak.

"Now, let's get down to specifics, Mother. What do you expect us to do that will make him jealous?" Avery looked up at his mother with false wide-eyed innocence, the rogue wanted her to say it! He didn't think she would be capable of laying out her scheme in explicit detail. He was quite mistaken.

"Don't give me that sweet-as-a-lamb look, child," Jane warned. "The three of you have sinned enough to fill the second circle of hell all on your own, and leave no room for others. You will do what you do with any gentle born lady. Compliment her. Seduce her. Fuel the fire deep within her. Lure her into passion. But do nothing to worry me in a month's time. Understood?" Had she been in a better mood she would have laughed at the flush of embarrassment on their faces.

"What? You expect me to play ignorant of such things? I gave birth to five children, and I assure you that I did not do that all on my own. Your father played a significant role in bringing your miserable existences about. There's that little book from India I believe you all own? The one with all the illustrations. Don't pretend you don't know it, because I've read it as well."

"Mother! For God's sake!" Lawrence begged, cutting his mother off.

Jane allowed a smile to curve her lips.

"It isn't as much fun when you are on the other end of unpleasant thoughts now, is it?" She clapped her hands together. "Now then, off to the ballroom. And remember, do what I charged you or you will beg for mercy, and I shall have none to give. I brought you into this world, and should you displease me, I shall happily remove you from it." She made the threat in such a sweet tone that all three of her sons shuddered.

THE MOMENT AVERY, LAWRENCE AND LINUS ENTERED THE ballroom, Lawrence turned to his brothers, speaking so he could not be overheard.

"What do you say we try the shell game?"

"Who will be the main player?" Avery asked in a low whisper.

Lawrence spoke up. "I will. You both remember what to do?"

The shell game was something the three of them had done together many times. No matter the form the game took, each knew his role. Linus and Avery nodded and the three of them separated. Linus went straight towards their unsuspecting prey, while Avery and Lawrence broke off opposite directions.

CHAPTER 20

oratia perched in a chair against the wall, listening to Lady Rochester's performance on the pianoforte. Cedric attended her, turning the pages as he followed her progress on the sheet music. Audrey was dancing with Gregory Cavendish, the two of whom seemed to be making the most of the wide expanse of the ballroom. Avery and Lucinda were dancing near them and Lysandra was dancing with her youngest brother.

A smile tugged at Horatia's lips. It warmed her to see Audrey so happily engaged. Her first season had been quite a disappointment after word of Cedric's overbearing nature circulated among the young bucks of the *ton*. Audrey had wept for days when no flowers or cards had been delivered to her. There was nothing so cruel as to watch one's sibling suffer. Marriage was all the poor girl wanted, and with Cedric's watchful eyes she simply didn't stand a chance.

Horatia spied Lucien across the room with Lawrence and their guests. He seemed much recovered, although still pale. There was a haunted look to his eyes that tugged at her heart. Lucien ran a hand through his hair, mussing the sleek red waves as he spoke to

John and Marie. Sir John laughed loudly, his voice carrying over the music.

Lucien had it in him to be a great, warm and loving man with a rare and irresistible charm. Horatia's eyes burned a little. She wanted to cry because he was hurt, and she wanted to weep with relief that he was healing from his injury.

She was so focused on Lucien she did not notice an entirely different Russell vying for her attention.

"Horatia?" Linus inquired, adding a polite cough.

He stood in front of her chair, peering down with an expression on his face that made her anxious. With him, schemes and pranks always followed that sort of look.

Horatia realized he seemed to be waiting for her to say something. "I beg your pardon?"

"I was asking you to dance. Would you like to?" Linus offered her his arm and a charming smile. It snapped Horatia out of her Lucien-watching daze.

"You wish to dance with me?" She hadn't meant to sound so incredulous, but Linus had never showed the least bit interest in dancing with her before. It made her wonder what exactly this prankster was up to.

"Of course! You are an accomplished dancer, and I've been known to dance a quadrille or two when the occasion arises."

He waggled his eyebrows, and she stifled a giggle. Linus was a devil, but a charming one.

"And a waltz?" Horatia asked as Lady Rochester's tune changed to a sweeping, light-hearted melody. "How do you fare with them?" At a formal ball in Almack's an unmarried lady would not be allowed to dance a waltz without the Patroness's permission. However, Lady Rochester didn't set such standards amongst friends. It was something she enjoyed about the Russell family and Rochester Hall. She was free from such plaguing social niceties.

"Waltzes are my specialty. You must let me prove it to you." Linus winked at her as though he was confessing a secret.

"By all means then. Let us take our places." Horatia took

Linus's offered arm. She still suspected that he was up to something, but couldn't begin to guess what.

He ushered her onto the floor and spun her in a slow twirl before pulling her back into his arms. She shoved a palm against his chest, attempting to put some distance between their bodies.

"I don't believe we have to dance quite so close," she cautioned him.

"Nonsense. A man never backs down from an opportunity to hold a pretty lady close."

"Pretty lady?" she echoed. "Really Linus, you are quite odd tonight. What game are you playing?" Her tone, while soft, warned him she knew he wasn't sincere. There had never been a hint before now that he was interested in her romantically.

"Sometimes a man wakes up one day and realizes what he's had in front of him all along." His eyes strayed away from her for the briefest second, a betrayal of his true thoughts. She was not the woman he longed for, but for some strange reason, he was pretending she was.

As the waltz gathered speed, Horatia became almost dizzy from the constant turns. She'd barely gotten used to the rhythm with Linus when he deftly spun her away from him and a different man caught her on the dance floor.

LUCIEN ENTERTAINED HIS GUESTS, ENJOYING THE PLAYFUL banter of the elder Cavendishes. Sir John had been a good friend of Lucien's father and hearing Sir John's stories of their reckless youth always filled him with a deep warmth. He very much missed his father and still mourned him despite the years that had passed.

"Your father would be proud of how well all of his children have turned out," Sir John nodded seriously at Lucien. "He loved each of you so much and must be smiling wherever he is."

Marie's eyes grew watery and she leaned against her husband. "Oh John, dear, you're making me very sad. You mustn't speak so, not on tonight of all nights." She curled her hand through the crook of Sir John's arm and glanced apologetically at Lucien.

"Are you excited to bring Lysandra to London next year for the season? I believe she will win many suitors."

Lady Rochester chortled. "She might win interest initially, but I doubt any gentlemen will interest Lysandra."

When Marie and Sir John's faces scrunched up with confusion Lucien laughed.

"She's a bit of a blue stocking. More interested in books. I think she'd rather conduct experiments on a suitor than dance with him."

Lawrence joined their group. "You're talking about Lysa?" He shook his head. "Woefully true, I'm afraid."

"Oh dear." Marie laughed softly. "But I suppose when the right gentleman comes along she will be as befuddled as the rest of us are when we fall in love."

The group dissolved into other discussions and Lawrence diverted Lucien's attention with an unexpected comment.

"Horatia's looking quite well tonight."

Lucien fixed his brother with doubting eyes. "Quite well? She looks spectacular, as always."

Lawrence's expression became unreadable. "Of course, you're quite right. That reminds me, Linus would like a private word with you. He's in your study."

"A private word? What does he want?"

His brother shrugged. "I believe he wishes to ask you to court Horatia. He knows she had feelings for you in the past, but he wishes to make certain you have none in return, so that he may pursue her."

"Like hell he will," Lucien snarled and stomped off to find his brother. Horatia was still dancing with Avery and would be safe enough from his youngest brother for now.

"Avery?" Horatia stammered in surprise at the new dance partner holding her. The middle Russell grinned back at her.

"And how are you faring, lovely Horatia?" The devil dared to charm her. He alone looked the least like his siblings who all favored their mother. Avery favored his father in looks and therefore always seemed one step removed from the rest of the Russell brood.

"I am well enough, and you?" She tried to keep her focus on the conversation, but her mind was on other matters.

"Perfect now that I have you in my arms."

Horatia gawked at him before she recovered herself. "Wha—what?" First Linus, now Avery? This was all very strange.

The waltz's tempo changed, and Horatia found Avery's hand delicately stroking her waist in soft but sensual sweeps that startled her into a deep flush.

"I believe my brother has been a fool. You have pined for him too long, my dear. Why not give another of us a chance to woo you?"

"Honestly, this is quite—" She couldn't finish because he cut her off.

"I see, you still care too much for him. Well, I suspected that might be the case. He is waiting for you in the hall. Do you care to meet him?"

She gave a little furtive glance over her shoulder and saw that indeed, Lucien had left the room.

"He really wishes to see me?" It was too much to hope that it was true.

"Of course. We convinced him that he shouldn't deny what was in his heart."

"Very well, then I should like that."

Avery drew them both near the ballroom's door, which was ajar and he twirled her through the darkened doorway. Horatia would have stumbled but a pair of arms caught her, clasping her to a hard, warm body. In the dim light of the hall she looked up at the man who held her scandalously close.

"Lucien?" she whispered.

The man who held her glided gently down the darkened hall with steps that still held the echoes of a dance to them. The servants hadn't lit the lamps—or someone had blown them out. A shiver of apprehension settled over her.

"Lucien, we shouldn't leave." She jerked at his hand, her slippers digging into the carpet as she tried to slow him down.

"Come now, Horatia. Lucien and I are not so alike, are we?" Lawrence's amused laugh froze her dead in her tracks. He tugged again on her arm, and she nearly stumbled.

"Lawrence, let me go. We ought to return to the ballroom. This isn't—where are you taking me?" Her pulse leapt as Lawrence chose a door halfway down the corridor and opened it, taking her inside. Horatia tripped over a wrinkle in the carpet and fell against the nearest piece of furniture, which happened to be a bed. Lawrence had brought her into a bedroom...alone.

"Lawrence, what's going on? Why did you bring me here?" She struggled to get up, hearing her gown rip at the hem as she tried to push away from the bed.

Lawrence ignored her questions. "This will do very well, I think. We don't have much time to do this and it must be done correctly."

Horatia righted herself and turned to face him. Her heart stuttered as he smiled and made a show of leaving the door open a few inches. There was no light in the room save for a pair of candles above the fireplace. Shadows fell across Lawrence's face as he stripped his overcoat off and dropped it over the back of the nearest chair. Horatia took two slow steps towards the door, but he mirrored her movements with an amused expression.

"Going somewhere?" he teased.

"Lawrence," she said softly, a new sense of uneasiness filling her. She was cornered and a little bit frightened. At that moment she did not trust him at all. "Let me leave." Horatia hoped he would listen to reason. "Surely you must see that this isn't at all proper, even for your family."

He leaned against the wall by the door, arms crossed over his chest as his eyes raked over her body. "My family is improper even at the best of times, and my dear sweet Miss Sheridan, you've become the newest toy for my brothers and me to fight over. Congratulations! Lucien is a fool not to want you, but I am no fool."

"You wouldn't... You couldn't!" Horatia watched in almost dazed shock as Lawrence removed his cravat and unbuttoned his shirt.

This couldn't be happening. He was a friend, someone she'd trusted and respected.

"You won't touch me. You won't." His widening smile made her shudder. "Come any closer and I'll scream..." Truth be told she'd do a lot more than that, but her instincts warned her to keep that intention to herself. No sense in warning the man what she was capable of.

He watched her with an expression so primitive that Horatia scrambled to get away as he pushed himself from the door and advanced upon her. She wished to God her hands would stop shaking. She knew his reputation was just as bad as Lucien's. She also remembered him in the Midnight Garden, and how he'd been seducing the woman he'd chosen that night. She would not be his next conquest. She could not!

Part of her was still stunned that it was Lawrence who would treat her this way. He'd always been so protective, almost as much as Cedric. What had changed in him that would bring about an attempt at forced seduction such as this?

As if reading her mind, Lawrence said, "I know it was you that night at the Midnight Garden. You were the beautiful woman on my brother's lap. I can still see that vivid blush beneath your silver mask when I shut my eyes. I've been haunted by dreams of your supple body beneath mine... It quickens your blood, does it not? The idea of that struggle for exquisite pleasure?"

Lawrence seemed to voice exactly what was happening in her body, but she was envisioning a different surrender to another man entirely.

Horatia was terrified now, and tried to do the sanest thing possible, which was scream at the top of her lungs. But the sound was strangled on her lips as Lawrence advanced on her. He grappled with her, curling one hand around her mouth, and she reacted.

Horatia bit down.

He yelled in surprise and stepped back. "Christ, woman! I'm not going to hurt you!" His look of genuine shock startled her, as though he hadn't really intended to touch her and even more stunned that she'd been frightened enough to bite like a cornered polecat.

"Horatia..." he said, as though trying to calm a startled horse. "Listen to me. He's coming. We need to pretend to kiss—" He lunged, catching her and pinning her against the wall.

She couldn't shake him off. Panic blurred her vision. He's coming? Was Avery or Linus going to join in this madness? She was trapped and helpless! He made no move to undress her, but his warm breath came out in soft pants.

"Just let me kiss you for one bloody second, woman! It's for your own good!" He ducked his head in towards hers.

Horatia slammed her head forward, her forehead colliding with his.

Lawrence staggered back a few steps, holding a hand to his forehead. "Holy hell! If you'd only let me explain..."

Horatia didn't fare much better from the blow, stumbling backward in surprising pain.

Just then Lucien burst into the room with a dark scowl the likes of which Horatia had never seen on him before.

"You bloody bastard!" Lucien's voice became a snarl as he lunged at his brother.

The two collided and smacked against the wall. Lucien had murder in his eyes, but Lawrence looked as though he'd been expecting Lucien to come into the room and throttle him.

Horatia shouted, "Lucien! Stop! Please! Just take me to my room...please."

Only the last word seemed to reach him. He released his brother, muttering a filthy string of insults. Lawrence straightened his clothes as Horatia walked up to him. Her palm itched to slap him, but not before she said what she needed to say.

"I don't know what you were trying to do tonight, Lawrence, but know this—you will face my wrath and it will make Lucien's fury look pale in comparison." She was barely able to keep herself from shouting at him. His eyes narrowed and the challenge snapped what control had remained. She slapped Lawrence as hard as she could, the harsh sound echoed through the room.

Despite the reddening mark on his face, Lawrence did not make a sound. Horatia raised her trembling chin high and marched to the door. She paused when she realized Lucien had not followed her. He still eyed his brother with murderous intent.

"Lucien, leave him. I need you."

He tore his gaze away and followed her to the door, pausing only to shoot one last furious look at his brother before he wrapped a protective arm around Horatia's waist and escorted her to her chambers. A footman stepped forward, a concerned look on his face.

"My lord, I heard a commotion. Do you or Miss Sheridan require anything? Shall I send for Miss Sheridan's lady's maid?"

"No. No need. It's Gordon, isn't it?" Lucien was still getting acquainted with his mother's new staff.

"Yes, my lord."

"Thank you, Gordon. No need to send for Ursula, but if you would be so good as to keep the other servants clear of my room and Miss Sheridan's. She needs to be attended to and I do not wish for her reputation to suffer."

The footman squared his shoulders. "Of course, my lord. I will take it up on myself to see that you are not disturbed." The footman bid them good night and slipped down the hallway, vanishing through one of the doors that led to servants' quarters.

The moment her door was shut Horatia fell into the nearest chair, body shaking with the aftermath of her scare. She had the sudden urge to cry, but choked down the sobs that tried to bubble up in her throat. She meant to thank Lucien for his intervention, but instead she burst into tears, unable to maintain her strength any longer. It wasn't so much what Lawrence had done, or almost done, it was something deeper, something more painful that she didn't fully understand. Looking at Lucien was like salt in a fresh wound. Why was she always falling to pieces around him?

◈

LUCIEN APPROACHED HORATIA, HATING THE DISTANCE BETWEEN them, and scooped her up out of the chair to hold her to his chest. She fisted her hands in his waistcoat and buried her face in the crook of his neck. The intimate seeking of protection and reassurance made his heart turn over. Even after being cold to her for so long, she still trusted that he would care for her. She amazed him.

Lucien banded his arms about her back, tightly grasping her to his body. He layered gentle comforting kisses on the crown of her hair, shushing her with warm soothing sounds. His rage at Lawrence and Linus was still strong, but Horatia was more important right now, and she needed him to stay with her. He would punish his brothers for luring him away when she needed his protection. Even Avery was involved somehow. They would all be dealt with on the morrow.

"Why did he...why did he have to do that? He has no interest in me, so why? He was cruel to toy with me, and to what end?" she asked between choked sobs.

"I don't know, love. I don't know." And for a long while after that neither of them said anything. He wished he had answers. He would by tomorrow, and Lawrence would be fortunate if he still drew breath once Lucien was done with him.

Lucien held her tight, amazed by how good she felt even now—every curve, every scent, every sweet breath she exhaled. He couldn't picture ever letting her go, or that he could exist in a world where she wasn't his.

SHE CRIED HERSELF OUT UNTIL SHE WAS EXHAUSTED. HORATIA sagged in Lucien's arms and he picked her up and carried her to her bed. Somehow being put on the bed banished her tears and the need to cry any further. Her thoughts drifted away from Lawrence and back to the eldest Rochester.

"Feeling better? Why don't I fetch Ursula to undress you and put you to bed?" Lucien suggested.

Her hand shot out and locked around his wrist. "No. Please stay."

"Someone needs to get you settled and undressed." He frowned, oddly even more attractive in the way he was determined to care for her.

"You can undress me." She smiled at him. "You've had plenty of practice."

"Horatia, you do realize how inappropriate it would be for me to..." He waved his hand up and down, gesturing to her clothes.

She rolled her eyes and sighed. "Inappropriate is your forte, Lucien. I want *you* to undress me. I trust you."

After he set her down, he began to undress her with tenderness akin to tending a newborn babe. There was nothing sensual or seductive in his movements.

Horatia wiped her tear-stained cheeks with the back of her hand, wondering if her complexion had become splotchy. She gazed down at Lucien's bent form as he removed her dancing slippers and slid his hands up her legs to unroll her stockings. His hair caught the lamplight so that the waves of dark crimson were glossy and inviting. She ached to thread her fingers through the strands, to see if they matched her memory of that night at the Midnight Garden.

Her fingers stretched towards him just as he moved to stand again. Horatia dropped her hand onto her lap as he began to slide her gown down over her shoulders. She was too weary to protest when he lifted her and dragged the gown down and off her until she was clad only in her stays and chemise. He reached out and unlaced her stays, peeled them off and let them drop to the floor. Her breath hitched as she crossed her arms over her breasts, hoping to hide her body with the filmy chemise.

Lucien then went to the armoire and searched through the clothes until he found a thick flannel nightgown and held it out to her. She took it and prepared to remove her chemise. He turned his back, uncharacteristically gentleman-like. It made her smile, if only a little, as she pulled the nightgown down over her head. He turned back around and the look on his face made her breath catch. He looked devastated, yet relieved, as though everything she'd been feeling on the inside was now painted across his handsome features. Her knees gave out and she sat down on the bed, thankful for the support it gave her.

As Lucian sat on the bed's edge beside her, he gently turned her sideways and began to pluck hairpins from her untidy coiffure with a gentleness Horatia had not thought possible. With the last hairpin set on the nightstand, Lucien wound his fingers through her wavy mass of dark hair with his fingers. The feel of him coaxing tangles loose and sweeping through the strands sent a wave of longing through her. When his hands finally drew away, Horatia faced him and his fathomless eyes.

"Lucien..."

"Yes?" The word wavered on his lips.

"Please don't leave me tonight." Her request shocked her. She'd only meant to thank him for saving her.

"Horatia, you know I ought not to stay..." His voice trailed off helplessly, but he didn't retreat. Instead he leaned down and stroked her hair away from her face.

"I would feel better if you stayed. Safer." She reached out and cupped his cheek with her hand and brushed a finger over his lips, recalling the way they felt on hers. He raised his hand and caught her wrist, rubbing his thumb over the sensitive skin of her inner wrist, just over her now racing pulse.

"Please stay. I need you here." Horatia felt like a child again, trapped in the shattered, splintered remains of her parents' carriage, hearing screams of pain, realizing later they were her own. She needed him to comfort her, to stay and hold her now as he had then.

Something in her plea made him nod, and he pulled back the covers of her bed.

"Go on then, get in." He urged her under the covers as he pulled them back. Lucien got up from the bed then and began to disrobe. Horatia's breath hitched as he removed his shirt and locked her bedroom door.

Usually, there was a natural air of control and command about him, but he seemed robbed of those qualities tonight. His legs shook, and he breathed more rapidly, as though he were being tested and found himself on the verge of failure.

The lamplight played over his sculpted form as he stood clad only in his drawers. She could spend a lifetime memorizing the feel, the shape, the taste of that body and it would never be enough to satisfy her. Lucien was a wicked addiction, and she had no hope, nor any desire to be free of the drugging influence of his body.

As he approached the bed she moved back a bit to give him plenty of room to join her. He blew out the lamp, enveloping them both in darkness as he settled into the bed next to her. He plumped a pillow behind his head and then without hesitation brought her body against his, his arms anchoring her to him.

For better or worse, he was here with her, comforting her in a way he had not done in seven years. It was worth Lawrence's rash actions to have been awarded this quiet, intimate moment with Lucien. She savored his warm breath fanning her neck and the heat of his body against her own. She was barely aware of anything except him as sleep crept in.

LUCIEN LAY AWAKE, ALL TOO AWARE THAT SHARING A BED WITH

Horatia was dangerous. Only her scare with Lawrence had allowed him to maintain his restraint for her. He focused instead on his brother. What the hell had Lawrence been thinking? Lucien knew his brothers better than he knew himself. Lawrence would never have hurt Horatia, or any woman. Why then had he put her in such a terrifying situation? A prank? That was more Linus's game. Lucien replayed the evening in his mind, searching for any hint, any detail to explain his brother's actions. Lawrence had lured him out on the pretext of meeting with Linus who supposedly had amorous intentions towards Horatia, but when he'd arrived at his study the room had been empty so he'd started back to the ballroom. When he glimpsed Linus ducking into a room at the end of the hall, he'd started to follow until he'd passed by one room that hadn't been occupied a few minutes before.

That was when he'd stumbled upon Horatia and Lawrence.

Lucien would never get that sight of them out of his head. Fear clawed at his insides and worry knotted his stomach. Whatever scheme his brothers had been involved in...tomorrow they would pay. Lucien would see to it, no matter the reasons. Horatia belonged to him, not Lawrence or any other man. And no one harmed what was his. A woman as wonderful and kind as Horatia deserved to be cherished, protected and...loved.

He pulled Horatia tighter against him. She shifted, murmured something and lay still again. It did not escape his notice that her body fit well with his, as though she had always belonged to him.

Only then did he realize that for many years now he had belonged to her, and this epiphany troubled him greatly.

Nothing good would come of feeling this way towards her. The rules of the League could not be broken, and friendships could not withstand such a trespass. Lucien didn't want to choose between Horatia and her brother. He silently prayed that he wouldn't have to.

CHAPTER 21

Lawrence flung himself into a deep armchair within a private parlor, his brothers flanking it on either side. His head hurt like the devil. He'd likely have a knot on his brow by the morning. Avery frowned and stared down at him while Linus paced back and forth. The rest of the guests had all gone to sleep and the three Russells were alone now to discuss the possible victory of their plan.

"Well, Lawrence, how did it go?" Linus asked.

Lawrence growled in response. He didn't want to think about what he'd just done. "I have a bad feeling that Lucien is going to put a bullet through me tomorrow. And if Cedric catches wind, it might be two."

"What?" Avery eyes widened.

"I went too far. It took Lucien too long to find us." Lawrence rubbed his eyes wearily.

"Just how far is too far exactly?" Linus asked.

"In trying to delay things I was perhaps a bit too convincing of my intentions and frightened the poor woman. She smashed her head into mine when I tried to kiss her. It was never my intent to scare her. I thought I could convince her to play along and kiss me back so Lucien would get jealous, but she panicked before I could explain." Lawrence flinched at the shock in his brothers' faces. "Lucien arrived just in time. Or at the worst possible time, I suppose. What the devil took him so long?"

"You really did that to Horatia?" asked Linus. "You almost..."

"Of course not. But she thought I was going to. She was terrified and I feel..." He scrubbed his hand down over his face. "God. I doubt she'll ever forgive me. I hope I didn't do her lasting damage. Lucien better marry her, or I've ruined a lovely friendship for nothing." Lawrence got up and stalked over to the nearest cabinet in the parlor and took out a bottle of brandy.

"I need a drink," he declared. His two brothers joined him, all grim over the spectacle they'd helped to create that night.

"Do we know how Lucien took it?" Avery asked Lawrence.

"No. He took her back up to her room. I haven't seen him since. I ordered the servants to stay clear of her room until after breakfast. I hope he means to stay the night with her. If he does, we'll most likely have won. We all know what a soft-hearted man he is, especially if he thought it would cheer up a disheartened lady."

"That's certainly true. He's much too tender-hearted to let her alone tonight after..." Avery trailed off.

"After Lawrence almost ravaged her?" Linus supplied helpfully.

"Russells do not ravage," Avery stated. "We're far too gifted in natural persuasion. There's no need to force a woman when after a few well placed caresses she'll give you whatever you ask for."

"Don't encourage the lad, Avery," Lawrence said noting the look on Linus's face. "He's in enough trouble already with Miss Cavendish."

Linus whipped his gaze from Avery to Lawrence. "What do you mean *I'm* in trouble?"

"After she saw you dancing with Miss Sheridan she took it rather personally. You did not ask her to dance, after all."

Linus's lips parted as he sputtered. "But we were...damn! Was she very upset do you think?"

Avery grinned. "I believe she spent the evening time glaring at you. I was surprised you didn't turn into a pillar of salt. I'm afraid you've rather bungled it." Avery patted Linus's shoulder in a rough but affectionate gesture. "Perhaps you can woo her again on the morrow?"

Lawrence continued to sip his brandy, watching the byplay with amusement, but his guilt at his actions from earlier still niggled at him.

"I suppose I'll have to. I mean, I owe the girl that, after kissing her. I suppose I ought to speak with her father as well. I know I'm a bit young to offer for her but... Perhaps we may enjoy a longer engagement period until I am ready to accommodate a wife."

The hopeful look on his youngest brother's face stopped Lawrence from re-filling his glass.

"Steady on, Linus!" Avery cautioned. "What's all this talk of making an offer? You need not, especially at your age."

Lawrence eyed his brother curiously. "But you kissed her?" The almost calf-mooned expression in Linus's eyes was a little disturbing. He'd seen it before, and always in the young.

"Yes. It was a rather chaste one, though. I believe it was her first," Linus mused aloud, a blush tingeing his cheeks.

"You like her!" Avery said shrewdly.

"There is...something undeniably sweet about her." Linus admitted.

Lawrence groaned. His brother was on the way to falling for a woman. One woman. But there were so many out there to taste and feel and explore. He shouldn't be limiting himself so soon. Linus had to be saved from himself.

"Sweet as she is, one kiss does not herald wedding bells," Lawrence said as he set down his brandy glass. "If it were, I would be married a thousand times over to a hundred different women. Fathers may expect offers after a single kiss, but we Russells do not go quietly into the leg shackles of matrimony."

"Then why are we helping Lucien with Horatia? Won't they end up married?"

"That is the plan," Avery said.

Linus frowned, entirely perplexed. "Then why—"

"Lucien is past his prime. He ought to settle down. It might as well be with someone who adores him. Miss Sheridan is the perfect young lady to prepare him to become a father to the much needed heir to the marquessate."

"We don't need an heir," Linus countered. "There are three more of us in line."

"Don't tell me that *you* want all that responsibility, Linus," Avery chuckled.

"Better that Lucien has a passel of boys and an army of girls," Lawrence said. "That way there's an heir and plenty of grandchildren for Mama to fawn over and the rest of us will be left to our own devices." The mere thought of Lucien having children eased Lawrence somewhat. What a wonderful sense of relief he would have when Mama finally left him alone. He'd do anything to achieve that freedom, even incur his brother's wrath. Though in light of recent events his liberty might be short lived.

"I suppose that does make sense, after a fashion. Mama would love all those grandchildren," Linus chuckled.

Lawrence poured brandy for his brothers and they raised their glasses for a toast. "To Lucien, Horatia and all the grandchildren Mama will ever want!"

୧✦୨

CHARLES BID HIS FRIENDS AT ESSEX HOUSE GOOD NIGHT BEFORE collecting his new servant, Tom Linley. Charles leaned back against the plush squabs of his coach as Linley scrabbled up to sit next to the coachman. He gave instructions to go to the house where Linley's baby sister was located. It was close to midnight and the baby's nurse would most likely be unamused at the disruption. Charles was prepared to pay to smooth any ruffled feathers that might arise from their late arrival. When Linley finally joined Charles inside the coach, he raised a quizzical brow.

"I asked him to take us to Bennett Street, my lord," Linley said.

"Bennett Street?" Charles sat up. "Where exactly do you live?"

"I rent a small room above the Dandy House, my lord."

"The Dandy House? You mean to tell me that you live above a gambling hell?" Gambling hells were not hellish, despite the title, but they were often rowdy and occasionally dangerous places. It was appalling to think of Linley trying to raise a baby in such a location.

"It was all I could afford, sir." Linley's face darkened and Charles felt he'd made a mistake in reacting.

"I was merely surprised you lived there. I will admit I have been to the Dandy on several occasions. Some of my friends and acquaintances are officers and they especially like the high stakes. It amuses them. I was just astonished to learn that you've been able to keep a child there."

Linley relaxed, but flinched when Charles tried once more to pat his arm.

"I'm sorry. I didn't mean to startle you."

"Tis my fault, my lord. My last master only touched me when he needed to thrash something to ease his temper."

"Who was your previous master before you came to work at Berkeley's?"

"I should not say. It would not be proper to speak ill of him," Linley protested.

Charles flung up his hands. "Easy, lad, I won't demand you reveal all your secrets. Not tonight anyway. We all have devils on our backs." Charles fell silent, a rare contemplative mood capturing him.

Neither he nor Linley said anything more until they reached Bennett Street. Linley tried to insist that Charles wait in the coach, but Charles leapt out and eyed the gambling hell with mild interest.

It had been awhile since he'd tried to gamble away his vast inheritance. Men in crisp red uniforms and those of an aristocratic bearing milled about the club's front entrance, talking and laughing. A few men recognized Charles and waved. He hailed them and followed Linley down the nearest alley and to a back door.

Linley went right inside and Charles followed, rather enjoying this curious little adventure. Charles listened to the raucous noises on the other side of the thin walls as they climbed the back stairs. There were shouts and the cackles of women, cheering on the winners and consoling the losers. Such things had never caused Charles concern before, but he was suddenly seeing his lifestyle through the eyes of the young lad ahead of him. Someone who was bearing a great responsibility by caring for his baby sister all on his own. It was admirable, and right now he felt quite the opposite.

Linley paused at a single door at the top of the stairs and rapped his knuckles in an odd pattern. After a moment the door opened a crack.

"It's me, Mrs. Bertie," Linley said.

The door opened more fully, allowing Linley inside. When Charles moved to follow him a rotund woman in her mid-thirties blocked his path.

"Eh, Linley, who's this, love? I thought ye stayed clear of them lords who fancied lads..." Mrs. Bertie's implication that he had such intentions made Charles wince.

Charles had no qualms with what other men did in their private lives, but abuse was easy to come by, and sometimes where wicked desires and vices were involved, people got hurt.

"That is Lord Lonsdale. He's an earl, Mrs. Bertie, so please be on your best behavior and let him inside." Linley strode straight for the wooden cradle against the wall. A bundle stirred where Linley bent his head over the cradle's edge. Mrs. Bertie eyed Charles with deep suspicion before stepping back and allowing him in.

"So, Linley love, ye were late, I expected ye hours ago. It'll be costin' ye double since I missed time with them gents downstairs."

Mrs. Bertie seemed unfazed by Charles's presence and turned her attention back to Linley who had started to gather his few belongings into a cloth sack.

"I...I can't pay you extra tonight Mrs. Bertie, but in a week I will have enough to settle my debt."

"I want my money now!" Mrs. Bertie hissed in annoyance.

Linley blanched just as Charles stepped between the woman and the lad.

"My dear, charming Mrs. Bertie, I am sure we can reach an agreement. The lad is now under my employ. I will advance him his wages to see you well paid for your services." Charles took Mrs. Bertie's hand and palmed several coins into her hand. Mrs. Bertie's eyes widened in shock before she leaned around Charles to look at Linley.

"Whatever he be using ye for lad, let him!" Mrs. Bertie whispered these last two words, but Charles still heard her and he raised his eyes heavenward, giving a silent plea for patience.

"Er, thank you for everything, Mrs. Bertie. But we really must be going now." Linley shouldered the cloth sack with one hand then scooped up the squirming bundle with a natural ease.

Linley juggled the babe and bag as he started towards the door. Charles followed him out, chuckling at the shocked expression on Mrs. Bertie's face as they headed down the stairs.

Once they were in the coach Linley dropped his bag onto the floor and saw to the care of the baby. The child's tousled golden curls were feathery light and seemed to shine, even in the dim light.

Charles ruffled a hand through the curls of the babe's head and continued to watch her the rest of the way back to his townhouse on Curzon Street. There was something about the baby, something familiar, just at the edge of his memory, but for the life of him he could not recall what it was.

The coach stopped out front of his townhouse.

A footman rushed out to meet them as they descended from the coach.

"Timothy, you look awful, what's happened?" Charles demanded as the white-faced footman took their coats.

"It's dreadful, my lord, dreadful. Come inside." Timothy led the way, all the while Charles felt his blood turning to ice in his veins.

When they entered the townhouse, several of the servants were standing there, all looking just as distressed as Timothy. A young upstairs maid stepped forward and held out a bundle of cloth.

"My lord, we found this in your tub." After he'd taken the bundle from her she wiped away tears and spoke again. "It was drowned, my lord."

Drowned? Charles peeled back the cloth and sucked in a harsh breath. A black cat was lying dead in his hands. The little body was stiff, cold and still damp. Despite all this, he recognized the cat's markings. It was Muff. One of the two cats from the Sheridan house.

"The poor thing!" Linley's eyes were bright as he held Kate's bundled body closer to his chest. The baby was asleep and Linley raised her higher in his arms as he spoke.

"Who would kill a cat?" Linley asked as he protectively shielded the baby.

"An enemy. An enemy who wants to send me a message."

"What message?"

"He wants me to know he can get to me and to my friends. The cat never left the Sheridan house. Someone grabbed him and brought him here. My enemy, the League's enemy, may be ready to strike."

"The League?"

"Yes. You might as well get used to the name. My friends, Viscount Sheridan, Baron Lennox, the Duke of Essex and the Marquess of Rochester and I are sometimes referred to by the society pages as the League of Rogues. We adopted the title in jest, but it seems to have stuck."

"So this enemy, he wishes to destroy this League?" Linley asked.

"Yes."

"Do you know who he is?"

Charles gave a slow nod as he looked down at the body covered in the cloth. He had a wretched feeling deep inside that Muff was the first casualty in the war that had been simmering for years.

"Sir Hugo Waverly. I believe he means to kill us all eventually," Charles predicted. A heavy shadow fell across Linley's face. "The worst of it will be breaking the news to Cedric and his sisters. They're damned fond of this little scamp. It's a blessing they're in Kent. I couldn't bear to watch the girls hear the news. Women crying is the worst thing imaginable. I never say or do the right thing to stop the blasted waterworks." Charles tilted his head back, heaving a sigh.

He tried not to think about how the cat had died. The choice of execution was no coincidence. Charles shuddered, remembering the sensation of cold water strangling him, smothering his nose and mouth, blinding his vision as he sank beneath the dark waters, weights attached his legs, and his hands bound so he couldn't swim. Yes. There was no doubt who committed this sin against an innocent creature.

"I wish we could bury him, but the ground is frozen. We'll have to cremate him. It might help console Lord Sheridan and his sisters to know that the poor creature was cared for," Linley suggested.

"That is a very considerate idea. We'll handle it tomorrow." Charles ran a shaky hand through his hair. Waverly was upping the stakes.

"It seems you may have chosen an ill time to take on a new employer, Linley," Charles muttered. Linley buried his face in the blankets around little Katherine, planting a kiss on the babe's forehead as though to ward off evil. But Charles knew better. Tender kisses and thoughts of love would not save anyone from Hugo Waverly.

CHAPTER 22

Dreams were wonderful things, no one could dispute that. But the moment when an intangible vision of one's desires becomes a reality? That is something infinitely more powerful and breathtaking than the moonlit inspired visions woven in the night. Now here Horatia was, waking beside Lucien. She blinked a few times to clear her vision and glimpsed snow falling outside the large window opposite her.

The flakes had clumped into penny-sized blotches, drifting down like feathers. It was still early. The light in the sky was reduced to a heavy gray by the voluminous winter clouds. Horatia lay nestled next to him, the heat of Lucien's body warming her back. She rolled over, settling deeper into the feather bedding as she studied him in the dim morning light.

Lucien was stretched out on his stomach. One hand was fisted around the bottom of his pillow, scrunching it up beneath his cheek. His other arm dangled off the side of the bed. The wide expanse of his shoulders and back were exposed as the sheets rode low on his hips. His face was turned towards her, his dark lashes spiking across his cheeks as he slept. Although Lucien was thirty-three, Horatia could see the boy in his features as they softened with sleep. She ached to brush her hand along his brows and trace the strong, straight aristocratic nose down to his sinful lips.

The lines of his body were carved with muscle. A long, pale pink scar dipped along the side of his chest and stopped at the top of his hip. Without thinking Horatia ran a curious fingertip along the raised surface of the mark. Lucien stirred at her touch, and his eyes opened. Horatia wished she knew the smallest details about him—the things a lover or a wife would know—such as whether he woke easily or not.

"Lucien, are you a light sleeper?" she asked.

His gaze warmed as he seemed to consider her question.

"Why do you wish to know?" He remained still, watching her, the closeness between them overwhelming her senses.

"I was curious," she hedged.

She realized her finger was still touching him near his left hip. She didn't pull her hand back.

I should stop touching him, she told herself. But instead she let the rest of her fingers splay defiantly on his skin, the touch intimate and possessive. Lucien did not shift his gaze away from her.

"I am a light sleeper. And you?" It seemed he was aware of the intimacy of the moment, and the conversation.

"Sometimes when I am worried or vexed I have trouble sleeping."

"You slept soundly last night," Lucien observed.

"That is because..." Horatia felt her cheeks flush.

"Because?"

"Because I feel safe when you are near." She could not tell him how she really felt. That being near him made her both restless and peaceful, that she trusted him with her body, heart and soul. When he was with her the dark memories that haunted her could not penetrate the ring of light he shone about her.

Lucien did not reply. Instead he propped his head up on one hand and removed Horatia's inquisitive hand from his hip. He studied her fingers and palm, his thumb teasing patterns on her skin. He spread her fingers and placed his own palm against hers, matching their hands, though his fingers were much longer than hers. Then he laced their fingers together and pulled her towards him.

Again, Horatia was struck by their closeness, and it left her struggling for breath. What if he pushed away again, as he always had before? The idea was unbearable. She had to emotionally take a step back through conversation.

"Lucien, how did you come by that scar?"

"Which one?"

"The...the one on your hip." She couldn't believe she was in bed with Lucien discussing his hips. If it weren't for her breathless fascination with his body, she would have laughed at the prudish shyness she was feeling.

"Oh that." Lucien laughed and placed a soft kiss on the back of her fingers.

Horatia shivered at the warmth of his lips. The man was irresistible. Her heart cracked at the seams, bursting with love and sadness all at once.

"I received that particular scar when I was at university. Ashton and I had only just met, and we didn't like each other."

"You and Ashton? But you are such good friends!" Horatia couldn't envision a world where Lucien and Ashton disliked each other.

"True. But at first, he and I did not see eye to eye. Ashton believes in rules and principles. To him I was the most unscrupulous fellow he'd ever met. I dare say he wasn't completely wrong about that."

She leaned into him, enchanted with the way he talked. "And what does that have to do with your scar?"

Lucien's face flushed uncharacteristically red. "Well, it is rather embarrassing."

"Well, now I must hear it."

"I was a student at Cambridge, and I got it into my head to seduce the young wife of one of our professors. He was interested in well...gentlemen, and she was quite lonely." Lucien grinned wickedly. "Call it payback for poor examination results I'd received. I don't know how Ashton found out what I meant to do, but he followed me one night. I was halfway up the trellis to the lady's room when Ashton jumped out of the bushes and startled me. I lost my hold and the wooden trellis sliced me open as I fell."

Horatia gasped. He chuckled at her shock.

"Quite. I was in a bad way when I landed, and Ashton was far too noble to abandon me. He helped me onto my feet and when he saw how deep my wound was he helped me to the nearest inn and found a doctor. Somewhere between my fall and the seven sutures I'd received without one drop of brandy to dull my pain, Ashton decided he liked me after all. He thought I ought to behave more like the gentleman I was, but he also knew I couldn't always fight my more untamed nature. He reconciled himself to the idea of our friendship and we've been as we are ever since." Lucien's mouth once more settled on Horatia's skin, this time on her wrist to kiss the sensitive skin where her pulse thrummed even more quickly.

She had a thousand questions, but when she felt his tongue flick out, all rational thought faded. With a slow sensual slide, he pulled her body flush against his.

"Horatia, I'm not good at this," Lucien whispered, his lips mere inches from hers.

"Good at what?" Her voice was a tad tremulous as she feared what he might say.

"Being a gentleman. In London I promised that you would be safe from me, yet I let Lawrence hurt you and now I'm sharing your bed, and having the most wicked sort of thoughts about you."

Her heart leapt inside her chest. "Oh?"

He let his lips brush hers, smiling as though he enjoyed her stunned response.

"Oh yes. I keep thinking about that night at the Midnight Garden and how brave you were to face me. How sweet you tasted! And right now, I wish it had been me last night who had you alone in a bedroom at my mercy." Lucien nipped her bottom lip and the spot between her legs ached.

"Lucien, I'm always at your mercy." Horatia brushed her hand through his dark red hair as he teased her further. "And you do have me alone in a bedroom."

"Mmm, I do, don't I?" He framed her face with his hands and plundered her mouth in a way that left her dazed and throbbing. "What do you say we—" Someone knocked at the locked bedroom door.

Horatia scowled. "Drat. That must be my maid, Ursula. She's early."

Lucien released her and slid out of the bed with a slow sigh.

"Perhaps it is for the best. I... Damn. This is a mistake, Horatia. I can never bloody think straight when I'm with you." Lucien's voice was hoarse as he quickly dressed.

WHEN LUCIEN OPENED THE DOOR THE MAID EYED HIM WITH disapproval. He'd faced far worse, however, he didn't want this woman bringing trouble to Horatia.

"I trust you will be silent about what you've seen here?"

"Of course, my lord," Ursula said without warmth. "My lady's reputation means everything to me. I dare not ask what your intentions are."

"My intention is to continue to see Horatia without anyone knowing. For her benefit, not mine. I am not ashamed to be with her, but her brother finding out would put everyone in a difficult position."

The lady's maid nodded. "Lord Sheridan would certainly be furious. I would not like to be the cause of his temper. I will keep silent so long as you treat her well."

Lucien nodded in farewell to Horatia, then slipped out into the hallway to ring for his valet, Felix.

He had to erase the image of her in bed from his mind. The way she looked so warm, soft and perfect, her hair tumbled in waves around her shoulders, her eyes still a little dreamy with sleep and her lips pink and ready for kisses... It was enough to drive a man mad.

After he'd bathed and dressed, Lucien stumbled upon his three brothers exiting the breakfast room and headed for the closest door that would take them outside.

"You three, stop!" he barked. It was time for a reckoning.

They caught sight of him and bolted like rabbits. Lucien managed to snag Linus by the collar of his long black greatcoat.

"Avery, help!" Linus clawed at his brother, who dodged away as he and Lawrence eyed Lucien the way one would a man-eating tiger.

A killing rage stirred in Lucien's blood and he was more than ready to unleash it after what had happened to Horatia.

"I want a word with you, Lawrence," Lucien growled. "*All* of you, in fact."

Linus kicked out but Lucien's grip had rendered him helpless. Avery and Lawrence looked to one another and nodded, coming back to Lucien. Lucien loosened his grip on Linus but did not release him completely.

"Last night. What you did, Lawrence, that had better been part of some silly plan you've concocted, because if I learn you meant to do Horatia harm you will never be welcome in this house again."

"Easy there, Lucien," Avery said gently, as though speaking to a spooked stallion.

"It was Mama's doing!" Linus gasped out. "She's to blame!"

"What?"

"Be quiet!" Lawrence hissed.

"Mama told us to seduce Horatia so you would become jealous and want her more." Lucien let Linus go, causing him to fall to his knees.

"You tried to make me jealous? The three of you kept her away until..." Lucien fixed his gaze on Lawrence, who gulped audibly.

"You were supposed to find the two of us much sooner!" Lawrence said. "I was trying to explain, but she kept... I never meant to take it so far."

"Tell that to the young lady you frightened. God, Lawrence." Lucien stepped past Linus. "I thought you had more sense. Did her pleas mean nothing to you?"

"I regret every second of it," Lawrence snapped. "But it's done. You stayed all night with her, just like we expected you to."

Lucien hauled back his fist when a voice from down the hall stopped him.

"Everything all right here?" Cedric asked as he came down the hall, pulling on his gloves and coat.

Lucien changed his movement to a stretch and rubbed his hair. "Yes. Everything is fine." Lucien scanned Cedric's heavy coat and gloves. "Where are you off to?"

"To build the forts. You know, for the snowball battle your mother arranged? Your brothers and I are to build two forts on either side of the garden. The ladies will be out in an hour or so to join us."

"The ladies?" Lucien was baffled. It had been ages since his family had a snowball fight, not since he was sixteen at least. What was she up to?

Cedric grinned. "Who else? Last night we decided that should we have a decent snowfall, we ought to have a battle. Men against women, of course. Even Sir John and Lady Cavendish have agreed to join in. The numbers favor us, but I imagine that a few of the gents will defect to the enemy side when our chivalry gets the better of us."

Thankfully it seemed Cedric hadn't overhead any of their discussion. Lucien could deal with his brothers later. For now he just wanted some peace and to spend time with Cedric.

"Well then, lead the way, Avery." Lucien called for a nearby footman to fetch his coat and gloves. Avery, Cedric and Linus headed outside, but Lawrence lingered behind.

"Lucien, about Horatia—" Lawrence began.

Lucien cut him off with a raised finger, but Lawrence threw out a hand and stopped Lucien from brushing past him.

"I would never have done anything more to her. I swear it.

She's...well, she's Horatia." Lawrence's tone conveyed his meaning where his words failed.

Lucien moved the hand aside. "Never, and I mean *never* touch her again. If you make her uncomfortable for even a moment..." He didn't finish his sentence because it would end with a threat and he didn't wish to ruin his day with such black thoughts.

Lawrence studied his brother's face. "Mother was right. You really do care for her. She's a good woman and will make a wonderful wife and mother."

The sudden vision of Horatia holding a child, *their* child in her arms stilled his heart. Pain, such sweet pain and longing, blazed to life inside him. But Cedric would never condone the match—he always seemed to forget that when he was near her.

"Speak of it no more. I expect you to find a moment later today to make your apologies to Horatia. And if you ever let mother coerce you into something so foolish again, I won't save you, whatever the consequences," Lucien warned.

"I'll apologize to her." Lawrence slid his coat onto his shoulders and looked as though waiting for his brother's permission to leave.

Lucien shoved ahead of him and donned his own coat and gloves. "Come along, Lawrence. These snow forts must be soundly built, and if we leave Linus in charge he'll make some delicate nonsense that will look impressive but blow over in a stiff wind." Focusing on the upcoming frivolities, he prayed he could shake loose the longing he had for Horatia. Last night couldn't be repeated ever again.

CHAPTER 23

An hour later, Horatia and the other ladies were assembled on the east side, admiring the fort the gentlemen had built for them. It was a waist high wall that arched around in a half circle about ten feet across, providing ample protection for the women now huddled behind it preparing their arsenals. The vast gardens behind Rochester Hall had been molded into a white battlefield ready for the coming war.

Lady Cavendish was helping Lady Rochester manufacture their ammunition. Horatia, Audrey, Lysandra and Lucinda were in a tight circle, all wearing red fur-lined cloaks with heavy hoods pulled up. Audrey had remarked that they were the most fashionable army in Europe. They discussed the various traps and places to avoid in the garden, areas where one might become cornered and savaged by the weapons of the enemy.

"Should we try to lure them out from their fort?" Lucinda asked.

Horatia glanced over her shoulder to the opposing fort fifty feet away. The men were hunkered down out of sight, save for the occasional surfacing head that glanced warily about. Her gaze met with Gregory Cavendish's as he peeked out over their fort's edge then ducked back down. They looked like a pack of squirrels, popping up and down like that. Horatia grinned at the thought of such noble gentlemen behaving so out of character.

"I think luring is not a bad idea," Audrey declared. "But we must go about it smartly. Only when one of them is decently separated should we set up a trap. Otherwise they could easily overwhelm us."

"And someone ought to be carefully guarding the fort," Lysandra reminded them. She broke from the group to show the other ladies something she'd covered in a brown cloth blanket. She pulled it back to reveal a simple yet cleverly constructed wooden trebuchet approximately four feet long that was counterweighed by a heavy pouch of stones. "This should help whoever is remaining here."

"Is that a trebuchet?" Horatia asked, both amused and appreciative of Lysandra's ingenuity.

Lysandra grinned, glancing in the directions of her brothers. "I thought we might need a bit of extra help seeing how they both outnumber us and can throw farther. I found a book in our library detailing its construction and I had a scaled down replica built last summer. I had a devil of a time keeping Linus from finding out."

She took a snowball from the ever growing pile her mother and Lady Cavendish were making and set it in the sling attached to the trebuchet's long wooden arm. Then Lysandra prepared the pouch of stones and as all of the ladies watched, she aimed towards the men's fort and then dropped the pouch. The trebuchet hurled the snowball in a beautiful arch before it crashed into a tree a few feet behind the men.

"Oi! Who threw that?" Linus's head popped up, scowling in their directions as he hollered.

Horatia bit down on her lower lip to keep from laughing.

"Sorry, Linus! We're just practicing." Lysandra waved a snowy gloved hand in his direction, then turned back to the ladies. "As you can see, we may need a larger snowball, but it's a decent way of forcing them to keep their heads down."

"Excellent thinking!" Lucinda said and the other ladies nodded.

Sir John Cavendish called out from across the garden at that moment. "I say, are you ladies ready to begin?"

"We are!" Lady Cavendish returned to her husband.

"Good, good. I've been informed that I must now state the rules," Sir John said. "Which are as follows: Whoever captures the enemy fort is declared the winner. Captives may be taken and marked with red ribbons provided by your side's leader. There is no bargaining for captives, they remain captive until the end of the battle and lastly...there are no other rules. Begin!" Sir John bellowed before ducking down below his fort.

The ladies fell behind their snow wall as a massive volley of balls came their way. Audrey shrieked as a slush of snow and ice landed on the top of her hooded head. There was a chorus of distant laughter from the other side. Audrey stood up to shout at them since the weapons were supposed to be fashioned of fluffy snow, not hard packed with slush and ice, but Horatia jerked her back down as another flurry was unleashed. The balls flew past the empty space where Audrey had been standing moments before.

"Why those wretched devils!" Audrey hissed as she crawled over to the trebuchet. "Quick, someone distract them while I add more counterweight."

"But the balls will fly too far!" said Lady Cavendish.

"Not necessarily."

Lady Rochester peeked over the edge of the fort, her face alight with a delightful smile.

"Tally-ho!" Lady Rochester whooped most inelegantly and waved her arms as she acted as a decoy so Horatia and Lysandra could return fire. Unfortunately the fifty feet of distance between the two forts seemed to ensure that their throws would fall short.

"See? We've nothing to worry about. They can't even reach us!" Linus taunted as he stood up brazenly to take his time in aiming at his mother. Audrey meanwhile adjusted the aim of the trebuchet and with a curt nod at Lady Rochester, Audrey dropped the heavier counterweight and let fly their snowy vengeance. The women watched in glee as a snowball the size of a man's head smacked Linus square in the chest, knocking him to the ground.

"What the deuce?" They heard feebly from behind the fort.

The ladies all burst out laughing.

LUCIEN AND HIS FELLOW WARRIORS WERE ALL GAZING AT LINUS'S prone body. At last he got up and brushed himself off.

"Didn't we pace it at fifty feet?" Lawrence asked. "I thought Avery said they wouldn't be able to throw anything that far?"

"Or that heavy," added Avery.

"Perhaps not that far," said Linus. "One of them must have snuck up closer and we didn't see them. Search the trees for scouts. Mother has a surprisingly powerful arm."

Sir John's lips twitched. "Do you mean to tell me that you lads purposely put the ladies at a disadvantage both physically and numerically?"

"Clearly you have never engaged our women in a snowball fight, Sir John," Lucien said with a low chuckle. "They cheat and therefore any measures we take are simply precautions to protect ourselves against the inevitable."

His brothers nodded in agreement.

"They are ruthless," Avery said in all seriousness.

"How should we go about getting them away from their fort?" Gregory asked.

Cedric peeped over the edge of the snow wall as he voiced an idea. "We ought to send a scout of our own. One who can see just how their supplies stack up and how they are organizing themselves. The rest of us can remain here."

"I'll go," Gregory volunteered.

"Head south and make a large sweep around back," Lucien advised. "We don't want them guessing what our game is."

Gregory had barely left when the women pressed their advantage. Several flanked from one side, distracting them from among the trees, and every so often out of nowhere either a white cannon ball or a storm of smaller ones rained down at once, seemingly dropped from Heaven itself.

A little while later, Gregory returned with a prize. Lawrence and Avery were the first to spot them and laughed at seeing Lysandra following behind with a red ribbon around her wrist.

"Got a captive on my way back from the enemy encampment," he declared and indicated for Lysandra to sit down behind a tree a few feet away. "Tried to sneak up on me, but her shot missed and I threatened to put my snowball down her hood if she didn't surrender."

"Well done. What's the status of the opposing forces?" Avery demanded.

"Lady Rochester and my mother are producing the ammunition. Luce and Miss Sheridan are the primary hurlers, but as we planned, they cannot reach us from there. They left the fort to flank you."

"We know. We've only just beaten those two back."

"So how the devil are they hitting us so hard?" Lucien asked.

"It seems the ladies have the use of a small trebuchet." Gregory stifled a laugh when his captive huffed.

"So that's how they're raining death upon us," said Linus.

A large ball hit the side of the fort, making the rampart buckle.

"Bloody hell. They'll be firing real cannonballs soon," said Lawrence.

Linus flicked a calculated glance at Lysandra, then studied the other men crouching down behind their wall. He then he dug out a white handkerchief from his coat pocket and leapt to his feet.

"What on earth are you doing?" Lawrence asked.

Linus jumped back a few steps and then bolted towards the ladies fort, waving the handkerchief as a sign of surrender. Lucien watched him tear off across the snow-covered lawn.

Traitor. He shook his head at his youngest brother's quick defection to the other side.

❦

"HAVE MERCY, LADIES! I SEEK SANCTUARY!" LINUS SHOUTED AS Horatia and Lucinda jumped up, ready to pound him with snowballs.

"You bloody traitor!" Lucien hollered across the garden.

"Got to follow the progress of technology! Why fight with sticks when the other side has bronze weapons?" He dove behind the cover of the ladies' fort as a vicious barrage of snowballs from the enraged men followed him.

Linus rolled on the ground and landed up on the balls of his feet like a practiced warrior. Horatia found it impossible to keep from laughing at him. He could be very impressive when he wasn't playing pranks, and she couldn't miss the excited gleam in Lucinda's eyes regarding their new ally.

Horatia shouted for them both to duck and they covered their heads as a barrage came crashing down on them.

"Always causing trouble, aren't you?" Lucinda giggled to Linus.

"I wouldn't be me if I didn't," he replied, then popped up to retaliate. "Take that, you cheating curs!" He hurled three snowballs one after the other. He was their very own knight errant ready to lay siege to his former allies.

Lucien bravely stood up across the yard. "Silence, pup! We'll capture your fort and you will have to surrender the lovely ladies whose skirts you hide behind!" He spoke like a villain from a comedy play.

But all Horatia felt was the love and joy she always had for him. Like drinking too much wine, she was light-headed and eager to find a way back into his arms. Even at a distance his answering smile was intimate, as though meant only for her. She uttered a silent prayer deep in her heart that the one dream she'd longed for most would come true.

The snowball battle lasted close to two hours but after that the excitement died down, and the chill in the air and the damp cold of the snow had started to set in. They declared the battle a draw and Horatia was happy that the others agreed they should return indoors. She wished she could have more time with Lucien—but it wasn't to be. She followed the rest of the party inside, her heart sinking lower with each step.

CHAPTER 24

The rider from London arrived in the early evening, just in time to prevent everyone from going to dinner. Lucien took the note, and he and Cedric returned to his study to read it in privacy. Horatia and her sister lingered in the corridor outside. She thought it might involve news from his friends in London.

Pressed against the wooden door to eavesdrop, Horatia flinched when she heard Cedric curse. There was a heavy thud, as though something had hit the wall. Lucien muttered something she couldn't hear, then there was a growl from her brother before footsteps approached the door. Both Audrey and Horatia scampered back, hoping to conceal their feeble attempts at eavesdropping.

When the door opened, Horatia's stomach clenched as she saw Cedric's face shrouded by a mask of pain and barely controlled rage.

"What is it?" Audrey asked as she glanced between Cedric and Lucien.

"Charles sent some bad news," Lucien answered carefully. He

glanced around, making sure that it was only the four of them. Horatia knew it must be a private League matter if he didn't wish for his brothers or anyone else to overhear.

"What happened?" Her throat constricted.

"Ashton was wounded when he and Godric were investigating the threats we overheard," Lucien said. "Someone shot him, but he'll be fine."

Horatia watched him closely. "That's not all, is it? You're not telling us everything." She'd been too afraid to ask her brother or Lucien, but she'd sensed there was more to this situation than either had let on. Were they all in more danger than she'd originally believed?

"I'm sorry. Someone killed Muff." Cedric's low sharp tone made Horatia flinch.

Audrey screamed. "No!"

"Waverly somehow managed to breach our home." Cedric's fists tightened as he spoke. "Someone killed Muff. They drowned him and left him in a tub at Charles's house."

"But why?" Audrey whimpered, tears threatening to spill over.

"Because he could. He wanted us to know our homes aren't safe. And he's succeeded. No one is going back until this is resolved." Cedric's tone was dark in a way that Horatia had never heard before.

"How do you know it was Waverly?" Horatia asked. Her voice cracked, but she got the words out.

Neither her brother nor Lucien replied for several long moments.

"We have no proof," Lucien said. "It's more of a feeling."

Cedric added his own dark thoughts. "He tried to drown Charles once. Now he's drowned a cat. It's obvious enough it's him."

There was a vengefulness in his brown eyes that frightened her. He was buried in a rage she understood all too well. She could barely think herself, the anger and grief churned to violence inside her.

Audrey threw herself at Cedric's chest and wept. Cedric folded her in his embrace.

"Take her to her room, Cedric," Lucien said. "I'll have dinner sent up."

Cedric nodded in silent thanks before leading Audrey, still sniffling, up to her bedchamber.

"Horatia?" Lucien was at her side now, weariness carved lines in his face. He'd always seemed confident and self-assured to her before, but his look now was entirely new to her. He appeared vulnerable.

"Yes?"

"Is there anything I can do for you? I know you were fond of Muff and that this news must be an awful shock to you."

"No...thank you. I would just like to be alone now." Her tone was dismally cool, she didn't have the strength to even feign that she was fine.

Lucien seemed hurt, as if that tone had been meant for him.

"Of course. I will leave you alone. Send for me should you need anything." Lucien left her alone in the dim hallway. The evening dinner bell rang, but sounded so very far away.

Heat surrounded her, a stifling kind that strangled her throat and made it hard to think. She broke out into a sweat and stumbled towards the door that led to the gardens. She needed fresh air. She couldn't breathe inside. She craved numbness. The cold winter air was the only way to achieve it. Without a coat or gloves, she forged a path through snow that was halfway up her calves. Just a few minutes outside and she could process this horrific news. Someone had broken into their home. A place of safety. What if it had been Audrey or her and not poor Muff? Muff...her charming companion. Gone.

She tried not to think but memories shot through her—Audrey's cherry red cheeks, so young and cherubic as she held up the pair of tiny kittens for Christmas. Muff falling asleep in Audrey's lap listening to Cedric sing Christmas carols. The black and white ball of fur struggling to climb the stairs behind Cedric—

little paws batting his Hessian boots for attention. She told him all the stories of the constellations and the charmer that he was, Muff would rub his furry whiskered cheek against her chin, purring loudly.

Horatia tripped in the snow, falling on her knees. Pain lanced up towards her heart. Her parents had given them to her and Audrey the Christmas before they'd died.

Muff was more than a cat. He'd been a part of her and one of her last connections to her parents. And now one more part of them had been taken away, violently. Would Audrey or Cedric to be next? Or herself? Which of her loved ones would be a target for one man's hatred?

Horatia lay down in the snow, too tired to care about the cold.

All I want is peace, please, let me have peace. Her dark lashes brushed across her cheeks as she shut her eyes.

But horrible thoughts haunted her. How scared had Muff been when his killer had captured him? Had the aging cat fought or had he been too weak in his grasp? Had his death been quick? She would never know.

A violent shudder shot through her at the thought. Who could be so cruel?

An explosion of panic and fear speared her through the chest. It wasn't just a way to hurt her family. It was a message, as her brother had said. He could get to any of them. She and her siblings weren't safe. No place was safe. He could always find them.

The vision of her parents dead in that coach flashed across her mind's eye just as the vision of a drowned cat, fur damp and body stiff merged with it. Her father's neck broken, her mother's pale pink lips coated with blood. Their bodies like a pair of broken marionettes abandoned by a child.

She'd touched them, her mother's cheek, her father's hand. But they'd been gone, and she couldn't bring them back.

Was her own life soon to be forfeit? Perhaps it was only a matter of days before hands would reach out of the shadows and snap her neck, leaving her lifeless body for Lucien or Cedric to find.

She struggled to breathe, but her gasping didn't help. There was only suffocating terror and pain.

"Horatia!" A soft cry, distant as the stars themselves.

Something yanked her up. She fought, screamed, bit, but she was so weak and cold that after a minute she had to yield. Noises intruded upon her numbed ears—the crash of wood, the scuffling of boots, the huff of breath. She felt cold softness beneath her. Horatia shifted uncomfortably while forcing her eyes open.

She was in a dark room, one she didn't recognize. The décor did not at all match that of Rochester Hall. A man huddled before the fireplace as he added few logs to the fresh burning kindling, stoking them with a poker. When he turned to face her, she saw it was Lucien.

Without a word, he came over to the bed where he'd set her down, and eased her onto her stomach. He dug his fingers underneath the neck of her gown and began plucking buttons out of their slips. His hands were hot, piercing against her cold flesh and Horatia winced.

"Does it hurt?"

Horatia shook her head as she tried to speak. "You're so warm," she managed at last.

"Good. That is the idea." He reached the last button of her gown and he peeled it away, easing her cold limp arms from her sleeves before he dragged the garment off her completely. Lucien did not stop there. He removed her stays, chemise, stockings, and slippers.

Ordinarily Horatia would have been clutching at a blanket to hide some of her nakedness but her inner pain and weariness had numbed her to such inconsequential concerns. Lying on her stomach, she gazed straight ahead listening to the sounds of Lucien stripping himself of his own clothes behind her.

There was nothing sensual in his movements. In fact, he nearly tripped getting his shoes off. The second he was down to his bare skin, he reached for a thick woolen blanket draped over the foot of the bed and he wrapped it around him like a cloak. Only then did he turn his attention back to Horatia as he scooped her up and carried her to the soft thick rug near the fire.

He sat down and braced her body back against his, securing the blanket around their bodies. Between the fire before her and the fire of his skin behind her, the chill in her bones melted away, followed by sharp prickling as her nerves came alive again. She shifted against Lucien and his hot breath quickened against her cheek.

"Easy, love," he whispered in her ear. "You have no idea how long you were out there, do you?" The tenderness of his voice, the soft endearment so pure on his lips had her quaking with bottled up emotions. "Let it out darling, let it all out. I'm here."

It was this promise, undiluted by the outside world and its concerns that crippled Horatia's protective barrier. She broke down, burrowing into him as though she could forge an unbreakable connection between their bodies and she never wanted to be without him or his comforting touch again. Her dry eyes pooled with hot, heavy tears and Lucien rubbed each drop of moisture away with his fingertips.

"It hurts," Horatia gasped as the weight of everything descended upon her. Like knife shards embedded in her lungs, each breath she sucked in was ragged and icy.

"That's a good thing, my love. It means your heart is still alive. Just let it all out." Lucien brushed his lips along her tear-stained cheek and absorbed her shaking with his body.

The two times in her life when she needed someone most, when she'd been her weakest, he'd been there. She'd often wondered why she loved Lucien and no one else, even when he'd been determined to be cold to her. This moment, this embrace, was everything that mattered. A man who would do this for her was the only man she could ever have, ever want.

As her shaking subsided, Horatia turned about in Lucien's arms. He gazed down at her in tender worry.

"Make love to me," she pleaded.

"No, darling, not like this." He feathered his lips against her temple and stroked her hair back from her face. "You've been through too much. I'll not add to that pain."

"I want you, Lucien. Each second you aren't kissing me is killing me inside." Horatia cupped his face. An auburn tinged night beard had started to graze his cheeks, and the roughness of it was an enticing contrast to the smooth skin of his chest.

Lucien smiled ever so slightly. "I know I'm a wonderful kisser but no one has ever perished from a lack of it as far as I can recall."

Horatia, her body filled with desire and a desperation for some sort of release, pulled free of his arms and stood up, entirely bare before him. She walked around him and approached the bed.

"I don't recognize this room," she said softly as she eased onto the bed.

Lucien followed her movement, his eyes focusing on the peaks of her breasts, the chill in the air tightening her nipples.

"I found you too far away from the house. I brought you to the gardener's summer cottage," Lucien explained. He got to his feet, blanket still loosely cloaking his body.

"The gardener's cottage?"

There was a hungry look in his eyes as he approached, but still it seemed he meant to resist her.

"Yes, it's always empty in the winter." Lucien's voice was even lower, huskier than before.

"So we are alone, without fear of discovery." Horatia started to reach for the blanket about his body.

"Are you trying to seduce me?" A wicked smile played about his mouth.

"That depends. Is it working?" Horatia ran her foot up against his calf and he tensed.

"Your feet are cold, love. Shall I warm them up for you?"

For an answer, Horatia tugged harder on the blanket. Lucien dropped it at his feet, baring his body before her. It seemed her entire life had been leading up to this moment. Bodies and souls finally bared to each other. She stared up at him, examining his finely formed body, at last able to see all the parts of him that had been hidden.

The inner savage in her was unbearably close to taking over. She held out a hand and Lucien took it, kissing the inside of her palm before she tugged him to the bed's edge. Horatia pushed back as he advanced, their bodies miming an ancient dance of conquest and submission as he crawled over her. Lucien dropped his head to hers, their mouths meeting in a slow kiss that lit fire to every nerve in her body. Horatia's hands slid up to his flexing biceps, clenching his muscles as he released her mouth to trail kisses down her throat.

"I didn't know a collarbone could be so desirable," Lucien murmured as he licked the grooves of her upper chest.

Horatia laughed until his mouth settled on the tip of one breast. He savored her, suckled her, teeth nipping her with sparks of pleasurable pain before he circled her with his tongue, leaving her writhing beneath him.

Horatia moaned as his lips danced to her other breast. She ran her fingers through his thick red hair, tugging as he feasted on her.

"Never let it be said that I neglected you, darling," he teased before taking her other breast into his mouth.

Her nails dug into his arms, Horatia's back arched, yearning for more of him. At the pressure of his hands on her inner knees, her thighs fell apart. A flash of déjà vu, a masked man, the devil of pleasure, an angel of sin between her legs.

"Oh God, if you do that...that thing again, I'll kill you," she gasped as his mouth trespassed down her waist and towards the dark triangle between her legs.

"You mean if I do this?" He assaulted her senses with a devastating lick, then fastened his mouth around that same tight bundle of nerves. Horatia bucked. Lucien pinned her deeper into the bed as he pushed her over the brink of sanity.

"You devil..." She forgot entirely what she meant to say as his tongue traced erotic patterns and she careened over the edge in a fall she thought would never end.

In time she became aware of Lucien moving higher, his mouth back on hers again. She could taste herself on him, the thought sinfully erotic. She groaned as his weight eased down over her. The pressure of his body was a welcome one; he pinned her to the bed when she felt light enough to drift away in the winter breeze. His shaft was hard against her inner thigh and he rocked forward, the tip of him sliding over her with a rhythm her body's instincts knew better than she ever expected.

"Yes, Lucien, yes."

"I don't want to hurt you, not ever again...and this might."

"If I never hurt again, I won't know I'm alive," she reminded him. She was desperate and needed to feel him. Her hands slid down the ridges of his hard abdomen until she wrapped her hand possessively about his length. He groaned against her lips with feral pleasure.

"You play with fire, darling, and I don't wish to burn you." He tried to pull back. Horatia slid a hand down to the base of him and back up to his tip.

"Burn me. Consume me, Lucien. It's the only thing I've ever wanted." Horatia kissed Lucien so deeply that her assault seemed to drive him wild. He snatched her hand away and confined her wrists above her head. Poised at her entrance, he began to work his way inside, gentle and slow, so unlike what she'd come to expect from him.

Horatia lifted her hips, forcing him too deep too soon and he muttered a curse and tried to lift away. She locked her legs around his hips, keeping him close. His hips jerked forward in a shallow thrust. The sudden intrusion of his shaft inside her burned and a piece of her was forever lost in the wake of his penetration. But she was glad. She was changed. She was his.

She ignored his apologies as passion sparked his movements into life inside her.

Lucien now held her prisoner beneath him, a slow steady pace of thrusts testing her limits. He feathered kisses across her cheeks, nose, lips and chin, as though unable to stop himself from branding his essence on her in every way possible.

The pain dulled in the wake of a tension that was steadily building. The sensation she'd once mistaken for nausea was back, stronger than before. Horatia reveled in it, understanding now what it meant and the throbbing between her legs eased with each of Lucien's thrusts.

Even though her wrists were trapped, she raised her hips, welcoming him deeper into her. Lucien released her wrists to glide his hands down her sides and underneath her, cupping her bottom, lifting it up. The angle changed things dramatically, and his shaft struck some new place deep within her. The cry that left her lips was one of startled surprise and Lucien hastened to repeat the move again and again, her cries a primal encouragement to continue. Sweat dewed on their bodies as Lucien's pace picked up.

"Lucien, I think I..." Horatia was silenced with a dominating and possessive kiss that ended in the most brilliant burst of pleasure in her life. She heard a scream and only later realized it was her own. Lucien shouted her name as he jerked against her. He continued to shake and rock, trembling above her. Horatia would never forget the look in his eyes—so bright with passion, fire, tenderness and confusion.

"My God, Horatia. I've never—didn't know—it could be this way." He seemed afraid, like a young boy faced with fear for the first time. Horatia ran her fingers through his hair and raised her head up to kiss him.

"Don't be afraid, Lucien. I'll hold you."

It was too soon to hope that he'd come to love her, but she knew that he cared. This was no casual affair. This was about making love, about forging a connection. Lucien settled in her arms, their bodies still linked as her hands brushed against him. He buried his face in her dark brown hair. A cool breeze tickled their bodies and Lucien disentangled himself from her.

"Please don't leave," she begged in a ragged whisper.

"Never, my heart. Never." He pulled back the covers of the bed so he could slip inside and join her, cocooning her body with his own. The only sounds were their mingled breathing and the snap and crack of the fire in the hearth.

Everything has changed. But what would Lucien do now? Not wanting to dwell on the possibilities, she burrowed into his arms and settled down to sleep.

CHAPTER 25

Ashton sat in his study on Half Moon Street. Letters of a financial nature were strewn over the surface of his oak wood desk. The numbers on the letters blurred as pain lanced up his left arm, which still hung limp and useless in a sling about his neck.

What a bloody nuisance being shot was. He had lost so much of his strength that his footman had to do many routine things for him and his valet, once a minor irritation, had become indispensible. He couldn't put a shirt on, let alone tie his neck cloth or button his trousers without assistance.

It was most humiliating. Everyone treated him like a child in leading strings and he was tired of it. And he'd only been injured a few days. The doctor had given him instructions to rest for the next *five weeks*. The idea was intolerable. He, of all people, could not afford to rest. There was so much to be done aside from his business; namely tracking down Waverly and ending this battle before it could progress to a full-fledged war.

With a heavy sigh, Ashton reached for the nearest letter, the movement sending a stab of pain through his bad shoulder. He pinned the letter down on his desk with his hand in the sling, ignoring the ache it caused and used his other hand to break the seal. He cursed under his breath until the seal gave way.

The letter was from his banker at Drummond's Bank, Mr. Jared Simms. Simms had given Ashton a detailed report of his funds currently tied up in the consols. It was a sound investment. Consolidated annuities were government bonds that paid three percent dividends twice a year.

Ashton had put fifty thousand pounds into them and the return had been a mighty fortune that he spent wisely and cautiously. Unlike his friends, he had not been born into money. His entire life he'd amassed a grand fortune so where his political clout could not win the day, his bank accounts could. Though he did not flaunt his wealth, he did not hesitate to use it when it could gain a clear advantage.

He was currently caught up in a bidding war over a company called Southern Star Shipping. Ashton owned his own shipping company, Lennox Lines, but acquiring Southern Star would put his ships deep into the Caribbean trade markets and the routes closer to Africa, an area he had yet to penetrate.

This was not his only interest in the line however.

For months he'd heard rumors that Waverly was involved in questionable shipments, bringing lord knows what into England. Ashton suspected slaves might be involved but it could be a number of things. If he could gain control of the line, he could clean up the ships, put new captains and crews on them that he trusted, and begin to eliminate Waverly's illicit sources of income, piece by piece. It was the one thing he knew he could do better than Waverly and if it was his best weapon, he needed to use it. A man couldn't hire killers to take out the League if he didn't possess any money.

He would have possessed Southern Star by now, but a rival shipping company had been matching him bid for bid. The end result was his solicitor, Mr. Danforth, contacting the owner of Melbourne, Shelley and Company to meet with Ashton in less than an hour to discuss the matter and come to an arrangement.

A knock on his study door made Ashton look up. His butler, Wimbley, a balding man of middle years, stepped inside.

"What is it?" he asked, looking back down at the investment report.

"There's a visitor to see you my lord. A lady," Wimbley clarified.

"If it is Her Grace, tell her I shall be with her shortly." He had no idea what Emily was doing here, except to berate him again for putting himself in danger.

"It is not Her Grace, my lord. She says her name is Lady Melbourne and that you are expecting her."

"Lady Melbourne?" Melbourne's wife had come? He'd asked to see her husband. "Show her into the Rose Parlor and have tea brought in. Tell her I will be with her directly." Still, he supposed he could work this to his advantage.

"Yes, my lord." Wimbley disappeared.

Ashton hastily organized his desk before checking his appearance in a nearby looking glass. His cravat was snug and his trousers unwrinkled. His silk navy blue vest was crisp and his shirt pressed. He looked decent enough for company.

Perhaps his hair was a tad long for the conventional styles favored among society but he'd been too busy of late to have it cut. His eyes, which had been glassy with fatigue and pain of late, were bright again with his irritation at having to deal with this proxie.

Ashton looked every inch the dapper rogue, save for the white cloth sling holding his left arm. Showing weakness in any way was not what he wished in a business setting, but his arm could not be helped.

He left his study and walked up the stairs to Rose Parlor. It was perhaps a bit improper to have a parlor on the same floor as his bedroom, but he only used the Rose Parlor for two things—intimate meals with his mistress, when he had one, and when he did not, it was a place of seduction.

He found that the dark hues of the room seemed to lull the ladies into a receptive mood. Rose-colored gauze curtains laced the windows, casting the room into tempting rosy dimness even in the morning. A fire was always lit in the hearth to keep up the impression of an evening rendezvous. The Rose Parlor had never failed to help him in his conquests.

If he was to deal with his competitor's wife, it seemed logical that a bit of seduction might help his cause. Ashton was no fool. Unlike other men, he learned long ago how powerful a woman could be in a man's world of business and how men underestimated them. However, if he played the charming rake, Lord Melbourne would be but a pawn in Ashton's game and Southern Star shipping would be his.

Ashton opened the door, expecting to find a gray-haired matron. What he found instead halted him in his tracks. A woman, who must have been in her late twenties, perched on the edge of the red velvet settee close to the fireplace. Her raven-black hair and almond-shaped gray eyes were framed by sooty dark lashes. She stared back, seemingly just as confused by him. It was clear that neither of them had expected the other to appear as they had.

"You are Lady Melbourne?" Ashton asked.

"Yes. Lord Lennox I presume?"

Her lips were a pale shade of pink and not as full as most women's, but their shape was somehow quite erotic. Rather than a pretty pout, she had a wide mouth, as though she was more inclined to smile, despite the cool gray of her eyes. Ashton rarely entertained thoughts regarding married women, but in her case he could make an exception.

"I am Lord Lennox."

"Good. We have much to discuss, my lord." There was a soft accent to her speech, a Scottish lilt. Not as heavy as a brogue and far more refined, as though she was trying to hide it. It was a revealing weakness and he acted upon it instinctively.

"What part of Scotland are you from, Lady Melbourne?" Ashton enjoyed watching her eyes widen. It was clear she preferred to hide her origins, something he understood only too well.

"I was born in Falkirk, my lord."

"Falkirk? *An Eaglais Bhreac*," he said with a smug smile.

"You speak Gaelic?" She looked doubly surprised.

"Only a few phrases and some cities and villages. I had an uncle who married a woman from Edinburough."

"Oh?" Lady Melbourne replied curiously. Ashton pressed on with his advantage now that she was off balance.

"What brings you here, Lady Melbourne? Not that I don't find your presence in my home charming, but I had expected to be meeting with Lord Melbourne."

"Lord Melbourne?" Her black brows rose in surprise.

"Yes. I had my solicitor contact the owner of Melbourne, Shelley and Company. Your husband, I presume, or perhaps father? It is he that I need to meet with. I assume he's related to William Lamb?" No longer surprised, her eyes seemed to glint with glee. He'd clearly missed some vital piece of information.

"I'm afraid *I* am the owner of Melbourne, Shelley and Company. My husband, only a distant relation to William Lamb, passed away last year. His company has been under my control for the better part of a year."

Ashton's jaw drop. A woman running a business? It wasn't unheard of...but still...

"You can handle business with the opposite sex, I presume?"

He didn't like that she'd gotten the better of him already. And the way she dressed was driving him to distraction. Her husband was dead less than a year yet she was not wearing the black crepe gown and veil expected of her. Instead, she wore a low-cut ruby dress that seemed to make her pale skin almost luminescent against the firelight. She looked more the seductress than the grieving widow. She knew her looks were an advantage and she wasn't afraid to use them. A dangerous lady. He'd have to remember that.

"And what of Shelley? Is he stationed in London? Perhaps I ought to meet with him instead."

A thin smile of victory teased her mouth. "That would be a waste of your time, my lord. I bought out Shelley's stock months ago and am now the sole owner of the company my husband founded. We will be changing the name before the next quarter. So it is in fact me you need to see." She punctuated this statement with no small amount of pride.

Ashton glowered. He was not one of those men who believed in discouraging women from the arena of business, but with Lady Melbourne he wished to make an exception. With her in the same room, he could not concentrate, not when his mind and body were conspiring against him like this.

"I've noticed that you are injured, my lord. Please sit. How did you come by such an injury?"

Lady Melbourne had the nerve to offer him a seat in his own bloody parlor? Oh, he'd sit down all right, and pull her body beneath his... Ashton locked the thoughts safely away in a dim corner of his mind, then he sought to regain his natural civility.

"Thank you." He seated himself in a chair opposite the settee. "In answer to your question, I was shot recently." He waited for her to show disgust or some form of feminine aversion to the mention of bloodshed.

She did nothing of the sort. Minor surprise transformed into open curiosity. Must be her damned Scottish blood.

"Were you dueling, my lord?" she asked bluntly.

"Dueling is outlawed. Do not make such quick assumptions about me, Lady Melbourne. I can guarantee you will be wrong on every account." His tone was so rough he barely recognized himself. It was the tone of his youth, before he'd learned to hone in his temper.

Lady Melbourne had awakened a very dangerous inferno in him. She raised her chin defiantly in a silent challenge to his temper, but the movement only brought her tempting lips closer to his. Ashton forced himself to back away from her as he spoke again.

"My apologies, Lady Melbourne. My arm twinges with pain and it has quite ruined my ability to play the polite host." It was the truth, though only part of it.

"I will accept your apology my lord—if you will satisfy my curiosity as to how you received your wound," she said. Her impertinence both infuriated him and astonished him.

"The business that led to my injury was personal in nature and I will not divulge it just to flatter your curiosity. Now come, let us speak of business, if you will."

She seemed as though she wanted to say something further, then thought better of it. "Very well," she sighed. At that moment a maid entered with a tea tray and Lady Melbourne took the pot from the tray and glanced at Ashton.

"May I pour?" It was usually a maid's job when a man did not have a wife or a lady of the house to perform the task, but the maid in this case took one look at him and scampered from the room without so much as a backward glance.

"Yes, of course," Ashton muttered curtly, once more resuming his seat as she poured two cups of tea.

"When your solicitor contacted my office I was informed that the business matter that concerned you involved the purchase of Southern Star Shipping."

"Indeed." Ashton didn't take his eyes off the woman as he took a sip of tea—and nearly spat it across the table.

The blasted woman had not added any milk, leaving it scalding hot. She seemed to be watching him for some reaction, some exclamation of pain, as he fought to remain calm and pretend that he hadn't just lost all feeling in his tongue due to sabotaged tea. The woman was ruthless.

"What puzzles me is why you crave the Southern Star ships." Ashton took another step in her direction, trying to recover lost ground. "As far as I can tell your business doesn't require them."

"Why does anyone want anything? I crave the power of the ships. And contrary to your no doubt thorough research on my interests, I do in fact need them for access to the Caribbean ports." It was a business answer, but not the truth, and for some reason her answer angered him. He could not negotiate with someone with such solid defenses around her. If only he could tear down those walls somehow.

"I propose a trade. If you tell me how you were shot I will cease bidding on the Southern Star."

This was unexpected. Another ploy to keep him off guard, perhaps? Ashton scrubbed his jaw with one hand, considering the proposal. Normally his affairs were kept private, especially those relating to the League, but he saw no harm in giving her a somewhat censored answer. He didn't trust her, however. Not one whit.

"You would relinquish the line to me that easily?"

She gave a graceful shrug of one shoulder. "There are other lines, of course. I have enough capital that I could build my own if I had to. Buying the Southern Star was simply a more efficient way to reach my goal."

Her answer satisfied him enough.

"I agree to your terms." He took a deep breath. "I was shot while investigating a place of ill repute for evidence that someone of my acquaintance had hired a man to murder my close friend. That same man found us there and opened fire before running off."

"You were shot trying to prove someone wanted to murder your friend?" Lady Melbourne seemed surprised.

"Yes." He would not tell her any more than that however.

Her reaction puzzled him further, as if his words had told her far more than he'd intended, and had told her everything she wished to know about him. "Very well. The Southern Star is yours, Lord Lennox. Enjoy the profits."

"Oh I will, Lady Melbourne," he assured her. If all such business could be conducted this cheaply he'd be twice as wealthy by now.

She gathered her reticule and Ashton followed her down the stairs to the door. He helped her put on her cloak before she turned to leave.

"It was interesting to meet you, Lord Lennox." She smiled that knowing smile again and he bowed over her hand, kissing it longer than was appropriate.

"And you, Lady Melbourne. I believe we may yet cross paths again." Their eyes met briefly and Ashton felt his world tilt on its axis. Lady Melbourne was going to be bad for his business.

When he opened the door for her, Charles stood there, hand raised as though to knock.

"Hello Ash, am I...er...interrupting?" His eyes darted between Ashton and Lady Melbourne.

"No." Both he and the lady replied in unison.

"Right, well, Ash, I need to speak to you straight away." Charles's stony gaze cut to the point. Something new had developed.

"It was...interesting to meet you," Lady Melbourne said and then hastened down the steps. He watched her depart for only a moment before Charles was dragging him by his good arm back inside.

"What is it?" Ashton asked.

Charles glanced about the house, as though searching for spies in every corner. Ashton's worry deepened like a gnawing pit in his stomach.

"I was going through my correspondence with Lucien's mother. They'd been building up for some time. You know how she writes to me about Lysa."

"Yes." Charles made few attempts to reply back to Lucien's mother since the letters more often than not included offers of marriage to Lucien's sister, which would never have gone over well with anyone for any number of reasons.

"Well, I noticed a strange pattern in her letters. She's been through several footmen in the last few months. Six in all. She writes about accidents, broken legs, being thrown from a horse, a few of them just up and left without any reason. I wouldn't have noticed except that I read all of the letters in one sitting and it struck me."

Ashton frowned. "What struck you?"

"The pattern, Ash. *The pattern.*" He slapped a handful of letters against Ashton's chest. "She said the last footman hasn't had any of the problems the others had and that the curse might finally be lifted."

"And you don't believe it is a series of coincidental accidents," Ashton said, seeing where this was going. "You think he took out the other footman to gain a secure position at the Hall?"

"Exactly." Charles paced the entryway, and his eyes again searched around them. "The question is why Lucien's house if Cedric is the target. Perhaps it was Lucien who was the target all along? The carriage did attempt to run him over after all. Either way, we need to warn them."

"You're absolutely right," Ashton agreed. "But we must be careful. After our message to them about the cat, if we show up without cause, the man might act rashly. We should send Lucien a letter but address it to his mother. If the man is under Hugo's control he'd likely be instructed to open any mail addressed to Lucien or Cedric. Best to do this carefully."

"Good plan," Charles said.

Ashton winced as his arm panged. "I'll have you write the letter, if you don't mind."

He led Charles to his study and prayed their letter didn't come too late.

CHAPTER 26

Cedric stretched stiffly in his chair by Audrey's bedside and rubbed the tight muscles in his neck with a weary hand. His sister was curled up in her bed fast asleep. Her delicate features and troubled expression made her appear like a fairy queen whose woes had followed her deep into the sacred realm of dreams.

Holding her had brought back horrific memories of years long past. He couldn't protect her from this, couldn't save her from all the hurts in the world. In many ways, he'd been both father and mother to her and Horatia after losing their parents, and perhaps the greatest cost had been that there was no one to hold him as he silently grieved.

The memories of last evening struck him all over again and Cedric shut his eyes. He'd been fond of Muff. The cat had been one of the last connections he and his sisters had of their parents before the accident.

The accident. How many years would pass before the sting of his parents' deaths would subside? A man could only endure so much before it finally broke him.

Audrey shifted restlessly and awoke to find Cedric staring straight through her, his mind still far away.

"Cedric?" Her voice was a little hoarse. She'd cried herself to sleep last night after he'd made her eat dinner and collapsed with exhaustion. A weak smile revealed she was doing her best to come to terms with events. She'd taken the death hard but had already begun to move on. *Good girl*, he thought silently.

"What is it, sweetheart?" He sat up straighter in his chair. Audrey smiled at him, but it was sad and wistful.

"I'm sorry that I've been so much trouble for you lately." She pushed back her covers and sat up to face him.

"You're a woman, Audrey. Troublemaking is the forté of your gender, like convincing Charles to go along with your scheme and thinking it wouldn't anger me. I don't mind, except when I end up strangling my best friend over it. We ought to talk about that, you know." Cedric found himself smiling despite himself.

"I suppose we ought to," Audrey agreed.

"Why didn't you come to me? You could have told me that you wished to marry. I had no idea you were in such a state of desperation."

"It is different for women, Cedric. I think that because Mama is not here that it is harder for you to understand. I want to marry. I want a husband and a life beyond Curzon Street. I dread a future like Horatia's."

Cedric slid to the edge of his chair. "And what future is that?"

"She's almost one and twenty and yet she will never marry because she's—" Audrey clapped a hand over her mouth.

The suddenness of her move worried Cedric. "Because she's what?"

"Oh I mustn't say. She wouldn't want me to betray her confidence."

Cedric was on his feet and looming over her. "You'd better tell me everything or I won't be very generous over the next few months for your shopping allowances."

Audrey scoffed. "Betray my sister for new gowns? Don't be silly."

"What if I doubled your allowance next month if you did?"

"Bribery? Never!"

"And what if I send you away to a place where there are no men of marriageable age?"

Audrey's eyes narrowed to slits, glowering up at him. "You play a cruel game, Cedric. I will tell you, but if Horatia finds out you learned it from me, I will find the next man on the street, be he a lamplighter or chimney sweep, and I shall run off to Scotland with him."

Cedric smiled. "You'd never marry a chimney sweep. The soot would ruin your fine gowns. Now, about Horatia? You know I only want to make her happy. Tell me and I will see that it is kept between us." His used his best cajoling brotherly voice, yet his sister seemed unmoved.

"Cedric, I shouldn't tell you. You'll get angry, and nothing can come of it regardless. Just forget I said anything." She pursed her lips as though resigned never to speak again.

"Do I ever get angry at you or Horatia? I know I threatened your suitors, but have I ever shown a temper with you or your sister?"

She cocked a brow, as though internally debating the matter. Finally with a heavy sigh, she relented.

"I suppose no more than any other brother might. But if I tell you, you mustn't overreact. She won't ever marry because she's still in love with Lucien. She's never loved or wanted anyone else."

Cedric's throat went uncomfortably dry. "Lucien?"

He'd known that long ago Horatia had developed a child's affection for Lucien, but he thought that had ended long ago. Now it all made sense. Horatia being upset every time Lucien was even mentioned, her odd behavior on the rare occasions when they'd been forced to be in the same room.

"You are sure she still loves him?"

"Yes and I believe that Lucien may be starting to return her feelings."

This was worse than he could have imagined. Lucien was like a brother, but if he was entertaining thoughts of an amorous nature towards Horatia... The League's rule existed for a reason. The last thing he or the others wanted was to fight over someone's sister, or pick up the pieces should the courtship sour. He could entertain thoughts of letting Audrey marry Jonathan because that man was young and didn't carry the weight of the sins the rest of the League did. But Horatia marrying Lucien was out of the question.

That man had a taste for wicked pleasures and Cedric would die before he let Horatia play a role in those dark fantasies. He could have any woman in the world, but not Horatia. Horatia deserved a gentleman who would care for and love her for the reserved and deeply loyal woman she was. She did not need to be burned in the wake of Lucien's fleeting passions.

Cedric shuddered as he recalled his discussion with Lucien in the billiard room the day before. Lucien had spoken of his changed feelings towards Horatia and foolishly Cedric had assumed his friend viewed her merely as a sister once again.

"What proof do you have of his feelings towards her?" Cedric asked.

"I'm not supposed to say..."

"Audrey," Cedric growled.

"Lucien bought her a gown for Christmas. It arrived yesterday from London."

"What sort of gown?"

"A lovely evening one to replace the one that was ruined. I helped him order it, since I have the best fashion sense in London."

"Naturally." Cedric's sarcasm was lost on his sister.

"But you mustn't be angry, Cedric. Nothing will come of it but...wouldn't it be wonderful if Lucien and Horatia were married?" Audrey smiled and clasped her hands.

The mere thought of Lucien in bed with his sister made a veil of red descend over Cedric's vision.

"Wonderful? Dash it all, Audrey! You're too bloody innocent. Lucien's not the kind to marry. None of us are, but *especially* not him." She didn't understand. Lucien would toss Horatia aside when the fires of passion burned down to embers. He'd seen it many times before, though always with women who found such terms agreeable. Horatia was no such woman.

"Is that any way to speak of your friend?" Audrey's eyes widened as though startled by his dark prediction.

"He's a friend, but he's also a devil. As am I. I know him only too well, and I know he won't marry her."

"You're wrong. Godric married Emily and he is much the same as the rest of you."

"Emily was different... She was a perfect match for Godric."

"And who's to say that Horatia is not Lucien's perfect match?" Audrey asked.

"If she is I dread to think what that says about our sister," Cedric muttered.

"You think that would mean she's a wicked, wanton woman, like Evangeline Mirabeau?" Audrey giggled at Cedric's horrified expression.

"Something like that. Certainly others would think that of her."

"Oh nonsense, Cedric. No one would think that of Horatia. She's far too sensible to do anything rash or romantic. She's Horatia," Audrey said as if that explained it all, as though there was no reason to worry.

"If Lucien is determined to have her, he won't let her be sensible. That's the entire point behind seduction. Men use passion to rob gentle bred ladies of their good sense. Just like Charles could have when he pretended to compromise you. He could have taken advantage of you, kitten."

"Firstly, brother dearest, *I* kissed *him*." The words caught Cedric unprepared. "And I had to do a great deal of chasing to achieve even that. Secondly, he knew you'd be angry. I had to beg him to help me no matter the cost. And thirdly, I was not nearly so swayed from rationality by kissing him as I was by kissing Jonathan."

Cedric froze in his pacing. "Jonathan? You mean to tell me that you've kissed him already? Is there anyone in Mayfair you haven't kissed?" he growled. His sisters were running amok like Whitechapel harlots. How long had they been doing this to him? Didn't they know it was his job to protect them, even if it meant protecting them from themselves?

Cedric collapsed back into his chair. "God in heaven. I think I may die from the shock of your exploits long before I reach old age."

Audrey watched him, warily. "Are you very angry with me?" Her voice wavered and Cedric winced.

"I'm not angry. But I am upset to learn you've become so determined on the matter. I want the truth now. Are you certain it is Jonathan you want to marry?"

Audrey gave a quick excited nod.

"Do you even know him? Audrey, you've only met him this September. I won't have you marrying a man for shallow reasons."

"How can I ever know a man when you threaten them all with pistols at dawn?"

Cedric huffed. "You exaggerate."

"Do I?" She raised one delicate brow.

He squirmed a little at her accusation. "Yes, it was only one time. The others fled before I could get that far in my shouting."

"And you feel this is helping your argument?"

"I like Jonathan, kitten, I do. The man cuts a fine figure, but that's no reason for marriage. You ought to marry for love." Cedric couldn't believe what he was saying. Somewhere along the way he'd managed to become his father. The words sounded like his.

The late Viscount Sheridan had been a noble man and he'd conducted himself with the highest levels of propriety and decorum. But buried beneath that he'd had a heart of gold that made him wise. It seemed some of his father's wisdom had developed in him, even if it was a little late.

"You're right, of course. But I know the way I feel around him, Cedric. I feel as though my life before him was merely an intake of breath before the true living begins."

"Oh God, you've been reading those dreadful gothic novels again."

"I have not!"

But the look in her eyes was so puzzling to him. It was as though she saw something he could not, a place that filled her with wonder and dreams. "I want to know him," she said. "I want to learn everything about him. But I cannot do that if you do not give me the chance. Will you consider him if I can convince him to court me?"

"If he needs convincing to pursue you, then he does not deserve you. But I will speak to him, and mention your interest. If he agrees, we shall arrange for you to see more of each other. Perhaps you might land a husband after all." He wouldn't have trusted any of his other friends with his sister. But Jonathan was new to their circle and didn't seem to be remotely as cavalier with his affections as his brother Godric had been at his age. There was something serious in the young man that Cedric found calming, far from the wilder valet he'd once been. It was as though Jonathan's new position in life had matured him rather than giving him airs.

"Oh thank you, Cedric!" Audrey slipped out from her covers and ran to him, wrapping her arms about his neck and hugging him.

"I will warn you that not all people in this world have the sweet and loving heart you do. If you believe you can withstand the gossip, then you may proceed."

She grinned impishly. "I think I can handle society and its gossip."

As always, he was completely at a loss as to how to say no to her. The troublesome little sprite was his world, just as Horatia was.

"You're welcome, my dear. Just promise me no more rash behavior. I need to handle this matter with Horatia and I can only survive one sisterly catastrophe at a time."

Audrey stifled a giggle as she released him. "I promise to behave."

"Why don't I believe you?" Cedric said with a theatrical sigh. "Why don't you get dressed and I shall return to take you down to breakfast." Cedric took his leave to give Audrey ample time to change while he went to his own chamber to freshen up. After that he had to find Horatia and see just how deeply her affections ran for Lucien, and whether the trouble was as bad as he feared.

Cedric had only just finished washing his face when he heard footsteps in the hall outside his bedchamber. He pulled on his boots hastily and went to open his door. Horatia was heading towards her room. She looked tired and rumpled and she wore the same gown as she had on last night. Worry ate away at him as he strode down the hall, catching her as she opened her bedroom door.

"May I come in, Horatia?" he asked softly. She nodded and let him follow her inside. "You did not sleep here?"

"No. After hearing about Muff, I rather lost my mind. It brought too many memories. I went out into the gardens and lost myself. I fell twice I think, and if Lucien hadn't found me I might have frozen to death. He rescued me, took me to the gardener's cottage and warmed me up by the fire then watched over me while I slept."

"My God," Cedric managed to say, torn between what she'd been through and the fact that Lucien had been with her all night.

"I had hoped I'd feel better or safer today..." She did not have to finish her sentence for him to know she did not.

Her tone was laced with pain of the heart. Cedric had spent last night holding one crying sister and he did not want to repeat the experience. But he was a brother first and a selfish rogue second.

"Come here." He opened his arms and Horatia buried her face

in his chest. She did not weep, the tears seemed to have drained from her long before. He rubbed one hand gently over her upper back in a soothing motion while stroking her hair.

"You don't always have to be so strong. Grief only rewards those who accept it, not those who fight it." Lucien had taught him this long ago, when Cedric had been convinced his life would end.

"You're right. But then who will be strong for you?" She gave a hiccupy laugh and pulled back to look up at him. "You are such a good brother, Cedric." She gently extricated herself from his embrace and he let her go.

Horatia approached her vanity and laughed at her mussed, wild, appearance. "Heavens, I look dreadful."

"Horatia, I'm afraid we must talk about something."

"Oh dear. I never like it when you use that tone. It makes me nervous." She tried to tease but her heart was not in it.

"You said Lucien found you and he stayed with you and watched over you last night."

"Yes," she answered cautiously.

"With another man, I might demand marriage if I felt he might have taken advantage of you."

"But not Lucien?" she asked, reading his tone correctly.

"No. That's why I am here. I know you still harbor some strong feelings for him and it has made me wonder whether Lucien has used them against you."

"Cedric, what exactly are you asking me?" Horatia demanded in frustrated exhaustion.

"Has he used you ill? You must tell me at once. I cannot allow him to do so."

"No. He has not." Horatia was slow to answer, but Cedric could not tell if she was deceiving him or not.

"I would not be angry with you if he had. Your feelings for him put you at a disadvantage. They make you vulnerable and he is cruel enough to—"

"Lucien is not cruel," Horatia protested. "He is your friend!"

"And I know him far better than you. Must I remind you of his treatment of you for the last seven years? He's done nothing but spurn you at every turn. Why you feel anything for him is beyond me."

"Cedric, if he changed—if he returned my feelings, if he cared about me, would you allow us to marry?" Horatia was never tentative, never hesitant about anything, yet now her very being seemed fragile and delicate.

"It would not matter what his feelings or affections were. I could never allow it," Cedric said bluntly.

"But why? Would it not be more to your liking to have a close friend as a brother-in-law?" Again she spoke with that damned hesitancy.

"Pick any man in all of England, but not *him*. I won't allow any sister of mine to be subjected to his desires. You know nothing about his amorous past, the countless mistresses, the nights at brothels. Not as I do. Even if I could overlook all of that, I could not forget how he treated you all these years, nor stop fearing that he might do it again later on. I am the head of our family. If I say you cannot marry Lucien, then you will accept my judgment and move on. Find a man more worthy of you."

"Why are you so quick to condemn him? Lucien has only ever supported you." Her words stung and Cedric wished he could silence her. "Need I remind you he was the one who brought me home that day when Mama and Papa died? He was the one who saved me, Cedric, and consoled you! To me that means something and if you are blind enough not to see his worth then please leave my room at once. We have nothing further to say to one another." Horatia marched over to her bedroom door and waited for him to leave.

He stopped halfway in the hall, studying her. Did she think that she could go against his commands? Surely she wouldn't be so brazen. He had to make it clear, she couldn't be with Lucien. That was final.

"You don't know him like I do, Horatia. He does things to his women that…well, I don't want to happen to you."

Her sudden blush had his anger rise like a tidal wave.

"What does it matter to you? What if I like the way I feel when I'm with him?"

Cedric pointed a finger at her. "You know nothing of his true self. As a friend, I can tolerate his behavior, even understand it, and I know there are those who would be more agreeable to his tastes. But you as a wife would not know happiness with him."

Horatia's eyes darkened with anger. "Not know happiness? Cedric, I *love* him. With every breath in my body, I belong to him and he to me. You cannot change that. It is done."

Did that mean what he thought? Had Horatia and Lucien…?

"My God," he breathed, stepping back. "You've been with him, haven't you?"

She didn't blink. Didn't say a word. She just gave one small but firm nod and his heart sank. If only she knew what Lucien was like, how he enjoyed tying up his women to the bed and dominating them and more. Horatia wasn't the sort of woman to want that in her life. But she was besotted. How could he break the spell?

"I meant what I said, Horatia. You will not marry him and if you think to let him drag you off to Gretna Green you will no longer be welcome in my house or my estates. You will be a stranger to me. Is that understood?"

It was a bluff, he could never disown her…but he couldn't have her thinking he would allow her to marry such a man.

"You have such a cold heart. No, I take that back. You have no heart at all," Horatia whispered sadly, her dark brown eyes misting with tears as she shut the door.

"Pardon me, my lord, do you require anything?" a footman asked as he walked out of a chamber close by, carrying fresh linens.

"Actually, yes." He paused studying the footman. "Have you seen Miss Sheridan going off alone with Lord Rochester at any point since we arrived?"

The footman hesitated, licked his lips nervously. "I'm sorry, sir, but it wouldn't be appropriate to speak of such matters. I hope you understand."

"I do. Thank you." The footman had as much as told him that Horatia and Lucien were meeting in secret.

There was nothing he could say to make his sister understand why she couldn't be with Lucien. She was ensnared in his trap, and few options remained to him. Everything Cedric had done was to protect her, even if it was from his own friends. It was only then, when he saw a passing footman carrying holly boughs, that he remembered today was Christmas Eve.

CHAPTER 27

The dining room was uncomfortably quiet that morning. Horatia ate only because she did not know what else to do. And even this she prolonged by prodding her food from one side of her plate to the other. Lady Rochester tried to engage her in conversation but Horatia's heart was too bruised to answer Lady Rochester's polite inquiries with much enthusiasm.

Horatia's gaze was torn between her brother at the far end of the table and Lucien who sat two seats away. It should have been a wonderful, joyous morning. She was a woman now, had crossed that threshold from innocent maiden to sensual goddess in Lucien's arms last night, yet she felt robbed of her happiness. Cedric's decree that she must choose left an unsettling pit in her stomach.

She raised her eyes from her plate to find Lucien watching her every move. All of the pain of her brother's words seem to fade. She made her decision. She would give Lucien time, let him decide how he felt. If in the end he wanted her then she would be with him. She loved Cedric and Audrey but someday Audrey would marry. Perhaps even Cedric would marry. If she chose them, she'd end up alone. And denying Lucien was like denying her body from breathing.

Lady Rochester at last broke that uncomfortable silence. "As you all know, tonight is Christmas Eve. In order to lighten our spirits, I believe we ought to exchange gifts this evening after dinner. Is that agreeable?" There were murmurs of assent and refreshed smiles. Horatia caught Lucien's eye and he offered her a secretive smile that warmed her blood. Footmen came to collect the plates and everyone rose to go about their day.

Horatia lingered in the hallway watching the flurry of activity with amusement until a footman approached her.

"Pardon me, Miss Sheridan. His lordship bade me to deliver this note to you and to show you a secret way to reach him when you are ready." He slid a slip of paper into her hand discreetly.

"Thank you, Gordon." She took shelter in a nearby alcove to read the note in peace.

Come to our cottage, my little stargazer.

Horatia's body began to hum with the promise of that single line.

Gordon cleared his throat. "If need be, I've been instructed to show you a passageway that would get you outside without the rest of the house being aware of it."

"Yes, I would appreciate that." She retrieved her cloak and made her way to the passageway that led to the gardens. She glanced over her shoulder to make sure she was not being followed, then quickly made her way to the distant gardener's cottage. The chimney of the cottage already puffed with fresh smoke, an inviting place of refuge. She found the door unlocked and the sight inside made her pulse race. Crimson petals littered the entry way and down the hall to the bedroom. The scent of orchids and other flowers filled her senses.

"Lucien?" she called out nervously.

"In the bedroom, love. Come to me." His sensual voice spurred her onward. She found him waiting in a chair by the fire as she entered the room. The flowers she'd smelled coming inside covered every surface. Horatia felt guilty even stepping on the petals that surrounded her lover and the bed like a crimson moat.

"How did you manage all of this?" she asked in admiration. "How did you find the time?"

"After I escorted you back to the hall, I roped a few footmen into helping me raid my mother's hothouse for the best flowers and had them brought here. You deserve for it to be warm and sunny and full of flowers, but I'm afraid this is the best I can manage in the middle of an English winter." Lucien stood, but she sensed the nervousness in him, as though he feared she would not appreciate his efforts.

"Oh Lucien, it is so beautiful!" She gave a bright and honest smile as she dropped her cloak on the floor, causing petals to ripple outward. She tiptoed her way across to him, gently put a hand on his chest and shoved him back down into his chair. His breath quickened when she slid onto his lap and wrapped her arms about his neck. Lucien waited as she leaned into him, rewarding him with a kiss. He growled in soft pleasure as her lips met his, but he ended the kiss too quickly.

"I have a present for you." He gestured towards the bed. It was only then that Horatia spied the large box sitting in the center of it.

"But we are to open our presents tonight," she reminded him in what she hoped was an admonishing tone. He merely dropped his head and nibbled her throat until she was ready to agree to anything he might ask.

"This gift is one I cannot give to you in front of others. Go ahead, my love. Open it now."

He gently set her on her feet and propelled her towards the bed. Horatia lifted the top off the cream box and peeled back the thin paper to reveal the most beautiful gown she'd ever seen. It was then that she remembered what he'd told her before—that he'd bought her a gown to replace the one that had been ruined.

The idea of the gown, which she'd once believed Lucien had bought to strike back at Waverly's attack, had a vastly different meaning now. She pulled out the gown and held it up to see it in its full glory. A melody of red and green silk with Belgian lace and delicate embroidery unfolded before her. A sprig of faux mistletoe decorated the décolletage in an almost scandalous manner. Lucien certainly had a hand in creating this, that was certain.

"Well?" Lucien asked, standing behind her. Heat emanated off him in intoxicating waves. Horatia briefly shut her eyes, savoring this private moment of paradise.

"It is too expensive. You ought not to have spent so much on me." Despite her chastising she clutched the gown to her chest and turned to face him, making it clear she would not willingly give back the gift.

Lucien's lips slid into a crooked smile. "If you believe it too valuable…I can always allow you to repay me in favors."

"Hmm…and what would these favors be, exactly?" Horatia wanted to sound like a cool and confident woman bargaining her charms, but she was unable to hide her desire.

"For one gown, I will charge you this morning and afternoon between the sheets. I demand tangled limbs, moans of pleasure and wild abandon." He plucked the dress from her hands, folded it and nestled it back into the box with a tenderness that had Horatia's body weak-kneed with pleasure, then set it on the floor out of the way.

"You wish to be paid now?" Horatia half-giggled until she saw the predatory look on his face. The savage lust in his eyes knocked the air from her lungs.

"Surrender to me now, Horatia. Let me have you a thousand ways, a thousand times." It was as close to pleading as Lucien had ever come and it aroused her in a way she had not expected.

She craved the power to make him plead, not from pain, but from desire and the need to control this passion, allowing it to slip only when she chose to. It was how he'd made her feel that night at the Midnight Garden and she wanted to experience it herself, before giving in to him again. When he looked at her like that it was like she was the last woman he would ever kiss, the only woman who would ever light the fire in his eyes and perhaps one day his heart...

"If you want me, it is you who will surrender to me, I think. I will have control." Suddenly she was holding out a hand and demanding the red silk she knew he kept on him. In a wordless look of surprise he turned the ribbons over to her. She pointed to his shirt and vest.

"Remove them," she commanded.

Lucien did so, but Horatia raised a hand. "Not too quickly now." Lucien's expression was dark and unreadable as she slowed down his movements. "Your boots next." Again he obeyed without a word, careful to take his time. Once he was clad only in his trousers, which hugged his muscled thighs like lovers, Horatia pointed to the bed.

"Lie on your back. Spread your arms."

He did as she commanded, and Horatia bit her lip as she watched the muscles of his back ripple like the sleek coat of a panther. He laid back and waited for her to come to him. With surprisingly steady hands she took one of his wrists and secured it to one bedpost. She brushed a few fingertips along his bicep, and his muscles twitched beneath her as she moved around to secure his other wrist. She left his legs free so he might have some mobility but no chance of flipping them over to be on top. He tested the bonds experimentally, his eyes still inscrutable.

When Horatia was satisfied that he could not get free, she positioned herself at the end of the bed and began to undress herself. Thankfully the gown she wore buttoned down the front. Lucien's tongue slipped out to wet his lips and Horatia imagined that tongue licking her but only if she allowed herself to be within reach. She had never felt so powerful, so aware of her hold over a man before.

With Lucien this felt right; she could do no wrong with him and he would never judge her again for sins not of her making. It was a freeing thought, to know that he was here with her and they were unburdened by the darkness of their past.

Once the gown was unbuttoned, she peeled it off her shoulders and slid it down off her hips in a teasingly slow move that had Lucien testing the strength of his bonds and bucking against the mattress. She dropped the gown to the floor and started to remove her stays and petticoats. Lucien's face flushed as she stood there, wearing nothing more than her chemise. Her breasts felt heavy and the nipples budded against the sheer fabric. Horatia caressed herself, enjoying the feel of her own hands along her body as much as the way it tortured Lucien.

She'd learned much about lovemaking in the few hours he'd had to teach her. They'd talked late into the night about the things a man and woman could do together. Horatia was intent on exploring some of those things now.

"Let me touch you, love," he begged. "Let me cup those perfect breasts."

"Silence, my lord."

She walked to the edge of the bed and climbed up between his spread legs. Horatia crawled over his body until she reached his mouth and she kissed him, thrusting her tongue deep, but withdrawing before he could catch it with his lips. Then she moved to his left ear, sucking on his lobe. Lucien groaned and writhed beneath her. She could feel the tension in his body, the need to capture her with his arms, but he was unable to do so. Lucien, the Marquess of Rochester, was at her mercy and it was good, so good.

"Be still, my lord, or you will be punished." She bit his neck playfully.

"Oh God!" he hissed. His erection strained between their bodies, even contained as it was by his trousers. Horatia eased a palm over the bulge, a slow exploring stroke that sent Lucien into a string of muttered curses. Horatia grinned and pressed another heated kiss to his lips. Then, inspired, she tweaked one of his nipples. He jolted up off the bed in response.

"Christ, woman! I'll be done if you do that again!"

"No, you won't. If you come before I say, then I'll stop and leave you here until you are ready to obey me." Horatia repeated the action on his other nipple, but this time with her teeth. He endured silently, tensing beneath her. She was satisfied that he kept his control, but her real satisfaction lay in torturing him. This was for every dark mocking smile he'd sent her way, for every punishing kiss, every rough caress meant to frighten her away from him. She wasn't afraid anymore. She would be his master.

Kissing her way down his chest, licking the taut planes of his grooved abdomen, she reached his trousers and began to unfasten them. When she freed him, his length sprang to full attention before her. She took the rigid organ in her hands, and with a chuckle she licked the hard length of him and circled her tongue around his tip. Lucien threw his head back, eyes shut, gasping as he sought to fight his body's response. The bed creaked as he tugged at his restraints.

"You may accept your pleasure now, my lord. I will allow it," she said before she took him fully in her mouth. She'd never done such a thing before, but she'd heard the upstairs maids talking about it and she decided it was worth taking a chance. He certainly seemed to enjoy it. He murmured encouragement and was barely able to breathe as he raised his hips towards her mouth.

"Yes, there, God yes! Don't stop. Please my love, don't stop..." Lucien's head thrashed back against the pillow as she sucked and licked him.

Shaking violently, he came in her mouth with a desperate shout. Surprise rippled through her as she tasted him. He was hers and she took a deeply carnal pleasure from that. Lucien's breath was fast as he slowly regained his composure, but Horatia was nowhere near done with him. She moved back up his body and claimed his mouth while her hands moved to his wrists and held them down tight.

"Who do you belong to, Lucien?" she asked between hot, drugging kisses.

"You my love. Only you." He answered without hesitation, his body relaxed beneath hers. His hazel eyes were still unfathomably dark but they held an unyielding truth behind them.

"Never forget that in this moment you were mine." She brushed her lips along his before she untied the silk and freed him. He lay beneath her for a time, unmoving as he recovered from his release.

"I've never trusted a woman to do what you've just done to me before," he said at last.

"Really?" Horatia, body still sprawled across his, looked down at him in surprise.

"I've never been able to relinquish control before. I never thought it possible. You're the first." There was an importance to this, but the full depth of it was beyond her at the moment. Her mind was too foggy with the passion they'd shared.

"And now, it is my turn." With a seductive smile, he rolled her beneath him, pulled her chemise over her head and tossed it away. Lucien captured her hands and tied her wrists together above her head, securing them to one bedpost. This position forced her breasts to rise up and her back to arch beneath him. He drew his fingertip along the seam of her lips and then down her throat to her breasts. That same fingertip teased circles around her nipple before he dropped his mouth to its peak. He bit the bud and Horatia gasped in both pain and pleasure.

"See how hard it is to control yourself when someone does that? I ought to punish you, my love, for being so bloody innocent that you nearly killed me with want." His warm breath fanned her skin before he dropped his head to her other breast, suckling and biting until Horatia was trembling.

Lucien parted her thighs and inserted a finger to find the wetness that awaited him there. He praised her readiness for him with soft words and caressed her inner folds tenderly before dipping deeper into her. After he tortured her for what seemed like an age, he spread her legs wider and moved back to set himself at her entrance. He did not even remove his trousers; the rough cloth slid against the silky skin of her inner thighs and she gasped helplessly at the sensation. When he thrust himself deep into her, Horatia cried out at the soreness mixed with the pleasure of him, the hard invasion that drove her mad with ecstasy.

Lucien moved to sit back on his heels, still deep inside her as he gazed at the point where their bodies united. He withdrew and thrust so hard that she arched off the bed, offering herself up. Lucien reached forward and clasped her throat with his hand, then slid that hand down between her breasts and over her smooth and slightly rounded belly to the apex of her thighs. That same wandering hand now circled the bundle of nerves he'd only teased before. He pinched and Horatia screamed at the responding climax that shook her to her very core. She felt like a shattered mirror, pieces of herself scattered in a thousand tiny reflections.

"Oh my God," she moaned as he pinched her again and she felt herself unraveling from the inside out.

"I prefer to be called Lucien."

Horatia was too lost in the thrill of being connected to him to share in his joke as he continued to pump deep into her. It was a savage claiming of her as his woman and she reveled in the ferocity as he held her captive to the hammer of his hips against hers.

He was close to coming, she could see it in his eyes. But suddenly Lucien pulled out and was turning her over onto her stomach. He reached over her and took two extra pillows and lifted her hips up to slide the pillows underneath them. Her bottom was up in the air and she felt terribly exposed.

"So beautiful, my lovely, sinful Horatia." His voice was low as he caressed her from the back of her neck down along her spine before reaching her bottom. He swatted her rump and she jerked in response. A tingle of fire shot up her body and a painful throbbing welled up between her thighs all over again.

"That is for torturing me. Consider yourself punished, love." He kissed each cheek, the sting of his blow turning into delicious warmth. Horatia was shocked how arousing this was. She could not see him, not unless she craned her head over her neck. She had to trust him completely from here.

"Lucien...please..." She shifted her bottom, desperate to entice him to enter her again. He moved over her, his chest sliding along her back as he kissed her neck. Then she felt one of his hands parting her folds, allowing him to push his way inside.

"Yes, yes, there!" The animal in her took over as she rejoiced when he thrust home. She met him with a push of her own hips. He was in to the hilt, his hands now braced on either side of her shoulders as each thrust struck some point deep in her that robbed her of all thought. She cried out as he ravished her, their skin slick with sweat and the aroma of their lovemaking clouding their senses.

That moment nearly robbed Horatia of her soul. When she came it was hard, earth shattering and primitive. She forgot who she was, who he was. There was only this moment, this explosion of the greatest pleasure she'd ever known. Vaguely she was aware of Lucien driving into her at a pace and harshness that would have shamed a stallion and even this thought sent her careening into another wild orgasm.

Lucien shouted incoherently and collapsed on top of her, their bodies still fused together. After a moment, he moved off her and she turned to face him. Limbs tangled and souls locked, they shared breaths and smiles. Words were unnecessary. The look of desire was etched so deeply into Lucien's face that Horatia felt her eyes burn with tears.

"I've been a fool to wait as long as I have." He gently untied her wrists and rolled her onto her back beneath him. She savored his warmth, enjoying the rapid beat of his heart against her cheek. "Please say you'll always belong to me." He kissed her mouth, her cheeks, her nose, her forehead.

"I always have." Her hands glided over his shoulders and down his arms in soothing strokes.

"I want to be able to do this to you every night and every morning. I want to share my life, my name and my soul with you, Horatia."

"I've only ever wanted your heart," she replied. Lucien smiled tenderly and feathered kisses along her jaw. But now she was shy and unsure. "All these years, when you've been with other women? Could you ever be satisfied with just me? How can I be enough?" She was terrified of how he might answer.

"I can't rid myself of my past, love, but know this—you've never been far from my heart or mind. Even when I was determined to be cold to you, you made it hard to do. It is impossible to be without you now. When I'm with you I cannot be sated, when you leave me I want you back at my side. I miss the scent of your skin, the silky texture of your hair against my lips, the blinding smile you hide from the world so often with your shyness. I crave your stories of the stars and your loyalty to those you love. I'm not sure the poets agree what love is, but I think I may have, somehow along the way, fallen in love with you. And I fear I've fallen hard. Can I trust you with my heart, Horatia?" Lucien's voice was shaky and had nothing to do with their recent explosion of passion.

"Oh Lucien..." She kissed him deeply. "Consider your heart safe in my hands." He slanted his mouth over hers, tongue delving between her lips. When Horatia was finally able to breathe again she remembered that not all was well.

"Cedric knows that we are involved. He gave me an ultimatum. It was to choose between you or my family. I cannot have both. He will never welcome me home again if I choose you." She tried to explain as calmly as possible but her throat constricted with sadness. What sense did it make for her brother to deny her this? She knew life was not fair, far better than most, but shouldn't her brother try and even the unfairness out with goodness in her life? Or at the least he should not deny her the right to make herself happy.

Lucien frowned. "I will speak to him. It isn't fair for you to choose. Neither of us should have to choose between our love for each other and him." Lucien pulled back the covers for them to slide underneath so that they could be warmer. Once she was tucked against his side, warm and drowsy in his embrace, he buried his lips in her hair, breathing in her scent.

"If we have to choose," said Horatia, "I choose you, Lucien. I will always choose you." She nuzzled his neck before sleep claimed her. She did not hear Lucien's quiet reply.

"And I you, my little stargazer. But I will do everything within my power to see you won't have to."

CHAPTER 28

Half an hour before Christmas Eve dinner, Lucien paced nervously inside the vast Russell library, waiting for Cedric to arrive. Gone were the last remnants of his misplaced coldness towards Horatia. All that was left was a deep seed of love. He'd spent years salting his soul trying to prevent that seed from taking root. But Horatia had become his sun, his water, and fed that deep seed. Petals were unfurling, roots coiling deep in his heart. He was going to have a long talk with his friend and Cedric would see the light and let Horatia be with him and that was that. There was no going back; he'd crossed the final bridge and burned it to ashes.

The library door opened and Cedric entered, looking as cold as the empty suit of armor that guarded it.

"I received your summons." His friend seemed to choose his words carefully.

Lucien tried to smile, but his nerves were on edge. "I did not mean to 'summon' you. I wished to discuss something of importance." His stomach felt as though someone had unleashed a bevy of butterflies. It was almost laughable to be so frightened, like a child standing up to their teacher.

Cedric shut the library door and approached Lucien with measured steps, hands clasped behind his back. "Here I am. What do you wish to talk about?"

Cedric's body language did not bode well, not at all.

"Over the past couple of months I've undergone a change of heart. A deep one. A very deep one." It was not the most flattering or elegant phrasing, but he had to begin this dreaded conversation somehow.

"I hadn't noticed." Cedric's voice held a fair amount of suspicion.

"It was not something I wanted anyone to see, Cedric. Look, what I am trying to tell you..." The words were there, but Cedric's hard eyes stilled them on Lucien's tongue, daring him to ask for something he had no right to ask for. Lucien drew a shaky breath before continuing.

"I seek your permission to marry Horatia." How unlike him, but he had to maintain his control for this brief moment and formality was the simplest way to go.

"So it's true then? You have your eyes set on my sister?"

Lucien knew Cedric in the way only true friends could and recognized that familiar edge of danger in Cedric's tone.

"I love her, Cedric..."

"Stop! You *do not* love her. You may love her body and the pleasure it gives but she will not be one more lady in the line of women you leave behind brokenhearted. Not my Horatia." Cedric's fists clenched at his side. Even twenty feet apart Lucien did not feel safe.

"Easy, Cedric. I am not that man anymore. Let me explain—"

"I will not listen to your lies, Lucien." Cedric stormed over and shoved a finger deep into Lucien's chest. "Save it for the next chit you fancy! You are breaking the rules our League was built on. I demand that you stay away from Horatia. That you won't even *look* at her."

"No." Lucien was weary of controlling himself. Cedric would listen to him, even if he had to bind him to a chair.

Cedric's eyes narrowed. "What?"

"I said no. We agreed to the second rule because we did not trust each other with the fairer sex, and rightfully so. But time changes us all. I love Horatia and I wish to wed her. I want a passel of children and her love in my life for the rest of my days. I have asked her to marry me and she has agreed. I came to you for the sake of our friendship and because you are her family. I do not *need* your permission to have her, because I already do." It was the worst possible to thing to say and Lucien realized it too late.

Cedric's fist drove into Lucien's stomach, staggering him back. Cedric followed and landed another solid blow to Lucien's chest, so hard that he fell back and struck a bookshelf.

"How *dare* you lay claim to her! She is not yours to take!" Cedric swung another fist and Lucien was struck yet again as he was cornered against the shelf.

"And she is not yours to lock away! Horatia always has and always will be her own person. She gifted me with her heart and though I do not even begin to deserve her, she wants me and no one else. So I will have her as my wife and do my best to be worthy. You may not support her decision, but by God you will not punish her for loving me." Lucien's body shook with rage as Cedric pulled him back and threw another fist into him. Cedric stumbled into one of the library's suits of armor, knocking it over with a clang and clatter.

"You've already had her, you blackguard?"

Lucien said nothing.

"She's warmed your bed. She could be with your child even now!" The accusation stung Lucien more from the truth than anything else. Cedric knew him too well.

"Yes," Lucien said. "And if there is a babe growing in her now, the thought fills me with a love I cannot begin to understand."

"You say that now. You may even believe it. But it does not matter. I know how you are, how cold you've been not just to her, but to other women. I don't care if my sister is your only chance at salvation, you will not have her. Not while I still draw breath."

The threat hit Lucien like a bolt of lightning. His senses frazzled as once more Cedric assaulted him with pummeling fists, again beating him back against the bookshelf. Lucien did not fight back. It would do no good.

"What do you mean by that?" Lucien asked.

Cedric puffed up his chest, as though addressing a condemned man. "I demand satisfaction, as is my right. Tomorrow at dawn. Choose a second and your preferred weapon."

"I will not duel with you, Cedric." Lucien could not believe it could come to this. The League often joked about Cedric being capable of such things, but none believed it.

"You will, or I will summon the rest of the League here and we will determine how to put you straight for breaking the second rule."

Lucien knew Cedric would be relentless on the matter, even if the others objected. The thought made his blood run cold. "Very well. I will be in the northern field at dawn with my second. I will bring my weapon of choice."

"Good." Cedric's eyes were filled with both anger and regret, but he said nothing more and turned to leave.

Lucien wanted to unsay the words that had brought them to this point, but Cedric was gone, and Lucien was alone in the library. Pain surged through him, reminders of all of the blows his friend had laid on him.

He stood next to the bookshelf for what felt like an eternity, catching his breath until he realized he was not alone. His sister, Lysandra, came out from behind the shelf he leaned against.

"How long have you been there?" He tried to sound harsh, but his words came out toneless.

Lysandra brushed a fingertip across her eyes, wiping tears from their corners. "Oh Lucien!"

She ran to him and he crumpled weakly in her arms. Falling to his knees on the wood floor, Lysandra was dragged down with him, still cradling him as he gasped for breath. What madness was this?

To love Horatia and in the process lose Cedric? It wasn't fair and he shouldn't have to choose.

"There, there," Lysandra said, stroking his hair in the way he'd done countless times for her. After a few minutes, he was able to control himself once more.

"You mustn't tell a soul, Lysa. No one must know what has happened here. Do you understand?"

"I do. Mother will never forgive you for fighting a duel on Christmas."

"I may not be around to suffer her ill humor." Lucien had no fear of death, even at his friend's hand, but the thought of all those years wasted without Horatia clenched his heart like nothing else.

"Dueling is illegal. You don't have to go through with it."

"It's a matter of honor. Of love."

"What good are those words on a tombstone?"

"Cedric won't let up just because I say no. He'll brand me a coward on top of everything else. Horatia cannot marry a coward. And though marrying a coward is not illegal, it should be."

"You're being ridiculous, and you cannot deflect a bullet with your wit."

Lucien gave pause at Lysandra's words. "Yes... Duels are ridiculous, aren't they? No matter. We do what we must, even when it is ridiculous." He looked over the mess the one sided battle had left in its wake. An idea began to form, and most certainly a ridiculous one.

"So you are going to shoot him?" Lysandra asked.

"I love him like a brother. So far I've never shot any of my real brothers, and I won't start with Cedric. He may be too foolish to understand the truth, but come what may, I will not fire my pistol at him."

❦

HORATIA WAS THE MOST BEAUTIFUL WOMAN IN THE ROOM THAT night after dinner. Lucien noticed this with a deep pang in his heart, regret and longing for a future he might never have now, left him quiet. All had enjoyed a wonderful feast marred only by Cedric and Lucien's silence towards one another. Now, family and friends were in the Russell ballroom dancing to a hired string quartet that performed Christmas music. The entire evening took on a greater importance to Lucien than ever before.

He danced with all of the ladies once, but kept returning to Horatia, as though keeping her in his arms would ensure that the night wouldn't end and dawn wouldn't have a chance to come. Cedric, for his part, kept his distance, allowing him this night like a final wish before the gallows.

Lucien's hand rested on the small of her back. He could feel the warmth of her body beneath his palm. Her gloved hand rested on his broad shoulder, fingers lightly curling in a tender possessiveness. Horatia wore his gown and it fit her perfectly, the embroidered silks clung to her in a way he wished he could. She held only radiant smiles tonight, and all sadness was banished by the merriment of the Christmas season. She had never looked lovelier in his eyes and he told her so.

"I am happy, Lucien. You made me so." She tightened her grip on his shoulder and his hand during their endless waltz.

"Would that I could always make you so happy, my love," he murmured too softly for her to hear over the music.

When at last the music faded Lady Rochester clapped her hands together.

"All right everyone, enough dancing. It is time for presents!" The announcement was followed by hearty cheers from the younger people in the ballroom. The group proceeded to the large parlor just off the ballroom where a roaring fire greeted them and refreshments of small Christmas puddings and freshly made wassail was ready to be drunk. Lucien's mind was not on Christmas puddings however. He did his best to ignore the concerned looks his sister kept shooting from across the room.

Just let me enjoy these last few hours...please, he beseeched fate helplessly.

Lucien felt almost reckless now, wanting to hold Horatia in his arms without a care as to who saw them. God, how he wanted her, how he loved her. Horatia seemed emboldened by the evening as they moved to a small settee. Under the waves of red silk from her gown his hand found hers and he gripped it like a man dying of thirst would a goblet of water.

From across the room Cedric's eyes were sharp, but he made no move against them. Lucien's body ached with the reminder of Cedric's righteous fury. Each breath, each twist of his body was a reminder of the animosity that had stolen Cedric's friendship from him like a cruel thief. It was agony, this choice which was no choice at all.

"Here, Lucien. This is for you," Horatia said in a breathless voice.

She looked as though she feared it would not be to his liking. Lucien smiled at her, thankful for the distraction as he took the package and opened it. In his lap he found a book titled *Astronomy and Mythology*. It was a history of the tales behind the constellations.

Grinning like the lovestruck fool he was, he opened the inside cover to find an inscription—*Happy Christmas, Lucien, may we forever share the stars*. He had never been one for poetry, but that single line had his heart both soaring and breaking. After the coming dawn there would be no more stars, no more tales, no more love...not without the cost of losing his best friend. The chances of dying in the duel were not as great as some made it out to be. That was the effect of pride on those who took part. But the truth was regardless of the outcome it would be devastating because it would tear the families apart. Horatia would lose him or her brother. No one would emerge from this unscathed.

"There's more." Horatia prodded with a cheeky smile as she pointed to the center of the book. He tugged a long slender strip of crimson silk out from the center pages. Too long for a bookmark, it was embroidered with silver stars and crescent moons.

"I thought you might find other uses for that." Horatia nibbled her lower lip with a gleam in her eyes. Damn the woman, she was perfect. Too bloody perfect.

The attention of the others in the room was diverted by Lucinda and Lysandra admiring Audrey's new fawn gloves.

"I love you," he mouthed silently

"I love you too," Horatia mouthed back.

"And this is your gift," Lucien said quietly, sliding her a small package behind the shelter of her skirts.

"But you already gave me mine," she said.

"When it comes to you, my love, I cannot seem to control myself." Lucien smiled as she began to unwrap the small gift, uncovering a velvet pouch. With a curious look she loosened the drawstrings and tipped it over. A slender bracelet of sapphires encircled by diamonds fell into her lap. Horatia's hands flew to her mouth.

"It was my grandmother's on my mother's side. She gave it to me when I was fifteen. She told me to give it to the woman who held my heart. I remember I laughed, telling her no one would ever have my heart, but the crafty old woman knew me better than I did myself. She told me to keep it and one day I'd know who to give it to.

"That night in the Midnight Garden when you spoke of the stars...I knew that this was meant for you. Even when I raged at you that night I still knew that you had to have this bracelet. You are the keeper of my heart. Take this gift and wear it when you think of me. These jewels are as close as I can get to stealing the stars and adorning you with them." Lucien took her right hand and gently secured the bracelet around her wrist.

Horatia marveled at the stunning glint of the gems in the firelight before Lucien slid her glove over the bracelet and covered it. Horatia gazed back at him wordlessly. She had never looked more beautiful, more wonderful. The angels paled in comparison, and no saints possessed brighter halos of innocence and purity of soul than his darling sweet Horatia.

"Lucien." She tried to say more but he could hear the break in her voice. She was overjoyed, filled with love and it humbled him.

When the last of the presents had been unwrapped, Sir John began to belt out carols in a deep rich baritone. His son, Avery and Lawrence all joined in while Lysandra and Audrey dissolved into giggles whenever the four men bungled the words. Linus stood by the fire fiddling with a woolen, navy blue scarf he'd received from Lucinda Cavendish. She joined him by the fire and with a small smile pushed his hands away and set about adjusting his scarf herself. Linus gazed down at her in open desire and admiration. Only Lucien seemed to notice when Linus set a hand on the young woman's waist and pulled her a few inches closer to him.

Hot cider was brought by a maid and once more conversation settled about the room like the distant hum of bees on a summer day.

"I wish it could always be like this," Horatia sighed dreamily.

Lucien agreed. There was nothing more wonderful than being warm and drowsy in a fire lit parlor surrounded by one's family and friends while snow laced the world outside.

"I do too." Lucien tightened his hold on Horatia's hand and drank in the sight of her and his own family—the twinkle of his sister's eyes, and the mischievous grins of his brothers. Even the reluctant grin of Cedric who was allowing Audrey to fuss over him while he tried on his new red hunting coat.

It was well past midnight when everyone decided to go to bed and the party reluctantly dispersed. Lucien retreated to his room and let his valet, Felix, prepare him for bed. Felix tried to hide a yawn and gave Lucien a weary smile as he went off to the servants' quarters. Lucien donned his nightclothes and was in the process of wrapping his dressing gown about his bruised body when there was a knock on his bedroom door.

He went to open it and found a nightgown clad Horatia peering up at him in the dim light of the hallway.

"May I come in?" She slipped past him before he could answer and went straight for his bed, climbing in between the turned down covers.

"What about Ursula? Won't she worry about you being gone?" He closed the door to his bedroom.

"She knows where I am and that she is to keep her silence on my whereabouts. I think she likes you, even if she does think you're a rogue."

"I am a rogue." He stiffened his spine and mock scowled at her.

"Of course you are," she answered in a tone one used to placate a fussy child and patted the spot on the sheets beside her. "Your bed is icy, my lord, come and warm me up." She spoke like a princess wanting her devoted knight to heed her every wish. And Lucien was that knight.

"Yes, my lady." He bowed with a mocking grin and she threw a pillow at him.

"It will take more than pillows to stop me, love." He blew out the remaining candles before peeling off his robe. He didn't want Horatia to see the bruises her brother had wrought on his body.

"Now, about warming you up." Lucien tugged her into his arms beneath the covers.

What followed was a sort of lovemaking he'd never done before. No restraints, no delving into darker passions. He was tender and slow, and he poured his soul into every kiss and gave her his heart with every caress. Horatia cried out again and again beneath him. Lucien painted her face in his mind, ecstasy ravishing her features in the moonlight. He wanted to capture the beauty that was Horatia's alone.

This...he thought as he finally allowed himself to reach his release close to dawn in her arms, *this is worth dying for*. He briefly shut his eyes, hoping to catch an hour of sleep before Felix came to wake him.

CHAPTER 29

"It is time, my lord," Felix whispered, rousing Lucien from his bittersweet dreams. With great care he disentangled his body from Horatia's. She remained asleep, but she spread one arm out unconsciously seeking his vanished warmth and Lucien felt her loss like a blow. He dared not touch her, dared not get too close or he'd wake her and never be able to leave.

Lucien donned a pair of trousers, then hastily pulled on a shirt and green waistcoat. Without bothering with a cravat, he pulled on his boots and left the room. With a single look back at his bed Lucien silently bid farewell.

"Sleep, my dear, and dream of the stars."

He slipped down the hall until he reached Lawrence's bedroom. He found the door unlocked and saw Lawrence lay sprawled on his stomach, entirely naked from what Lucien could see. He approached his brother's bed and shook his shoulder.

"Wake up, Lawrence."

Lawrence swatted a hand in Lucien's general direction.

"Five more minutes, Tom." Tom was Lawrence's valet. Lawrence tried to roll over and face away from him. Lucien returned the favor by smacking the back of his brother's head.

"Get up, Lawrence. I have need of you."

"Hmph...Lucien?"

"Come on. I need you to come with me to the North field straight away."

"The North field? What on earth for?" Lawrence sat up, rubbing his eyes and blinking.

"I have an appointment with a pistol," Lucien replied. That got Lawrence's attention and he leapt out of bed.

"What?"

"Get dressed and I will explain along the way." Lucien stood impatiently by the door as Lawrence threw on his clothes. Only when they were outside in the hall did Lucien explain about the duel.

"You are seriously going to duel Sheridan? I don't believe it. Not you two."

"Believe it, Lawrence. I blame Mother. If she hadn't worked towards forcing my hand with Horatia I might have been able to introduce the idea of courting Horatia to Cedric slowly without the volatile reaction."

Lawrence winced. "This is my fault. I can explain it to Sheridan. Maybe he'll see reason and not continue with this nonsense."

Lucien kept walking, his brother keeping pace. "Better that I alone face his wrath. I'm hoping he'll have cooled down during the night. If not..."

They walked quietly through the halls and Lucien paused just outside the library doors, handing Lawrence his great coat.

"Wait here, I need one more thing before we go."

When they reached the northern most field, where Cedric waited along with a confused and drowsy Gregory Cavendish. Lawrence and Gregory shared concerned glances as Lucien held out a boxed pair of pistols. Gregory and Lawrence assumed the duty of inspecting the weapons for any faults or tampering. Once the seconds determined the pistols were in fine working order, the men stepped back. Cedric and Lucien each took a pistol and then faced each other. The silence between them was only enhanced by their cloudy puffs of breath in the pale predawn light.

"Last chance to call this off, gentlemen." Gregory waited, but neither side attempted to put a stop to the duel.

Cedric shifted on his feet, his lips parted as though he wanted to speak, but then gave a little shake of his head.

"Twenty paces each," Cedric said.

"Agreed," Lucien replied. His heart screamed inside his chest as he turned and began to measure out his paces. *Please God, let him come to his senses.* He made sure to take slow, measured steps, wincing each time the small clinks and creaks betrayed his best hope for surviving this should sanity not deliver him.

When the two were forty paces apart they raised their pistols in salute, waiting. Lucien slid his index finger out of the metal loop that enclosed the trigger, so that if he was hit he would not involuntarily fire his weapon.

The cold air shot through him like fire, his every sense on high alert. The smell of dead grass and the fell of crisp snow beneath his boots, the biting chill of the air and the endless gray skies melding with vast fields of virgin snow. *How sad that this last vision is so cold and lifeless.*

"You will fire at the call of three," Gregory called out, his tone carrying across the field.

"One..."

Back down, you fool, Lucien thought, and angled his body sideways to give Cedric as little of a target to aim at as possible.

"Two..."

Cedric dropped his pistol down to aim. Lucien dropped his arm farther, aiming his pistol instead towards his feet. Lucien's mind flashed across every moment of last night. He willed himself to summon his last ounce of emotional strength to stand firm for Horatia.

"Three..."

Cedric's hand visibly shook, then he cursed and fired.

Ptang!

The bullet struck Lucien's shoulder and ricocheted, grazing his head. Lucien sighed with relief, even though the pain was agonizing. He hadn't died. The pain lessened slightly. Good, he was going to be fine, what was a flesh wound after all?

"You must return fire," Lawrence called out grudgingly. There were rules to these things.

Lucien fired his pistol into the ground. It was done.

As if the act had somehow released him, his body suddenly felt light and weak. He collapsed to the ground, clanking loudly. Maybe his head wound was more serious than he thought.

"You bloody fool!" Cedric tossed his pistol at Gregory before rushing over to where Lucien lay.

"Help me get this off." Lucien dug his hands into his coat, hoping to remove the metal armor plates underneath.

"Good God, what on earth…" Gregory asked as he caught sight of the armor on Lucien's shoulder, running down the length of his arm.

"That is what you retrieved from the library?" Lawrence examined his head. "Really, Lucien, where do you get these ideas? That's almost as bad as the time you snuck of out of Lady Godfrey's house right past her husband, dressed as a footman."

With a pained chuckle, Lucien nodded. "Perhaps. But that had also saved my life. Cedric's a fine shot and I didn't want to risk it." He glanced down at his shoulder.

Crimson stained the shiny metal where blood dripped from his temple. "Though I may have miscalculated somewhat." He looked to Cedric. "You damned fool. You actually fired!"

"Why didn't you fire back?" Cedric's voice was filled with despair. Was the wound even worse than he thought?

"I did fire back."

"Yes. Into the ground. You should have shot me."

"And what would that accomplish?" Lucien sighed. "I wagered my life that you would back out, or misfire. I'd hoped you would reconsider or calm yourself before it came to this. The armor was a desperate plan in case all that failed. It seemed I was right to do so."

Cedric looked pained. "I didn't mean to fire at all. I meant to stare you down until you yielded. When you lowered your pistol it unnerved me, and my hand...it shook."

Lucien's smile withered and he grew serious. "No matter what you think, I meant what I said. I love Horatia more than anything...but I could never kill my closest friend, nor the brother of my greatest love." Lucien tried to ignore the burning pain in his head. It felt like someone was branding his skull.

"You...you really love her?" Cedric asked. The pain in his eyes wounded Lucien more than the bullet.

"She is everything to me. Always has been. I just couldn't face that before. I tried to push her away." Lucien winced. "I don't deserve her." He shut his eyes as pain overcame him. A cold darkness swept over his limbs, numbing him to any other sensations.

"Help me get him up!" Cedric shouted at their seconds.

Lucien opened his eyes and tried to laugh. "I always knew she'd be the death of me," he said before he went numb again.

"You die on me and I'll kill you," Cedric growled as Lucien's eyelids fell heavily shut once more.

"Not planning on it," he said, but his spiraling vision warned him otherwise.

Memories of Horatia clouded his mind as he sought to focus on the best moments he'd had with her. But death was cruel he supposed, because only the sad and awful moments rose to his mind. Shouting at her in the Midnight Garden. His harsh words, forced kisses and scathing glances. *Such a damned fool I was*, he thought as he was swallowed by darkness.

❧

Horatia woke to an empty bed and frowned. Something was wrong. A sense of foreboding rippled through her like the remnants of a nightmare teasing the edges of her waking mind. She slid out of bed and slipped her shift and dressing gown back on. She wanted to seek out Lucien immediately but it seemed better to be fully dressed, should she have to canvas the huge mansion to find him. She trod down the hall and slipped inside her room.

She selected a gown that buttoned down the front, so as to avoid summoning Ursula. A moment after fastening the last button, she heard the distant crack of a gunshot. Horatia bolted to her window, which faced the northern field. She saw four distant shapes and a second crack cut across the field. One of the figures collapsed to the ground.

A duel! Why hadn't she questioned Lucien? She'd sensed something was amiss last night, but she had ignored it. Why had she done that? In her panic she barely heard the door open behind her.

"A terrible thing, is it not, Miss Sheridan?" a voice said softly from just over her shoulder. She tried to scream as an arm banded about her neck, choking her while a hand clamped over her mouth. "But I'm afraid I'm now running short on time and there is still much to do." The voice was strangely familiar. But even as Horatia thrashed against her captor she still could not see his face.

"I never would have guessed a quiet little chit like you would drive men to duel. Perhaps I will taste you for myself, just to see what the fuss is about." A tongue flitted around the shell of her ear. Horatia tried to claw at his arm, but it only squeezed her throat tighter. Black and gray spots blotted her vision as she fought to breathe.

"Fiery little hellcat. Didn't expect that from the likes of you."

Horatia saw a brief opportunity and abandoned her attempt to claw his arm. Instead she pushed her head forward and then threw it back, colliding her skull with his. Her attacker cursed and loosened his hold. Horatia dropped to her knees, escaping the arm wrapped around her neck. She turned just in time to see the face of the man who'd assaulted her.

"You!" she breathed in shock.

A blow struck her temple, and Horatia saw no more.

CEDRIC CURSED AS HE AND LAWRENCE CARRIED LUCIEN'S BODY between them across the field and into the house. Gregory had sprinted ahead to alert the house and have someone ride to Hexby. As Cedric and Lawrence were nearing the stables they learned that someone was Gregory himself.

"I'm off for the doctor," he shouted and streaked past them on a dappled gray stallion. Avery and Sir John were the first two people to meet them at the front door.

"Good God!" Avery gasped at the bloody wound on Lucien's head and Cedric's grief-stricken expression.

"You were dueling?" Sir John growled. "Fools." He relieved Lawrence of Lucien's feet to help carry the unconscious Marquess up the stairs to an empty bedroom. The second Lucien was on the bed Lady Rochester burst into the room, fire in her eyes.

"Is he dead?" she asked, panic creeping into her.

"The blow glanced his skull," Lawrence said. "He may still live."

"May? Oh, he will not die. I want to kill him myself and he will not deny me that." But when she caught sight of her firstborn bleeding on the bed, she crumpled to her knees. Avery caught his mother before she could faint dead away.

"Get her out of her here, lad," Sir John barked. Avery obeyed, half-carrying his mother out of the room. Sir John turned his attention back to Lucien and started to rip off his shirt and remove the armor to see the damage better. The men winced at the bruises that ranged from Lucien's collarbone down to his hips.

"Who in the bloody hell did that?" Lawrence asked.

"I did," Cedric's said, void of emotion. "We fought last evening before dinner."

"What on earth possessed you to engage in fisticuffs and then a duel?" Sir John growled in such a way that he established himself the dominant male in the room of young foolish boys.

"He bedded my sister," Cedric defended, but there was little heat in his tone.

"You're a damned fool, Sheridan. Lucien loves her," Lawrence said.

"I realize that...now," Cedric admitted.

"Now may be too late," Lawrence shot back.

"You think I don't regret it?" Cedric snapped like a wounded animal and Lawrence saw the despair in his eyes. "I didn't even want to shoot him but my hand shook so badly and I..."

"Then why duel at all?" Lawrence asked.

"I'd hoped he'd back down. I was too afraid to trust him with my sister's heart. I could not let her be hurt. Not again."

"I think you ought to go and wake your sister, Sheridan. She should be prepared for the worst." Sir John put a steady hand on Cedric's shoulder and pushed him towards the door.

"You're right. Horatia must know." He left the room where Lucien lay bleeding and unconscious. What could he possibly say to her?

"Cedric?" Audrey's timid voice cut through his grief. She and Lucinda Cavendish were at the other end of the hall, clad only in nightgowns and robes.

"Where is Horatia?" he asked as they met halfway.

"I haven't seen her. Is it true? You shot Lucien in a duel?" Audrey's voice was tremulous and her eyes on the verge of tears.

"Yes."

"It's all my fault!" Audrey wailed. "I shouldn't have told you about them. Lucien will die and Horatia will never be happy and you will be hung for murder!" She reached for Cedric, seeking comfort from him but Cedric angled her towards Lucinda.

"I'm sorry. It is far more important that I find Horatia right now," he apologized. He had to put Horatia before Audrey today of all days.

She wasn't in her room. The bed was unmade and empty, and her nightgown abandoned on the floor. Her wardrobe was open and Cedric guessed she must have dressed before leaving. He turned to search for her elsewhere but a slip of paper caught his eye resting on her pillow. He retrieved it and read it hastily.

To the victor of the duel: Congratulations! Your prize awaits you and you alone at the gardener's cottage.

There was no name signed. The ambiguous wording was much like the note after the carriage incident. A threat veiled in civility. He did not know who had his sister, but knew who had to be pulling that man's strings. With a curse, Cedric crumpled the note and tossed it to the floor before running out the door. He prayed he could get there in time.

The house was in a buzz as servants flitted through the halls. Cedric tore past them to the stairs and out the back door to the gardens. Lucien's fate was out of his hands now, but he could still help Horatia.

He had no plan and no weapon. It had to be a trap, he knew, yet somehow it felt like the devil's due. When at last he reached the cottage his breath was ragged. He practically wrenched the door from its frame as he stormed inside.

The cottage was dark and quiet but he heard a pained whimper down the hall. Cedric immediately regretted the noise he'd made in entering. No doubt his sister's abductor knew he was here. There was a muffled shriek and Cedric rushed headlong down the hall.

He burst inside and found Horatia crumpled in a heap on the floor next to the bed. Rose petals strewn the floor and bed around her, mixing with the blood on her lip and the slashes on her arms. A man stood with a pistol in one hand and a knife in the other. He raised the pistol at Cedric's chest.

"So glad that you could join us, Lord Sheridan. Do have a seat. That chair." The man pointed to a chair by Horatia.

Before him stood one of Rochester's footmen, Gordon, dressed in the green livery of Rochester Hall. The same servant who had indirectly confirmed to him that Lucien and Horatia had been stealing away together.

"Sit down. Now," Gordon said, cocking the pistol.

"Cedric, get out of here!" Horatia hissed.

"I'm not leaving you." Cedric did not sit down, but he made no move to leave.

Gordon calmly swung the pistol towards Horatia.

"The situation is quite simple. You will sit in that chair, Sheridan, or I will splatter the wall with her brains."

Cedric slowly took a seat and waited. Gordon kicked a coil of rope towards Horatia.

"Bind his hands and feet to the chair. Bind him tight, or else." Horatia took the rope with shaky hands and got to her feet.

"It's all right," Cedric whispered. "Just do as he says." Cedric remained outwardly calm, but the fury in his eyes warned her that he had not given up yet. Horatia tied the rope around his boots and wrists. Cedric stretched and flexed against his bonds once she was done and the murderous look he gave Gordon made the footman smile.

"To be honest, this is not how I wanted to handle this commission at all. If it was up to me, I'd have killed you your first day here and been off before anyone woke. But I'm afraid my instructions were quite specific on a number of points, such as prolonging your discomfort."

"Who hired you?" Cedric demanded.

"I believe you know," Gordon replied simply. "And if you don't, well, it won't really matter much longer. Now, Miss Sheridan, be so kind as to lie down on the bed. I wish to enjoy you while your brother watches. It is Christmas, after all."

Horatia stumbled away from the bed in horror.

"Don't you touch her!" Cedric shouted, yanking on the ropes. "You have me already, just finish me and be done with it."

Gordon put on a theatrical performance of confusion. "Oh? I'm sorry. You must have misunderstood. My instructions regarding prolonged discomfort and death were for your sister. I was instructed not to kill you unless absolutely necessary." Gordon started towards Horatia, a gleam in his cold gray eyes.

"Run! For God's sake run!" he shouted at his sister.

HORATIA MADE IT HALFWAY DOWN THE HALL BEFORE GORDON caught up with her. He grabbed her by the hair and yanked her backward. She shrieked as Gordon pulled the knife back against her throat, drawing a trickle of blood. Horatia ceased fighting him then, and he dragged her back into the bedroom.

"Please. You may do with me what you will...but do not make my brother watch."

"I believe my employer would prefer it if he did." Gordon shoved Horatia onto the bed. She grunted in pain and rolled onto her back just as Gordon charged towards her.

"Lucien will kill you," she promised.

He only laughed. "I very much doubt he will. I'll be long gone before he comes here, assuming he survives at all. You really mustn't worry over him much though, it is you that you should be concerned about."

"How bad was the wound?" Horatia asked Cedric. "How badly did you hurt him?"

"I am not sure. When I left the house he was unconscious and bleeding heavily," Cedric said, looking away.

Gordon smirked at Horatia. She was silent for a long minute eyeing the dying embers in the fireplace. "It seems the hellcat has lost her hellion ways. How easily defeated you are."

Then she got to her feet and to both Cedric and Gordon's confusion she added a few logs to the fire.

"What are you doing?" Gordon asked suspiciously. "Back over here, now."

Her face was so bleak and dispassionate that Gordon glanced at Cedric as though ascertaining whether there was some plan at work here between the siblings. But Cedric's face only burned with shame and defeat.

Horatia whirled on him with the poker just as Gordon raised his pistol. The shot went wide as the sharp tip of the poker raked his chest. She struck his arm with the poker before he could pull out his knife. Gordon cried out in pain as his arm bent unnaturally, but before she could land a second blow he wrenched the poker from her with his good arm.

"That was very stupid." Gordon struck her across the head with the poker. Stars burst across her eyes before everything went dark.

☙❧

GORDON FROWNED DOWN AT HORATIA. HE TORE OFF A LENGTH of her dress and fashioned himself a hasty sling.

"Well, there's no point in taking her now. In truth, I have no wish to linger here any longer. But a contract is a contract. But now that we're alone, I have to ask. Whatever did you do to earn such enmity? What sin earns a man this level of personal attention?"

Cedric said nothing. He didn't give a damn what the man had in store for him. He focused solely on his sister and the way she laid in a crumpled heap against the wall.

With no answer forthcoming, Gordon strode over to the fireplace. He used the poker to drag a log out of the fireplace and onto the floor. Slowly flames began to lick at the edges of the floor. Then he came over to Cedric and with his good arm cut his bindings. Before Cedric could fight him, Gordon rammed the pistol into his stomach.

"Move. I want you to walk out of this cottage ahead of me. I may need you if others have arrived."

"I'm not leaving my sister," Cedric snarled.

"Yes, you are, or I put a bullet through you and you won't be able to save anyone. You still have one sister left. Are you going to leave her as well?"

Fear exploded through Cedric, but he wouldn't give up on Horatia. He would *never* give up on her.

"Horatia! Horatia wake up!" he hollered as he was pulled away.

The flames from the log began to creep along the floor and up the curtains of the window.

Horatia did not stir. Blood trickled from her forehead. She had to be alive, she had to be! While the small fire danced, the crimson rose petals lit up one by one, flames devouring them in flashes like fireflies. As they exited the house, Gordon stumbled on the bottom step.

Cedric turned and grappled with him over the pistol. Cedric shoved against the footman's broken arm, causing him to cry out and drop the weapon. Cedric kicked it away and pushed the man back. He had mere seconds to either fight the villain and turn the tables, or to run back into the cottage to save his sister.

The choice was clear.

He dove back into the darkened doorway, rushing headlong towards the fire.

CHAPTER 30

Thoughts drifted through the murky waters of Lucien's mind, jumbled and hazy. Horatia's soft smiles and shivery sighs, Cedric's haunted stare as he raised a pistol at him.

His eyes wouldn't open and he couldn't move.

"Lawrence, try this," a feminine voice said.

Something sharp penetrated Lucien's nose and shot straight to his brain. His eyes flew open and he surged upright, a pounding headache and pain in his side nearly making him cry out. Smelling salts. One never got used to them.

Lucinda and Lawrence along with Sir John all stood watching him, eyes wide and worried.

"Cedric!" he shouted. Fear for his friend exploded into him as he remembered the duel. He was alive? Where was he now? His bedroom.

"Easy, Lucien, he's fine." Lawrence tried to still him with a firm hand but Lucien knocked it away. One thought formed more clearly now. He'd been too damned distracted to pay attention until now.

"Let me up, damn you! Where is Cedric? Where's Horatia?" He

fought to be free of the tangling bed linens and fell to the floor. Pain tore through his head and he felt a large bandage bound around his head where the bullet had struck him. Sir John gripped his good arm and hauled him up onto his feet, angling him back towards the bed.

"You need to rest, Lucien," Lawrence said.

Lucien cursed and clutched a hand to his head but kept walking towards the door.

Avery and Linus ran into the room from the hallway.

"The gardener's cottage is on fire!" Avery shouted. "We need to get buckets and water. Everyone come with me to the kitchens."

"Has anyone see Horatia?" Lucien bellowed as everyone rushed towards the kitchens.

"No…" Audrey came running to him, breathless. "Her room was empty but there was this." She pressed a scrap of paper in his hands and he hastily scanned it.

"She's been kidnapped!"

The words on the page confirmed his worst fears. Horatia had been taken as bait to lure either him or Cedric to the cottage.

"Damn, we may be too late! Tell the others!" Lucien took off at a run. He had to get to the cottage! He nearly fell down the stairs in his haste as people were rushing past him to find buckets to fill. When he burst out into the gardens he saw inky black smoke in the distance.

"Please be alive," he breathed as he raced towards the cottage. The question he couldn't answer was who had done this? It had to be someone on the staff, he knew it. No stranger had appeared out of nowhere, this was the act of someone who'd waited in the shadows for the right moment.

When Lucien was within twenty feet of the cottage he saw the house's new footman exiting from the front door, forcing Cedric in front of him with a pistol aimed at him. Gordon tripped and the two men struggled before Cedric fled back into the burning cottage.

The footman stared at Lucien. "I thought you were dead,

Rochester. Good for you." Lucien took a step forward, intending to restrain the fiend, but Gordon raised a finger on his good arm. "Your friend went back inside to rescue your lady love. I didn't come here to kill him, but the fool will likely die all the same. What do you think?"

Gordon sidestepped Lucien and walked on past, but Lucien didn't care. Cedric and Horatia were inside the burning cottage. He plunged inside the smoky interior without a second thought, dropping as low as he could, and covering his face with his blood soaked shirt.

"Cedric! Horatia!" he shouted.

"Lucien?" A ragged voice answered from the end of the hall, followed by a hoarse cough.

"Cedric!" Lucien ran down to the open bedroom. He was repelled by the heat of the flames before him. Coughing, he waved his hand in the air, trying to shift the coiling smoke and he glimpsed Cedric, on the floor, barely conscious, and Horatia was much closer to the fire, crumpled on the floor.

"Get her out of here," Cedric groaned.

"I'm too damn selfish to give up either of you," Lucien shouted. He first ran to Horatia, dragging her body far away from the sprawling flames, then helped Cedric up. "I should think that as my friend, you should know me better by now."

"I'll try to follow," Cedric coughed, staggering for the door. "Go. Get her out of here."

Lucien knelt and lifted the unconscious woman in his arms, biting back the pain that still lanced through his head. Horatia's body was drenched in sweat; the limp feel of her in his arms made him sick with dread.

"Just keep moving," Lucien said through gritted teeth as he started for the door.

He met Cedric's gaze across the hazy expanse of the room. They both knew he wouldn't make it out on his own. Something wrenched in Lucien's heart as he witnessed the grim resignation in his friend's eyes.

"Take care of her for me," Cedric's voice was barely audible above the groaning of the house around them.

Lucien managed a nod and tightened his grip on Horatia as carried her out. When he reached the door he ran a good distance away from the cottage before falling to his knees. A small crowd of servants and guests were forming a bucket line, throwing pails of water on the far side of the cottage where the blaze was largest.

Horatia rolled out of Lucien's arms and onto the snowy ground, leaving a sooty trail of black in her wake. He bent over her and cupped her face between his shaking hands and kissed her. She stirred beneath him, then coughed violently.

"Lucien?"

"I love you. Never forget that," he said, kissing her once more before he ripped himself away and started back into the cottage.

"Lucien!" Horatia cried out.

He paused at the entrance to the cottage, looking back, then plunged into the swirling smoke.

Lucien put his bloody sleeve back up over his face and ducked as low as he could. He was halfway down the hall when the beams overhead shrieked. One of them shifted and crashed down behind him as he crossed the threshold of the bedroom. He found Cedric slumped on the ground before him.

Lucien swatted a few flames that had latched onto his leg. The fire burned him, but he stamped the flames out and crawled over to Cedric.

Another beam crashed down by the fireplace. Sparks shot up around the two men and Lucien shut his eyes and flinched away from the flames until the heat receded. A moment after he'd hoisted Cedric up, a massive chunk of the ceiling fell and struck Cedric from behind, sending Lucien toppling to the ground, the beam on top of them both. Lucien yelped in pain as the beam trapped his legs and pinned Cedric down by his back. Lucien clawed at the wood, even though flaming splinters dug into his raw palms. He glanced up, hoping to find anything that might help him when he saw a shadow at the end of the hallway.

"Leave us!" he screamed in desperation. "The roof is coming down!"

But the shadow drew closer, revealing itself as Horatia wrapped in a wet heavy cloak. She hopped over flaming wood and stones until she was kneeling by Lucien's legs and using the wet cloak to cover the flames, heaved at the beam with all her might. Lucien dragged himself out and he and Horatia both worked to pull the debris off of Cedric.

They each grabbed one of Cedric's arms and carried him towards the exit. More than once the flames and smoke almost won, but finally the three stumbled out of the cottage with Cedric just as the entire roof collapsed. Relief and pain swept through Lucien as the last bit of adrenaline in him finally expired.

He collapsed next to Cedric and was lost to the world.

CHAPTER 31

Horatia lay curled up against Lucien's body as he slept in his bed. No one dared to point out the impropriety of it and if they had Horatia would have screamed. As it was, everyone was very polite, even the doctor from Hexby, whom Gregory had returned with ten minutes after she, Lucien and Cedric had escaped the cottage.

Lucien's injury from the duel had indeed been minor, a scratch. The doctor had assured them that head wounds, even grazes tended to bleed profusely. The concussion had been of far more concern, but that too had passed. Unless Lucien suffered an unexpected infection, he would be fine. Horatia hadn't left Lucien's side since they'd returned to the house, other than to quickly bathe and change. Now the doctor was attending to Cedric, who was resting in the room across the hall. Horatia stroked Lucien's hair back from his forehead and placed a delicate kiss to his brow.

"I cannot believe that Gordon escaped," she whispered. The idea that the man who had tried to kill her was still out there was terrifying.

"He won't be back," Lucien said with such certainty that she pulled away a little to stare at him.

"How do you know?"

"We know who he is and what he was hired to do. We are safe from him." The implied *but not entirely safe* hung heavy in the air.

"Horatia? The doctor would like to speak to you," Lady Rochester said quietly from the doorway. Her eyes settled on Horatia and Lucien, but she didn't say anything, a sad smile crossing her lips.

Poor Lady Rochester was pale and the lines around her eyes, which had once been only there from joy and laughter, seemed to age her with concern over her son.

"Is everything all right?" Horatia asked, sitting up.

"He...the doctor has news regarding your brother."

Horatia slid from the bed and steadied herself. "Bad news?"

Lady Rochester's hesitation worried Horatia. "Yes. He wishes to speak to you and Audrey alone. Cedric is sleeping right now. The doctor will see you in his room."

Horatia couldn't seem to move. Her body felt as though it had turned to marble. She couldn't take much more of this. It was as though her entire body was strung like a harp's strings and she was seconds away from snapping.

Horatia crossed the hall and found Audrey and the doctor waiting for her in the other room. She shut the door behind her.

"You have news?" She was unable to look away from the sleeping form of her brother.

The gray-haired doctor cleared his throat. "Yes. It seems that Lord Sheridan has suffered a very serious injury to the head. I'm afraid that he has lost his sight...completely."

Audrey clung to a bedpost for support. Tears began to roll down her cheeks but she said nothing.

"He's blind?" Horatia asked.

"I am not sure if the condition is permanent, but I thought I should advise you immediately so that you might prepare for the worst. Life for someone without sight can be very difficult, but made easier by the support of one's family..."

The doctor droned on but Horatia ceased listening. Her head

turned back towards Cedric. A strip of gauze had been wound around his head, over his eyes.

Blind. Her brother was blind. Her own vision seemed to spot and darken before she remembered to breathe and her vision cleared.

"Thank you, doctor," she said. The doctor then left her and Audrey alone for a while.

"Audrey...why don't you go have some tea brought for us?" Horatia suggested, and her bleary-eyed sister dashed out of the room. It would be best for Audrey to have her time to cry. Horatia could not think logically with her sister in the same room. She sat down on the edge of the bed and nearly jumped when Cedric spoke.

"Don't cry, Horatia. Please. I'll have enough of that from Audrey." Cedric shoved at the bandage, pushing it away from his face as he opened his eyes and gazed in her general direction, but there was an unsettling blankness in his gaze that ripped open Horatia's very soul. How much of a person's life existed behind their eyes? So much expression, emotion, and understanding was lost to Cedric now. She bit her lip to keep from weeping.

"I can't stand to have my eyes covered, even if I can't see. Come closer. Let me have your hand," Cedric said gently, his right hand seeking the comfort of hers. Horatia threw herself against her brother's chest and he wrapped his arms about her. He kissed the top of her head and held her tight. That simple, sweet act tore her open. There was no stopping the tears. Funny thing that comfort often made her cry. It was as though she was only strong when alone, or perhaps it was that she only trusted those she loved to allow herself such feelings. Who would care for Cedric? He would have her and Audrey...but it wouldn't be enough.

Her brother's hand stroked her hair. She tucked her head into his shoulder as she'd done when she was younger, only this time she hoped it was him who was comforted.

"Please forgive me, Horatia," his voice broke. "I've made so many mistakes of late. I did not trust your judgment and I did not have faith in Lucien's heart. He asked me to believe in his love for you but I couldn't. I have failed you both and it has cost us all a great deal."

"Don't say that," Horatia began but Cedric shushed her.

"I must, Horatia. The truth is that Lucien loves you and he deserves you for a wife. I give my blessing freely. Any man who is stubborn enough to care about both of us even when the world is burning down around him...that man is allowed to marry my sister."

"Oh Cedric."

Guilt warred with her joy over being able to marry Lucien. It wasn't fair to feel such happiness when her brother faced a lifetime of darkness.

"I asked you not to cry," he said, his hands wiping tears from her face.

"May I cry from happiness?" she asked.

"I suppose I can suffer tears of joy." Cedric chuckled. "You will be happy with him. Lucien, I mean?"

"Yes. He loves me and when I am with him I feel free. Gloriously free to just be myself. I love him so much." She wished Cedric could see the truth of it in her eyes, but knew it carried in her voice as well

"Then there is nothing more to do but place the banns in the papers and ready St. George's. Your marriage to Lucien won't be as bad as I feared. He is one of my closest friends after all and now to be a brother-in-law." Cedric laughed as though genuinely amused. "What an odd notion that is. But it is no longer an unwelcome one."

"Will you walk me down the aisle?" Horatia asked after a moment.

"You wish a blind man leading you to the alter? Sounds like a bad omen, my dear."

Horatia hugged her brother and pretended not to see the tears streak down his face. In that moment, she would have given her life in exchange for his sight.

"You don't have to lead me. Just hold my arm and trust me to guide you. You've always cared for me. Now let me care for you."

Cedric's smiled trembled. "Then guide me, because I will most certainly be there to give you away."

"You could never give me away. We are stuck with each other. In marrying Lucien I don't believe you'll ever be rid of either of us again." Horatia sighed, thinking of how happy Christmas Eve the night before had been. "Happy Christmas, Cedric."

Her brother chuckled. "I hope to God next year we have the dullest holiday ever."

Audrey returned with a maid bearing a tea tray, her eyes still red and puffy.

"Anyone care for some tea?" she asked with a falsely bright tone that might have fooled a small child.

Cedric moved to sit up. "I would love some."

When he released Horatia, she joined her sister to help with the tea tray. Audrey's hands trembled so badly that Horatia took the offered cup and saucer before it rattled to pieces. Horatia prepared Cedric's tea just as he liked before she returned to the bed and reached for his hands. She placed the cup in his open palms and he slowly raised it to his lips. He sipped carefully so as not to spill.

"Well...that was easier than I expected. Thank heaven for small favors," Cedric remarked. The maid returned and addressed Horatia.

"His lordship is awake and is asking for you, ma'am."

Horatia looked at her brother's face, and even though he could not see her, he must have sensed her gaze upon him.

"Well, what are you waiting for? Go and see the man." Cedric shooed her out of the room. "Lucien abhors tardiness."

Horatia rushed back across the hall into Lucien's bedchamber. He was sitting up, his bare chest bandaged around his lower waist. His hazel eyes lit up like topaz stones when he saw her.

"Thank God you're all right," she said.

He held his arms out for her and she curled up in his embrace as though she'd never left him. He grunted and winced.

"That might be overstating my condition a little." He chuckled.

Lucien kissed her gently, a compassionate expression of his love, but it soon burned hotter, threatening to consume them both. After a long delicious moment he freed her lips and just held her close.

"Cedric has given us his blessing. If you still want me..." Horatia was suddenly uncertain. Maybe Lucien would not want her because of all the trouble she'd been. Duels and assassins were not exactly easy obstacles to dodge.

"After all I've endured to have you? If you think I'll just let you escape after that, you are quite mistaken. I plan to marry you as soon as possible and if that requires tying you to my bed I most certainly will." Lucien's hands slid down her back to cup her bottom teasingly. Horatia tried not to grin.

"You already have tied me to your bed, and I quite enjoyed that experience. Should I feign escape to ensure that you do it again?" She stroked his chest, relishing the feel of his warm skin. She would never get over how easy it was to be with him, to tease and play in a way she'd always longed for.

"That sounds like a game I should certainly like to play, as soon as I am no longer at the mercy of my mother." Lucien winced. "Or the doctor."

"You had better heal soon, darling, because I am in desperate need of you." Horatia brushed her lips lightly across his. "All of you..."

"And what of Cedric?" Lucien asked Horatia. "No one has told me how he is."

Horatia tensed in his arms, and a darkness fell over her.

"What's wrong?" His heart lodged in his throat as he saw tears glimmering in the corners of her eyes.

She bit her lip and looked away. When she still didn't answer, he caught her chin and turned her face back towards his.

"What is it, my love? Just tell me."

Her shaky nod tore at him. "Cedric is alive but...he is blind."

"Blind? God in heaven!" Lucien cursed. He couldn't begin to comprehend the torture of that affliction. To never see anything ever again? Lucien's arms tightened about Horatia.

"Is there nothing we can do?" he asked her.

"The doctor does not know if it is temporary or permanent. We need to be there for him. Support him. Life will be difficult for him from now on and he will need his family and friends to see him through this."

"You are always so brave, my love. And you are right. He will need us now more than ever." Lucien shut his eyes and held Horatia, to let her know that he would never let her go again.

"You know, when I went out to the field this morning, I thought to myself that my greatest regret was all the time I wasted without you," he whispered into her soft brown hair.

"Don't worry, Lucien. I plan to make up for it." Horatia kissed him with all the love she'd been holding for him and him alone.

When their mouths parted, he cupped the back of her head, pressing his forehead to hers.

He was like a man viewing his first sunrise and seeing its striking beauty, that was how it felt to know he and Horatia would be happy. He was awestruck knowing how fortunate and blessed he was to have her in his life and in his heart. They had fought through the very fires of hell itself to be together and now they deserved joy, great joy.

Perhaps it wasn't so bad, to be a rake redeemed.

He smiled and stole another kiss from his love.

There are only good things to come, he silently promised her with his lips and with his heart.

EPILOGUE

Anne Chessley always seemed to forget how to breathe whenever she was near Viscount Sheridan. With short breaths she watched him walk down the aisle in St. George's. Light pierced the stained glass at the front of the church, showering a rainbow of colors onto the altar and the people gathered in the pews.

Miss Sheridan and her brother moved arm in arm down the aisle. His free hand gripped a cane that he swept over the floor ahead of them. Music echoed off the walls and floated to the ceiling in a roar of wondrous sound. At the front of the church, near the altar, the Marquess of Rochester waited to receive his bride.

A wedding of the ages. A rake reformed—or so the *Quizzing Glass* had reported—and a quiet, beautiful woman, blossoming with love. Anne felt a little ache in her chest as she wished to be so fortunate.

All too soon her attention was pulled back to Cedric. Even thinking of him made her so happy. Yet sadness lingered at the edges of her joy like shadows. Cedric's dark eyes roved over the crowds, unseeing. Anne fisted her fingers in her handkerchief.

Blind. The man she'd spent many dreams with during the night was blind.

Her father leaned down to whisper in her ear. "Brave man, that Sheridan. Always liked him before, but now, well, he's damned courageous."

Anne agreed. She closed her eyes, wondering if she would be as brave as him to walk down the aisle without being able to see?

No. The very thought of it terrified her. To be that helpless... that dependent. How did he bear it? She wasn't that brave. Cedric had no choice. He had to face that eternal darkness every second of every hour of every day. A shudder wracked her body and she moved closer to her father. He put an arm around her shoulders. He was such a good man, a good father.

Anne knew how lucky she was to have him. Her mother had died so long ago, but her death hadn't broken him. He'd doubled his love for Anne and they had become inseparable. It was a good thing she never intended to marry. She could not bear the thought of leaving her poor papa alone.

Her eyes found Cedric again, unable to look away from him for long. She adored the way he offered his sister a sheepish smile and kissed her cheek before stepping back to allow her to join Lord Rochester. Lord Lennox stepped up from the front pew, whispered something to Cedric and then with a guiding hand, helped him find his way back to his pew to sit.

The sight moved Anne. The League of Rogues had always fascinated her with their scandalous ways, but what she admired was their kindness towards each other. Like a large family. She only wished she could be a part of it. Alas, that path was not for her. She wasn't like Emily, the Duchess of Essex or Horatia, the soon-to-be Lady Rochester.

The ceremony itself was a blur for Anne. Instead she had focused on Cedric. The way his chestnut hair was a tad too long and curled at the ends. He was so handsome to look at, and yet somehow his personality, even his soul, came out through his expressions as well.

Cedric was different. There was a warmth to his smiles. The faint laugh lines around his eyes and mouth would crinkle when he grinned and laughed. Watching him, adoring him, knowing he would never belong to her was bittersweet. It was rather like stumbling upon a painting in a secret gallery. She could look, admire, love from afar but never step through the painted canvas into that world.

If only you were mine, Cedric. If only I was yours...

⚜

CEDRIC LEANED AGAINST THE RAILING OF THE LAST WOODEN pew at the back of the church, speaking with the final guests as they trickled out and onto the steps outside. Lucien and Horatia had already gone on ahead in a carriage to Lucien's townhouse to prepare for the wedding breakfast.

A chasm opened up in Cedric's chest at the thought of returning home to find Horatia's empty bedchamber. It would be just Audrey and him for now...and Mittens of course. The poor old cat missed her littermate Muff terribly. The first few weeks following his death she wandered the house at all hours, crying, yet never heard Muff's answering call.

After a month she'd given up and taken to stalking Cedric at night, finding him wherever he was and eventually settled down to sleep, whether it was his bed, a settee in the parlor or elsewhere. At first he'd hated her direct attentions, especially the way she'd pounce on him without warning, claws digging into him as she kneaded herself into a blissful state of contentedness. But once he'd grown used to Mittens' impromptu nightly appearances he'd settled in with her and relished the warmth of her small body and the steady purr she made. The sound was perhaps the most comforting aspect of the arrangement. It reassured him that nothing loomed out of the darkness to harm him when he could not see it. His enemies would have no chance of sneaking up on him, not while Mittens manned her post.

Audrey slipped her hand in his, pulling his attention back to their guests.

"Lord Chessley! Anne!" Audrey greeted eagerly.

"Miss Sheridan." Lord Chessley's deep baritone voice was full of amusement. "For now you are indeed Miss Sheridan, since your sister is now married. What a lovely ceremony, wasn't it? Anne and I were thankful you thought to invite us."

"Of course!" Audrey replied without hesitation.

"Yes, we were very happy to come," Anne said.

Cedric's breath hitched. He'd always loved the sound of her voice, warm like a glass of fine brandy.

"Thank you so much for inviting us. Your sister looked so beautiful. I can tell she and Lord Rochester will be very happy."

Audrey laughed. "They had better be, given all that has happened."

Cedric detected the note of anxiety in his sister's tone and gently nudged her ribs to remind her to be silent. The news of his blindness had been unavoidable. However, the matter of how he'd lost his sight—other than 'in a fire'—was a matter best left unremarked upon returning after the holidays. If only he could shake the nightmares, rid himself of the horrors of the lost memories. What was worse was knowing that Charles suffered the same sort of dreams, had for years now. He relived drowning in the River Cam far too often. Could a man ever come back from that? Perhaps not.

"Well, Anne and I must be going. Thank you again for allowing us to come. Lord Sheridan, Miss Sheridan." Lord Chessley bid his goodbyes.

Cedric extended his hand, shaking the other's and then he waited for Anne to take his hand as well. A moment of hesitation, then Anne slid her gloved fingers into his grasp, which he raised to his lips, brushing a soft kiss on the backs of her knuckles. A tendril of longing spun in him, like a fine gossamer thread and as delicate as a bloom after a harsh frost.

In another life he would have claimed her for a dance at the ball where they had first met. In another life he might have been the first and only man to kiss her lips, to see her smile and hear her laugh.

In another life, she could have been mine...

HUGO WAVERLY WAITED INSIDE HIS COACH JUST OUTSIDE THE church. The door opened and Daniel Shefford slid in. Waverly rapped his cane on the roof and the coach started forward. He settled the cane on his lap, a gloved finger running over the silver head. Once he'd had a cane with lion's head. A gift from his father, a gift that Cedric Sheridan had stolen from him when they'd been at Cambridge. Now his cane bore a wolf's head. The creature's teeth were bared in a silent, menacing snarl. For that was how he saw himself. A wolf amidst a flock of insipid sheep. It was only a matter of time before he feasted upon his prey.

"What have you to report?" he asked Shefford.

"Mostly good news. Gordon made it to your ship in Brighton. He's heading out first thing for Spain. He'll be of good use there because he is fluent in the language."

"Excellent." Hugo hadn't been too disappointed by the report of Gordon's failure to kill Horatia Sheridan. After all, the true purpose had been achieved. The League knew that their loved ones were no more safe than they were themselves. The exercise had been a fruitful one because it revealed the League's weaknesses. Ones he could exploit over time until he was ready. And he couldn't deny the pain he caused along the way was pleasurable. Like a cat beating a mouse senseless but staving off the death blow, fascinated with the stunned little creature lying limp beneath its paws.

"Sir, Avery Russell has been active in our office these last few months. Should we reassign him elsewhere while we engage in this current business?"

"No, leave Russell where he is. We can use him to keep an eye on his brother. He might even become useful to us later. I want you to focus on our Brighton connections. There's a small bit of an underground slave trade that I wish to remove from the port."

"Slaves?" Shefford scowled.

"Yes."

"Very good, sir."

Waverly settled back in his seat, his mind ever turning with possibilities.

"How was the wedding by the way?" he asked Shefford.

Shefford shrugged. "Nice, I suppose. I don't much care for them. Since Sheridan has lost his sight, he's become a source of pity by most of the *ton*. They avoid him when possible."

"Do they now?" Waverly couldn't repress a smile. What a delightful little turn that had been, to learn of Sheridan's blindness. A fitting end for the thief. The fact that the *ton* had turned their backs on him was an added reward.

"I believe there is one who overlooks his condition. A woman named Anne Chessley. She and Sheridan were speaking just before I left."

He'd heard of the Chessleys. Her father was a baron, a wealthy one. That situation would bear watching. He would not let Sheridan have a bride. He didn't deserve happiness. Perhaps he could make use of the slavery situation in Brighton before he had it shut down. Weren't there always markets abroad for genteel bred ladies with fair skin? If Sheridan ever married, it wouldn't be for long.

THE END

*BE SURE TO TURN THE PAGE TO SEE EXCLUSIVE ART OF HORATIA and Lucien waltzing!

Thanks for reading *His Wicked Seduction*. I hope you enjoyed it! You've just read the 2nd book in the League of Rogues series. The other books in the series are *Wicked Designs, Her Wicked Proposal, Wicked Rivals, Her Wicked Longing, His Wicked Embrace, The Earl of Pembroke, His Wicked Secret* and *The Last Wicked Rogue*. More books with the League are coming soon!

The best way to know when a new book is released is to do one or all of the following:

Join my Newsletter: http://laurensmithbooks.com/free-books-and-newsletter/

Follow Me on BookBub:
https://www.bookbub.com/authors/lauren-smith

Join my Facebook VIP Reader Group called Lauren Smith's League:
https://www.facebook.com/groups/400377546765661/

OTHER TITLES BY LAUREN SMITH

Historical
The League of Rogues Series
Wicked Designs
His Wicked Seduction
Her Wicked Proposal
Wicked Rivals
Her Wicked Longing
His Wicked Secret (coming soon)
His Wicked Embrace (coming soon)
The Seduction Series
The Duelist's Seduction
The Rakehell's Seduction
The Rogue's Seduction
Standalone Stories
Tempted by A Rogue
Sins and Scandals
An Earl By Any Other Name
A Gentleman Never Surrenders
A Scottish Lord for Christmas

Contemporary
The Surrender Series
The Gilded Cuff
The Gilded Cage
The Gilded Chain
Her British Stepbrother
Forbidden: Her British Stepbrother
Seduction: Her British Stepbrother
Climax: Her British Stepbrother

Paranormal
Dark Seductions Series
The Shadows of Stormclyffe Hall
The Love Bites Series
The Bite of Winter
Brotherhood of the Blood Moon Series
Blood Moon on the Rise
Brothers of Ash and Fire
Grigori
Mikhail
Rurik

Sci-Fi Romance
Cyborg Genesis Series
Across the Stars (coming soon)

ABOUT THE AUTHOR

USA TODAY Bestselling Author Lauren Smith is an Oklahoma attorney by day, who pens adventurous and edgy romance stories by the light of her smart phone flashlight app. She knew she was destined to be a romance writer when she attempted to re-write the entire *Titanic* movie just to save Jack from drowning. Connecting with readers by writing emotionally moving, realistic and sexy romances no matter what time period is her passion. She's won multiple awards in several romance subgenres including: New England Reader's Choice Awards, Greater Detroit BookSeller's Best Awards, and a Semi-Finalist award for the Mary Wollstonecraft Shelley Award.

To connect with Lauren, visit her at:
www.laurensmithbooks.com
lauren@Laurensmithbooks.com